SPEAKER OF TONGUES

ALSO BY CHRIS TULLBANE

THE MURDER OF CROWS
See These Bones
Red Right Hand
One Tin Soldier

STORIES FROM A POST-BREAK WORLD
The Stars That Sing
The Storm in Her Smile
A Sure Thing

THE STORM WHO RIDES
The Queen of Smiles
The Queen of the Road *

THE MANY TRAVAILS OF JOHN SMITH
Investigation, Mediation, Vindication
Blood is Thicker Than Lots of Stuff
Ghost of a Chance
The Italian Screwjob
A Dead Man's Favor
Godswar *
John Smith Doesn't Work Here Anymore *

THE (SECOND) LIFE OF BRIAN
Speaker of Tongues

*Forthcoming

SPEAKER OF TONGUES

CHRIS TULLBANE

GHOST FALLS PRESS

NEVADA

First published by Ghost Falls Press 2024
Speaker of Tongues. Copyright © 2024 by Chris Tullbane.

GHOST FALLS PRESS

Publisher's Cataloging-in-Publication Data
provided by Five Rainbows Cataloging Services

Names: Tullbane, Chris, author.
Title: Speaker of tongues / Chris Tullbane.
Description: Henderson, NV : Ghost Falls Press, 2024. | Series: (Second) life of Brian, bk. 1. | Also available in audiobook format.
Identifiers: ISBN 978-1-955081-15-3 (paperback) | ISBN 978-1-955081-14-6 (ebook)
Subjects: LCSH: Coming of age--Fiction. | LitRPG (Fiction) | Extraterrestrial beings--Fiction. | Portal fantasy fiction. | Fantasy fiction. | BISAC: FICTION / Fantasy / Dark Fantasy. | FICTION / Fantasy / Epic . | FICTION / Science Fiction / Alien Contact. | FICTION / Coming of Age. | GSAFD: Fantasy fiction.
Classification: LCC PS3620.U45 S64 2024 (print) | LCC PS3620.U45 (ebook) | DDC 813/.6--dc23.

Book cover design by Jake @ jcalebdesign.com

This novel is entirely a work of fiction. The names, characters, places, and incidents portrayed in it are either the product of the author's imagination or are used fictitiously, and any resemblance to actual persons, living or dead, events or locales is entirely coincidental.

FIRST EDITION

For Nami,
the reason for everything

Acknowledgments

This is my tenth full-length novel, and there are *so* many people to thank:

My angel-wife, Nami, who keeps our life, our home, and my heart going.

Johanna, my dearest friend, who deserves every joy in the world.

My brother, Jamie, who had to field far too many emails about class and leveling mechanics.

Claudia, Denise, Kerri D., Mark E., Sam, and Scotty B, who are all fabulous authors and even better friends.

Cory, Mitch, Montie, and Tom, who went way, way above the call of duty this time by beta reading a monster of a book in not-so-bite-sized pieces.

Anthony, Charity, Deanna, Joe, Kerri K., Kevin, Lara, Lynn, Mark S., Mike, Reid, and Ziggy, who continue to support this little hobby of mine.

Keith and Shawn, who remain trapped in a chat-channel hellscape of their own making.

And always last but never least, my parents.

Here's to the next ten books!

Book 1: Chosen

"They come from the void,
burning their way across the midnight sky,

and with their passage
the world is changed forever

Call them savior or doom bringer,
hero, villain, or agent of chaos

Call them Chosen."

-Excerpt from *The Pride of Lachesia*

1

I knew something was wrong right away. It was too quiet. No hum from the window unit or refrigerator. No ticking from the wall clock in the living room. The silence was as thick as the comforter I must have kicked off sometime during the night.

As I opened my eyes, I added another oddity to that list. It was dark. Really dark. Whether I had fallen asleep on the couch or in my fifteen year old bed, there should have been *some* source of light: the digital display of the ancient DVD player, the neon glow of the Santa Claus nightlight Dad had bought me that first Christmas after Mom left, or even the too-bright streetlights, penetrating the tattered blinds of our double-wide mobile home.

There was none of that, only darkness. *True* darkness, pitch-black and all-consuming. I blinked my eyes to make sure they were open and waved a hand in front of my face. Nothing. I could feel the passage of air but couldn't pick out the motion. Apparently, the whole trailer park had lost power and clouds had rolled in to hide the distant moon and stars.

Just another beautiful morning in Midton, Ohio.

There were two things I always did upon waking up. The first was to check the time. I was regularly *blessed* with the morning shift at

Pritchard's Coffee & Baked Goods, and the list of things I needed to do before leaving was a mile long: look in on my dad, empty, wash, and replace his bed pan, clean any leftover dishes, shower, shave, and dress, and last but not least, tidy up the trailer before Mrs. Cho arrived to assume caretaker duties.

With the power out, I'd have to find my phone to see the time, but the lack of light from outside told me it was early. So, I turned to my second morning ritual, extending my unseen hands in the air above me. I wiggled each finger, then the attached hands and arms, followed by my toes, feet, and legs. *Symptoms* usually presented first in the form of weakness or a loss of muscle control. And while the doctors said I should have *at least* a decade of asymptomatic life left, self-evaluations had become as much a part of my mornings as the thoroughly regimented schedule of caring for my dad.

Like father, like son isn't always a good thing.

I'd learned that lesson early.

I was halfway through my daily forms, every muscle in my body aching as if I'd been run over by a truck, when my mind finally woke up, breaking through the darkness that clouded my brain as much as the room around me. I squeezed my eyes shut as the events of the previous day came back with a vengeance.

A funeral and a firing meant I no longer needed to worry about taking care of my dad, any more than I needed to get ready for my shift at Pritchard's. I'd never have to worry about either one ever again. That realization hit me like a two-punch combo, followed by a strange mixture of grief, panic, and relief.

The grief was all for Dad, Chuck to his very few friends, and Mr. Fieldings to the handful of others who had bothered to visit during the final stages of the disease that took his life. The panic was *mostly* financial; in-home care had been more than I could honestly afford, even after going outside the system to find a retired nurse like Mrs.

Cho, and running a register at Pritchard's had barely even covered the minimum payments on my credit cards. Dad was gone, but the bills remained, and without a job, I didn't know how I'd be able to pay them.

And the relief? What about that, Brian?

I didn't want to think about *why* I felt relieved. Not now, four days after Dad's death, and less than one after the ceremony where he'd been laid to rest in front of me, the mortician, and the tiny collection of people in our nothing town who gave a damn. It was better—healthier, even—to focus on other things, like why it was so dark and...

Where the hell am I?

Because, as more details started to filter in despite the ever-present darkness, there was one thing that was becoming apparent: this *wasn't* our trailer. *My* trailer, now. The surface beneath me was cold and hard, missing both the lumps from my ancient twin bed and the hard springs from our equally venerable couch. And it felt like rough stone instead of aged carpet or the cracked linoleum tiles that had transformed our small kitchen into a chessboard where both players inevitably lost.

With a groan that echoed more than it would have in a double-wide, I forced myself upright. Whatever truck had run me over had apparently shifted into reverse and come back for a second pass; every muscle in my body had its own individual hangover.

And speaking of hangovers...

I vaguely remembered returning to the trailer park in the rain, long after both the funeral and the afternoon shift where Mike Pritchard, in all his puffy-faced benevolence, had shitcanned me on the same day I buried my dad. Our double-wide had seemed too large, empty without my father for all that he hadn't left his tiny bedroom in years.

Wet and tired, I'd sat in our living room, a plate of Bug's brownies in my lap. *Special* brownies, made by my one friend as an apology for his absence at the funeral. They'd been the only thing in the refrigerator, and although I'd never tried edibles—couldn't afford to spend the time or the money on them, really—I'd been hungry. Hungry and, for the first time since my very early teens, free of responsibilities.

But after that?

I shook my head, ironically the only part of me that *didn't* hurt. The first brownie had gone down smooth and chocolatey, but I hadn't felt a damn thing. So, I'd had another. And another. And… Everything following that fourth brownie was either a blur or a blank, but given the stone beneath me, I must have left the trailer. Which meant I could be literally anywhere in Midton.

Focus on the immediate issues. Find a light. Figure out where you are. Get ready to apologize if you broke into someone's basement.

The last bit seemed unlikely, as I would have had to leave the park entirely to find a basement. Still, it *would* explain the lack of light.

I bit back a second groan as I stood, arms extended above me in case the ceiling was too low even for me. My hands found only air and empty space. Cold from the stone floor radiated up through my feet in the first sign that I'd forgotten both socks and shoes during my brief career as Hallucination Houdini. A quick check of my pockets told me I hadn't brought my wallet, keys, or phone with me either. No doubt, they were back in the trailer on our thrift-market coffee table, next to whatever was left of the plate of brownies.

Bug was going to laugh his skinny ass off when he heard this story. And there was no way in hell I was ever taking edibles again.

Being upright didn't do much to improve my situation. The darkness was still so thick that it swallowed everything around me but sound. Judging by the echo, the room I'd wandered into was large and mostly empty, but any further details remained a mystery. With a shrug, I took a cautious step forward—

—and found nothing but air under my outstretched foot.

Arms flapping like a flightless bird trying to change its nature, I fell onto an equally hard stone surface a few feet further down. Through the grace of a God I had long since stopped speaking to, I didn't land on my head. Still, the impact blasted the air from my lungs.

When I could finally breathe again, I didn't stand back up. Instead, I rose onto my hands and knees, groaning from the pain of the fresh bruises I'd just earned. This time, I *crawled* forward, testing the ground in front of me as I moved. The new surface continued for a while, suggesting that maybe *this* was the floor and whatever I'd originally woken up on had been some sort of table or raised surface.

A crudely carved stone table? In the middle of a pitch-black room? Because that's *not ominous or anything.*

I kept crawling. Ten feet later, I found another drop-off. This one was shallow, the next level only a foot or so below, and it was followed by another and then another. *Stairs*, I quickly realized, though they were both deeper and wider than most.

And what kind of basement has stairs going down?

The fifth step proved to be the last, but as I crawled on, my confusion only grew. This place was bigger than I'd thought… far too large to be a basement or cellar for any of the houses on our side of town. So, where was I? And why did the space around me feel almost familiar?

It took another minute of crawling to answer that second question. In the years before Dad's diagnosis—and for a few short, despair-filled months after—we'd been faithful members of the local parish of St. Augustine's. The layout of this room reminded me of that church's main chapel: a large room with wide stairs leading up to a raised dais that in turn held some sort of altar on it.

This *wasn't* St. Augustine's—their chapel had hardwood floors, stained glass windows, and rows of pews rather than endless empty space—but there were too many similarities for me to ignore. Unfortunately, St. Augustine's was one of only two churches in town and the second one was not only seven long miles from the trailer park... it was significantly fancier.

Which this place clearly isn't.

For the first time, the thought surfaced that I might *not* have wandered in here on my own. Had someone taken me instead, snatching me off the streets in my edible-fueled delirium?

Unknown kidnappers. A hidden chamber containing a secret chapel. No lights to speak of. I did the mental math and didn't like the answer that equation gave me:

Cultists.

Admittedly, Ohio wasn't known for its history of satanic practitioners. Still, before dementia had taken hold of my dad, we'd watched our share of scary movies together—first from the living room couch, and then, after movement became a challenge, on the smaller television I set up in his bedroom. And this... *whatever* this was... felt just like the setup for one of those movies.

Before she'd left for NYU, my ex-girlfriend Kate had liked to say that Midton had a dark underbelly, but I'd assumed she was talking about the growing opioid epidemic.

Clearly, I'd been wrong.

Just like that, the all-consuming darkness felt threatening; no longer empty, but rife with unseen dangers. I sped up, scurrying across the floor like a human-shaped beetle, ignoring the scrapes I was accumulating on my hands and knees. Maybe I was panicking for nothing, but if I *had* been kidnapped, I needed to get the hell out of here before the cultists came back and moved on to the human sacrifice portion of their religion.

Finally, I encountered something new: a wall. It was the same stone as the floor, worked just enough to not be wholly natural, and it extended to the left and right, far beyond my admittedly limited wingspan. I climbed to my feet again, kept one hand on the wall as I turned left, and started walking.

Find a wall: done.

Follow the wall: in progress.

Find a door and exit through that door?

It was a simple plan, but simple was good. Simple had gotten me through high school and way too many years as a barista under the world's shittiest boss. Either I'd come across the door I was looking for, or I'd find myself in a corner, and would reverse direction.

Assuming there is *a door. Assuming whoever kidnapped you didn't just dump you into some sort of bomb shelter or underground cellar for human sacrifices.*

Before that deeply disturbing thought could take root, I reminded myself of the altar. Nobody built an altar in a room they couldn't access. And unless the cultists were CrossFit enthusiasts, that access point would involve something more functional than a rope ladder from above.

Fifteen steps later, I was starting to question my assumptions. On the sixteenth step, I froze, as two things happened almost simultaneously.

First, the hand I'd kept on the wall touched something that wasn't stone, something smooth and almost slippery. Not wood, unless it had been heavily lacquered, but not metal either. Plastic, maybe? Or bone? Whatever it was, I was pretty sure it was the door I'd been searching for.

Unfortunately, I was no longer sure I wanted to go through it. Because the second thing that happened was me hearing a deep coughing roar, coming from somewhere on the other side of the wall. That noise set the door vibrating in its frame.

We didn't have many bears in Ohio, but whatever had made that sound was a hell of a lot bigger than a bobcat or any of the other wild animals that occasionally found their way into town. It wasn't something I wanted to face, with or without my socks.

On the other hand, I told myself, *waiting around for your kidnappers to return isn't a winning plan either. Better a beast that you can avoid or outsmart than a whole congregation of killers with opposable thumbs.*

I ran my hands across the door's surface, looking for a handle. Eventually, I found a knob—metal, surprisingly cold to the touch, and almost a full foot higher than I'd expected. In fact, it was practically level with my unseen forehead. I was notoriously short, but the doorknob's placement would have made it abnormally high for *anyone.* Unless they played basketball for the Cavs.

Still, it served its function. When I pulled, the door—nine feet tall if it was an inch—slid smoothly open to reveal an adjoining hallway.

It wasn't until after I'd slipped out into that hallway that I realized I'd been able to see the door as it opened. For the first time since I'd woken on the altar, there was light. Not the *sunlight* I'd been hoping for, but a more fickle, ruddy light. It came from somewhere out of sight, bouncing off the walls to send shadows dancing down the long passageway I'd just entered.

The floors here were tiled, in contrast to the chapel's stone, and that only added to the growing list of questions in my mind. Actual *tapestries,* faded and impossible to decipher, hung on the walls, giving the impression that the cult's hiding place was at least as old as Midton itself. To my right, the hallway ended in a stone wall and even more decrepit artwork, but to the left, it ran twenty to thirty paces before making a sharp turn towards the unseen light.

Only one direction to go. That makes it easy.

Of course… it also means whatever made that roar will be somewhere ahead of me.

At least I'd see it coming?

ooo

The light turned out to be from torches. *Literal* torches, like you'd see in an old *Indiana Jones* movie or on unfathomably long-running reality survival shows. Strange metal rods—black like cast iron but flecked with orange flakes—were fitted to brackets in the walls and had been wrapped in oil-soaked cloth and then set ablaze. There was quite a bit less smoke than I remembered from my brief forays into pyromania as a kid, but the flames provided ample, if inconsistent, light. Tongues of fire danced as I moved past them.

As welcome as the light was, the torches were a concern. They were more proof that I wasn't alone here. *Someone* had lit them and, judging by the amount of cloth still left to burn, it couldn't have been that long ago.

The second hallway, just like the one I'd originally entered, had only one room off it, but its door was gone. I snuck closer and glanced into a well-lit chamber. Fragments of the missing door were scattered across the floor, each piece sharp-edged and layered like the shells Kate had brought back senior year from her trip to Virginia Beach. Torches lined the room's interior, illuminating *another* chapel, one whose steps led up to a primitive iron altar draped in blue cloth.

Normally, my first question would have been why any group of cultists, regardless of their numbers, fanaticism, and undeniable resources, needed *two* chapels, but this once, my mind was focused on more important things. Because the altar wasn't the only thing in the room. There was a *body*, or what was left of one, an arrangement of sickening bloody lumps almost lost within a hooded robe that was every bit as blue as the altar's runner. And above that body, bending down to take another bite—

I mostly managed to hold back my scream, but the *thing* spun toward me anyway. All I got in that initial glimpse was an impression of legs. More legs than any mammal should have. More legs than *anything* that size should have.

And then I was running for my life.

ooo

One minute and two additional halls later, the thing—*the monster,* my mind informed me—hadn't caught up, but I could hear its pursuit, a steady, tireless progression of clicks as it flowed across tiled floors. Despite my best efforts, it was getting closer.

Not just big, but fast. Or at least faster than I am.

My fourth and most recent hallway had been the first to offer multiple doors, but I'd already seen how little protection the shell-like barriers offered. I kept running, looking for anything that screamed *exit,* no longer even wasting energy on wondering just how big this facility was.

Facility, because whatever that thing was that was chasing me, there was no way it was natural. And that meant either my kidnappers dabbled in bioengineering… or occultism was way more real than I'd ever believed.

Or hell, maybe it was both?

I rounded yet another corner at top speed, bouncing off the far wall. This time, I only managed a single shaky stride before I slipped in a pool of liquid, my aching bare feet skating out from under me. I toppled to the tiled floor, mere inches from a second body. This one, too, was hidden beneath torn blue robes, but given the discrepancy between the robes' size and whatever remained beneath them, some of it had already been consumed.

Whatever was left of Bug's brownies threatened to make a reappearance as I recognized what the liquid I'd just slipped in was.

Get up. Move!

The words echoed in my head, but my body refused to listen. The creature hunting me had slowed, seemingly content to match its pace with mine. Its too-many legs beat out a slow march, the steady cadence of inevitability.

Maybe it was still the edibles in my system, but the coughing roar that came from just around the corner sounded almost smug to my ears. Smug like Mike Pritchard had been when he fired me after Dad's funeral. Smug like ancient Mrs. Applewood at that same funeral, wearing her threadbare Sunday best and treating the whole thing like a victory party, as she outlived yet another of Midton's residents.

It was those memories—only a day old and still raw as hell—that got me back up onto wobbly legs I could barely feel, my lungs burning with every breath. I had just turned to run when I spotted yet another element that defied explanation:

The dead person had a spear.

Why *any* Ohio native, even a demon-summoning, bio-scientist cultist, would favor medieval weaponry over a hunting rifle or nine-millimeter was something I couldn't answer, but I'd solve those mysteries when I got home. *If* I got home. For now, I wasn't going to refuse something sharp and poky. I scooped up the spear and took off again in a dead sprint, energy restored as much by my own anger as the momentary rest.

The spear's shaft was taller than I was and wooden, although something about the grain seemed odd. The spearhead was forged from the same black metal as the door hinges and sharp on the edges, flaring out before it narrowed again into a wickedly sharp point. It was an ugly weapon, primitive and simple, and it made my flight through the unfamiliar halls that much more difficult, but it never occurred to me to toss it aside. If the monster caught me—*when* it caught me—it would be better to be armed than not.

Just be sure to stab it with the pointy end.

Another hall, and the sounds of pursuit continued, the monster's pace now unmistakably calculated to close the distance between us without ending the chase too quickly. My second wind had already guttered out like a candle flame and my speed flagged accordingly. What had briefly been a sprint became a jog and then a shamble. Still, I kept putting one foot in front of the other, my eyes fixed on the far end of the hallway that turned yet again to the right.

Maybe that next hall would contain the exit, or maybe the remaining cultists would be assembling there in force to attack the demon they'd foolishly summoned or created. Either way, I just had to get to—

An arm reached through an open doorway as I shambled past, almost clotheslining me. Before I could react, I was pulled inside and tossed to the floor like a bale of hay. Even as I belly flopped onto the shaft of the spear I'd been carrying, the person who had intercepted me was shutting the hallway door. Then they were above me, their hand a gentle pressure on my back.

"Stay down and remain quiet," they murmured into my ear, voice a breath on the non-existent breeze, low and unmistakably female. "The sluthari hunt by sound, not smell, and it *will* come in after us if you are heard. I do not know whether the door will hold."

Having seen the fragments left of similar doors, I could have given her the answer to *that* question, but I followed her instructions and said nothing. Maybe it was because she sounded even younger than I was and almost as scared. Maybe the tiny part of my brain still functioning realized I'd have a better chance of escaping a single cultist than the nightmare her sect had summoned or engineered. Or maybe I was just so exhausted that the idea of *moving* filled me with almost the same level of existential dread as the creature hunting us. Whatever the reason, I focused on my breath until it matched that of the woman above me. Face down on the floor, and unwilling to risk changing positions, I shut my eyes and *listened.*

Clicking became audible even through the now-closed door as the creature made its way down the hallway. Without my own noise distracting me, the sound of far too many legs seemed even more horrific, the alien *wrongness* of it sending shivers down my spine. There was nothing natural about a grizzly-sized millipede.

Please keep going, I prayed, over and over again. *Go eat some other cultists and return to whatever hell you were summoned from.*

As if it could hear my unseen words, the creature paused outside our door. I stopped breathing entirely and the woman above me tensed. We both waited for a sign we'd been discovered.

Finally, the clicking resumed as the predator flowed further down the hallway, leaving our hiding place behind. I waited for the noise to fade entirely before taking my next glorious gulp of air. Oxygen filled my body, and I sagged against the tiled floor.

The cultist who had saved—but also presumably kidnapped—me waited a few seconds longer. When she spoke, her voice remained a whisper I could barely hear. "Keep quiet in case it doubles back. If we are fortunate, it will make its way back out into the hills in search of fresh prey." Something shifted in her tone as she stood, removing the weight from my back. "And perhaps you can tell me what one of the Nor is doing so far west. Are you a refugee? Shouldn't you be with the rest of your kind at Whitehall? The primarch has promised your nation's citizens food and shelter there."

"I'm sorry?" I did my best to emulate her whisper as I pushed myself up onto my hands and knees to reclaim the spear beneath me. We were in yet another chapel, the third so far if my count was accurate. This one was brightly lit, much like the second had been, but considerably less bloody. Wide stairs led up to an altar formed from polished white marble and almost entirely hidden beneath folds of orange and crimson of cloth. "I didn't understand almost any of that. What's a *Nor*? Where are—?"

The words died in my throat as I finally got my first look at the woman next to me. Her robes were orange and red instead of blue, matching the runners on the nearby altar. More importantly, her hood was down. Torchlight reflected off the metallic threads in the patterns woven across her robe… and then again off the *white scales* that covered every inch of her exposed and hairless face. Glowing orange eyes lacked both iris and sclera, and her—no, *its*—teeth were as white as its scales, sharp and terrifying.

Grown-ass adult and proud son of Ohio though I was, my scream hit a note well beyond the high range of most sopranos.

2

An indecipherable look crossed the robed lizard's alien features before it covered my mouth with clawed fingers, both muffling my screams and extending them. "What are you doing?" it hissed. "You will bring back the—"

The chapel door shuddered as something heavy slammed into it from the outside. The lizard squeezed its eyes shut—a clear membrane came down first, followed by a more human-like, if scaled, eyelid—and it let go of me, running to brace the door.

"Look for something we can block the door with," snapped the cultist, all attempts at stealth forgotten, as it leaned its full body weight against the shaking portal. "Please, son of Corros. Move!"

My legs felt like Jell-O. A large part of me was still busy freaking out, but at least this time, the screams were only in my head. Bipedal lizard or not, this… creature… seemed intent on saving both of our lives while the *whatever* out in the hall had other plans. And that meant I needed to help if I could.

Granted, *not screaming* would have been good, too.

Unfortunately, the chapel didn't have any refrigerators or convenient bookshelves on hand. It didn't even have much in the way of furniture beyond the two black iron candlesticks that flanked the altar. *Heavy* candlesticks, but I muscled them over to where the lizard was doing its best to keep out something six or seven times the mass of both of us put together.

The gleaming altar was solid marble and far too heavy to move, and the cloth runners on top were of no use at all, so I headed for the sole remaining piece of furniture in the chapel, a small wooden cabinet. It wouldn't be more than a speed bump for the monster, but we weren't exactly spoiled for choice. I pushed it to the door, turned it on one side, and tried to wedge it against the frame under the candlesticks. One last scan of the chapel confirmed that I'd run out of items, so I picked up my spear and went to stand next to my savior and presumed captor.

"What are you doing?" asked the lizard. Another blow to the door sent it rocking back on bare feet every bit as scaled as their arms and face, clawed toes scrabbling futilely against the tiled floor. "We need more!"

"There's nothing else here!"

It turned to scan the chapel and came to the same conclusions I had. "Then help me hold the door!" The lizard did that strange double blink. "What techniques do you have?"

"Techniques?"

"For combat!"

I frowned. Growing up without a mom and with a sick dad had taught me how to throw a punch, but the emphasis the creature had put on the phrase made *technique* sound like some kind of kung fu code. And what did a reptile know about martial arts? I was pretty sure *Teenage Mutant Ninja Turtles* hadn't been a documentary. "I don't know what you're talking about!"

The lizard sagged and turned back to the door. "Then we must hold this entryway at all costs."

It made space for me to join it at the door, and I took advantage of my lack of height to lean under the candlesticks, putting my body weight against the shell-like surface. Every blow threatened to knock us both to the floor, but I was far more concerned about the door itself. So far, we'd been able to hold it shut, but if the shell-like material shattered like the door I'd seen earlier…?

We would be dead and eaten.

Hopefully in that order.

"What now?" I asked, not even surprised that the lizard, as young as it seemed, still loomed over me, at least the size of a very tall woman. A human woman, that is. It was stronger than me too, judging by the way it had yanked me into the chapel.

"We hold for as long as we can." The lizard staggered as a particularly strong hit to the door sent shockwaves through our bodies. "Should the shrine guardians still live, they will gather and do what they can to drive the sluthar away."

I liked the sound of *any* kind of guardians, given our predicament, but— "Are they… people like you?"

"Synossians? Yes. But whereas I am a Priestess of Aurea, they are Warriors and focused entirely on combat."

I ignored all the words I didn't recognize and focused on the few I did. The two bodies I'd already encountered appeared in my mind like blood-soaked postcards. I'd *assumed* they were human but hadn't checked to be sure. With a sigh, I held my spear up in front of the self-proclaimed priestess.

"Did they carry weapons like this?"

It blinked again, looking closely at the spear for the first time. "Where did you get that?"

"I came across bodies in blue robes."

The lizard's double eyelids squeezed shut. "How many?"

"Two. One in a chapel like this, and one in a hallway." I winced as the door almost popped *out* of its frame, battering my already aching shoulder. "I didn't stop to look for more."

"Ours is a small shrine, with only four guardians to accompany me," the lizard said, its feminine voice now flat and small. "And if the other two were still alive, they would already be here."

"What does that mean for us?"

"That you chose a poor location to take refuge in. The shell of a kresshac," it added, nodding to the door, "is durable but has its limits. And when it breaks, it will be the pair of us against a monster out of the mountains. I do not know what gods your kind pray to, with Corros and his ilk long banished, but I suggest you begin doing so now."

Kresshac? Corros? Once again, I understood *most* of the words the lizard was saying, but that didn't do anything to help me parse their meaning. "You're saying you guys *didn't* summon this thing? How the hell has a creature like that made Ohio its home without any hunters noticing? And what mountains are you even talking about?"

"I have never heard of an Oh-hi-oh," it told me, "but the Ironscale Ridge is less than a seven-day's ride to our north. How… how do you not know that? Your nation's lands sat just beyond those mountains until you became refugees seeking sanctuary in our primacy!"

"I'm starting to think," I said slowly, "that you're *not* cultists who kidnapped me off of Midton's streets while I was high on brownies."

"Cultists?!" Any questions I'd had about the lizard's gender were put to rest by the amount of scorn and indignity that it—no, *she*—managed to lace into that single word. "We are the scions of Synos, the Father and Creator! We trace the lineage of our civilization back to pre-Framework days when your kind were still learning to wield tools and fire. In fact, it was you humans, the *children of Corros,* who—"

A loud snap interrupted her tirade. We turned to the door we'd been bracing and saw that a wide crack had appeared in the glossy shell. The next blow sent that crack spreading outward in multiple directions.

Time was running out.

"The door will not hold," she told me, outrage already forgotten. "Take a position to the left. When the creature breaks through, I will attempt to blind it from the right. You… see if you can strike while it is distracted. I can only pray that your skill in the spear will prove sufficient."

It sounded like a *horrible* plan… but given that it was mostly my fault we were facing certain death, I didn't argue. I waited on one side of the door, glancing at the lizard woman across from me. I couldn't read any emotions on her strange, scaled face, but I'd worked retail for half my life, and her body language said she was as scared as I was.

"I don't know what's going on," I admitted, "let alone where we are or how I got here, but I'm sorry I ruined your hiding spot. And that all I have is a spear instead of something high caliber with a bucket of ammunition."

"And I regret that the Shrine of the Family could not be a sanctuary for you in its final days. For either of us," she amended. "I am Miko Nesari, priestess and shrine keeper. May Aurea guide your spirit to its rest."

"Brian," I replied. "Brian Fieldings. And I don't know who or what Aurea is, but I'll take any help I can get."

Before she could reply, the door exploded inward. Fragments of shell blasted past us and into the otherwise empty chapel and the candlesticks we'd used to block that door clattered to the ground, one of them warped beyond recognition. The monster surged inside, crushing the small cabinet into so many splinters, and I finally got a good look at what had been hunting us.

It was straight out of a horror film, all gruesome, glistening practical effects instead of CGI. Its lower body was segmented and insectile, with dozens of spear-like legs on each side acting like oars on a boat to push the squirming mass forward. Instead of the expected, if horrifically oversized, upper thorax and head, the creature's top half looked like something between a bear and a cougar… if that unholy hybrid had then been skinned and dipped in acid. Multi-jointed arms, as pale as maggots, jutted from its chest, ending in hooked claws, and a bulging expanse of way too many eyes of varying sizes and shapes crowned the upper hemisphere of the creature's misshapen head.

I could *feel* the moment those eyes locked on me and the weapon in my hands. Its maw dropped open, revealing multiple rows of needle-sharp teeth.

The hell beast rushed forward but Miko was there, charging in from the flank to thrust a clawed hand toward the vastly larger beast's face. Given their respective heights, I could tell that her attack would come up woefully short, but something impossible happened: a small whorl of glowing white appeared at the center of her outstretched palm. That light flew forward, as if borrowing Miko's momentum. and struck the creature's hideous face, blossoming into an eruption of brilliance.

Even shielded from the worst of the effects by the monster's own body, I was half blinded. Thankfully, the creature had it so much worse. It rose onto its rear segments, head scraping the chapel's high ceiling and forelegs waving wildly in the air.

I didn't know what Miko had done, let alone how, but I recognized the opportunity she'd given me. Blinking tears from my squinting eyes, I rushed forward and drove my borrowed spear into the creature's underbelly.

The weapon was every bit as awkward to wield as it had been to run with, and I didn't honestly expect to hit anything. Jefferson High hadn't offered electives in medieval weaponry, after all… probably for the best, given the sheer number of assholes in our student body. Still, the sluthari was temporarily blinded and even more temporarily frozen *and* it was roughly the size of a Vanagon.

My spear pierced the pale, fleshy mass of its belly and sank in all the way past the spearhead to the shaft.

The monster didn't seem to notice.

I kept pushing forward, trying to use my spear like a lever to flip the creature onto its armored back, but it was three times my size, four times my mass, and even now, had a stable base, thanks to all those legs. Basic physics was *not* on my side, and all I managed to do was drive my spear in a few more inches.

That and finally get the creature's attention.

I didn't see the legs that hit me, but I *felt* them… like two baseball bats—aluminum, not wooden—to my arm and chest. There was a noise of something snapping, like when the chapel door had exploded inward, and then I was soaring through the air.

I'm pretty sure I lost consciousness, somewhere mid-flight, but I woke right the hell back up again when I crashed into the nearest wall. Another bright flower of pain unfurled in my body to join the already colorful bouquet and I crumpled to the tiled floor, too stunned to even scream.

Twenty feet away, Miko was in full retreat. She was apparently all out of high-tech flashbang grenades but had recovered the least deformed of the two candlesticks and was waving the mangled thing about in front of her, trying to fend the monster off.

It went as poorly as my plan to flip the thing over.

The sluthari brushed aside the candlestick like it was a pool noodle, ripping it from Miko's hands and flinging it across the room.

The priestess ducked and rolled under a second leg, only for a third to drive down like a spike, sending her back the way she had come. Every move she made was answered by legs as tall as I was, and even my untrained eyes could see that the creature was boxing her in.

I looked at my spear, still protruding from the monster's underbelly. The shaft had snapped in two, and thick liquid was dripping down the embedded fragment to puddle on the floor. Maybe I hadn't done any serious damage, but I *had* hurt it. Our best chance— our *only* chance—rested with that spear and the wound that had already been made.

I needed to get up.

I needed to get over there.

I needed to—

The world went white as I rolled onto one side and every flower in my bouquet of pain opened its petals to scream bloody murder. By the time I could see again, Miko was pinned to the floor, two of the creature's forest of legs having snared the priestess by her brightly colored robes. The sluthari's segmented lower body scooted forward until its animal-like upper half loomed over the struggling lizard. Those two horrific upper arms reached downward.

Miko slashed at her own robes with her claws, cutting through the cloth that had her pinned, but before she could scoot away, the monster was there again, its legs forming a cage around the lizard as it almost languorously reached for her. It seemed to be savoring her struggle.

I'd never encountered a lizard person before, let alone a hell beast intent on eating them, but there was something distressingly familiar about the feeling that went through me as I lay there on my side and watched the monster draw out Miko's final moments. I'd spent years watching someone die, utterly helpless to stop it, and now, less than a week later, it was happening again.

Maybe it was that thought that gave me the strength to move again. Or maybe it was the reminder of Dad's final years and the ticking time bomb buried in my own genetic code. After all, what was something that breathed and bled—even something as monstrously alien as this—compared to the horrific inevitability of disease?

I forced myself up with my one functional arm, blinked away the whiteness that again threatened to swallow my vision, and staggered toward the desperately struggling Miko.

I was ten feet away when the monster paused, the lizard woman now suspended in the air before it like a dress it had been thinking of trying on. Its scarred, skinless head turned in my direction, a multitude of eyes narrowing and widening in jerky, out-of-sync patterns. It roared and spittle spattered the tile between us.

I didn't stop. With every step, I swayed from side to side like I was drunk, but the sluthari didn't notice or care. All that mattered to it was that *prey* was challenging its dominance, presenting a more obvious threat than the barely twitching body held in its claws.

A distant voice in my mind was left to wonder exactly *how* I'd deduced any of that information. While I had watched my fair share of nature specials with Dad and Bug, National Geographic had never covered a beast like this.

Still, there seemed to be something to it; the sluthari dropped Miko and spun on me with another roar. The self-titled priestess was in motion as soon as she hit the floor, crab walking backwards in a scramble for safety.

This time, I did stop, all of my energy going to keeping my legs stable beneath me. As the sluthari charged toward me, my mind was nothing but static… curiously empty of emotion, let alone illusion. I could barely stand; there was no way in hell I'd be able to weave between the monster's many legs to reach the spear I'd left in its underbelly. But the longer I held the monster's attention, the more time Miko would have to reach the door and flee. She knew this shrine better than I did and seemed more mobile too. Of the pair of us, she had the only realistic chance of escape.

Given that part of me still believed she was the reason I was here, I wasn't sure why her survival mattered to me, but it did.

The only problem was… Miko didn't run. When the sluthari was almost upon me, she appeared right behind it, warped candlestick swinging down like the wrathful sledgehammer of an overly enthusiastic home renovator on demo day.

To the dismay of every would-be DIYer, the jury-rigged weapon bounced right off the armored carapace of the monster's lower half. Still, her blow distracted the sluthari yet again, giving me just enough time to stumble out of its path. It wheeled about, lower body coiling in upon itself so that its forward momentum transferred into that spin, and just that fast, the sluthari was headed back toward me. Miko scrambled to flank it, but this time, the beast refused to be distracted, ignoring the priestess and her makeshift club.

It roared as it came forward and I roared back, putting everything I'd bottled up over my life into that yell. Eight years of being part student and caretaker, twelve years of shocked realization since the initial diagnosis, twenty years since I was old enough to understand that Mom had left for good. Rage and grief and pain, all of it justified, but also resentment, hatred, and contempt, along with the self-loathing that had always swiftly followed those last sentiments.

The sluthari came toward me like an avalanche, and I held my ground, my one working hand bunched into a fist, as if punching the thing would work where actual weapons had failed. I was yelling a mix of obscenities and nonsense when I threw the looping overhand right that had gotten me suspended twice in high school, a desperate power-bomb that didn't have a prayer of even making the monster flinch—

—only to find myself airborne again, a fraction of a second before the sluthari's arrival, as someone or something tossed me away as easily as if I was a child.

I dropped and rolled, my roar morphing into yet another scream as the pain from that landing radiated out through what were almost definitely broken bones. This time, the sound of my pain was drowned out by something else, high-pitched and discordant, like a dozen tea kettles left to boil.

The sluthari was screaming.

A stranger stood before the monster, as wide as a linebacker and at least two feet taller. They were dressed in grey robes, but torchlight shone off blue scales so dark they were almost black. They held a spear in their hands, and both warrior and weapon were moving almost too quickly to see, batting aside insectile legs with a bone-crushing force that put Miko and my attacks to shame.

The monster reeled back from the frenzied assault, and the spear wielder stepped forward smoothly into the vacated space. One clawed hand pointed toward the recoiling sluthari, while the other pulled the spear back, as if chambering a bullet in a gun.

Light coalesced around a spearhead as dark as the starless night, and for a moment, the world went still: the hard, gleaming light I couldn't explain, the length of shadow in the shape of a spear, a faint smell of ozone and blood, and a lone fighter facing down a monster out of H.R. Giger's nightmares.

The world took a breath. The spear flashed forward.

The sluthari's second scream was somehow even worse than the first, so piercing that I covered my ears with my only working arm to block it out. When the sound finally faded, the monster was writhing on its armored back. More than half of its far-too-many legs were broken, splayed out to the side, and the newcomer rode its undulating underbelly like a surfer navigating the gentlest of swells.

The dark spear lanced down a half-dozen more times, opening effortless, bloody wounds in the creature's thick skin as the wielder walked their way up the insectile lower body to the bestial upper half. The sluthari's clawed arms offered even less of a defense than its multitude of legs, and a final ruinous thrust buried the spear right in the center of the cluster of eyes.

A few legs continued to jerk and sway, but I'd come across enough dead centipedes in my life to recognize post-mortem twitching when I saw it.

3

The spear-wielder turned to the chapel's doorway where a slightly smaller robed shadow appeared. "Sergeant Loris, send Berys in. Not everyone is dead, praise Kal." Their voice was brisk and deep, the kind that would carry over a crowd at ballgames. From the sound of that voice, I was guessing they were male, although the reptilian features made it almost impossible to know for sure. "Then take a few scouts from the claw and make sure the rest of the shrine is clear."

"At your command, Wind Walker." The figure bowed and left.

A dozen feet from me, Miko's gasp was audible. She scrambled to her feet, robes in tatters around her scaled form, and offered a bow of her own, scaled face contorting with the pain of her movement.

The lizard who had just been named Wind Walker waved away the show of deference. "We are in the field, shrine keeper. Save the formalities for Whitehall. Are you hurt?"

"A few cracked scales and maybe a bone or two as well," managed Miko. She remained hunched over, her voice breathy as the lizard version of adrenaline drained from her body. "I thought we were dead—"

"And yet you survived and having done so, will grow that much stronger under the gaze of the Father and his children," rumbled the big lizard. Eyes a blue only slightly lighter than his scales turned to me. "As for you, young Nor… I have seen acts of bravery in the face of certain doom—far too many, as of late—but this is the first time I can recall seeing anyone face down a charging sluthar without even a weapon."

Sluthar instead of *sluthari.* I didn't know if Miko had misnamed the monster, or if the latter was the plural form of the word. Either way, I was struggling with my own adrenaline dump and too weak and pained to do much more than shrug my only working shoulder.

"I am Riok Diocil, called Wind Walker by some, and leader of the 9th Claw, on detachment from Fort Ilcindal. We were headed for Whitehall when we came across tracks out of the mountains." He slapped a heavy fist to his chest, ringing off some sort of metal armor under his robes, and gave a bow that was significantly shallower than Miko's. "We met and destroyed most of the sluthari in battle two days ago but have spent the time since hunting down the survivors. I regret that we were so late in arriving to eliminate the last."

It took a moment for the words to sink in, and then I felt my eyes widen, surprise momentarily drowning out the pain. "There was more than one of these things?"

"Much like gyr beasts, the sluthari travel in packs," said Miko, handling her own injuries far better than I was.

"The unnaturally long winter has driven them down from the mountains," explained Riok. "Even the northern forts have suffered the occasional assault. Now, may I have the pleasure of your name, brave Nor, that I might spread the tale of your valiant stand?"

There was nothing threatening about his body language or demeanor, but the combination of size, alien nature, and the spear he'd used to shish kebab a minivan-sized monster had me nervous.

"I'm Brian," I finally said, "Brian Fieldings. But I don't know what a Nor is."

The lizards lacked any of the facial tics that I'd become accustomed to when deciphering a person's reactions, but Riok seemed confused as he cocked his head. "I did not think there were any other children of Corros on this continent."

"I don't know who or what that is either."

"Just as we synossians are the mortal children of Synos, you humans are considered the sons and daughters of Corros," said Miko, her tone almost scholarly. "The Nor are—or were—a nation of your people."

It was the second time Miko had used the word *synossian*. If that's what they called themselves, I'd need to remember it. And it was probably less offensive than calling them lizards. "So, *children of Corros* means anyone who looks like me? Humans?"

If anything, Riok's puzzlement only grew, but he nodded anyway. He turned to Miko, and something vaguely sibilant colored his words. "I apologize that I do not know your name—"

"Miko Nesari, honored Wind Walker." Her voice had adopted that same sibilance. I couldn't tell if the two lizards had simply given up on enunciating their words or if something else was going on. Either way, it was strange.

"Shrine Keeper Nesari, who is this person who is ignorant of even the most rudimentary of things? How and when did he come to seek refuge in your shrine?"

"I do not know," she told him. "He was running from the sluthar when I pulled him into Aurea's chapel." She paused, and her tone went flat. "He was running *toward* the exit when I found him, which means he came from deeper in the shrine."

"Perhaps he had been hiding within? But if so, why? With respect, I would not feel comfortable leaving you with someone who could well be a madman or liar."

"I woke up on some kind of altar," I told them through gritted teeth, any positive feelings towards Riok vanishing in a fresh wave of pain. "In a pitch-black room a few hallways away. And if you're going to call me a liar or a lunatic, you should at least do so where I can't hear you."

Both lizards had gone still, Miko's eyes so wide that the orange dominated her face. Her inner eyelids flicked up and down in a spastic twitch.

"You speak the High Tongue?" asked Riok, the sibilance gone from his words.

"I don't know what that is either."

"It is one of our primacy's two main languages," said Miko, "the other being Common. While the second language is used by each of the seven nations, the High Tongue is generally known *only* to our people."

My latest attempt at a shrug sent more pain racing through my body. Either these two were running an elaborate con on me, or something very odd was going on. Synos? Corros? Nor? Some sort of primacy? It was starting to feel like *I* was the alien here, which made the question of how I'd arrived even more urgent.

That said, the armed lizard staring at me took priority.

"I'm sorry," I said. "I'm not sure what's going on exactly. Like I said, I woke up on some sort of rough stone altar in the darkness. I ran into the sluthari—sluthar?—as I was trying to find a way out."

Miko was still looking at me like I'd told her the sky wasn't blue. Which, I suddenly realized, it might *not* be to lizard eyes.

And wasn't *that* the sort of thing to blow a man's mind?

"An altar in a fully dark room? The chapel of Synos?"

I shrugged, not knowing the answer. As far as I could remember, there hadn't been any signs posted.

"Before that, where were you, Brian Fieldings?" asked Riok.

"I…" For the first time since the battle, my brain kicked into action. There was something solid about Riok, something that made me want to trust him, but I didn't know him or Miko at all. Telling a bunch of apparently militant lizard aliens too much might have dire ramifications and the last thing I needed was to end up on a lab table somewhere, being dissected by instruments every bit as sharp as that spear.

"I don't remember," I said instead. It wasn't hard to adopt a confused expression, given the circumstances. "I just woke up… and…"

"You said something about an Oh-hi-Oh when we first met," said Miko, "and accused me of being a cultist."

Crap. So I had. "Did I? I'm sorry. I was confused and… well… scared, I guess. If I've ever met one of your kind before, I must have forgotten it."

"Along with many other things, apparently," concluded Riok. "I have seen it happen with head trauma. When Berys arrives, he will do what he can to assist."

"Thank you." I swallowed and asked the all-important question. "Where are we?"

"In the northern reaches of the Synossian Primacy," said Riok.

"And that's…"

"On the southern shores of the continent of Issandryl." When I stared at him blankly, he continued. "Which you have clearly never heard of either. Do you at least remember Eos?"

For some reason, the name struck a chord, but damned if I knew why. "Yes? I think? What *is* Eos, exactly?"

There was a moment of silence.

"It is the shining jewel in the gods' cosmic collection," Riok finally said. "The home of all who live in its soil, soar on its winds, or navigate its seas."

It took me a bit to parse my way through language way more figurative than anything I'd heard in Midton, but once I had, I just stood there in shocked silence. Eos was a *planet.* I was on an entirely different *world.*

This was *not* how I'd expected to spend my weekend.

"Wind Walker? You sent for me?" Another synossian entered the chapel, pale eyes taking in the three of us in a single glance. His voice was deep, but he lacked Riok's sheer size and gravitas.

"Berys, yes. Please see to the wounds of Shrine Keeper Nesari and her… guest, Brian Fieldings."

The newcomer crossed over to a barely upright Miko. He raised both hands, palms cupped and hovering above her midsection. Light manifested out of nowhere to bathe the shrine maiden in soft hues of lavender. A moment later, the light was gone, but Miko stood straight, no longer pained by the blow she'd taken to her side.

Riok had told Berys to see to our wounds, but I'd expected him to be some kind of field medic. I *hadn't* expected the lizard to stand there and heal Miko without even touching her. And yet, I'd just seen it with my own eyes. Either the lizards' technology was so advanced that their tools operated on a microscopic level—and given that they were wearing armor and wielding medieval weapons, that seemed unlikely—or Berys had cast an honest-to-God *spell.*

Between the healing, the flashbang Miko had made from nothing, and whatever the hell it was that Riok had done with his spear to end the fight, one thing was quickly becoming clear:

On Eos, magic was real.

○○○

Miko waved Berys off when the healer went to recast his spell of healing. "I am able to treat the remainder of my wounds," she told him. "Please see to the—to Brian Fieldings."

I eyed the healer warily as he approached. Berys was a full head shorter than Riok, and half the other synossian's width, with heavy leathers under his robe instead of metal armor, but he still loomed over me like a giant facing a toddler. "What are you going to do?"

"As a Priest of the Pure, I have been granted some small measure of Etriska's power," said Berys, his voice soft.

Behind him, Riok snorted. "*Small measure*, he says. Such humility is unwarranted, Berys. Kal teaches us that there is no sin in justly earned pride."

"And Etriska teaches that there is strength in softness, Wind Walker. Perhaps one day you will give it a try." Berys' words were mild, and when Riok snorted a second time, something told me this was an argument the two had carried on many times before. He turned back to me, pale grey eyes scanning my form. "How significant are your injuries?"

I pointed at my injured arm, wincing as the motion sent pain through ribs that had to be at least cracked. "I think my arm is broken, and something's wrong with my ribs too. Other than that, it's mostly just cuts and scratches."

"The son of Corros also suffers from memory loss," said Riok.

"I will treat that last," said Berys, casually invading my space as he bent to bring his face within a few inches of mine. Like Riok, Berys' scales were blue, but a paler blue that only slowly darkened as they moved from the faint suggestion of a lizard-like snout toward his shoulders and neck.

"No blood on the lips or in the breath," he murmured to himself, forked tongue tasting the air. "Your lungs appear to be intact. Still, even *Light Healing* will not suffice for injuries of this nature."

He looked to Riok for some reason, receiving a slow nod in return, then took a step back and raised his hands—four fingers and a thumb, just like mine, if tipped with dangerously sharp claws and covered in pebble-like scales. Before I could think to flinch, light washed over me, sweeping away first my tension and then my pain. I could feel my bones literally knitting themselves back together but for some reason, that sensation didn't disturb me.

When it was done, I took my first full breath in minutes. "I don't know who Etriska is," I told him. "But thank you and thank him."

"*She* is the youngest of Synos' celestial children," said Berys, bowing. "And has no doubt already heard your thanks."

"Great." From what I gathered, Synos was the head god of their people. That made a celestial child… what? A younger god? A demigod? A high-ranking church functionary? Given my own non-relationship with the Catholic God back home, I wasn't sure what to think.

The healer held out his hands again, but this time positioned them to either side of my head. Both sets of Berys' eyelids closed, and the glow that coalesced about me was brighter than any halogen bulb. After a moment, he let his hands fall away.

"If there is a physiological root to your memory loss, it is beyond my ability to heal." He took a step away and gave me a small bow. I wasn't sure if I was just projecting, but it *seemed* apologetic.

"Is he healthy enough to travel?" asked Riok. Another lizard in grey—the Sergeant Loris that Riok had sent to search the shrine, I thought—had returned and now stood beside him.

"His injuries are healed," responded Berys, "though I would suggest an easier pace for what remains of the day. We are taking him with us to Whitehall? There are specialists in the church who might be able to help with his head trauma."

"We are taking them both," said Riok.

Miko twitched. "With respect, Wind Walker, my post is here. Mother gave me the assignment herself."

"Your guardians are dead," Riok told her, his tone kind even if the words were not. "And the primarch, blessed be her name, has issued a summons. The villagers you serve have already left for the capital; it is time that you do the same. The Voice would tell you the same thing, were she here in my stead."

Whatever words Miko had been about to say died on her forked tongue. She dropped her head in acknowledgment.

"What is Whitehall?" I asked. Miko had mentioned it once, before our near-death experience, but hell if I could remember what she'd said.

"It is our capital city and the ancestral seat of the primarch herself."

"And I'd be welcome there?" I didn't love the idea of going to an alien city, but after coming face to misshapen face with one of the things that roamed the countryside, a little civilization sounded pretty good.

"Refugees from the kingdom of Nor have swollen the city's population over the last few moons," said Riok. "You will not be the only child of Corros walking the streets, I promise."

"I see." This time, my shrug didn't hurt at all. As impossible as this whole situation seemed on the surface, it was feeling more and more real with each passing moment. "I have... a lot of questions."

"It is a full seven-day's travel to Whitehall," said Riok. "You will get your answers. For now, I ask that you assist Shrine Keeper

Naseri in collecting her things. Berys and I will wait for you below with the rest of the claw."

"I don't have much," said Miko, in a voice suddenly made small by fatigue.

"Then I suspect you will be swift."

4-Interlude

Riok waited until the sounds of the shrine keeper and her strange guest faded, then turned to the synossians at his side. "I would hear your thoughts."

"He lacks any wounds consistent with head trauma or memory loss," said Berys, words mild.

"A liar then?" said Riok. "Or a spy?"

"I found traces in Synos' chapel," said Sergeant Loris. "The human *did* emerge from within. Perhaps he first snuck in through the shrine to take up camp there, but…"

"But why?" Riok nodded, turning back to Berys. "Has Etriska shared any of her wisdom with you, old friend?"

"You know it does not work that way. The gods watch, they judge, and they bless, but they do not directly interfere. Not anymore." The Priest cocked his head, thick scaled ridges tightening around his eyes in a thoughtful expression. "This Brian Fieldings is flesh and blood. That much is clear. As for the rest? I know little more than you."

"If he is an agent of the Buried," warned Loris, "do we dare take him to Whitehall?"

"He would not be the first spy to sneak in amongst the greater mass of refugees."

"Even so…"

"What if he is not associated with the Buried at all?" countered Riok. "What if he is something more?"

"Something more—" Berys clicked his teeth shut, turning to look up at Riok, inner eyelid fluttering shut in a show of astonishment. "You think *he* might be Chosen?"

"It has been three moons since I watched the heads of our churches perform their ritual, and there has been no sign of the summoned savior. Now, a stranger appears on the altar of Synos himself, a child of Corros who knows nothing of us or this world and who wears apparel I do not recognize. I do not claim certainty, but the possibility exists."

"A Chosen appears, and *our* claw is the one to find him?" Berys sighed. "It has the makings of a quality story. However, the most potent lies are ever those we tell ourselves."

"Why would a Chosen need to be saved from a mere sluthar?" asked Loris.

Riok turned back to Berys, who shrugged.

"It is difficult to say. In the fullness of his power, such a minor creature would obviously provide little challenge, else he would be incapable of saving our people. But if he truly did just arrive from beyond the Veil, perhaps he has yet to be awoken? Perhaps his powers will remain unrealized potential until the Dreaming?"

"So, today's field mouse might wake up a cosmic devourer tomorrow?" Loris chewed on that idea like it was a stone to crack between his teeth.

"No one who faces a sluthar with only their clawless hands is a field mouse," said Riok. "Whatever else can be said of this Brian Fieldings, I will honor the courage of his stand."

"Unless he *is* an agent and was never truly under threat at all."

The Wind Walker paused and then tapped the scales of his left arm in acknowledgment of that reality. "Regardless, we have a full seven-day to determine whether he is spy, refugee, or something altogether greater. Loris, assign someone to observe him. Perhaps he will let more slip during the journey."

"What about the shrine keeper?" asked Berys. "Do we inform her of either our suspicions or our hopes?"

"No. Let her proceed in ignorance. Miko Naseri and Brian Fieldings have shed blood together and in doing so, formed a bond. She can serve as his guide to Eos. If he is what we hope, then she will only benefit from the association."

"And if he's not? She is but an acolyte, Riok. The risk—"

"Our people stand upon the precipice of annihilation, Berys." Riok's smile was as sharp and humorless as the spear at his side. "Every *breath* is a risk. At least the shrine keeper will have the protection of our claw nearby. It is more than most in these dark times can claim."

5

Miko's room was located off the hall where I'd encountered the second corpse and picked up my now-broken spear. The soldiers Riok had sent to search the shrine had apparently moved the body somewhere else, but the young synossian stiffened as she saw the pool of blood. For a long moment, she simply stood there in silence.

"Are you okay?" I asked.

She didn't answer, but my question broke her stasis. She moved to the third interior door, opening it to reveal a small cubby that made my bedroom back home look like a palace. Blankets were piled atop a rough cot made from strange, light-colored wood, and a simple chest built of that same wood took up most of the remaining available wall space.

Miko went to the chest, retrieved an empty pack from within, and started to shovel the chest's remaining contents into the pack, pausing to replace her tattered robe with a fresh one that was every bit as orange. She was done packing in a matter of moments, and I didn't know whether to be horrified or impressed.

"Is that all that you own?" Kate, my ex, had packed *three* suitcases just for a weekend visiting colleges on the East coast, whereas Miko's entire wardrobe wouldn't fill a single carry-on.

"Most of my possessions are kept back at the nest in Whitehall," she said, pulling the blankets from her cot and stuffing them into the pack on top of the clothing. "As an acolyte, I recently served a cycle in the field with the legions. Afterward, I was assigned further service at this shrine, where I could share the blessing of Aurea with nearby villages. It was deemed necessary to travel light."

I wasn't sure what a cycle was, but I mostly got the rest of what she was saying. "So, you usually live in Whitehall, but have been performing mandatory military and religious service abroad?"

"Precisely. Although it appears the latter has ended early." She slung the pack over one shoulder like it was an alien rucksack and gave me yet another look I couldn't interpret. "You truly do not know of this? Even Eos itself?"

"Like I said, the name sounds familiar somehow, but…"

"Do you even know what you are?"

"I'm a human." It took a moment but the phrase they'd all been using came to me. "A son of Corros, I guess, although I'm still not sure who Corros is."

"A betrayer," the lizard told me darkly. "Corros the Corrupted. The last of the Elder Gods and the worst. It was he whose actions broke the celestial peace as he struck down Synos the Creator and ignited a war that spanned the heavens and scoured the very surface of Eos."

"He killed your… god?"

She tapped her right arm with a scaled finger in a gesture that was probably supposed to mean something. "Deities cannot die—not truly—but Synos' consciousness was spread across the cosmos. He slumbers, every eon but an echo of his heartbeat."

"And Corros?"

"His bloody rebellion failed when the remaining Elder Gods joined forces with their offspring—Synos' celestial children among them—to fight back. Corros and those who sided with him were cast into the void between realities where they remain imprisoned to this day. The gods made a pact to end direct interference on Eos, lest another such war destroy what was left of their mortal creations."

"When you say celestial children—"

"I speak of Aurea the Dawn Maiden, Kal the Oathkeeper, and the twins, Etriska the Pure and Shan the Trickster. Each a Younger God, born of Synos' soul, and keepers of the pact with his people."

As mythologies went, theirs was at least somewhat inventive. It raised a bit of concern though.

"If the god of my people attacked the god of yours, does that mean we're enemies? Because I want to make it clear I wasn't a part of that."

Miko flashed sharp teeth at me, and I flinched before realizing it was a smile. "Of course you were not. These events occurred in the Age of Creation, when Eos itself was still young and the Framework had only just been built. You and the rest of your species have had eons to become your own people, forming a multitude of nations, some good, many evil. The Nor kingdom, of which I suspect you are a member, is our ally, or was before it fell upon hard times."

I relaxed slightly. Whatever was going on and however I'd gotten here, at least I wasn't public enemy number one. "What happened to them? The Nor, I mean?"

"The Wind Walker and his claw would be best equipped to tell that tale," she said, and despite our differences, I could hear the somber note that had entered her voice. "After all, they were there at the end."

"And we can trust him, right? It sounds like you know him?"

"I had never met Riok Diocil before today, but everyone knows *of* him, Brian Fieldings. He and his claw are legends. Heroes in a time where our peoples need them most." She waved a clawed hand to the door. "And we should not keep them waiting."

○○○

I *should* have had a hundred questions to ask as I followed Miko back through the shrine. Even more to the point, I should have been freaking the hell out, as befit someone who'd just almost died only to realize they were somehow on an alien planet. Instead, my emotions were curiously distant, my mind once again empty of anything but static, like a television without its digital antenna. Even forming a thought was a struggle. It wasn't until we'd passed the chapel where I'd first met Miko—empty now of even the sluthar's disgusting corpse—that I finally found my voice.

"I'm sorry about your… coworkers? The shrine guardians, I mean."

"As am I." She hunched her shoulders, as if to keep the pack from sliding off. "Had we been together—had I not hidden in the chapel of my goddess—perhaps things would have been different."

"Or maybe you'd have died along with them. And then I'd have joined the rest of you when the sluthar got tired of playing with its food."

"Perhaps." If my words had touched her at all, it wasn't apparent in her body language.

Two more turns brought us to a wide chamber and a pair of double doors that opened onto a cloud-stricken sky. It was almost shocking to realize how close I'd come to the exit in my panicked flight. Not that it really mattered. After seeing the monster's true speed, I knew I would never have made it to safety.

The entry room held the smashed remnants of tables and benches. Two more pools of blood marked where the final pair of Miko's shrine guardians must have fallen. Those bodies, too, had been removed, but a spear, the twin to the one I'd left broken and buried in the monster's underbelly, had been cast aside. I made a beeline for the weapon and picked it up. It felt every bit as unwieldy in my hands as the last one, but remained better than nothing.

I turned to find Miko staring at me.

"Is this okay… I mean… should I leave the spear behind?"

She shrugged, her voice still small. "Better that it sees use in the hands of the living than be buried with the dead, I suppose."

It wasn't the most enthusiastic of approvals, but if I was going to be stuck on Eos for any foreseeable length of time, I wanted a weapon. I kept the spear and followed Miko out into the open air.

The shrine had been built into the side of a steep hill, the embankment descending far below us to where a collection of lizards—synossians, I reminded myself—milled around what looked like horses. To one side, the bloody corpse of the sluthar had been discarded, and to the other, four bodies had been laid out and wrapped in blue robes.

I shivered, as much from the sight of the dead as from the cold wind that cut through my shredded sweats and t-shirt. It had been early summer in Ohio, but I could see snow in the distant peaks to my left, and the clouds hanging over us were thick and heavy, threatening a storm. There wasn't any clear sky for me to tell if it was blue or not, but the air was fresh and clean, crisp in a way that reminded me of camping trips with my dad when I was a child.

"Brian Fieldings?" I shook away my introspection and turned to find Miko back at the doors leading into the shrine. "Could you assist me in closing these? While I have a premonition that I will never return, I would still leave the Shrine of the Family protected from the creatures of the forest."

She didn't mention the wreckage or blood pools inside, and neither did I. Cleaning up both would take days, and by the looks of the preparations happening below us, we didn't have that sort of time. I set my spear aside and leant my weight and strength to pull the massive gates closed.

I'm not sure I added much to the effort, really.

"How are you so strong?" I asked, huffing and puffing as the second door boomed shut.

"Next to someone like the Wind Walker, I am a hatchling at best," said Miko. "But our people tend to be stronger than yours, just as some other species are hardier. It is simply the way of things. One might as well ask why the skyborn made for stronger Mages."

"Mages?" I asked, recovering my spear. "There are magic users as well as priests?"

"Of course. Pursuits both divine and arcane, although the energy which ultimately powers them both remains the same, of course."

I didn't really understand what *that* meant, but even with the empty fog that filled my brain, I knew one thing: in a world where magic was real, I absolutely wanted to be able to cast it.

"How do I become one?"

"How do—" Her mouth dropped open, exposing needle-sharp teeth, and her inner eyelids flicked up and down. After a moment, she shook her head. "You have forgotten even the Framework?"

It was the second time—at least—that I'd heard that word, and I still didn't know what it meant, but the way she said it told me it was important and probably capitalized. "Yes?"

"And yet you speak our languages as flawlessly as one born to them."

The spear in my hands made my shrug that much more awkward. "I know; it's weird. Still, anything you can tell me would be a huge help. Unless *this* is something I should hear from Riok too?"

She shook her head again. "Priest Berys, perhaps, but in truth, I was training to be a scholar before I was called to Aurea's service. This much I am suited to do. However," she added, hefting her pack back onto her shoulders, "we should walk as we speak."

I was happy to agree to that. It had to be warmer down below instead of up on the hill, exposed to what felt an awful lot like winter. As we began our descent, I picked my steps with care, all too conscious of my bare feet and the rocky terrain.

"Before we discuss the Framework," said Miko, adopting a vaguely professorial demeanor, "can you bring up your personal record?"

"My what?"

She did the double-blink again but didn't bother asking the questions I could almost see in her strange, sclera-less eyes. "Simply will it and it should appear before you, like a scroll in the air that only you can see."

I waited for one of her sharp-toothed smiles, but it never came. Apparently, this *wasn't* a joke? As we picked our way down the steep hill, I did my best to follow her directions.

Nothing happened.

"Maybe I'm not doing it right," I said after a minute of futility.

"There is no trick to the action. It should just happen." She slipped on a loose rock in the soil, then shot me a look as she readjusted her pack. "You are the first Nor I have ever met. Are you of age among your people?"

"I'm sorry?"

"The Dreaming occurs upon reaching adulthood. On the eve of our tenth cycle, we sleep. When we wake, our initial path has been set. As a newly awoken Aspirant, we are then finally able to view our own record."

"I don't... know what to say," I said. "Or what most of that means. I'm an adult, yeah, but I'm not even sure what a cycle is."

"A cycle consists of eleven moons, each of which is made up of five seven-days."

"And a seven-day is… seven days?" It seemed obvious, but I wasn't going to take anything for granted.

"Each of which consists of thirty glasses, yes."

"And a glass is…?"

"It has been roughly a glass since we first met."

Which meant a glass was about an hour… or close enough to count as one in the absence of watches or phones. So, a day was thirty hours long? And a moon was thirty-five of those days, but a *year* was only eleven moons long instead of twelve. That meant a cycle was…

I did the mental math, aided significantly by the fact that I'd been doing our household budget since I was twelve. I was pretty sure ten cycles would be roughly equivalent to thirteen years on Earth. That meant I was *definitely* of age. The math to figure out my actual age in Eos-units was a little bit trickier, but…

"I think I'm about eighteen cycles old," I finally concluded, wincing as I stepped on another rock. By that time, we were a quarter of the way down the hill, and I was starting to think I'd be lucky if my feet were intact by the time we reached the bottom. Still, I appreciated that Miko had stayed quiet, letting me run the calculations on my own.

"If that is the case, you should have had your Dreaming long ago." I had no hope of interpreting the glance she shot my way, so I just ignored it. "Perhaps Priest Berys will have a better idea of what might be wrong. In the meantime, I can at least explain the theory behind the Framework."

"Please. You said you studied to be a scholar?"

"Yes. When Aurea chose me to be one of her clergy, those plans changed, of course." She paused. "I apologize in advance if any of this seems condescending or overly rudimentary. Without knowing exactly what you know—"

"Don't worry about it. Just assume I know nothing at all. About the Framework or even Eos in general."

"Very well." She shifted her pack to her other shoulder and held up three fingers. "We are taught that reality consists of three separate realms. They all exist beside one another but do not overlap. The first is that of the physical. It contains what you see, what you think, and what you feel. Eos and all its mortal creatures, yes, but also the many stars in the sky. Life in all its grief and triumph."

"What about the second?"

"It is the realm of the spirit. As sentient beings, a piece of us exists in that second realm as well, the piece that extends beyond mortality, that accepts and absorbs the lessons of each of our lives before it births the next."

The latter bit of that sounded a lot like reincarnation, which meant…

"Are you talking about souls?"

"The portion of each individual that is eternal, yes. So, that much you *do* remember?"

I coughed. "I guess I'm familiar with the general concept." Whether I *believed* in that concept was a whole different question entirely. "But how does it work?"

"Which part?"

"Well, if I have a soul—" A big if, in my opinion, but that was neither here nor there. "—but it's not part of this realm… how is it even mine? And for that matter, is the spiritual realm just kind of a big, formless amoeba of people energy?"

Miko lit up in a way I hadn't yet seen, her reptilian features coming to life. "I asked the same question when I was a hatchling! The truth is that none of us really know *what* the spiritual realm looks like. What we do know is that, even before the Framework, we were connected to our souls. Metaphysically connected, that is. Upon death, when the connection to a mortal shell was severed, some portion of life experience was transmitted back to the soul, and when the person was born again, their new life would reflect those changes."

So instead of the body being a container for the soul, it was just a temporary puppet with a pipeline back to it? That prompted all sorts of weird imagery in my still-fuzzy brain, but I nodded to show I was following along. "So, if I learn a lot in this life, I might be more academically capable in my next one?"

"That is how it was believed to work, yes. The creation of the Framework changed all of that."

By that point, we were at the base of the hill, and rock had given way to a clay that was far less painful on my aching soles. A few of Riok's men turned our way as we approached. What I had taken for horses ended up being almost as alien as the sluthar—or the synossians themselves. They were strange beasts with equine heads but fur instead of hair and six legs rather than four. In place of hooves, they had enormous paws, and claws that dug furrows in the reddish clay. Only the fact that they were grazing placidly on the surrounding grass kept my fight-or-flight instincts from kicking into overdrive.

As we arrived, Riok appeared before us, his presence an almost physical weight that seemed even more impressive—if not *oppressive*—out in the open space.

"Brian Fieldings," he said, "am I correct in assuming that you are unfamiliar with the dalysi?" It was another word I'd never heard before, but context—and the fact that he was pointing to the six-legged mounts—made translation simple.

"I don't remember seeing them before," I admitted.

"Then I will have you ride with Shrine Keeper Naseri." He waved over a synossian with a massive round shield strapped to their back over grey robes. "Niaci will see you to your dalys and provide more appropriate traveling garb."

"My honor, Wind Walker," said the other synossian in a voice that was feminine despite its deep tones. She offered Miko and me a shallow bow and escorted us to a mount with tiger stripes in grey and black. It already had both a saddle and saddlebags; Niaci reached into the latter to pull out a grey robe that matched what the rest of the claw was wearing.

"It will be… somewhat large for you," she warned me, "but should at least be warmer than your current apparel."

"I'm used to things being too big; I'll take whatever I can get." I pulled the robe on over my head. Excess fabric pooled around me like I was a child trying on his parents' clothes, but the change in warmth more than made up for it. "Thank you."

She glanced down at my previously exposed feet and shook her oversized alien head. "While I know your people are accustomed to having footwear, I fear we do not have anything to suit you. However, we will be stopping for the night at one of the villages along our route; perhaps they will have supplies more suitable for one of your kind."

"That would be great." Now that we had stopped, my feet were *really* beginning to hurt. I didn't think I'd actually cut them or anything, but hiking down a hill barefoot in winter hadn't been fun either.

"Oh!" said Miko, coming closer. "I did not even think of your feet being unprotected. Allow me."

Before I could react, she had placed a clawed hand against my chest. The light that came as she focused was a far cry from what I'd seen with Berys' spell, but the warmth that swept through my body was the same. When she dropped her hand, my feet no longer hurt. In fact, the slight ache in my muscles from walking down uneven terrain was gone too.

"That's still incredible," I muttered.

"What is?"

I looked up to find both Miko and Niaci looking at me, the young priestess dwarfed by the soldier beside her, for all that she was at least six feet tall by Earth measurements.

"Healing."

"Do your kind's remaining gods not grant healing techniques?" asked Niaci, dark eyes intent on my face.

"I… don't know?"

"He doesn't remember," supplied Miko.

"I see." Niaci cocked her head, then shrugged. "Now that you are both here, we will be departing shortly. Be warned: our claw rarely stops unless it is to make camp. If you get hungry or thirsty along the way, you will find travel rations and a waterskin in your saddlebags."

"We are grateful, Shieldbearer Niaci." Miko offered a bow that was considerably deeper than the one we'd merited.

"Just Niaci." The larger synossian gave us the terrifying expression that I was starting to see as their species' version of a smile. "I prefer to leave the titles—and the responsibility—to those like Riok and Loris."

"That's Sergeant Loris to you, Niaci, unless you want ditch duty *yet again* tonight." The synossian who had originally accompanied Riok into the shrine passed by us on his way to another mount, moving quietly for all that he was built like a brick wall and clearly wearing armor beneath his robes.

"Sir, yes sir," said Niaci, banging a clawed fist against her own metal breastplate. She dropped her voice as she watched him go. "I swear, that one's got the hearing of a gyr-beast and almost as much stealth. Kal should have made him a Rogue instead of a Warrior." She shook herself, almost like a wet dog, and turned back to Miko and me. "Let's get the two of you mounted so that we can be on our way."

The dalys—apparently the singular form of *dalysi* in something even I was starting to recognize as a pattern—was larger than any horse

I'd ever seen, with a back so broad that my thighs ached just looking at it. Thankfully, it stayed calm and quiet as Niaci helped first Miko and then me up onto its back. My borrowed spear slid through a series of leather loops that kept it from tangling with the creature's many legs. The saddle was—just barely—large enough to accommodate two, but it left me pressed up against Miko from behind.

As the only one of us who had any experience riding at all, let alone on a furred beast like this, I was more than happy to have her be responsible for driving. Or… whatever it was called.

"We won't be traveling at full speed on account of your recent healings," said Niaci, "but if the pace still proves too fast for comfort, let me know. I will send word up the chain of command. We can't have either of you falling out of the saddle."

I carefully avoided looking toward the ground. I wasn't afraid of heights, but it was a very, very long way down. And if I fell beneath the dalys' giant paws, I'd probably be dead before Miko even realized anything had happened.

Around us, the rest of the claw mounted up, leaving only Riok and Berys on foot. The pair approached the shrine guardian bodies that had been laid in the grass. Berys bowed his scaled head, and upended a metal flask, splashing the four corpses with its contents.

"Blessed firewater," explained Miko. "For when the full funeral rites cannot be performed."

If we'd been on Earth, I would have assumed that *firewater* meant alcohol, and would have questioned the purpose of pouring it over the dead. But we were on an alien planet, and one that had magic… as far as I knew, the name might be literal.

If it was, the fire part needed a bit of external assistance. Berys tucked the flask into his bag and pulled out a metal rod and a block of black stone. Scraping the two together generated a surprising quantity of sparks, and those sparks cascaded down onto the now-drenched corpses. Moments later, flames ignited, blue instead of orange.

"May their souls serve forever in Kal's immortal legion," murmured Niaci, her words echoed by the mounted soldiers around us. "May their strength find its way back to this land and our people."

"Watch over them, Bright Lady," added Miko, in a voice so quiet I could barely hear it even pressed against her back. "They were brave men and women, stalwart and true."

I didn't say anything, but simply lowered my head, one hand brushing the spear I'd claimed as my own.

The strangely colored fire burned fast and didn't spread. Barely a minute had passed before the bodies were gone and the flames had guttered out. Berys bowed a second time and headed for his mount. Riok stayed a moment longer, murmuring words I couldn't parse. When he finally turned away, his hard blue eyes swept across the force assembled around him, carrying a weight that had even the dalysi shifting where they stood.

I shivered, despite the warmth of my robe. I didn't know what Riok had done to earn his title—or Miko's awe—but the man had an aura about him that was practically tangible. Even if I *hadn't* seen him easily slaughter a monster straight out of my nightmares, even if I'd met him under better, happier circumstances, something told me I'd have known, soul deep, that he wasn't someone to mess with.

I really, really didn't want to end up on his bad side.

6

We were underway soon after, fifteen armed synossians, one human in grey robes, and the shrine keeper in crimson and orange. I spent the first twenty minutes of that ride wishing Niaci had strapped me down like our saddlebags. The dalys' strange gait had me pitching from side to side and a part of me was convinced I was going to fall off entirely.

"It appears you were not a rider before you lost your memory," said Miko, speaking over her shoulder.

"I guess not." I was doing my best to mimic her riding motions while giving her as much personal space as I could. It was going about as well as predicted.

She reached back and pulled one of my hands forward to wrap around her midsection. "You will want to hold on and move as my body does. If Niaci's warnings were correct, we will be moving at a greater speed soon."

I did as instructed, trying to ignore how *different* the woman in front of me looked and felt, from the lack of ears on the side of her head, to the firmness of scales under my hand, noticeable even through the thick robe's many layers. I held on tightly and tried to sync my movements with hers.

Eventually, I found a groove… or at least no longer felt like I was going to be tossed off the dalys' back with every stride. I was finally able to spare attention for the countryside we were traveling through: hills and stone, for the most part, without a tree to be seen. The air was clean, but thicker than I was used to in Ohio, somehow humid while still cold. The dalys covered an inordinate amount of ground as it ran, claws leaving deep channels in a ground that, save for the stiff stalks of grass cropping up here and there, seemed more clay than dirt. Above us, the sun remained hidden behind increasingly dark and heavy clouds.

It clearly wasn't *home*—the lack of trees told me that much—but it was still hard to believe I was in another world. Frankly, it was easier to think of the synossians and other creatures as aliens visiting Earth. First contact without the anal probes.

Except that Earth didn't have magic.

Our mount was quieter than it would have been with hooves instead of paws, but I still had to raise my voice to be heard. "You were telling me about the Framework?"

"I was, yes." Miko gently disengaged my hands from around her waist and then, in a move that would have had circus performers back home applauding, pulled her knees up to her chest and spun about on the back of the moving dalys. When she was done, she was facing me and now riding our mount backwards.

I blinked, so startled that *I* would have fallen off if she hadn't reached out to steady me. "That's a neat trick. How did you learn to do that?"

"As I said, I served in the legions for a cycle. While much of that time was spent behind the walls of my fort, I also joined my assigned claw on patrol. Riding is a skill like any other, and I was fortunate enough to gain it. I would not want to attempt such a maneuver at higher speed, but at our current pace, it was simple enough."

I would have to take her word for it. I peeked over her shoulder. Our mount didn't have reins, nor did it seem to care that its primary rider was now facing the wrong direction. Instead, it loped along, following the path set by the other dalysi.

"Hopefully, I can learn from your example," I said. The saddle wasn't designed for us to sit facing each other, but even with me doing my best to keep our legs from tangling, it was a hell of a lot easier to talk face-to-face.

"With luck, you will, soon after your Dreaming."

I didn't understand the correlation and said as much.

"We were talking about the soul, yes?"

"Yeah." My head was mush, a combination of exhaustion and mental fog, but that conversation was still fresh in my mind. "And the idea that it grows with each physical incarnation."

"With each death," she corrected, "although that growth then manifests in the next life."

I nodded. It seemed like the same thing, but she would know better than me. "And you said the Framework changed that somehow?"

"Yes. As I mentioned, our legends speak of a time before the Framework, where an individual's capacity for growth was limited by their physical forms. True advancement occurred only upon death and rebirth, and even then, the gains were small at best. It was during this time that the Elder Gods looked upon Eos and saw their peoples struggling to survive against beasts and monsters both stronger and more numerous than they. Synos proposed the change, but it took all the Elder Gods together—even your own—to create the Framework." She held my gaze with her strange orange eyes. "Its purpose was two-fold. First, it strengthened the connection between body and soul, allowing for information and energy to be conveyed bidirectionally between the two."

She gave me time to puzzle over that one.

"Meaning someone doesn't have to die for their soul to get stronger?" I guessed.

"Or be reborn for that growth to be transferred back to the mortal shell, yes."

That… seemed impossible… even *if* I bought into the existence of souls in general.

"The second purpose of the Framework," continued Miko, "was to both amplify and quantify that growth, channeling the energy into defined pathways with outsized, real-world impacts."

"You lost me there," I said. "It did *what?*"

"Riding is a perfect example," she said. "I gained the skill during my initial training for the legions. As I continue to practice, that experience strengthens my soul, and the Framework interprets that growth into something concrete and measurable: an improvement in my riding skill."

I still didn't get it, and if Miko had been any more familiar with human expressions than I was with synossian ones, I was pretty sure she'd have realized as much. Learning skills and improving on them was a fundamental part of human existence. And synossian, presumably. What did the *soul,* or this *Framework,* have to do with anything?

"Skills are, of course, merely a single thread in the tapestry," said the shrine keeper, "although my teachers would argue they are the foundation for all the rest. Classes, levels, techniques, professions… even traits and titles are a part of the progression system that the Framework established. Thanks to it, our capacity for personal growth is almost limitless."

I seized upon a few of the words that stood out. "When you say classes and levels…"

"I mean exactly that. I am a fourth-level Priestess of Aurea. At my level, the Bright Lady has granted me two of her blessings as techniques or spells, *Flare* and *Minor Healing*."

I was guessing Bright Lady was another title for Aurea, the goddess she worshipped. "*Minor Healing* is what you cast to fix my feet… and *Flare* is the thing you used on the sluthar back at the shrine?"

"Yes. We achieve level one in whatever class we are granted during the Dreaming and receive our first technique. *Flare* was mine, whereas I was able to select *Minor Healing* upon reaching level three."

Huh. "But how do you level?"

"Primarily through combat."

"Seriously?"

She nodded. "While *professions* can be leveled through repetition and diligence, it is said that growth in your *class* requires the sort of strain that even the soul can feel. The risk of death is among the most profound of such moments."

I *really* wanted to ask what professions were, but managed to resist the obvious tangent, focusing instead on the ugly truth she'd just dropped on me.

"So you have to fight—and kill?—to get stronger?"

"It is the way of the world, Brian Fieldings."

I shook my head. Classes, levels, skills, traits… even experience as something tangible rather than just a general concept. *None* of this sounded like reality. In fact, it sounded almost like a…

"I can assure you; this is no game," said Miko when I voiced my thoughts. Her inner eyelids fluttered in what appeared to be a sign of agitation. "This is *life*. We grow or we falter based on the choices we make and on the collective strength we harness as a people."

"I wasn't…" I coughed. "I wasn't making a joke, I promise. I just… don't get it. I mean, I don't understand," I clarified, in case the idiom hadn't translated.

"Which part?"

"All of it?"

She took a long breath and then blew it out, scaled nostrils flaring. "This should be common knowledge, even to one who has forgotten their own face. Perhaps we would be better served with you asking questions and me providing answers?"

"That might be helpful," I admitted.

"Very well. What is your first question then?" Still riding the dalys backwards, she settled in to give me her full attention.

"What's a class?" I asked. "Like… what does it even mean? And how does it differ from a profession? And why are they both a thing?"

○○○

An hour later—or a *glass*, by Eosian measurements—my head was swimming, flooded with new information. As far as I could tell, Eos and its Framework really *did* resemble the pen and paper RPGs I had played with Bug in high school. There were four foundational classes—Warrior, Mage, Priest, and Rogue—and a person received their class during the so-called Dreaming. Leveling that class earned them new abilities or spells, both called techniques here on Eos, as well as allowing for further improvement in their skills.

Skills were pretty much the same as they were back on Earth: proficiencies in specific tasks or actions. Except on Eos, they were somehow both quantified and regulated. The numbers tied to them indicated how good you were at doing something… and there were even rarity levels that indicated how common a given skill was, or I guessed, how deep your understanding of it was.

Skills were also, as Miko had said, the foundational core of the whole system. Leveling in a class required more than just combat experience; it also required ranks in a subset of skills that were class-related—Minor and Major skills, Miko had called them. Those skills had hard caps that increased with each new level, while non-class skills had far less capacity for growth.

None of that had made any more sense to me than the talk of souls until Miko provided examples. As a Priestess, *First Aid* was a Major skill for her, whereas something like *Riding* wasn't a class skill at all. Because of that, she would only ever be able to raise the *Riding* skill to the tenth rank, whereas the max rank of *First Aid* went up with each level. What's more, the rate of improvement or advancement was significantly faster for class-related skills. So, while she had a three in *Riding*, and might never reach ten without cycles of serious, dedicated training, her *First Aid* skill was already at rank twenty-three, two away from her current level's cap.

To my brain's dismay, I'd done even more math and figured out that meant the cap went up by five every level for Major and Minor skills, with all skills starting out capped at ten at level one.

Unfortunately, it only got more complicated from there. Skills were not only both required for leveling and directly impacted by the same... they *also* played a role in your *options* for advancement. The new techniques you could choose upon reaching an odd-numbered level in your class were sometimes impacted by the skills you'd been advancing as well as the actions you'd performed while leveling. There were even advanced classes that only became available with a certain mixture of skills raised to their maximum level.

Niaci, riding nearby, had come through with an example on that front when Miko faltered. She had pointed to one of the synossians riding far ahead of our column. Slanit had been granted the Rogue class in his Dreaming, but his focus on *Riding, Tracking*, and a few other skills—many of them belonging to the pool of General skills—had opened up the Scout advanced class when he'd reached fifth level. As a Scout, *Riding* had even become a Minor skill, no longer subject to the ten-rank limit.

The possibilities, according to both of my would-be instructors, were theoretically infinite. Skill, class, and level all came together to form an ever-shifting matrix that tailored advancement to the individual. In practice, it didn't quite work that way. Skills could degrade if they went unused, and so there was a limit to how broad anyone's training base could be… as well as to how much time, effort, and energy anyone cared to expend trying to find new workable combinations. The archives in Whitehall had a few very closely guarded advancement paths that focused on known routes for leveling, and most of those who Miko called Aspirants—people who focused on leveling their classes–followed one of those prescribed paths.

Riok's claw, for example, consisted entirely of Priests, Warriors, and Rogues who had developed their classes along known routes. Slanit was one of several Scouts, and although Berys was the claw's only Battle Medic—a specialization of Priest—the Warriors who had advanced sufficiently were all either Spearmen like Riok or Shieldbearers like Niaci.

It was a lot to take in, and I still wasn't sure how it really worked. Or why I didn't seem to be part of it. I was well past the age when the people on Eos were awoken, after all. If and when I went to sleep, would I experience this Dreaming for myself? Would I find myself integrated into the so-called Framework?

And did I even want to be?

The answer to that last question came to me quickly: *yes,* underlined twice, with at least three exclamation marks behind it. I didn't know how I'd gotten to Eos, and an increasingly small part of me was *still* convinced I was having a brownie-fueled hallucination, but if any of this was real, then being part of a system that allowed me to not only get stronger but cast literal magic was an absolute no-brainer.

As for the whole fighting and killing thing… I'd figure that out when I had to. Maybe there was another way to advance.

I grappled with the idea of an omnipotent program that somehow both quantified and enabled progression beyond physical possibility. Bug had been the bigger gamer of the two of us, courtesy of worn manuals and rulebooks passed down from father to older brother to my friend himself, but I'd taken part in enough of his haphazardly assembled campaigns that the concept was familiar.

The *mechanics* though? They were far harder to accept, let alone understand. It was one thing to have a character sheet with stats scrawled in pencil that was meant to approximate what your fictional creation could do; it was another thing entirely for those numbers to influence reality. If Miko was to be believed—and I was already so far down the rabbit hole that it seemed stupid not to believe her—then I had a character sheet of my own, with attributes like strength and intelligence or charisma or whatever? Were those values representative of who I was? How did improving one of them, as people apparently got to do at even levels, even work? Would it fundamentally alter who I was?

Neither Miko nor Niaci were much help there, saying simply that it *did* work. Miko had at least added that there were Sages in Whitehall who made the study of the Framework their primary focus. Sages were, apparently, a profession instead of a class, although we hadn't gotten to how the two differed just yet. It was the Sages who had helped catalogue the known advancement paths as they worked to delve into the mysteries of the underlying system itself.

"It is, by all accounts, a frustrating pursuit," said Miko. "They believe the Framework itself appears to resist investigation."

"How so?" I'd long since gotten used to the sight of the young synossian riding backwards on our mount. "Is it… alive?"

"No." She paused, her eyes doing that strange double blink. "I mean… I don't *think* so? By all accounts, it has no will of its own. But it *is* both vast and complex, and it operates on rules that have proven difficult to identify let alone test. Worse, it seems like there's an intrinsic element of randomness involved."

"How is something that provides structure *random?*"

"Take skills, for example," said Miko. "You gain a skill by performing the action associated with that skill, yes?"

"From what you've told me, yeah."

"And yet the legions have found that, when a full scale of prospective soldiers undergoes the same training, only a portion will learn the requisite skill."

A *scale* was yet another synossian military unit… in this case one made up of five claws. I tried not to sigh as I did the math.

"Wait… so seventy-five people take a riding class, but only thirty of them actually gain the *Riding* skill?" At her nod, I frowned. "How?"

"We do not know. There could be some underlying potential required at the spiritual level that is not enumerated or exposed on the personal record… or there might be some minute variance in how the action is being performed amongst the individual trainees. Or it could very well be random chance."

"I don't think nature's supposed to be random."

"The Framework is not natural," said Miko. "Remember: the gods created it after the fact. The Elder Gods. And while *our* pantheon is renowned for its steadfastness, honor, and courage, there are other gods—"

"Like Corros?"

"Not just Corros and his allies. Most species have their own pantheon and many include a trickster or agent of chaos. Who is to say that such irresponsible deities did not infuse the Framework with their own disorder, ensuring that it would remain impossible to truly comprehend?"

"Didn't you call Shan a trickster god?"

She looked away. "That's different, of course."

Of course it was. Still, I wasn't here to start a holy war. "If there's chaos built into the system, I can see why Sages have a hard time of things."

"Yes. A happy Sage is like a sunny solstice, they say. Altogether rare and unlikely to last more than a single day."

Beside us, Niaci snorted, the noise surprisingly cute. Miko spared the other synossian a look and then turned back to me.

"The challenge extends beyond just skills, of course. Traits, titles, even achievements… they all seem to vary between individuals, which makes any true study that much more problematic."

"Because there are too many variables," I realized, hearkening back to one of my dimly remembered high-school science classes. In order to test for something, you had to eliminate every other variable from the experiment. It sounded like that wasn't possible here.

"Exactly!" She gave me a considering look. "Perhaps *you* were a scholar before you lost your memory? A Dedicated instead of an Aspirant?"

This time I did sigh. "A what?"

ooo

Dedicated, it seemed, was the name given to those who leveled their profession, while an *Aspirant* focused on their class. Another hour—*glass*, I reminded myself yet again—of discussion made it clear that the Framework supported dual roles: the class you were given and the profession you chose. However, most people opted to focus exclusively on one or the other due to the difficulty of maintaining and advancing the skills necessary to level both.

As the unseen sun slowly charted its path to the horizon, I let the idea of the Framework bounce around in my head. I didn't make much progress in truly understanding how it worked—probably wouldn't until I became a part of it and could see some concrete examples—but at least the exercise gave my tired mind something to focus on.

Riding on the back of a six-legged zebra, surrounded by armed and armored lizards and marooned on an alien world, I found myself suddenly grateful for the strange emotional distance I'd felt since surviving the sluthar. The last thing I needed or could afford was a public breakdown. I had to focus on the here and now, learning whatever I needed to survive this new world.

Anything else—*everything* else—was secondary.

At some point in my silent reflection, Miko had spun back around on our mount. Whatever energy had filled her at the opportunity to share knowledge had long since left, and she rode slumped forward in the saddle. I couldn't have read her expression even if she'd still been looking my way, but her body language told me she was back to thinking about the guardians we'd left behind.

Niaci had given the shrine keeper a long look—one I chose to interpret as compassion, but which could have been literally anything else—and allowed her own mount to fall behind us. She still rode close enough to fulfill her evident role of shepherd or escort, but far enough away to grant the illusion of privacy.

With nobody to talk to, and the Framework still a deeply confusing mystery, I turned my attention back to the world around me, munching on a piece of hard bread I'd found in the rightmost saddlebag. Eos was just close enough to normal to mess with my mind. As I'd already gathered, it was winter, and the grass that blurred by under our mount's paws seemed dry and stiff as befitting the season. That grass *was* a different shade of green than I was used to—how I'd always imagined Kentucky bluegrass to look—but not *so* different as to stand out as truly alien. The air was clear in a way I'd never noticed even on hikes outside Midton, but even that made sense, assuming the synossians weren't polluting their surroundings like we did on Earth.

The absence of trees remained one of the most obvious differences from home. The shaft of my spear and the bows on the back of some of the scouts suggested the synossians had *some* kind of lumber, but the doors in the shrine and at least some of the furniture had all been made from that strange opalescent material. What had Miko called it? A kresshac shell?

Which brought up another oddity that my mind latched onto as a ready distraction: how was I able to communicate with everyone—apparently in multiple languages—and why were there words that *didn't* seem to translate?

I had no answer at all to the first question—at best I had to assume it was some sort of Framework-empowered weirdness that would reveal itself after my Dreaming. As for the second… the best I could come up with was that whatever translation was happening only worked for words that had English analogues.

Sluthari and *dalysi* and *kresshac*—or should it be *kresshaci*, if we were talking about them in plural?—all seemed to be names for creatures that didn't exist on Earth. Maybe there was nothing to translate those words to in English? Maybe that's why I was being fed what seemed like a random assortment of consonants instead? Did that mean I was hearing—and speaking—the actual words, or was my brain just making up noises that the translation scheme accepted?

It was the sort of puzzle Kate would have loved to work on, but the more *I* thought about it, the more my head hurt. I was physically and mentally drained. As for emotionally?

I shook my head and bit down on another piece of bread.

7

Darkness fell as we rode on, the dalysi apparently seeing far better than I could. While my eyes had found little in Eos that was recognizably different from Earth, my ears didn't have the same problem. Every cry or animal call in the night was something I'd never heard before, and my imagination was all too happy to conjure up terrifying imagery of the unseen creatures around us. Things that made even the sluthar seem almost pleasant.

There was a limit to how much of *that* I could stand, so headache or no headache, I leaned in against Miko again, pitching my voice so she could hear me.

"You said that reality has three realms," I reminded her, "but only mentioned the physical and spiritual ones. What's the third realm?"

"That which we call the Veil, the realm of the transcendent," she replied. "It is the home of the gods, both elder and young. As mortals, not even our souls can reach it."

"Then how does anyone know it exists?"

She paused to consider the question. "We don't. But we know that the *gods* exist. They no longer manifest in the physical realm and only ever seem to touch the spiritual realm during the Dreaming, which suggests they ultimately dwell elsewhere."

I let that roll around in my head a bit. Maybe it was the stresses of the day catching up with me, but her logic almost made sense.

"I didn't realize the gods took part in the Dreaming. I thought that was just the Framework."

"It varies between individual, really. Occasionally, a god calls someone to serve them directly, such as when I became a Priestess of Aurea. I didn't actually *see* the Bright Lady or anything, of course, but I felt her presence. Even before I woke and checked my personal record, I *knew*."

"Do the gods then decide what classes we get?"

She nodded. "I believe so, even in those cases where the freshly awoken did not report any sign or sense of a deity's presence. It is held as truth that the Framework is powered by the energy the gods invested, first the Elder Gods who created it, and then the Younger Gods who added their might to fill the void when Corros and the others were banished. Whether it was Aurea herself who entered my dream or merely the part of her that she infused into the Framework is ultimately irrelevant, I think."

I followed that idea to its logical conclusion. "That explains how those trickster deities you mentioned could inject some randomness into the whole process. The Framework is literally running on the various gods' energy or power."

"Exactly."

"Then is there any way to stack the odds in your favor if you want a particular class?"

"Of course! The skills and training and knowledge that you accumulate in your first ten cycles of life play a part, as does your personality and temperament."

"So, if *someone* wanted to be a Mage—"

"Scholarship. Academic excellence if you have access to tutors. Even a focus on languages might help. The skills you gain in your Dreaming reflect the life led beforehand, and that helps influence the class you receive. If I had not been called to serve Aurea, I might have been a Mage instead.

"That said," she continued, "there are fewer Mages in our primacy than any other class. The legions are the backbone of our nation and our class demographics reflect that. Warriors are by far the most common class awarded, followed by rogues. Priests are a distant third and Mages… well, it is rare that an entire legion will have more than a single claw's worth of arcane casters."

That gave me a lot to think about. How well would my high-school education stack up with Eosian academics when it came to determining my class? I hadn't been a great student—more from the knowledge that I couldn't go to college than from a lack of intelligence, I thought—but even so, Earth was a modern world. What I *had* learned almost had to be impressive compared to what passed for education in a pseudo-medieval society, right? I mean… we had electricity, and interior plumbing, and guns, and water parks…

For a brief moment, I envisioned myself as a one-man Industrial Revolution on Eos, introducing all the conveniences of a technologically advanced society while carefully pruning away the inventions that had gotten us into trouble. Trains and mass transit: yes. Social media: no. Reality tv… a *definite* maybe.

That dream lasted the few seconds it took me to realize that I had no idea how to create *any* of those things… and that they all relied on resources and manufacturing methods that probably didn't exist on Eos either. Methods I was *also* clueless about.

Which left me with magic. The whole 'kill things to level' seemed barbaric as hell, but combat had to be more palatable when hurling lasers from a safe distance, right? Especially with people like

Riok standing between you and the many-fanged monster. If I could become a Mage in a nation where they were a rarity, I'd have value right out of the gate. Assuming my first spell—or technique—was a good one, I might not even have to level to make a comfortable life for myself here.

Of course, it was clear there was a lot more going on than what I'd been told so far. The human nation both Miko and Riok had mentioned—the Nor—had apparently fallen, its refugees swelling Whitehall's population. Worse, Riok had said the synossian leader had issued a summons to the primacy's rural towns, which suggested the calamity was ongoing and poised to impact their nation as well. I needed to learn more about that crisis and what it meant for me before I made any real plans for the future.

Does this mean you're planning to stay?

That thought brought me up short. Did it? I had no idea how I'd even gotten to Eos, and until I did, I would have no idea how to get back to Earth. But if I could figure that out...? Would I go back?

I don't know.

I'd already almost died once since waking, and it was clear to me that the sluthari were just the tip of what was likely a terrifying iceberg. Here on Eos, I was free of the debts that had piled up back home, but I also had nothing but the clothes on my back... and even those were borrowed. I'd be starting from scratch, and I had to imagine there were limits to the synossians' charity. *Especially* if they were already dealing with refugees. Once Riok and Miko said goodbye, I might find myself struggling with poverty far beyond anything I'd experienced to date.

But even so... this was a whole new *world*. I'd been trapped in Midton, trapped in Ohio, trapped with my—

I swallowed.

—and none of that was true anymore. I was starting from scratch, yeah, but that was better than digging myself out of a hole back on Earth. Kate was gone. My *family* was gone. The only thing left in Midton was Bug, and we barely saw each other anymore. Once he left, the town would be empty of anything but memories, many of them bad. If Whitehall was a good place to live… if Miko or Riok or someone could help me get settled… if there were enough other humans around to keep me from feeling like the lone Earthling in an alien zoo…

Why not *stay?*

As if that thought had been some kind of signal, a dalys came up beside ours. From the darkness, Niaci spoke.

"We are closing in on the town of Ilya. Its citizens have already answered the primarch's call, but the scouts have secured shelter for us for the night. We'll stable our dalysi there and start out again in the morning."

"Thank the Bright Lady," said Miko. "I was starting to fear we would be sleeping in the saddle."

"Only when time is *truly* of the essence."

Sadly, I couldn't tell if Niaci was joking or not.

"When we arrive, please see to your shared mount, shrine keeper," continued the soldier. "Rooms will be set aside in the inn for each of you."

I swallowed. A room meant sleep, and sleep meant a definitive answer to whether this Dreaming thing was real or not… and whether I was going to continue to be ignored by the Framework. If I ended up unable to advance at all… well, bills and debt were preferable to being the lone mundane person in a world of magic.

Soon after, the town came into view, its nearest buildings illuminated by the torches that Slanit and the other scouts were carrying. Most of the column made a beeline for a large building on the near edge of the town. The stables, presumably.

"I can help with the dalysi," I offered. "If we're going to be traveling for days, I might as well learn while I can."

"I will show Brian Fieldings what to do," agreed Miko. "We can care for your mount as well, Niaci."

"After a day like this one, I will not say no. I should report to the Wind Walker directly and find what duties he and Loris have bestowed upon me for the evening." The larger synossian dismounted, pulled a few items out of the saddlebags, and patted her dalys. "When you are done, ask one of the others to guide you to the inn. And thank you both."

We watched her go, moving swiftly for all her size. As she passed the well-lit stables, she vanished into the shadows that still cloaked the remainder of the town.

Miko rose in the saddle, swung one leg over the dalys' back, and slid to the ground, her movements casual and well-practiced. She waited for a long moment and then looked up at me. "It will be easier to stable the dalys if you dismount."

"I'm working on it." There were no stirrups, so I wasn't sure how she'd stood up in the first place. When we'd mounted, Niaci had basically thrown me onto the creature's back like I was a saddlebag. Without that aid, getting down seemed a much more daunting task.

Finally, I placed both of my hands on the front of the saddle where Miko had been sitting. I leaned forward and swung my left leg out and up behind. Lying face down on the furred back of the not-horse didn't feel like much of an improvement. Trying to avoid the spear still in its loop, I swung that same leg further until both of my legs were together on one side and I was clinging onto the saddle to keep from dropping.

Despite the difference in our species, the snort that came from behind told me Miko found my attempts to dismount almost as absurd as I did.

"Simply let go," she instructed, not even masking the mirth in her tone. "There is nothing in your path, and your feet are not far from the ground."

That was easy for *her* to say, already being on the ground, and being six feet of reptilian muscle besides. Still, I didn't see any other option, and I worried I was starting to test even our mount's remarkable levels of patience. I held my breath, swallowed a curse, and released my death grip on the saddle.

Not far from the ground apparently meant slightly different things to Miko than it did to me, but when my feet hit dry, packed earth, the Priestess' clawed hand was there to keep me from stumbling.

"The sooner I get this *Riding* skill, the better."

"On that, we are both agreed. Now, if you follow me, I will show you how it is we care for these great beasts."

I staggered after her, my legs on fire as muscles I didn't even know I had voiced their protests over our multi-glass riding session. Either Miko didn't notice, or she was out of magic... either way, my pathetic waddle didn't prompt a second healing spell.

Something else to ask about, I realized. *How do techniques work? Is there a limit on their usage? In Bug's terminology, is this a mana-based system or a per-rest system? Or some blend of the two?*

The building we had stopped by was, in fact, the stables. Members of Riok's claw were already there, caring for the mounts that had been led into open stalls. I followed Miko and our own dalysi to the far end of the building. Despite the lack of reins, they wandered into two stalls of their own accord.

"How intelligent are they?"

"Roughly the same as your average two-or-three-cycle hatchling," offered Miko, forgetting that I had no frame of reference for what that meant. "They accept training very well, however, and their temperament makes them reliable even in battle." She accompanied me into the stall with Niaci's mount and tapped its saddle with a clawed finger. "Before the dalys can be cared for, we must first remove the saddle and bags."

I followed along dutifully as she went through the handful of steps, from undoing the strap beneath, to untying the leather cords that kept the saddlebags from shifting at higher speeds. Once the saddle was off, she dug into those same bags and passed me a thick, bone-handled brush. I groomed the beast while she checked its enormous paws.

"Do we need to provide food?"

"Someone else will take care of that. No doubt, there are supplies here in Ilya, left behind when its people headed for Whitehall. If I remember correctly, they kept those supplies behind the inn."

"You've been here before?" Clearly, Niaci hadn't realized that.

"A few times, yes. Ilya was one of the towns we supported from the Shrine of the Family. Most recently, I came to perform a nesting ceremony." Her voice softened. "The entire town was decorated, bright and sparkling as the stars in the sky."

"Does its evacuation have anything to do with what happened to the Nor?"

"All things are connected, yes."

"Very cryptic."

"Ha!" She bared her sharp teeth at me in what I was coming to recognize as a grin. "To be truthful, I *was* channeling Mother just then."

"Mother?"

"The Voice of Aurea and the head of the Bright Lady's church. She is revered and wise and all-too-often maddeningly cryptic. I didn't realize until now how much fun it can be."

"I guess it comes with the class?"

"It must." Her smile flickered and disappeared. "When we are done here, we should find the Wind Walker in the town's inn. I promise you will have your answers."

"I appreciate that."

We moved to the second stall, where we repeated the whole routine, and I stashed my spear in the corner of the stall. By the time we were done, I was guessing a half-glass had passed. Despite the cool night air, I was sweaty and tired. I also had a better appreciation for why Niaci had been so quick to take up Miko on her offer to care for the dalysi. I'd only been here a day, but life in the Middle Ages seemed to involve an awful lot of physical labor. Someone needed to learn a spell to handle this sort of thing.

At the same time, I couldn't deny that it felt good to have done *something*, after having spent an entire afternoon and evening being carted around while I asked questions that probably seemed inane to my two companions. Giving back just a little wasn't a bad thing.

I tucked the brush into one bag and reached into another to get more food for us both. The synossian version of bread was clearly made from some grain that didn't exist back on Earth, but it was filling. Miko's sharp teeth tore into the crust with ease while I mostly just put it in my mouth and let my saliva work on it until it was soft enough to chew.

By the time we were done, our dalys was eyeing us both, as if to ask why we were still there, and when *it* was going to get some food. The answer to that second question became clear as we left the stables; a grey-cloaked synossian was pulling a cart of dried grass in from the street. He—or she, I still couldn't tell until they talked—gave us a silent nod as we walked past.

In the darkness, I couldn't tell how big the town of Ilya was, but the inn was only a block from the stables and was the lone two-story building we'd encountered so far. Like the others, it had been built from clay instead of brick or wood. On the bottom floor, we found a large common room with a bar and a door behind it that I assumed led to some sort of kitchen as well as the back yard. To the left, stairs of hardened clay led up to the second floor.

As we started up the stairs, Miko stopped and turned to me.

"You can trust the Wind Walker," she told me.

I blinked. "Okay?"

"What I mean to say is… you are safe with him. With me. With all of us, really."

"I'm not sure what—"

"Though I sorely lack Berys' levels and experience, I've treated head trauma before, Brian Fieldings. On the rare occasions when memory loss occurs, it is almost never all-encompassing. Nor have I ever seen it impact learned capabilities as well as knowledge."

I felt my face heat up. "Look, I don't—"

"Your truth is your truth," she told me, voice still soft for all that she sounded a lot older than she was, "and Aurea teaches that patience is its own reward. But you and I saved each other's lives, and Riok Diocil saved us both. There is a bond there, I believe. If there *is* more going on, we will do what we can to help. *I* will do what I can. This I swear to you. But it requires trust on your part."

She nodded toward the stairs. "I am of little importance in the primacy—simply one acolyte among many—but the Wind Walker is a ranked Aspirant and known for his sense of honor as much as for his skill. Trust in him to help you find the answers you seek."

Given the unsubtle reminder of just how much the synossians had already done for me, I couldn't help but feel like an ass. If Miko— younger and far less experienced than the veteran members of Riok's claw—had seen through my amnesia defense, Riok and Berys must have known I was lying from the very start. Yet they'd still given me food, clothing, and passage on one of their mounts, after both saving my life and healing me.

"You're right," I admitted. "Trust has to start somewhere."

8-Interlude

Leaving the shrine keeper and Brian with the two dalysi, Niaci headed straight for the inn, trading nods and the occasional friendly retort with the legionnaires she passed along the way. *Sergeant* Loris was by the stables, directing the organized chaos and ensuring that the town would be defensible in the unlikely possibility of an overnight attack.

A cycle ago, she'd have found that sort of single-minded focus laughable. After all, who needed guard posts and embankments in the heart of the primacy? Now, Niaci felt almost guilty that she wasn't pitching in with the work. But she had her orders.

The inn's common room was empty, and would likely stay that way, but torches had been lit. She made her way up the nearby stairs and down the long hall that served as the backbone of the inn's second floor, stopping in front of the final door.

Before she could knock, she heard Riok speak from within.

"Come in, Niaci."

She eased the door open, amber light spilling out into the hallway. The Wind Walker and Berys were both within, crouched around the wide table that dominated the room. Clay cups on that table's surface held a liquid she could smell from the door. *Kallnor*, no doubt.

"Reporting as ordered, sir!" Niaci came to attention and banged a hard fist against her armored chest.

"Are we doing this again? Truly?" Riok shook his head.

"You never know," she replied, the crisp formality disappearing as swiftly as it had appeared. "At some point, being an officer might really go to your brain. *Sir.*"

"If it does, I will make certain that you are the first to know."

Niaci wasn't sure if that was a threat or a promise, so she just nodded, closing the door behind her as she pushed into the room. "Shrine Keeper Naseri and Brian Fieldings are stabling their mount and mine. I suspect we have a glass or less before they finish."

"Have a seat," suggested Berys, finding another cup and filling it with a generous pour. "It was a cold day for riding."

"We've had worse, but I won't say no," she said, crouching to sit on her heels before she picked up her glass. She'd been right: it was kallnor, hot and warm and soothing the way only a concoction blessed by the gods could be.

"How are our two guests doing?" asked Riok, after giving her time to savor the drink.

"Miko Naseri is a better rider than I would have expected after a single cycle in the legion," said Niaci. "Her situational awareness is sorely lacking, however."

"You've said the same thing about me, from time to time." Berys kept his features blank, but she caught the twinkle in the man's pale eyes.

"Because it's true. It's a miracle you haven't ridden straight into an ambush yet."

"I would never dare claim divine providence," answered Berys, "but if the Pure *does* wish to look out for me, it would be churlish to refuse."

Trying to win a war of words with a Priest was every bit as futile as trying to outrun a skyborn. Niaci just shook her head and turned back to her commanding officer.

"She grieves, of course, and is smart enough to be troubled by the doom which faces us all, but otherwise, the shrine keeper seems resilient enough. I would not want her in our claw—not without significantly more training—but I would be proud to call her a fellow legionnaire."

Riok nodded, his features guarded. "And the son of Corros? Brian Fieldings?"

"If he is a spy, he is a terrible one. The questions he asks have little to do with our primacy but instead focus on things every hatchling already knows. Not to mention that this whole approach has only brought additional attention to him, something a spy would surely want to avoid."

"Do you then believe in his memory loss?" asked Berys.

She cocked her head. "You said he didn't have a head injury."

"Ignore that truth for a moment."

"Memory is a strange thing." Niaci took a second sip of kallnor and clicked her teeth. "I lost a nest-brother to the grey wasting once."

Berys and Riok stilled, all traces of amusement vanishing.

"By the end of it," she continued, voice low, "Tarl didn't know my face. He didn't know his own name. He had forgotten the entirety of his life, from egg to legion to sickbed. But the *Framework* never forgot *him*. Amnesia or not, Brian Fieldings should show signs of having awoken, given his age. And yet…"

"And yet he doesn't," finished Riok. "Because he has not yet done so, having only arrived in Eos today."

She tapped her claws against her left forearm in reluctant agreement. "Do you really think this human who struggles to even mount a dalys could be *Chosen?*"

"We are running out of alternate explanations," said Berys.

Riok's cup remained untouched on the table in front of him, his dark blue eyes practically glowing with the intensity that identified him as a ranked Aspirant. "Chosen or not, what are your impressions of Brian Fieldings as a person?"

"Well, clearly he is a liar—"

"Beyond that."

The scent of kallnor was too tempting to ignore for long. After another long sip, Niaci sighed, letting her tension dissipate with the breath.

"He is… odd," she admitted. "He offered to help care for the dalysi without any prompting. He made no complaints over the course of the ride, despite clearly having never ridden before. His dialogue with the shrine keeper was insightful if not altogether esoteric. If it were not for his lack of knowledge, I might take him for a scholar of some sort. He certainly *speaks* like one." She darted a glance at a blissfully relaxed Berys. "Or a Priest, I suppose. But—"

"But?"

She shrugged. "I'm not as familiar with the children of Corros as either of you, but his emotions seem muted, especially for someone you believe might have only just crossed the Veil."

"You think he's hiding something?" asked Riok.

"Beyond the head injury he *didn't* suffer?"

"Yes."

She shook her head. "I think… he might be heart-blighted."

Riok rocked back on his heels a bit, eyes distant.

"Would that change anything?" She directed the question to Berys as much as the Wind Walker. "As far as him being Chosen?"

The Priest shrugged. "While their numbers are ever small, there have been heart-blighted in every society, and to my knowledge, they are as capable as any other individual, for all their differences. At worst, it would merely inform our future interactions with him."

"The worth of a person should be divined from their actions," said Riok, "and not whether they feel too deeply or even at all. As for Brian Fieldings—"

A knock came at the door.

"Speak of him and he shall appear," murmured Riok.

"You don't mean—"

"I do." The Wind Walker raised his voice. "It is unlocked. Enter and be welcome, the both of you."

The door swung inward to reveal the diminutive form of Brian Fieldings, almost lost within the borrowed robe he wore. Behind him stood Shrine Keeper Naseri in the brightly colored garb of Aurea's faithful. Both younglings were dusty from the road and their work in the stable, but beneath the streaks of dirt across the human's strange, scaleless face, Niaci saw something different: determination.

"I have something to tell you," he said.

9

For a room large enough to comfortably fit four synossians and me, there was a surprising lack of furniture. One huge table, two cots, and zero chairs. A darker patch on the hard-packed floor indicated where a rug must have once been laid, but even that was gone now. Whoever had owned the inn, they'd taken everything they could when their town was evacuated.

Although… judging by the easy way everyone else was squatting around the low table, maybe *chairs* had never been part of the furnishings to begin with.

"There are no formalities here," said Riok in that deep rumble of his. "Please, be seated."

Behind me, Miko practically squeaked. "Is that kallnor, Priest Berys?"

"It is. I only just finished brewing the last of my supply." The grey-robed synossian reached into his bags and pulled out two more clay cups—halfway between bowls and stemless wine glasses. "Would you like some?"

"Please!" The shrine keeper pushed past me while I was still trying to guess what kallnor was and why it was steaming. As Berys poured a small measure into both our cups, a pungent smell filled the air. It wasn't *coffee*—too many years at Pritchards' had made me something of an expert—but the aroma was kind of similar.

I lowered myself next to Miko—kneeling instead of crouching due to my lack of height and already-aching joints—and took my first sip. It wasn't alcohol, which had been my first assumption, but it wasn't coffee, tea, or hot chocolate either. Instead, it was a mélange of unusual flavors, heated almost to the point of boiling. Sadly, it did nothing at all to take the edge off my growing headache from caffeine withdrawal.

"It's uh… earthy," I managed. "With some fruity notes and something else that gives it a kick."

"Well divined," said Berys, filling his own cup with the last of the pot. "The earthiness is from the tubers used to create a base. The fruit notes come from the berry of the tulalla bush, found primarily along our eastern border. And that *kick* you noticed comes from the scat of the beetle that makes its home in the soil beneath those bushes."

I started to nod along. Then stopped. "I'm sorry… did you just say *scat?*"

"Yes. Both fruit and droppings are surprisingly rare, not to mention difficult to process. I fear you won't see another cup of kallnor before Whitehall."

"And even then, it will cost you a moon's wages." Niaci, silent until then, finished off her cup, her lizard tongue flicking out to lick a few wayward drops from her teeth. "It was generous of you to share with us, Berys."

He bowed his head in acknowledgment. "It was a cold day and a hard one. We bid farewell to four of own today."

Riok nodded. "Though they were not members of our claw, they were still brothers and sisters of the spear. The primacy is weaker for their loss."

I bowed my head along with Miko. When I looked up again, four sets of strange double-lidded eyes were fixed on me.

"You had something you wished to tell us?" prompted Riok.

"Oh. Right." I took a deep breath, placing my half-full cup of kallnor back on the table. "This is going to sound crazy, but I promise you: it's true. All of it. I…"

"You do not have memory loss," said Niaci, when my pause showed signs of turning into simple silence.

"Right. Well, actually, I do, just… not in the way I made you think. The truth is…" I swallowed. "I don't know anything about Eos because I'm new to it."

"New how?" asked Miko, head cocked to one side like a bird instead of a lizard.

"He means he came from across the Veil," said Riok, and something in his tone caught my attention.

"You already knew?" I asked him.

He tapped his scaled forearm for some reason. "I suspected, yes, and shared those suspicions with Berys and Niaci."

Berys nodded. "Your garb was strange even for a child of Corros."

This was going a lot better than expected. Although I'd clearly been an idiot to think anyone would buy my story.

"But how? And why?" asked Miko.

I turned to her. "You didn't know?"

"That you were hiding something, yes. But to cross the Veil is…" She gave a full blink, inner eyelids preceding the outer ones. "Are you a god?"

Ignoring the primary lesson of my dad's favorite movie, *Ghostbusters*, I shook my head.

"Not a god, but a Chosen," said Berys.

"A what?"

It was Miko who answered, her voice falling into its academic cadence even as she visibly wrestled with the revelation. "Throughout the history of Eos, there have been records of individuals from other realities. Forces great and terrible, who crossed the Veil to make their mark upon our world."

"They are called Chosen," added Berys, "because only a god can ensure their passage across the Veil. It has been a thousand cycles since the last Chosen appeared. It was she who signaled the Retreat and ensured that the remnants of the synossian people survived to reach Issandryl."

Issandryl, I reminded myself, was the name given to this continent. As for the rest of what he'd said, there were a *lot* of phrases and terms that I didn't get, but before I could ask for more, Miko had turned on Berys and Riok.

"According to the archives, the Chosen were vanishingly rare, even before we left the Great Wilds. With so many other, more likely explanations for Brian Fieldings' presence, why would you assume he was a figure from our own mythology? He could have been a spy, a traitor, or simply a witless coward!"

"Maybe not *witless*," I argued. "Still, while we're asking questions, I'd love to hear who it was that chose me, as well as how and why."

"You do not remember?"

"No. I had a—" I swallowed again, for a very different reason. "A terrible day back home—on Earth, where I'm from."

"Earth, and not Oh-hi-Oh?" asked Miko.

"Both, technically. Midton was a town—like Whitehall or Ilya, I guess—whereas Ohio was a state. A territory, maybe? Part of a nation called the United States of America. But *Earth* was the name of our planet."

"You named your world *Dirt?*" Niaci side-eyed me over the dregs of her kallnor.

"*I* didn't name it, but… yeah? I mean, I guess so? Why? What does Eos mean?"

"In our scriptures, it is the jewel in which transcendent consciousness resides," said Miko. "The home of the soul, now writ large to serve as the home of all mortal things."

Okay; that did seem at least a little bit cooler.

"You were having a bad day on your planet…" prompted Riok.

"Right. So, I sat down on my couch—" I coughed. "It's like a bed, but for sitting not sleeping."

The Wind Walker nodded. "I have seen such furnishings in my time amongst the other species."

"Okay, good. Anyway, that's the last thing I remember. I was sitting on the couch, eating some food, and then… I don't know. The next thing I remember is waking up in the darkness on what turned out to be Synos' altar."

"I see." Riok took a slow sip of his mostly full glass and set it aside, spearing both Miko and I with a single glance.

"The answer to both of your questions lies in the fate our people currently face. Shrine Keeper Naseri is familiar with some of what I am about to tell you, but not all. And though some have accused me in the past of having only a passing familiarity with brevity—"

Next to him, Berys snorted and took another sip of kallnor.

"—I believe you should hear the full tale of our calamity." Blue eyes met mine. "We face an enemy that devours all in its path. Seven nations stood on this continent and now, only we and our allies under the mountain, the Brushan, remain intact. Winter's snow has kept the enemy at bay, but not even our greatest wizards can halt the changing of seasons. When the snows melt, the northern passes will clear, and the final hammer strike will fall upon our people. Representatives from the Brushan are marching even now to Whitehall to speak with the primarch, blessed be her name, as our nations finalize our defenses and the contingency plans for our young and noncombatants."

Of all the things that I'd expected him to say, *that* had not been one of them. "So, you're at war," I summarized. "And losing?"

"Simply stated, but yes."

"And who is this enemy?" I asked.

"I will get to that, Brian Fieldings. As I said, this land once held seven nations. We were the last to arrive, roughly a thousand cycles ago upon the completion of the Retreat that Berys mentioned. From the very day of our landing, we were by far the mightiest, veterans of a war in which we were beaten but not broken. Even in our weary and bedraggled state, we had sufficient might to conquer our new neighbors, yet we have never been infected with that particular lust or greed. Instead, we sought only to live without persecution. We made peace with our immediate neighbors, the Brushan and the Nor, and then with the nations beyond them, the Keelona, the Shumen, the Torash, and even the reclusive skyborn, who are not so much a nation as a loose grouping of their species."

"Seven countries, living in harmony. Got it."

"What no one knew was that there was an eighth nation, ancient kin to the Brushan, who dwelled beneath a second mountain range on the far shores of our continent, past the plains and the great woods. Where the skyborn soar on the winds, seeking to embrace the heavens, this other nation, much like the Brushan themselves, delved into the earth."

Bird people and dwarves, my mind supplied helpfully, even though I didn't know if either was truly a thing on Eos.

"One day, their digging uncovered something more than simple stone; they found a chamber buried deep below their mountain, its doors bound in a metal that did not match any ore previously encountered. They turned their energies toward opening that chamber, and to the sorrow of us all, they succeeded."

Miko finished off the last of her kallnor and set the empty cup down with a mournful sigh. Clearly, this part of the story she already knew. I nudged my own cup over to her but stayed focused on Riok's tale. This was sounding an awful lot like *The Lord of the Rings*, and while I owed Riok—and Miko—my life, there was no way in hell I was up for fighting a balrog. And if any *god* had chosen me to do so, I would have some serious questions about their divine intelligence.

"What they found inside," he continued, "were the slumbering forms of five of your kind. Three sons and two daughters of Corros, each of them naked, filthy, and wrapped in chains of that same foreign metal that had once bound the door. Even asleep and imprisoned, their auras were so powerful that the diggers fell to their hands and knees, as if greeting gods made flesh."

"Those we now call the Buried eventually woke and repaid their saviors with subjugation," said Berys. "This was twenty cycles ago, as far as we have been able to determine, and the unnamed nation was only the first of their conquests. By the time word reached our primacy, the Torash too had fallen, and the skyborn were being hunted to their last nest. Both peoples were broken and then bent to the wills of their new masters, though we do not know how the latter was accomplished so quickly."

"I thought *I* was telling the story?" Riok's tone was heavy with dry humor despite the solemnity of the subject.

"By all means," said Berys, offering a bow that even I could recognize as mocking, "speak on, Wind Walker."

"Such is my duty and my burden." The massive synossian turned back to me. "When word finally spread of the war being waged across our continent, across Issandryl, the other nations looked to us for leadership. Kal ever teaches duty and vigilance, and so we had maintained our military, whereas they had little more than local militias and hunters to command."

A lizard species with a standing army. Just the idea would have sent a shiver down my spine if I hadn't recently been rescued by them.

"It was decided that we would meet our foe in battle with the combined might of the five remaining nations. And so we gathered on the plains to the north of the Lapskil mountains," said Riok. "In Issandryl's history, there has never been a greater force assembled: archers from the Keelona, cavalry from the Shumen, heavy infantry from the Brushan, and scouts and skirmishers from the Nor. At the heart of that army stood the battle-tested legions of the Synossian Primacy; Warriors, Rogues, Priests, and even Mages gathered as one."

He took a second sip from his cup, and even though his alien features remained unreadable, I recognized the thousand-yard stare in his cold blue eyes.

"What happened?" I finally dared to ask.

"Tradition dictates that there be five legions," said Riok, "one for each of the members of our pantheon. Now, only two remain, and only because they stayed behind to man the forts and guard the primarch, blessed be her name."

"The enemy won? How?" By my math, the Buried would have conquered three nations by that point—the dwarf-alikes who first unearthed them, the bird people, and… whatever the Torash had been. In facing five countries, they should have been vastly outnumbered, *especially* if the synossians had had the only real army on the continent.

"Seven-day after seven-day, our training told the story against the Torash, the skyborn, and the unnamed people of the eighth kingdom, may their faces be forgotten. We held firm, too, against the wild beasts who had been brought under the enemy's banner, creatures darker and more dangerous than a hundred sluthari. After almost a moon of battle, we threatened to rout the enemy's forces entirely. Until *they* took the field."

"The Buried?"

"Yes. Five children of Corros, each shining like dark stars made flesh. They shattered our formations… tore the land, ruptured the sky, and then stood back again as their forces fell upon our broken lines, watering the plains with the blood of thousands. When the order to retreat was finally given, it was almost too late. Our scale lords were dead, our legions were broken—"

"Yet one ranked Aspirant remained," said Niaci, her words iron wrapped in velvet. "In the midst of chaos and despair, he found a weak spot in the forces that encircled us. He led our claw and others out of that deathtrap and defended our flanks during the subsequent retreat over the mountains. There but for the Wind Walker would we all be buried."

Riok dropped his head. "It is no less than each of you did on our flight. No claw has ever been through more or done so much."

Still seated, the other soldier gave him a salute, massive fist clanking off the mail shirt hidden beneath her robes.

"During our flight, we sent word of the slaughter to our northern forts," continued Riok in a quiet rumble once we were alone again. "They passed that word on to Whitehall, where the High Circle—the greatest of our too-few Mages—spent their energy and their lives summoning an early storm to choke the mountain passes with snow and ice. Without that spell and their sacrifice, the enemy would have arrived moons ago. As it is, they wait beyond the mountains. They wait for spring, their numbers swelled by the Nor who did not flee in time."

Silence fell, three synossians studying the table as if it held answers while Miko held my cup of kallnor in her hands, not daring to take a sip and break the quiet.

I kept silent too, mostly because I had no idea what to say. I was just a barista from Ohio. I'd only left Midton twice, and both times had been for house parties one town over. What did I know about genocide or continent-spanning war? And how did I factor into any of what Riok was telling me? What did any of this have to do with how I'd ended up in Eos?

"That much, Shrine Keeper Naseri knew already," said Riok finally, "if perhaps in more general terms. She may also be aware that, over the last few moons, the primarch and her council have been pursuing contingency plans. The Brushan have offered sanctuary under their mountains, but that space is limited, and our people are ill suited to a subterranean lifestyle. The enormous ships upon which our ancestors fled the Great Wilds, in that migration known as the Retreat, were disassembled long ago, the materials repurposed for our new home, but the art of the shipwright is not one that was entirely forgotten. Dedicated have been working to build new fleets and the first waves of those ships have already departed." He shook his head. "Nobody thought we would ever return to the land we were once driven from, but in the face of annihilation, even the impossible must be considered."

"Is that what the summons to Whitehall is about?" I asked. "Getting everyone together so they can be shepherded to safety."

There was a long silence. It was Berys who broke it, his voice soft but kind.

"Whitehall is in the center of the primacy," he said, "more than two seven-days from the harbors along the coast."

"Then why…"

"It is a reality of numbers," said Riok. "Numbers and logistics. The Brushan can only take so many. Our shipwrights can only build so fast, and as enormous as their new creations are, each ship can only hold a set number, given the need for supplies on a trip that took multiple long cycles the first time. While there are other avenues of escape being explored, they have yet to prove viable. What our people need most is time."

"And you're trying to give that to them," I realized.

"Yes. A third legion is being formed from volunteers. Able-bodied Dedicated, retired Aspirants, even those among the refugee species who are willing and able to fight. We have two moons until the snows melt enough for the mountain passes to open again, and Whitehall prepares for the war that will come."

A war that even I, as a stranger and military moron, could see they would lose. Two legions plus a volunteer army couldn't possibly compare to the force that had already been crushed on the other side of the mountains. Especially considering that the enemy had likely added the rest of the Nor to their forces.

"What only a small tithe of people know is there was a final contingency that was explored," continued Riok. "One of our Sages discovered the bare bones of a ritual, etched into the margins of one of the oldest volumes in our Archives. It took a moon to interpret the steps, a seven-day to amass the materials required, and a second seven-day to wait for the prescribed time to arrive. On the darkest night of Wintermarch, the heads of our churches—the Fist, the Heart, the Voice, and the Whisper—came together with the primarch and the lone surviving Mage of the High Circle to enact that ritual."

"It was a cry for aid," added Berys quietly. "A prayer designed to carry the words of our people beyond the physical and spiritual realms to the Veil itself, to the Gods who, since that first terrible celestial war, have agreed to let Eos' people face their own fates."

"They asked," said Riok, eyes glowing with their own steady light, "for a savior from beyond the stars."

10

I took my mug back from Miko and had a long sip of beetle-feces tea to give myself time to think. It didn't help. By the time I was done, I still hadn't come up with a diplomatic way to voice my response.

"You don't… I'm not…" I took another sip, which burned almost as much as the first two. "I don't get it. You think *I'm* supposed to save you? I almost died ten minutes after appearing on this planet. Shouldn't you have asked for someone that was… I don't know… level one million or something?"

"The Framework is, as we understand it, unique to Eos and this reality," said Berys, "but the life led before a person's Dreaming has a direct impact upon their awakening. For those who come from beyond the Veil, the experience and wisdom they have already accumulated should manifest in a more direct manner, translated and quantified by the Framework."

"In simpler terms," said Riok, "the greatness achieved in their former reality will translate to levels and power in this one."

"And so," agreed Berys, "the ritual was designed, with the gods' aid, to seek out an individual beyond the Veil who had reached a certain level of spiritual enlightenment."

"So, Mother Theresa becomes a level ninety-nine ass-kicker," I reasoned. It *sort of* made sense, given what I'd been told of the Framework so far. Strong souls made for strong people. There was just one problem. "Why did it pick me?"

Four synossians traded glances.

"You were clearly a learned individual," offered Niaci, "judging by what I overheard of your conversation with Shrine Keeper Naseri."

"Were you not a person of importance on Earth?" asked Miko.

"Definitely not."

"A renowned ascetic or philosopher then?" suggested Berys.

"A combatant of great fame? Or infamy?" Riok shrugged his massive shoulders at the look Berys shot him. "Kal honors strength, Berys. You know this as well as I do."

"I wasn't any of those things," I told them. "Yeah, I graduated high school, but... after that, I just took care of my father and sold coffee and pastries."

"Coffee?" Miko sounded out the unfamiliar word.

"And pastries," I reminded her.

"There is honor of a sort in serving as a merchant," reasoned Riok. "And to finish your studies at the highest of schools at such a young age surely means—"

"High school isn't..." I shook my head. "Never mind. We can cover the American education system some other time. The point is: what if your ritual made a mistake? What if the wrong person was chosen?"

"The gods work in mysterious ways," said Berys, echoing one of my least favorite religious sayings back on Earth. "They brought you to us. We must trust in their plan."

"Tonight, if all goes well, you will experience the Dreaming," agreed Riok. "Once you have been awoken, we will know more about that plan."

"So, the hope is that I wake up tomorrow able to crush armies with my bare hands? What if that *doesn't* happen?"

"Then we will press on," said Riok. "To Whitehall, where those who performed the summoning ritual reside."

"Mother will know what to do," said Miko.

"And Councilor Kresslock has the *Analyst* trait," added Riok. "It gives him a limited ability to read another person's record. Class and level, if nothing else. If you have already awoken even now, and the problem instead lies with accessing your record and techniques, he will tell us so."

I rolled my neck, wincing at the sound of crunching cartilage, and turned to include all four lizards in my field of view.

"So, either I have my class and can't see it, or I'll get it tonight when I sleep and the gods visit my dream."

"Likely just a single god," said Riok, "and it is less a visitation than a gentle touch."

"I found myself sitting in a grass-filled meadow beside a stream," said Berys. "The light sparkling upon the water's surface told me that Etriska was with me. When I woke, I was one of her servants."

"I found myself marching at the head of a legion," said Riok, "my hearts beating in time with the footsteps of a thousand brothers and sisters."

Niaci shrugged and drained her cup. "Whereas some of us didn't even get that much. I saw a shield and then I woke up. Sometimes, our personal record is all we have to go by."

○○○

Less than a glass later, I was heading for bed, or at least a cot in a room down the hall from where I'd discovered I was supposed to save an entire species. I'd already learned most of the basics of leveling and such from Miko, and Riok had tabled further discussion of those mechanics until the next day. After all, the Framework would make a lot more sense once I had a personal record of my own to use as a reference. And once I had my class, they'd have a better idea on how they could help me adjust.

Assuming I even needed that help—as the first Chosen they had heard of in over a thousand cycles, nobody was entirely sure how this worked.

If I ended up as a Warrior, Rogue, or—*god(s) help me*—Priest, someone in Riok's claw would talk me through using the techniques and abilities they recognized. If I instead won the lottery and became a Mage, I'd have to wait until we reached Whitehall to learn how to unravel the very forces of creation. Either way, the expectation was that the techniques granted to me would be both more numerous and far more powerful than anything possessed by those in Riok's claw. And that would mean learning most of my new abilities through trial and error.

Given my lack of enlightenment, fame, or spiritual significance back on Earth, I was less optimistic. Regardless, that was tomorrow's problem. All I had to focus on tonight was falling asleep, so I could receive a sign from the gods who had brought me to Eos and earn the class that was my ticket to this strange, codified system of personal advancement.

I spent a long time on the uncomfortable cot trying to do just that, my borrowed robe wrapped around me like a comforter. The lack of central heating and air made the room I'd been given both stuffy and too quiet for comfort, magnifying what few sounds filtered in from the hallway. I'd long since abandoned any hopes that this was a hallucination, but despite my near-death experience, the muscles that were now sore from riding, and even my still-throbbing headache, the whole situation felt unreal. Like I was more witness than participant, floating through someone else's story.

I'd just buried my dad and now I was… what? A messiah summoned from another reality? It was all I could do not to laugh. Or cry, maybe. In the end, I just stared up at the ceiling of the dark room and let my thoughts wander of their own volition.

The longer I lay there, the more sleep seemed like an impossibility. Part of me wondered if *not* sleeping on my first night in Eos would screw things up with the Framework even more. Assuming I was a candidate for this Dreaming at all, would it wait for however long it took me to finally pass out, or was there some sort of unseen timer out there in the spiritual realm, slowly ticking down to zero?

Somewhere in the middle of all that wondering, the longest day I'd ever lived—starting with my dad's funeral and ending with me in the empty inn of an abandoned town on an entirely different world— finally took its toll. Sleep snuck up behind me like a silent assassin and pulled me into oblivion.

○○○

I knew it was a dream from the start.

I was standing in our kitchen, staring at a pile of dirty dishes in the sink. The dishwasher had broken years earlier, and we didn't pay Mrs. Cho, the retired nurse who watched Dad, nearly enough to also clean. I was the only one who used the kitchen these days, so I tended to let things slide until we had run out of dishes entirely.

Thankfully, we weren't quite there yet; I poured some milk into my dad's plastic sippy cup, screwed on the lid, and carried it through the nearby doorway.

Dad was in bed. He was always in bed these days. A year or so ago, I'd set a chair next to him and an ancient CRT on the table at the far wall so we could both watch whatever the airwaves decided to grace us with on a given day. Mostly golf and soap operas because network TV was the absolute worst.

"I don't need to see this," I said aloud. "I was here. Day after day, I was here. I lived this."

"That was your first life," said my dad in someone else's voice. For the first time in years, he turned his head under his own power and looked at me, his eyes open windows into a starless sky.

I frowned as the events of the day rushed back into my mind. Funeral. Firing. Drug brownies. Eos.

"Who are you?"

"Who and not what?" Their voice was dry sandpaper scraping against Styrofoam, sending a shiver down my spine.

"This is Eos, and it's my first night here, so I'm guessing this is the Dreaming and you're a god."

"And yet you stand instead of kneeling."

"Whoever you are, you're not my god."

"And if I was?"

I frowned again. If he was—

"Would you prostrate yourself before me or would you hold me accountable for all that happened in your first life? For all that you know is yet to come?" Not-Dad's smile was sharp and almost hungry.

"If you know about all that, you already know my answer."

"Yes."

I thought through what little I'd learned from Miko of her deities. This clearly wasn't Aurea or Etriska, both of whom were female, insofar as gods had gender. Synos was, by all accounts, still spread across the cosmos. That left either Kal the Oathkeeper, who seemed like a poor match for someone wearing my father's skin like a suit, or—

"Shan?" Miko had called him the Trickster, and that seemed to fit this being far too well.

"If you wish."

"Huh. So, gods really do exist here."

"Do they? Or am I something that your mortal mind has conjured to rationalize what comes next?"

"You mean me getting my class?"

"As you say." He swung Dad's legs over the side of the bed and sat up, and even though I knew it was a dream, I still had to blink away tears at the sight. *"Your all-important class assignment. The singular event that will set the course for your second life here on Eos. Are you ready, Brian Fieldings?"*

"Yes. Absolutely. I mean… would it matter if I wasn't?"

"No."

Neither of us moved, but Shan was suddenly seated behind a desk and wearing a suit as slick and sharp as shark skin. I found myself standing in front of that desk in the clothes I'd worn to Dad's funeral, clutching a resume I'd never written. The office barely qualified as such; it had neither walls nor windows but was instead surrounded by an endless empty void.

"So then, Mr. Fieldings," said the Trickster, *"let's talk about you. Where do you see yourself in five years?"*

"What?"

"This is an interview, Brian. The most important interview of your life. Please do try to keep up." He glanced down and my resume was now spread across the desk, every page blank. *"I would have started with the usual nonsense about work experience, but clearly we can skip that this time around."* He glanced at an empty page and moved it to one side. *"Middling grades. Few extracurricular activities to speak of."* Another blank page. *"Other than the fights, I suppose. You did get into your fair share of those, didn't you?"*

"I was the smallest kid in class. I didn't have a mom, and Dad—"

"Yes." A shark's smile came and went. "Well, I suppose I've seen what I need to see. Perhaps you can do me the favor of answering my question now?"

"I'm sorry?"

Those empty eyes caught mine. "Once again, where do you see yourself in five years?"

Maybe it was because it was a dream, but I had a much harder time stuffing down my frustration than usual. "Given that there's apparently an unstoppable army coming to kill everyone, I'll probably be dead."

"And if you were to survive?"

"I don't know yet. I literally just got here."

Shan wrote down something on a yellow notepad that hadn't existed until just then. "Lacks short-term goals. Interesting, if somewhat expected. What about long-term goals?"

I met those terrible eyes, and this time I didn't flinch. "You already know that answer too."

"Yes." All traces of life left my father's face. "The question is whether you choose to go down swinging or to die a shell of a being like this skin I am wearing."

Two quick steps took me around the desk. "My father fought," I said, looming over the god in a way I could only ever manage in a dream. "Every day and every night, for as long as he could. Wearing his body doesn't give you or anyone else the right to judge him."

If Shan was bothered by my defiance, he didn't show it. Instead, that same hungry smile crept across his face, widening far beyond human dimensions. "Question asked and answered."

Just like that, I was back on the far side of the desk. My resume was stacked a hundred sheets high on the desk, even though it had only been a few pages long when I'd held it.

"So," he continued, voice now smooth as melted butter, "what shall we make of you? Perhaps a Caretaker again?"

"No." That answer came from somewhere deep in my chest, surprising me with its vehemence. I coughed. "Look, if you want to know what class I prefer, I'm happy to tell you."

"Mage," he said, pulling my answer out of the void. "But why?"

"Because your people face annihilation, and I don't think one more person with a sword or spear is going to change that."

"And?"

"And magic is cool," I admitted. "And probably safer than the alternatives."

"Interesting, if ultimately irrelevant," said Shan, tapping the stack of papers.

"How is what I want irrelevant?"

"Because class is a function of what you are and not what you desire."

"That's—"

"You have no relevant work experience. No short-term goals other than survival. No long-term goals whatsoever. Scrape away the fear that pollutes your shell and what is it that remains?"

"I don't—"

"Nothing," he answered, ignoring my reply. "You are a blank slate. An unfilled chalice. Potential equal parts unearned and unrealized."

"You're the one who picked me," I reminded him.

"That much is true." The shark's smile widened even further, grotesque on my dad's face. "Although it was you who chose to accept."

"What? Like hell I did!"

My dad's body cocked its head, and Shan pulled a blank page off the stack that was my resume. Scanning it as if it contained text, he tsked.

"I see nothing here about memory issues. I must warn you that falsifying your resume is something that prospective employers take..." His grin disappeared. "...quite seriously."

"I still don't know what you're talking about."

"Perhaps your passage through the Veil is to blame. Or maybe it was the entire plate of brownie edibles you consumed." He pretended to consider the matter at length, too many teeth glittering in my dad's mouth, and then finally tapped one of my dad's misshapen fingers against his skull. "You know what? I'm starting to believe it was the edibles."

"What—"

Before I could finish my question, Shan was in front of me, face inches from my own, my dead dad's breath hot and wet on my skin. Those impossible alien eyes filled with a grey light, cold and piercing, drowning out the world.

A second later, that light was gone. We were in the living room of our double-wide, Shan resting one hand on the larger television I watched when Dad was sleeping. In the way of dreams, I found myself suddenly seated on the couch, shoes off, keys and phone on the coffee table in front of me. And in my hands...

The plate of Bug's brownies.

"There's no way I'm eating those again," I announced.

"You have no choice in the matter. What happened will happen as it must," said Shan, his smile flipping upside down into a tooth-filled scowl. "Even I remain constrained by those rules."

I wanted to protest, but my hand was moving of its own accord, another brownie—the third by the looks of it—making its way

to my mouth. It was like experiencing a movie while being stuck inside
the body of the main actor. Only somehow even less fun.

I settled back—metaphorically speaking—and watched as the
me I was inhabiting polished off the plate. In real life, I remembered
them being chocolatey… almost excessively so. In this dream, they
tasted like ash.

Four more brownies slowly disappeared, each laced with
enough THC—and, knowing Bug, maybe something extra—to get a
rhino high.

"This," said Shan, as the world around the mock living room
began to shift and warp, "is where things got unusual. For all that you
were not in the proper frame of mind to appreciate it."

The television came to life, its screen black and white instead of
color, flickering between channels as the stars of a half-dozen shows
argued with one another. The walls of the living room wept, and I
couldn't tell if that wetness was rain or blood. Our twelve-year-old
coffee table fled from the couch, scampering away like a scared dog and
carrying my phone and the now-empty plate with it. Our carpet shifted
and bubbled, transforming from worn shag into hot molten lava.

And in the middle of it all—

"Is that a pop-up window?"

It was. Largely innocuous in the midst of the greater chaos, it
hovered in mid-air, looking like an artifact from the 90s or the ancient
browsers still used in Midton's only public library. Grey, flat, and ugly,
it had two buttons—Accept and Decline—in the bottom center. Above
those buttons, in sparse block letters, was text:

```
Brian Fieldings, as someone who has achieved a level of
enlightenment seldom witnessed on this plane of existence,
you have earned an all-expenses-paid, one-way trip to the
magical land of Eos.
```

[Accept | Decline]

I watched myself wave a hand at the pop-up window a few times, as if to shoo it away, and then the body I was in leaned in close, lips moving soundlessly as I read the text again and again. It was the sort of thing even an eighty-year-old grandmother who routinely sent checks to Nigerian princes would find suspicious, and not just *because it was literally suspended in the air where nothing should be.*

"Huh," said a voice that was mine and also not mine, the word drawn out as if my batteries were running down. "I wonder."

Don't do it, you idiot! *The words thundered in my brain even as my body refused to voice them. I watched my hand rise into the air again, this time with purpose. The index finger extended and then, weaving back and forth through the air like a snake trying to strike after a three-day bender, it lurched forward.*

The pop-up window shouldn't have even been there. It shouldn't have been able to ignore the laws of gravity. And it most definitely shouldn't have responded to a person's touch, no matter how high that person happened to be.

The [Accept] button depressed with an audible click.

And just like that, I was back in control, back in the half-made simulacrum of an office, looking at the Trickster who had regained his seat behind the now-empty desk.

"I was clearly baked out of my mind on edibles," I said, unable to deny what I had just seen and experienced.

"Truly. It is the only reason the ritual found you at all."

The discussion with Riok and the others, held what seemed like hours earlier, came back to me in a flood. What they had been searching for and why. The synossian ritual had sought out an enlightened being, under the belief that such enlightenment would in some way translate into quantifiable power on Eos. But even if weapons-grade pharmaceuticals had pushed me to what passed for enlightenment on Earth, I highly doubted the Framework would give me any credit for my brownie-fueled trip. Especially now that I was sober again. Which meant—

"We are almost done here," said Shan, voice once again knifing through my thoughts and leaving both them and me adrift.

"Already?" Even for a sham interview, this had been quick.

"Time and energy are two more limits we have yet to transcend." My dad's face twitched into another scowl. "Rules. There are always rules."

I didn't know what that meant, but my thoughts were almost as chaotic as the emotions I suppressed so easily during the day. Keeping hold of them was like trying to pluck a bird from the sky with only my brain.

"And so," continued Shan, "I have but one question left for you, Brian Fieldings, scion of Earth, son of a dead man, and sole heir to his inevitable grief."

I did what I could to ignore the anger that came. "I already told you my answer: Mage. I want to cast spells."

"Management will naturally give your demands the consideration they merit, but my question lies along a different path. Class aside, what is it that you truly want?"

"I'm sorry?"

He said nothing, eyes now gaping pits of unsettled darkness, leaving me to puzzle my way through both question and answer.

I frowned. "I want to—"

"No." His voice was final.

"Then at least—"

"Again, no."

I threw up my hands. "What are you looking for?"

"Truth."

"That's—"

"Not what you think I wish to hear. Not what you hope will net you a prize. Forget your first life. Forget your shallow and meaningless former existence. Forget those you failed and how each of them failed you first. Forget the feeble whisperings you call wisdom."

His voice hollowed out, then expanded until it filled the void around us like a howling wind. Each word became its own distinct symphony, each syllable a funeral dirge for the death of whole universes. Dad's skin melted like hot wax and what was left behind was something infinite and inconceivable, something that was not merely crouched behind the desk but consuming it, breaking the flimsy bonds that defined shape and structure.

That presence approached, and I felt my own sense of self start to splinter, cracks spreading outward through my soul.

What.

Do.

You.

Want?

My dream body crumbled under the weight of the god's words, falling into the void, but even as light became sound and sound became a flame that could not sustain itself, the answer came to me, unbidden, one word that resonated with whatever was left of my shattered core.

Though I lacked a mouth to voice it, that answer tore its way out of me, stretching beyond the void's reaches.

Much like the concept it embodied, it refused to be caged.

Freedom, *I said/thought/screamed.* Freedom to choose. Freedom to live. Freedom to be and to grow and to—

The bitterness of a wind that was not wind stilled.

A god's unknowable form became briefly whole.

I heard Shan's voice, like a whisper in my missing ears.

"Yes," it mused. "You will do."

11

I woke into darkness. Too much darkness. Whether I had fallen asleep on the couch or in my fifteen-year-old bed, there should have been *some* source of light: the digital display of the ancient DVD player, the neon glow of the Santa Claus nightlight Dad had bought me that—

Wait. I'd done this before.

Slowly, the events of the previous day came back to me. There were no lights because I wasn't home. I was on an alien planet, Eos. I had been rescued from a monster by a lizard species facing annihilation and we had stopped at the inn of an abandoned town to sleep for the night.

To sleep… and for one of us, at least… to dream.

I could only remember fragments from my Dreaming, but I did my best to reassemble those pieces as I went through my morning forms, verifying that I still had my usual coordination, that my fingers and toes and everything in between continued to function the way they were supposed to, smoothly and easily and without so much as the hint of a tremor.

Contrary to what Riok and Miko had suggested, I'd *met* a god. Shan. The Trickster had seemed content with playing the part of an asshole, for reasons I couldn't understand. On the one hand, I wasn't the world-famous saint or guru the ritual had been intended to find, which meant bad things for Shan's mortal worshippers. On the other hand, the god hadn't been particularly bothered by that fact.

In fact, from what I could remember of his speech, my lack of qualifications had almost seemed like a positive.

Maybe, I reasoned, *it gave him more leeway within the Framework to shape my class and level to be whatever the synossians need?*

My morning forms completed, I sat up. The room I'd slept in didn't have a window, so I had no idea if the sun was up yet, but sounds from the hallway told me Riok's claw was active. I badly needed to pee, but that was only second on my list of priorities. At the very top...

Show me my personal record, I silently commanded.

A screen appeared halfway through the mental order, manifesting without any effort at all.

Much like the one I'd seen in my Dreaming, it resembled something from the computers of my childhood—grey and crude and aesthetically unappealing. This time, I ignored the shoddy presentation, my eyes focused on the words contained within:

```
Name: Brian Fieldings
Class: Warrior (Common) - 1
Profession: None
Deity: None
Ideal: Freedom

Attributes:
Strength: 10 / Finesse: 10
Vitality: 12 (+2) / Intellect: 12
Discernment: 10 / Will: 14 (+2)
```

```
Skills:
Major: None
Minor: None
Professional: None
General: Brewing (1/10), Caretaking (2/10,
Mercantilism (1/10)


Techniques: Lunge (C)


Achievements: None
Titles: None
Traits: Speaker of Tongues, ???, ???
```

Two things leapt out at me in the sea of unexplained text: my class—Warrior—and the number that followed it: one. Given the lack of any other fields for level, it didn't take a rocket scientist to realize that's what that number was meant to represent.

Which meant I'd been screwed twice over, by Shan and the Framework both.

Not only was I *not* a Mage, like I'd specifically requested, but I was a first-level Warrior. One with a single technique and apparently zero class skills to my name.

"How the hell will *this* help save anyone?"

As if my words were a signal, a knock came at the door.

"Chosen?" said a voice I already could identify as Miko's. "Are you awake?"

I pulled on my borrowed robe and crossed over to open the door. "Yeah, I'm up."

Miko started at my sudden appearance, then dropped into a shallow bow. "Good. Sergeant Loris says that we will be departing in a glass. If you would follow me, I can show you where to bathe?"

"Bathe?"

She paused. "It means to cleanse oneself. I thought you might wish to do so before we head back out on the road. Is… is bathing not a thing where you come from, Chosen?"

"No. It is. I just…" I shook the cobwebs of sleep and disappointment from my brain. "I guess I just didn't realize you all would have indoor plumbing."

"Indoor what?"

"Never mind. And please… call me Brian, not Chosen." I finally remembered to return Miko's bow with one of my own, although, by the fluttering of her eyelids, and the way the scales around her eyes tightened, I probably did it wrong. "It would be great to be clean. I also need to…" It was my turn to pause. Did lizards have euphemisms for going to the bathroom? Did *synossians* even *have* to go?

"Expunge waste?" suggested Miko.

"Thank you. I don't know how this translation stuff works, but it's clear it doesn't function as well for some idioms and words."

"There is a chamber pot in your room," said Miko, "but there will be one at the bathhouse as well. Like most small towns, Ilya lacked the funds to purchase enchanted goods, so you will have to empty the bowl yourself after using it."

"Okay." I didn't know what that meant, really. Were there such things as self-cleaning chamber pots? And if so, how did they work, with plumbing being a word and concept that didn't translate at all?

Eos was going to take some serious adjustment.

Miko led me down the hall to the first floor and then out through the common room. It wasn't until we'd stepped out into a crisp, cold day, the sun still hidden behind a thick layer of clouds, that she spoke again.

"I see you show no signs of wear from yesterday's travel."

"That…" My voice trailed off. By the time I'd gone to sleep the night before, the soreness of muscles I'd never used had only been exceeded by the headache pounding away in my skull. This morning, both pains were gone. That didn't make sense… experience told me I was still a day or two away from kicking caffeine withdrawal, and after a night of sleep—especially on that uncomfortable cot—I should have been *more* sore, not less. "Huh. You're right. That's weird."

"When we level, minor injuries and ailments are often healed. Am I correct in assuming that you had your Dreaming?"

"Yeah. I had it alright."

Miko's exhale was audible. She let both sets of eyelids flutter shut for just a moment. "Thank the gods. Are you able to see your personal record now?"

I nodded, but she just looked at me expectantly.

"If it's okay with you," I suggested, "I'd prefer to go over it after I use the chamber pot and bathe. Both Riok and Berys are going to want to hear this too."

"You are right." Miko dropped her head. "Mother always said I needed to learn patience."

She looked like a kicked puppy, for all that she was a foot taller than me, but I held firm. It was already going to hurt to have to reveal the supreme disappointment that was my level and class… I didn't want to do it twice. I would tell her, Riok, and Berys at the same time so that they could all grieve together.

I keyed in on Miko's last comment as we started walking down the dirt street. "You said she's known to other people as the Voice, right?"

"The Voice of the Dawn, yes. High Priestess of Aurea, just as the Fist, the Whisper, and the Heart each represent their patron deities."

"Only four high priests?"

"The Father is revered, of course, but until he returns, he will not have a church."

That made sense, sort of.

"What is she like? The Voice, I mean?"

Miko's voice softened. "Wise. Thoughtful. Caring and compassionate but never weak."

"And patient?"

I'd meant it as a joke, but the shrine keeper nodded. "There is a story told from many cycles ago, when she was making her ceremonial pilgrimage after having been anointed as the Voice. During her solitary journey, she came across a dispute between two competing herdsmen. Upon seeing her robe and youthfulness, they took her to be an acolyte, and demanded that she mediate their argument."

"Over the course of a full seven-day, she listened, seldom speaking, as the inciting quarrel slowly revealed itself to be merely the latest in a chain of such disagreements. Mother unraveled each incident as they were recounted to her until at last the two herdsmen had arrived at the true heart of the matter, a cycles-old slight that had been allowed to fester."

"What did she do?" I asked, interested despite myself.

"She had the offended party speak aloud of that slight, of the words that had been said and how they were taken. When they were done, she allowed the other herdsman to speak on the same subject, explaining their thoughts and their intentions. As the two came to recognize each other's position, they realized that the sum totality of their ill will had arisen from a simple misunderstanding. The offending herdsman bent his knee in apology, only for his compatriot to do the same. A cycle later, it is said they had become business partners, their combined herds feeding a fifth of the Eastern Reaches."

"I don't know what's more surprising… that it took seven days to unravel the whole thing or that it all came from one basic misunderstanding."

"The clergy of the Pure have a saying: *a wound left untreated infects the body.* We who worship Aurea say instead: *every tree is born of a single seed.*"

"Did the herdsmen ever find out that they'd detained the head of one of your churches to mediate their own private argument?"

"They did. When Mother failed to reach Whitehall on schedule, three claws from the primarch's own legion were dispatched to locate her. They rode into the distant town at the tail end of the mediation, where they found the Voice of the Dawn, a woman who had already given sermons to whole cities, seated in the dirt, listening to two bitter old herdsmen." Miko grinned as she led me to a one-story building that occupied most of its block. "Needless to say, the herdsmen were mortified when they realized who they had detained. Mother said only that she had encountered them while following the sun's path across the sky and that even a Voice must listen when Aurea speaks."

"She sounds impressive."

"She is what all her children aspire to become. As a Chosen, you will meet her for yourself in Whitehall."

I followed her into the building we'd been headed for. There was a small vestibule at the front, beyond which lay an open room. Inside, steps led down into a tiled basin, several feet deep and roughly as wide as our entire kitchen back in Ohio. Three buckets of water had been placed on that basin's edge.

"I will wait outside," said Miko, passing over a cloth-wrapped bundle and leaving me to figure the rest out on my own.

In retrospect, it wasn't all that complicated. The buckets of water were there to wash with as I stood in the basin that was the synossian version of a sunken tub. At the sloped center of that basin, there was a crude but functional drain that could be toggled shut with a metal lever. In lieu of the expected drainpipe, it simply opened onto a dirt pit below. I left that drain open, so I didn't end up ankle deep in water dirtied with my own filth.

With buckets and tub both figured out, I turned to the bundle Miko had given me. The grey cloth matched the robes I wore but was about half the size. I unwrapped it and set it aside with the plan of using it as my towel.

The two objects that had been held in the bundle were a little bit more difficult to parse. One was a glass vial filled with some sort of liquid. Soap? Oil? Tea? Hell if I knew… it didn't smell like much of anything when I opened it. The second object was a brush, its handle carved from the bone of something that no doubt happily consumed poor unassuming Chosen in their sleep. The bristles on the brush were stiff and coarse. I was pretty sure it wasn't for styling hair, given that the synossians didn't have hair, but its actual purpose eluded me.

I shrugged to myself. I'd figure it out as I went.

I tested the water with one finger and found it only mildly warmer than the air outside. Cold showers were something I'd had to deal with far too often in the past for comfort, but now that I was awake, I could *smell* the previous day on me, from sweat to blood to the… musk… of the dalys we'd ridden.

Cold is clearly the lesser of two evils.

I lifted the bucket over my head, letting its contents cascade down my body. It was the least comfortable shower I'd ever taken, and I was shivering by the time the bucket was empty, but the first layer of dirt and dust was already vanishing down the drain.

Next, I poured some of the contents of the glass vial into my hand. It was oil, still odorless but viscous enough that it clung to my fingers. A little went a very long way, and I spread that oil across my skin. I vaguely remembered from a history book that the Romans had used something similar in their bathhouses. Unfortunately, like everything I'd been taught in high school, the how and the why remained indistinct.

Once I had finished oiling up like the world's shortest and poorest exotic dancer, I poured the second bucket of water over my head… and that was when I encountered my first problem. Unlike Earth soap, the oil didn't want to just rinse away.

I looked around the bath house for anything that I could use to scrub it off, but the only things in evidence were the buckets, the towel, the vial, and…

Oh man, this is going to suck.

I grabbed the brush and ran it across my chest. The bristles were every bit as rough as I'd feared, and I took a layer of skin off my torso before I found a pressure level that scraped away the oil *without* removing the flesh below with it.

By the time I was done, I was clean, tired, and had developed a new fear of bathing. I poured most of the last bucket over my head, trying not to wince as water found its way into fresh abrasions. With the final bit of water, I did my best to wash the brush clean. Oil that had clung to my skin rinsed from its skin-devouring bristles without issue.

Toweling myself off was, thankfully, much less of an *experience,* but even when I was dry, it was hard to stop shivering. My t-shirt hadn't survived a single day on Eos, and the less said about my boxers the better. My sweatpants, at least, were mostly intact, so I pulled those on, but if it weren't for my borrowed robes, I'd have looked like the bare-chested, commando-going reject from a budget harem movie.

The robes in question seemed even more practical after the bath; the thick fabric both wicked away moisture and locked in heat like a down-filled puffer coat. Of course, it wasn't until I was fully clothed that I remembered I *still* had to pee. So, I stripped back down, searched for a pot that looked like it had been designed for… use… and in the phrase my dad liked to use when I was just a child, drained the lizard.

Which, now that I thought about it, was a phrase I should probably *never, ever* say aloud here on Eos.

When I was done and clothed yet again, I looked at the pot and then to the drain in the middle of the tub.

Nope.

Even if nobody ever returned to Ilya, pouring urine down the hole in their town bathtub seemed like a solid way to lose whatever respect I might have earned with the synossians. So, I instead headed back out into the street, bowl in one hand and bathing supplies in the other.

Miko was still there, waiting. I handed her the towel, brush, and oil, and nodded to my half-full chamber pot.

"Where should I dispose of this?"

"There's a freshly dug pit behind the inn that someone will fill in before we leave," she said, her free hand guiding me in that direction.

Not that I really needed the help… in the daylight, the town's only two-story building stood out in a way it hadn't the previous night.

"How was your bath?" she asked.

"Cold, but otherwise okay. The brush took some getting used to though."

"The brush—" She came to a dead stop in the street, looking down at the bathing supplies I'd given her. I was pretty sure synossians couldn't blush… or that the scales at least hid it, but her body language screamed embarrassment. "Bright Lady save me from myself."

"I'm sorry?"

"Both the brush and oil are for your… scales," she said, words almost tripping over each other. "Which of course, you do not have. It is a miracle you did not tear your fragile pink skin to shreds."

I must have shifted in place or made some kind of noise in response, because the next thing I knew, Miko was muttering what sounded like a prayer and warm light was washing through me, healing my recently acquired scrapes.

"You didn't have to do that," I told her. "There were just a few scratches. Besides, without the brush I'd have never gotten the oil off, and without the oil, I don't think I could have gotten clean. It all turned out okay."

"Even so…" She placed a fist against her chest and bowed. "I am not at my best in the mornings. It did not even occur to me to look for alternate supplies."

"Given the ongoing absence of shoes, I'd have been surprised if you found soap and a loofah," I told her.

"I do not know what that last word was."

"I guess they don't exist here then. That's a bummer." I'd never actually used a loofah, but they had always looked luxurious in commercials. "Anyway, I'm getting the idea that this town—Ilya— didn't get a lot of foreign visitors."

"That is true. Whitehall will have accoutrements more suitable for your species, I promise." She nodded to the still-full chamber pot I was now cradling in both hands. "And speaking of Whitehall… shall we dispose of your waste and speak with the Wind Walker and Priest Berys about your Dreaming?"

I didn't see any way to avoid it. "Yeah. I think it's time."

"As you wish, Chosen."

"Brian," I reminded her. "Just call me Brian."

12

After dumping my chamber pot's contents, I rinsed out the container with a bucket of water from the town well, and then left both bucket and pot out in the sun to dry. Miko led me back around the inn, but instead of going inside, we headed for the stables.

The massive form of Riok stood in the middle of the road, conversing with the slightly smaller—if still monstrously big—Sergeant Loris. As we approached, Loris banged a clawed fist to his chest and spun away, barking orders that sent nearby synossians into motion.

"Brian Fieldings. Shrine Keeper Naseri. Well met." It had only been a few hours, but I'd somehow forgotten the sheer weight of Riok's presence. I still couldn't put my finger on what it was. I mean, sure he was an eight-foot-tall mass of inhuman muscle expressly designed by his people's gods for the purpose of war, but... so was Niaci, and she didn't make me want to find the nearest hole and bury myself in it.

Except when she smiled. Synossians had a *lot* of teeth.

"Riok," I said, finally getting my tongue unstuck. "Do you and Berys have a moment? We need to talk."

Riok's grin, at least, was no more terrifying than that of anyone else from his species. "It happened then? The event we discussed?"

"Yeah." As far as I could tell, only a few people in the Claw knew about me, and from the way Riok was dancing around the subject, I guessed he wanted to keep it that way. I was curious if that would remain the case once he heard what I had to say.

Berys, it turned out, was *not* working with the rest of the claw to prepare the horses and remove all traces of our stay in Ilya. Instead, he had found a seat in a house across from the stables. We found him crouched beside the sitting room's only table, a cylinder of what looked like charcoal in one hand and a loosely bound book of thick-sheeted pages in the other. He finished as we came in, sprinkled some kind of powder over the freshly written words, and closed the book, placing it on the table.

"Berys writes the reports of our claw's actions," explained Riok, catching my interest in the leather-bound book. "Each legion runs on supplies and communication both."

"Is literacy common in the Synossian Primacy?"

"Writing and Reading are skills like any other," said Berys, sparing Riok a mild glance. "Some work at them harder than others."

"Some of us must wield weapons other than words," agreed Riok. "However, the sun is already in the sky and time is short. The floor is yours, Brian Fieldings."

It took me way too long to realize he meant that figuratively and not literally. I cleared my throat.

"I had my Dreaming last night."

Riok grinned his terrifying grin again, but Berys was watching my face with an intensity even I could decipher.

"And yet you seem troubled," he said.

"I'm a Warrior," I told him. And then, before Riok could enthuse about the class—and based on half a day of familiarity with the big guy, I was pretty sure he would—I dropped the *real* bomb. "And only level one."

Miko audibly gasped, but Riok went still, like an armor-clad statue. After a long moment, he turned to Berys. "What does it mean?"

If he were human, I was betting all the color would have drained from Berys' face. As a lizard, I had only the shakiness of his voice to tell me he was genuinely shocked. "I will seek guidance from the Pure herself, but… I do not know. It is said that even before the betrayal, Synos helped those who helped themselves. Maybe… maybe this is something *we* as a people are supposed to solve?"

Riok nodded simply, but shoulders broad enough to carry a house drooped, as if the best and perhaps last hope for his people hadn't just been crushed. "I see."

"I'm sorry to be the bearer of bad news," I told them all.

"We can only be who and what we are," said Riok. "This is not on your head, Brian."

Given my brownie gluttony, it sort of *was*, but I wasn't going to mention that. Now or ever.

"What can you tell us about your dream?" asked Berys.

"It was kind of like a job interview," I said. "I was back on Earth, more or less, and we were talking about my past experiences and what I'd gone through." It was my turn to scowl. "I said I wanted to be a Mage, but apparently he had other plans."

Riok and Berys exchanged glances.

"Are you saying you spoke to someone during the First Dream?" asked Berys, his words quiet yet pointed.

"What? Yeah. Shan, apparently." I shook my head. "I'm not here to blaspheme or anything, but between the sham interview and him wearing my dad's dead body as a suit, I can't say I'm a fan."

Berys and Riok were still looking at each other, and even if I couldn't read lizard expressions, I could tell that a silent dialogue was taking place.

"What is it?" I asked, inserting myself into that conversation.

The big soldier motioned for Berys to take the lead, and the Priest of Etriska turned back to me, ducking his head in momentary apology.

"In our recorded history, the number of Dreamings that included more than a basic sense of one of the pantheon's presence is miniscule. I told you of my dream with Etriska."

"And I of mine," said Riok. "The cadence of several hundred brothers and sisters marching filled me with pride even as the responsibility of leading so many souls weighed upon me. I knew Kal had spoken and chosen me to be one of his spears."

Which was pretty and symbolic and all, but…

"Neither of you spoke with your gods? Or met them?"

"I would have to consult the Sages to say with certainty, but to the best of my knowledge," said Berys, "you are the first. Ever."

Riok nodded. "Your lack of levels is undeniably troubling, yet you spoke directly with one of our gods. Whatever is happening here is clearly not for me to understand. Thankfully, there are those who are better versed in such matters."

"The primarch?" murmured Berys.

"Yes, blessed be her name. Perhaps she or the council will be able to divine the path forward."

"I'm not following," I admitted.

"You are Chosen for a reason," said Berys. "Shan is famed for schemes that are nigh impossible to decipher until they have reached fruition, but wiser heads than ours might have a better idea of how you fit in the coming days. And for that, we must reach Whitehall." He paused, and something almost apologetic entered his tone. "If you still wish to accompany us, that is."

"I have a choice?"

"You are a sentient being," said Riok. "Of course you have a choice. Your fate is your own, to make as you see fit."

Any doubts I had about the synossians pretty much disappeared then and there. If history was anything to go by, my government back home wouldn't have been anywhere near as generous.

As for whether I would still go with them? That wasn't even a question. I was a level-one Warrior in a strange world filled with things that could kill and eat me. The pack of sluthari that had come down from the mountains might be dead and gone, but I was sure the lowlands had their own predators. And it wasn't like I knew how to forage for food and water, let alone defend myself. Hell, I didn't even know of any cities to go to, *except* Whitehall. Being escorted there by a bunch of armored badasses who had food and tortuous shower brushes was a no-brainer.

Still, my dad hadn't raised a complete moron.

"What happens if we get there and the primarch and the others still can't figure out my purpose? What if I'm exactly what my… uh… *personal record* suggests?"

"Then you will have a choice to make. Recruits are gathering to form a new legion in defense of the capital. You could join them and lend your spear to the cause."

Different species or not, I kept my face very, very still. Riok had saved my life, and so had Miko, but there was a big difference between going into battle against an unstoppable enemy as a gods-anointed, high-level Chosen, and doing the same thing as a rookie recruit who didn't even know how to use the spear he carried.

"Alternately," said Berys, "you could join the rest of our people in flight. The great river runs from Whitehall to Kronask, jewel of the southern coast. That city is one of several ports where our shipwrights have been at work these past few cycles. Though the first fleets have already departed, I believe the primarch would see to it that you were given space on the next."

So, I would have a chance to run away with all the other non-combatants. Part of me felt like I should be ashamed of how appealing that sounded.

"You could also join those of our people who will take refuge under the mountain with the Brushan," added Riok. "Life in the cave kingdom will not be easy, but their nation is designed for self-sufficiency, and once they collapse the entrances, the enemy will never reach them. The ocean crossing, by contrast, will take multiple cycles and the journey, according to our records, is neither easy nor safe."

"That's... generous," I said. And it was. "Especially if I turn out to be a complete nobody."

Riok shrugged his massive shoulders. "Kal teaches that aid given with the expectation of reimbursement is not aid at all, but simply a merchant's transaction. If you had been merely another of the Nor, hiding in the shrine, we would still have offered our assistance. It is the right thing to do."

I bowed my head. "If I *can* help, I will."

"That is all any of us could ask of you." He flashed another toothy grin, and if it was less exuberant than the one he'd greeted me with that morning, the fact that it existed at all said something. "The gods brought you to our world, and I will choose to believe they had their reasons for doing so. Perhaps saving the primacy was not their focus. Or perhaps your strengths will become clearer as we travel. Either way, I will put my faith in them... and in you."

"We must be in Whitehall to meet with the Brushan in a little more than a seven-day, but we will have time after we make camp each night. Be certain to collect your spear from the stables, and I will see that you are familiar with it before we reach our destination. Perhaps you will surprise even yourself with your rate of advancement. And if not, then knowing the fundamentals should still serve you well, regardless of the path you choose."

Given what I'd seen Riok do with a spear, I couldn't argue on that front. And if I *was* going to be a Warrior, the weapon seemed like a great choice for my continued survival… something to keep whatever attacked me as far from my delicate bits as I could possibly manage. I'd already seen one monster up close and personal and had no desire to repeat the experience.

"We have a brief time still until our departure," added Berys. "If you wish, we can review your record. I know that Shrine Keeper Naseri briefed you upon the fundamentals of the Framework, but now that you have more information in front of you, I suspect you might have questions?"

I summoned my character sheet again and scanned its largely incomprehensible contents. "Yeah. You could say that."

○○○

A quarter glass wasn't a lot of time, but my character sheet was mostly a wasteland of valuable data; we managed to cover the whole thing before our departure. As I'd already learned from Miko, my class determined the Major and Minor skills available to me. The fact that my sheet didn't show any of those wasn't quite as bad a sign as I'd feared. Instead, it simply meant that I hadn't earned any ranks in class-related skills yet.

Given my performance against the sluthar, I could kind of understand that. A Warrior's Major skills encompassed most weapon types, different kinds of armor, and various other combat-related abilities, while their Minor skills had more to do with physical prowess, from athletic activities like climbing to more personality-given capabilities like intimidation or even inspiration. None of which had really been much of a focus in my previous life on Earth.

Ranks in those skills would come swiftly with training, according to Riok, for at least the first few class levels.

As for my General skills… I had a skill point in *Mercantilism,* another in *Brewing,* and two in *Caretaking,* which I figured was the Framework crediting me for both my job and my time looking after Dad back on Earth. Why I only got a single point in the first two skills, despite literal *years* as a barista, was another open question, but I chose to believe it was a meta commentary on Pritchard's general shittiness rather than an honest critique of my own abilities.

Apparently, if I wanted to make Brewer my profession—and I wasn't sure I did—I would need to first increase the *Brewing* skill to its default maximum of ten. I would also have to advance a handful of related other skills, like *Milling* or *Mashing* before the profession became available. Once I qualified as a Brewer and chose to become one, I would then be able to level the profession, with the associated skills becoming Professional skills instead of General ones.

It was basically like how classes worked, but with an extra step in between, where you had to learn what you were doing first instead of having a god just stick you with a role you didn't want. The same rules held true if I wanted to become a Merchant, but there, I'd be focused on the *Mercantilism* skill as well as skills like *Appraisal* and *Haggling.*

As for whatever profession was tied to *Caretaking?*

No. Just no.

I'd already lived that life since my mid-teens. Never again.

As Miko had said, there were Sages at Whitehall who worked to research what Riok called advanced path formulas, the ways in which some skills, professions, and classes worked together and influenced each other to define a particular development path. Formulas were necessary because the possibilities seemed otherwise infinite. Worse, the Framework offered no guidance at all. I'd already noticed that I couldn't tap on the labels of *anything* in my character sheet to get help text. Apparently, that was just how things worked.

"The elder gods created the Framework so that we would have the opportunity to improve ourselves," Berys said, "but every mortal must make their own journey. If the primarch permits it, I highly suggest you speak with a Sage about the paths available for Warriors. Perhaps, you will find one that suits you."

Given that my desired path had been to stand back and drop fireballs on the bad guys' heads, I didn't see much hope on that front… but maybe poking things with the pointy end of a stick would grow on me by the time we'd reached Whitehall.

What I *was* excited about was the general idea of leveling at all. Not only did Eos give me the fundamental ability to improve myself, it *measured* that improvement. I mean… I'd been able to progress on Earth too, technically, but here, development was tied to numbers and visible at any given time. The idea of seeing those numbers go up in a concrete way excited me in a way a gym membership never had.

Even if I could have afforded the gym back in Midton.

My attributes were, apparently, largely average. Ten was a base line for each stat, adjusted by racial bonuses or even penalties. As a child of Corros, I had a racial bonus to Vitality and Will, represented by the +2 in parentheses next to those attributes' number. Ignoring the bonuses, I had a slightly higher Intellect and Will than the bog-standard average human, with a base stat of twelve in each, and an adjusted stat of fourteen in Will.

I wasn't sure what that did for me—I certainly didn't *feel* any smarter after waking up—but there wasn't time to ask about how stats worked. And the Framework, once again, was no help on that front.

The two components I *hadn't* covered with Miko were Ideals and Traits, and the fact that I had both was something of a big deal, given the way Riok's terrible smile widened.

"Ideals," he said, somehow conveying the capitalized word with his tone alone, "are something each Aspirant or Dedicated must develop on their own. They are a central truth that speaks to you and, in accordance with your class and skills, shapes the options provided to you upon leveling. Yours is not a common Ideal, but the fact that you have it already at level one speaks well of you."

Traits, on the other hand, were exactly what they sounded like: innate qualities that differentiated an individual from those around them. One example was *Analyst*, the trait Riok had mentioned that allowed one of their councilors to view the classes and levels of those around him.

Speaker of Tongues was clearly the reason I could communicate with the synossians at all. The fact that it had also given me knowledge of their High Tongue made it that much more powerful of a trait.

"It is possible," said Berys, "that you will even find yourself able to speak more than just *our* languages. In Whitehall, we can experiment to find out for sure."

As for the traits currently represented by question marks…

The Priest shook his head. "I have neither seen nor heard of such a thing as a trait whose name remains hidden. Truly, you are a mystery, Brian Fieldings."

"We must assume your traits will reveal themselves according to some schedule known only to the Framework and Shan himself," agreed Riok. "Keep an eye upon them but do not let their mystery distract you from your goals."

"Right. My goals."

"Fret not, son of Corros." His clawed hand engulfed my shoulder. "The day is young, the sun still burns, and spring remains moons away. We have time, and with time and will, all things are possible."

13

As I climbed up and onto the dalys behind Miko, I was thankful all over again that she had healed my shower scrapes. I'd have spent the whole day with my abraded chest pressed up against her back otherwise. Instead, I felt like a new man.

Magic did not suck. At all.

Which just made it that much worse that I was a Warrior.

We soon left Ilya behind, the hills becoming sparser as they were replaced by rolling plains. After a glass or so, Miko finally stirred ahead of me. She swung around on the back of our mount to fix me with her bright orange eyes. Her voice was low, barely carrying over the sound of our passage.

"You really met Shan?"

"Apparently so, yeah."

"What was he like?"

I coughed. "He was kind of an asshole."

Either the swear word translated into something inoffensive, or Shan's reputation was well known, because Miko just nodded.

"If my goddess Aurea is the light, it is said that Shan is the darkness, working through shadows and secrecy to protect us all."

"Well, I wish he'd opted to share his plans with me. Or at least given me a few more levels. And maybe a skill rank or two in *Riding*."

"Those will come with time," she said. "Until then, I can heal you each night when we make camp, if you'd like? Between the day's ride and whatever training you are given in the spear, I think you might need it."

"I'd appreciate it." I cocked an eyebrow. "How do spells work, anyway? I'm guessing since you didn't just keep spamming *Flare* back at the shrine, there's some sort of cooldown or limit?"

I don't think all my words translated—*spam* was probably something totally incomprehensible to a synossian, just like sluthari was to me—but Miko got the gist of what I was saying. She was unconsciously chewing on a claw in a manner that would have been terrifying twenty-four hours earlier, but now seemed almost cute. "*Flare* does no damage, and the sluthar had already been blinded to the best of my limited abilities. If I'd chosen to upgrade the technique at level three instead of choosing a new blessing, I could have added a fire-based component to it… but being able to heal seemed more suitable for my role as shrine keeper. I thought I would always have my guardians to look over me and protect me."

She bowed her head, doing that strange double-blink, and I gave her a moment. After a time, she lifted her head and continued speaking, as if nothing had happened. "That said, there *are* limits to technique usage, and those limits hold true whether the technique is martial, arcane, or divine."

"Like what?"

"A technique can only be used so often, although that period depends upon the technique itself as well as the Intellect and Discernment attributes of the caster. Some upgraded versions of a technique can reduce that time even further, but there is always a cost."

So, cooldowns, like I'd thought, with some sort of attribute-based modifiers. And it sounded like more powerful abilities had correspondingly longer cooldowns.

"Additionally, every time a technique is used, it requires energy from your soul, and that energy cost scales with impact. The *Greater Healing* that Berys cast on you earlier drained him significantly more than the *Light Healing* he cast on me. Again, this can be mitigated through improved versions of a technique and even further by improving the Vitality and Will of the caster."

"So, why not boost those four attributes and then choose technique upgrades that also improve efficiency? That way, you would pretty much never run out of techniques."

"That is *one* path, although it would require more levels than I believe are possible. As a Warrior, focusing on Strength and Finesse to improve your ability to do damage with and without your techniques might be a better choice. Every decision made with the Framework has its benefit and its cost. For example, if I had chosen to upgrade *Flare*, I would have a better version of that technique, but no healing whatsoever. There are times when flexibility is more valuable than a single strong technique, and other times when the path of balance leaves you comparatively weak in *every* area."

"One-trick ponies versus jacks-of-all-trades," I said, and then immediately had to explain what both sayings meant.

"Precisely. There are volumes as thick as a dalys written on the subject, but the Sages say that there is no single answer that suits everyone. The Framework gives us the ability to grow along the path we choose, but it is up to us to choose it."

"Huh."

"What?"

I shook my head. "Nothing. I can see why you were planning to take the Scholar profession. You're really good at explaining this stuff in a way that even someone with a twelve Intellect can understand."

"A twelve Intellect is nothing to be ashamed of."

"No? What's yours?"

Miko looked away. "Somewhat higher," she admitted.

"That's what I figured."

"A fourteen Will at level one, on the other hand… *That* is impressive."

She was definitely trying to boost my ego—or salve my pride—but I decided to take what I could get.

For the hundredth time in the past hour—the past *glass*—I opened up my character sheet, as much to marvel at how easy it was to make something appear out of nowhere as to look at the numbers I'd already practically memorized. Currently, I had one technique, *Lunge*, that was of Common rarity. That realization had been a downer until Riok explained that everyone started with a single common technique at level one.

If I wanted to upgrade *Lunge* or add a second technique, I would have to reach level three in my class. Meanwhile, I could improve one of my attributes at level two. That was the basic blueprint for life as an Aspirant: odd levels got you spells or flashy moves while the even levels let you improve your mental and physical foundation.

Of course, before I could reach level two, I had to max out at least a few of my class skills… and before I could do *that*, I had to first gain those skills. To hear Riok tell it, a hard moon of training would be enough to get me there. Unless, of course, I proved my worth as a Chosen by showcasing an absurd leveling rate or other, previously hidden, gifts.

So far, even *Riding* had proved elusive. I felt better situated on the dalys behind Miko, but my character sheet stubbornly refused to reflect that improvement. For now, I remained a level-one Warrior with basic proficiencies in brewing caffeinated beverages and selling things, and a slightly more advanced ability to take care of dying dads.

Even for a fake Messiah, this is sad.

Beneath us, the dalys made a strange chuffing noise, as if to voice its agreement.

ooo

I'm not sure what Miko was doing as we rode on the dalys through the early morning hours. Meditating, maybe? She kept her head tucked into her scaled chest, and other than those initial words, stayed quiet, leaving me to my own thoughts. Between the loss of her shrine and my less than satisfying *greatness*, it was entirely possible she was just depressed… and I couldn't really blame her for that.

We didn't stop for lunch but ate in the saddle. Just bread again, although I'd been told there would be something called tusker for dinner. When I got tired of the seemingly mundane terrain, I turned my attention back to my character sheet yet again.

My level made sense, even if it sucked. My attributes made sense, even if being rated mostly average seemed like yet another Framework-spawned insult. The lack of high skills—Major, Minor, *or* Professional—all made sense too. And even though I didn't know how to use it or exactly what it did, my single technique, *Lunge*, made some basic sense as a starter move for people doomed to engage in melee combat. And while I didn't really understand how Ideals worked yet, mine was at least proof that my conversation with Shan had actually happened.

Freedom. I wasn't sure where my answer had come from, in the dark depths of that dream, as my body and soul were both disintegrating around me, but I couldn't deny that it fit. I'd never had much choice in my life… first as a motherless kid, and then as the caretaker of a sick dad. There was an undeniable allure to the thought of being free to choose my own path, but… what did that even mean?

For as satisfied as Shan had seemed with my answer, the situation he'd placed me in didn't seem to support it. Here I was, with a massive, unstoppable army just a few months away from crossing the mountains and destroying everyone in its path. And I had the option to… what? Fight and die against that army, or run away and probably still die?

Freedom isn't free, muttered a voice in my head.

Super helpful, I fired back.

Finally sick of staring at numbers that refused to change, I closed my character sheet, only to find that Miko had once again turned around, reptilian mouth open with a question of her own.

It was not one I'd been expecting.

"Why did you scream?" she asked.

"What?"

"In the shrine. After I had saved you and the sluthar had passed by. It's the one thing I don't understand. I had already told you the creature hunted by sound… so why did you scream?"

Oh. That.

I coughed. "Up until that point, I'd thought I was still on Earth. Kidnapped by demon-summoning cultists, maybe, but on my planet at least."

"So, there *is* magic on your planet?"

"No. Well…" I shrugged. "I guess it depends on who you ask. There are a lot of stories, but I think they're all just that. Still, the idea of being transported to a whole different planet was even *less* believable."

"And the scream?"

I didn't know Miko well, but I liked what little I did know. At the same time, she seemed young when she wasn't going all scholarly on me, and she was *also* a lot bigger than I was. And probably stronger, too. It wouldn't take much of a push from her to send me right off the back of the dalys.

But lying hadn't been a winning strategy so far. I sighed. "We don't have synossians on our planet. We mostly just have humans, like me. So, when I saw that you were uhm… different, I just uh…" Her eyes had narrowed to slits, and it was my turn to raise my hands, though I was trying to ward off a blow rather than cast a spell or blessing. "It wasn't my finest moment."

"Are you saying that *I* scared you?"

"Kind of? Imagine you'd never even heard of humans—children of Corros—let alone seen one, and then *I* popped up out of nowhere. Wouldn't *you* be scared?"

"I would be cautious," she replied, "but I wouldn't scream."

"Like I said, it wasn't my finest moment."

She shook her head, eyes still narrowed. Her mouth fell open to reveal those rows of sharp teeth, but instead of the expected mockery or even wounded feelings, I heard… giggles?

They weren't *human* giggles, but if the occasional barks I'd heard from Riok's men and women were laughs, this was the higher-pitched, softer, and borderline adorable little cousin.

"Sixteen cycles old, barely a shrine keeper, and without even a weapon to call my own, and yet *you* were afraid of *me?* I can't wait to tell Kai!"

I didn't know who Kai was, so I focused on the important stuff. "And I almost got us both killed in the process."

"Almost," she agreed, "but through the grace of the gods and their mortal servants, we survived. Still… maybe *don't* scream in the future when stealth matters?"

"I'll have to work on whatever skill's associated with that. *Stoicism*, I guess?"

For some reason, that invited a fresh round of giggles. Some of Riok's claw looked in our direction to see what was going on, flashing their own versions of the lizard smile to see the young shrine keeper happy.

Given that she'd just lost her guardians a day earlier, the burst of humor seemed a bit sudden, but I didn't say anything. I didn't know what was going on inside her head… and besides, there was something about her giggles that made *me* want to smile.

I waited for the moment of hilarity to die down and asked the first question that came to mind. "You said you're sixteen cycles old? So, I'm older than you?"

"You are." Miko shook her head again, her giggles finally fading. "I would never have guessed it, given your size." Before I could even reply, the Priestess squeezed her eyes shut and shook her head. "I ask for your pardon, Brian Fieldings. That was not something I should have said."

"Well—"

"There are times I think Mother sent me to the Shrine of the Family precisely *because* it was so far from civilization."

That seemed like a dick thing for a mom to do, even one who ran an entire church, but at least *Miko's* had stuck around past her infancy. That made the elder synossian a saint in my mind, completely independent of any actual religious connotations.

"Are the Nor taller?" I asked, already knowing the answer.

"I've never seen a Nor in person, and I'm sure there is some variance within the nation's people, let alone your greater species, but most are reported to be a few fingers shorter than my height."

Which put them somewhere around the upper ranges of five feet and the lower ranges of six. Meanwhile, I was anything but. Even after changing worlds and maybe realities, I was fated to remain a shrimp of my species.

Except…

Riok was huge, even for a synossian, and while I still didn't know what level he was, it was clear he was more powerful than the rest of his band. Had the attribute points he allocated through leveling physically changed his size?

Miko didn't know the answer to that when I asked, but I settled back on our dalys and let the idea of it wash over me. I'd been in competition for the title of shortest adult male wherever I went back in Ohio, but maybe that didn't have to remain true?

Maybe belonging to a class that depended on physical attributes wasn't such a bad thing after all.

14

By sundown, the northern mountains, which I thought we'd been paralleling, had grown so distant they were hard to spot. I helped Miko with caring for our dalys—removing the saddle and gear and brushing it down in the absence of a stable's other tools—and then we both followed the others over to where shelters were being erected. Unlike tents back home, these were low to the ground, barely tall enough for a synossian to slip under. Given the lack of trees, I assumed it made sense to keep a lower profile.

I pitched in with the… uh… pitching… which won me a few smiles of thanks. I even earned a heavy pat on the shoulder from a Spearman who went by the name of Kato. Through some kind of miracle, I managed to keep my feet, but it was a close call; the man had almost definitely moderated his strength, but it had *still* felt like being punched with a brick.

When the last shelter was done, Riok approached us, dark spear in hand. "Though we are in friendly territory, we will continue to travel under wartime code. That means no fires tonight, and the meal will be served cold. As ever, security remains paramount." He turned to me. "I would teach you something of the spear."

Kato, lurking nearby, stiffened in apparent shock. "There is no need to trouble yourself, sir. The son of Corros can join our training ranks for the evening, or I can put him through his steps instead."

Riok shook his scaled head. "Brian Fieldings faced a sluthar with his bare hands. For his sake and my own conscience, I will teach him the basics of the weapon he has chosen to wield."

"As you say."

"Train the claw while we are absent," Riok said to Sergeant Loris as the other man stepped out of the shadows. "When I return, I will spar with all who wish it."

That got the attention of more than just the handful of synossians already present. Heads popped up across the camp, eyes wide and practically glowing, as if Riok had just announced an early Christmas.

Loris banged a clawed hand against his chest and nodded, then spun away to bark at the rest of the claw. "You heard the Wind Walker! If you are not on watch, get your duties done and fall in for training. Tonight, you will cross weapons with a ranked Aspirant!"

Riok seemed unaffected by the sudden fervor with which people threw themselves into their assigned tasks. He gestured to me to follow, and we left the camp, traveling until we had passed through the scouts' perimeter. There, he stopped, and scanned me head to toe.

"Where is your weapon, Brian?"

"I left it with the dalys."

"Then let this be your first lesson." His voice was deep and grave, empty of the occasional humor he'd shown so far. "Your spear goes where you do. Always. My people have their claws and teeth to fall back on, if all else is lost, but you have few natural weapons of your own." He extended his spear and pointed to my head, hands, elbows, knees, and feet. "These will avail you in some situations, yes, but you are best served with an implement that provides both reach and penetrating power. Now, go and fetch your spear. I will wait."

Feeling like I'd already disappointed my own personal—if reptilian—Mr. Miyagi, I trotted back to camp. I could feel the eyes of every synossian there on me as I made my way to where the dalysi were munching on winter grass. My spear and saddlebags were still off to one side where I'd left them. I took both with me and hurried back. Upon reaching Riok again, I froze, my mouth dropping open.

The Wind Walker was waiting for me, as promised, but he was far from idle. His spearhead glimmered darkly in the late evening sun, etching lines through the air as he whirled and thrust, both man and weapon always in motion, always in harmony. The action was too fast to follow, but something told me this was far from Riok's top speed, that whatever he was doing was as much about meditative contemplation as killing a thousand unseen enemies.

A moment later, the dance was over. Riok's spear butt planted itself in the earth as the man himself came to attention. His stance was easy and controlled, his breath light and unhurried despite the dance of death he'd just performed. He found me across the empty space and nodded.

"The second lesson," he said, going right back into his instruction, "is a simple one. The spear points at your enemy."

I blinked and waited for more, but he had gone quiet, deep blue eyes fixed upon me.

Oh. Right.

I set down the saddlebags and took my spear in both hands. It was identical to the one I'd lost to the sluthar and felt heavy and unwieldy in my hands. Nothing at all like the bladed feather Riok had made of his own weapon. Carefully, I extended the spear until it was pointing at the other man.

"Now then," he said, "let us begin."

○○○

By the time we were done, the sun was low in the sky, and I was caked in sweat, despite the chill. I'd taken off my borrowed robe about five minutes into the longest hour of my life since junior-year SATs, and even my sweat pants were soaked through.

Forget *breathing hard*, I couldn't say with certainty that Riok was breathing at all. The man was clearly a scaled automaton, sent back from the future to extinguish any hopes I had of ever knowing how to fight, and that spear in his hands was somehow both as light as air and an unstoppable force.

We'd spent the entire training session on Riok's second lesson—*the spear points at your enemy*—with a few remedial courses on the first lesson—*the spear goes where you do*—every time I dropped my weapon; a result of baby's first failed parry or my fingers simply not keeping up with the increasingly frantic orders my brain was screaming their way.

"How the hell did *three legions* of people like you lose a battle?" I said, trying not to wheeze.

"Numbers matter," he said, the words coming slowly, as if each had to be individually mined, "but strength matters more. A cycle ago, I was one of several dozen ranked Aspirants spread across three legions. Now, those of us who remain could fit into a single claw. And while I have earned some acclaim for my skill and power, the Buried put mine to shame."

"What does it mean to be *ranked?* Do you all have some kind of yearly tournament or something?" It wasn't the first time I'd heard the phrasing, and this seemed like as good a time as any to ask about it. Especially if it gave me more time to catch my breath.

"Tournaments are—or were—a part of our culture, yes, but *rank* is another artifact of the Framework." Riok took a seat in the circle of grass we'd long since trod into dirt and waited for me to join him. I brought my spear with me. "The higher your level, the more difficult it becomes to advance, with skills rapidly becoming the primary impediment rather than deeds or experience. However, when—or if—an individual reaches level ten, they inevitably plateau, finding their progression stalling out."

"Why?"

"I am not a scholar," he reminded me, "but—" He paused again and visibly changed courses. "On your world of origin, do they have the concept of something called a soul?"

This was familiar territory. "Yeah, although I'm not sure anyone has proved it exists. Miko said that on Eos, the soul exists in the spiritual realm, and that the Framework is some kind of a conduit between soul and body, right?"

"Precisely."

"What does that have to do with ranking?"

"At level ten, the block faced by every Aspirant and Dedicated—and overcome by far too few of either—is not one of intellect or physical prowess. It's a question of your soul itself. Each person must find their sense of self, their purpose and their philosophy, and refine it."

I chewed on that for a bit. The sound of the other synossians training back at camp was clearly audible now that our own training had ended. "Does that tie into someone's Ideal?"

"It does, and it doesn't. Your Ideals, if you have any, are a starting point. What they mean to you, how you choose to interpret them and pursue them in your life, all this and more." He barked the synossian version of a laugh. "When I first dreamed of taking up the spear, I didn't realize there would be philosophy involved."

"What is your Ideal? Or is that not a polite question to ask?"

"It is not so much impolite as slightly intrusive. Yet we are brothers of the spear, are we not?" He seemed to take my silence as agreement. "My first Ideal was *honor*. Soon after I ranked, I found another: *duty*."

Huh. Those fit. "So, ranking is about refining the core of who you are? That sounds complicated."

"Our academics believe that the process intentionally resists explanation, so that we each must find our own paths forward. Most who reach level ten are unable to take that step at all. It took me three full moons of seclusion to achieve my breakthrough and even now, I remain unable to adequately describe the journey. I became more *me*, I believe. More certain in my path, more secure in my beliefs, just… *more*. My soul was reshaped and through the Framework, my physical being responded to that reshaping."

It all sounded very mystical, so naturally, I distrusted it immediately. Still, I couldn't deny that Riok had an aura that none of the other synossians could match.

"Is that why you feel the way that you do?" It took a few tries to explain what I was talking about, but once I had, Riok nodded.

"What you are experiencing is what any individual feels when confronted with someone ranked above them. You know that there is no way to see another's personal record without the *Analyst* trait, yes?" At my nod, he continued. "That makes any encounter with strangers a dangerous situation, precisely because there is no way to easily judge level or capability. But if you encounter someone whose presence bears down upon you, you at least know that they are ranked above you and not to be trifled with."

"And the Buried?"

He sighed. "Scale Lord Garlos, who leads the legion at the northern forts, is the strongest person left in our legions at seventeenth level. The Fist of Kal, who leads the Oathkeeper's faithful back in Whitehall, is a few long-sought skill gains from twenty. Their presence does not weigh upon me; we are equal in rank if not level. But the

Buried, the terrors who broke the sky and routed our forces… it was all I could do to even stand against them. Until that battle, it was widely believed that there was only a single rank, and that it was reached at level ten… that the stories of our ancestors and their enemies walking the Great Wilds like demigods were only myth. Our slaughter on the plains taught us otherwise."

"So, the Buried are… at least level twenty?"

"If I had to guess from their auras, I would say higher. Much higher." His words were quiet, barely carrying over the sound of unseen bugs in the distance. "According to legend, my people once fielded entire scales of Aspirants at level twenty or above. A thousand cycles later, and we lack even one such person. I was trained from hatching to hold a spear. For ten cycles, I have marched in Kal's legion, in the finest fighting force assembled upon this continent, and yet I cannot help but wonder what we lost when we fled our ancient home. Maybe all these generations of peace have made us soft, or maybe our enemy would have overrun our honored ancestors as easily as they have us. I do not know."

"But you're going to fight them anyway?"

"Our goal is not victory, but time," he reminded me. "Every seven-day, more ships sail for the Great Wilds. We will buy as many moons as we can with our blood."

I was glad I was already sitting down because that admission weighed almost as heavily on me as his presence.

"Having said that," he continued, his voice shedding some of its dark tone, "numbers *do* matter. A single unranked individual obviously cannot stand against a highly ranked competitor, but a hundred of them? A thousand? Whatever level the Buried may be, there are only five of them and as mortals, they must tire. The solution is to bleed them, to drown them in an endless flood of attacks. Our strategy, hatched with our allies, the Brushan, will be to focus our strikes and our defenses upon the Buried themselves as they thread their way through the mountain passes. Slow those few and their armies will grind to a halt. Destroy even one of the five and their collective power will be dramatically reduced."

"You're talking about a war of attrition."

He tapped his left forearm, a gesture I was starting to gather indicated agreement. "Our mistake was in meeting them in the open field, confident in our own superiority. Instead, we will harry them from the shadows, from the woods and the hills. And in doing so, we will also prolong a war that might otherwise end in a single day of traditional combat."

None of which changed the reality that Riok, his soldiers, and the other Aspirants in the empire were preparing to *die* in the next few months, their lives spent to give the rest of the nation a chance to make the deadly ocean crossing back to the Great Wilds they'd once fled.

It was sacrifice on a scale I could barely comprehend, all of it just to ensure that *somebody* survived.

The primacy's only chance of victory would have entailed finding someone strong enough to go toe to toe with the elites they called the Buried. Instead, thanks to a plate of pot brownies, they'd gotten me. Even as drained and empty as I was, that hurt.

"I'm sorry I wasn't what you were all hoping for."

"You spoke face to face with Shan in your dream," said Riok, his words firm. "That means something. Whatever the Trickster's reputation, he is Kal's brother and has always been a protector of our people. I have faith that his latest plots will bear fruit."

I didn't know what to say to that.

"And on that note," Riok continued, "it is time we move on to the most important lesson of the night."

"More important than *your weapon goes where you do?*" I patted my spear.

"Indeed. Because this lesson is the key to advancement."

That got my attention. I straightened up from my tired slouch. "I'm listening."

"I believe Shrine Keeper Naseri told you already that advancement requires two things?"

"Yeah, first, you have to level two Major and two Minor skills to their limit. And second, you have to get enough experience to strengthen your soul."

"Correct. Both can be accomplished through training, but gains are most often seen through combat itself. After all, it is through life and death struggles that the soul is truly put under pressure."

Miko had told me much the same thing. As a Warrior, it'd be faster to level through killing things than with endless practice sessions with the spear. I still didn't *love* that, but I wasn't surprised either. Maybe it was because of the sluthar that had greeted me upon my arrival, but I'd gotten a feeling that Eos was a particularly bloodthirsty world.

"Skill gain requires focus, which is why even my veterans train as hard as they do. In the early levels, each rank will be swift, but the more skills you have gained, the slower the progress will become. Given that skills can also degrade, it is wise to focus on only a handful of skills and to build your class around those skills. To become a true lord of the spear, for example, you must always be pushing yourself, improving your understanding of the weapon and expanding your knowledge of how to best utilize it. If you focused on learning every weapon, you would surely master none of them."

I just nodded again, even though some of it was information I already had been told. I needed to learn everything I could about how things worked on Eos, and if high school had been anything to go by, repetition was a key part of my learning process.

"You have yet to see any skill gains since this morning, yes?" It was phrased as a question, but something told me he already knew the question.

"Yeah. Honestly, I'd expected to get a point in *Riding* at the very least."

"And this is where we return to the discussion of souls. Everything you've done since arriving in Eos has been a physical action, from battling the sluthar to riding and caring for your dalys to tonight's training. However, your actions must now be internalized and transmitted to your soul before the Framework will calculate any gains."

I blinked. I needed to learn things with my *soul?* What did that even mean? "Is there, like, an established process for doing that?" I finally asked.

"This would be a poor lesson if not." Riok's teeth gleamed blood red in the light of the slowly setting sun. "As with everything in the Framework, the method is the individual's to choose, but I will show you what has worked for my people. To start, find a seat in a quiet place as we have already done. Rest your hands, palms-up on your legs and knees, let your eyes close and empty your mind."

I'd gone through something like this almost four years earlier, with my ex-girlfriend, Kate. "Are we… meditating?"

"You are familiar with the practice then?"

"The concept, at least."

"Excellent. The goal is to separate yourself from the present moment. Once you have freed yourself from your mortal body, you let your experiences flow through you, part of you and yet distinct from your mortal self. As those moments are digested, some amount of each will be sent to your intangible soul to be absorbed."

"And once my soul has absorbed enough, the Framework recognizes my gains by ranking up the associated skill?"

"And sometimes attributes as well, yes."

That set me back a second. "I thought we only improved our attributes when we reached even levels?"

"What you speak of are the bonuses gained through leveling. They are in addition to, not in place of, the ability to naturally improve your attributes through related training."

"So, I could lift weights and boost my Strength, and then boost it again by choosing to upgrade it when I reach level two?"

"Of course. Though it should be noted that natural gains can be lost, just as a skill can degrade. Bonuses assigned through levels remain, regardless of what might come in the future."

"Huh."

It was a sad thing to admit, even to myself, but of my tiny circle of friends back on Earth, I was easily the *least* suited for this new life on Eos. Bug would have figured out the underlying mechanics of the Framework in a matter of hours and would already be trying to break its rules, while Kate would have taken to the meditation side and all this talk of souls like a duck to water. Meanwhile, I was a mediocre gamer and about as spiritual as a binge-drinking Spring Breaker in South Beach.

Meditation just wasn't something I did. Even sitting there with Riok was enough to remind me that I was shirtless and starting to get cold again, that some of my muscles were sore from riding all day, and that the rest were sore from trying to hold off a master of combat with nothing but a sharp stick.

"It may take some practice," admitted the other man. "I would suggest you make it part of your nighttime rituals. This is a foundational aspect of advancement, so it must be learned by anyone with a class or profession." He rose to his feet smoothly, finally tucking his spear back down by his side. "By the sounds of it, Sergeant Loris' training is winding down, so it is time for me to join them. You are welcome to watch our sparring sessions, but if you would rather, you can get your evening meal and call it a night."

He paused and his next words were almost apologetic. "In the absence of a town to shelter in, we will be sleeping in tents, as you already saw. Unfortunately, our supplies are limited. As the two smallest individuals, I have you and Shrine Maiden Naseri sharing space."

"If she's okay with that, then so am I." Something about us being entirely different species kept the whole thing from feeling even vaguely taboo.

"Excellent." He pulled me to my feet, hand so large that it engulfed my arm with room to spare. "Let us return. And Brian?"

"Yeah?"

"The world is not yet lost. As long as we breathe, we can fight."

It would have been more reassuring if I knew *how* to fight.

○○○

I was slow in following Riok back to the camp, and by the time I arrived, he was already engaged with the first of the night's challengers. I took a seat in the grass, close enough to see, but far enough to be safely out of the way. As I watched, the burly Spearman dispatched every synossian in his path.

I'd seen Riok in action once, against the sluthar, and between that, his spear dance, and our own training, I thought I'd had a pretty good handle on his capabilities. The next half-glass of sparring showed me otherwise. He never used a single technique, as far as I could tell, and yet nobody could touch him. Almost as impressively, I could sense he was adjusting on the fly to the skill level of whoever he was facing, making sure that each spar would be a true contest instead of just a beat down.

It quickly became apparent that the claw had ordered themselves from the least skilled to the most, and by the time Riok and

Loris clashed, their movements were too fast to follow. I did my best to just let it all soak in, as if their skill was something I could absorb through osmosis. If I was going to use a spear to survive, I needed to know more than the footwork Riok had started showing me; I also needed to understand the ebbs and flows of combat.

By the time their match ended, with Loris crouched defensively and Riok's spearhead humming a mere inch from the other man's throat, I wasn't sure I'd picked up on anything that would contribute to my own progression… but watching hadn't hurt anything either. If nothing else, it was motivation. Someday, assuming we didn't all die horribly, that could be me up there, looking like some kind of superhero.

Spear and saddlebags in hand, I fetched my cleaning supplies and went to find a place to clean off. Before I shared the small confines of a tent with anyone, I had layers upon layers of dust, dried sweat, and dirt to remove.

The water, somehow, was even colder this time, the *bath* was an open field upwind from the hastily dug latrine, and the brush was just as brutally rough as it had been that morning, but I still felt better when I was done. Cold, sore, and tired, yeah, but being clean was its own reward.

It didn't take long to find the tent I'd be sharing with Miko. She was already inside, seated upright and with her scaled head bowed. I crawled to the opposite side of the low tent, trying to give her time and space for whatever it was she was doing, but she opened her strange orange eyes and turned to me.

"Brian Fieldings."

"Shrine Keeper Naseri," I returned.

"I have left my appointed shrine," she corrected, and even if the shape of her mouth made a frown difficult, there was something of the expression in her voice, "and thus should no longer hold to the title of shrine keeper. In formal circumstances, I would be Priestess Naseri. Here on the road, I am just Miko."

"Right." I coughed. "What can I do for you, Miko?"

"How was your training with the Wind Walker?"

"Good? I guess?" The last vestiges of daylight had finally faded, leaving us as two darker shadows in the tent's pitch-black interior. "I think we proved I'm not any kind of prodigy."

It clearly wasn't what she wanted to hear.

"I see. Well, there is always tomorrow."

"Yeah. We're going to tackle techniques in a day or two, apparently. In the meantime, Riok taught me how to meditate for skill gains, so I think I'm going to give that a try."

"Would you like a healing first?"

"I'm never going to say no to that," I admitted. All of me hurt, even my head. I wasn't sure how much of the latter was still caffeine withdrawal and how much of it was trying to learn how to fight with a weapon taller than I was, but either way, I was ready for it to be gone.

Either synossians had better night vision than humans, or Miko's other senses allowed her to pinpoint my precise location, because a moment later, light bloomed in the small tent, and I realized she had positioned herself directly in front of me.

Energy flooded my body, washing away the strains of a full day of riding, a glass of fumbling about with my spear, and my second full day without caffeine. Even my shivering from the cold bath rapidly became a thing of the past.

"Thank you," I said, blinking my eyes to adjust to darkness that seemed that much more complete now that the glow of her spell—or divine technique, technically—had passed.

"May I ask you a question, Brian Fieldings?"

"Just Brian," I reminded her, trying to find her in the darkness. "And yes, of course you can."

"Are you heart-blighted?"

"I'm… sorry?" I was starting to get used to hearing words that I knew without being able to grasp their actual meaning.

"You said that you were not considered a person of great renown back on Earth, yes?"

"That's right."

"Nor were you wise or particularly successful?"

This felt less like a question than an endless series of putdowns, but I knew where she was going with this.

"That's right," I finally said, waiting for the inevitable question: *why had the ritual chosen me?*

"Then how," she asked, "are you handling all that has happened to you so calmly?"

I blinked. *That* was not what I'd expected her to ask.

"What does *heart-blighted* mean?" I asked.

"There are those who simply cannot feel things deeply. It is not a true affliction, despite the name, and they can be productive members of society, yet they often find it more difficult to fit in with their nest-brothers and sisters."

"And you think that might be me?"

"I think that if *I* had woken up in your Oh-hi-oh, had found myself taken across the Veil to someplace new and entirely alien, I would have struggled to function at all. Yet you appear entirely stable."

"Huh." Maybe it was the darkness hiding both of our faces, but it was easier to talk to her in the tent than it had ever been on the back of the dalys. Easier to share, maybe. "I don't think I'm as stable as you think. I'm just trying to focus on what I can control and leaving everything else to be dealt with later."

"And that works?"

"So far." I waited for a reply, and when one didn't come, shrugged, and turned back to my bunk. "I'm going to try to meditate now, I think. Unless there's anything else I can do for you?"

I don't think I was supposed to hear her reply, but the hushed words traveled across the tent like someone had hand delivered them to my ears.

"Just make all of *this* have meaning."

I didn't have any reassurances to offer.

ooo

Meditation is a scam, I decided, much, much later. *Either that or my soul is off on summer vacation by itself, resting next to a pristine lake that my body will never get to see and sipping something warm and alcoholic.*

I pulled my borrowed robe back around me and lay down in the darkness. Somewhere to my left, Miko was already asleep, and given the likelihood of yet another early morning, it was past time I joined her.

15-Interlude

Berys was waiting outside Riok's tent. The Priest stood as the Wind Walker approached, his visage lost in the darkness. "No wounds to heal this time, I see."

"These were mere spars, Berys," rumbled Riok. "More instruction than actual combat."

"Spoken as if you hadn't cracked three scales and almost lost an eye in another such spar."

Riok sent the smaller synossian a look that not even the darkness could fully hide. "I was thirteen cycles old!"

"Were you?" He shrugged. "It still resonates in my memory."

"I'm sure it does." Riok snorted and moved to his tent. "Is there something you need, *old* friend?"

"I come under the auspices of the Pure," said Berys, bowing deeply, "to offer her wisdom and my own counsel."

"Meaning you want to know how Brian Fieldings performed."

"It sounds less majestic when you phrase it that way." Berys shrugged. "But I do confess to a certain curiosity."

The Wind Walker's voice dropped to a whisper. "Either his skill with the spear is so great that he is able to mask it even from me, or he is every bit the novice he appears to be."

"Well, we did not think he was lying about his inexperience."

"We did not, though I find myself wishing that he had." Riok's sigh filled the night sky. "He is not the worst student I have taught."

"High praise from—"

"I did not intend it as such. He is that much further from being a hidden genius. With time, he could make an adequate spearman, but we both know that time is something that eludes us."

"The gods chose him for a reason," said Berys. "If his starting position does not impress, maybe his rate of advancement will?"

"Perhaps. Or perhaps he was sent to do something other than fight our war for us."

"Strange to have a Warrior suggest such a thing."

"I blame the company I keep." Riok's smile, lost in the darkness, made itself known in his voice. After a moment, even that small vestige of humor fell away. "I do not know why Brian Fieldings was Chosen, or how one such as he could deliver salvation to our people, but he is here, and we are the ones who found him. I will train him as best I can and deliver him to the primarch, blessed be her name. Perhaps she and her council can divine a path forward."

"All is not yet lost, my young friend. Have faith."

"Faith is your domain." He tapped his massive fist against the armor under his robes. "I will focus upon my duty."

"As it ever was," murmured Berys.

"As it ever shall be," came the reply.

16

The next day went a lot like the first—long hours in the saddle, followed by a night of training, cold food, a colder shower, and a total lack of progress when it came to gaining skills. I *felt* like I was growing more capable—with the synossians, the dalys, and the spear—but the Framework stubbornly refused to confirm those gains.

On the third day out of Ilya, four things of interest broke up what was already starting to feel like an endless routine. The first was Slanit and another scout riding back to our small column with word of tracks ahead. Before I could even try to convince Miko to go see what was going on, our dalys was on its way to the front. Apparently, she was as curious as I was.

"Heavy treads and soled shoes," Slanit was telling Riok and Berys as we arrived, his words brisk as he used as few words as possible. "Brushan. Day or two ahead."

"Earlier than expected, but we still will reach Whitehall in time for the planning sessions," said the Wind Walker. He turned to Sergeant Loris. "Still, we'll extend today's ride by a glass to make up some ground."

"Yes, sir."

Riok turned to the second scout who was still crouched over the tracks, shaking their head. "Is there something else?"

"No, sir. I mean… yes." This synossian's scales were an odd patchwork of red and blue, but her voice was steady. "There are more tracks than I'd expect for an ambassador's entourage."

"She's right," agreed Slanit after a moment of inspection. "Full scale's worth instead of a paired claw."

It took me a moment to remember that, in the synossian system of military units, a scale was equal to five claws. So… roughly seventy-five people?

"It is a long journey from the mountain," reasoned Berys.

Riok tapped his left arm. "These are dangerous times and the Brushan know that the winter has been a hard one. I don't think we should begrudge the ambassador choosing to augment his own guard. An escort of such size will keep all but the most desperate of creatures away, yet it still represents a small force compared to the garrison at Whitehall. Our leaders should find neither harm nor insult in the decision."

"As you say, sir," said the red and blue scout.

I leaned into Miko and kept my voice low. "Ambassador?"

"The Brushan are traveling to Whitehall to finalize our defensive strategy," she murmured back. "Riok's claw was recalled from the northern forts to participate in the meetings. As veterans of the first battle, their words hold weight."

"Indeed," said Riok, coming over to join us as the scouts rode away. "Brian, we will need to find a quiet moment before the beginning of those strategy sessions to introduce you to the council. Perhaps they will have a better grasp on how your presence here might change things. In the meantime, we can only keep on as we have been doing."

"More riding." After having oriented my schedule around my dad's care for years, there was something deeply disquieting about having long blocks of time to do nothing but sit astride a furry six-legged horse.

"The dalysi are not always comfortable, but they *are* sturdy. And at least there will be something of note to see today." Before I could ask what he was talking about, he turned to Miko. "Shrine Keeper Naseri, it is my understanding that you plan to join the provisional legion being formed in Whitehall?"

"Yes, Wind Walker."

I couldn't help but notice that Miko didn't correct *Riok* about the form of address he'd used.

"Might I suggest you join my claw in training tonight then? Even a Priestess should be able to defend herself."

Miko bowed her head. I'd been training with Riok, but she had spent the past few evenings alone in our tent. "Yes, sir. Though I did not bring weapons with me to the shrine."

Seated behind her, I tried not to react. *Lesson #1* remained all too fresh in my mind.

"What weapons do you favor?"

"The sling and the short staff."

Riok nodded, turning to Loris. "Sergeant, make sure the shrine keeper is supplied with both. She will work with our scouts tonight."

"Understood, sir."

And that, apparently, was that.

ooo

The second big event came sometime after we'd eaten lunch in the saddle. After multiple days on Eos, the lack of toothbrushes had gone from a mild inconvenience to an outright concern, but Miko had directed me to a pouch of dried leaves in the saddlebags. I had assumed it was the synossian version of salad and had avoided it accordingly, but when chewed, the leaves turned into a minty sort of liquid paste. I had just finished gargling with said paste and spitting it back out again, trying not to watch the long, long, *long* arc it made from the top of the dalys all the way down to the ground below, when Miko stiffened.

"What is it?" We'd been winding around a series of hills, the treeless landscape having long since lost my attention, but she was looking ahead. All I saw were more hills and dark clouds looming with the promise of a storm that I hoped would bring rain instead of snow.

"One of the ancient wonders of Issandryl," she told me. "I wasn't sure we would pass it on our way back to Whitehall."

It took another glass or so to even guess what she was talking about, in part because I'd been looking at the ground instead of the sky. The black clouds grew ever more prominent as we rode forward, but instead of traveling with the wind, they seemed fixed to one location. Lightning flashed silver and gold within the storm, though the accompanying thunder was curiously absent.

"We'll circle to the south," said Niaci, still our silent escort, "but the hills there will provide a vantage point as we pass by."

Neither would give me any more information than that, so I kept my eyes on the strange storm as we rode on. It wasn't until we climbed the hills Niaci had pointed out that I finally saw something that firmly separated Eos from Earth.

Beneath black, circling storm clouds was a pit that descended hundreds of feet. Still, we had canyons and sinkholes and such back home. What made this weird were the islands suspended above that pit, craggy masses of a strange blueish stone hovering in the air above and around each other, forming multiple layers of floating sediment in the sky.

It was almost like someone had tossed a blue ceramic plate in the air and smashed it with a hammer, only for the pieces to find their own gravitational equilibrium instead of tumbling back to the ground.

"What is it?"

"We call it the Fall," said Miko. "It was here when our people first reached Issandryl and has remained unchanged in the time since. Our ancestors believed it to be a remnant of the war between gods, fragments from the transcendent realm that somehow found their way to Eos and have remained fixed ever since."

"Has anyone ever tried to see what's up there?" It was hard to judge scale from this distance, but many of the islands seemed large enough for people, if too distant from one another to make ascending them possible. "One of the other races on the continent has wings, right?"

"The skyborn." Miko nodded.

"Many have tried," added Niaci. "There has always been some fool who believes they alone are fated to reach the top. With the skyborn suborned, I guess the most recent attempt was truly the last."

I winced. The doom hanging over the Synossian Primacy was a subject that seemed impossible to avoid entirely.

"What happened to the would-be explorers?" I asked, trying to steer the conversation back to safer topics.

"Most found themselves plagued by weakness as they neared the Fall," said Niaci. "Of those who ignored that sensation and pressed on anyway, the vast majority ended up plummeting from the sky when their wings gave out."

"And the others?"

"Fell to the guardians of the place." Miko pointed out a flock of birds lazily flying about within the storm, so high that I only saw them because they moved in a contradictory pattern to the clouds themselves. "It is said that their wingspans are thrice the length of a full-grown dalys, and their talons are not bone but a metal that puts our own alloys to shame."

I blinked and dramatically reassessed the scale of what I was seeing. If those birds were each twenty-plus-feet wide, then the land masses they were flying about were enormous… vast swaths of stone hanging in flagrant disregard of gravity's embrace.

"What about the pit below?"

"That *has* been explored," said Miko, "to some extent, at least. Those who have flown down and returned never found a bottom. It is as if a hole was bored, not just through Eos but through the fabric of the physical realm itself."

I didn't know what to say to that. It sounded impossible, but so did bus-sized birds and islands hovering in the air.

"Perhaps," mused Niaci, "we could lure the Buried here and toss them in. It would be just to see them go from being entombed in one hole to falling forever in another."

Given what Riok had told me about the Buried, it didn't seem feasible, but Niaci no doubt already knew that. And it was always good to have options.

◠◠◠

The third thing of interest didn't happen until we'd finished riding for the day, the Fall now hours behind us. I took care of our dalys as Miko went to train with the scouts. Once camp was set, I stripped down to my sweatpants and had my own training session with Riok. After thirty minutes—a half-glass—or so of training, he stopped, his blue-eyed gaze falling on me like an anvil.

"Still no skill gains?"

"I'm trying."

"I know you are." For a long moment, he was a statue, the cool breeze toying with the ends of his robe. "Perhaps we should move on to techniques then. I prefer to leave them until the trainee has at least a small foundation of skill in their given weapon, but time is not our friend."

"You're going to teach me how to use *Lunge?*"

"I am." He paused again. "Despite being a common-ranked technique, judicious application of it can change the tide of battle, or even end a battle entirely."

Techniques, he'd told me a second time the previous day, almost *always* started at common rank. While every even level granted a person an increase in the attribute of their choice, every odd level came with a selection of three techniques. At least one of those options would be an upgrade to techniques the person already had, while at least one of the others would be an entirely new technique. It was how Miko had been able to choose between augmenting her spell, *Flare*, or getting access to *Minor Healing* instead. As a technique was upgraded, its rarity changed accordingly.

"At its core, *Lunge* is a weapon-based movement technique," said Riok. "It assists you in crossing the space between two points."

I wasn't entirely sure what that meant, but decided I'd rather find out for myself than ask. "Okay. What do I do?"

"First, stand in striking position," instructed the giant lizard. "Body bladed to your target, spear in both hands and aimed accordingly."

This much came easily after three days, though it still felt awkward. "And now?"

Riok took up position across from me and then, after a few moments of consideration, took several long steps back. "Now, strike while calling upon your technique."

Which was almost as helpful as telling me to stop thinking so much during meditation. I arched an eyebrow like I was the Rock and waited for more detailed instruction.

"Your body is a reflection of your soul," he said, in another oft-repeated bit of phrasing that didn't help me at all. "Don't think. Don't act. The Framework has already seen to it that you know this technique. You just need to let it flow through you."

Kate really *would* have been five times the fake savior I was, but I was here and she was in NYC. So, I nodded and tried to follow his advice. Don't think. Don't act. Just flow.

Predictably, nothing happened.

"Should I… shout out the technique name or something?"

"Only if you want your opponent to know what you're doing before you do it," he said, voice bone dry. "Remember, *Lunge* is a technique that thrusts you forward through space. Your weapon becomes the singular point of that thrust, and everything else follows suit. As you strike, try focusing on that concept becoming reality."

A few failed thrusts later, it was becoming clear that this might not be the sort of night for concepts to magically become reality.

"Would a demonstration help?"

"It couldn't hurt."

Riok nodded and moved to stand at my side. "While many attributes can impact aspects of a given technique, actually activating that technique requires little more than an act of Will." He mimicked my stance, his spear cocked back like it had been before he skewered the sluthar. "I do not create the strike; it has existed since the first spearman desperately charged a distant foe. My role is to simply unleash it, to let it once more manifest in this reality."

He thrust forward and as he did so, his entire body blurred across the clearing like a fiery meteor. A mournful howl followed his passage, the displaced air moaning as he carved through space itself, that dangerous spearhead leading the way.

It was just as terrifying as it had been the first time I'd seen it and knowing that it was some sort of upgraded version of my own technique didn't lessen the intimidation factor at all. Still, I tried to focus on what I'd seen and not just the way it made my knees tremble.

Unleash the technique. Let it flow through me. The soul already knows what to do.

I breathed in slowly, focused on a point across the clearing, shifted my weight, and thrust. Exactly as I'd done literally a dozen times before.

Only this time, something changed.

As I drove outward with my spear, the clearing blurred about me, like I was sprinting forward instead of taking a single step. Riok had been a good ten feet away, but he was suddenly in my path, my spearhead rocketing toward the center of his chest. I tried to pull my strike, but it was too late—

And then he moved smoothly out of the way, slapping my spearhead aside with one clawed hand and keeping me from tumbling into the earth with the other.

"What the hell was that?" I asked as time caught up with us.

"You tell me." He set me back on my feet. "What did you do?"

"Shifted my weight?"

That won me a laugh. "Is that really it?"

It wasn't, but I couldn't really verbalize what I *had* done. "That was *Lunge?* I did it?"

"Yes." Four days together had taught him to read my expressions in a way that I still hadn't mastered with his. "Perhaps being a Warrior is not so bad after all, hmm?"

"That. Was. Awesome!"

"The question," he asked with a toothy grin, "is whether you can do it again?"

The answer, apparently, was no.

Not at first, anyway. It wasn't like summoning and dismissing my character sheet. I had to figure out what I'd done to trigger it and then reproduce it exactly. And considering I was already tired from the day's ride and our training, it wasn't easy.

"Remember," he said. "Focus on the result you desire, and let the Framework do the rest. A technique *wants*—"

I *Lunged* toward him, once again feeling that sense of exhilarating speed. Even in mid-speech, Riok was ready. And this time, he took the spear from me, and tossed me over his hip into the dirt.

"—to be used," he continued, as if nothing had happened. "And that makes all the difference."

Once I had gathered myself again, the third time came even easier than the second, just over a minute later. It was as if I was now following a path I'd successfully found with my earlier attempts. But the fourth attempt…

Nothing happened. I took a step and stumbled, only the butt of my spear saving me from face-planting in the dirt.

"What happened?" I wasn't tired, but I was… drained. Like after a particularly long shift at work or when Dad was having one of his episodes. I felt paper thin.

"A technique can only be used so frequently."

Right. I had forgotten about the cooldown effect Miko had mentioned. That explained why it had taken me a solid minute between technique activations, even once I knew what I was doing. But this felt different. More like—

"In addition, each usage saps your energy. The magnitude varies from technique to technique, or even between variations on the same technique, but a single attack can be as tiring as a quarter-glass of mundane combat. I've seen Aspirants drop where they stood from using advanced techniques they lacked the energy to invoke. Our High Circle gave their lives doing the same."

"Which is why you think you can grind the Buried down?"

"We will grant them no rest or respite. We will force them to unleash their techniques again and again until their souls are so exhausted that we can swarm them and bring them down."

"And you think that's possible?"

He was silent for far too long. Finally, he shrugged. "In two moons' time, we will find out."

As incredible as training *Lunge* was—and truly, learning to rocket around a meadow with my spear was the closest I'd felt to being a superhero since making it across the monkey bars in elementary school—training with Riok was only the second-best thing that happened that day. Because later that night, after we'd eaten yet another cold meal, and Miko healed both of our sore muscles, I found myself once again trying to meditate.

The tent was cramped, its ceiling low enough that even I couldn't stand upright. The ground beneath the heavy canvas floor was cold and hard. Miko was an ever-constant presence to my right, shifting in the darkness as she tried to get comfortable enough to sleep, and my mind was a strange mixture of excitement and exhaustion.

Yet none of those external details mattered.

I found the events of the last few days floating through my mind unbidden, observed and experienced by a part of me that was somehow both past and present. *Three days on the back of a dalys, the wind harsh in my face when I stopped using Miko as a windbreak. The great beast's muscles churning beneath us as terrain blurred past. Even taking care of that same mount at the end of the night, pushing aside its curious snout as I ran a brush through thick fur.*

And then there was the spear. Always at my side or in my hands. Even now, it rested next to me, its shaft close enough to touch. *Hours holding the weapon, taking careful steps to keep Riok in sight as the Spearman stalked me. The way my weight shifted to my lead leg as I thrust forward. The wan light of the bloody sun as it caught on the spearhead. Even the moment of impact when I'd driven a different spear, days earlier, into the body of the sluthar.*

I'd been on Eos for three and a half days, and for just a moment, the tent around me disappeared as those days flowed through me. I didn't have to think about them because I'd lived them. I just had to accept them and then send them on their way again.

And somewhere in all that, my soul, the Framework, or both, woke up and finally took notice.

I opened my eyes to find a dialogue box in front of me, perfectly visible despite the darkness of the tent's interior.

```
You have increased the following skills:

Major skills:
Light Armor [+1]: 1/10
Spear [+3]: 3/10

Minor skills:
Athleticism [+1]: 1/10
Avoidance [+1]: 1/10

General skills:
Animal Behaviorism [+2]: 2/10
Riding [+1]: 1/10
```

I yelled so loudly that Miko sprang to her feet, hit her head on the tent, and fell back to the ground. Shouts from outside the tent told me guards were on their way but that was a problem for future-Brian to deal with. Even the questions I had about a few of the skills I'd gained seemed irrelevant. All I wanted to do was look at the glowing notification window and smile.

I knew how to use my one and only technique and now I was finally—*finally!*—improving my skills too.

Life was looking up.

17

The rest of the camp was considerably less delighted with my recent skill-ups... or at least with having been woken up by my shouting for what were, in the end, relatively rudimentary gains. Synossians didn't have fur or feathers, but the lizards sure acted like I'd ruffled both, even as Sergeant Loris ordered them back to bed or the watch.

By the next morning, most of that ill humor had passed. Niaci even gave me a nod of acknowledgment when she found me already up, bathed, and helping ready my dalys for the day's ride. In some ways, that minor recognition felt almost as good as my gains the night before. It had been a long time since I'd earned anyone's respect... and almost as long since I'd cared about doing so.

But that had been in my old life, on my old world. This was Eos, and even if I was only a first-level Warrior with limited skills, the Framework gave me a means to improve every single day.

I wasn't *stuck*. The future was wide open.

Except for the massive army bearing down on the synossian empire and threatening to wipe everyone out, including you, said the voice in my mind.

Details, I shot back. *The synossians will figure something out over the next few months. And if all else fails, I can hitch a ride on the next outgoing fleet.*

You've never been on a boat before!

That just means I've got skill points to gain in Sailing.

Even the pessimistic part of my brain had nothing to say to that. Maybe I wasn't the savior everyone had anticipated, but I was growing. Who knew what I could be in a matter of weeks, let alone months?

My first clue as to how skills worked in the real world came as I prepped the dalys Miko and I would be riding. Little cues I'd missed the previous day were now evident: the way it shuffled its rear sets of legs when I approached from the right instead of the left, the soft chuff it made when I scratched behind its wolf-like ears, even the almost imperceptible grumbling when I pulled it away from the grass that was its breakfast.

I was pretty sure that increased awareness came from my new *Animal Behaviorism* skill. What I couldn't figure out was why that skill was ranked so high—above *Riding* and only one rank below *Spear*. I'd spent three days traveling on the back of a dalys and three nights getting one-on-one training in the spear with an acknowledged master. Meanwhile, I'd spent a comparatively small amount of time trying to help care for my mount.

If I'd been a vet or worked at an animal shelter back in Ohio, having two ranks in the skill might have made sense. As it was, I was just left with more questions.

That seemed to be a common issue with the Framework. No help text. No instruction manual. Nothing but questions and poor, hapless mortals trying to fumble their way to answers.

Thankfully, neither my body nor the dalys itself seemed to care exactly how or why I'd improved the skill. All that mattered was that I had. By the time Miko had made her way over, both our mount and I were ready to go. The Priestess, on the other hand, looked like she could use an extra-tall cold brew with a triple shot of espresso. *But hold the whip because I'm on a diet.* After multiple nearly silent mornings riding together, I had finally realized that Miko was *not* a morning person.

Being woken up in the middle of the night by her tentmate probably hadn't helped either.

As we left the campsite behind, my gains with the *Riding* skill were a little less obvious. I simply felt a touch more comfortable in the saddle, adjusting to the dalys' awkward stride and finding a stability in my seat that had been missing previously.

Even so, Miko noticed the improvement immediately.

"You gained the *Riding* skill, didn't you?"

"How did you know?"

"When our dalys started trotting, you didn't grab on to me as if I was the only thing keeping you from toppling to the ground." She threw me a toothy smile over one shoulder. "Is *that* what had you hollering like a phloxl in mating season last night?"

I had no idea what a phloxl was, but it didn't sound like a compliment. Then again, I kind of deserved it. I'd had to leave the tent to talk down Riok and the guards who'd come rushing in like there was a murder happening, and by the time I returned, Miko had been asleep again. "Yeah, sorry about that. I finally figured out the whole meditation thing."

"What did you get?"

I filled her in on my gains. None of them were particularly surprising, considering my activities since coming to Eos, but she at least pretended to be impressed. Even better, she had an answer about why I'd gained two points in *Animal Behaviorism.*

"The sluthar." When I didn't say anything, she elaborated. "You distracted it from more defenseless prey—me—by challenging its dominance. I don't have the skill myself, but from what I've read, it isn't just about taking care of domesticated creatures; it's about intuitively understanding the thought processes or attitudes of their wild cousins. Your actions with the sluthar and your work with the dalys likely both factored into your improvements. And since the first happened in combat with an opponent far stronger than either of us, it must have carried extra weight."

"Huh. That makes sense. Sort of." It was another General skill that would remain limited to ten ranks unless I found a profession that made use of it, but I didn't hate having it either. Especially since it already been useful when saddling the dalys that morning. And who knew? Maybe it would even factor into the techniques or advanced classes I was offered in the future? Everything felt so much more achievable now that I'd seen actual, physical proof of progression.

"Speaking of your actions with the sluthar," said Miko, interrupting my dreams of future deeds, "I should have thanked you back then for saving my life."

"We saved each other's lives," I pointed out. "And it was Riok really who saved us both."

"Well, yes, but—"

"And you wouldn't have needed saving at all if I hadn't screamed and brought the thing right to our door."

"I was not going to mention that again," she said, almost primly.

"I'm just glad we both made it through. And if I got some skills out of it too, I'm not going to complain."

"We likely earned a small bit of experience toward our next level too. The Wind Walker did most of the killing, but even surviving a situation like that has its benefits. Beyond the obvious, of course."

"Yeah, I guess I'm grateful for that part too," I teased. "Leveling must be difficult for the dead."

"I think it depends on the person," she said.

Even after four days with Miko, I couldn't tell if she was joking.

○○○

We traveled for another three days, and we never did catch up with the Brushan ambassador. That was saying something, given that we were mounted and they appeared to be on foot. Either the Brushan marched a hell of a lot faster than the rest of us, or they hadn't been stopping every night to make camp and train. Still, we would arrive in Whitehall with plenty of time before the diplomatic summit kicked off.

That was the good news. It was also kind of the bad news. By early afternoon on that final day, we were only a few glasses out of Whitehall. Which meant time was running out before my meeting with the primarch—*blessed be her name*, that voice in my brain unconsciously muttered—and her council.

I didn't think the nation's leaders would be impressed by my recent skill gains… or by the fact that their so-called Chosen was only a level-one Warrior, and *that* was enough to finally banish my unreasonably good mood. More than a week after my dad's death, a whole jumble of emotions had started to accumulate, like limbs strewn across a battlefield.

Hold it together, I told myself. *At least until this is done. There's nothing you can do about not being their savior, and most likely, there's nothing any of them can do either. So, just do your best and keep your mouth shut when it comes to religion, and you'll be okay.*

Or as okay as everyone else could be with an army bearing down on the country.

To distract myself, I took another glance at my character sheet:

```
Name: Brian Fieldings
Class: Warrior (Common) - 1
Profession: None
Deity: None
Ideal: Freedom

Attributes:
Strength: 10 / Finesse: 10
Vitality: 12 (+2) / Intellect: 12
Discernment: 10 / Will: 14 (+2)

Skills:
Major: Light Armor: 3/10, Spear: 5/10

Minor: Athleticism: 2/10, Avoidance: 2/10

Professional: None

General: Animal Behaviorism: 3/10, Brewing: 1/10,
Caretaking: 2/10, Mercantilism: 1/10, Riding: 2/10

Techniques: Lunge (C)


Achievements: None
Titles: None
Traits: Speaker of Tongues, ???, ???
```

The only changes were to my skills. Over the last few days, I'd gained two more points in *Spear* and *Light Armor*, and one in each of *Athleticism*, *Avoidance*, *Animal Behaviorism*, and *Riding*. The claw was split on whether my advancement rate was slightly faster than normal, or whether I was simply benefiting from the personal instruction of a ranked Aspirant. Even if it was the former, it was a far cry from the meteoric improvement Riok and Berys had been hoping for.

The mystery around exactly *what* I was supposed to do to help the synossians was only growing as my apparently mundane nature continued to reveal itself every day. I worked my ass off—and was lauded for that fact—but nothing about my progression screamed *exalted savior.*

A glass later, we were starting up what Miko had promised would be the last hill before Whitehall, when one of the scouts came galloping back to the column. By the time the Priestess had guided our dalys to the front, Riok, Berys, and Loris were already there, following the scout up the hill. We joined in without asking permission.

Beyond the hill, as Miko had promised, was Whitehall. The primacy's capital city dominated the valley it had been built in, nestled into the hills on the north side and occupying both banks of what appeared to be a massive river. I hadn't been sure what to expect, but Whitehall checked off a lot of the boxes on my list of expectations for a medieval city: tons of mostly one-story buildings built along narrow roads and alleys, bridges crossing the river's sparkling ribbon of light, and a wide wall surrounding the urban sprawl. Outside of that wall and about halfway between the city and us was a second cluster of buildings, laid out in a uniform pattern within their own wall.

What surprised me most about Whitehall was the amount of smoke rising from the city itself. I was pretty sure the synossians hadn't had an industrial revolution just yet, and that was a lot more smoke than I'd have expected from whatever factories they *did* have.

"Is there a fire?" asked Miko, apparently as puzzled as I was.

"If so, it started in multiple locations," said Riok, pointing out the distance between smoke plumes. "Slanit, can you get us a closer look?"

"Lots of smoke, but I will try."

Before I could ask Miko what that meant, the scout turned back to the distant city and spread his hands in front of him, like someone opening a window. The air in front of him shimmered, forming a pane of hardened air several feet wide and just as tall. Within that pane, the view of Whitehall magnified far beyond anything my phone back home could have managed.

Magical telescopes? Now I'd seen everything.

"Another technique?" I asked Miko.

"*Farseeing,*" she murmured back. "One Scout in every claw is meant to have it, although Slanit has upgraded his version to allow for group viewings."

Now, I kind of wished I'd been a Rogue instead of a Warrior. *Lunge* was badass, yeah, but so was this.

For a moment, there was nothing but smoke in the viewing window, but as Slanit panned it around the city, details started to filter in through the heavy cover. Houses with windows smashed, cobblestone roads with carts overturned, and…

"Are those bodies?"

It was a rhetorical question, and nobody bothered answering me, too focused on the scene of devastation before them. Here and there, robed synossians lay sprawled in the streets next to their carts, dalysi, or storefronts. Nor were the lizard people the only bodies evident—I saw humans and a couple of winged creatures… skyborn?— lying amongst the fallen as well. Given the size of Whitehall, it was barely a fraction of the greater population, but even so—

"The primarch's keep, Slanit." Riok's words were as hard as railway spikes. He pointed. "Look to the keep."

Moments later, it became clear what he had seen. To the north end of the city, a rocky promontory rose above the buildings, a narrow causeway leading up to a white-stoned keep at its top. That causeway was packed with a mob of people—hundreds, maybe more, carrying torches and weapons. As Slanit focused in, the synossians around me shifted uncomfortably. More than a few hard eyes turn my way.

The mob that looked intent on storming the keep seemed entirely made of humans.

"The Nor refugees?" breathed Miko in a voice gone thin with shock and horror. "But why?"

"We took them in," growled Kato, the last of Riok's claw to join our viewing party. "We clothed them, sheltered them, even fed them and this is their repayment?"

"Calm yourself, Private," said Loris. "The how and the why can wait until the action is done."

"Where do they think they are going?" asked Berys. By now, Slanit had turned his focus all the way to the gleaming keep at the top of the causeway. Gates that looked massive even at this distance were shut, and the mob's vanguard was milling outside, robbed of any opportunity to vent their inexplicable rage.

"The wall atop the gatehouse." At Riok's urging, Slanit adjusted the focus again and a handful of figures swam into view, climbing an interior staircase to regard the mob from above. The first nine were all synossians, a white-scaled figure in gold robes followed by four in black, and another four who each had robes in their own color scheme.

Miko's breath caught as the last of those figures ascended the wall, a person wearing robes of crimson and orange that matched her own. "Mother! And the primarch!"

Which made the four in black the primarch's council and the final three the other religious leaders.

In Slanit's viewing panel, a second group of figures joined the primarch on the wall. These weren't humanoid lizards at all, but albino dwarves—stocky and pale-skinned, their hair and beards gleaming like precious metal even in the wan afternoon sunlight. The lead figure was draped in rich robes in silver and bronze, while those accompanying him wore sturdy clothing still dusty from the road.

"At least the ambassador made it to the keep before this began," said Riok, some of the tension leaving his voice. "I do not know when or why this riot erupted, but it will take a mob like that time to breach the keep's walls, time they don't have with the city garrison no doubt mobilizing."

I gave Miko a questioning look and she pointed to the orderly set of buildings outside the city proper. "Most of the Primarch's Legion is stationed at Fort Noska," she whispered, "but a detachment is permanently garrisoned outside Whitehall, probably amplified by recruits for the auxiliary legion."

"The rioters will be caught between hammer and anvil," added Kato, and after seeing the bloody bodies in the city, I couldn't blame him for the satisfaction that colored his words. "And utterly destroyed."

"A loss of life that serves nobody," said Berys. "And which the primarch, blessed be her name, appears intent on preventing."

Slanit's technique didn't include sound, so we couldn't hear what the synossian leader, flanked by her council and religious heads, shouted to the crowd below, or what, if anything, they shouted back. I didn't envy her having to negotiate with the mob that was even now attempting to storm her keep, but she was at least operating from a position of military strength. The fancily robed Brushan made his way past the other synossians to join her, lending his political support.

"It will take a glass to reach Whitehall's gates and another to make it to the keep. By then, this will surely be over, but we can lend our strength to whatever cleanup action is required." Riok turned to Loris. "Sergeant, call the rest of the scouts in. We will proceed to the garrison at speed."

"Bright gods, no..." breathed Berys in a voice I'd never heard from the Priest, his words barely more than a whisper. At the same time, gasps and at least one moan erupted around me.

"Berys?" Riok spun back to Slanit's magical telescope to see what the rest of the claw had already witnessed.

The primarch had stumbled forward to collapse across the parapets. As we watched, the Brushan ambassador pulled a bloody weapon from the synossian's back and turned to launch himself at the nearest councilor, black fire igniting around both that weapon and the albino's pale form. The other Brushan charged the stunned synossians from the rear, weapons flashing in the afternoon sun.

One councilor fell to the unexpected treachery, then a second. They might have been overrun entirely in those first few moments if it hadn't been for one of the Priests, an enormous synossian in a deep blue robe. He held off a dozen Brushan single-handedly, laying about with a sword as tall as they were. Every stroke of that two-handed weapon took a life, but also earned the Priest wounds of his own from the assassins attempting to overrun them. With a roar we could see if not hear, he lashed out again, and this time something more than just steel hit the wave of attackers, a thunderclap of force that blew the remaining Brushan right off the wall to plummet into the unseen courtyard below.

"Ware to those who would stand against the Fist of Kal," said Riok, his voice almost reverent.

The blue-robed synossian spun to the wall to seek out the Brushan ambassador who had literally stabbed the primarch in her back, but the battle there was already over. A third councilor had been slain, but the ambassador was dead. The synossian in pale lavender robes knelt above the primarch's body, hands extended and a familiar purple glow beginning to shine.

"If there is a spark of life left in the primarch, the Heart of the Pure will save her," whispered Berys, eyes fixed on the distant pair. "She is the greatest healer we have."

"Where is the Royal Guard?" asked Miko, her tone anguished. Her mother had made it through the quick battle atop the wall in one piece, but I could only imagine what the young Priestess was feeling, close enough to watch this horror unfold, but too distant to be more than an observer.

"There were far more Brushan in the ambassador's column than those few we see on the wall," said Riok, his words firming as he spoke. "I suspect they are even now engaged with the guard. All of this was planned. If they can reach the gatehouse…"

As if his words had been a signal, one of the great gates cracked open. The mob raised a cry we could almost hear from our distant hill, and figures started to slip inside.

Up on the wall, the remaining synossians seemed almost frozen. The Heart of Etriska was crouched over the bloody body of her primarch. The only living councilor remained on their hands and knees, caught in mid-scramble for whatever safety their panicked mind had identified, and the blue-robed Fist of Kal was heading for the stairs, footsteps slow but resolute. Miko's mother and the fourth Priest—this one in a robe of mottled grey and black—turned to follow, leaving the Heart of Etriska to tend to the primarch.

If those two were even half as scary as the Fist of Kal, I was pretty sure the remaining Brushan were in for a really bad day. The only question I had was whether it would be enough. The gates were open, and according to Riok, numbers could wear down even ranked opponents. Fifty or more Brushan along with five hundred or more traitorous refugees against four Priests, one terrified councilor, and whatever was left of the primarch's guard?

I didn't want to solve that equation.

"Who is that?" asked Miko, pointing to Slanit's viewing window. A man had emerged from the mob outside and was climbing the keep's exterior wall like they were part spider monkey. The newcomer was bald and shirtless, but recognizably human, his skin bronzed except for a pale patchwork of scars. As the stranger rolled over the parapets and onto the wall, I saw—in excruciating detail—that he had empty sockets instead of eyes, but that lack didn't seem to impact his vision.

"Kal defend us," murmured Loris in a voice of broken glass. Even my limited knowledge of synossian expressions let me decipher the despair that washed over the faces of Riok's claw.

Almost as soon as the stranger's bare feet hit stone, he was standing above the High Priest of Etriska and driving a fist into—and through—her scaled head, spreading brains and bone matter across the already bloody stone. The Heart of the Pure collapsed in a boneless heap, lifeless corpse sprawled across the primarch she had been unable to save.

Berys sagged in his saddle, too stunned to speak.

The last councilor joined the others in death before the three remaining Priests could turn to face this new horror. The Fist of Kal stepped toward the attacker, a step that lengthened and lengthened and then lengthened even more, the synossian's body swelling to titanic proportions. The priest's sword had grown to match his proportions and now thundered down with meteoric force.

The bald human stepped almost casually to one side, letting the strike slide past him, somehow ignoring even the force of the weapon's passage. A shower of sparks erupted as darkened metal struck polished stone, and an entire segment of the wall fell away to come crashing down on the mob streaming into the keep. By the time that light show had ended, the enemy was at the synossian's flank. Bare hands tore through blue robes and the oversized greaves beneath them to savage scaled flesh.

His leg a bloody ruin, the Fist of Kal dropped to one knee and spun about, bringing his massive blade across faster than physics should have allowed. This time, the air around that weapon distorted in an epically oversized repeat of the technique he'd used earlier to annihilate the Brushan forces.

The bald human started to dodge again, but a grey-and-black-robed figure stepped out of the man's own shadow to strike him from behind, wielding a blade that seemed as much smoke as steel. Over by the stairs, Miko's mother now stood alone, her scaled hands raised to the sun.

A twist of the human's hips sent the second Priest—the Whisper of Shan, I was guessing—tumbling aside, but that momentary distraction proved costly. The Fist of Kal's sword hammered into the bare-chested man's body, driving him into and then *through* the interior battlements.

I sighed in relief, and heard Miko echo me, but the members of Riok's claw remained fixated on the scene below. The viewing window started to cloud and fade, nearing the end of its apparent duration, but we all saw the attacker emerge again on the wall, bruised and bloody but otherwise whole where he should have been a mass of broken bones.

The Whisper appeared again in the enemy's shadow, teleporting across the battlements in a single step, but this time his opponent was ready. In a blur of motion, he spun, catching the synossian's descending wrist. A second shadow knife formed in the Whisper's other hand and drove forward, but the human was already twisting away, tossing the priest through the air and into the Fist of Kal.

Eyeless sockets focused on the two Priests, one battered and barely able to stand, the other clutching an arm now hanging by bloody threads from its shoulder.

And that's when Miko's mother, the Voice of Aurea, finally entered the battle. A second sun appeared in the sky above the keep and fire poured down to savage the area atop the battlements. In front of the Fist of Kal, Shan's head Priest erected a shield of darkness, but even that barrier wavered against the all-encompassing power of whatever spell the Voice had cast. Stone melted like magma to form a deadly shower that savaged the mob below.

The keep's entire wall shuddered.

By the time any of us could see again, Slanit's viewing window had shrunk to the size of a hand mirror, but even that was sufficient to show a human-sized shape, somehow still standing in the center of molten ruin. Eyeless sockets turned toward the Voice, whose scaled hands were now ringed in nimbuses of golden light. Serpents of pure sunlight struck at the enemy, but he wove his way through the storm like a man walking in the park, actually deflecting the last of those attacks with a bare hand as he reached the Priestess herself. Just before the viewing portal snapped shut, we saw the red and crimson robed figure crumple on the keep's distant wall.

Miko's choked sob tore at something inside of me.

"To the garrison," snapped Riok, his normally dominant presence somehow subdued. "The keep may be lost, but it appears only one of the Buried came with the Brushan through their kingdom's pathways. That arrogance will be his doom." He spun on the other soldiers, many of them shell-shocked and staring at the empty space where Slanit's technique had once been. "Damn your scales, children of Synos! Honor your ancestors and *move!*"

Even before his words had faded, the Wind Walker was gone, charging his dalys down the hill's sharp incline. Berys was close behind, and the rest of the claw, stirred to action, followed in a ragged line. Miko and I were the last in that column, and even as I used every scrap of my recently earned skill to stay on the dalys' rolling back, I found myself staring at the dialogue window that had just appeared in front of me, as primitive looking as my character sheet and the pop-up window that had brought me to Eos.

```
NEW QUEST: Escort Priestess Miko Naseri to safety.

[ Accept | Decline ]
```

In our days discussing the Framework, nobody had warned me about *quests.* Worse, the screen made it impossible to see where we were going, which taxed my fledgling *Riding* skill to its max. Holding onto Miko for dear life, I accepted the quest with a thought.

I'd figure out what it meant and how the hell I was supposed to accomplish it later.

18

I t took us more than ten minutes to reach the valley's edge, and through some minor miracle, or the dalys' many, many legs, nobody died on the insane charge downhill. As I watched the garrison wall creep closer with each passing minute, I couldn't help but question what I was doing, riding towards an angry, army-sized mob and the bald monster who had just single-handedly decapitated the synossian hierarchy. My new quest wanted me to get Miko to safety. Wasn't this the exact opposite?

Unfortunately, *I* wasn't the one controlling the dalys… and I was pretty sure pulling us both off the back of a galloping not-horse was just a different way of committing suicide. So, I held on tight, using Miko's larger body as a windbreak as we hurtled toward the garrison.

Riok's a ranked Aspirant, I reminded myself. *There's no place safer than with him and his claw. Add in however many soldiers are in the garrison and this is the smart move. But… maybe I can convince Miko not to join the attack on that eyeless monstrosity?*

Any last thoughts of being a true Chosen had been extinguished along with the Voice's flames. The now-dead High Priests had *all* been ranked Aspirants, yet one man had torn right through them. An

Earthborn ex-barista with a borrowed spear wasn't going to even give him pause.

Maybe the legionnaires can wear him down, like Riok said?

Unfortunately, as we reached the garrison, it became apparent *that* wasn't happening either. The fort's gates were wide open, revealing a courtyard where dozens upon dozens of bodies were strewn across the dirt. Some had fallen still organized into columns, suggesting they'd been in marching drills and hadn't even had time to react before their deaths.

It seemed the eyeless monk had made a pit stop at the garrison before assaulting the keep. And Riok's whole attrition strategy had just become a lost cause.

The Wind Walker wheeled his dalys about and I could read the grief even on his alien features. A breath later, and it was gone again, buried beneath determination. "Berys—"

Something hummed through the air and Slanit was thrown from his dalys, a thick bolt impaled halfway through his scaled head. Within seconds, another dozen bolts were in the air, and it wasn't until the screams started that I spotted the Brushan who had been hidden atop the garrison wall.

I dragged Miko off the dalys with me, and just in time, as a bolt flew through the space we had recently occupied. The projectile buried itself in the back of the dalys instead, and our mount stumbled, its multiple sets of legs suddenly unsteady. The albino who had missed us adjusted her aim and fired again.

This time, the bolt rebounded off a heavy shield. "If there is any secret you have been keeping in reserve, Brian Fieldings," Niaci said in a voice like ice, "this is the time to show it."

I dropped my head. "All I have is *Lunge.*"

Something stronger than a mere crossbow bolt struck Niaci's shield, rocking her back, and she let her inner eyelids drift shut for just a moment, before nodding.

"Then stay down until we have cleared the wall."

I felt like a failure and a coward rolled into one… but I wasn't going to argue with a strategy like that.

Riok's claw was responding like the professional unit it was. Niaci wasn't the only synossian with a shield out to protect the others, and our scouts were taking advantage of those bulwarks to return fire with bows and slings. Meanwhile, Berys was bent over one of the wounded, and the glow surrounding his hands told me we'd have at least one casualty back in the fight soon enough.

Either Miko had noticed the same thing or her own military training was taking over. Her orange eyes darted about until she located another fallen synossian. Kato was flat on his back, but still somehow breathing even with two bolts sprouting from his chest.

"Niaci," she hissed. "If you can get us over to Kato, I can at least keep him from bleeding out."

The synossian above us just nodded, twisting slightly to deflect another bolt that streaked down from above. "Move in lockstep with me, both of you. Follow my cadence."

One step at a time, we scuttled to the right, using Niaci's shield and the wounded dalysi to shield our path.

We were five feet from our target when one of the crossbowmen adjusted their aim. The bolt that struck Kato in the head made our intentions moot.

Miko made a sound halfway between a sob and a snarl. I froze, staring at the blood and skull fragments spread across the dry earth.

Still, while the Brushan's ambush had hit us hard, they weren't faring nearly as well now that true combat was underway. Pale bodies toppled from the garrison wall like dominoes, struck down by arrows, stones, or lances of light or darkness that could only be techniques in action. The majority of the Brushan took cover behind the parapets, but the claw's salvo served a greater purpose.

It gave Riok time to reach the wall.

If the Buried at the keep had been a spider monkey, Riok was a grasshopper, taking two strides toward the garrison and then launching himself into the air. He cleared the fifteen-foot wall with room to spare and landed between two Brushan, his wicked spear bringing death to both crossbowmen in a single fluid movement. The enemy refocused on the attacker in their midst, and the other synossians used the sudden respite to push through the open gates, seeking out the internal stairways that led up to the walls.

I pulled my spear from the side of our dying dalys and followed Niaci and Miko inside.

The carnage from the garrison's massacre was horrifying. Blood and scales and vital fluids were everywhere, armor and flesh ripped apart by a single man's bare hands. From the lack of bolts in those corpses, it seemed that the Brushan who had ambushed us hadn't taken part in the slaughter.

They simply hadn't needed to.

In addition to the crossbowmen on the wall, a number of Brushan were lurking below, these ones wearing boiled leather vests and wielding curved knives the length of my forearm. They outnumbered the remnants of Riok's claw almost two to one, but the synossians didn't even slow, charging their enemy with shield and spear and even truncheon.

Heavily armored career soldiers fighting in tight quarters against what appeared to be assassins or marauders… it wasn't a battle but a slaughter, the Brushan overrun and savaged by their larger, stronger, and better equipped attackers. Sergeant Loris tore one of the enemy's arms right out of her shoulder, and bludgeoned a second albino to death with it even as the hammer in his other hand danced to its own rhythm, brutally shattering bones with every strike.

I forced down my rising gorge and turned away from the carnage, holding my spear in front of me as if I was watching for a second ambush from deeper in the garrison and not just trying to save myself from future nightmares. I doubted anyone who noticed bought the fiction, but they didn't call me on it either. There was blood to be spilled and so many deaths to avenge.

Unfortunately for me, the rest of the courtyard was nightmare fuel all on its own, and the fact that the bodies there were *already* dead didn't do much to change that fact. I was so busy trying not to look at *anything* that I almost missed the motion in front of me. Near the center of the courtyard, one of the synossian bodies was pushing itself to its feet. Any joy I felt at finding an unexpected survivor guttered out as soon as I saw that the body didn't have a *head.* Bone poked through visibly broken arms, but it rose up anyway like a puppet or one of the poorly animated creations in low budget zombie films.

"Niaci—"

By the time she had turned to see what I was pointing my shaking spear at, a dozen corpses were on their feet and shambling toward us. Behind them, a second pile of bodies practically disintegrated, limbs skittering away like rats deserting their nest to reveal a seated figure who had been hidden beneath the dead.

Her hair was silver at the roots, but darkened as it passed the brow. By the time it reached her bony shoulders, every strand was blood red, and as it neared her too-narrow waist, the ends were as black as the dress she wore. Unlike the killer at the keep, she still had her eyes, but they were empty and wild, black pits in a pale white face. Her smile was overly wide, exposing black teeth that were as sharp and pointed as a shark's, and even though she was barely taller than I was, her shadow flooded the surrounding courtyard.

If Niaci's soft moan hadn't already told me all I needed to know, the dark presence that suddenly unfurled to hit us like a titan's maul would have made it clear:

Riok had been wrong.

The garrison wasn't our salvation, but our doom… and more than one of the Buried had come to Whitehall.

○○○

With our small group now beset on two sides, the battle's momentum shifted, even as the strange woman seemed content to sit and watch the dead do her bidding. The zombies weren't fast, but they were every bit as strong as they had been in life—maybe even stronger—which put them on a whole different level from someone like me.

I waited for Niaci to smash one of the dead to the side, breaking at least a few more of its bones with her heavy mace, and then darted in to stab with my spear. Every step was a struggle under the weight of the Buried woman's presence, but the zombies weren't at all focused on their own defense. My spearhead knifed into the creature's stumbling form, and I pushed forward, driving the zombie off its feet entirely. I pulled back again, withdrawing my weapon as I retreated.

It wasn't *Lunge*, but it was effective. Five ranks in a weapon skill made a noticeable difference.

Niaci took my place again a moment later and obliterated the zombie's legs. The dead thing was *still* moving, but without functional limbs, it was at least temporarily out of the fight.

Sadly, there were more where it came from. A lot more. Around the courtyard, additional corpses were coming to life. Another ten, then twenty. A quick glance behind me showed the remaining Brushan had mounted their own counterattack. Individuals on both sides flickered or enlarged or burst into flame as techniques popped off like fireworks.

What had already been chaos to my untrained eyes became absolute bedlam.

The zombies were threatening to overrun our defensive position. Miko was busy healing another soldier and beyond her, Berys was doing the same. To Niaci's left, the only other soldier on our line went down, buried by four of the walking dead as he struck down a fifth. This time, I *did* trigger *Lunge*, driving into the pile of living and dead, my spear piercing through the topmost zombie.

I'm not sure it even noticed. It *definitely* didn't care, more inconvenienced by the length of the weapon that had impaled it than suffering from whatever damage I had dealt.

Gripping the spear shaft in both hands, I tried to lever the zombie off the fallen soldier, but weight, strength, and position were all against me; I barely even shifted it to the side.

Niaci was there a moment later, her mace far more effective than my spear, but the soldier at the bottom was dead by the time we could free him. Dead… and yet beginning to stir as the blood-haired woman finally rose and took her first step toward us.

Niaci crushed the skull of her former claw mate, snarling as she brought her mace down, and for a moment, there was space to breathe. The synossian threw her bloody mace aside, and took her shield up in both hands, strange synossian eyes blazing bright blue.

"Make for the gate and the remaining dalysi," she told me, eyes fixed on the mob of oncoming corpses and the small woman who wore a shark's smile while mincing along beside them. With a roar that I could feel as well as hear, Niaci slammed down her shield, stabbing it into the earth like a spade or a pick.

A glowing wall sprang into being, twenty feet high and twice as wide, a hundred shields overlapping and spreading out from the purely physical one in Niaci's hands one to create a barrier between us and the oncoming horde.

"Niaci!" roared another voice, Loris by the sounds of it.

"Go!" she shouted back, bracing her shield. Her massive form was already shaking as dozens of undead fists beat on the wall in their path.

Maybe a true Chosen would have stood by the synossian to face down certain death. *I* joined Miko in fleeing for the gate. Of Riok's original claw, there were *seven* left, including Niaci, but Sergeant Loris had managed to clear a path out of the garrison that threatened to become our tomb.

I'd taken three steps when the air rang like a bell, a singular sound that drowned out the noise of the battlefield and drove me to my hands and knees.

The Buried woman had reached Niaci's shield wall. As I clutched my pounding head, she reached out and tapped it with a nail painted in dried blood. Another gong, and this time, several of the glowing shields that made up the wall shattered, fragments of light falling into nothingness. That damage spread like a chain reaction, and soon, the wall was gone. Only Niaci remained, down on one knee, the broken remnants of her original shield still clutched in both clawed hands.

I was ten feet away from Niaci, and almost thirty from the gate. I wasn't any kind of savior and I sure as hell wasn't a hero, but the synossian had been kind to me, and a part of me refused to watch her die. I'd done too much of that, even before coming to Eos.

I triggered *Lunge.*

Not a damn thing happened.

Cooldowns were an absolutely *bullshit* mechanic, and in my third life, I'd be sure to tell everyone so.

A roar from behind me told me that someone—Loris again, most likely—was on his way, but whatever techniques the sergeant had, he either lacked a movement ability or had already used it. And that meant neither of us had a chance in hell of arriving in time. The Buried woman's smile widened to grotesque proportions and her bone white hand lashed at Niaci with an almost languorous flick of the wrist—

—only to be batted aside by a blast of wind that sent dirt whipping about the courtyard. When the dirt had settled, Riok was there, the dark spear in his hand glowing with its own light.

The enemy necromancer cocked her head, mouth bleeding as she chewed through her lips with those horrible teeth. Loris stepped past me to stand beside Riok, followed by the remainder of the once-mighty claw. A visibly exhausted Berys knelt over Niaci, the glow of his healing spell sputtering like a candle flame in a hurricane. Even so, it was enough to get the Shieldbearer back on her feet.

"Is this it?" The Buried woman's voice was sweet and almost childlike, a terrible match for her appearance and her words. "*This* is the might of the pre-eminent empire on this puny continent?" She cast her eyes upward. "How far has Eos fallen, Father!"

Riok hadn't had time to teach me more than a handful of things in our short journey. The first was to always keep my weapon with me. The second was to point that weapon at the enemy. The third lesson, like the others, had been little more than common sense: there was a time for talking, and there was a time for killing, and mixing the two was a great way to end up dead.

As the necromancer looked theatrically to the heavens, the Wind Walker's spear streaked for her exposed throat. Loris and Niaci moved to strike from opposing flanks, and Berys somehow mustered the energy to cast another spell, fireflies of lavender light darting out into the clusters of walking death. Even Miko joined in, casting *Flare* on our opponent.

The result of Berys' spell was apparent first, groups of zombies immolating as each lavender firefly erupted. But by the time I blinked the tears from my eyes, it was already too late. Had clearly already been too late the moment we'd charged down into the valley like we were heroes in a book.

Loris was falling back, blood spurting from the empty socket of his shoulder, war hammer still clutched tightly in the hand of the arm he'd just lost. Beyond him, two other synossians were motionless heaps in the dirt. Outside of Miko and me, only Riok, Niaci, and Berys remained upright.

The necromancer was smiling again, her only visible wound the one she'd caused with her own teeth. She batted aside a spear strike that was too fast for me to even see, tossing Riok to one side as she gestured with her free hand toward the gate. The groan of recently killed people, Brushan and synossian both, rising to their feet, told me that the exit had been cut off behind us, that our escape had always been an illusion.

Berys was either out of spells or the energy to cast them. The Buried woman shattered the club he used as a weapon and drove her hand *through* his leather-armoured chest, spinning back to spit a cloud of something dark and malignant into Niaci's face. The dead surged forward, dozens of walking corpses swarming Riok even as he tore them apart.

Miko darted through the crowd to reach Berys, on the small chance her Minor Healing spell could help. At the same time, Niaci fell to her knees, screaming and clutching at her throat. The scales on her face steamed and fell away, leaving nothing but bloody ruin behind, and then she too was gone.

Wind as sharp as any I'd felt in the western hills arose, tossing Riok's undead attackers aside like broken driftwood. The man's robes were in tatters, the armor beneath battered and torn, but the spear he pointed at the enemy necromancer hummed with energy. The miniature cyclone that had torn apart the pile of dead surged forward like a wave, sweeping bodies, carnage, and steel before it until the whole untidy mess washed over the smaller woman.

You can dodge a spear. You might even be able to dodge a wrench. But good luck dodging an avalanche.

Riok was right behind the attack he'd unleashed, but his flashing spear slid off a wall of bone that formed from the bodies he'd just tried to bury the woman with. He swept past the necromancer instead, landed in a twisting roll, and came back to his feet, spear darting at her like a needle, yet finding only air.

"Xor would enjoy playing with you, synossian," said the woman, paying no attention to the gore that had drenched her dress. "A shame he's busy decapitating your shabby government. By the time he rejoins us, there shan't be enough of you left to fill a jar."

As far as horrifying speeches went, that one ranked pretty high up there. It told me the name of the eyeless killer we'd already seen— Xor—but even more importantly, it told me that our enemy *still* hadn't learned Riok's third rule.

I triggered *Lunge* and this time I felt the air around me shiver as I warped forward. With Riok on the far side of the necromancer, she'd thought nothing of giving me her back, and while I doubted my Common-ranked technique would do more than annoy her, it might give Riok the opening he needed.

And if not, then at least I'd die doing the closest thing to magic that Eos and Shan had seen fit to provide me with.

At first, it went exactly as planned. The woman sensed me coming, somehow, but as she stepped to one side and lashed out, shattering the wooden shaft of my spear like it was a hundred years old and riddled with termites, Riok was in motion. I don't know if he saw me coming and anticipated which way she would dodge, if he was just that fast, or if the whole thing had come down to simple, blind luck, but as I crumpled to the ground, next to a blank-eyed Miko trying to fight off Berys' animated body, Riok finally landed a hit. The sharp head of his spear took the Buried woman right beneath the shoulder blades, sliding up and through her ribcage to burst forth from her narrow chest.

And that was when things went the rest of the way off the rails.

The necromancer stumbled in my direction, but the anticipated shower of blood never occurred. Instead, her blood poured *up* the shaft of Riok's spear, stealing the weapon's glow with every inch swiftly traversed. The Wind Walker tried to toss the spear aside, but even his speed proved insufficient. A tide of blood washed over his hands, then his wrists and arms. More fluid than any one being should have in their body surged out of the necromancer like a crimson-waved ocean and enveloped the Aspirant who had dared land a blow.

Two breaths. That's all it took. One moment, Riok was stabbing the necromancer, the next he was coated in her animated blood. Then that shroud fell away again, reversing course to return to the necromancer's body, leaving only the stained shaft of a once-magnificent weapon behind.

And if the *spear* had suffered from the mere touch of the woman's blood, it was so much worse for the weapon's wielder. What was left of Riok Diocil, Wind Walker and ranked Aspirant, fell in wet, thick clumps to be lost in the puddles of gore already soaking the courtyard.

There wasn't enough to fill a jar.

I didn't scream and I didn't cry. I didn't even throw up, somehow. I just lay there on my back, listening to Miko's screams. I watched the Buried woman pull Riok's spear the rest of the way through her chest until she held the oversized weapon, dark and stained now, but curiously free of blood, in her small hands. The endless darkness of her eyes turned in my direction, and that spear leapt forward.

No words this time.

Apparently, she *had* learned the lesson.

○○○

It wasn't like in the movies. My life didn't flash before my eyes… not that it would have made for much of a movie anyway. Music didn't swell up in an angelic orchestra that told the viewing audience that my (second) death would have true meaning. I didn't even get a Morgan Freeman voiceover.

But the closer the spearhead got to me, the slower it traveled. By the time it was a few inches away, that weapon and the world around me had slowed to a crawl that would make even a snail seem swift. I wasn't spared from the effect either, the next best thing to frozen and unable to move, only my thoughts traveling at anything approaching normal speed.

"Seven days?" asked a voice I recognized from my dream, hollow and biting at the same time. "I go through the trouble of bringing you to Eos and you can only survive seven days? As impossible as it is to believe, you have managed to limbo right under my already low expectations."

I tried to reply, but it was difficult with a mouth that might take an hour to even begin to form a single sound. Besides, Shan was still talking.

"This won't do," he decided. "One more chance. That's all you get, and all I can manage. And since you apparently *cannot* be trusted to abstain from charging headlong into battle with enemy champions, I'll dump you somewhere else instead." Something dark filled that endless voice. "Too much has been invested in you, Brian Fieldings, and now that investment *doubles*. If you die, I will extract payment from whatever remains of your soul. Go and make something of yourself."

The god's presence, somehow both more and *less* domineering than that of the necromancer doing her best to kill me, dissipated like smoke on a breeze. Time didn't fully resume, but it *did* come unstuck, the spear creeping toward me again. My skin crawled, as if covered by ants, and I could feel my feet start to warp inward, collapsing into fractal patterns of amber light instead of flesh and bone.

I didn't know what was happening, or why Shan had chosen to save me instead of the species that literally worshipped him, but it looked like I'd be gone before the spear reached me, escaping death by an endless fraction of milliseconds, an inch shaved down to a sub-atomic sliver.

I'd be alive and *somewhere else*, leaving only death in my wake. The people who had found and helped me, every last member of Riok's broken claw, even the population they had hoped to save… all dead. Like the sluthar at the shrine. Like the Brushan who had ambushed us. Like my dad. And there wasn't a thing I could do about any of it.

Or was there?

Out of the corner of an eye only now remembering it needed to blink, I saw Miko, struggling under the risen body of Berys, her formerly crimson and orange robes dark with dirt and blood. The Priestess' eyes were wide, sharp teeth bared in either fury or despair, and her claws were digging into the hands the zombie had wrapped around her scaled throat.

I didn't know why Shan had brought me to Eos. I was no Chosen. No messiah. I couldn't do a thing to stop the monster who had murdered Riok, let alone save the people of Whitehall and the larger population of the Synossian Primacy. But maybe—

As the pinprick of a thousand needles crept up my legs like bugs under the skin… as the dark, corroded head of Riok's spear slowly cut through the air…

I reached for Miko.

It was like pushing through molasses, the very air fighting my motion. Worse, I could feel that resistance weakening the further I pushed, time starting to catch back up, my first heartbeat echoing through my body, the spear's crawl already visibly quicker than it had been a lifetime ago. Only the slow march of the invisible insects up my body remained the same, as if my actions were disrupting whatever Shan had done to give me time to be transported elsewhere.

For a moment, I hesitated. If I kept this up, would I be signing my own death warrant, condemning myself to whatever endless torment Shan had promised? Did I even know that I could save Miko at all?

I didn't.

But I was going to try anyway.

I reached for her, and time continued to accelerate, now almost a tenth of its usual speed. I could tell now that both my hand and the necromancer's spear would reach their targets before my body collapsed entirely into fractals.

This is going to suck.

I couldn't both avoid that spear and reach Miko, so I did my best to twist and take the weapon's hit somewhere less fatal, my body sluggishly reacting to the commands screamed by an increasingly terrified brain. And then whatever Shan had done snapped like a rubber band stretched past its breaking point and the world lurched into motion.

I screamed as the stained spear of a now-dead hero tore *through* my shoulder, pinning me to the dirt of the courtyard. The necromancer's black eyes went wide as she saw that her killing blow had somehow gone off-target, but before she could withdraw the spear and stab a second time, two things happened:

First, my outstretched hand grabbed one of Miko's flailing legs.

And then my body dissolved into shards of broken light.

Book 2: Refugee

*"I do not fear the Witch King and all his fell powers
nor the blighted and the madmen who brought them into being.*

*I do not fear the monsters of the deep
or the beasts of the dark woods.*

*But a man with a weapon and nothing left to lose…?
That, my friend, is another story indeed."*

-Armsmaster Briglin, *On War*

19

This time, I *didn't* wake in darkness on top of an altar to a god I'd never heard of. That was the good news. The better news? I was alive and my hand was still holding tightly to a scaled ankle. Shan's teleportation had worked, and I'd apparently brought Miko with me.

Unfortunately, Riok's spear had come along for the ride too, and it remained embedded in my body, if not the dirt beneath me. A strangled scream worked its way through clenched teeth as pain came rushing in, the world going white around me even though I had yet to open my eyes.

"What? Where—?" Miko's voice, sleepy and befuddled, came from the direction of the ankle I was holding. I wasn't sure if I had woken her, or if she'd regained consciousness on her own, but before I could release my grip, she jerked away, the claws on her feet leaving deep rents in the flesh of my arm.

This time, there was nothing strangled about my scream.

A moment later, more movement came from her direction.

"Brian Fieldings? What happened? Where are we?"

I'd have loved to fill her in on everything that had gone down, but I was now busy bleeding out from *multiple* wounds.

"*Help,*" I croaked.

I heard a gasp as Miko finally saw the enormous spear driven through my body, and maybe even the damage she'd just done freeing herself from my grasp. My eyes were still stubbornly refusing to open, but I could sense her above me even before she pulled the tattered remnants of my robes aside to expose that intersection of spear and flesh. Her ensuing hiss of dismay somehow only fueled my pain.

"I need you to lie perfectly still, Brian. Pulling the spear out will increase the blood flow, and I'll need to close the wound immediately after. Can you do that?"

Lying perfectly still was one of the few things I was confident I *could* do. In fact, I didn't even want to nod. Thankfully, she took my muttered response as the *yes* I had intended it to be.

"Bright Lady preserve us." Instead of the hand I'd expected, something hard and bony pressed against my chest. A knee, maybe? Miko took hold of the spear and even that movement sent a fresh wave of pain through my body.

"On the count of three," she said, voice faint over the rush of blood in my ears. "One, two…"

I guess her people had the same stories we did, because she tugged on two, instead of three. My latest scream put all the others to shame and despite my barely verbal assurances to the contrary, I spasmed uncontrollably, twitching like a fish on dry land. My eyes popped wide open, and only the knee in my chest kept me down.

Miko tossed Riok's spear aside where it clattered on rocky ground, and the now-familiar glow gathered around her outstretched hands. Warmth flooded through my shoulder, softening the pain if not healing it entirely. Wherever we were, it was evening and I could make out the snarl on the Priestess' face, an expression I'd started to recognize as the synossian equivalent of a frown. She tore three strips of cloth from my borrowed grey robes, wrapping one around the wrist she'd savaged, and pressing the second and third into the still-bleeding entry and exit holes in my shoulder.

"I will have to wait briefly to cast *Minor Healing* again," she said tiredly, pulling my right arm across my body until its hand was resting on the makeshift bandage. "For now, keep pressure here."

I blinked away the tears in my eyes. My wounds were already a hundred times less painful than what I'd woken up to. Magic might not be able to fix everything, but I was grateful as hell that she had it.

"Thank you," I managed.

"I am but a servant of Aurea," Miko murmured, the words almost ritualistic. She scanned the area around us and then turned back to me, orange eyes intent. "What happened?"

"Shan happened. He decided it wasn't my time to die."

"And me?"

"I made sure you were included in the bargain."

"It is a good thing that you did, given your wounds."

I didn't tell her that I'd only been stabbed *because* I had chosen to save her. What was done was done, and if I had the chance to do it all over again, I was pretty sure I would.

I tried to sit up, and a fresh wave of pain washed through my body. *Okay, maybe 85% sure.*

"Stay down, you stupid phloxl!" hissed Miko, returning her knee to my midsection moments after I had already sagged back against the earth. "I haven't been able to stop the bleeding yet, and you moving about will just open the wound further!"

Make that 65% sure. I still didn't know what a phloxl was, but I recognized an insult when I heard it.

The fact that she'd prefaced it with *stupid* tipped me off.

"So, the Trickster saved you, and you saved me," she concluded, several uncomfortably quiet moments later.

"Yeah."

"And the spear?"

"Apparently, whatever I was touching came along for the ride. Including that." For the first time since waking up, I winced from something other than pain. "It was Riok's."

Miko's eyes closed—first the transparent inner membrane, and then the lightly scaled lids—and she sagged above me. "And the Wind Walker himself?"

"I'm sorry."

"The others?"

I shook my head, the words not wanting to come.

For a long while, we stayed silent, me flat on my back and still bleeding, her pinning me to the dirt and drowning in her own thoughts.

"We need... we need to figure out where we are." Her voice firmed as she spoke. "I see trees, which would suggest the coastline. Whitehall has... has fallen, but if we can reach Kronask or any of the other port cities, we can spread word of the primarch's fate, and get as many of my people to safety as possible."

"On the ships they're currently building?" From what Riok and Berys had said, it had seemed like the construction of those fleets was the primary bottleneck. I wasn't sure any news we shared could change that, but I also wasn't a shipwright.

Yet, I amended. I wasn't a shipwright *yet.* I hadn't chosen a profession, after all. And maybe that was true of other people in the port cities. Maybe if enough of us took on the profession and gained its relevant skills, we could accelerate matters?

Assuming the problem was labor and not materials.

"If the Brushan have turned on us, the ocean voyage is our only remaining escape route." Miko shivered, even though it was unseasonably warm. "To think we would choose to return to the Great Wilds after all this time. The stories say that our previous journey took multiple cycles and that the losses were significant. Still, any chance of survival is better than none. One moment."

Before I could ask her what Miko needed that moment for, she was casting another *Minor Healing*. This time, the warmth washed away the pain in my shoulder entirely. She finally withdrew her knee from my ribcage and stood.

"Berys…" She swallowed and tried again. "Berys could have healed you entirely and in a single casting, but there are limits to what *Minor Healing* can accomplish. I have closed the wound, but there may be internal damage to the underlying muscles. Please alert me if you encounter any mobility problems or unexpected pain, and we will seek out a Priest more talented than me to treat it. Thankfully, there *are* temples within each major city."

"I'm just glad to not be bleeding out anymore." I felt weak, but past experience told me at least some of that was from being healed. A meal or two would hopefully work wonders.

Which raised an unfortunate point. Miko and I had brought our clothes with us—or the remnants of them, in my case—but the claw's supplies were back in the garrison by Whitehall. We lacked shelter, toiletries, and most troubling of all, food and water.

"I assume there are skills for hunting or gathering?" I asked.

Miko scanned the clearing around us and came to the same realization that I had. "There are, and it appears one or both of us will need to gain them. There are fields in the north where we could simply harvest the growing food, but along the coastline, it is—"

Her words cut off with a choked gasp, and this time, nothing kept me from clambering up to a seated position. The Priestess was looking off into the distance, where the Eosian sun hung on the distant horizon, painting the verdant carpet of trees in red and purple tones.

It was the first time I'd seen it clearly since crossing the Veil. It seemed bigger than the Earth's sun, somehow.

"What's wrong?"

"It's almost sunset." Her voice was faint and so strangled that I almost thought she was speaking in another language.

"And?"

"And that makes this direction west," she said, facing the sun, and then turning a half-step to the right. "So then, why is the ocean to our north?"

I stood on two shaky legs, looking about us. Our surroundings were wildly different than what I'd experienced so far in Eos. In place of grass, rolling hills, or even snow-capped peaks, there was thick forest in almost every direction. The rocky terrain we'd been transported onto provided a thin border to those forests, lichen-covered stone pockmarked with holes and grooves that reminded me just a bit of Swiss cheese. And to the north, white-feathered birds pinwheeled above an endless expanse of water, where rolling waves glowed in the rays of the setting sun.

What I knew of my new world's geography could fit onto a postage stamp, but from what I'd been told, the Synossian Primacy sat with the ocean on its southern border and mountains to the north and west. I could see why the massive body of water to our north had Miko concerned.

The primacy is just part of the continent of Issandryl, I reminded myself. *Maybe we're on the northern coast... or maybe that's not an ocean, but a lake that puts even the Great Lakes back home to shame.*

Except... the Buried had already conquered the rest of the continent—and had originally emerged in the north—so Shan sending me there didn't make much sense. And if the primacy's territory had included landlocked bodies of water this large, I was pretty sure Miko would have at least heard of them.

I'll dump you somewhere else, Shan had told me, and so far, the trickster god had yet to lie. Which made me think we might have traveled further than Miko was guessing.

"Is there any sort of divination you can cast to find out where we are?"

"I am *level four.* You've already seen the two techniques the Bright Lady granted me." With the sun setting, I could feel the wind off the ocean, but Miko's sudden glare was enough to keep me warm, if not exactly set me on fire like she had intended.

Right. *Flare* and *Minor Healing.* So far, I was a much bigger fan of the second.

"So, what do we do?"

"Shouldn't a Chosen already know?"

I'd dealt with enough angry customers at Pritchard's Coffee & Baked Goods that I knew snapping back at her wouldn't get me anywhere, no matter how much I wanted to. "Wherever we are, I'm guessing—"

"We wait," she decided. "When the sun sets, I will seek out known constellations in the night sky and determine our position from them."

"Another skill?"

"Call it education," came the clipped response.

As the person who had recently been stabbed by a necromancer with acid blood, I was rapidly rediscovering the temper that had mostly eluded me since my father's death. Still, I reminded myself that Miko had just watched the leaders of her country die. Not to mention her *mother.* She had every right to be angry, and if she wanted to take that anger out on me, well… that was her prerogative.

Then again, I didn't have to stick around and give her an easy target either.

"I'm going to take a look around before then," I said instead, hoisting Riok's spear for the first time. Whatever the necromancer's blood had done to it, it was still heavier than the spear I'd trained with, and despite the visible corrosion, it seemed sturdy. It was also the only weapon we had. "I won't go far."

The young Priestess of Aurea, the closest thing I had to a friend on Eos, said nothing as I headed out.

The first question was where to go. As much as we needed food, I wasn't entering the woods, not with night drawing near. I'd already seen the sort of things that lived in the mountains, and I was guessing Eos' forests weren't any better.

Giant spiders, my mind conjured unhelpfully. *And maybe wolf hybrids with steel fur and lanterns for eyes.*

Yeah, the woods were out. For now, at least. But the birds I'd seen over the ocean had to nest somewhere, and the rocky coastline we'd found ourselves on seemed a likely option. Nests might have eggs, and eggs would make for a better dinner than air. How we'd cook those eggs was a problem for future-Brian to solve.

That meant I could go east or west, and it wasn't a choice I dwelled on for very long. To the west, the terrain got rougher as it climbed above the forest. To the east, things stayed level.

Obviously, I went east.

The rock was hell to walk on with bare feet, uneven and filled with sharp angles. I angled north as I went, looking for an easy path down to the ocean, but finding instead a cliffside that plunged hundreds of feet. Far below was a beach we had no way of accessing. That beach—dark rock like the cliffs themselves—stretched in both directions until it was lost from view, but beyond that was water, touching every horizon until I struggled to distinguish it from the evening sky.

If this *wasn't* an ocean, it was doing a great impression of one.

Wind tugged at me, as if to pull me over the edge, and I took a careful step back. And then, as I rethought the brilliance of walking atop a cliff in the looming dark, another several dozen steps. My hopes of finding the ingredients for an alien omelet had faded as soon as I saw the scope of these cliffs. In all likelihood, any bird nests would be a fair way down that rocky wall and out of reach of any *real* predators, let alone pretenders like me.

I sighed and turned back. With the cliffs a bust, the surrounding forests were our only source of potential food—and water—but I was exhausted from the day and my healing. Worse, as night truly started to fall, I was starting to reconsider how good an idea it had been to explore on my own. Especially since I'd left Miko without even a weapon.

In the morning, maybe we could *both* look for something to eat and drink. For now, safety was more important.

I was maybe halfway back when the sun finally fell below the distant trees, plunging the world into grainy twilight. The darkness thickened with every passing second, far beyond anything I'd ever experienced back on Earth. Soon, I couldn't see a damn thing. I extended my spear butt in front of me to tap against the stone, a blind man trying to avoid stepping right off the cliff.

To my surprise, the darkness lessened a few minutes later.

My first thought was to look up at the stars—where I also got my first glimpse of what appeared to be *two* moons—but the light was coming from the rock beneath me instead, soft and scattered, a hundred pinpricks of light slowly strengthening.

It's the holes, I realized. *The pockmarks in the stone. Either the rock itself is glowing or… Or something within that stone is.*

I had never been much of a film buff, but I'd seen enough horror movies to know that *glowing things coming out of the ground* was rarely a good thing. I hurried onward, moving faster now that I could mark the location of the cliff's edge by the *absence* of illumination. As I went, the glow continued to intensify, a highway of light that stretched along the top of the cliffs.

I had been walking for another few minutes when I heard Miko scream. A moment later, the bright ember of her *Flare* spell triggered, killing whatever night vision I had left, but by then, the glow was strong enough that I could run, bare feet be damned.

Miko was crouched low, clawed hands extended outward as she spun about, her orange eyes reflecting the glow surrounding her. Either the process had started earlier here, or the pockmarks and tunnels were shallower this close to the forest. Either way, the source of the light had already emerged, long, phosphorescent tendrils, almost like tentacles.

No, I realized, as one emerged entirely, creeping forward across the stone, ten inches long and as thick as my pinkie finger. *Not tentacles. Worms. Thousands of glowing worms.*

With a bestial hiss, Miko leapt back as another worm emerged, directly beneath her. More and more worms came out into the open, individual forms melded into a wriggling mass that somehow straddled the border of beauty and horror.

I spun Riok's spear in my hands. My shoulder twinged, but it was nothing that would keep me from striking. For all the good the weapon would do. Hitting something wouldn't be a problem, but a spear was the wrong tool for the job. What I really needed was a mallet or some kind of juicer.

Except… the worms were ignoring Miko and me both, squirming toward the lichen I'd spotted earlier.

Giant-sized bear-cat centipedes: carnivorous. Oversized lantern worms: not so much? Got it.

I made my way to Miko, who had come to that same realization. We retreated down the hill from the worms' night-time feast, our bare feet eventually finding grass instead of stone. In the light of the worms' phosphorescence, the lichen appeared to be visibly growing, spreading across the rock surface only to be consumed by the creatures responsible for its growth.

I was pretty sure that wasn't how things worked on Earth.

Kate would have known for sure.

"Have you ever heard of these things?"

She shook her head. "Not even in stories. I think we may be further from home than I realized."

That wasn't possible for *me*, given that everywhere on Eos was either light years or an entire reality away from Earth, but I nodded anyway, my eyes still on the worms.

"Do you think they're edible?"

She cocked her head, then shrugged. "If not, then the lichen should be. Assuming there is any of it left after this feeding frenzy."

That had me frowning. How *was* there still lichen on the rocks? And for that matter, why hadn't the worms' population exploded from what seemed like the perfect incubation chamber for them: a combination of safety and readily available food?

I found my grip on Riok's spear tightening. Maybe it was my skill points in *Animal Behaviorism*, but to me, the most likely explanation was that we weren't the only ones thinking about having worms for dinner.

"We should—"

Shapes swooped from the sky, invisible until fractions of a second before they struck, wings furled tightly to narrow bodies, then snapping open again at the last moment as they returned to the sky, wriggling invertebrates caught in their razor-sharp talons. *Birds.* Maybe even the birds we'd seen flying out over the ocean earlier… the same birds whose nests I'd been hoping to find.

I didn't have the *Hunting* skill, but I did have five points in *Spear*. And that was going to have to do.

Another bird—the sixth or seventh I'd seen so far—dive-bombed the carpet of worms below, but this time, I was waiting, my spear stabbing out at a potential meal that would put worms, lichen, and even eggs to shame.

I went too early and missed, because Eos and its many gods clearly hated me, but the bird's dive was thwarted, at least. It spread its wings to catch an updraft, and that moment was all I needed to trigger *Lunge*.

Whatever the necromancer had done to Riok's spear hadn't impacted its utility as a weapon: the spearhead caught the bird beneath its breast feathers and punched right through, spitting the bird as easily as it had impaled my shoulder an hour or so earlier.

I pulled back, struggling to balance even the comparatively light weight of the carcass on the tip of my spear.

"Well done." Miko tugged the bird's body off the spear, careful to avoid the weapon's tip. "But I think we should retreat further down the hill."

I looked back and realized what had been a few birds had turned into an entire flock's feeding frenzy. The one I had killed was large enough, but some of the creatures now diving would have been mistaken for eagles back home. Any bigger and *we* might start to look like suitable prey.

"Yeah, let's go."

20

We found a camping spot halfway between the worm colony and the still-unexplored forest, and that was that. There were no tents to set up nor dalysi to care for. It would make for a tough night sleeping under the stars, but as Miko started to pluck the bird with her claws, I realized that was the least of my concerns.

"Do you know how to cook that?"

"*Cooking* is not one of my skills, no. Not yet, at least."

"So then…"

She tossed something to me and I only caught it thanks to the glow of the worms uphill from us. Given the smell and the slippery warmth of it, I was pretty sure I knew what it was, but I forced myself to ask anyway.

"It's dinner," she answered.

"It's *raw.*"

"Yes." She tore into her own piece of bird, sharp teeth doing exactly what evolution had bred them to do. "I have a fire-striker on me, among a few other supplies, but we lack tinder or wood, and I would prefer *not* to alert enemies to our presence."

"If the *Flare* you cast didn't already do so, you mean."

She shot me a look, but we were far enough from the worms that I could pretend I didn't see it. "You had departed with our only weapon. It was the quickest way I could think to summon you back."

I could hear the embarrassment in her voice, and that, more than anything, convinced me to let it go. When it came to panicking, I wasn't going to throw stones, not after the mess with the sluthar or me freezing back at the garrison. Besides, neither of us had known what the worms' capabilities were and I'd been prepared to go Rambo on the things myself.

Which left me back where I had started, holding a piece of raw, bloody bird. I pushed down my rising nausea and tossed it back over. "Thanks, but I'd rather not eat."

"For how long?"

"One night, at least." I could get wood from the very same forest I had already sworn not to explore until after sunrise. And it wasn't like I had been all that hungry, even before my only companion started chowing down on raw bird. In fact— "Now that I think about it, I'm feeling kind of... full? Maybe Shan fed me when he teleported us?"

That was enough to have her staring at me across the empty space where a campfire should have been. "How would you describe your feeling of fullness? Be precise."

"I'm sorry?"

"It matters, Brian."

I shook my head, rolled my eyes, and then, for good measure, did both at the same time. How did someone describe being full? "I don't know? Kind of a warmth in my stomach, I guess? I don't feel like I've overeaten, but I still feel... full. Like I would after a satisfying meal."

"And you didn't eat anything while you were away exploring?"

"No. Nothing since we broke camp this morning, actually."

"Then I think what you're experiencing may be what we call pre-level satiation."

"Pre-level what?" Before she could reply, I put it together. "You mean I'm ready to advance to level two?"

"Only once you've maximized two Major and Minor skills each for the current level. Remember, you must do both."

That took some of the wind out of my sails. Last I'd checked, even *Spear* was a long way from its current limit of ten. "But how did I get enough experience to level?"

"Actions in accordance with your class invite advancement, and combat magnifies that gain. After multiple days of training with the Wind Walker, you just survived combat with a creature even more highly ranked than him."

"Only because a god decided to teleport me away."

Up the slope, the surviving worms had begun to retreat into their holes, and the light was diminishing accordingly; I heard her shrug even though I couldn't see it.

"Survival matters, Brian. And we both contributed to the battle before that point."

"Does that mean you're ready to level too? Or, you know, are you feeling *satiated*, at least?"

"I'm fourth level," she reminded me. "You'll find the effort needed for each new level increases significantly. Don't expect level three to come anywhere near as swiftly as level two has; if you reach it within the next cycle, I would be surprised and impressed. At my level, no single battle, regardless of how fraught it might be, is sufficient for advancement."

"And I have to make it all the way to third level before I get another technique?"

"Or an upgrade to your existing technique, yes."

"But even level two requires me to rank my skills up first." Miko had just said that, but I was talking to myself more than her at that point, rehashing what I'd been taught. "I guess I should practice the spear now."

"Perhaps you could wait until daylight?" She coughed. "As the only living person in range of you and your spear, I would hate to be accidentally stabbed."

"That's… fair. I guess I'm going to try to consolidate any skill gains I already got then."

"I will stand watch while you do," she said, crossing over to scoop up the spear at my side. "And then perhaps you can do the same for me. My nest-brother used to say that battle provided fertile soil for every kind of advancement."

"I hope he was right. And yeah, of course I will." I couldn't see a damn thing, but with the birds gone, I was pretty sure I'd at least be able to *hear* something coming.

Unless it was another, even bigger bird. In which case, we were just screwed. But there wasn't anything I could do about that, and futility was something I'd gotten used to a long time before coming to Eos.

Focus on what you can control.

I was already seated, but I let my eyes drift shut, hands open and palms skyward the way Riok had taught me. I let my mind drift back over the horrors of the day and the actions I'd taken: our mounted charge toward the Whitehall garrison; pulling Miko out of the path of an enemy crossbow; being saved from the same by Niaci's shield, then returning the favor in our desperate stand against the Buried woman's undead hordes.

The fight against the necromancer herself occupied a special place in my thoughts—and no doubt, my impending nightmares—but I tried to let the emotions of those desperate moments pass by me, focusing on the experience itself. Not just what *I* had done but what Miko had done, what poor dead Berys, Riok, and the others had all done. Actual combat, I now realized, was more than just the combatant and their foe; it was the flow of everything around them, opponents rising and falling and even switching as the action dictated.

If there was some sort of greater understanding of combat beyond that, I didn't have it, but I'd experienced all of two battles since saying goodbye to my life as a barista. Maybe greater enlightenment waited out there somewhere… or maybe I was getting carried away with this whole meditation thing. What mattered was that when I opened my eyes, minutes or maybe even hours later, I saw the message I'd been hoping for.

```
You have increased the following skills:

Major skills:
Formations [+1]: 1/10
Light Armor [+3]: 6/10
Spear [+4]: 9/10
Tactics [+1]: 1/10

Minor skills:
Athleticism [+3]: 5/10
Avoidance [+2]: 4/10
Pain Tolerance [+1]: 1/10

General skills:
Animal Behaviorism [+1]: 4/10
Danger Sense (R) [+1]: 1/10
Hunting [+1]: 1/10
Riding [+1]: 3/10
```

Once again, I wasn't entirely sure how my actions correlated with the gains I saw. *Riding, Spear,* and *Light Armor?* Sure, assuming my tattered robes counted as light armor. But why had *Athleticism* gone up three ranks? Why had *Avoidance* gone up two? I'd quite literally *failed to dodge* the only strike that came my way.

Of the five new skills included in my list—*Formations, Tactics, Pain Tolerance, Danger Sense,* and *Hunting*—only two of them made much sense. *Hunting* had no doubt leveled up from me getting our dinner, while I was guessing *Pain Tolerance* was a consequence of getting stabbed and clawed. But the others? I didn't even know what they *did*, let alone how I'd gotten them. And why did *Danger Sense* have an R next to it? The synossians had said that skills, like techniques, had quality levels... did that make that skill Rare instead of Common?

More questions for Miko, although I was starting to think that the Framework was purposefully obtuse in its operations.

Leveling required at least two Major skills and two Minor skills to be at the Aspirant's current cap. Which meant I needed ten ranks a piece in four skills before I could become a level-two Warrior. I had multiple Major and Minor skills already, but *Formations, Tactics,* and *Pain Tolerance* were all only rank one. I had no idea how to advance the first two and wasn't at all interested in what I'd have to do to advance the third.

That left *Spear, Light Armor, Athleticism,* and *Avoidance,* which were each anywhere from one to six ranks away from the current cap. I felt confident I could get my last rank of *Spear* through the training exercises Riok had taught me, but the rest were a mixed bag. Did what was left of my robes still count for *Light Armor,* and if so, how could I raise the skill quickly *without* getting into another fight that would likely kill me? Would running or carrying things help *Athleticism*? How much did the danger I faced amplify whatever gains I made in *Avoidance*?

Character development was so much easier in games.

As I moved from math to questions about training, an external noise finally intruded on my reverie. It wasn't a giant bird of prey descending from its aerial kingdom for a Brian-sized snack. It was something even worse:

Miko was crying.

She was making an effort to stay quiet, huddled in on herself, a shadow visible only against the backdrop of stars that had finally emerged, but the night was dead quiet now that the birds had left again, and her muffled sobs filled our campsite.

"Are you okay, Miko?" I brilliantly asked the young woman who had just lost her mother, her nation, and whatever friends and siblings—nest-brothers, she'd called them?—she might have had.

"They're all dead, aren't they?"

I was glad the darkness hid my wince. It was like she was reading my mind. "The people in Whitehall may be, but—"

"I'm talking about the entire primacy!" She waved at the sky above us. "Look at these stars, Brian Fieldings. What do you see?"

"I—"

"The Tears of the Lady are halfway across the sky from their expected position," she answered for me. "The Shield of Kal isn't even visible, and yet Corros' Black Heart is ascendant!"

"I don't know what any of that means," I reminded her.

"Of course you don't! Because you know nothing at all and are capable of even less!"

That was accurate, but still kind of hurtful.

"It means," she continued, grief giving way to anger as she bit off her words like they were bloody scraps of raw bird, "that we have either found ourselves in a different time entirely or are thousands of leagues south of where we should be!"

"Ah."

"You knew?"

"I… suspected? Shan said he was sending me somewhere I could progress. If he'd meant one of the primacy's port cities, why wouldn't we have woken up there instead of in the middle of nowhere?"

"I have *many* questions about all that the Trickster has done as of late," said Miko. "Most of all, what *your* purpose is, given that it clearly *wasn't* to save my people."

She wasn't the only one with questions, but even though Shan had gotten me into this mess in the first place, he was also the only reason I'd survived it. Insulting a god out loud where he might hear it seemed, as my crotchety old English teacher would have said, *imprudent.*

As did dwelling on my failures as a so-called Chosen.

"So, assuming we *are* that far south…" I prompted instead.

"There is only one place we could be. The same hellscape my people fought to escape over a thousand cycles ago and the continent for which our newest fleets recently set sail again."

"The Great Wilds?"

"The Great Wilds."

On second thought, how will Shan ever grow as a god without at least some constructive criticism?

As if reading my mind, Miko continued. "The Great Wilds are not a *place to progress*, Brian Fieldings. They will be your death and mine, and no one will know to even mourn our passing."

"Would you rather I had left you behind in Whitehall?" The words slipped out before I could stop them, and I was glad the darkness hid my wince. "Not that I would have—"

"I would rather none of this had happened," she said, all emotion gone from her voice. "Yet decisions of fate are seldom ours to make."

By the time I'd come up with something to say to that, Miko had retreated back into her own thoughts. A minute later, she announced that she would be meditating, giving me no choice but to reclaim Riok's spear and keep an ear out for predators.

An hour after that, she stirred again, but instead of saying anything, she simply lay down and went to sleep.

We'd agreed to keep watch for each other's meditation but hadn't gotten around to discussing sleep schedules. Still, I wasn't as tired as I should have been, so I made myself comfortable in my borrowed robes and shredded sweatpants.

I held Riok's spear across my lap and kept my vigil.

If there was a skill for doing more than my share, I was going to damn well level that bastard.

ooo

I woke to a hand on my shoulder. By the time my eyes were open, Miko had retreated to the other side of our small campsite. Clouds had driven all traces of blue from the sky, but the fact that I could see at all told me it was morning.

I'd fallen asleep. Not only was I *not* a true Chosen, I was apparently that moron who always ends up dying first in zombie movies. It was a miracle we'd lived to see the dawn.

Another miracle? The purple and blue berries piled in front of me. I looked over at Miko.

"I found them at the forest's edge," she said. "An apology for my behavior last night. And for leaving you to stand the watch alone."

Which was either far more mature than I'd have expected from someone her age *or* an insidiously clever way to trick me into eating poisoned berries.

Given that she could have just smothered me in my sleep, I decided it was probably the first thing.

"You don't have to apologize. Frankly, I'm amazed you're keeping it together as well as you are. You just lost… everything. I think you're entitled to be upset and angry about it."

"The same could be said for you."

I stopped in mid-head shake. Technically, she wasn't wrong.

"Priest Berys—" This time, Miko barely stumbled over his name. "He asked me to keep an eye on you and to support you as we traveled. *Brian has left behind all that he ever knew or loved,* he told me. *It is the sort of shock that no individual, no matter how enlightened, can adequately prepare themselves for.* Yet you continue to take everything in stride, my own visage notwithstanding."

"It wasn't your *face*, exactly—"

"I saw armed conflict in my cycle of service with the legions—it is how I am level four, after all—but what we witnessed at Whitehall was bloodshed and loss on a scale far beyond any I had experienced. And yet you, who by your own words, were a merchant who never saw combat in your old world, not only survived that battle, you remain untouched by its horror."

"I'm not untouched." I swallowed. "I'm just *numb*."

"Your wound?" She was headed toward me before I could wave her off. "Why did you not tell me—?"

"The shoulder's fine. Mostly," I amended, wincing as I rotated my shoulder. "I'm talking emotionally numb."

And I feel like a whiner even mentioning it, I didn't add.

"Because of what you have experienced since your arrival?"

"Not really. Not entirely, anyway." I gave myself a moment to gather my thoughts, popping a handful of berries into my mouth. They were both tougher and sweeter than any I'd had back home. They didn't *taste* poisonous.

After a moment, I sighed. "I buried my father on the day I was summoned to Eos. He died earlier in the week, but it took a while to take care of the arrangements—getting the obituary in the paper, handling the funeral, rearranging my work schedule, canceling our hospice care. Just… everything."

"And grieving, of course," she added.

"I…" I swallowed and looked away.

"You didn't allow yourself to grieve?"

"I didn't have *time* for it. There was too much to do. Then I found myself in Eos, and we were fighting for our lives against the sluthar. When that was done, Riok named me Chosen, and just like that, I had an entire species I was supposed to save. Even after the shitshow that was my Dreaming, I've been trying to come to grips with my new reality."

"I see." Miko crouched next to me, resting a scaled hand on my uninjured shoulder. "I am sorry about your father."

I coughed, pushing down emotions I didn't want to feel. Couldn't afford to feel. "It's okay. We knew it was coming eventually, and by the end, I don't know how much of him was left." I ducked away from the emotion that filled Miko's orange and eyes. "Anyway, I'm sorry too. About your mom, I mean."

"My… mom?"

"Sorry, mother." When she still didn't react, I raised an eyebrow. "The Voice of Aurea?"

"My blood-mother was a farmer, I believe, though I never met her. My nest-mother passed three cycles ago, either to sit at the Bright Lady's side or to have her soul returned to Eos for renewal in a new form. *Mother* is simply the title that Aurea's clergy give our High Priestess."

"Oh." I coughed. "Even so, I shouldn't be whining about my circumstances given all that your people are facing."

"Trauma is not a competition. One tragedy does not invalidate the other." From the change in her intonation, I knew Miko was quoting—or at least paraphrasing—something she had read. "If only the most disadvantaged are granted space to heal, wouldn't everyone eventually end up broken?"

"I think everyone *is* broken. We all just push things down and focus on taking the next step forward."

"Maybe I should expect no better from a people who called their world *Earth.*" She shrugged, dismissing the notion. "So, the truth of it is that I am struggling to contain my feelings while you are doing all that you can to ignore yours?"

"Seems like it, yeah."

Miko sighed. "And now we are lost in a land I know only from nightmarish legend, with few levels and a single weapon between us. Am I missing anything?"

"We have food," I pointed out, scooping up another handful of berries. "And we have each other. We also know that at least some of your ships left port already for this continent."

For a moment, she just stared at me, and I was left wondering what else I had said—or done—wrong. And then, her mouth dropped open.

"You're right! They are on their way, even now!" For the first time since our escape, there was a spark of energy in her voice. "According to the stories, it took multiple cycles to cross the ocean, but that simply means we have time."

"Time?"

"To prepare for their arrival!" She was on her feet, scanning the land-locked portion of our horizon. "Maybe… maybe *that* is why you and I are here? Maybe the primacy was always doomed to fall, but Synos' celestial children intended for us to shepherd the rebirth of our empire on the very continent our ancestors fled?"

There were a *lot* of holes in that theory, but since Shan hadn't told me his plans, I let it go. Besides, Miko was right. Having people on the ground long before shiploads of refugees arrived had to be a positive, right? And if we were talking a journey of *years*, we would have ample time to lay the foundation for their return.

Assuming we could figure out where we were, where that landing might eventually occur, and a whole bunch of other things, naturally. Still, those were just additional problems for future-Brian to deal with. In the short term, we needed drinking water, a destination, and—most importantly of all, in my mind—levels.

One of those issues was more easily resolved than the rest. As I rose to join Miko, she pointed westward. Far away, beyond the virtually endless carpet of trees, smoke lazily curled its way up into the sky to mingle with the clouds above.

"Wildfire?"

"Too stable for something naturally occurring, and too much smoke for a simple campfire. A town maybe? It might be less than a seven-day away. If we can reach it, we could look for work or at least information."

"But what if the inhabitants are hostile? Didn't your people leave the Great Wilds because they were being persecuted?"

"They did." She threw her hands in the air at the doubt she saw in my face. "What other choices do we have? You are level one, and I am level four. Even if we could hunt or gather sufficiently to stay fed, all it would take is a single encounter with something like a sluthar to end us both. We will scout the encampment upon arrival, as we must, but civilization *is* the safer option."

Twenty-plus years of watching action movies told me otherwise—that *people* could be far more dangerous than any monster—but I didn't have a better suggestion.

"West it is."

Maybe they'd have indoor plumbing.

21

The forest that had seemed so ominous at night *still* seemed plenty ominous during the day, but to my great surprise, we spent the first few hours of our hike without anything leaping out to kill us. The deeper we went, the bigger the trees became, trunks as wide as my badly worn couch back home, with bark that was purple and silver instead of brown. High above us, too high to climb even if I *did* want the skill, branches fanned out to form a multi-layered canopy that kept the forest floor in perpetual shadow.

I could hear *things* chittering within that canopy, but so far, they seemed content to stay up there. That suited me just fine.

With the sun hidden, keeping our course had been the first challenge. I'd never been a Boy Scout, and Miko's woodcraft wasn't much better than mine. We did our best to parallel the rocky cliffs to the north even as we descended below them. Eventually, we hoped, those cliffs would give way to a beach, and we'd be able to travel along the coastline instead of through the forest itself. It would probably add miles to the journey, but it was still better than getting turned around and lost in the woods.

With a decent idea of our general heading and an absence of creatures trying to kill and eat us, the lack of supplies and clothing became our primary concern. The berries Miko had gathered from shrubs on the forest edge only lasted through lunchtime, but at least we'd eaten. Water was a bigger problem, but even that worry was outweighed by my lack of shoes. Neither of us had footwear, but Miko had scales. Terrain that didn't even give her pause had me looking for different pathways, trying to avoid the rocks and roots that threatened to cut my feet to ribbons. Twice now, the Priestess had been forced to recast *Minor Healing*, and yet I could already feel fresh lacerations forming on my soles.

"It'll be getting dark in a couple of hours—or glasses—I think," I said, licking dry lips as I eyed the canopy above us. "We'll need to find somewhere to camp. Preferably someplace where things won't creep down and kill us in our sleep."

"We need water first," countered Miko. I wasn't an expert in synossian biology, but she looked even more dehydrated than I felt. "Better that we find it now than spend a second night without."

I winced as a blister popped. I wasn't in combat, which meant there was no chance of amplified skill gains, but if I didn't get at *least* a rank in Pain Tolerance from this, the Framework and I would have words. "In that case, I might need another healing. Please."

"I have only a few left before I am out of blessings," Miko warned.

"Right. Your cooldowns are fine, but your soul energy is low." I frowned. "It doesn't come back as we travel?"

"It does, but not at any great speed. A full night of sleep will ensure that I am restored. Everything else is… like taking a breath between runs instead of a nap."

"Well, I've got *Lunge* locked and loaded, for all the good that it will do us." I blinked at Miko's sigh. "What?"

"While the words you speak are in our language, the way they are arranged often makes no sense."

"Oh, right." I coughed. "Those are sayings from my world. I guess my trait doesn't know how to translate them."

"Then maybe you should *stop speaking them*." Her words cracked like a whip.

"I can do that."

She didn't offer to heal my feet, and I didn't press the matter as we traveled on in silence. Maybe I was better off forming calluses until my skin was as tough as a synossian's. Or maybe I'd decided to walk my feet down to the bone rather than give Miko another opportunity to complain about me.

We'd been in the Great Wilds for less than a day. I was tired, I was in pain, and I was thirsty. Worse, I was heartily sick of Eos in general, and more than a little pissed off at Shan and his so-called celestial siblings.

What the hell kind of god saves someone from certain death just to dump them into extremely likely *death?*

And why does a level-one human from Earth matter more to that same god than the very people who worship him?

I didn't know, and once again, there was a conspicuous lack of help text or lore drops to clarify the issue.

A half-glass later, Miko stopped and turned to face me. "I did not mean to snap, Brian Fieldings. You and your unintelligible idioms are not the source of my temper, and you do not deserve to bear its brunt."

It was kind of annoying how easily and *well* she apologized, but that was probably just my bloody feet talking. "It's fine. I understand. And I'm sure it's irritating as hell having to hear idioms that mean nothing to you. Kind of like when you use a word that doesn't translate into my language."

"Like what?"

"Sluthari. Dalysi. Phloxl. I'm sure there'll be more."

"Names of creatures, one and all."

"Apparently." I shrugged. "I need to know them if this is going to be my new home, so I'm not complaining. I'm just saying that the frustration goes both ways. And that it's not *really* about the language for me either."

She nodded, curving around a tree while keeping an eye to the cliffs we could barely see now to our north. "Somewhere in my past few cycles, I have become too reliant on others. My shrine guardians. Priest Berys. Even my fellow Priests of Aurea. It is humbling to realize that, even at level four, I remain so poorly prepared to be traveling on my own."

She technically *wasn't* on her own, but I got what she was saying. "We'll figure it out together. If nothing else, this is what Riok would have called an opportunity for growth, right? I gained the *Hunting* skill last night thanks to the bird I killed. Who knows what else we'll have learned by the time we reach town?"

She brightened and nodded. "If you can deliver us more meat, maybe I will try my hand at cooking. This deep in the forest, we should be able to at least mask the smoke of a fire."

"I know you said you have a fire-striker, but... have you ever used it to start a fire before?"

Her silence was answer enough.

"Then I guess one of us will be learning how." Assuming my *Caretaking* skill didn't already cover that, I might have another new skill soon.

It hurt to smile, but I did it anyway. As tired as I was and as awful as the past two days had been, I still felt a visceral sort of thrill at the thought of actual, tangible advancement.

Miko didn't reply, but I could see my words take hold. Her chin lifted, her spine straightened, and she took each new step with a renewed energy that I could only envy.

Ten minutes later, we found water.

It was a tiny stream, so narrow I could have easily stepped across it, bubbling up from underground to chart a course that, much like us, meandered in a westerly direction. One at a time, we knelt to slake our thirst, then repeated the process to take longer, slower sips. The water was ice cold, and I could taste minerals, but judging by the vibrant green vegetation growing along the stream's edge, it was probably safe to drink.

As Miko knelt for her second drink, I headed downstream to examine the muddy shoreline. Color aside, the plants were a dead ringer for cattails on Earth, looking like fuzzy sausages on long stems. In between a thick cluster, I found the first evidence that we weren't alone down here on the forest's floor: tracks from some kind of animal.

A day ago, I didn't think I would have even noticed them, but maybe *Hunting* was useful for more than just the actual killing. The skill didn't tell me what the creature was, or even anything as general as its size or species; it just alerted me to the tracks' existence. Either there was another skill that handled the rest, or I needed to get my *Hunting* up to a more respectable rank.

Like *two*, for example.

I turned back to Miko and almost fell over. Yellow roots, closer to string than something you'd see from a tree, had tangled around my right foot. As I watched, additional roots sprouted from the soil at an impossible speed, binding the foot to the earth beneath it. Worse, I could feel *something* scraping against the bottom of that same foot, tearing into its already blistered and bloody sole.

With a shout, I tore my foot away, ripping through the net of roots that was forming. Where my foot had stood, several thorns now poked up through the dirt, glistening with fresh blood.

I didn't know if I was being attacked by a carnivorous plant, an animal, or an unholy hybrid of both, and I didn't care. I took another step back, spun Riok's spear in my hands—*lesson one* remained a winner—and stabbed it into the dirt, right in the center of those still-questing thorns.

The ground shuddered, and several of the neighboring cattails lashed about, striking the soil with blows far heavier than I would have expected—if I had ever expected cattails to move at all. I leaned on my spear, driving it further into whatever had the dirt pitching and rolling like a localized earthquake, then pulled it out and stabbed again. And again. Either my attacker *wasn't* a plant, or plants had vital bits just like the rest of us, because my third strike caused the crawling yellow roots, the flanking cattails, *and* whatever was under the soil to stiffen and collapse.

I gasped for breath, winded even though the whole fight had taken maybe five seconds. Miko was only now reaching me, water dripping from her scales, orange eyes wide as she took in the scene.

"What happened?"

Instead of answering, I used the butt of Riok's spear to scrape aside the dirt I'd already torn into with my attacks. What lurked beneath was an eggshell-pale blob of rubbery flesh. It had neither eyes nor ears, but a circular tube extending upward from the center of a circular array of thorns almost had to be its mouth. Thick tendrils splayed outward, some narrowing and splitting to become the strands that had tried to trap me, others forming the root systems of the cattails I'd thought were independent plants.

"It's all one creature," I said, announcing the obvious, "or one plant. My weight or my blood must have triggered it."

"I would like to borrow some of your emotional numbness right now," said Miko in a very small voice.

"I'm screaming inside, trust me." Somehow, I dredged up a smile. "But I recently learned that it's best *not* to make loud noises where predators might hear them."

For the first time all day, we shared grins, but Miko's vanished almost immediately later. "Wait. What do you mean your *blood* triggered it?"

Before I could reply, she was one knee, lifting my foot like I was a horse—or a dalys, I guess—and hissing at what she found.

"Some of that was from the thorns."

"And the rest?"

"I figured we should save your blessings for when they mattered. After all, our resources are limited—"

"And I was being the opposite of approachable."

"I wasn't going to say that."

"But it's true, isn't it?"

"That's water under the—" I coughed. "Sorry. Idiom. I meant to say that it's all in the past. We talked through it."

"Okay." She murmured the words of her blessing and warmth swept through my foot as flesh knitted itself back together for the third time that day. "Then I hope you will not take it poorly when I ask that you be more insistent in the future should you require healing. Treating your wounds is not just about your comfort or even a means for me to work towards my next level. It is also common sense."

"How so?"

"What do you think predators use to track their prey?" Happily, she didn't wait for my answer because I'm sure it would have been disappointing. "Hearing and sight, yes, but also scent. It is bad enough that we both smell like we slept in a butcher's shop; your blood is a marker that a hungry beast will track with great intent, knowing that its prey is already injured."

A trail that led right to where we were standing. "I guess we won't be camping here then?"

Even with lizard features, the look she gave to the dead plant thing I'd just killed spoke volumes.

"I didn't mean *on* the shoreline."

"I think it would be best to travel further downstream," she agreed. "Before we do so, we might want to take care of our stench as well. If we are prey, we should at least do our best to remain elusive."

Neither of us dared the water until I'd stabbed the remaining plants along the shoreline. Five minutes later, we stood in the middle of a massacre that future plant generations would speak of in hushed whispers, but we also knew for a fact that we were safe and alone.

Although... I leaned over the spring and drove my spear through the water itself, past the shallow flow and into the basin below.

Nothing moved or reacted.

Okay; *now* I was sure.

Miko bathed first, while I stood watch with spear in hand. She set aside a few items that had been held in an inner pouch and then pulled off her stained robes entirely, revealing nothing but white scales beneath. Once again, it didn't even occur to me to be embarrassed. The synossian Priestess was *so* alien that sexual attraction didn't enter the discussion.

Captain Kirk would have to walk that road alone.

Still, to offer her the privacy she didn't seem all that concerned with, I kept my eyes on the stream and the terrain around us, watching for threats as Miko washed first her robes and then herself.

"I wish either of us had managed to bring oil and a brush," she muttered, halfway through.

"Agreed on the oil. The brush I could do without." I shivered theatrically. "It felt like I lost a layer of skin every time I used it."

"No doubt, we will be able to find you an alternate solution once we reach civilization. I struggle to believe that soft skins are unable to properly bathe—" She stiffened in the stream and sent me a deep bow. "I apologize again."

"For what?"

"For calling you a soft skin."

"I don't have scales or fur or anything. I'd say it fits."

"Even so."

I dipped the butt of my spear in the water and used it to splash her. "Yesterday, you called me a *stupid phloxl!* I have no idea what that is, but I'm betting it's both more offensive and less accurate than *soft skin*. Now, hurry up, would you? This scale-challenged Chosen wants to get clean."

By the time we were dressed again, the scant light that made it through the gaps in the forest's ceiling was gone. Still, we pushed on for another glass or so, following the water instead of the cliffs we could no longer see. I went first, hoping my *Danger Sense* skill would warn me of any encroaching threats, despite its failure to do so with the plant monster.

Eventually, Miko announced that we had gone far enough. After moving another dozen paces from the stream, we made camp. Which, in the absence of supplies, mostly just involved sitting down.

"We need a tent," I said. "And waterskins or canteens." My stomach rumbled. "And something to eat other than berries."

"I suggested bringing the riverstalker," Miko pointed out, using the name she'd coined for the thing that had attacked me.

"And *I* still think eating a vampiric plant monster that neither of us has ever heard of is a bad idea. We can't afford to come down with food poisoning."

"Then berries will have to do. Although if you *do* hunt something more palatable, or less creepy looking, I will see about cooking it."

"I'll do my best." With nightfall, the sounds from the trees above us had gone from creepy to truly sinister. For all we knew, this was when the forest's inhabitants descended to feed, kind of like the birds back on the cliffs. "Do you want to meditate first this time?"

"Yes. When we are both done, I will take watch for a few glasses, so that you may get some sleep."

"And then I'll stand watch until sunrise," I agreed. "See? We're working together better already!"

I couldn't see the glare Miko sent me, but I could practically feel it. I could also tell it had a lot less heat behind it than it would have a few hours earlier.

"Just warn me if there is trouble," she said.

An hour miraculously passed without any real excitement. Soon after that, she stirred again.

"Anything good?" I asked her.

"Little of immediate value. Given the lack of excitement today, I am unsurprised. If I had taken part in the battle with the riverstalker…"

"Your claws are plenty sharp, believe me, but I think we should get you an actual weapon before you enter combat."

"Perhaps we can find a fallen branch or something for me to utilize as a club." I heard the rustle of robes as she shrugged. "But first, it is your turn to meditate."

22

"**B**rian." Miko's voice was hushed, but the hand on my arm—my bare arm, because after five days in the woods, my robe was basically ribbons—was tense, her claws thoughtfully angled away to avoid piercing my skin.

"What is it?" I didn't move an inch as I woke. While I wouldn't say either of us was ready to quit our careers and become park rangers, we'd come a long way, both figuratively and literally.

We'd had to leave the stream a few times over the past few days, because it turned out to be a magnet for trouble. Still, our inescapable need for water had meant we kept coming back as it slowly curved to the north and the unseen ocean. Five days of travel added up to a lot of miles, even when taking the terrain into account.

That was the literal distance. The figurative distance was all about our skills. Our first night in the forest had taught us that its inhabitants *did* hunt at night, including ape-like things that climbed down to feed from the forest floor. Multiple encounters with those creatures had left us battered and bloody but rolling in potential skill gains.

Unfortunately, it had been days since I'd been able to meditate and see those gains realized.

"I heard a noise. Distant but coming closer."

After two straight days of this, I was pretty sure we both knew what it was, but I felt compelled to ask anyway. "From above, I hope?"

"No; iron scraping against bark."

"Shit. Did we piss this thing off in a past life or something?" The apes had turned out to be the least of the problems we would encounter. At the opposite end of the monster hierarchy was a black-scaled serpent with a body as long as multiple school buses and as wide as one of the forest's great trees. As far as we could tell, the apes were its preferred prey, and our handful of clashes with those creatures must have gotten its attention. Two days later, it was *still* chasing us.

I hurried through my forms, then climbed to my feet, grabbing both my spear and the primitive sack Miko had fashioned from the sleeve of her robes. "Any ideas?"

"Run through the night and then shorten our rest times even further?" Miko sounded as exhausted as I felt. "It may be slower than we are, but it is relentless."

I didn't love the idea of traveling at night. Eos' two moons didn't offer much illumination, thanks to the thick forest canopy, and running in the dark felt like a good way to get killed by dangers we wouldn't see until far too late. But I didn't have any better ideas either. While we'd found Miko a makeshift club, neither of our weapons would even inconvenience the titan on our trail.

"Okay. Let's go."

Miko's night vision was better than mine, so she took point, crude club in hand, and I did my best to follow the patch of greater darkness that I knew was my companion. She was right about one thing: as swift as the serpent was in battle, its sheer size worked against it when traversing the forest. Without clear cut trails, it was forced to wind its scaled bulk through trees that we could simply run past. That both slowed it down and generated the noise that Miko had once again heard.

We hurried through the woods for hours, the air burning in my lungs. Miraculously, I managed not to break my neck in the darkness. Which wasn't to say I didn't fall; I did, and lots of times. Even *Miko* fell once or twice. But one of us was always there to help the other up, and by the time my legs simply refused to keep going, the serpent had once again been left far behind.

Even better, from the sound of the songbirds that remained above us and out of sight, it was approaching daytime. The one thing we had gathered over the past two days was that the serpent, much like the ape things it hunted, was nocturnal.

"What now? Meditate and sleep during the day and then travel at night?" It would slow us down even further, and make finding our way that much more difficult, but at least we'd be able to get some rest.

"Let's keep going a while longer," said Miko, forked tongue flicking the air as she panted for breath. "If more slowly. We can take the afternoon to recover before we head out again. I want as much space between us and that creature as we can get before we try to sleep."

I was *exhausted*, having not slept at all, but I nodded. I didn't know what Miko's Vitality was, but the Priestess had to be suffering as much as I was. If she wanted to keep going, I could hardly do less.

For another few hours, I focused on putting one foot in front of the other, staggering forward as much as walking. By the time we stopped again, the infrequently seen sun was high in the sky, and it was a struggle just to keep my eyes open. When Miko cast *Minor Healing* on both of us, aching muscles unknotted and warmth suffuse my body, but the exhaustion remained. In some ways, it even deepened.

"Healing does not restore energy," she explained. "In fact, it uses some of the recipient's energy as fuel. But our bodies would take too much time to heal on their own, whereas a good nap should at least partially help restore our reserves."

"I'm not complaining," I said, almost mumbling.

"You meditate first," she said after one look at my face. "Maybe it will help you stay awake when it is my turn."

I wasn't even sure I'd be able to stay awake while *I* was meditating but didn't bother saying so. I collapsed to the ground, not even trying to sit how Riok had taught me. My spear was in reach, my pouch next to it, and either I'd learn to meditate while lying on my side, or I'd get an hour of sleep before I had to stand watch for Miko.

Shockingly, it ended up being the first one. After the events of the past few days played out in my brain, I opened my eyes to see the now-familiar screen in front of me:

```
You have increased the following skills:

Major skills:
Light Armor [+3]: 9/10
Spear [+1]: 10/10
Tactics [+2]: 3/10

Minor skills:
Athleticism [+3]: 8/10
Avoidance [+2]: 6/10
Pain Tolerance [+5]: 7/10

General skills:
Animal Behaviorism [+2]: 6/10
Danger Sense (R) [+2]: 3/10
Meditation [+1]: 1/10
```

It didn't surprise me to see that *Pain Tolerance* had gained another five ranks over the past two days, in addition to the one I'd gained since entering the forest. Miko had turned my sweatpants into a loincloth and used the rest of the fabric to wrap my feet, but the journey had still been anything but fun. To say nothing of the wounds I'd taken in our various battles.

Pain Tolerance had even leap frogged *Avoidance*, which said terrible things about my combat style.

I took a quick peek at my full character sheet, but as expected, none of the other skills had improved at all. Still, I was getting closer. One more rank in *Light Armor* and a few points in *Athleticism, Pain Tolerance*, and/or *Avoidance*, and I'd finally be able to level.

And then we'll turn around and show that serpent who's boss, insisted the part of my brain intent on getting us both killed.

"Did you know *Meditation* has its own skill?" I asked Miko, finally opening my eyes. I didn't feel rested, exactly, but I was less ragged than when we'd first made camp.

"Of course, although I don't think I've ever seen anyone learn it while lying on their side like that."

I fought back a yawn. "If it works, it works... although I'm guessing I picked it up sometime in the previous days' attempts instead. Everything okay?"

"Dead quiet," she agreed, not even having the grace to wince at her choice of words. "My turn?"

I took hold of my spear and nodded. "See you soon."

An hour later, she opened her orange eyes and smiled. "Finally."

"Something good?"

"Ranks in *Cooking, Tailoring*, and *Orienteering*, in addition to some minor gains in my class skills."

"*Orien*-what?"

"Pathfinding. Keeping to a given route. I'm only at rank two, but it should make our journey a little easier."

That would come in handy, but I was way more interested in her *Cooking* gains. I hoisted the sleeve sack that had earned Miko her first rank in *Tailoring*. It was half full of badly burned gorilla monster meat. Starting a fire had turned out to be the *easy* part of cooking. "Does that mean we don't have to eat *this* anymore?"

"That depends on if you manage to kill anything fresh tonight, oh exalted hunter." Miko flashed another sharp-toothed smile my way. "Now, get some sleep. The sooner you're done, the sooner I can start."

Three days of relying on each other had altered our relationship in a way that traveling with Riok's claw had not. I'd come to discover that the young synossian possessed a sharp tongue that would have been cutting were it not counterbalanced by what appeared to be genuine sweetness. At the same time, Miko had never complained after those first terrible days. I could still hear her crying herself to sleep more often than not, but she woke up each morning ready to press on, and when battle found us, her skill with the makeshift club easily eclipsed mine.

Club is one of my class's Minor skills, she'd told me, after our first encounter with the apes left monkey brains splattered across the forest floor. *If you should reach my level, your skill with weapons will almost definitely surpass mine, but for now… watch and wonder!*

The further we traveled together, the more the real Miko shined through, and frankly, she didn't suck. If we'd met on Earth, and she hadn't been a white-scaled lizard beast that my fellow Americans would've probably shot on sight, I'm pretty sure she could have been friends with Bug, Kate, and me. I didn't know what she thought of me—the Chosen who had *not* saved her nation but *might* have been sent to save some small portion of its people—but the Priestess treated me like a companion rather than a burden.

And together, we were staying alive.

ooo

When evening fell, we were on the move again, as refreshed as a few hours of sleep could make us. Miko promised we'd stop at sunrise to meditate and get more sleep, assuming we didn't encounter our hunter again in the interim. As we traveled, I found myself dreaming of fluffy pillows and luxurious white bedding—the kind you'd see in one of those high-end hotels I'd never gotten to visit. Did Eos have room service? Or spas? I'd never experienced either of those things back on Earth either, so I could only hope.

Judging by our time in the forest so far, we'd instead be settling for dirt and at least one tree root perfectly placed to make *every* sleeping position uncomfortable, but even so, a full night—or day, technically—of sleep sounded heavenly.

We marched on into the night, not running, but not dawdling either, doing all that we could to stay ahead of the monstrosity on our trail. In the darkness, I stumbled just as much as I had the night before, but my gains in *Athleticism* made themselves known in small but tangible ways, allowing me to regain my balance more often before I faceplanted into the dirt. As a result, our pace was only marginally slower than it had been when we ran.

Everything stayed calm until sometime after midnight. I was a few paces behind the darker shadow that was Miko when something in me twitched, like an electrical charge running right through my body. I halted, mid-step, and raised my spear as a dark shadow pounced from the branches above.

Sadly, I was facing the entirely wrong direction and didn't hit a damn thing, but my unexpected stop had at least messed up the timing of the creature's leap; it landed where I should have been and missed me entirely. I turned and stabbed out with my spear, rewarded with an ear-splitting yowl that sounded like nothing so much as a pissed-off barn cat.

"Miko!" I had *Lunge* ready, of course, but had to see where I was going to trigger it, and in the darkness, that wasn't happening.

Thankfully, this wasn't our first nighttime battle together. Light flooded the clearing as Miko cast *Flare*, and just like that, our attacker was stripped of its nighttime camouflage. Black fur and vaguely feline features supported my initial *big cat* impression, but as with everything I'd encountered on Eos, this thing had taken a hard right into Crazy Town. Its hindquarters were armored with some sort of carapace, and a sinuous scaled tail ended in a solid ball twice the size of my fist. It was like someone had married a panther to an ankylosaurus.

If I'd been a guest at that wedding, I would have 'spoken now' and stopped the whole thing in its tracks.

"Watch the tail!" I shouted.

"Beware the claws," Miko shouted back. "And teeth!"

So… everything. Got it. Even as the random thought skittered across the surface of my mind, I was triggering *Lunge*, taking advantage of the creature's *Flare*-induced flinch. I hurtled through empty space, spear leading the way like the vanguard of some unstoppable army.

Whatever this new monster was, it was quick and it was nimble. It flowed around my technique and turned to swipe a paw at my now-exposed back. Before it could strike, Miko was at its side, hammering the creature with her club.

A loud crack split the night. I expected the beast to go limp, spine snapped by the Priestess' hit and a Strength attribute that, even without additional ranks in it, almost definitely outmatched mine. Instead, it was the club that broke, leaving Miko holding a shard of wood about eight inches long.

Lunge wasn't off cooldown yet, so I charged the beast the old-fashioned way. This time, the creature was slower to dodge. Thick fur gave way to the deadly sharp spearhead, and blood gushed from the creature's flank. I pressed my advantage, using the full length of Riok's spear to avoid the creature's flailing claws. *Nail it to a tree and let it bleed out*, whispered a voice in my mind. *Don't risk getting within range of those things.*

I didn't know when my inner voice had taken a crash course in combat, but as far as tactics went, this one made sense. My arms were already tiring, but I churned my legs forward, driving toward the nearest tree.

That was when the beast reminded us all that it had more than just claws and teeth.

The ball on its armored tail whipped around like an Olympian's shotput, and although I—somehow—managed to get out of the way of its destructive arc, my spear wasn't that lucky. Despite its corroded and decrepit appearance, Riok's former weapon held strong, but my grip gave out. The spear flew free to clatter off a nearby tree.

Which left me unarmed, facing a pissed off panther dinosaur.

As the creature opened its cavernous maw, revealing *way* too many teeth, a second burst of golden light triggered in its face. Miko's second *Flare* didn't have the same impact as the first, but it *did* give me enough space to duck and roll. And that was all I had time to do; as I made it back to my feet, the creature's crystalline eyes were already blinking away the sting of two light sources. It focused in on me immediately, stalking forward like the creature it approximated.

If Shan had just made me a Mage, this thing would already be dead, I raged, backing away as I tried to circle around to my lost spear. *Fireball, Bigby's Big Bad Booty, whatever that wilting spell was, and poof.*

An entire reality away, I wondered if Bug was experiencing a moment of inexplicable pride, somehow unconsciously aware that I'd remembered so many random details from the games he'd taught me to play.

Sadly, I *wasn't* a Mage. I was still a good twenty-five seconds from being able to use *Lunge* again too. This cat thing, while vastly weaker than the serpent hunting us, had to be higher level than the apes we'd killed so far. And that was… problematic.

When the cat rushed forward, I simply wasn't fast enough to dodge the charge entirely. Claws raked down one of my arms as I ran for my dropped weapon. I couldn't hear the creature land behind me, but that feeling I'd started to associate with *Danger Sense* told me I'd never make it to my spear in time.

Instead, my questing hands found the item I'd dropped back when combat first began.

As the panther leaped again, I swung my sack of burned ape meat and caught the creature in its misshapen feline head. There was no crack or yowl of pain, but the blow knocked it off course, and *that* gave me the handful of seconds I needed to finally reach my spear again. I rose into a crouch and Miko joined me, the jagged remnant of her club now held like a dagger.

"You're bleeding," she said. "Again."

"It's kind of my thing." I tossed her the food bag. "Throw it when it leaps? I'll try to attack from below and hit something vital."

"And then I'll take it from behind once you have it distracted."

"Just watch the—"

"You already said that." For just a moment, so quick that I almost doubted I'd seen it, Miko grinned.

And then, the panther was on us.

○○○

"The bleeding has stopped," announced Miko, leaning back on her haunches and rubbing her scaled face. "Finally."

Lacking both the element of surprise and the darkness it preferred, the creature had gone down relatively easily in the end, but I'd taken yet another hit along the way. It was a testament to my slowly growing *Avoidance* skill that so far, the wounds I'd received in the forest had been mostly superficial… or at least shallow enough for Miko to heal with repeated castings.

Unfortunately, between the two *Flare* spells Miko had cast and our post-battle healing, she was low on energy yet again. We'd seemingly left the apes' territory behind us but neither of us was willing to bet that there was only a single ninja catosaur ahead. And while I thought we would survive a second encounter, we'd almost definitely end up bleeding out from any wounds we took in that fight.

We couldn't afford to stop, but we didn't dare keep going.

"Does *Orienteering* help with figuring out which way is north?" I asked.

"It would be easier in the daylight, but…" She examined a tree I couldn't see now that darkness had reclaimed the area. "Yes. What are you thinking?"

"I want to try to find the cliffs again. If we're lucky, they'll have finally descended to meet the rest of the forest. Maybe we can get out from under these trees and an entire ecosystem that wants us dead."

"And if we are not lucky?"

"The cliffs will give us protection from one side."

It was Miko's turn to accept a not-so-great plan due to the absence of a better suggestion. "We'll still need water."

"Yeah. We can come back south to find the stream again, or maybe following the beach will take us to where it dumps into the ocean. But for now—"

"Yes. For now, we should keep going." I felt more than saw her crouch in front of me, followed by a tearing sound I'd become uncomfortably familiar with over the past week. "I'll leave most of the carcass behind, but between the meat I've already cooked, and this flank, we should have enough to reach our destination."

"Assuming we don't die first."

She didn't even grace my comment with a reply.

It was almost dawn before we stumbled out from under the forest's all-encompassing canopy, the sound of crashing waves music to my tired ears. Above us, stars twinkled and glittered next to one of the two moons. Their light shined down upon the rocky beach we'd finally reached.

It was peaceful as hell, which told me there were probably nightmarish things lurking in the watery depths.

I was onto Eos' bullshit.

"Brian, look."

At Miko's urging, I turned away from the water and the sky above it, and looked to the west, down the length of dark beach. At some point, the forest encroached again, a handful of trees making an ill-advised sally onto rock and earth poorly suited for supporting life, but past that, in the distance…

"Is that light?"

"I believe so. Still distant enough that we wouldn't see the source in the daytime, but—"

"But we're getting closer to the town you spotted."

"Another night of travel, I think." The Priestess patted my shoulder, her strange eyes reflecting the stars above us. "And then we can truly begin."

23

We traveled onward through the morning, as the sun crept up over the horizon behind us, and although I was sure the beach and ocean had their own dangers, nothing bothered us on our journey. Finally, through silent, mutual agreement, we came to a halt. I gathered up pieces of driftwood that had washed onto the beach and dried in the sun, and Miko collected a small pile of brush from the forest's border to serve as kindling.

The Priestess' fire-striker was basically flint and steel, like I'd assumed, although the 'steel' portion was black and shot through with flecks of some other mineral, much like the hardware at Miko's abandoned shrine. It worked like a charm, whatever it was. Next to Riok's spear, it was the most valuable thing in our possession, in terms of simple survival, if not money.

Miko's improved *Cooking* skill meant the catosaur ended up only partly burned. That was a huge improvement over previous attempts. The meat was tough and kind of gamey, with no spices to counteract its acrid taste, but I could chew it without spending long minutes softening it with my own saliva, and that was huge.

Hopefully, it wouldn't cause any digestive issues. The lack of toilets in Eos was already bad enough as it was.

We were chowing down when Miko went stiff, turning to stare at the fire with wide eyes. It took me a moment longer to realize what she was thinking, then I too traced the thin trail of smoke that rose from our fire into the cloudless sky.

"Crap." We'd set several fires over the past week, but they'd been within the depths of the forest, where the smoke would presumably be partially dispersed or hidden entirely by the many layers of leafy ceiling above us.

Out here on the rocky beach, we didn't have that luxury. While the light of the fire might be lost in the morning sun, its smoke was an unmistakable sign of our presence. I helped Miko scatter the embers, but even after the fire was out, we shared a long look of concern. If anyone in that town had been looking our way, the damage was already done.

"Back into the woods?" I asked.

She shook her head. "We don't know if your *catosaurs* are nocturnal or if we just stumbled into one who found itself hungry."

"Fair. I have a hard time separating my complete guesses from insight potentially granted by *Animal Behaviorism*."

Miko spared me a considering glance. "How tired are you?"

That was a loaded question if I'd ever heard one, but I just went with the truth. "Pretty tired. We've gotten about eight hours of sleep over the past three days; I'm surprised I'm not actively hallucinating by this point. Still, I can keep going if we need to."

The Priestess shook her head. "Exhaustion will kill us as swiftly as anything else. Let's camp here for now. We can meditate and then sleep until nightfall. If anything approaches, we will be able to see it coming from a league away."

To be honest, the only part of her speech that I really heard was *camp here*. I went back to the forest's edge, found a relatively soft patch of dirt, and doubled down on my new, patent-pending, meditation pose.

An hour after that, a familiar dialogue screen was in front of my eyes, but I didn't bother reading it, too tired to do much more than roll over and go to sleep.

Hours later, I realized my mistake, waking up with a muttered curse. Miko sat nearby, orange eyes open as she scanned our surroundings. She turned as I jerked my way up.

"Good afternoon, Brian Fieldings."

"I'm sorry, Miko. I was supposed to let you meditate before I passed out."

"You were more tired than I was," she said, a yawn belying her words. "When you started to make that racket of yours, I recognized you were asleep and no longer meditating."

"It's the pollen or something." I rubbed at my nose. "I don't usually snore."

"I was happy to stand watch," she said, rightly ignoring my excuses. "However, if you are now awake?"

"Yeah, no, totally. I'm awake. Please, get your meditation and sleep on. I'll wake you up at… sunset?"

"If nothing occurs before then." Unlike me, Miko adopted the seated position that Riok had demonstrated, bowing her scaled head as she let her eyes drift shut. I felt bad about screwing with the usual watch schedule but couldn't deny that the hours of sleep had done me good.

Once she was meditating, I went and took care of my daily business, making sure the ever-present ocean breeze didn't send my piss right back at me. What was left of my clothing was a disaster, but I still had *some* pride. And according to both Miko and *Animal Behaviorism,* urine would attract predators as readily as blood. Maybe even more so.

The speed with which my bladder emptied made it clear that I was riding the edge of dehydration, but that was a problem for later. I retreated from the water's edge to take up my watch near the meditating synossian. Now that I was awake, I realized my skill-ups dialogue screen had disappeared. Was there some sort of timer that nobody had told me about? It wasn't like I had an actual HUD or anything, with a flashing notification or button to click on.

Although… that *did* give me an idea. The skill-up window had always popped up automatically upon skill gain after I finished meditation, but maybe I could summon it manually, like I did my character screen?

A fraction of a second later, the missing screen appeared in front of me. Once again, I didn't bother reading it, but this time it was because a thought had just struck me like a lightning bolt from one of Miko's gods: if the Framework gave me on-demand access to *two* screens, who was to say there weren't even *more* of them out there, just waiting to be summoned?

For the next ten or so minutes, I tried to conjure every possible screen I could think of, from *inventory* to *help topics* to even a detailed combat log. None of it worked, which either meant those screens didn't exist on Eos or they had to be summoned in some other way. I was guessing it was the former… but wouldn't be too broken up to learn otherwise. Some form of theoretical spatial storage that the synossians hadn't known about would make life *so* much easier.

I ran through another dozen possibilities before I finally gave up and re-summoned my skill-up screen instead. Technically, the character sheet contained the same information, but I preferred the more focused view. Not only did it filter out any skills that hadn't leveled—something I could see becoming ever more useful as I gained additional skills—it also told me exactly how many ranks I'd gained in the skills that *did* level.

And that saved me from having to remember any of it myself.

You have increased the following skills:

Major skills:
Light Armor [+1]: 10/10
Tactics [+1]: 4/10

Minor skills:
Athleticism [+2]: 10/10
Avoidance [+1]: 7/10
Pain Tolerance [+2]: 9/10

General skills:
Animal Behaviorism [+1]: 7/10
Danger Sense (R) [+1]: 4/10
Meditation [+1]: 2/10

It was a shorter list this time, thanks to the relative quiet of our night's journey. The catosaur had been tough, yeah, but it had been the *only* opponent we fought, and that was going to impact skill gains as far as anything combat related was concerned. Additionally, skills were starting to cap out for my level. *Spear* had hit rank ten the day before, and now *Light Armor* and *Athleticism* were capped too. That meant any potential gains in those three skills would be lost while I was stuck at level one.

That sucked, especially since skill gains slowed as a person leveled. Still, any sour apples I was feeling faded quickly in the face of another realization:

One more rank in Pain Tolerance, and I'll be level two!

Of all the skills I possessed, *Pain Tolerance* was unquestionably the one I *least* enjoyed advancing, but I didn't hate its increasingly noticeable effects. More importantly, I was looking forward to the extra attribute point I would earn at level two. Health and mana—or energy, as everyone called it—remained weirdly abstract, thanks to the lack of numbers on my character sheet, but I would presumably see some gains there through leveling. And even though *Lunge* wasn't quite the game changer I'd thought it was, it would be awesome to have it usable more than four times over the course of a day.

My General skills were less exciting, but *Danger Sense* had already saved my life at least once, and even if the Rare skill remained deeply unreliable, I didn't hate seeing that number go up. *Animal Behaviorism* would be less useful once we reached civilization, but maybe I could turn that into a job working with pets or horses or something?

With our destination only a day or two away, my thoughts couldn't help but turn to what came next.

It had been more than two weeks since my dad's death and the emotional numbness that had carried me through my introduction to Eos was starting to wear off. The complicated jumble of thoughts and feelings about my dad's fate was still neatly packed away somewhere, where I didn't have to think about it, but I was finding myself struggling more with recent events. The battle with the sluthar. The dead guards at the shrine. Our front-row seat to Whitehall's fall. And, most of all, Riok's spear, the same spear that I now carried, coming at me in a blur, wielded by a pale woman with blood-tipped hair and a shark's smile.

I had nearly died in my first week in Eos.

Twice.

Add in the serpent chasing us, the riverstalker, and maybe even the catosaur, and it seemed ludicrous that I had stayed alive, even *with* a god's direct intervention.

I have *to get stronger.*

Not just for Miko and her people, but for me. I'd told Shan I wanted freedom, but on Eos or Earth, true freedom didn't exist without power. The stronger I grew, the fewer constraints I'd be faced with. I'd be free to act as I wished, both to help the synossians or pursue my own goals.

Until you go symptomatic, at which point all bets are off.

I shoved that voice down; if Dad was any indicator, I had years left to me still. I would use that time to take advantage of the nearly unlimited potential for growth on Eos.

Miko and I hadn't discussed exactly *how* we were going to prepare the Great Wilds for her people's arrival, but if my time as a so-called merchant had taught me anything, it was that any plan we devised would require money to succeed. If this continent was as big as it seemed, the synossian fleets might make landfall at ports that were literal months or even years away from us. Or moons and cycles, as the people on Eos said. Either way, we'd need some sort of messaging network in place to alert us to their arrival, and some means to ferry them to whatever destination we'd helped prepare. And all of that would cost.

Thankfully, my first life on Earth had taught me that wealth, too, was the province of the powerful. So, my personal goal of getting stronger would help there. Levels led to power. Power led to wealth. Wealth would help us secure a safe arrival for Miko's people.

As for minor details like *how?* More problems for future-Brian. We weren't even sure if the settlement we were headed for would be friendly. If the Great Wilds were as bad as Miko's people remembered, our destination could be a coven of devil worshippers just waiting for two new sacrifices. Or even the home of the catosaur's slightly more intelligent cousins. Detailed plans could wait—would *have* to wait— until we had more information.

For now, I kept my goals simple: *Get to where we're going. Help Miko however I can. Grow in power until eyeless monks, necromancers with acid blood, and nightmares about both are yesterday's news.*

Everything else would take care of itself.

○○○

By the time night fell, there had been no sign of a response from the distant town. Either they hadn't seen our campfire smoke, or they had dismissed us as someone else's problem. I didn't know which it was, and I didn't care. Miko and I had gotten a solid afternoon of sleep, and we closing in on our destination.

"Forest or beach?" I asked.

"I would prefer the beach, given the lack of predators so far, but we still need water."

"The stream we were following in the woods hasn't reached the ocean yet. What do you want to bet the place we're heading to sits on some sort of port and the stream feeds into it there?"

"If so, that would mean the stream will continue to curve north," she said, picking up what I was putting down. "We could travel along the beach and only occasionally detour into the forest to look for water."

"Exactly. Anything we can do to reduce the chances of running into more catosaurs, right?"

She gave that some more thought, chewing on a slightly charred strip of meat. "I agree. Let's take the beach route for a few glasses, then look for water. If we find it, we can drink our fill and then come back and make the rest of the journey out here. If we don't find the stream where we expect it to be, we'll need to stay in the forest and keep looking for it, regardless of the danger." She gave my filthy footwraps a look. "The forest floor will also be easier on your feet than this stone, if not by a lot."

"I'm one point in *Pain Tolerance* away from leveling," I told her. "I'm pretty sure I'll earn it whichever route we take."

As usual, Miko's plan made sense, so we walked along the rocky beach, Eos' two moons rising into the sky behind us. Unlike the cliffside we'd originally found ourselves on, the stone here was solid, the colonies of glowworms nowhere to be found. It made for a dark, somewhat treacherous path, but at least we didn't have to worry about things leaping down on us from above. And the huge birds we'd seen before seemed content to stay to the east, where food was both readily available and showed up for dinner each night with its own soft light.

Eventually, we reached the spot we'd seen earlier, where the woods extended out onto the beach's stone. The trees here were sparse and spindly compared to those in the forest's depths, and as we pushed through the narrow strip, we got our first real glimpse of the settlement we were headed for.

As we'd guessed, it had been built beside a river—no doubt fed by smaller tributaries like the stream we'd been following—which then dumped into the ocean. A low wooden wall surrounded an indeterminate number of buildings, and lights along that wall allowed us to spot a handful of small boats that had been pulled up onto the shore. I didn't know anything about boats or sailing, but the lack of masts told me they were probably used for fishing rather than travel.

Although if someone had water-based magic, maybe they wouldn't *need* sails?

If we'd had a boat ourselves—even one that relied on oars—we could have reached the village in a matter of hours by traveling across the water. If we'd had wings or some sort of magic to fly with, the journey would have been made in minutes. As it was, the coastline turned to the south from our small promontory before turning back westward again, and then slowly curving north to meet the village that sat on the ocean's edge.

I didn't need Miko's soft sigh to recognize that we were still over a day away, no matter how close our destination appeared to be. In the light of two moons and at least a thousand stars, I could even see the slump in her scaled shoulders—both bare now that she'd replaced my footwraps with her second sleeve.

"The good news is that they have a wall," I told her, squinting at the distant village. "And people of some kind up on that wall with lights. That sounds like civilization to me, and that means they should have food and supplies." I shook my increasingly worn makeshift pouch, now filled with an equal mix of burned ape meat and half-burned catosaur.

"I have a small quantity of chits," she said, tapping the pouch that also included her fire-striker. "But we don't know if they will honor the currency here. And we have nothing else we can afford to trade."

I just nodded. If we'd been thinking, we could have tried skinning the things we'd killed along the way. Neither of us had the skill, meaning the early results would have been disastrous, but by this point, we might have improved sufficiently that the hides would have had some limited value.

Of course, we'd spent most of that time running for our lives from a serpent that would give Godzilla pause, so I wasn't going to give myself too much shit over it.

"We'll figure something out," I said instead. "For now, should we look for drinking water?"

She spared another glance for the settlement, so near and yet so far, and nodded. "We'll need it. Stay close? Your *Danger Sense* skill may be the only thing that gives us warning."

I hefted Riok's spear and squared my shoulders, no doubt looking ridiculous in the tattered remnants of my borrowed robes and loincloth. "Even with four points in it, the skill seems flaky as hell, but I'll do what I can."

For an hour or two, our journey took us more south than west, as we veered away from the coastline in search of water. By the time we encountered the stream, half again as wide as it had been the last time we saw it, we'd already run afoul of a second catosaur. This one had gone down easier than the first, even if *Danger Sense* hadn't given us any warning.

"Won't carrying that attract more predators?" I asked Miko, as she lowered the catosaur's bloodied corpse to the ground near the stream's shoreline. I'd already verified that the area was safe, the remnants of a dozen apparently normal cattails ample evidence of my caution.

"It might," she admitted. "But these creatures seem to have their own territories, so I'm hoping we can make it back to the coast without attracting more attention. And this," she added, patting the corpse, "could bring us money if we sell its meat and give the hide to a tailor."

I couldn't quite hide my skepticism as Miko stepped up to the stream to drink her fill. I'd stabbed the catosaur a half-dozen times before it finally died, and I was pretty sure all the damage we'd done had left the hide a patchwork of fur and skin that wouldn't make a pouch the size of the one Miko kept under her robes.

Plus, it *stank*.

Miko was facing away, bending down to scoop up more water in her hands, but somehow, she knew what I was thinking.

"Just be grateful that you're not the one carrying it."

"Oh, I am. Believe me." I wrinkled my nose as I stepped past the dead beast to have my first drink. "Which is not to say that I won't help if you need it. It's just that you're a lot stronger than I am—"

"I have a Strength of twelve."

"Which is more than this sad excuse for a soft skin can claim. Frankly, it's amazing I can even hold my spear up as we walk." I grinned at the reluctant sparkle in her orange eyes, then sobered. "But seriously, if you need help carrying it, I'm willing."

Especially if there was a *Carrying* skill that I could gain ranks in. Truly mundane things didn't seem to fall under the Framework's purview, but you never knew.

"That spear remains our best defense," said Miko, "and you are the only one with ranks in the associated skill. Still, if the carcass gets too heavy, I will accept your offer. In the meantime, we should bathe. Who knows if we will get another opportunity before our arrival."

I glanced at the dead catosaur, currently leaking fluids into the dirt, and raised an eyebrow. Whoever was carrying it would find them filthy again in virtually no time at all. "Is there any point in bathing?"

"It will make me feel better, however briefly." She flashed the smile that had terrified me when we'd first met. "And at least *you* will smell better."

I clutched my chest in mock-hurt, mood briefly restored through basic hydration. "Bold words for someone relying on my good will to not push her into the stream as soon as she turns her back."

"With a ten Strength?" She scoffed, but I could hear the laughter in her voice. "An unlikely tale, Brian Fieldings of Earth. A most unlikely tale."

24

I dodged aside as another catosaur tore through the air. It landed on all fours and spun on a dime to menace me, but my spear was already in position, a length of stained metal topped by an unfailingly sharp head that had already left bloody furrows in the creature's hide.

I was *still* level one, but this was our third catosaur of the night—our second since leaving the stream—and our tactics for dealing with the beasts had improved with every fight. Between Miko's senses and my *Danger Sense* skill, we'd gotten better at anticipating and avoiding the initial ambush, and the catosaurs' reliance on stealth and tendency to hunt alone made the resulting fights almost predictable.

I darted in with my spear, not bothering with a *Lunge* that the catosaur would just dodge. As it flowed away, it found Miko waiting on the flank. The Priestess' newest club was substantially larger than the previous one, more oversized baseball bat than anything I'd feel comfortable carrying, let alone wielding. The thud it made when impacting the catosaur's side was accompanied by a yowl and a series of smaller cracks and pops.

Something had just broken.

Probably ribs.

As the catosaur told the world of its pain, I didn't hesitate, finally triggering *Lunge*. My technique did more than just speed up my passage; it added power to my strikes that was far beyond what my thoroughly average attributes alone could account for. Riok's spear blasted into the creature, tore past the mess Miko had made of its ribs, and pierced something vital.

After that, the fight was mostly academic, the creature lacking the strength or leverage to do much more than weakly paw in our directions. I did my best to ignore the swell of pity that rose out of nowhere.

It attacked us. We'd be dead and dinner if it had its way.

That knowledge helped, but somehow not as much as I'd wanted it to. We'd killed enough animals in the past week—sometimes for food, but mostly in self-defense—that I should have been inured to it, but watching the cat-dinosaur hybrid flail about bothered me in a way I struggled to put into words.

I guess I'm not a closet serial killer after all?

I frowned at that thought, withdrew my spear, and struck again, this time ending the catosaur's life for good.

"No point letting it suffer."

"Well said." Miko waited for the creature's last spasms to fade and then eyed the corpse. "This body is in better shape than the last."

"You want to swap carcasses? Again?" Our first catosaur kill of the night, the one she'd carried all the way to the stream and part of the way back, had been discarded for the second kill, which she'd declared to be far more sellable.

"I was thinking we could bring both." She cast *Minor Healing* on me and waited as I rearranged the ribbons that made up my robes. Despite our recent baths, the cloth was once again spattered with blood, some of it mine. "If you were serious about your offer to carry one."

"I was, but—" I waved at the corpse she'd been carrying and that of the cat we'd just killed. "We keep getting ambushed. If I'm carrying one of these, I'm going to be hampered the next time a catosaur comes out of nowhere to attack us."

"This should be the last such attack."

"What? How can you be sure?"

She cocked her head, the scaled features now almost familiar. "I can hear the waves of the ocean. Can't you?"

I couldn't, which was honestly annoying, given that I was the only one of the two of us who even *had* ears.

"I *do* have ears," retorted Miko when I made the mistake of sharing that observation. She tapped a small indentation on the side of her head with one claw and then repeated the gesture on the other side of her head. They were little more than holes in the scaled expanse, but apparently led to whatever the synossian version of an ear was. "And they clearly function better than yours, while also being far less vulnerable."

"Yeah, yeah, whatever. Don't get your tail in a knot."

Miko went still. If she'd had fur like the creature we'd just killed, I was pretty sure every single inch of hers would have been raised. As it was, her eyes practically blazed as she spun on me.

"That…" She took a long breath even as I stepped back, hands tightening on my spear. "That is not the sort of thing you should say to one of my species, Brian Fieldings."

I forced myself to relax the spear I had unconsciously raised to defend myself. Miko was the closest thing to a friend I had. She wasn't going to attack me. "I'm sorry. Sore subject, I take it?"

"Yes. It is said that our ancestors' ancestors, when Synos first raised us to sentience, had tails," she finally said. "It has been many thousands of cycles since that point, and to speak of a synossian's tail is to say they are acting like the primitive species we ascended from."

"I didn't know."

"Nor could you have." Miko blew out a breath and deflated. "And I know that. Just… be aware? If you should say something along those lines to one of my fellows, they will likely challenge you on the spot, Chosen or not."

"We'll have time to review any potential minefields—err, sensitive subjects—while we prepare for their arrival," I told her. "But for now, let's just accept that your hearing is better than mine. And if the ocean is that close, I'm fine with doubling our potential sales."

I stabbed my spear into the dirt and knelt to toss the catosaur's disgusting body across my shoulders. It was heavier than it looked, and I only made it back to my feet with the aid of the spear I'd just planted. Still, once I was upright, the weight was manageable. I tugged the spear out of the dirt and took an experimental step.

It wasn't fun, but I could do it.

"Shall we?"

At least I'd find out if there was a *Carrying* skill.

ᑐᑐᑐ

Even with our burdens, we might have been able to reach the settlement at some point during the following day. However, Miko rightly suggested we'd have an easier time scouting the settlement at night… and that with a near straight shot of coastline between us and our destination, traveling during the day would make our presence obvious.

So instead, we stopped when dawn arrived, finding a spot to rest just inside the tree line. This time, I let the Priestess meditate first. Once she was done, it was my turn. I was less exhausted than I had been the day before, despite our three fights, and managed to meditate the *proper* way for once. I sat with my legs crossed and my palms facing the sky that we could clearly see through the sparse canopy at the forest's edge.

I was getting used to the process of meditating and wasted no time in letting the thoughts and experiences of the night flow through me. The slight twist I'd made with one spear thrust to help spin the sharp head past a catosaur's ribs. The whistle of air from a claw strike that should rightly have taken my head off. The ache in my feet from miles—or *leagues*—of hiking without shoes mixed in with the white-hot bursts of pain when I'd been too slow to dodge or had no choice but to accept a strike to improve my own positioning. Even the warmth of the sun on my skin had its moment in the meditation, a sensation felt by a body I was both part of and yet entirely separate from.

I wasn't sure what, if anything, any of that might do for my soul, once the Framework finished its analysis, but that wasn't up to me. I let the night pass through my mind and my heart, let what I'd done, felt, or experienced be absorbed and then set free. And when I opened my eyes, I saw just what I'd been hoping for.

```
You have increased the following skills:

Major skills:
Tactics [+1]: 5/10

Minor skills:
Avoidance [+1]: 8/10
Pain Tolerance [+1]: 10/10

General skills:
Animal Behaviorism [+2]: 9/10
Meditation [+1]: 3/10
```

Either there was no skill for *Carrying* or there was a trick to gaining it that I hadn't learned yet. I tried not to let that bother me as I reviewed my skill gains. I didn't know why *Danger Sense* hadn't advanced this time, or why Miko didn't even have the skill. Nor did I know why *Animal Behaviorism* had gone up *two* points, where everything else had only managed one. Gains in *Tactics*, *Avoidance*, and *Meditation* were all things I was happy to see, but the real gem was the skill I most hated leveling.

Pain Tolerance had finally reached rank ten.

Energy filled me, similar to when Miko or Berys had cast healings in the past, but somehow richer and more vibrant, full of something that felt wild and free. The shoulder I'd been stabbed in *still* hurt a bit, but the other minor aches and pains were gone. I dismissed my skill-up screen and wasn't at all surprised to see another window replace it.

```
Congratulations, Warrior.

You have reached level 2!

You have one point to allocate to an attribute of
your choosing:

Strength: 10 / Finesse: 10
Vitality: 13 [+1] (+2) / Intellect: 12
Discernment: 10 / Will: 14 (+2)
```

The numbers in parentheses, I reminded myself, were my racial bonuses… but why was there a +1 in brackets next to Vitality? I motioned to Miko, not even bothering to hide my grin. "If you've got a moment or two to spare, I have some questions about leveling."

"You've reached second level already? That was swift for someone who started from nothing." She settled next to me, just barely visible out of the corner of my eyes with the screen obscuring my vision. "What are your questions?"

"I think my Vitality went up a point on its own? It shows a plus-one inside brackets, in addition to the racial bonus." I shaped my hands into their best approximation of brackets.

"And?"

"How did that happen? Is it all the hiking we're doing?"

"It *is* possible to improve attributes through study or exercise, yes, but there are limits and it takes far more than a week in the woods." She shook her head. "Every even level, your Vitality increases on its own."

"Oh. Okay." So, technically, I didn't get one attribute point on the even levels… I got *two*. Except the Framework automatically allocated one of them to Vitality. Given that the stat seemed to have to do with things like stamina, toughness, and even the energy I used for techniques, I wasn't going to complain too much. "So the brackets…?"

"Indicate points to the given attribute that were gained through leveling. While one's attributes can be improved through effort and practice, they can also deteriorate. Only the points added through leveling remain fixed."

"Wait. What do you mean *deteriorate?*"

I could almost hear her frown. "Injuries that are not healed, age that falls more heavily upon some individuals than others, even a lifetime of sloth rather than hard effort… all of these things can impact one's attributes, although in the last case, it is an effect felt over the course of cycles. I know you lacked the Framework on Earth, but surely this much at least was similar?"

I really didn't want to think about age and the effect it would have on my life, so I focused on the rest of what she'd told me. "You mean if I lost an arm, it would be reflected in my attributes?"

"Yes. But attribute increases gained through leveling would remain untouched."

That was perhaps the most game-like thing I'd encountered yet on Eos, but it only amplified my desire to reach higher levels. At tenth level, I'd have a full five points in Vitality and another five spread between attributes of my choosing. Even better, nobody would be able to take those improvements away from me.

My mind flashed on the image of a shell of a man, bedridden for months and unable to even feed himself.

"Brian?"

I shook my head. "Just thinking."

"Did you have any other questions?" I could hear the curiosity in Miko's voice, but she was kind enough not to press.

"Uhm, yeah, actually." I coughed. "What attribute should I increase?"

"That is up to you." She shrugged. "Many Warriors focus on Strength, Finesse, or even Vitality again, depending upon their prescribed advancement path… and assuming they do not have to overcome a crippling deficit in Intellect or Discernment."

Since I didn't *have* an advancement path, that was less helpful than it could have been. And there was one attribute she had left out entirely. "What about Will?"

"Will is important in its own way, but if I recall correctly, it is also already your highest attribute?"

"Yeah."

"Then I would suggest focusing on whatever you think will help you most, both now and in the future."

Again, that didn't clarify things much. Without one of the advancement path recipes that had been kept in Whitehall's archives, I was working blind. From my perspective, I needed to improve *everything.*

"Strength, Finesse, and Vitality are all pretty self-explanatory, but what do the other attributes do again?"

She ticked the remaining stats off on three clawed fingers. "Intellect improves your memory as well as reducing the length of time it takes to reuse a technique. Discernment helps with reuse too, although it's primarily about social skills and allowing you to notice details that others might miss. And Will improves your focus, while both it and Vitality slightly increase your pool of energy for technique usage."

Once again, they *all* sounded good. Even Discernment. Still, if I could only focus on one attribute for now, the one that let me hit harder and carry more stuff seemed like a good option.

I dumped my point into Strength and waited.

Nothing happened. No sudden burst of light or angelic music. No new muscles suddenly bulging. Judging by the comparative length of the scraps of clothes I was still wearing, I hadn't even gotten taller. I opened the attributes portion of my character sheet again, just to make sure I'd done it right:

```
Name: Brian Fieldings
Class: Warrior (Common) - 2
Profession: None
Deity: None
Ideal: Freedom

Attributes:
Strength: 11 [+1] / Finesse: 10
Vitality: 13 [+1] (+2) / Intellect: 12
Discernment: 10 / Will: 14 (+2)
```

"Try lifting something," Miko suggested. With my meditation over, it was time for her nap, but she was watching me instead, invested in my progress. "Something you've carried before."

We didn't have a ton of things *to* lift, so I turned to the disgusting cat carcass and hoisted it onto my shoulders.

It was… easier? Not *easy*, not even close, but the corpse felt lighter than before, and my motion to lift it was more fluid than I recalled it being. And yeah, as I lifted, I *maybe* noticed a little more definition in my bare legs than I remembered seeing before.

I wasn't Superman. Hell, I wasn't even Jimmy Olsen on gym day, but I was stronger than I'd been seconds earlier.

I was *more*.

"Do you want to go hunt something?" I suggested. "Just to see how much this helps my damage?"

She scoffed. "Second level and he considers himself a predator. I am going to *sleep*, Brian Fieldings. I ask that you keep watch instead of testing your newfound might against creatures still quite capable of killing us both."

When put like that, she kind of had a point.

ooo

For the first time since our encounter with the monstrous serpent, I felt rested upon waking. The sun had only just left the sky and Eos' two moons were lost behind a wall of clouds building to the east, making for a night as dark as anything we'd faced our trek through the forest. Even at dusk, the nearby water was more audible than visible, the low murmur of waves ceaselessly lapping against stone.

"We should go," said Miko, waiting for me to lift my designated catosaur. "As long as those clouds outpace the greater moon, we will have all the darkness we need to travel along the shoreline."

"And in doing so, we'll avoid further catosaurs."

"Or whatever creatures' territory comes next, yes."

Assuming nothing new went horribly wrong, she thought we'd reach the village sometime after midnight, which would leave ample hours to observe the place under the cover of darkness. No doubt there was some sort of *Scouting* skill, but even without it, I figured we could just rely on the old-fashioned approach of using our eyes. And if *that* didn't work, Miko would probably have another idea.

But first we had to get there.

As we hiked, I was reminded of what a difference the terrain made. The forest had brought with it the occasional wayward root, trees that made orientation difficult, and the near-constant risk of attacks, but the shoreline had its own issues. Mostly that it was all rock, and uneven rock at that. It would be smoother down by the water, where even stone could be worn down by the water's endless appetite, but we didn't know what, if anything, lived in that ocean. All we needed was some giant shallows squid plucking us both right off the beach.

And yeah, *shallows squid* seemed like an impossibility, but so had catosaurs, glowworms, and riverstalkers.

The added burden of our still-bloody kills only added to the difficulty of navigating the terrain, but I found myself slipping just a little bit less than expected as we walked. That threw me for a loop at first: wouldn't *Finesse* be the attribute that lent itself to things like balance and stability? Or did my higher Strength mean I was more easily able to adjust the weight as needed?

Hell if I knew. I'd talked to Miko at length about the Framework since our arrival in the Great Wilds, but the huge gaps in knowledge continued to frustrate me. The Priestess knew a hodgepodge of information, from things she'd been taught as a hatchling to things she'd read and tales she'd overheard, and while the synossians were certainly greater experts on the subject than me, even Miko admitted that at least some of what she told me was probably hearsay.

The Sages who dedicated their lives to learning about the Framework tended to share that knowledge only with a select few, and none of it was accessible to us now, given both the ongoing invasion and our location thousands of *leagues* away.

Once we have money, I need to see if I can find a Sage here on this continent. An advancement path formula, detailing the skills and actions needed to unlock a specific advanced class, would be fabulous, but more information regarding the Framework's underlying mechanics would be even more helpful.

After all, knowledge was just another form of power, right?

It was a shame I hadn't subscribed to that philosophy during my life on Earth. College had never really been an option, of course, but I'd spent countless hours—endless afternoons and evenings—sitting next to Dad's bed, where I could have been doing *something* other than watching television. Maybe I would have arrived in Eos as a fledgling engineer and not just a failed *merchant?*

I shook my head, almost violently. That was in the past. *Earth* was in the past, and I was more than happy to let it stay there. I needed to focus on the future, on what came next, and on how we'd stay alive in the interim.

The discordant yowl of a catosaur brought that point home. Miko and I both froze, and while it was too dark to see much more than her general shape, I was pretty sure she was looking toward the woods, just like I was.

"That was a good distance away," she said quietly.

"And it sounded pained rather than angry."

I still couldn't see Miko, but her robes rustled softly, and I could *feel* the weight of her gaze.

"What?"

"You can tell what it's feeling based on one roar?"

"I think it was more of a yowl, really."

That unseen gaze intensified.

"Right. Not important." I shrugged. "*Animal Behaviorism* is my highest ranked General skill. I guess it's good for something."

"Whereas I still don't even have a rank in it. *Danger Sense* is one thing, being a Rare skill, but *Animal Behaviorism?*"

"The Framework works in mysterious ways, young Miko. Mysterious ways indeed."

"Now, *that*," she eventually admitted, "was *very* well said."

It seemed *some* idioms translated.

25

It was still dark when we approached the village. Time was a nebulous thing without a watch or phone, especially with the clouds in the sky hiding both the stars and moons, but Miko thought it was around midnight, and that was good enough for me. We had a few hours to observe the place and to determine our next steps.

We'd headed south into the forest upon our arrival, knowing that any break in the cloud cover would otherwise expose us on the rocky shoreline. Unfortunately, the woods ended a good three to four hundred yards from the village, the shift from forest to meadow far too abrupt to be natural. That left multiple football fields of open space between us and our destination, and I didn't need Miko to tell me that the space could easily transform into a killing ground if the villagers were hostile.

Equally problematic, the darkness that made us essentially invisible to the residents made scouting their home equally difficult. There were torches set atop the wooden palisade, but that light didn't carry far. We could hear rushing water, so different from the metronomic repetition of the ocean's waves that it almost had to be the river, but without stars to reflect off its surface, not even Miko could see well enough to spot it.

"We have to get closer," said Miko. "I'm not sure what we can learn from all the way out here."

"But if the moons shine through while we're sneaking, the people on the wall will spot us. Maybe we should wait until dawn instead? Even given the distance, we'll be able to see more in daylight."

"Very well." It was the opposite of what Miko had originally suggested, but I didn't think she'd anticipated the difficulty of scoping out an unknown location at night. If either of us had been Scouts, we might have had a technique, like Slanit's *Farseeing*, or some sort of active stealth that would make the whole thing moot… but we weren't and we didn't. As usual, we'd have to muddle through on our own.

Another yowl sounded, somewhere behind us, and Miko shifted closer to me. "Pain again?"

"And fear, I think?" It was the fifth or sixth such noise we'd heard during our night-time trek, and while *Animal Behaviorism* didn't help me track things, it *did* tell me that each yowl had likely been made by a different catosaur.

"That one was closer," Miko said, her words almost mild enough to mask the tension that had leaked into her voice. "What do you think is going on?"

"I don't know. Territorial disputes, maybe?" A second yowl followed, right on the heels of the first. "Whatever it is, as long as it doesn't spill over to us, we should be fine. I hope."

"Even the watchmen appear to have taken notice," said Miko, eyes on the distant, poorly illuminated village.

"I didn't realize you could see anyone on the wall."

"Just shapes," she admitted, proving once again that her eyesight trumped mine, "but they are clustering together near one of the torches. Whatever is going on is unusual enough to have them spooked."

"Or excited." We knew nothing about them, and that made judging their reactions and motivations almost impossible.

"Even so, maybe we should—"

Something burst out of the woods behind us, moving at reckless speed. Before I could even try to bring my spear to bear, it was past us, a darker shadow moving on silent paws even as it abandoned all other attempts at stealth.

"Was that a catosaur?"

"Look," said Miko, pointing back toward the village. Someone on the wall had summoned a glowing orb that put the torches' illumination to shame. As we watched, that orb floated over to hover above the empty fields.

Someone gasped, and I'm pretty sure it was me.

There were *dozens* of catosaurs in the field, all of them running flat-out. We watched two smack right into each other, becoming a ball of flesh and claws like you'd see in a cartoon. Just as quickly, it resolved back into two catosaurs, fleeing in opposite directions.

"Something is very, very wrong," I said, stating the obvious.

On the wall, the guards, now recognizably humanoid according to Miko, were reacting, shouts of alarm rising even as a handful of bows were lifted. A bell began to ring from somewhere inside the wooden palisade.

"What could they have done to incite solitary hunters to come at them in a pack?" mused Miko.

I frowned. Everything we knew about the catosaurs said that they were careful killers who relied on stealth and ambush tactics. Nothing about what we were seeing fit their usual behavior. Granted, my *Animal Behaviorism* skill was barely nine, and we'd only encountered our first catosaur a few days ago, but even so...

The catosaurs were a dozen yards from the fort when it clicked.

"They're not attacking." I pointed out a few cats who had veered off course, headed north along the river we could only now see. "They're running away. Fleeing something in the forest."

Which… left an obvious question.

Unfortunately, it was all too soon answered.

The next yowl came from maybe a quarter mile behind us, and this time, it was accompanied by the unmistakable sound of trees falling. This far west, those trees weren't the giants that grew in the heart of the woods, but they were still decades old and sturdy enough to hold a catosaur with ease. For something to be knocking them over like bowling pins…

Miko turned to me, and the distant glowing sphere was just bright enough for me to make out her widening eyes. "Is that—?"

I nodded, the words stuck in my throat.

Apparently, the great serpent hadn't given up its chase.

ooo

The village's defenders were attacking catosaurs as they neared the walls. Here and there, the occasional light show signified a technique being unleashed, but for the most part, the growing number of people atop the palisade were using ranged weaponry—bows, crossbows, and slings.

In the darkness, there was a chance the townsfolk might mistake us for cats, but we'd have to risk it. The wooden palisade and its cluster of hopefully high-level defenders were our only hope of survival.

"Run for the wall," I said. "Yell once you're in range and maybe they won't shoot us!"

"What about our kills?"

I pointed at the battle happening next to the village. More and more of the beasts had been pulled into combat by the defenders, now striking back at the people who, in their ignorance, hadn't thought to just let them pass. Already, a half-dozen catlike bodies lay still outside the wall.

"I think the market for catosaur is about to be flooded!"

I wasn't sure if that was yet another idiom that didn't translate, but Miko saw the bodies and put two and two together all on her own. She nodded and kicked into a run, club in hand and catosaur carcass left behind.

I was right on her heels, fear giving me speed that my Finesse attribute might have not otherwise warranted. Additional creatures were pouring into the open fields, not just catosaurs but smaller horrors with spikes instead of fur, too many limbs, and even more eyes. None paid us any mind as they tore past, and more than a few were sporting injuries of their own.

If the serpent laired at the heart of the woods, the creatures here on the outskirts might have never even encountered it before, never realized that their forest was home to a true apex predator.

But they were sure as hell learning now.

In some ways, our sprint across that open meadow was even more harrowing than the ride downhill towards Whitehall. On the one hand, I wasn't on the back of a dalys, struggling to even stay on, but on the other, we were not just running *into* danger but *away* from it at the same time. If one of us fell... well, the serpent was still behind us somewhere, but the animals fleeing alongside us might very well run right over our flailing bodies, and the damage from their claws and spikes would be just as deadly for all that it was inadvertent.

My *Athleticism* skill was no doubt helping me in unknown ways, but I was deeply regretting not having raised Finesse instead of Strength.

Two-thirds of the way across, we reached the river, and there, I stumbled to a stop. Flowing to the ocean, its waters created a natural barrier between the forest and village. The river was also easily fifty times the width of the stream that had been our water source for the past week, and while it proved little obstacle to the wildlife surging through, it was big enough to give me pause.

Miko dropped her club, shucked her robes, and then scooped up both weapon and clothing and dove into the river's night-black depths, cutting through the water as easily as if she'd been born in it. Given her talk of hatching, I didn't *think* she had been, but she had never said for sure.

I swallowed and followed her example, stripping down to my soiled pants-turned-loincloth and wrapping my tattered robes around Riok's spear. I didn't know if undressing was necessary—with the robes now mostly ribbons, it seemed unlikely that they would create too much drag—but it had been literal *years* since I last swam, and I'd never been particularly great at it.

I waded in instead of diving, feeling the muddy shoreline clutch at my bare feet, and set off after the synossian once the water reached my shoulders. One hand paddled while the other pushed the spear and my robes in front of it. It went about as well as I should have expected; even the slow current carried me downstream several feet for every foot of forward progress I made.

Twenty seconds into my swim, I started to panic, which further slowed my progress. With the ocean so close, there was every chance I would be swept out to sea before I could reach the other shoreline.

Should I dump the spear? It wasn't all that heavy, but it was almost as big a reason for my plight as my own limited swimming abilities. If I dropped it, I would make the shore. Maybe after all of this was settled, I could come back and recover it. Assuming it hadn't been swept out to sea.

No, said a voice inside of me, stubborn and resolute. That spear was my only weapon. More importantly, it was the only evidence that

Riok Diocil, known to his people as the Wind Walker, had existed. Hell if I was just going to toss it aside.

I kicked and paddled even harder, sputtering as water forced its way into my nose. The waves I was creating made it that much harder to see where I was going, let alone judge distance or direction, but I was pretty sure I'd passed the halfway point.

That was when something large brushed past me under the waters, spinning me to one side. For all my noble sentiments, I almost dropped Riok's spear then and there. Whatever it was that had hit me never surfaced, but by the time I recovered, I'd been swept even further downstream, my forward momentum blunted by that moment of shock and surprise.

I was at least thirty or forty feet from the shoreline, and despite the summer warmth, my arms and legs felt like icicles, heavy weights that only sluggishly responded to my brain's commands.

I'm not going to make it.

I swallowed a mouthful of river water and coughed it right back up. It was all I could do to stay afloat as I spun in the river's eddies. Still coughing, I spread my limbs wide to counter that spin and focused on the distant shoreline.

The second lesson, Riok had told me, *is a simple one. The spear points at your enemy.*

I pointed my weapon toward the far side of the river and triggered *Lunge.*

If anyone on the wall was looking downstream, I bet I made for quite the sight, a mostly naked man soaring forward, the force and power of my passage carving a path through the river's murky waters. It worked better than it should have, better than I could have hoped for, and if I'd just been able to chain-cast the technique, I would have reached the shore without issue.

Instead, *Lunge* gave out almost fifteen feet from my destination. The water I'd been cutting my way through flooded in on top of me and drove me down into the darkness.

There was a time for nostalgia and a time for survival, and in my inexpert opinion, the latter *always* trumped the former. I tried to cast aside Riok's spear, but my ice-cold fingers refused to respond. I tucked the spear close to my body instead and kicked up toward what I thought might be the surface, pulling at the water with my one free hand as if I was digging through wet sand.

It felt like I'd only been underwater for a matter of seconds, but my lungs were burning. My mind screamed at my body to open its mouth and suck in oxygen, ignoring that there was only water around me.

This was a really stupid way to die.

I was still crawling through the water, going nowhere fast, when a light burst into being, white and diffused, a few feet to my right and slightly below me. Even in my panic, even through the water's distortion, I recognized a spell I'd gotten very familiar with over the past week.

Flare.

But why is it all the way down there?

I was puzzling through that, my limbs doing little more than going through the motions as my brain began to close up shop for the day—to hurry home from Pritchard's before Mrs. Cho's shift with my father was over—when the light reflected off of white scales and orange eyes. A clawed hand reached up and grabbed my ankle, pulling me deeper into the river's depths.

I struggled, the last bubbles of air escaping my mouth, but after however long I'd been underwater, even a Strength of eleven barely ranked. Inexorably, Miko tugged at my form, avoiding the spear still caught in my hand, and dragging me down.

It wasn't until we broke the surface and I breathed in the sweetest air I'd ever tasted that I realized I had gotten turned around in my panic, that I'd been swimming toward the riverbed and not up to the surface.

The warmth of *Minor Healing* washed through my body as Miko pulled me to my feet. "We have to go!"

"What?"

"Brian!" She turned me toward the village and gave me a shove that almost sent me sprawling. "Run!"

During my time in the river, what had been a mostly one-sided battle between villagers and monstrous wildlife had taken a turn. Several catosaurs were up *on* the palisade and at least a few of the motionless bodies outside the wall now were wearing clothing. More people had come to the defense, and while some of them were dealing with the catosaurs in their midst, techniques now as prevalent as weapons, the others were pointing toward the forest.

I didn't need to look to know what they were pointing at, but I did it anyway.

A vast swath of destruction had been torn through the woods' edge, saplings and even old-growth trees splintered and shattered, and the monster we'd already fled once was making its way into the open fields. At least half of the serpent's great body remained in the forest proper, but that left almost thirty feet of serpent exposed, wide as a barn and as tall as a monster truck. Without trees to slow it down, its speed was horrifying; every undulation sent that great scaled head forward a dozen paces or more.

The creature swung in our direction, and even with a river and another hundred yards separating us, I could swear the thing focused in on me.

I turned back to the village, tucked my head, and ran like my life depended on it.

Because it did.

We were twenty feet from the wall, yelling like madmen to let the defenders know we weren't on Team Snake, when the last of the catosaurs went down. Seconds later, we reached our destination, hurtling twitching and still corpses alike along the way. The gate was half again Miko's height, wide enough to admit a wagon, and so solid that I bounced right off it.

I hadn't *expected* it to be unlatched, not with an entire forest on the warpath, but I'd kind of been *hoping*. Miko and I banged on the gate, screaming for the inhabitants to let us in, but nothing happened. Either we were impossible to hear over the sound of everything else, or the villagers had decided they had bigger things to worry about.

Literally bigger things.

My fingers finally decided to start working again, and I almost dropped my spear as the monstrous serpent left the forest entirely and we got our first look at its true size.

It was the length of four school buses, bumper to bumper, with eyes like bonfires, teeth as large as I was tall, and midnight black scales that seemed to absorb the light of the glowing sphere that hovered on our side of the river.

Whatever we'd done to piss off this thing—this king of the forest that had hunted us for literal days—I really wished we could rewind time and take it back.

"Maybe… we can dodge aside when it strikes," I suggested. "So, it will hit the gate, or the wall, or both?"

"And then?"

"We escape while it's stunned?"

Miko looked from the giant serpent, already nearing the river that we'd lost so much time crossing, and back to me, her expression saying everything.

"Right. Plan B then. You cast *Flare* to blind at least one of its eyes, and I'll see if I can make it to the other one with *Lunge*." I was pretty sure it had been long enough since I'd used the technique in the river.

"I have a better idea." She swallowed and pointed up at the wall above us. "I saw how you used *Lunge* in the river. Can you use it to get up onto the wall?"

I hadn't thought of that, no doubt because of the water still sloshing around in my brain, but saw one immediate downside.

"I can't take you with me."

"I know." She took a step away from me and bowed low. "Bright Lady watch over you, Brian Fieldings."

Yeah, the hell with that. Miko and her people were too damn honorable for their own good. And I hadn't saved her from the Buried just to lose her to an oversized garter snake.

That said, me getting up onto the wall *did* make sense.

"I'll come around and open the gate from the other side," I told Miko. "Shouldn't be more than a minute."

I didn't wait for her nod but stepped away from the gate to look up at the wall. It was at least fifteen feet high and, like the gate itself, made out of wood likely harvested from the land they'd cleared. I didn't think I'd have been able to climb it even *with* a rope, but if I targeted the space just above the palisade with *Lunge*, maybe…

I'd never tried going *up* before, but there wasn't time to second-guess the idea. I picked a destination, triggered *Lunge,* and was in motion, still mostly naked, my filthy rags wrapped around the extended spear.

When the technique gave out, I was still in mid-air, my momentum swiftly reversing as gravity regained its hold on me. Much like in the river, I hadn't traveled as far as intended, but the top of the palisade *was* in reach, if only barely. I tossed Riok's spear onto the ledge behind that palisade and stretched my arms out as I started to fall. My left hand found no purchase on wood worn smooth by the elements, but my right grabbed hold. A scream I barely recognized as my own erupted as my entire body came to a precipitous halt and my shoulder promptly dislocated.

Whatever strength was in my grip deserted me in an instant. I had just started to fall again when someone reached over the wall to catch me. My second scream was more of a whimper as they pulled me onto the narrow ledge on the palisade's interior side, but Miko stayed fresh in my mind. I called on *Pain Tolerance* to keep me conscious and rolled to one side to make my way down to the gate.

Only to find the point of a long blade at my neck, wielded by the man who'd just saved me.

"I don't know who you are, stranger," he said, "but you're not going anywhere until this is over."

"Snake!" I gasped up at him. Like me, he was human, if older, at least a foot taller, and significantly cleaner. A thick black beard hid his frown and dark eyes glittered in the torchlight, giving away nothing.

"Yes, Nikkaali is difficult to miss, even in darkness." He bared teeth in what could only charitably be called a smile. "If Valestia can drive him off, she'll want to speak with you about why exactly the titan of the woods is so far from home. If she cannot, you will die along with the rest of us."

He withdrew the sword from my throat, stepping away and giving me space to rise. At the same time, his position put him between me and Riok's spear. As casual as the man's motions seemed, something told me he'd cut me down before I could even *think* the word trouble, let alone cause it.

Was it *Animal Behaviorism* or half a decade working the counter at a coffee shop? I didn't know, but I wasn't going to second-guess that knowledge; I left Riok's spear where it had fallen.

"I have a friend," I said instead. "She's still below. If you can open the gates—"

"It is far too late for that." He waved to the field I'd just left.

The serpent—Nikkaali?—was longer than the river was wide, its great head emerging from the water even before its tail had entered.

"It took six moons to clear the land here and build Harborton's first walls," said the man, voice almost conversational as he watched our doom slither closer. "But we did it anyway, because the soil was fertile, the ocean was close, and the Snake River flowed to our east as a shield against external threats."

"With respect, it doesn't seem to be working."

"It was meant to slow down raiders or beasts, boy, not stop ancients like yon serpent," he snarled. "And even so, it serves as a defense in more ways than just one."

A dozen feet from us, a steel-haired woman rose to look out over the parapet. I could feel her presence manifest out of nothingness, like a flag unfurling. That weight was as strong as anything I'd felt from Riok, if still feather-light compared to the Buried necromancer. Flanked by two burly villagers, the old woman waved her hand, thin and fine-boned, and mouthed a word I couldn't hear.

Just that quickly, the serpent lost its sinuous grace, thrashing about in the river so wildly that a full thirty feet of neck and head rose into the air. The glowing sphere, summoned long minutes earlier, floated above, its light catching on the thick black blood that now trickled down the monster's glistening scales.

The woman—Valestia?—waved her other hand and the serpent thrashed again, but whatever wounds she was inflicting seemed comparatively tiny to the creature's greater bulk. Sweat beaded on her brow like tiny jewels in the torchlight, and this time, she raised both hands to the night sky. Water surged about the serpent, rising from the river's basin to craft a tower two dozen stories high.

"The Tower of Hybellus," murmured the man at my side. "Jewel of our homeland before it was razed to its foundations. Lost but never forgotten."

For a moment, that strange watery building held its shape, all gleaming columns, arching balustrades, and a dozen other fancy architectural terms I couldn't remember. Then, the woman swung her hands downwards, and the building went with them, crashing into the serpent in a hammer blow whose impact was so strong that we could feel it on the wall.

26

I could hear a handful of prayers from others on the wall, and even the start of what sounded like a cheer, but as the fog of spray cleared, something immeasurably large stirred where the tower had fallen.

"Erlund!" Valestia turned and locked eyes with the man looming next to me. Her grey hair was plastered to her scalp with sweat, and she looked like she had aged twenty years in a single minute. "We have no choice!"

The other man met her eyes and nodded. Turning to the serpent that was already starting to uncoil, its great bulk battered but whole, he unlatched the pouch at his waist and pulled free what looked like a Faberge egg, sapphire blue with gold filigree.

"May the nine demon gods consume you and your *friend* if you were the ones who brought Nikkaali to our doorstep." He turned to two of the nearby villagers. "Watch the stranger until I return. If he moves, kill him."

Erlund stepped up onto the parapet and off into open air, plummeting to the earth. Moments later, he was back in view, racing toward the monstrous serpent and showing no ill effects from what had been a twelve-foot drop.

On the wall, Valestia cast a fourth spell, but this time, Nikkaali barely flinched, its head weaving back and forth as it focused on the two-legged meal foolish enough to come its way.

Two-thirds of the way to the serpent, Erlund stopped. He took a slow breath I could see even from the wall, and then hurled the egg towards the serpent like it was some sort of grenade. As soon as it left his hand, he was sprinting back toward the wall at a pace that would make your average Olympian jealous.

The serpent, cautious after Valestia's earlier attacks, swayed backward, as if to dodge the incoming projectile, but the egg fell far short, landing in the open field a dozen feet from the river's edge. It didn't explode, and it didn't erupt in a storm of fury and light.

It simply... broke.

I spared a glance at my would-be captors, but they remained transfixed by what was happening out on the fields. I heard it then, a humming, emanating from where the egg had fallen, low-pitched but so resonant I could feel it in my bones.

Nikkaali reeled backward, its station-wagon-sized tongue flicking into the air. It didn't seem injured by the noise, but more... *troubled*, assuming *Animal Behaviorism* was worth the time I'd accidentally invested in it. As the noise swelled, the prey it had hunted for multiple days was forgotten. To my shock, the great serpent and so-called king of the forest turned tail and fled, heading for the forest at a pace that made clear its earlier advance had been a mere shadow of its true speed in open land.

Even after the snake had disappeared into the forest, the humming from Erlund's egg continued to increase, growing not so much louder as more *present*, rhythmic music that existed on wavelengths other than mere sound. The world shuddered, twisting to reach an equilibrium with that vibration, and I stumbled, falling to one knee. Others collapsed entirely, hands clutching at something they could not see.

Even so, we were the lucky ones, a hundred paces or more from that sound's point of origin. Erlund, for all his jaw-dropping speed, was far closer. He managed a dozen steps, his body rippling like a reflection in the water, then five more, each slower than the last. Finally, he collapsed in the empty field, a marionette whose strings had been savagely cut.

Atop the wall, Valestia's anguished cry was lost beneath the cacophonous noise. She took a step toward the wall, only to be wrestled down to the platform by the villagers at her side.

Below us, a figure in dirty orange and crimson robes darted from the questionable safety of the walls. Miko crossed the space to the fallen man, grabbed hold of his outstretched hands and pulled, her slim form wavering in the face of the noise Erlund had summoned.

I forced myself back to my feet. *Lunge* was available, my spear was nearby, and even with a dislocated shoulder, I was off the wall again before my captors knew I was gone. I ran to help Miko, only to realize that the sound was already fading, the reality warping howl now a chorus, now a hum, now a whisper.

As fast as I was, the old woman known as Valestia was somehow even faster, appearing next to Miko like she'd been wished into existence. She brushed the synossian aside with casual strength and fell to her knees, taking Erlund's head in her delicate hands. "I'm sorry," she murmured, voice thin and empty. "It should have been me."

Erlund's skin had gone grey, his eyes had rolled up in his head, and the breath rattled in his chest like a baby's toy, but he *was* breathing. I gave Miko a look.

With a nod, the Priestess approached the grieving woman. "I can only cast *Minor Healing*, but with your permission, I would—"

The look that the old woman turned on Miko had the synossian taking a step back, the sheer weight of a ranked Mage's presence doing its level best to crush us both into the ground. "If you must speak, beast," she said, her worn voice tight with grief and rage, "do so in a civilized tongue that we understand."

Which was when I finally realized that the two of them were speaking entirely different languages.

And I could understand them both.

○○○

I stepped between Miko and Valestia, drawing the latter woman's attention and ire. At some point, I needed to figure out just how many languages *Speaker of Tongues* gave me access to. But first, I needed to defuse the current situation.

I focused on the way first Erlund and now Valestia had spoken, letting their words, tones, and mannerisms roll around in my head. So far, I'd only ever unconsciously replied to someone in the tongue they had addressed me in. This time, I needed to be purposeful. The old woman looked to be a handful of seconds away from killing us both, and even with the river a good distance away, I was painfully aware she could do so with ease.

"This is Miko Naseri," I told her. "She is a Priestess and was offering her assistance with your… husband?"

"Brother," murmured Valestia, one hand unconsciously stroking the sweat-drenched hair out of Erlund's face. "The youngest of eight and the last who remains. As for healing—" She broke off and turned a jaded eye on Miko, eyeing the synossian up and down.

"What is happening, Brian Fieldings?" asked Miko.

"I'm translating your offer." This time, I just replied, letting my trait handle the choice of language for me.

"What level is the beast?" Valestia shook her head. "No, I withdraw that question, too rude even for such a creature. Besides, if you or it were Tin, I would feel it. And if either of you were higher, you would not have chosen to huddle outside *our* gate for safety."

Tin? Beast? I buried my confusion under the pleasant mask I had worn as a barista. There was no way I would give a potential enemy Miko's level—let alone mine—but the Priestess *had* offered healing.

"Her talents lie in other areas," I prevaricated, "but she has access to *Minor Healing*, and offers it freely to aid in your brother's recovery."

Valestia barked a laugh, sharp and without humor. "You think *Minor Healing* can counteract even the merely conceptual echoes of the Swarm?" She waved a hand at the surrounding field. "Every blade of grass in this field will remember that presence and fade into obscurity. Nothing will grow here for a dozen years or more. With water a purifying agent, the river, at least, will recover quickly, but dead fish are even now being swept out to sea. Though we have escaped the doom you brought upon us, Harborton will now pay the price for its survival. And my brother—"

Miko looked back and forth between us, and only two weeks of knowing her allowed me to read the confusion in her reptilian features. Not being able to understand any of this must be maddening.

"I'm sorry," I told Valestia. "We're just travelers, seeking safety and shelter. We fled from Nikkaali, like everything else in the forest. I promise that none of this was—"

"A debt is owed." She stood, lifting her heavily muscled brother in her arms as easily as I had a catosaur.

"What is she saying?" hissed Miko.

"That we owe her a debt."

"Meaning?"

"I'm still waiting on that part." I turned to Valestia. "A debt?"

"There are dark places beneath the southern woods where a plant called the nilwort grows, its roots nourished by the fires of Eos' burning heart. Three sprigs of nilwort, ground into powder with a finger of shademoss and diluted by ocean water within a seven-day of its harvesting will create an elixir of purification. The elixir, much like the harvested nilwort, loses its potency all too swiftly, but if fed to Erlund in time…"

"It will cure him?"

Another harsh laugh. "There is no *cure*, boy. What is lost to the Swarm stays forever lost; a dozen years or more gone and never to return. But it will ameliorate the residual effects. Erlund will wake, and though my youngest brother is now my elder, he might at least speak again."

"I understand." I swallowed. There would be other times to ask what the hell the Swarm was, and how the *conceptual echo* of something could be stored at all, let alone in an *egg*. Other times and better times. "Miko and I will go fetch this nilwort and… shademoss?"

"No, you will not." She started toward Harborton, an imperious look over one shoulder the only indication that we should follow. "If the two of you are as weak as it appears, you would never survive the journey, even *if* you made the attempt in good faith instead of fleeing the moment our village was out of sight. No, I will put out a call for *true* adventurers. You and your beast will repay your debt in other ways."

"Other ways?"

"Erlund was not the only one wounded in the attack that you either directly provoked or had some hand in, and we have dead to bury, besides. While we wait for the adventurers to arrive, your beast can see to Harborton's injured and give funeral rites for those whose families permit it."

I didn't think Miko would complain about helping. Healing was her vocation, after all, and given her class, she'd probably even earn experience from it. As for funerals… well, again, she *was* a Priestess.

The whole *calling her a beast* thing was a little bit weird, but the Great Wilds hadn't seen synossians in a thousand cycles; I was guessing they had other animalistic humanoids on this continent and they weren't well regarded.

And at least *the old woman* hadn't screamed.

"What about me?"

Valestia paused outside the slowly opening gates to look at the man in her arms. "You will be tasked with my brother's wellbeing. He will not wake unless—until—he is fed the elixir, but in the interim, he must be fed, cleaned, and cared for."

I stumbled, catching myself at the last minute and hissing at the pain that radiated out from my dislocated shoulder.

"What?"

"You and your beast are responsible for his condition. You will be his caretaker until that condition is resolved." The gates opened before us with a torturous creaking, and Valestia stepped forward, missing the complex mix of emotions that had just run across my face. "You will be fed, housed, and—" She spared a glance for the rags that were all that remained of my borrowed robes. "—clothed while you are working off your debt. Harborton operates under the duke's charter, and that means you will be treated fairly, if not warmly. Nevertheless, what is owed *will* be repaid."

"What is happening, Brian?" asked Miko, perhaps the only person in the village even more miserable than me.

"This place is called Harborton," I told her. "We're going to be stuck here for a while."

○○○

The village wasn't much to look at. It had maybe twenty-five buildings in total, all but one of them single story. The main road led down to the shoreline, where several small fishing boats had been pulled onto the beach. As we walked, I filled Miko in on the conversation with Val. The young Priestess was predictably happy to heal, but less than thrilled by our new status as indentured servants. Still, we didn't have much choice, being both outnumbered and outpowered, and we *had* been at least partly responsible for the attack on the village.

What passed for a main square was just the intersection of the village's primary two pathways, but the village's lone two-story building flanked that intersection, the sign hanging above its open door depicting a crudely carved mug. "The inn," explained Valestia, her words clipped. "You'll meet Lomas at some point, but unless you have coin, and a lot of it, I wouldn't recommend frequenting his place of business."

She handed Erlund off to a pair of individuals still returning from the wall and then took us across the street and into a neighboring building. A handful of people in bloody bandages had already been laid on the dirt floor, and a man, as tall as Miko and skinny as a rail, was walking from patient to patient.

"Tantalas!" She called him over and motioned to Miko. "Found a beast who can *heal*. It will be your assistant for the time being."

Tantalas was the first person I'd seen in Harborton who wasn't human, but I wasn't entirely sure what he was. Pointed ears and a too-angular face said *elf*, but the shaved head and scalp tattoos said *biker gang member*, while spindly fingers with an extra joint just said *freak-show alien*. Still, the smile he flashed at Miko was one-part welcome and nine-parts relief.

"Praise the Twelve," he said, in a voice both more and less high pitched than I'd expected. "My supplies were already low after the recent accident, and there are limits to what a well-crafted poultice can do. A true healer could make all the difference, regardless of their origin and nature."

"You're an Herbalist?" I asked him.

"That is my profession, yes."

"And your class?"

"Is none of your business," interjected Valestia. "Folks come to Harborton to get a fresh start. Most focus on their professions instead of classes, while the rest of us see to the village's defense. The luxury of a choice like that is one of the benefits of living in civilization."

If this was what passed for civilization, I was starting to think Miko's description of the Great Wilds had been *too* complimentary. Still, it was a positive sign that even a place like Harborton could support and be supported by noncombatants.

"This is Miko," I told Tantalas, translating my words back and forth so they both could understand. "She—*not it*—doesn't speak your language but is eager to help."

Miko nodded, and offered the other man a short bow, which he returned. The herbalist either didn't share the older woman's hostility towards the synossian or was too grateful for her unexpected assistance to care.

"Meanwhile, this boy has a hurt shoulder," Valestia told the herbalist, her tone brusque. "If you can reset it, we'll be out of your way."

Pain Tolerance must have been working its magic because I'd almost forgotten my dislocated shoulder on the walk from the gate. In fact, it barely hurt at all, except when I walked, breathed, or tried to move it.

"This will be uncomfortable," Tantalas warned me. "I would ask your… companion… to heal it, were *her* energy not needed to help save lives."

It was all I could do to grunt instead of moan when the herbalist set my shoulder, the strength in his too-long hands far beyond what I'd expected. Lights swam beneath eyelids I didn't remember closing, and the world went sideways for a second, but I kept my feet.

"Ouch," I finally said, opening my eyes again.

Something in Valestia's severe expression shifted but whatever it was disappeared a moment later. "And now on to our assignment, boy."

"Brian. Brian Fieldings."

"I will remember your name," she told me, ice in her words, "when my brother is awake, and not a Waste-cursed moment before then. Now, come."

I took a step outside and came to a halt, momentarily resisting the old woman's efforts to pull me along. A screen had appeared in front of me without any intent on my part. More importantly, it reminded me of something I'd somehow forgotten in the past week of desperate survival.

QUEST COMPLETED: Escort Priestess Miko Naseri to safety.

Just that. No fanfare or flash of light, let alone mention of a reward. Still, any remaining doubts I'd had about leaving Miko with Tantalas disappeared. If even the Framework decided she was safe, who was I to argue?

"Are you still damaged, boy?" Much like the herbalist, Valestia had more power in her wrinkled, wiry limbs than I expected. She spun me around and peered down into my face.

Yes, *down*. Even in a village mostly populated by humans, I was still the shortest person in view.

"I'm fine. I just—" I shook my head. "Never mind. I'm fine."

From what I'd seen in Harborton so far, one's interactions with the Framework were considered private. I didn't need to know Tantalas' class or level, and Valestia didn't need to know I'd just finished the quest I'd received on an entirely separate continent.

Nor did she need to know that the very instant the dialogue window had closed I'd felt full again.

No, not just full… *satiated.*

Miko had said the amount of experience to reach level three was significant—far greater than that for level two—but it had only been a day since my last level, and here I was, a whole bunch of skill gains away from doing it all over again.

I didn't know what that meant, but it didn't suck.

The old woman gave me the eye for a long while, waiting for me to volunteer more information, but I'd never had a mother and was immune to their brand of witchy magic. Finally, she nodded.

"Erlund has been taken to our home. I will escort you there and explain your duties. At night, I will return to watch over him, and you and your beast—"

"She's a person."

"*You and your beast* will bunk in one of our empty storage buildings. I will expect you back on duty by first light. And should you try to run…" Her smile was as cold as the river I'd almost drowned in, far more dangerous than the spear I still held in one hand. "I promise you will live to regret it."

27

I spooned the last bit of fish soup into Erlund's open mouth, holding his head steady as I waited for him to swallow. When he had done so, I set the bowl aside and took up the pitcher of water instead. I would return both dishes to the service door of Lomas' inn on my way back to the warehouse where Miko and I slept.

But with dinner served, it was first time to prepare the comatose man for the night. I dipped a soft rag into the pitcher, soaking the cloth in what was left of the water, and wiped away the day's accumulated dust from Erlund's face and body. A second rag towel followed, drying any remaining beads of moisture. Even indoors the wind off the sea was a persistent presence, and the last thing any of us needed was Valestia's brother catching pneumonia.

I set both towels aside and carefully covered the man in two blankets, one a length of what looked like patterned wool, the other a quilt in colors so bright I could practically see them with my eyes shut. With Erlund once again tucked in for the night, I breathed out a long sigh.

With every day that passed, it felt more and more like I hadn't left Earth at all. Like I was back in our double-wide, taking care of my dad all over again. Erlund looked nothing like Dad—tall and strong and healthy-seeming beyond his white shock of hair and the coma from which he hadn't stirred even once—but my duties were almost identical. Clean. Feed. Clean some more. I'd traveled to an entirely different reality, only to find myself back in the role of caretaker.

The routine was almost comforting, a return to normalcy and schedule, but I didn't want that comfort. I wanted a chance to live, to help, and to see the world I'd found myself in. I'd told Shan I wanted freedom, yet here I was, two full seven-days into my time at Harborton, doing all the things I'd learned how to do at my father's bedside years earlier.

The adventurers Valestia had summoned still hadn't shown up.

With another sigh, I turned to light the candles that flanked Erlund's bed—candles meant to ensure that if and when the man woke, it would not be to darkness—and froze. Valestia stood in the doorway, her steel grey hair a skullcap atop her wrinkled face.

"I'm sorry. I didn't see you—"

"This is not your first time caring for someone, is it, boy?" Two weeks in, and she still refused to call me by name, but her tone had softened over time.

"No."

She looked at me for a long time, reading something in my face. I waited for the inevitable questions, questions I didn't even want to think about, let alone answer, but instead she stepped in to take the fire-striker from my hands. "You may go. Deliberations finished early tonight, and I will watch over my brother until the morning. Perhaps you can spend time with your beast before sleeping."

I remained *boy* and Miko remained *beast*, but at least Valestia had kept her word so far. We'd been worked hard, but also fed and clothed, and the worst we'd received from the other villagers were dirty looks, and maybe a few muttered curses as they passed me on the narrow streets.

That said, a comfortable cage was still a cage.

I didn't ask about the adventurers, because Harborton was the very definition of a frontier village, and it didn't get many visitors beyond the occasional traveling merchant. I'd have heard if any strangers had arrived. Instead, I squeezed by the old woman and out into the narrow hall of the house she and her brother shared.

"Boy," called Valestia, waiting for me to stop and turn. "Whatever it is that happened to your last charge, Erlund will survive this. He *will* live."

Her voice thinned out just a bit at the end, but her eyes were chips of polished glass, daring me to disagree.

I just nodded and left.

The sun was still visible above Harborton's western wall, which meant that Valestia had released me from my duties a full glass earlier than usual. I'd already gotten my one meal of the day—stew and a dry, gritty bread made from locally sourced grain—but carried Erlund's empty dishes back to the inn, placing them on the mat outside the rear door. I'd yet to meet Lomas himself, but the young woman who brought me Erlund's meals each day was polite enough, if overly tall and oddly cheerful. I waved to her as I left, thinking about what to do with my sudden free time.

For two weeks, Miko and I had been worked to the point of exhaustion. By the time we made it back to our assigned sleeping quarters, we'd both been too tired to do more than trade a few words before flopping onto the low cots and passing out. Some nights, I hadn't even meditated, not that there'd been anything in the way of skill gains to realize.

An hour—a full glass—of free time changed all of that, especially if I could get Miko off work early too.

I left the inn behind and went down to the road that paralleled the shoreline. With the casualties from the battle now either healed or buried, the Herbalist had returned to his usual place of business, a house that served as both storefront and living quarters. It wasn't the biggest house on the street, but it was well maintained, its wooden walls freshly painted in defiance of the salt-ridden winds that came in off the ocean.

For all his apparent youth, Tantalas was a person of consequence in Harborton.

I pushed through the front door, feeling like I was walking into a garden as much as a store, and found Miko and Tantalas leaning over a table along the rear wall, conversing as they sorted through piles of dried herbs. Two weeks in, their conversation remained mostly nonverbal, but the former shrine keeper had discovered that Harborton's primary language, called Trade, had a few similarities with synossian Common. She was making progress with her vocabulary by the day.

Rapid progress; I was pretty sure Strength wasn't the only attribute of hers that dwarfed mine.

"Brian!" she said in the High Tongue, the warmth in her voice a balm to the exhaustion I felt in my bones. "What are you doing here? Is everything okay?"

I nodded, consciously switching back and forth from her language to one that the Herbalist would understand. "Val dismissed me early. I wasn't sure if Tantalas could do the same for you? It's been a long time since we talked."

She turned expectant eyes on the man at her side, and he waved his hands dismissively.

"Go. You've done more than your share today. Just stay out of trouble, yes? Those you have helped treat will recognize your value, but…"

He didn't finish the sentence, nor did he have to. Harborton had more non-humans than I'd first realized, but Miko was of course the lone synossian, and Valestia wasn't the only one who called her *beast*.

"I'll watch out for her," I told the Herbalist, receiving a solemn nod in return.

I doubted Miko had gotten more than half of the Herbalist's words, but she nodded anyway, flashing the sharp-toothed smile I'd grown accustomed to. Threading an arm through mine, she pulled me out of the shop.

We made quite the pair as we walked through the streets: a white-scaled, humanoid lizard and a much smaller human, both clad in coarse grey pants and equally coarse, if significantly looser, long-sleeved shirts. A short length of rope served as a makeshift belt for each of us, with the waist of my pants folding down over mine. I was pretty sure our clothes had come from one of the dead villagers, one who didn't have any relatives to claim their belongings. Nothing fit, not really, but it was still a massive improvement over what I'd arrived in.

With one exception: I *still* didn't have shoes. Probably because shoes would have made it easier to run away; trust remained in short supply. That said, I'd built up enough calluses on my soles that the hard-packed dirt streets didn't give me too much trouble.

"Where to?" I asked Miko, ignoring the glare one of the village's fishermen sent our way.

"Home would be best." She'd lost both her smile and her cheer, which told me she'd seen the fisherman too. "We can talk before meditation for once."

Our temporary home, just off one of the two main streets, usually served as a warehouse, holding the supplies and items that would be sold when the next trade caravan arrived. As we headed over, I waved to the town's Tailor, a woman who couldn't be much higher level than me, judging by the distinct lack of fashion in Harborton. She waved back, which was a first. Another seven-day or two and I might even merit a smile.

Once we reached the warehouse, I followed Miko inside, past the sparsely populated shelves and to the interior corner where we'd placed our cots.

"How are you doing?" I asked her, keeping my voice low. I didn't *think* listening devices existed on Eos or that anyone in Harborton could understand the synossian High Tongue, but there was almost definitely magic that could make up for both of those things, and the warehouse was empty enough that noise carried. "Is everything still okay with Tantalas?"

"He is strange but kind," she murmured back, "and generous to offer up his knowledge to a stranger. While I have not yet acquired any herbalism-related skills, I believe I am close. Such skills will prove valuable when we depart."

We traded glances. I knew Miko had to be as frustrated to be stuck in Harborton as I was. We had a *lot* of time before the first refugee ships would arrive, but we had just as much that we needed to accomplish before that time. Indentured servitude in a frontier fishing village wasn't getting us anywhere closer to achieving our goals.

"Have you discovered anything more about the Great Wilds?" she asked me. "The communication barrier with Tantalas makes anything but small talk and practical instruction difficult."

"Whereas Valestia rarely talks to me at all." I shook my head. "Erlund has a couple of books on a shelf in his room, but the handwriting is abysmal. I can only read for a few minutes before I get a headache."

Miko perked up at the mention of books, reminding me that she had at one point wanted to become a scholar. "You can read them? What are they about? Can you smuggle one back here for me?"

"I am pretty sure they're all in this continent's Trade tongue," I told her, "so I doubt they'd do you much good."

"They could serve as language primers," she pointed out. "I will eventually have to do more than simply *speak* the local tongue."

I winced. I wasn't particularly happy with Shan for the plans he'd mired me in and failed to explain, but I *was* grateful for the *Speaker of Tongues* trait I'd been given. Especially since I hadn't done anything to earn it in my former life on Earth. I would have struggled a lot more than Miko to learn another language at all, let alone how to read and write it.

"One book seemed to be a travel journal," I said. "Maybe Erlund's? The other is a history of a place called Hybellus."

"Is that the nation we are in?"

"I don't think so." Erlund had mentioned Hybellus, up on the wall, saying something about a tower and a jewel. "I think it's where Valestia and Erlund came from originally."

"I see." Miko was silent for a long while in the dim interior. When she spoke again, her voice was even more hushed. "Perhaps we should seek it out when we are freed?"

"Assuming we ever are." I heard her twitch of a reaction and felt her orange eyes on my face but stared off into the shadows rather than meeting her gaze. "I'm just saying... it's been two seven-days already and nobody's seen any sign of these supposed adventurers. What happens if they never show up? What if Erlund dies?"

"I do not agree with Harborton's leader—this human called Valestia—that we are at fault for her brother's fate," said Miko, the words coming slowly, "but we do share *some* responsibility. Aurea teaches to act in the night as we would in the light, and that every moment is an opportunity for growth."

"Meaning?"

"Unwanted though it may be, our forced servitude in Harborton provides us with food and shelter. Additionally, we have a safe space to learn about the land Shan sent us to. These are not bad things."

"That's a pretty enlightened attitude for someone your age."

"This is far from my first time serving," she reminded me. "A cycle in the legions and most of another at the Shrine of the Family. Did they not have such duties on your dirt world?"

"Some countries did," I said. "I think so, anyway."

"Then why does this chafe at you so? If Valestia is a harsher taskmaster than Tantalas, perhaps I can have him speak to her on your behalf…"

"No. She's crotchety, short-tempered, and worried to death about her brother, but honestly, I barely see her. As far as I can tell, she's running herself ragged just to keep this whole place operational. Especially with multiple acres of farmland now unusable."

"What is it then? Does your frustration have something to do with your Ideal?"

"I… kind of?"

She simply waited, wielding silence as deftly as her club.

I swallowed. "I told you about my dad, right?"

Miko straightened, something somber entering her tone. "Yes."

"He was sick. Sick for a very long time," I said quietly. "With something our doctors—our healers, I guess—couldn't cure. As it progressed, he lost more and more of his basic capabilities. To eat or relieve himself. To talk. To function as a person."

"So you took care of him."

"Yeah."

"Which explains why you have the *Caretaking* skill."

"Of everything the Framework added to my personal record, that one was more than earned." I coughed and cleared my throat, blinking my eyes even though there were no tears to fall. "When he died, I was sad, of course. But—"

"But you were also relieved." Miko shrugged at the look I sent her. "It is not so uncommon a sentiment, Brian Fieldings, even here on Eos. Your life was trapped in a sort of stasis as you cared for another, and his death freed you to pursue a future of your own."

"I guess so. Only I ended up on Eos instead."

"And now you bear the weight of an entire species' future on your back."

"I think we're carrying that weight together."

"Even so, it is another wall between you and your freedom."

"Yes… and no? We have a long time before the first fleet reaches us. I don't see any reason why working with you to provide for their arrival has to clash with my own plans or goals."

Whatever they are.

"Then why is it that—" Her words trailed off. "The human male. The brother. Erlund. You are back to being a caretaker, having thought yourself free of such a role."

I frowned. "Was it Intellect or Discernment that let you figure that out?"

"Some combination of both, I suspect, accompanied by multiple cycles listening to the petitions of Aurea's faithful. I *am* a Priestess, remember? Whether stationed at a shrine or in the Cathedral of the Dawn itself, my role was to offer counsel."

"I assume there's a skill for that?"

"If there was, it would be telling me that your sudden interest in the mechanics of the Framework might be an attempt to redirect us to safer subjects." She placed a clawed hand on my arm. "It is your choice, but I suspect you will feel better for speaking."

After a moment of silence, I shrugged. "Honestly, being a caretaker again is *easy*. There's a structure to it. A sameness of schedule.

I spend each day doing what I'm supposed to do, come back here, fall asleep, and then repeat it all the next day. And I guess that's kind of the problem. I don't like how quickly I've fallen back into a routine I never wanted in the first place. Not when there's so much to do."

"How is your shoulder?"

Frowning at the non-sequitur, I shrugged again, the ease of the movement giving my answer. "I'd say it's back to normal."

"Something that would not have been possible without this time free of conflict, where you have had to lift nothing heavier than a pitcher of water or a wooden tray of food."

"You're saying our stay here is a *good* thing?"

"Even with the Framework, some healings take more than techniques, Brian. They take time. If you were not a caretaker for this Erlund, you would be out in the boats with the fishermen, looking for fresh fishing grounds as the river's dead continue to flow out to sea. Or tilling the western fields with the farmers. Neither would have done your shoulder any good. Look at this time as a gift, a temporary reprieve from which you will emerge stronger."

The setting sun streamed in through the glassless window to paint the synossian's scales in colors reminiscent of the torn robes she'd carefully folded and put away. I'd only known her for a month or so, but it was already hard to remember the panic and horror I'd first felt on seeing her. Now, she was just Miko, the closest thing to family I had in this reality.

"You're pretty good at this guidance stuff," I admitted.

"Really?" Every trace of solemnity vanished. "My instructors always felt I spoke too much and listened not nearly enough."

"Well, I'm just one guy, but I think you're doing great. And I guess you're right; as much as I hate this role, it's one that gives me a lot of free time. Time I should be putting to better use."

Miko cocked her head, waiting.

"I'll start by asking Valestia if there's anything I can do while watching over Erlund. Apparently, I can read and write in Trade, and I'm betting that's not the case for everyone in Harborton."

"You want to become a Scribe?" I could hear the capital letter that told me that was a Framework-recognized profession.

"Not particularly, no, but it would give me steady access to information, and that's something we don't have right now. Until you're fluent, I think I'm our best chance at learning about the world outside Harborton."

A part of me—the part that forever seemed stuck back on Earth—was shrieking in horror. Study had never been high on my list of interests either, and now I was suggesting I add that to my caretaking duties?

The rest of me—the increasingly louder part of me that couldn't resist pulling up my character sheet on an almost hourly basis—wondered what sort of growth I might get from focused study. An earned point of Intellect? More General skills?

Hell if I knew, but I wanted to find out. Maybe the most magical thing about the Framework was how it made even the mundane seem rife with possibilities.

"I think that is an excellent plan," decided Miko. She hesitated, then continued. "On another subject, I have a request to make."

"Yeah?"

Miko's posture was always perfect, but somehow, she found it in herself to straighten up even further. She waved to the window above us.

"Five nights from now, both Lakshi and Tirsa will be hidden. The moons," she explained, deciphering my confusion. "In their absence, it is tradition to bid farewell to those who have been lost to us."

"Like a memorial service?"

"Yes. I was not able to say the words or light the pyres for those who fell at Whitehall."

I nodded. "Makes sense. But… you said you had a request?"

"Yes." Her strange eyes darted around the interior of the warehouse, looking at everything but me. "Would you stand with me during the ceremony?"

The easy answer was, of course, *yes*, but…

"What would that involve?"

"Simply bear witness," she said. "And if you feel compelled to do so, share some words about the fallen."

Oh. "Yeah. I can do that."

She turned to me. "Are you certain?"

"It's not a big ask, Miko." I shrugged. "Shan aside, I'm not a part of your religion, but I owe a lot to Riok and his claw. If this will help their souls rest easier or whatever, how could I say no?"

"Thank you." Her inner eyelids fluttered up and down. "In truth, the ceremony is as much for those of us who remain as it is for those who are lost."

"I get that."

"Do you?"

"We have funerals on Earth, remember? Although sometimes, they feel more like…" I shook my head, remembering Mrs. Appleton's grim smile as she watched Dad's coffin go into the ground. "Closure's not always in the cards, I guess."

"In the cards?"

"Sorry; I mean it's not always easy to come by."

"I see."

Despite my tiredness, I stood back up, feeling a need to *do something*. I retrieved my spear from where I'd leaned it against the nearby shelf. "I think I'm going to practice the forms Riok taught me."

"You remember your weapon forms after only a few days of training?"

"I… remember *some* of them," I admitted, looking about for an open space other than the one where we'd placed our cots. "Or *pieces* of some of them anyway. With my shoulder healed, I'd like to try to improve my *Spear* skill."

"I wish you good fortune in that," said Miko, dropping into a meditative stance on her cot. "In the meantime, I will see if I have finally gained a skill related to the Herbalist profession."

A glass or so later, I let out a frustrated sigh. I remembered bits of the footwork Riok had shown me and some of the simpler hand placements and shifts but stringing them together into anything approximating a form was apparently beyond me. I'd found myself focusing on our desperate fights in the forest instead, first against the apes and then the catosaurs, trying to think how I could have improved my performance in each with a step here or a careful retreat there.

It was all theoretical, because I didn't know enough to guess how my changes would play out in reality. What I needed was a teacher. *Another* teacher.

In the meantime, however… I had a technique I could continue to try to master. I wiped the sweat from my forehead and hefted Riok's spear again. In the forest, I'd used *Lunge* as an empowered attack, a way to reach my target with speed and greater force than strength alone could provide. Crossing the river and scaling the wall had shown me I could use the technique simply for movement as well. And that raised some interesting possibilities.

I only had a handful of uses of the technique, each separated by the minute-long cooldown, but I spent those uses propelling myself around the warehouse. By choosing my target as a place instead of an enemy, I could vary some parameters, like distance and angle of movement. I could even *Lunge* directly up into the air, although—as I had already discovered—that left me at gravity's mercy when the technique ended. I couldn't push through spaces I'd be unable to move through normally, and I also had to be able to see where I was going, but even so, the technique was amazingly flexible.

The few battles I'd been in had shown me how much positioning mattered. With *Lunge* my only technique, I'd be foolish to waste it on *not* striking an enemy, but once the cooldown was shorter or I had other techniques to utilize in tandem?

Common rank or not, there was something there.

As I settled down to meditate, I resolved to add technique training to my nightly list of activities. I couldn't lessen the cooldown without improving my attributes or upgrading the technique, but the more I familiarized myself with *Lunge*, the better I'd understand it … and the greater my chance of a higher-rarity upgrade being offered at level three.

When I finally emerged from my meditation, another glass later, Miko was snoring quietly on her cot. Harborton was silent and still around us and there was a skill-up message waiting.

Just… not the one I'd been hoping for.

```
You have increased the following skills:

General skills:
Caretaking [+1]: 3/10
```

The adventurers couldn't arrive soon enough.

28

Five more days passed and Erlund's condition didn't change at all. Any doubts I'd had in Valestia's original diagnosis were gone. Her brother's recovery hinged on the missing elixir and the adventurers who'd been summoned to retrieve its ingredients.

Unfortunately, those adventurers were still nowhere to be found. I fell back into the schedule I had been trying to escape, repositioned my patient as frequently as possible, and kept an eye out for bed sores. An ointment provided by Tantalas helped some on that last front, but I was resolved to bring Miko in if true healing became necessary.

As much as magic had caused this whole mess—magic and whatever the Swarm was—I couldn't deny that it made the aftermath a little bit easier too.

Along the way, I gained another two points in *Caretaking*, bringing my total to a deeply irritating five. I even picked up the *Scribing* General skill, thanks to the bookkeeping work Valestia had agreed to loop me in on. *Spear*, on the other hand, remained stuck at ten, despite being a Major skill.

Clearly, my late-night training sessions weren't doing much.

My limited work as a scribe—small S, because I didn't have the profession—helped fill the endless hours watching over Erlund. Even better, I picked up a lot of useful secondhand information as I reviewed Valestia's documents and wrote letters on behalf of the villagers using a sludge-like chalk that hardened when it dried. There were four actual books in the entire village, all of them handwritten, and I was making my way through each one, building a better understanding of the land to which Miko and I had been dispatched.

Harborton was less than ten cycles old, established under a charter that Val and Erlund had purchased from Grand Duke Willerton, who apparently owned more property than Warren Buffett. The village sat on the easternmost edge of the duke's vast territories, multiple days' ride from the next small outpost of civilization. Its location at the mouth of the aptly named Snake River at least explained why the settlers had pushed so far: access to farmland, freshwater, *and* the ocean all suggested a bright future, assuming the place could survive its initial birthing pains.

Even the horribly unimaginative name had been chosen as a form of advertisement, telling both potential settlers *and* future trading partners what they could expect.

"Eventually," said Valestia, in one of our infrequent and always brusque conversations, "there will be settlements up and down this river. We will be perfectly suited to serve as the trading hub for all of them."

Eventually was doing a lot of heavy lifting in that sentence. Currently, there were just under thirty-five adult residents in Harborton, not including Miko or me. I'd heard Valestia mutter under her breath that the number was far too small … but then, I'd *also* heard her complain that the loss of the western fields made feeding the existing population a struggle.

There was a lot of muttering going on, really. It was hard not to feel personally responsible for some of it.

While the siblings were the village's founders and unofficial mayors, Harborton officially operated under a council. Tantalas and the innkeeper, Lomas, had seats on that council, as did representatives from the fishermen, farmers, and craftspeople. Valestia's daily work seemed to involve keeping the peace among the various groups, a job made more difficult by the crisis we'd brought upon the village.

Apparently, Erlund had been both a steady voice of reason *and* the head Hunter, so his absence was felt keenly by all sides. And explained why my daily allotment of stew almost always had fish instead of meat.

I flipped to the final page of my borrowed book on Hybellus. As I'd told Miko almost a week earlier, the text told the history of that small nation… which was fitting, because history was all that was left. Hybellus had been conquered repeatedly in what were called the Kingdom Wars—a series of prolonged conflicts involving a half-dozen different countries that had emerged from what had once been an empire. The Kingdom Wars had only ended because of a sickness that swept through the land, a plague that ignored borders and sapped nations of both their armies and their will for conquest.

As informative as the book had been, its focus was narrow, its information was old, and the bias of its author was undeniable. What little I knew of *current* events had been pieced together from Erlund's travel journal, what I'd read and written as a scribe, and a few innocuous questions I'd asked Valestia while trying to mask the extent of our ignorance.

The unnamed nation that had taken Hybellus was eventually conquered in turn, but decades of warfare had left the country's original inhabitants scattered and broken. Valestia and Erlund had fled as refugees to the Kingdom of Elthor, one of the few nations that

hadn't engaged in the repeated cycle of Hybellus' pillaging.
Unfortunately, they had arrived in the capital, Elthoris, just ahead of
the plague. Huge swaths of the population had died, including several
noble houses, and the entirety of the royal family. The Kingdom of
Elthor was now formally divided into four great duchies. According to
Erlund's journal, those dukes were the country's true rulers and the
king who sat on the throne in Elthoris was little more than a
figurehead.

Miko and I had spent the last few nights discussing all that I'd
learned. We'd even formulated the beginnings of a plan. Once we were
free again, we would make our way to Grand Duke Willerton's capital,
Trynfall, where we would try to build connections with those in power
to help prepare the way for the synossians' arrival. Exactly *how* we were
going to contact those people, let alone get their support, was still an
open question. Miko wanted to petition the duke directly, while I, as
the resident human, was certain we'd need money to grease the wheels
of bureaucracy.

We would presumably be able to leverage Miko's healing and
my literacy to bring in some funds, but if we could instead find or form
an adventuring party of our own… well, personal power *and* wealth
definitely trumped just wealth.

Sadly, we didn't have a lot of information to go on when it
came to adventuring parties either. If it weren't for Erlund's condition
and our forced servitude, we wouldn't even know *adventurers* were a
thing. In the Synossian Primacy, that sort of thing was organized by the
government and run through the military. In this continent,
adventurers seemed closer to independent contractors, roaming the
untamed wilds, plundering ancient ruins, and performing missions on
behalf of benefactors.

I didn't hate the idea of delving a dungeon and walking away
with an armload of magical gear and a few chests of precious gems…

but I was also *level two*. Unless there were missions for clearing rats out of cellars or something equally mundane, I was likely too weak to be considered by any party of significance.

Some settlements had mission boards where tasks were posted for adventurers, or even guild houses where adventurers would congregate. Harborton was too small for any of that. Instead, Valestia had sent a messenger and two guards to make the week-long journey to Madea, the largest town in the region and the only one big enough to support a chapter of the Adventurer's Guild. With luck, they would eventually locate adventurers willing to accept the mission and whatever money Val had been able to scrape together as reward.

By the time the older woman returned home, the sun had long since fallen. I gathered up Erlund's dishes along with my spear and headed to the inn, meriting a single, severe nod from Valestia on the way past.

My welcome at the inn was warmer, not that the bar was particularly high. I passed the used plate and cup off to the barmaid and received a wide smile in return, causing dimples to appear out of nowhere in what seemed almost stereotypically rosy cheeks. Her smile only grew when, for the first time since I'd come to Harborton, I followed her to the inn's side door instead of turning away into the darkness.

"Here to grace us with your presence, are ya?" Her voice was rough but pleasant enough, the humor obvious in her tone.

I nodded. Miko's memorial service was scheduled for midnight and Tantalas had slipped her some bent copper bits so that we could spend the time beforehand doing something other than huddling in our warehouse dorm. "We thought it was about time we came over and said hi. I'm Brian."

"I know that. *Everyone* knows. I'm Halletia." She was at least five years older than me but miraculously only a few inches taller, her curly hair up in a bun and her skirts and short-sleeved blouse both modest and mostly clean. Her accent differed from Val's or Tantalas', but that seemed to be par for the course; as a new settlement, Harborton was a collection of cast-offs. "Wait… did ya say *we?*"

"Yeah. Miko will be coming too."

Halletia's smile vanished, and the evening seemed darker for its absence. She leaned in, dropping her voice. "Best be careful there. Tempers are always high of late and whatever the duke's laws, there aren't so many who look kindly upon the beasts, ya know? You'll have to convince Lomas that she won't be a problem if you want him to let her stay."

I gave her a smile for gendering Miko at all, let alone correctly, and nodded. "I'll do that. And maybe you can find us a table that's out of the way or something? We don't want to start trouble."

"Out of the way? You've clearly never been inside. Still, I'll do what I can." Mischief crept into her hushed whispers. "If Lomas lets ya stay, I'll see about watering the ales tonight, too, so the usual suspects don't get too rowdy."

"Don't go to any trouble on our account—"

"Nonsense. Your healer assisted old Tantalas with my littlest one just the other day. Cleared his nasty cough right up! Helping ya both in return is the neighborly thing to do." She wrapped her free arm, tanned and freckled, around my shoulders and guided me in through the service door. "Now come on. I'll take ya to see Lomas before I get back to slinging mugs to grumpy men."

"Any advice?"

"Be honest and brief, if ya can. He's a fussy old curmudgeon at the best of times, that one, but most especially now. Many of the eastern fields were his, growing crops to be used for the inn's cooking and brewing."

The eastern fields that wouldn't grow anything for at least twelve cycles, thanks to the fabled Fabergé egg of utter desolation. I did my best not to wince.

Sadly, Halletia worked in the service industry too and was *at least* as good as I was at reading body language.

"He doesn't blame ya," she said, opening the interior door and escorting me through a kitchen that looked nothing like what you'd find on Earth, from the live fires under metal pots to the absence of refrigerators or faucets. Along the way, Erlund's dishes were deposited in a metal trough that served as their sink. "Or at least I don't think so. Just… be aware."

"Of course. And thank you. If there's anything I can do for you, just let me know."

She paused, one hand on the door leading from the kitchen to the common room, the other toying with a strand of curly dark hair. "This was supposed ta be about *me* paying back the two of ya, but…"

"But?"

"Is it true that ya know yer letters?"

"Thankfully, yes."

She brightened. "I have a sister in Madea…"

"And you want to write to her?"

"If possible. I need to let her know that there's space in Harborton now for her, her man, and their little ones."

I wasn't sure if that was because of all the people that had died on the wall, and I didn't ask.

"I can provide ya with the parchment, I think," she continued, "but I never learned ma letters."

"I'd be happy to write a message for you," I assured her. "Why don't I stop by tomorrow night when I return Erlund's dishes again? That way, you can tell me exactly what you want the note to say?"

It was her turn to wince. "Could it be in the morning instead?" She nodded to the closed door and the noise coming from beyond it. "Nights are busy times, ya know?"

"That'll work too." I had to come to the inn twice during the day to pick up meals anyway—my one and Erlund's two—so it wouldn't even be a hardship.

"Great!" She nudged open the door with a well-practiced move of her hip and ushered me into the common room, where we were both hit by a wall of light and sound. Harborton might have only had thirty-five adult residents but almost half of them appeared to be at the inn, four of the six available tables overflowing with people and their food or drinks.

Mostly drinks, I couldn't help but notice, although here and there, bowls of stew were being spooned into open mouths.

"That's Lomas over there," said Halletia, leaning in to be heard and unaware of the way her lips at my ear sent inadvertent shivers down my spine. "I've got to get to ma tables."

The man she'd pointed out was standing behind the bar, the only person in the entire room shorter than me. Lomas wasn't human or… whatever Tantalas was… but something else entirely, with an overly wide head, the barest hint of a neck, and shoulders like a defensive end. He was hairless right down to the eyebrows, his skin brown as the soil in the western fields. Dark eyes settled on me as I made my way across the crowded room.

I gave him a bow when I arrived, doing my best to emulate Miko's courtly manners without poking him with Riok's spear. "Good evening. I'm—"

"I know who you are, outsider. I was on the wall when you brought yon snake god down upon us." Lomas' voice was rough and hard to parse. Marlon Brando with a mouthful of marbles.

"We were just running away, like everything else in the forest."

"Perhaps. Suppose I can't blame anyone who flees a monster like that. But then you bring a weapon into *my* inn?"

"I was taught that the spear goes where I do."

"In larger cities, I suppose. This is Harborton."

"I'll… uh… keep that in mind for the future." I wasn't going to argue, but I wasn't forgetting Rule #1 either.

"See that you do. Now, what is it that you want? You don't look like you've got a copper to your name, and nothing in my inn is free."

"Nothing?"

"Even the lunches you've been getting are coming out of the siblings' coffers." He smiled at whatever he saw in my face, exposing teeth as grey as wet cement. "Didn't realize that, did you?"

"Not really, no." Although it *was* just one meal a day; I was pretty sure Valestia was getting that expense repaid and more from Miko's healing alone. "Anyway, my companion is bringing the money."

He scowled and spat something entirely too large and dense for comfort onto the floor behind the bar. "You mean the scaled one?"

"Miko's a person, just like you and me."

"I suppose that depends on who you talk to."

"She won't cause any trouble," I said, trying a different approach. "Neither of us will. I can promise you that."

His eyes wandered past me and his voice shifted into something even more guttural. "What do you or any of these mud dwellers know of oaths or honor?"

"I know a person is only as good as their word," I told him, too confused by the *mud dweller* comment to take offense. "And that—"

I stopped, mid-sentence. Lomas' mouth had dropped open, and his brown skin had gone pale like oat milk.

"Dust take me…" he whispered, voice still guttural even as it lost its harsh edge. "If you would, say something more."

"I'm not sure what you want to hear," I managed. The people around the closest table had turned to watch us, their murmurs lost beneath the inn's general noise.

"Anything," said Lomas. "And everything. It has been too long since I heard the words of stone and wind from a voice other than my own. Never did I think to find such in a village like ours."

Which was when the looks we were getting from everyone—and the last twenty seconds of conversation, in general—finally made sense. Lomas had switched to his native tongue to insult me, and I, unknowingly, had switched right along with him.

"Miko Nesari is a good person," I told him, now consciously trying to ensure I didn't revert to the Trade tongue. "Kind and generous, almost to a fault. You can trust her."

The innkeeper didn't seem to have heard a word I said. He shook his head in wonder. "You speak like one born from the Waste itself. Like my sire's sire, even. How is this possible?"

"I have a gift for languages," I told him, skewing uncomfortably close to the truth.

"A gift indeed, and one I would shame my ancestors were I to refuse." He cleared his throat. "He who brings the language of my home inside these walls will be forever welcome."

"And my companion?"

He hesitated, then turned to the watching patrons, the change in intonation the only thing that told me he had switched to Trade. "The outsider and his—his companion—are to be welcomed as guests in my inn." He scowled at the murmurs that arose and glared down the closest table, eyes glittering in the wan light. "Any who have a problem with that can go to another Brewer for their ale!"

I lowered my voice, still speaking what Lomas had called the words of stone and wind. "Harborton has two Brewers?"

"It does not." Lomas flashed his concrete teeth. "My closest competitor is days away and produces watered-down vermin piss." He motioned me to one of the few empty tables in the common room. "Take a seat and set your weapon aside. I will have your—I will have this *Miko* escorted to your table."

∘∘∘

When Miko arrived, bearing a small purse and a handful of copper bits, the public reception was… muted, at best. Still, under Lomas' unblinking stare, nobody made a stink about her presence. A handful of people even sent her nods, likely men and women who had benefited from her healing over the past few weeks.

The two of us spent the next few hours in the common room, drinking clay mugs of what tasted like a thicker, more bitter Guinness. Despite still being summer, the wind off the ocean was perpetually cool, and the roaring fire in the room's hearth did a lot to dispel its chill. Somewhere after the second drink, I felt something deep inside of me unclench. It was the first time we'd had to relax since our arrival in the Great Wilds, and though we were more observers than participants in the revelry, I soaked up the light and the laughter like it was water in the desert.

The farmers and the fishermen were the first to depart, owing to their early morning schedules, but by the time midnight rolled around, only a handful of customers remained. Miko paid for our drinks and I said goodnight to Lomas in the language whose name I still didn't know. As we left the inn, we found Tantalas outside, the slender herbalist shivering in the cool night air despite the multiple layers of clothes he'd wrapped himself in.

"Is he joining us?" I asked Miko. I was aiming for *her* continent's base language, Common, but ended up speaking the synossian High Tongue instead. I only knew four languages—five, including English—and it was already getting confusing.

"He is, if that is acceptable to you." She then switched to Trade, her words already flowing more smoothly than they had a seven-day prior. "Tantalas wish to learn my people… is it death… custom?"

"Close," said the other man. "Memorial ceremonies."

"Memorial ceremonies." Miko nodded as she repeated the words. "Yes."

"Given that there is a fire element to those ceremonies, I also thought the guards would take comfort in a council member's involvement," added the herbalist, waiting for me to translate the few words Miko seemed stuck on. "Come along; I have set up a place by the water, safely away from the boats and pier."

We followed the other man through Harborton's quiet streets. As small as the village was, *everything* was just a few minutes' walk, and that included the ocean. Tantalas led us to a carefully stacked pile of wood, looking out of place on the rough stone shore. As promised, we were a good twenty to thirty feet from the closest fishing boat, a small two-person craft that had been pulled up onto land for the night. Past it were several similar-sized boats and then the pier itself, where larger boats could safely dock.

"Not that we've seen any of them yet." Tantalas' voice was soft, but the sound carried over the rhythmic ocean waves. "But once we are more established… that pier will be the key to Harborton's role in maritime trade."

"Smart," I said.

"At least someone thinks so. I had young Neddard gather deadwood from the western woods. Will this suit your purposes, Miko Nesari?"

"It will, Tantalas Khailleson." The two of them exchanged bows, like rival dignitaries trying to out-courtesy the other. After their contest ended in a draw, Miko pulled out her travel pouch and the fire-striker within. Despite the dampness in the air, the wood caught easily, and soon there was a small fire cheerily blazing away in front of us, its light almost as great a balm as the heat it gave off.

The Priestess stared into the flames for a long moment, quiet and still. I didn't know if she was praying, counting, or just trying to remember how things went, but eventually, she stepped forward and spoke once again in the High Tongue.

"Even in darkness there is light," she said, voice reverent. "The fire of the Dawn Maiden, Synos' first daughter, who watches over her people, who warms us, cares for us, and welcomes us home when our days are done."

She lifted her arms and turned her scaled head upward to the dark sky, to a sun that was not shining and the moons that were lost. "Aurea, I ask that you hear our words tonight. That your light provides a beacon for the souls who fell to treachery and betrayal. Grant them a place at your side where they can bask in your warmth or return them to Eos as instruments of your will."

She stepped to the left, circling the fire, and stopped again, holding one hand out to me.

Thankfully, she'd briefed me on what the ceremony would entail, so I was ready; I passed Riok's spear over, feeling a strange reluctance to see anyone else wielding it, even for just a moment.

"Even in chaos there is order," said Miko, words now ringing in the darkness. "The strictures of the Oathkeeper, Synos' eldest child, who keeps his celestial father's vigil and forever holds to the dual truths of honor and duty."

She turned the spear horizontally and held it above the small fire. "Kal, I ask that you hear our words tonight. That you see the souls who stood in the face of tyranny, who recognized their own deaths and fought still when hope was gone. Give them a place of honor within your immortal legions or return them to Eos as instruments of your will."

Miko returned the spear to me and took another step around the fire, the ocean now at her back. This time, she held up a waterskin, the container filled almost to bursting. Her words gentled, losing their martial rhythm.

"Even in death there is life. The breath of the Pure, Synos' youngest, who knows that all things heal, even pain such as this, who sees worlds and bodies and souls reborn, each strengthened by their struggles."

She turned the waterskin over and loosened the latch so that a stream of cool water poured onto the fire below, spattering off the rocks, and thickening the small plumes of smoke rising to the night sky. "Etriska, I ask that you hear our words tonight. That you see the weary souls huddled upon your doorstep and bid them welcome. Grant them succor at your hearth, that they become another wind in the breath of life, or return them to Eos as instruments of your will."

As she finished, she released the latch entirely, the remaining water flooding out to drown the fire below. The shoreline plunged into darkness, the only light the village behind us.

"Even in silence, there is a whisper," said Miko, her voice hushed and now coming from the right side of the extinguished fire. "The words of the Trickster, Etriska's twin, who finds space between each moment, who dwells in darkness to protect his siblings' light."

If she made a gesture or held anything out this time, I couldn't see it. The Priestess was just a shadow in the darkness, everywhere and nowhere at once. "Shan, I ask that you hear our words tonight. That you defend these fallen souls from the dangers only you can see. Guard them in their passage and give them parts to play in your eternal machinations or return them to Eos as instruments of your will."

For a long moment, there was only silence. Tantalas shifted, somewhere to my right, but before he could speak, Miko's voice filled the air again.

"I honor Riok Diocil, known as the Wind Walker. Youngest of the primacy's ranked Aspirants and a hero a dozen times over in his life. May his memory never be forgotten, and his light never extinguished."

Another pause, this one briefer than the last. "I honor Berys Komoto, Priest of the Pure, who healed with both blessings and words, whose wisdom brought comfort even in these dark times."

She continued down the line, naming each person in Riok's claw before continuing on to the primarch, her councillors, and the High Priests at Whitehall. The last name she gave wasn't really a name at all.

"I honor Mother, the Voice of the Dawn, who led the goddess' faithful for longer than I have lived, and who, through her actions and her presence, served as a reminder of Aurea's light. I do not know why I was spared, and she was not, but I will never be alone while the example she set lives in my heart. And that is what made her a mother to us all."

I waited for the closing words, but instead Miko approached me. Her voice, still slightly sibilant with the High Tongue's intonation, was a breath in my ear.

"I know that we are not on your dirt world, that your own gods are absent, and that much time has already passed, but if you wish to speak of your father, please know that my gods are listening. What peace they and I have to offer is yours tonight."

This had *not* been part of the briefing. I coughed, already struggling with a throat that had gone tight during the recitation of names, so many of whom I'd ridden with but never actually spoken to.

"I... uh..."

"This grace is freely given," she added, "but it is a gift only; there is no fault in saying no."

Part of me wanted to jump on the out she had just provided. It had been a long day—a long month-plus, really, dating all the way back to Earth—and I was tired and would have to be up in a matter of hours to empty Erlund's bedpan and change his clothes. I didn't have time for this.

Right?

Unfortunately, all those rationalizations somehow faded away in the darkness. The stars above were hidden, the fire was nothing more than a few embers, and in the stillness of the night, in the dwindling moments of Miko's memorial scene, there was no space for anything but truth.

Truth and words I'd kept inside for too long.

I focused on my *Speaker of Tongues* trait and did my best to switch to the only language I'd known in my first life, the language my dad would understand if souls were a thing and his had impossibly made the journey with me. My voice was thin and weak, but I spoke into the night.

"I honor Jacob Fieldings, my dad, who fought longer and harder than anyone should have to under the shadow of what he knew was coming, as he tried to give me a normal life and normal family." I shook my head, glad the darkness hid the tears I felt running down my face. "I'm sorry I didn't thank you for that when you were still well enough to understand. Sorry that I could only think about myself. My loss, my frustration, my own inescapable end. You did the best you could, and I love you."

I don't know how much time passed in silence before Miko spoke again.

"Children of Synos, we ask that you welcome these of whom we have spoken as well as those who fell without any left to mourn their passage. For though our shells are mortal, our souls live forever. May they grow in the light of your celestial presence."

Miko began to sing, a low, wordless melody that carried out over the unseen tides, taken by the winds to worlds we might never see. When she finished, there was a long pause. "It done," she said, switching to her broken Trade. "I never perform all parts before. I hope is good enough."

"I think it was beautiful," said Tantalas. "What little of it I could understand, anyway. Thank you for sharing the ceremony with me."

Miko's bow was mostly lost in the darkness.

There wasn't much to say after that. The herbalist escorted us to our makeshift dormitory and bid us goodnight. I stayed quiet as I bunked down for the night. I could still see the little campfire burning when I closed my eyes, still hear Miko's words as she circled it.

Thoughts of my dad, before and during his illness, filled my head. Our life together had been far from ideal, but that hadn't been his fault. It hadn't been mine either, no matter how much my brain tried to convince me otherwise. We'd both done the best we could, trying to fill the time instead of just marking it. And now that he was gone… and I was technically *also* gone… that would have to be enough. It was time to look forward, to make the most of whatever time *I* had left.

"Goodbye, Dad."

If anyone heard me—person, soul, or Trickster god—they didn't reply.

And I was okay with that.

29

Another two weeks passed, and we fell back into our rhythm: work, train, and sleep. When possible, I met with Miko at the inn, but she was the only one getting paid for her work, and that coin didn't go very far with Lomas' ale. Most nights were still spent in our warehouse dormitory, meditating or talking. I trained every night with the spear, for all the good it did me; I had yet to see a single gain in the skill since reaching Harborton.

Miko, on the other hand, was making real progress on her next level. She'd capped out the required skills and was now inching towards the requisite amount of experience needed to advance. With such experience hard to come by outside of combat or soul-pressuring stakes, it seemed unlikely she'd level in Harborton, but *her* day-to-day job involved class-related activities, and that meant progress.

I continued to care for Erlund, and my increases in the *Caretaking* skill soon produced tangible results. I found myself handling each small task that much more efficiently… even the ones I'd performed for my dad for years. It wasn't just a matter of being *better* at it… I also had a greater understanding of what to do and when, almost like a doctor learning to read his patient.

Back in Midton, it had felt like there was never enough time at night to both take care of my dad and do my own thing. Here in Harborton, I found myself with the opposite problem. What scribing I'd been doing had already started to tail off. The letters I'd written wouldn't go out until the next merchant came through town, and nobody had received new mail for the same reason. I'd read all four of Harborton's books, cover to cover, multiple times, and had long since gleaned what information I could from each of them.

I spent more of that suddenly plentiful free time in my own head than was probably healthy, but the other alternative was repeatedly pulling up a character sheet that I knew wouldn't change until meditation. And maybe not even then, really… the only skill I'd improved other than *Caretaking* was *Scribing*. I still didn't have access to the Scribe profession because a profession required you to have maxed at least three of its associated skills, and without a Scribe to apprentice under, gaining those skills was as much about luck as repetition.

In fact, *Scribing* was the only new skill I'd gained since coming to Harborton. Lomas swore there was a General skill for *Alcohol Tolerance*—and one night of watching him work his way through his own inventory made it clear the man had considerable ranks in that skill—but so far, I had yet to earn it myself.

At least the people in Harborton were slowly warming to our presence, courtesy of Miko's healing and my pro bono work as a scribe. Few of those who had died in Harborton's defense had had families, so there was less outright resentment than there might have otherwise been, and most of the remaining defenders were whole and hearty thanks to Miko. Those who hadn't fought on the wall had been a slightly tougher nut to crack, but the crafters in town were starting to come around. The bigger surprise was the farming families; while they had been directly impacted by the loss of the western fields, a few visits from Miko—accompanied by Tantalas—had them treating her like an actual person instead of a pariah.

The fishing families, on the other hand… they were civil enough under Lomas' roof, but any encounter in Harborton's streets was usually accompanied by muttered curses, dark looks, and at least one gesture that Tantalas claimed was a ward against evil and not the obscenity it had looked like. I didn't know what we'd done to them, and they weren't saying.

Still, while they were a large coalition, they were far from the majority of the village. It was a nice change to walk the streets and be greeted by smiles or waves. I'd even spoken with Agnes, the village Tailor, about a thank you gift for Miko. I hadn't had any money to offer, but her eldest daughter wanted to learn to read and write and I'd convinced Valestia to give me a glass every other day to see to those lessons.

The fact that it would provide Harborton with a potential future Scribe when I finally departed no doubt factored into the old woman's agreement.

With another sigh, I spooned the last of Erlund's stew into his mouth. It was a good thing his autonomic functions remained intact, or I'd have spent this past moon watching him slowly starving to death instead. As it was, the man had already lost a fair bit of muscle during his convalescence.

Erlund wasn't the only one dropping weight. One meal a day wasn't much, even if I spent most of that day sitting around. In fact, the last time we'd gone to Lomas' inn, Miko and I had bought extra servings of bread and stew instead of ale. It had been worth the innkeeper's indignant glare to feel halfway full, for the first time in literal weeks.

Training with the spear at night was adding some muscle onto my frame, and the one Strength point I'd purchased on leveling had added some more, but I was leaner than I'd been at any time since high school. Between that and my height, I'd had several different villagers mistake me for one of the town's few children from behind.

One woman had even tried to chastise me for carrying a weapon about. She'd realized her mistake as soon as I turned around, but the moment had stuck with me. While Harborton's population was mostly human, and thus far shorter than the synossians had been, I felt my lack of size more keenly here, where even my own kind still towered over me.

I'd like to say that Lomas being even shorter *didn't* factor into why I spent as much time with the man as I could… but I'd be lying. It was a heady feeling to loom over another adult for once. Assuming a few inches made for looming, and I was convinced they did. It didn't hurt that the man was always happy to see me and always gruffly polite to Miko when she showed up too.

Much like Val and Erlund, Lomas was a refugee from another land. The place he had once called home was not so much a country as a collection of small tribes eking out a living where few could even survive. For reasons that remained private, Lomas had left the Waste behind, crossing a good quarter of the continent to reach the war-torn northern territories. Here, he served for years in one army or the other before eventually retiring. He'd used the lion's share of his savings to apprentice with a Brewer in Elthoris, and then, when he had finally earned the skills needed to unlock the profession, his remaining funds to purchase the stock, lumber, and manpower to start the inn in Harborton.

Some days, Lomas seemed happier about that decision than others. Still, the man clearly loved alcohol—both brewing it and drinking it—and he could talk for hours about his experiments with different strains of yeast and grains.

As for *what* he was, I never worked up the nerve to ask the man himself. Thankfully, his chief—and only—barmaid, Halletia, had been happy to share.

"They're called wasters around these parts, on account of being the only people who live in that desolation, but I heard ol' Lomas once refer to his people as dunsmen instead."

"Why dunsmen?"

"*Dun*no." She had grinned at her own wordplay. Halletia was an odd one, and not *just* because she was a service worker who was also somehow perpetually cheerful.

Given how far away the Waste was, there weren't a lot of dunsmen in the kingdom. There were even fewer in the duchy. Somewhere underneath his general grumpiness and beer obsession, I could tell Lomas was deeply homesick, and his reaction to my fluency in his native tongue had started to make more sense. I made a point to speak the language as much as possible with him.

To date, it hadn't even gotten me a discount, let alone free drinks, but hope sprang eternal.

ooo

"I think we're done for the day," I told Nala, taking the chalk square from her in exchange for a damp rag that she could wipe her slate down with. "You're making really good progress."

I wasn't saying that just to be nice. Agnes' daughter had come a long way in her literacy journey in just a few sessions. In fact, she'd somehow picked up both the *Reading* and *Writing* skills, even though *I* didn't have either one.

Miko had theorized that my *Speaker of Tongues* trait made such skills unnecessary in the eyes of the Framework… but it was still weird.

"Thank you, senior!" Nala went beet red at my compliment, and she fumbled the rag I'd just handed her. That was… well, par for the course, really. The young woman was just past thirteen cycles in age, which made her around eighteen and a half Earth years old, according to my probably faulty calculations. *Everything* seemed to make her self-conscious, especially me. "Mama is pleased."

"I'm glad. She's still giving you time to practice, right? I know your apprenticeship comes first, but—"

"I practice for a full glass every night, senior!" Indignation accomplished what my friendliness had not; Nala actually met my eyes. "I will not shame you… I mean, it is not… I uhm…"

Somewhere in there, she realized she was looking me in the face, and her words trailed off. She ducked her head again, cheeks still flaming.

I tried not to sigh, but it was really, really hard.

"That's good," I told her. "It's only been a short time, but I've been really impressed with your dedication."

In truth, Nala was a better student than I had ever been back on Earth. Part of it was probably that the Framework made progress tangible and more rewarding, and part of it was that, as far as I could tell, Nala wasn't sure she wanted to be a Tailor, like her mom. The skills I was teaching her gave her other options.

That said, I'd never wanted to be a teacher back on Earth, and my time on Eos hadn't changed that fact. Nor had these lessons with Nala; she was a nice girl and an attentive student, but the whole exercise was just… kind of dull. Too often, I found myself daydreaming about being back out on the road with Miko, the open world before us, danger, treasure, and most importantly, *excitement* lurking around every corner.

I wasn't sure what it said about me that I *missed* fleeing for our lives through monster-infested woods, but I kind of did.

Nala didn't respond to my latest compliment, the half-cleaned slate clutched in one hand and forgotten. Pale blonde hair peeked out from under the bonnet she wore—one of the few I'd seen in the village, again courtesy of her mother—and her eyes were looking anywhere but at me.

Yet again.

Thankfully, Val chose that moment to come home. The older woman stalked through the front door, her every movement brisk and economical. She glanced at the blushing young girl, rolled her eyes, and then dragged me out of the sitting room and into Erlund's bedroom.

"I fear for the future of Harborton if our young cannot even *speak* to the other sex," she muttered.

"It's a tough age," I said, ignoring the fact that Nala was almost nineteen Earth years old, not twelve. "She'll grow out of it, I'm sure."

"I will bow to your evident experience."

I was *pretty* sure there was an insult in there... just not sure enough to respond. It seemed the day's meetings had gone poorly.

"How is he doing?" Val asked, voice softening as she turned to her brother's still form in the bed.

"No change. He's fed and washed, and I changed the bedding, but..."

"Yes, I know." She brushed a strand of prematurely white hair out of her brother's face and said nothing else.

"Are you sure you don't want Miko to try *Minor Healing*? I know he needs an actual cure, but a casting or two a day couldn't hurt." After all, as I'd found with my shoulder, progressive healing *was* a thing.

She swallowed what would have almost definitely been the sort of retort that could flay a man's skin at twenty paces and shook her head. "As your beast has no doubt told you, the basic healing spells are limited in their function. They will not even address maladies like poison or curses, and the Swarm is an affliction of the soul as much as the body."

"I still don't know what the Swarm even is."

"So you've said." She sent me a look halfway between suspicion and irritation but volunteered no further information. "Regardless, Merchant Jessup should arrive in Harborton sometime within the next seven-day. With luck, he will bring word from Madea. If we are *truly* fortunate, he will be accompanied by the adventurers we have requested."

"And then Miko and I will be free."

"You will be free when my brother stands on his own two feet again." Her voice had gone iron hard. "And *that* will not happen until the adventurers have returned with both nilwort and shademoss."

"Hey." I warded off her angry glare with both hands, trying not to think of the watery tower she'd collapsed on Nikkaali the serpent. "That's what I meant."

Maybe if I'd had the *Deception* skill, she'd have bought it.

ooo

The next night found Miko and me back at Lomas' inn, in our now-standard table along the right wall and near the stairs leading up to the building's rentable bedrooms. I hadn't been up those stairs, but I was pretty sure the bedrooms were a hell of a lot nicer than our current sleeping arrangements. Then again, they were also no doubt a hell of a lot more expensive too.

For now, they were empty. If Merchant Jessup ever showed up, that would presumably change.

Miko had practically poured her mug of ale right down her throat, but even without the *Alcohol Tolerance* skill, she seemed none the worse for wear. Meanwhile, I was nursing my mug, once again conscious of the early morning that awaited us both.

"—and when we were done, we had a poultice that should slow bleeding and help prevent infection," Miko was saying. "It could be useful when I am out of healings."

"Do you think you'd be able to recognize the herbs you used in the wild? Aren't the ones in Tantalas' shop already dried and prepared?"

She tapped her left forearm in acknowledgment. "Most should look the same, but there are a few that could be tricky. Which is why I asked to join the next gathering expedition."

I looked up from my beer. "They're letting you leave Harborton?"

"With Tantalas… and a guard," she admitted. "Still, it will be nice to smell something other than fish and ocean, even if for just an afternoon."

"Do you think I could come along too?"

Synossians couldn't really wince, but her inner eyelids fluttered. "I can ask, but…"

"But Val won't let it happen," I finished for her.

"In fairness, if we were both outside the walls, we *could* flee."

I sighed. "I'm starting to think my Ideal is some sort of sick joke. Instead of Freedom, maybe I should have chosen Communal Service. If my friends could see me, they would laugh: 'You crossed reality to a world of magic and are doing the exact same thing you did here on Earth?'"

"It is temporary," she reminded me.

"I know. And you were right, anyway; the break *has* been good. For both of us. But—"

She pushed her empty mug away from her. "One more moon."

"I'm sorry?"

"I have prayed on the matter. Should adventurers never come at all, one more moon of service will more than pay our debt."

It was a nice thought, but… "Val is pretty adamant that we have to stay until Erlund recovers."

"Be that as it may. We have much to do. And we cannot accomplish it here."

I lowered my voice, as if anyone could have heard us over the noise of the inn. "You're talking about running?"

"We are free people, Brian Fieldings. There is service owed, yes, and perhaps rightly so, but Val is not the final arbiter of moral justice."

"I'm not sure I *believe* in moral justice."

Miko cocked her scaled head, orange eyes unblinking. "And yet it exists."

"Fair enough." I gave the idea of escape some thought. "With the eastern fields a wasteland and the woods beyond home to the cause of this whole mess, I'm guessing you and Tantalas will be heading west to gather herbs?"

"I believe so, yes."

"Then maybe you can take the opportunity to scout out the path for when we do leave?"

"There is still the matter of the wall and its guarded gates."

"That wall doesn't extend into the ocean." We'd seen that much during the memorial service. "We could always take one of their boats."

She dragged her claws across the tabletop. "I would not add theft to our list of transgressions. Not without dire need."

"I'd say the very future of your people counts. I wasn't suggesting we steal it though… just use it to get to the shore on the other side of the wall."

It was a short enough distance that we could just swim it, but between my experience in the Snake River and my ongoing concerns about what might be living in that ocean, staying dry seemed like the better idea. Especially if we were carrying supplies.

"That could work." Her long tongue darted out to taste the air. "Are you familiar with boats from your dirt planet?"

"You can just call it Earth, you know."

"It's the same thing. That's what makes it so funny."

Every now and then, Miko reminded me that, for all the responsibility heaped upon her white-scaled shoulders, she *was* still young.

"No, I don't know much about boats. The only body of water we had in Midton was the community pool. Which was… basically, a big bath or a manmade lake, except cleaner and filled with chemicals."

Miko's inner eyelids fluttered, but she didn't ask the obvious question of how something could be both clean *and* filled with chemicals. Which was good, as I didn't have an answer.

"Still," I added, "it shouldn't be that hard."

"Then it is settled. One moon to collect more information and pay our debt. And then we will be on our way."

I raised my mug in a silent toast. Maybe it was my Ideal talking, but I liked the sound of that.

"You seldom talk about your… about Earth," Miko said, sometime later. "Do you not miss it?"

"Not really? I mean… I do miss its conveniences. Indoor plumbing. Electricity. The internet."

"You've tried to explain indoor plumbing before, but what are the other things?"

"Light available at the touch of a button. Access to information on a global scale."

"Illumination enchantments and scrying." She nodded. "We have those, though Enchanters were a rare profession back home, and true Seers are an even rarer class."

"That's not…" I let it go. I wasn't qualified to explain electricity, let alone what the internet was and how it worked, and Lomas' strong ale had sapped me of any desire to even try. "Anyway, life on Earth was more convenient in some ways, but I don't know that it was all that much easier."

Miko nodded, not saying anything, her eyes almost glowing in the firelight.

"I miss a few people, but… Kate had already left Midton, and Bug… I know he'll do fine without me."

"Bug?"

"It was a nickname. His parents named him Bartholomew and well… he decided that was never going to stick."

"And Kate? Was she your blood-mother or your nest-mother?"

"Neither, I think? She was my ex. Ex-girlfriend, I mean."

"A mate?"

"Sort of." Apparently, synossians didn't have boyfriends and girlfriends. Good to know. "She left to see the world and get further education. I didn't have that option."

"I see."

I didn't ask if Miko missed the Synossian Primacy; I already knew the answer. As much as we'd both felt… lighter… following the memorial ceremony, there were still nights when I fell asleep to the sounds of the Priestess' quiet weeping. I'd lost three people in my unexpected move to Eos, and two of them were at least still alive to pursue their own dreams. Miko had lost damn near everything.

"We're going to make a new home for your people," I said.

If Miko was confused by the non-sequitur, it didn't show on her face. But then… even after more than a month, I was better at reading her body language than her expressions. Still, she nodded.

"One moon. Let's continue to learn while we are here to improve our odds of success when we depart."

"One moon," I agreed. "Maybe I'll even gain a point in *Spear* by then."

30

T hree things happened over the course of the next few days. First, my sarcastic prediction improbably came true. A few hours after talking with Miko about Earth, I emerged from meditation to a welcome dialogue screen:

```
You have increased the following skills:

Major skills:
Spear [+1]: 11/15

General skills:
Caretaking [+1]: 7/10
Scribing [+1]: 4/10
Meditation [+1]: 4/10
```

I sat in the warehouse's darkness for a short time, just basking in my accomplishment. No teachers and no actual combat, but my amateurish training attempts had still resulted in an increase in *Spear.* Only four more, and I'd be capped for level two.

That exhilaration faded almost as quickly as it had come. It had taken me well over *a month* to gain a single point in one of my Major skills. To reach level two, I needed *nine* more points to cap my two highest-ranked Major skills, and *ten* more points to cap my two highest-ranked Minor skills. At my current rate, that would take more literal years.

That wasn't going to cut it.

The improvements in *Caretaking* and *Scribing* were almost expected by now, the new point in *Meditation* only slightly less so. I did spend significant time every day doing all three, after all. Of those skills, two were foundational skills for professions I wasn't interested in, while the third just made my nightly experience upload a little bit easier.

None of them had a damn thing to do with adventuring or the 'get rich and powerful quick' schemes Miko and I had hatched… but that was life in Harborton. Safety had a price.

The second development came a day later, when Nala arrived for her lessons at Val and Erlund's home bearing a bundle of cloth. With a wide grin, she passed it over, Agnes' payment for the lessons I'd been giving.

"Mama finished last night," she told me.

The cloth was far softer than the sturdy clothes worn by the villagers, a tight weave that, for the first time, spoke to Agnes' true skill as a tailor. I held it up and let the fabric unfurl, revealing robes in the style of Miko's people. Agnes had based the garment on the scraps I'd scavenged from my companion's old set and the cloth was even dyed in colors of crimson and orange. The robes were way too big for me, of course, but looked like they'd fit Miko just fine. She could finally look like a Priestess of Aurea again.

"The Hallorans provided beetroots for the red dye," said Nala, referring to one of the farming families. "The orange dye…"

"Yes?"

"Are you sure you want to know?" She wrinkled her slightly crooked nose. "It's kind of gross."

"Knowledge is power."

"It is?"

"That's what I've heard. You're not going to gross me out."

"Okay. There's a type of worm that lives in the soil on the edge of the western woods. When you collect enough of them and crush them into paste…"

"I get it." Given that the synossians had made a ceremony for drinking beetle feces, I was pretty sure Miko would be okay with dye made from worm guts. "Please tell Agnes she did a beautiful job."

"Mama says the scaled aren't as bad as everyone says. That they're blamed for lots of stuff just because they look different than us."

"It's the way of the world, unfortunately," I said, examining the clothing I'd traded multiple lessons for. "Many worlds, I guess."

"Anyway, I have my slate with me," said the young woman. "I was struggling last night with a few words and was hoping you—"

"Wait… what do you mean by *the scaled?*"

Nala intently studied the floor. "The… b-beasts? People like… like Miko? I mean, some of them probably *are* bad—my friend Ellie says you can't have a bushel of apples without at least a few rotten ones showing up—but that's no reason to be mean to the whole species, right?"

I didn't know who Ellie was, and I wasn't sure what apples had to do with anything, but… "Are you saying there are others who look like Miko here?"

"In Harborton? No, of course not! Maybe not even in Madea, although they seem to have *everything*. Unlike those of us stuck out in the middle of nowhere." She rolled her eyes, and for a moment, we could've been back in Midton, Ohio, enviously discussing Columbus.

"But Grand Duke Willerton is one of the few to offer safe harbor to the scaled, so Mama says our duchy has more than its share."

"And they look like Miko?"

"I mean… I've never seen one before, but… I… I think so?" My impromptu interrogation triggered Nala's ever-present self-consciousness. "Did I… did I say something wrong?"

I dialed it back before she had a stroke. "No, not at all. I'm not upset. I'm just surprised. How long have they been around? The scaled, I mean."

"Wouldn't your friend know better than me?"

"We're not from around here," I reminded her.

"Oh, that's right. Mama says you came from the east, from outside the kingdom." She shook her head, bonnet wiggling atop her messy pile of hair. "Did you know Innkeeper Lomas came from outside the kingdom too?"

"I did, yes."

"He came from the south, not the east. That's where the Waste is, after all." She beamed at me. "Anyway, what were we talking about?"

"How long these other scaled have been around." From the journey Miko had described, we were still cycles away from when the first of her people would reach the Great Wilds' shores.

"Oh… forever, I think? Old Togur says they even had a country of their own a long time ago, before the Kingdom Wars and even the Waste, when the Endless Empire was still a thing. Still, nobody listens to him much." She wrinkled her nose again and adjusted her skirts. "He's drunk *all the time* and even grumpier than Miss Val."

There was a lot to say and even more to ask, but I had lessons to give in payment for Miko's new robes. So, we spent the next glass going over Nala's homework. I corrected a few words she'd either misspelled or misused, and filled in the gaps of the very basic note she was writing. It was apparently intended for her friend, the Ellie I hadn't even known existed a day before, and full of rambling, stream-of-consciousness gossip and jokes. Ellie wouldn't be able to read the note, but Nala assured me she'd happily read it aloud to her friend so everything would be fine.

That leap of logic left me feeling way older than I was. In the end though, it was a good way for her to practice—both writing *and* reading—so I let it go.

Somehow, I made it through the lesson, despite my distraction. I now had *two* gifts for Miko instead of one. First, the robes that Agnes had made on my request, and second, the knowledge that my companion *wasn't* the only synossian here in the Great Wilds. It sounded like some of her people had stayed behind a thousand cycles ago, and while they didn't seem particularly well loved, they had at least managed to survive to this day.

We had allies out there waiting for us… maybe a lot of them.

All we had to do was find them.

And just like that, a dialogue screen that I hadn't seen in a long time popped up, filling my vision:

NEW QUEST: Help Miko Naseri make contact with the native synossians.

[Accept | Decline]

Needless to say, I hit Accept.

○○○

The third event happened two nights later. It was our first time back in the inn in several days. With our newly planned breakout weighing heavily on our minds, we were trying to save up as much of Miko's pay as possible ahead of time.

Still, she and Tantalas had just returned from their herb hunting expedition, and it had gone well enough that he'd given her a bonus of four copper bits. Two of those went into her savings, and the other two paid for bowls of stew for each of us.

Currency was one more thing we had gotten a handle on. In the Kingdom of Elthor, bits were the lowest and most common denomination. Ten bits made a plug, ten plugs made a tower, and ten towers made a crown. The first two were copper and the third silver. Crowns, on the other hand, were gold, although it was rare that anyone outside the nobility or the most powerful merchant houses had ever even seen one. According to Erlund's journal, Harborton's charter had cost eight towers and represented almost the entirety of the fortune that he and Val had smuggled out of fallen Hybellus.

I didn't know how much of that fortune had been theirs to begin with, and how much had been *rescued* along the way, and the journal made a point not to say.

Over the past moon, Miko had saved up fifteen bits, the equivalent of a plug and a half. By village standards, it was a *lot* of coin, testament to both Tantalas' generosity and the money-producing potential of the Herbalist profession.

With so much of Harborton's day-to-day trade working off barter, most of that coin had come from Tantalas' own stores. However, he would more than replenish those funds once Merchant Jessup arrived, by selling both his own wares and the goods he'd received in trade from the villagers.

It was easy to see why the Herbalist had a place on the council.

So far, I had made a grand total of *no* money, testament to Val's lack of generosity, but Miko's robes would have cost a fair bit in coin, so I felt like I was at least contributing something. And while the

Priestess had chosen to wear those robes only on special occasions—like when we went to the inn—the clear comfort she took in having something that reminded her of home was gratifying.

There were only two of us, yeah, but we were a team working toward a common goal, and that didn't suck.

I was sopping up the last of my stew with a piece of bread that Lomas had slipped me in secret when the front door creaked open. There was nothing unusual about that; people came and went throughout the night according to schedules that only they knew. What was different this time was *who* came through the open door.

Or maybe *what?*

The man was so tall he had to stoop to pass under the header and he was gaunt in a way that seemed unnatural. His features were curiously elongated, human-ish but not quite human, and his skin was not merely pale but pure white. His clothing was dusty and travel-worn but still nicer than anything in the village other than Miko's new robe. A sheathed sword, axe, and several daggers dangled from the belt around his waist, and a larger weapon poked up from behind his shoulder, wrapped in some kind of shroud.

Several feet away, Lomas sucked in a breath. "Dust take me," he muttered in the words of stone and wind.

"What is he?" I asked him, speaking in kind.

"Reaver," he murmured back. "They are giant spawn. Raiders from the south, dwelling in the mountains and steppes beyond the Waste. Though this one," he added, scanning the stranger a second time, "has seen better days. First reaver I've ever seen who looks like he could be blown over by a stiff breeze."

The newcomer seemed oblivious to the shock his appearance had caused. He glanced around, located the bar, and made his way over, long strides eating up the space in a handful of steps.

Lomas was there to meet him. "Welcome," he said, switching back to Trade, his mannerisms as gruff as ever for all that the reaver was twice his size. "What can I do for you?"

"Food. Drink." The man's voice was empty and his words economical, far from the savage snarl I'd have expected from Lomas' brief description.

"One bit for stew, another for ale. Two if you want some of my recently brewed special reserve."

"Water?"

Lomas barely hid his scowl. "Water's free, but you'll have to fill it yourself from yon barrel." The innkeeper nodded to the large cask by the fireplace.

"Three stews, one water, one ale." The big man cocked his head, and for the first time, some vague hint of emotion colored his words. "And one special reserve."

"That'll be six bits." Just like that, Lomas was all smiles again, his concrete grey teeth not putting the other man off at all.

The thunk of the coin the reaver placed on the counter spoke of its weight even before I saw it and as he pulled his overly long fingers away, I knew I was seeing my very first copper plug. It looked… a lot like the copper bits, to be honest, just fatter.

"Six for meal," explained the newcomer. "One for peace between our ancestors, dunsman."

For the first time since I'd met him, Lomas seemed at a loss for words. Still, the plug disappeared from the bar like magic, replaced by three bits, the bowls of stew, and three mugs, one empty, one full, and one reeking of something I could smell from a half-dozen feet away.

"Are ya here with Merchant Jessup, mayhap?" asked one of the men sitting at the crafters table.

"Yes. Arrived with wagons half-glass ago."

That set off a commotion as customers left on the spot, hurrying out into the night to take care of whatever last-minute business they had to finish before trading with Jessup. Lomas' scowl returned and grew with every departure.

The villagers who remained were almost inevitably the ones who'd been drinking for hours already.

"Never seen anyone so tall before," one farmer said to his drinking partner in a whisper that carried through the inn.

"That there's a reaver, Kres," replied the other, just as drunkenly. "Terrors of the southern steppes, or so they say."

"How come I never heard of 'em then?"

"Cause you're dumber than that herd beast you call a phloxl," said a third man.

"Nah," said the second man. "It's 'cause they don't dare come up past the Waste. They know there's Kingdom bronze waitin' for 'em here and that *our* men don't scare so easy."

"That's enough out of you, Tyrus," said Lomas, black eyes darting from the stranger at his bar to the tableful of drunk farmers. "Best get home to your wife while the moons are still in the sky. The morning waits on no man."

Tyrus burped, swaying back and forth as he rose to his feet. He patted his buddy, Kres, on his shoulder and turned to go, then stopped.

"What I can't figure out," he said, turning back and staggering over to the bar, "is why yer okay with strangers bringing their arms into yer place of business, Lomas. First the little one and his oversized spear, now this pillar of skin and bone? Don't sit right with me."

"What I allow in my inn is my decision and mine alone." All geniality had disappeared from the innkeeper's voice, and for the first time, I felt it: an aura of weight and pressure emanating from his squat form.

Lomas, much like Riok, Valestia, and Erlund, was ranked.

Even drunk, Tyrus bent under that pressure. His voice broke, becoming a whine. "Come on, Lomas! A rusty spear is one thing, gods know, but the reaver has a whole armory around his waist. Not to mention *this* monster on his back."

Tyrus reached for the wrapped weapon and froze, his hand somehow already trapped in the reaver's oversized grip. Despite the half-giant's frail build, he easily held the husky farmer in place, a predator pinning its much smaller prey.

"Tempest is my burden to carry, friend. Be grateful that it is not yours."

"What?" asked a rapidly sobering Tyrus, but it was the reaver's sudden eloquence and the confused look on Lomas' face that told me the stranger had spoken in a language neither villager understood.

My *Speaker of Tongues* trait remained undefeated.

"He said 'don't touch the stick or you'll make him angry', dirt farmer," drawled a laconic voice I'd never heard before. It came from the other side of the inn, where two more strangers had just entered. The speaker, wearing leathers made grey by dust and dirt, was a woman, with skin as jet black as her hair, the red beads in her braids the only color to be found other than her eyes.

Behind her was a slim figure in a mask and cowl, their clothing a grey that blended easily with the dust. A man's voice, dry and creaky, emerged from beneath the mask.

"I keep telling you, lass, you can't just go around calling everyone farmers. It's not polite."

"I *am* a farmer," said a very confused Tyrus, still unable to move his arm.

"Oh." The masked man shrugged and headed for an empty table. "Carry on then."

"If your friend—" started Lomas.

"Skaal," said the woman.

"If *Skaal* would release Tyrus, I do believe yon farmer has learned his lesson about touching other people's property."

"We'll get him home," said the unnamed third villager, standing with the still-drunk Kres. "Back to his doting wife who, pray to the gods, never hears *this* particular tale."

Given all I knew of small-town life, that prayer had as much chance of being answered as… well… any of mine ever had back on Earth.

"I may have… uh… had a bit too much to drink," said Tyrus, now undeniably more sober than he had been even a minute earlier. "No harm intended."

"Is good," said Skaal in Trade, letting go of the man's arm and patting his shoulder. "Go in peace."

The three farmers made their way out of the inn. As the reaver carried his purchased food and mugs over to the table that the woman and masked man had claimed, I buried my minor irritation that Tyrus had referred to me as *the little one.*

Drunks can sober up.

Idiots can find education.

But height… height doesn't change.

○○○

"Could you feel that?" Miko lowered her voice, adjusting to the reduced volume of the nearly empty inn. "I had no idea that Lomas was a ranked Aspirant all this time."

"Val and Erlund are too. Apparently, the Buried aren't the only ones who know how to hide their auras."

She shook her head. "That reaver—Skaal, did they say?—didn't even flinch. Does that make *him* ranked as well?"

We traded glances and I now knew her well enough to identify concern in the way the scaled ridges around her eyes tightened. Riok had been one of a handful of ranked Aspirants in the entire Synossian Primacy. Meanwhile, we were in some backwater village and had already run into at least *three* such people. Maybe more.

"I'm starting to understand why your people fled the Great Wilds," I told her.

"And *I'm* starting to wonder just what we lost in doing so." Her inner eyelids flickered shut. "First, you tell me that some of my people remain on this continent, and now this?"

"A thousand cycles is a really long time, Miko. Between that and the nature of your ancestors' ocean crossing, it's not *too* surprising that some things would be forgotten."

"I think you are being overly generous. In our time on Issandryl, we thought ourselves the lords of our domain, and yet the meanest village on this forsaken continent holds strength to rival Riok's claw and more. How much has our arrogance cost us?"

"Riok asked a similar question before Whitehall."

"Truly?"

"The Buried had made him realize there were levels far beyond twenty… and probably more than just one rank as well. But he seemed to think it was the centuries of peace that had weaned your people away from constant advancement."

"Is apathy better or worse than arrogance?"

"I… don't know?"

Miko gave my reply more consideration than it deserved. Eventually, she nodded. "Before I was called to Aurea's service, one of the first lessons we were taught as academics was that learning never ends. There is clearly far more to the Framework than my people understood or have conveyed, but that is just another opportunity to expand my knowledge."

It was a distinctly Miko way of looking at things. I was pretty sure she would've been on the honor roll back at Jefferson High.

Still, she wasn't wrong.

"The more we know, the stronger we can get," I added.

"And the stronger we are, the better we can prepare for my people's return." She glanced at the table of strangers. "If these are the adventurers Valestia requested, our time in Harborton may at last be coming to an end."

"Maybe." The reaver was calmly drinking from his mug—the one filled with water, I couldn't help but note—but his companions were arguing, the woman in leather running roughshod over the masked man's careful rebuttals. "They don't seem thrilled though."

"Can you tell what they are saying? Between the language barrier and the other noise, I can at best grasp one word out of five."

"Not from here." I gathered our empty bowls. Normally, Halletia would come by to clear the table, but if I took them back to the kitchen myself, I'd walk right past the adventurers' table. "I'll be right back."

I took my time, and Miko was practically vibrating with impatience by the time I settled into my chair again.

"What did you hear? Are they not going to take the mission?"

"The guy in the mask is worried. Apparently, he's heard of the region they'll have to reach to retrieve the nilwort, and he's not confident in their ability to do so."

All the air went out of Miko. "It's that dangerous?"

"Yeah." I let the moment build and then grinned. "But only because they don't have a healer."

Miko's eyes locked onto mine and rows of sharp teeth flashed in the terrifying synossian smile.

"Oh."

"Exactly."

31-Interlude

The problem, thought Lace, was that Mordecai was a pompous ass. Worse, he was a pompous ass because he was so frequently right. Convincing him that this was *not* one of those times was like trying to persuade him to pursue water magic instead of fire.

It just wasn't happening.

On the other hand, it had taken a full seven-day to reach this nothing little town, and guard work for Merchant Jessup had barely covered their expenses. A return trip to Madea would exhaust their funds entirely and leave them right back where they had begun, fighting for the scraps the larger adventuring companies didn't deem worth their time.

They needed the mayor's promised coin badly. They needed her letter of recommendation even more. If that meant going into certain danger without a healer, then so be it. They were adventurers, damn it, not peace-loving dirt farmers!

As if her angry thoughts had summoned him, one of the villagers approached their table, this one wearing a badly fitting gray shirt and trousers. No shoes, which said all that needed to be said about Harborton, as far as she was concerned.

He was almost comically small, and slight in a way that suggested a lifetime of light labor, but his face was well-formed beneath a mop of shaggy hair and an equally shaggy beard. A half-span of additional height, broader shoulders, and significantly more muscle all over, and Lace might have debated taking him captive had her clan ever raided as far north as Harborton.

She frowned at the thought. The hells with the clan. The hells with all of them.

"What can we do for you, lad?" asked Mordecai.

"My name is Brian," he replied in a voice that made it clear he was an adult for all his lack of height, "and I couldn't help but overhear your… discussion."

Mordecai just nodded, while Skaal remained… well… Skaal. As imperturbable as a mountain and half as talkative. But Lace was tired and she was dirty and the innkeeper's special reserve was the first thing she'd found in ages that merited her full attention. The last thing she needed was another distraction.

"Save the con for those whose minds move slower than your tongue, villager. We're not interested."

If this Brian took offense, he did a great job at hiding it. He simply nodded, eyes moving from Lace to Mordecai and then finally landing on Skaal.

"Fair enough," he said. "My Priestess friend and I wish you luck in retrieving the nilwort."

He was walking away when Mordecai spoke.

"Did you say *Priestess*, lad?"

When he turned back, Brian's smile was wide and friendly, and there wasn't a trace of smugness to be found, no matter how hard Lace looked for it.

"I did. Miko is a Priestess of Aurea, goddess of sunlight, fire, and…" He smiled again. "…healing."

Well, damn.

"Let's say we are interested in knowing more," said Lace. "Where can we find your... friend?"

"She's seated over there wearing the colors of her goddess."

Mordecai glanced over and sucked in his breath. "A scaled?"

The stranger's face went hard and for the first time, he looked like something other than a half-grown man playing dress-up. "Is that going to be a problem?"

"I don't see why it would be," answered Lace. The scaled weren't a thing south of the Waste and she had yet to get an adequate explanation of why they were so reviled here in the north. "Assuming she truly is what you say she is and wants to join."

"We *both* want to join."

Lace gave him a second look and found herself just as unimpressed as she had been the first time.

"She's a healer. What do *you* do?"

"I watch her back." After a moment of silence, he coughed. "And serve as interpreter."

Which was about as useful as extra testicles on a phloxl when it came to retrieving the nilwort.

"We're a package deal," added Brian. "Take it or leave it."

For an interpreter, he had an odd turn of phrase. But so did a lot of the people she and Skaal had encountered in the Kingdom of Elthor. This was what happened when a nation chose to arm itself with words instead of weapons.

"I think we should—" began Mordecai.

"Speak on it as a group," interjected Lace, with a significant glance at the spellcaster. "Alone."

Brian nodded again, almost as unflappable as the mountain guzzling water next to her. "You know where to find us."

"Ten strides away? Yes, I think we'll manage."

She watched him leave, waited until he had settled next to the scaled woman in robes, and then turned to her companions. When she spoke, it was in Gorash, as much to irritate Mordecai as to keep their conversation private. The man prided himself on his education but was still learning the communal language of the south.

"Thoughts?" she asked.

"We need a healer," said Mordecai.

"That Priestess isn't even Tin." She glanced at Skaal and got a small nod of confirmation. "Neither of them are."

"True. They both seem as green as spring's first blossom. I suspect we'll be the ones doing most of the killing, but that's hardly new. Even limited heals will keep us alive long after our medical supplies have run out."

Lace frowned. "What medical supplies?"

"Exactly my point. We ran through them like water during last moon's failed assault."

He wasn't wrong, but Lace scowled anyway. It had been the perfect mission right until everything had gone horribly wrong. If it hadn't been for Skaal, their stories would have ended then and there.

"So, you're a yes?"

"I'm a *this is the only way you'll convince me to go at all.*" Mordecai moved his mask aside just enough to take a sip of ale. "But yes."

"Skaal?"

"I am curious about the spear."

"What?"

The reaver nodded to where the two would-be adventurers were seated. Leaning against the wall behind them was a black spear crafted entirely from metal and unmistakably tarnished.

"The spear. It's unusual."

Lace swallowed a particularly inventive oath. "We're not talking about weapons, old man. We're talking about the people who will be wielding them."

"We need to complete this mission," said the reaver. "If that means bringing the Priestess, then so be it."

"And the boy?"

"Is a man, regardless of his stature."

"Not what I was getting at."

"Yet it remains true." Skaal's pale eyes twinkled, even as his face remained carved ivory. "And if he goes where she does, I would say our choice is already made for us."

Exactly as the villager had intended. Lace buried her frustration deep inside, where it had far too much company. She was supposed to set traps, not walk into them.

"I'm not convinced," she said, "but I'm also not looking to miss out on another reward. Let's bring them over."

She waved to the boy—to Brian—and his Priestess, but the former was already off his stool and coming over, almost as if he'd known their decision as soon as they did. The scaled was on his heels, towering over her human companion, the firelight painting her white scales in the same hues as her robes. She tapped her clawed fingers together and bowed, the movement surprisingly graceful.

"This one is Miko Nesari," she said in halting Trade. "We greet."

Okay, so maybe the Priestess *did* need an interpreter.

"I go by Lace. The big one is Skaal, as you no doubt heard. Don't ask him for the rest of his names or we'll be here long after the moons have set. Wearing the mask is our spell weaver, Mordecai. Don't ask him anything at all, or we'll be here a full seven-day."

She wasn't sure how much of that Miko had gotten, but the scaled nodded and pulled out a stool next to Brian.

"As you clearly already know," Lace continued, spearing Brian with a glare, "we *are* in need of a healer. However, we have questions that must be answered before we can agree to take you on as provisional members of the party."

Provisional was a good word. She'd stolen it from the Adventurer's Guild, which used a thousand words where only a few would do.

"Of course," said Brian. "Ask away."

"Are either of you members of the guild?"

"The *Adventurer's* Guild?"

Gods. She needed another mug of the innkeeper's special brew. "That would be the one, yes."

He shook his head. "We're new to the Kingdom of Elthor. To the whole region, really."

"You're not southerners."

"No. We came from the east."

Mordecai coughed. "Wait, are *you* the two who caused this whole mess in the first place?"

Skaal, who had skipped the meeting with the village's harridan of a mayor, turned to the caster for an explanation, but Lace beat Mordecai to it.

"Two strangers passed through the eastern forest and roused the great serpent who lairs at its heart. It was in driving away that creature that the mayor's brother was struck down. Which you would have known," she added in Gorash, "if you had come with us instead of heading straight for the inn."

"And yet I came straight to the inn and now know the tale anyway," he replied in kind.

If she didn't owe him literally everything, Lace would have stabbed Skaal in his sleep a long, long time ago. Hells, she was still sorely tempted, even now.

Brian's eyes had darted between the two, almost like he was attempting to follow their conversation, but when he spoke, it was to answer Mordecai's question.

"That was us, although we didn't *cause* the issue, really. We were just in the wrong place at the wrong time."

"And now you want to make it right?" asked Mordecai.

Lace tried not to roll her eyes. The man had read far too many books at that school of his and come away with a titan-sized soft spot for lost causes.

"Yes. Although we're also hoping to find allies for the future. We aren't members of the guild, but we intend to join as soon as we can. And while we're new to adventuring, Miko did serve in the military before this."

"What about you?" asked Lace.

"I… served."

There was something he wasn't saying, but then, she had no intention of telling *her* life story either. Not without significantly more ale and the warmth of a few good kills pumping through her veins.

"Neither of you are Tin." She phrased it as a statement of fact, leaning heavily on Skaal's confirmation. "And I'm confident in saying you're not Copper or Iron either. So I'm going to do something that's considered the height of rudeness in these lands."

Mordecai's sigh was almost lost behind his mask.

"I'm going to ask your levels and classes," Lace continued.

Brian and Miko traded looks.

"You'll keep the information secret?"

"I swear so on the nine rosy breasts of the Night Hag herself."

Both strangers swallowed and Brian went a little bit pale. Apparently, Hashoggath was every bit as feared in *their* homeland as she was in the north.

The world truly had gone soft.

For a few seconds, the two traded glances, as if speaking directly into each other's brains, and then the scaled woman nodded. Brian turned back to Lace.

"Miko is a Priestess of Aurea, as I already told you."

"And her level?"

"Four, although she is approaching level five."

Mordecai had himself a bit of a coughing fit. When he was done, his voice was thin and reedy.

"Level *four*? She has only two techniques! Are either of them even heals?"

"I have *Minor Healing* and *Flare*," said the scaled, apparently just fluent enough to reply.

"That's…" The Mage sighed. "Better than *nothing*, I suppose. If only just." He tugged his mask partly aside and took another long swig of ale.

"And you?" Lace asked Brian.

"I'm a Warrior."

The spear had kind of given that away, so Lace just waited.

"And I'm level two."

Half the ale Mordecai had just sipped came right back up, drenching his cloth mask.

It was the funniest thing Lace had seen since leaving Madea.

"I just need to get my skills up," said Brian defensively. "Once I do, I'll be ready to level."

For some reason, the scaled gave him a sharp look.

"A level two and a level four want to explore a region that anyone below Copper will find a challenge." Lace shook her head, braids swaying. "We would have to be mad to take you on."

"Or desperate," added Skaal in Gorash.

"Or that," she replied in kind before switching back to Trade. "We leave in the morning. Do you have anything that must be done before then?"

"You… could say that," said Brian.

32

"A bsolutely not," said Valestia, her voice a hiss that would have put the serpent Nikkaali to shame. "Your service is not over until my brother is cured. That was the deal, and the deal has not changed."

A single candle was all that lit the entry room. The older woman had been clearly readying for bed when I knocked on her door. She had a heavy coat on over her sleepshirt, softening her usual rail-thin lines, but there was nothing but steel in her voice.

"I understand," I said, trying to find the right words, "but the adventurers you summoned aren't going anywhere without a healer, and Miko is the only healer around. Can Erlund afford to wait another few moons for a second adventuring party to answer your call?"

She scowled. "That explains the beast's inclusion. It does not explain yours."

"She's my friend. I go where she does."

"Then we are at an impasse. You have duties here."

I held back my sigh. This had seemed simpler back at the inn. Sweet-talk our way into joining the adventurers, then turn around and parlay *their* acceptance into permission from Valestia. That first step had gone well—surprisingly so—but the second was proving difficult.

 CHRIS TULLBANE

"You don't really need me," I tried again. "Tantalas can look after Erlund while I am away. Or Nala, even… she's certainly watched me take care of him enough during our lessons. Meanwhile, I'm the key to Miko joining the adventurers… and she's the key to your brother getting his cure."

"I could simply order her to go."

"Forcing someone who isn't even Tin into a region that anyone below Copper would find a challenge?" I didn't really understand what any of the words I was saying meant, but they'd seemed important to Lace. "With respect, you don't get to do that."

"Yet you both would choose to go there on your own?"

"If accompanied by Lace and the others? Yeah."

"Why?"

I frowned in confusion. "Because Erlund needs the nilwort?"

"I see."

Honesty forced me to continue. "And frankly, we need the experience. Harborton is just the first stop in our journey and we're going to have to keep growing as we go."

"You would walk the path of an Aspirant." Most of the fire had gone out of Valestia's voice. She seemed older than ever and tired.

"We don't have much choice in the matter, but yes."

"And what assurances do I have that you and your—you and Miko—will not abandon the party as soon as you have passed beyond Harborton's walls?"

"Is my word not good enough?"

Her scowl was my only answer.

"You trust me with your comatose brother every day, Valestia. Maybe you should also trust that I don't want him to wither away and die?"

"How can I?"

"I…"

"Is that what happened to your last patient?"

It felt like she'd just punched me in the chest. I swallowed, and then when that didn't help, swallowed again. "Yes."

"And what were they to you?"

"*He* was my father."

"Oh."

I stood there in silence, unsure of what to say. I'd said my goodbyes to my dad, twice, and truly felt like I'd made my peace with his death, but even so…

"It was recent?" asked Valestia, voice quiet.

"A few seven-days before we came to Harborton." I shook my head. "I took care of him for yea—for cycles, unable to do anything but watch him degrade. If there had been a cure available, I would have paid anything, done anything, promised anything…"

I stopped and shrugged. "Erlund has something my father never did, a chance at recovery. Please believe me when I say I want to see that happen."

She studied me for a long while, the candle's flame leaving most of her face in shadows. Finally, she nodded.

"The five of you will come here in the morning. I would have words with all of you before you depart."

And just like that, I was out in Harborton's quiet streets again, the sky above me lit by a thousand stars and the slivers of two moons. I hoisted my spear and made my way back to the warehouse dorm, passing dark houses and closed storefronts along the way.

Are you sure you know what you're doing? asked the voice in my head.

I didn't answer. We needed money, we needed power, and we needed connections. This was our best shot at all three, the best shot we'd get for at least another moon. And if I could help cure a dying man in the process…

I didn't see how we had any other choice.

That will be cold comfort when your corpse is rotting in some cave system far below ground.

For some reason, the thought made me laugh.

Death is waiting, I told the voice. *I've known that since I was twelve. Freedom isn't about living forever; it's about living the life you want.*

I guess we'll see how that works out.

I rolled my eyes and stepped into the darkened warehouse where Miko was waiting for me. My inner voice always had to have the last word.

It kind of reminded me of Shan that way.

○○○

The next morning, Miko and I made our way to the inn to meet the others. I was surprised to find the adventurers already up, washed, dressed, and looking significantly more imposing in the daylight.

Lace was in black once again, but the beads in her hair were gone, braids pulled back into a thick knot at the base of her skull. Her silver eyes glimmered against skin that was a true black rather than the shades of brown we had on Earth. Mordecai wore a new mask, this one a darker grey, while Skaal looked unchanged; far too thin for his height, his over-long face hollow and gaunt. The morning sun picked out thin scars across his bone white face that the inn's shadows had hidden. Once again, he had a small armory around his waist, and the larger weapon—*Tempest,* he'd called it—swaddled in cloth and strapped to his back.

"The mayor has asked that we stop by her house before leaving," I told them.

"Is that where you stored your supplies?" asked Lace. Each of the adventurers had a full pack slung across their shoulders, Skaal's so large it seemed a miracle he was able to carry it.

"Supplies?" asked Miko.

"Shelter, food, extra clothing and… shoes?" she added, glancing at my bare and callused feet. "This will not be a pleasure hike."

Mordecai sniffed, his expression still hidden behind the mask. "As if there were such a thing."

I glanced at Miko. She had her clothes on under the robes I had bought her, along with the small pouch that contained our coin and the remainder of her possessions. I only had Riok's spear and the clothes on my back. For some reason, it hadn't occurred to either of us that we'd need more, like backpacks and a tent, or rations and extra gear.

"We'll pick supplies up after speaking with Valestia," I said, already picturing our small pile of bits dwindling to nothing. "We're not going to slow you down."

"You will *unquestionably* slow us down, lad," said Mordecai, "but I believe *Minor Healing* to be worth the tradeoff."

Lace seemed less convinced, but she just shrugged.

Valestia was waiting in front of her house, outfitted more nicely than I'd ever seen her in a deep green dress with black embroidery. She held a scroll in her hand—one that I *hadn't* worked on—but it was the two packs at her feet that surprised me. They were smaller than those the adventurers carried, but well made, leather exteriors bulging with whatever had been stashed inside. And next to one of those packs was something that made me want to cry.

A pair of boots.

Harborton's leader addressed Lace first, holding out the scroll. "Your copy of the commission, including both the terms of the mission and the rewards we agreed upon. Three sprigs of nilwort and a finger of shademoss, each to be delivered within six days of the former's harvesting, that they may be fashioned into the required elixir. In exchange, you will earn fifteen plugs and a signed letter of recommendation to the contacts we still have in Madea and Trynfall."

There was an undeniable eagerness to the way Lace snatched the scroll out of Valestia's hand, but the dark-skinned woman was careful as she added it to her pack. By the time she was done, Valestia had turned to me.

"For more than a moon, you and your *companion* have worked in Harborton to repay your debt, and while *many* would say that debt stands until my brother is cured, the village council believes your efforts merit recognition. In lieu of coin we do not have," she continued, ignoring both the money Tantalas had been giving Miko *and* the veritable fortune Lace and the others would be receiving, "we have pooled our resources to provide you with supplies, that you may leave our village with more than you arrived carrying. Put them to good use, first in assisting these adventurers with their mission, and then in taking your own steps along the path of an Aspirant."

"I don't know what to say," I managed. "I didn't expect this."

"I was outvoted," she said simply.

That made a little bit more sense.

"Thank you," said Miko in perfectly respectable Trade. She stepped forward and dropped into a low bow. "Your faith is be rewarded."

Valestia didn't seem to know how to take that, but she returned Miko's bow with a nod. "Fare well on your mission," she eventually said, speaking to the four of us who weren't scaled. "I expect to see you again before the next moon."

Which gave us roughly eighteen days to find the nilwort *and* shademoss and bring both back to Harborton.

"The boots are yours, Brian Fieldings. Cobbler Relsson swears they will fit. Take it up with him if they do not. Now go," she added. "I have work to do."

Without another word, she walked down the road, leaving the packs and my new boots behind.

"Charming woman," said Mordecai.

"She has her moments." I passed one heavy pack to Miko and took the other for myself.

"Lad, if you are going to travel with us, you will have to learn to recognize and appreciate sarcasm when you hear it."

I nodded absently, pulling on my new boots. I hadn't met the cobbler, but he did good work: the boots fit as well as anything I'd had back on Earth. The leather was well-stitched, and the soles were supple while still thick enough to protect my feet from the sort of damage they'd taken on the journey to Harborton.

"How long does it take to make a pair of boots?" I asked.

"For a high-level Cobbler? A glass, at most, unless they are crafting something special," said Mordecai. "But anyone who would live in a place like *this* probably requires a day or two at a minimum."

Which meant the boots had been made for me *before* the adventurers arrived. And given that Cobblers, much like Tailors and Innkeepers, didn't work for free, I could guess who had shouldered that cost on my behalf.

Valestia really *did* have her moments.

ooo

As small as Harborton was, it only took a few minutes to reach the eastern gate, through which Miko and I had first entered the village what felt like years earlier. Each of the two gates had one guard on duty and this one couldn't quite decide whether to salute or bow to the adventurers with us. Eventually, he gave up entirely, and just pulled the gate open.

"Fortune to you all," he said, mopping sweat from his uncovered head. "Me and the others on duty will keep an eye out for your return."

"Rest assured," said Mordecai, "the deed is already as good as done. You have an Adept of the Crimson Needle on the case!"

"Uhm… that's… great?" asked the guard.

Mordecai seemed put out by the lack of adulation, but we were already being waved through. Lace took the lead, followed by Skaal and the spellcaster. Miko was next, but as I started to follow behind, I heard someone calling my name, and the sound of bare feet slapping against dirt. I turned to find a young woman tearing her way down the road towards us.

"Nala? What are you doing here?"

"I heard… that you… were leaving." She was breathing heavily, like she'd just run all the way from her mother's shop. In place of the pretty but modest dress and bonnet she wore to class, she had on work clothes. In her hands, she held another wrapped bundle, this one smaller than the one that had contained Miko's robes. "Is it true?"

"It is, but we'll be back soon," I said, hoping it was true. "I'm sorry about our lessons. Things happened quickly."

"It's fine. I have my slate and your exercises to practice. But…" She shifted from foot to foot, suddenly finding the dirt particularly fascinating.

"But what?"

"Imadethisforyou. It'snotmuchbutIreallyhopeyoulikeit," she said, all in one breath, throwing me the bundle in her arms. I was still trying to parse her words when she turned about and fled, running back down the road.

My companions had stopped to take in the scene, their expressions ranging from bemused to concerned.

"I know we're in the country and all that, but she's too young for you, lad," said Mordecai.

"What?"

"I come from a storied line of heartbreakers myself and I must tell you: there *are* boundaries."

"She's like five cycles younger than me, Mordecai."

"Precisely my point."

"Brian teach her letters," said Miko in her broken Trade.

"Ah. Then it's just a schoolgirl crush? Fair enough. You'll want to let her down easy when we make it back, lad. To an adventurer, friendly harbors are almost as precious as silver."

"She's not—" I sighed, taking off my pack and slipping Nala's gift inside without unwrapping it. The bundle had barely weighed anything at all, but the pack somehow still felt heavier when I pulled it up onto my shoulders. "Whatever. Let's just go."

"Well done, Mordecai," said Lace, in the odd language she and the others used when they didn't want Miko or me to understand. "We haven't even left yet and you're already irritating our new recruits."

"One must always make the proper stand where propriety is concerned, lass. It is but one of the many valuable lessons we were taught in—"

"Save it for the road," she said, this time in Trade. "We have leagues to travel before night falls."

By the time the gate shut behind us, we had turned south, paralleling Harborton's exterior wall. A few hundred yards away, the Snake River carried its water north to the ocean, seemingly untouched by all that had happened just a moon earlier. The fields were a different matter entirely. Where once had been fertile soil and sunbaked sprouts, there was now just cracked earth and dust.

"This is a place of death," muttered Lace.

"Worse," said Skaal, striding alongside the smaller woman. "Emptiness."

"We arrived from the west," Lace told Miko and me, spinning around to walk backwards so she could face us. "There, the land between your village wall and the woods was practically overrun with growing crops. But this… is this where the village fought the serpent?"

"Yeah. And where Valestia's brother released an echo of what they called the—"

"We should not speak of it here," interrupted Mordecai. "I would put a full day's distance between us and this place ere anyone speak its name."

His obvious discomfort, even behind the mask, was enough to restore Lace's good humor. With a grin, she bowed in his direction, still walking backwards as easily as if she had eyes in the back of her head. "As you wish, mighty Mordecai. As you wish."

If the masked man heard the gentle mockery in her voice, he chose not to respond. Instead, he tugged his cowl down more closely around his head, hunched his thin shoulders, and hurried onward, doing all he could to ignore the desolation to our left.

It didn't take long to leave the stricken area behind. We passed beyond the southern perimeter of Harborton's wall soon after. Vegetation made its return, followed almost inevitably by bugs—small gnat-like things that buzzed about in clouds as we marched through. Another few minutes of walking and the foreboding silence was broken by distant bird song and the occasional animal cry, although both came from the woods to our left and right.

We followed the river south, the terrain getting steeper as we went. Ahead of us, the two forests crept towards one another until they became a single expanse of trees.

"We'll parallel the river for a few days' travel into the woods," said Lace, speaking for the first time in almost an hour. "Eventually, we'll have to find a crossing and head east, but we should be able to stay well out of the territory of anything as dangerous as your serpent king."

I didn't like Nikkaali being *our* serpent king, but let it pass. "You have a specific destination in mind then? All Valestia told us was that nilwort grows deep underground to the south."

"We have a map, purchased in Madea," said Lace. "Someone reported a system of caves to the south and just a day's walk east of the river. We'll look for the nilwort there first."

"And the shademoss?"

"Stays fresh far longer than the other herb," said Mordecai, "when properly harvested. I'm not an Herbalist, but I should be able to figure out how to preserve it if we come across any early."

"I have *Herbalism* skill," said Miko, joining the conversation. "And single rank in *Gathering*."

"And just like that, you have become my favorite person in this party," said Mordecai, conveniently ignoring his own reaction to her race the previous night. "After retrieving the nilwort, we'll see if we can find some rare harvests to supplement our income, yes?"

Miko looked to me and switched to the High Tongue. "He wants my help?"

"To gather herbs that can be sold for a profit," I explained.

"Oh." She turned back to Mordecai, swapping back to Trade. "Yes. I help."

"For a share of the profit on any sales, of course," I added.

"What were you, a merchant in your last life?" muttered Mordecai in a language that was neither Trade nor the secret unnamed language the party used. He beamed a wide smile at both of us as he continued in Trade. "Of course! I would never have dreamed of suggesting otherwise."

Up ahead of us, Skaal grunted.

Book 3: Warrior

> "*We do not rend the evening sky,*
> *cannot speak with the servants of the void,*
> *or harness the energies of creation.*
>
> *We march, we fight, we die…*
> *weapons in hand until the end,*
>
> *and on our shoulders rest*
> *the pillars of civilization.*"
>
> -Creed of the Swordbearers of Lost Hybellus

33

By the time we stopped for the night, still a good hour or so from the southern forest, I was a sweaty mess. My beard itched, my hair was plastered to my skull, and my pack felt like it was stuffed with rocks instead of supplies. Riok's spear had gone from a weapon in my hands to a walking stick for me to lean on, and I didn't even have the energy to feel bad about that fact. Eos' longer days made for correspondingly longer hikes.

Miko wasn't much better off, though she bore it with her usual stoicism. Only the hunch of her shoulders and the tightening of the ridge of scales around her eyes gave clues to her condition.

Of our remaining three companions, Mordecai was the only one who looked as tired as we were. Lace could have been out on that pleasure hike she'd sworn this wouldn't be, still full of energy and breathing lightly. And Skaal, despite perpetually looking like he might keel over if someone sneezed in his direction, barely seemed to be breathing at all, entirely unaffected by the day's travel.

"We'll stop here. Skaal will secure the camp," announced Lace. "Mordecai, help the greenhorns with their tents and supplies. I'm going to scout along the forest's edge."

Skaal stiffened and turned to her, but she waved off whatever protest he'd been intending to make.

"I'll be fine," she promised. "And swift and silent aren't exactly your watchwords." She nodded to Mordecai. "Hold off on a fire until I'm back and night has truly fallen. We don't need the smoke attracting attention if there's anything intelligent in the area."

Just like that, she was gone, vanishing into the gathering dusk at a speed that far outpaced ours, her quiet steps a marked contrast to the noise the party had made traveling.

"What did she mean by anything intelligent?" I asked Mordecai. So far, all we'd seen were bugs and the occasional bird, although Skaal had pointed out a variety of animal tracks to Lace as we walked.

"Out here? Could be anything from scarsworn to blighted to everyday bandits." He reached under his mask to scratch his face. "Further east, there are colonies of the treefolk too, although I'm sure you encountered them on your journey."

"Ape-like things? Live in the trees and hunt at night?"

"That would be them. Not quite developed enough to be considered an actual civilization, but they are close. There's plenty of other intelligent wildlife in the wilds, creatures that straddle the boundary between animal and monster."

I shifted, clutching Riok's spear more tightly, and the Mage laughed.

"If there were anything waiting to pounce on us, Lace or Skaal would have noticed it already. We just want to avoid attracting attention if we can. Now, why don't you set down your packs and see if that mayor provided tents?"

In the end, it looked like Miko and I had only one tent between us—mine. I didn't know if the villagers had intentionally excluded her or just assumed that we would continue bunking together.

It didn't matter too much because while the assembled tent was barely tall enough to reach my waist, it was amply wide to accommodate us both. I placed my pack at one end, where I could use it as a pillow, laid my spear next to where I would be sleeping, and finally turned my attention to the bundle Nala had given me.

Miko had crawled into the tent on her hands and knees and now watched me unwrap the package from just a foot or so away, her orange eyes curious.

"Is that a shawl?" she asked, speaking in the High Tongue.

"A scarf, I think. See how it's long and thin?" Some kind of wool had been dyed in a geometric pattern of black and grey. The weave was reasonably tight but still a far cry from the understated elegance of Miko's robes. "I'm pretty sure she made this herself."

"A gift made with the hands and given from the heart," said the Priestess. "I only understood some of your words with Mordecai at the Harborton gate but… you do not have an interest in mating with this woman, do you?"

"No. And I'm pretty sure that even here on Eos, there are a lot of steps that people go through before… you know… mating."

"Like what?"

"Dating? Talking? Meeting the parents, maybe? I wouldn't be shocked if there's even some element of gift-giving—" I stopped dead.

"Unless I am mistaken, you have done two of the four already. And now she has given you a gift."

"Yeah, well. It's not happening." It wasn't even just that Nala would have been a senior in high school back home, whereas I was in my twenties. There was a reason Kate and I had parted ways, and that reason hadn't changed just because I landed in Eos. "I don't know how she feels, but to me, she's my student. Nothing more. And we'll be leaving Harborton again almost as soon as we return."

Miko nodded, the motion almost lost in the growing darkness of the tent. "Then may I suggest we find an appropriate gift for you to give her in return?"

"Like I said, I don't *want*—"

"One that clears any debt between you while also making it clear that your desires lie elsewhere."

"Oh. Yeah, that sounds like a good idea." It also sounded like a lot of heavy lifting for a present to do, but Miko seemed to have a better grasp on the whole situation than me. "Is this how things work with synossians too?"

"No. In our culture, someone makes their interest known through a common acquaintance. If that interest is returned, the pair may seek shared postings or even cohabitation. But unlike mammals, we only mate at certain times of the cycle, and only when our bodies are deemed ready by the gods."

I blinked. "I… don't know what that means."

I couldn't see her face, but I could hear the shift in her tone. Embarrassment, maybe? It was hard to know with Miko sometimes.

"There are three seven-days a cycle when an adult synossian woman's body prepares itself for mating. We will either take medicine to bypass this period or sequester ourselves with the mates we have selected. Any eggs from those unions will be contributed to the greater nest. There, individuals who have felt the call to serve as nest-mothers see to their hatching and basic education."

I hadn't been an expert on lizards back on Earth, but I was pretty sure *their* reproductive habits had been wildly different. And a lot less collaborative. One more reminder that the synossians weren't really lizard people, no matter how much they looked like it.

"So your nest-brothers and nest-sisters aren't related to you by blood?"

"Some may have been, but there was no way of knowing for sure. What matters are the relationships we build after hatching. From what I have read of the Nor and seen of the people in Harborton, your kind concern themselves with blood-focused bonds?"

"Yeah. We call it family."

"Whereas we have community instead."

Someone jostled our tent from the outside.

"If you two are done in there, Lace has returned," said Mordecai. "I'm going to start a fire and we'll see who's cooking dinner tonight."

"We'll be right out," I replied in Trade. Before we joined them, I turned back to Miko, switching easily to the High Tongue. "I'm not trying to be intrusive, but… do we need to find someone to make this medication for you?" I didn't know what a synossian going into heat looked like, but I was pretty sure it would be a distraction for her, especially if we were out questing.

"You need not worry." There was a rustle of fabric as she presumably pulled out her small carrying pouch. "We are a few moons from the next occurrence, and I have sufficient medicine. If I can continue to advance *Herbalism*, I may even be able to recreate the formula myself. I will not be a burden."

"Nobody who knows you would suggest otherwise." I grinned, even if she couldn't see it. "Especially when they find out you *also* have the *Cooking* skill."

"Perhaps tonight could be your opportunity to pick it up as well?" she teased. "I would not want to rob you of such."

"Whereas I wouldn't want to take away your chance at advancement."

She barked a quiet, distinctly synossian laugh, and pushed me out of the tent.

I didn't see how Mordecai started the fire, but it was already burning when we reached him, its steadily growing light sending shadows racing across the walls of the tents clustered nearby.

"The fire will attract some creatures and ward off others," he told us, "but Lace didn't find signs of anything we should truly worry about."

"It will be different once we enter the forest itself," said the woman herself. "This will likely be our last hot meal until we are back out again."

"I have *Cooking* skill," Miko offered.

"As does Skaal. With all respect, I'd rather not eat anything that you or Brian makes until we know each other better."

Miko looked confused, and only partly from the language barrier, but I put two and two together pretty quickly.

"You think we'd poison you?"

"I think you're strangers who wanted out of Harborton. I'm reserving judgment about everything else for now."

"I help then?" asked Miko.

Lace sighed. "It's your call, Skaal."

"Come," said the reaver, his voice a low rumble. "Need water."

The two disappeared into the darkness, and it was my turn to struggle with paranoia. I didn't love the idea of Miko heading off into the darkness with someone who'd already proven himself dangerous.

"Maybe I should go help too," I decided, starting to rise.

"Skaal won't touch a scale on her pretty bald head," said Lace. "That man has a thing about protecting the helpless."

"Like you said, we're strangers. How do I know that's true?"

Lace's voice barely carried over the cracks and pops of the small fire. "If it weren't, I wouldn't be here."

That told me nothing at all, but something in her tone convinced me. Either she was a far more subtle liar than she'd demonstrated so far, or she was being genuine.

I sat back down. "It sounds like there's a story there?"

"The world is full of stories. Some more private than others." She took a seat next to the fire and stretched like a sleepy cat. "And speaking of stories, I would hear more about this so-called Swarm, Mordecai. Assuming we are far enough away now for your sensibilities?"

"I sometimes question whether any distance would be sufficient, but this is as good a place as any, I suppose. What did you wish to know?"

"Anything? Everything? I've heard the name a few times since Skaal and I first crossed the southern peaks into the Waste and came north, but I have yet to be told what it is or how it came to be. And I would dearly like to know how the echo of *anything* could do the kind of damage we saw this morning."

"The *conceptual* echo," I clarified.

"What does that mean?"

I didn't have an answer to that.

Mordecai waited until he was sure we were done. "I can't tell you anything about what the townsfolk unleashed or how they came by it, but if you wish to know the *origin* of the Swarm, we should wait for the scaled to return."

"Why?"

"Because it was her people who loosed it upon the world." Something must have showed on my face. "You didn't know?"

"There's a lot I don't know."

He harrumphed. "So it seems."

That kind of killed the mood, to the extent that there had been a mood to begin with. We sat in silence for a few long, awkward minutes before Skaal and Miko came back, the two speaking back and forth in equally broken Trade.

"Told you," said Lace. "Old man's as reliable as they come."

I didn't think the reaver was all that old, but his strangely sickly demeanor admittedly made it hard to know for sure.

"Is he... okay?" I asked.

"That's another story. Live long enough and one of us might share it with you."

"The reaver is stronger than he looks, lad," said Mordecai. "Have faith in that much."

"I'm not big on faith," I admitted.

"Then ask your companion instead." Lace rose gracefully to her feet. "By the looks of it, they're bringing back dinner as well as water."

Apparently, her night vision was a hell of a lot better than mine, for all that we were both presumably human. It wasn't until Skaal had entered the circle of firelight that I saw he had a carcass slung over one shoulder. Behind him, Miko carried a small pot and a string of bulging waterskins.

"Predator," said Skaal simply, patting the carcass. "Will butcher away from camp and bring meat to fire."

"You didn't want to do it down by the river?" asked Mordecai.

"Butcher meat or protect under-leveled. Not both."

"Fair enough. We'll watch the Priestess."

Skaal grunted and moved past us into the darkness. I didn't get a good look at the carcass he was carrying, but the number of legs reminded me uncomfortably of the sluthar that had nearly ended my stay in Eos on the very first day.

Miko placed the copper pot full of water on the side of the fire and sat next to me.

"Are you okay?" I asked her in the High Tongue.

"It was over before I realized we had been attacked," she said, sounding truly shaken. "The creature didn't even have a chance to make a sound."

"Did he use a technique?"

"I… don't think so? He just caught it in mid-leap and snapped its spine in the same motion." Orange eyes mirrored the dancing flames as they met mine. "These people are far more dangerous than we realized."

"That's why we need them… almost as much as they need you."

She took a long breath and nodded, her inner eyelids fluttering once or twice although I couldn't tell if it was from the smoke or her own emotions. "I'm sorry; I was just startled."

Lace obviously couldn't understand what we were saying, but she'd been watching us from across the fire. "It's like I told you," she said. "Nothing was going to harm your Priestess while Skaal was at her side."

"And now I have proof instead of faith," I said. Miko shot me a questioning look and I shook my head. "I'll tell you later."

"Now that Miko has returned," suggested Mordecai, "perhaps *she* would share the story of the Swarm? If you don't mind translating on her behalf, lad; it is clear she still struggles with Trade."

"The Swarm?" asked Miko.

"He says your people caused it. Or loosed it. Or something."

"What?" She turned from me to Mordecai. "How? When?"

"I… assumed you would know that story better than I." Even with the mask hiding his expression, it was clear Mordecai was confused.

"We're from a small village in the middle of nowhere," I said, sticking to the story Miko and I had agreed upon. "Several seven-days past the eastern forest."

"Hard land, according to the few explorers who have ventured out that far."

I nodded, as if I had any idea what he was talking about. "Yeah. Our village was self-sufficient because it had to be. Since making it to Harborton, we've found that much of the history we were taught is inaccurate. To be honest, even our knowledge of the Framework is less comprehensive than we thought."

"Yet you are clearly learned," said Lace. "You speak two languages."

"So do you." I shook my head. "I'm good with languages, yeah. That's partly why I'm here, after all. But for the rest of it? Miko and I are both trying to learn everything we can."

"Ask them why they think the synossians had anything to do with the Swarm," pressed Miko in the High Tongue, "and what it is, for that matter."

"She wants to know more about the Swarm," I translated. "And why you think her people had something to do with it."

"Because they did." Mordecai sighed. "Many cycles ago, long before this kingdom existed, when the Endless Empire that preceded it was still in its infancy, the scaled ruled their own domain. A militant people, they regularly waged war against their neighbors. Eventually, that aggression went too far, and several of those neighboring lands, along with the burgeoning empire itself, joined forces to rid the land of their threat."

I quietly translated for Miko, the synossian growing more and more still with each passing word.

"The scaled were strong individually," he continued, "and for all their bloodthirst, they were disciplined as well, but the numbers arrayed against them proved insurmountable. The allied armies fought their way to the capital city. There, they prepared for a siege that would never come to pass."

"What happened?" asked Lace, seemingly enthralled.

"The specifics are hard to come by," Mordecai admitted. "The meisters at the Crimson Needle believe the scaled reached out to their gods, begging for intercession. This, despite the divine laws that have forbidden such actions since the Godswar. When their calls went unanswered, they reached deeper, into the space between stars."

"They sought the Father himself," murmured Miko. "He who slumbers in the darkness. Synos."

Mordecai looked to me, waiting for a translation. When I waved him on instead, he shrugged, and took up the tale again.

"Instead of a god, they made contact with… something else. Something that *was* the void yet also existed within it." He coughed, clearing a throat that had gone rough. "The only witnesses to the event were scouts who had been posted to the rear to watch for a flanking maneuver that never came. Only a handful of them lived to reach safety, and they were all withered and broken, old before their time. Each spoke of a being with a thousand voices and none. Desolation that spread outward in hideous waves. Ten thousand nails clawing at the weave of reality itself. They called it the Swarm."

For a long moment, the only sound in the campsite came from the fire itself.

"None of those scouts lived long enough to bear witness to the allies' responses," said Mordecai. "Over the next few cycles, multiple squads were dispatched south to seek confirmation of the strange tale. None returned. Nor were the original armies ever seen again. An agreement was forged, and the kingdoms and empire all pulled back their respective borders, deeming the land of the scaled condemned and inviolable."

He sighed and pulled his mask just far enough away to drink from his waterskin. "It was almost five decades before someone broke that treaty, a treasure hunter named Mar with more greed than sense.

He and his team found a land swept clean of life, nothing left behind but dirt and wind. For two seven-days, they crept through the desolation, their goal the site of the final battle. But when they reached the capital city, they found only more of the same. Of both the scaled and the armies that had once besieged them, nothing but weapons and armor remained… and what should have been a fortune in bronze crumbled into dust when touched. Instead of treasure, they came away with only a story. That and confirmation that, while the thing that had caused the desolation, this so-called Swarm, was gone, the land itself was forever ruined."

"Emptiness," said Skaal from behind us. He moved to drop some leaves and a few small bulbs—turnips maybe?—into the copper pot. Making his way around the fire, he planted sticks into the earth so that the bloody strips of meat impaled on each were positioned over the flames "You speak of the Waste."

"Precisely. It has been almost nine hundred cycles since the battle that never happened, and in that time, much has changed. The dunsmen either migrated into the Waste or emerged from beneath it, suited to survival there in a way that few of us are. A handful of merchant caravans have learned to brave the passage to make contact with the people of the southern peaks. Of those, a *very* few have attempted to cross those peaks and bring trade to your respective lands," he added, nodding to first Lace and then Skaal.

"As for the scaled, they were broken as a power, their leadership and military might wiped out by the same horror they unleashed upon their enemies. Still, some of the people remained… refugees who had fled the war long before the desolation. In small villages like your own, I suppose a few have managed to hide away from the world and find peace. In the greater nations…" Mordecai shook his head again, directing his words to Miko. "There are few who actually remember why the scaled are reviled, but even as kingdoms have risen and fallen, the attitude toward your people has stayed constant, lass. This duchy is one of the few regions in the north that even allows your kind to own property and doing that much has earned Grand Duke Willerton his share of discontent and unflattering nicknames."

I was pretty sure Miko had gotten the gist of things from the way her slim shoulders had slumped over the course of Mordecai's tale, but I finished translating anyway.

"Do you think it true?" she asked me, speaking Trade for everyone's benefit. Nine hundred cycles meant Mordecai's story took place *after* the founders of her primacy had fled the continent, but clearly there was more history behind that flight than she had been told. *Especially* if they'd left behind an entire nation of their own people.

"Maybe. Maybe not," I told her. "Remember, history is written by the winners."

"There were no winners in this tale," said Mordecai soberly.

"The survivors, then."

"It doesn't matter," said Lace. "All that matters is what people believe, and *that* means little Miko's going to have a tough time showing her scaled face anywhere outside the duchy."

"Little Miko? She's bigger than you are," I said.

"Is she? I hadn't noticed." Her teeth flashed white in the darkness of her face, more snarl than smile. "Thank you for the story, Mordecai, but now that we are all present and dinner is cooking, we need to speak on more current concerns."

Skaal grunted, taking a seat across from Mordecai and between Lace and me.

"Tomorrow, we enter the woods," the woman continued. "We should be fine for at least the first day, with Mordecai and I flaring our auras to keep away the predators, but the deeper we go, the more those auras will serve as lures rather than deterrents."

"Why's that?"

"More danger deeper we go," answered Skaal.

"No, I get that. I was asking about the aura stuff."

"The heart of progress is conflict, lad," said Mordecai. "That holds true for the beasts and monsters of this land as much as it does us. Only a truly desperate unranked creature would attack someone who has reached Tin, but the monsters have their own progression. To Tin-equivalent beasts, we would represent a challenge and opportunity for growth. Anything Copper or above would see us as convenient snacks."

"What is Tin?" asked Miko. "Or Copper?"

"Does it have to do with being ranked?" I wondered.

Lace shot me a look. "I think you understated just how remote your village was. But yes. A metal for every rank, starting with Tin if you pass your tribulation at level ten. Then Copper at twenty, Iron at thirty, Bronze at forty, and so on, to heights neither you nor I will likely ever reach. The kingdom of Elthor exists on the fringes of civilization, this particular duchy even more so; it's unlikely you'll find anyone over Copper anywhere but in the capital cities."

"Meaning the dukes?"

"Maybe." She shrugged. "Here in the north, it is rare that the strongest rules."

"Why?" That flew in the face of most fantasy novels I'd read.

"Numbers have own strength," said Skaal.

"Exactly," agreed Lace. "Gather more than a hundred people together and even a Copper has to pay attention. Cities of the size you northerners prefer require management, and that management is best handled by the appropriate professions. Often, the strongest Aspirants you'll find in cities are army veterans and retired adventurers who have settled down to spawn a bunch of brats while leading a given ruler's personal guard."

"There *are* exceptions," said Mordecai. "The Witch-King of Hybellus was one of the greatest before that nation fell. Even now, you have the Council of Nine in the west, the One Alone somewhere deep beneath the Waste, and the Lady of Stars—"

"*Of course* there are exceptions," interrupted Lace. "There are *always* exceptions. But I'd like to get back to the point before our dinner burns to a crisp." Skaal gave her a flat look that she ignored. "What was I talking about before all of this?"

"Forest," said Miko. "We have day before things get bad."

"More dangerous than outright bad if we're lucky. But yes, the day after tomorrow is when we'll start doing our best to actively avoid attention. Tomorrow, we'll work on teaching the two of you just that."

I didn't bother pointing out that we'd made it all the way through the forests east of Harborton on our own… because *technically* we'd brought a massive snake down on the town in the process. Worse, Nikkaali had to be *at least* a Copper equivalent monster, given that two of Harborton's Tins had barely even scratched it.

"Shouldn't we know about your classes before we go into danger?" I asked instead. "Or at least your roles? Miko and I will need to know how we fit in."

"When it comes to combat, you both need to stay back and out of our way," said Lace.

"What if that's not possible?"

"Then we're in serious trouble and likely to end up spitroasted over Hashoggath's fires, cooking for all eternity."

I didn't know who Hashoggath was, or if he or she had any relation to the nine-breasted hag Lace had sworn by the previous night. What I did know was that the deities of the Great Wilds made Shan seem like a cupcake.

"Still," Lace allowed, "we will be sharing a camp for at least the next moon, so I guess it's a reasonable request. I started as a Rogue, graduated to Skirmisher, and am now a Marauder."

I blinked. I hadn't even known there *could be* multiple class evolutions. "What does that mean?"

"It means that I'm quick, I hit hard, and you're not finding me in the dark."

"At the cost, alas, of a certain caliber of social deftness," added Mordecai dryly. "Which is not to say that you're not a charming companion in your own way, lass."

"Skaal," continued Lace, her voice gaining an edge, "was a Warrior, like you. Don't ask what his current class is, because it doesn't exist outside the steppes and therefore doesn't have a translation."

That threw me for a loop. It hadn't occurred to me that people's records would be in their own native languages.

"Regardless, if I were light infantry, he'd be the heavy equivalent. Just… without the turtle-like armor people favor in the north. In most battles, he'll be facing the strongest opposition and yet require the least assistance."

"Which brings us to me," said Mordecai. "I am an Adept of the Crimson Needle, second in my circle, endowed with the secrets of—"

"He's a Mage," said Lace. "Specializes in fire. Exclusively fire."

"A Flameweaver," corrected Mordecai. He gestured to the campfire between us all, and a writhing tongue of flame split away, constrained by nothingness as it floated to his outstretched hand. "Fire control and manipulation as well as outright evocation."

"Yes. That. He's the least likely to get hit, but the first one Miko should be healing when it happens," said Lace. "Outside of yourselves, I suppose. When we travel, I'll range ahead as a scout, while Skaal stays with the rest of you. Priestess and Mage go behind the reaver, and our other Warrior will play rear guard."

"I'm only level two," I reminded her.

"You have a spear," she shot back. "And you're a hell of a lot less vital to our success than either of them."

"No worries, lad," said Mordecai. "Miko can heal your wounds while I teach a lesson in flame to whatever dares attack us from behind."

It was my turn to grunt. Either *Danger Sense* would have to get a lot less flaky or I was in for even more increases in *Pain Tolerance*.

Was it weird that I kind of wanted both?

34

Dinner was far better than it had any right to be, given that it consisted of freshly killed mystery meat cooked over an open fire. The sauce Skaal had mixed in the pot gave a bit of a tang that contrasted the earthiness of the meat and none of it was as tough or as chewy as I'd expected.

If the reaver didn't have a *Cooking* skill well above Miko's, my name wasn't Brian.

Food aside, it was a quiet affair. Lace held a mostly one-sided conversation with Skaal, while Mordecai seemed contemplative behind his mask. As for Miko… I didn't have to be an expert in synossian facial expressions to know that Mordecai's story about the Swarm had troubled her. As tough as my last few months had been, hers had been even worse, and since we'd reached Harborton, she'd come across far too many signs that her knowledge base was either incomplete or badly skewed.

I hadn't gotten to meet the synossian leadership before they were wiped out but based on my experiences with Riok and the others, I found it hard to believe that there had been an intentional misinformation campaign going on. Deceit seemed almost antithetical to the pillars of their culture.

Well… outside of Shan's faithful, at least. I kind of had to assume lying was par for the course for anyone who worshipped the Trickster.

Knowing what I did of *Earth* history—which admittedly was less than my high-school teachers would have preferred—I was betting that the long ocean crossing and more than a thousand years of pseudo isolation on the new continent were to blame for the inconsistencies in their history and the obvious gaps in their understanding. Still, while *I* was just having to unlearn a few weeks of recent education, Miko was having to change her entire perspective.

"Are you okay?" I asked her in the High Tongue once we had both finished our meals.

"I am troubled," she said simply, orange eyes staring into the fire's depths. "I would speak to you later tonight, if you are willing."

"Of course. After meditation?"

"That will serve. Thank you, Brian Fieldings."

"We're in this together, Miko Naseri."

Unfortunately, Lace scuttled those plans almost immediately.

"We need to talk watch order," she announced, having finished her quiet conversation with the reaver. "Brian, I'd like you to take first watch. Skaal will take second, while I take third."

"I get a full night of sleep for once? I'm already seeing the benefits of a larger party," said Mordecai.

"I help watch too?" asked Miko.

The dark woman shook her head, braids swaying. "We'll rotate watches from night to night, but in general, I want our melee combatants in that role. Once we reach the deeper forest, Mordecai will lay down wards, but I need you recovering your heals as early as possible each night, in case we're attacked."

I was starting to think that Shan giving me the Warrior class had screwed me in more than just the usual ways. Other than *maybe*

Miko, everyone in the party had significantly higher Vitality than I did, due to their levels, yet I was still being voluntold to give up a full third of my sleep every night.

"Keep your back to the fire, lad," said Mordecai, "and focus on your hearing as much as your sight. When you hear something—and you always will—please, if you love the face of your parents, try to judge whether it is a threat *before* you wake us all."

"Sounds like the voice of bitter experience," laughed Lace.

"Truly. I adventured with a greenhorn who sounded the alarm seven times over the course of their very first watch. Turned out they had never spent a night in the forest and were convinced every sound they heard meant bloodthirsty bandits were sneaking up on us. Needless to say, we parted ways with him at the next town."

"Right," I said. "Don't look at the fire and don't wake anyone up unless something is about to eat or rob us."

"Close enough," said the Flameweaver, hoisting himself to his feet. He didn't move with anything approaching Lace's grace, but he didn't grunt or groan on the way up either. That put him ahead of most of my teachers at school. "And with that, I'm going to avail myself of the wilderness and then retire to sleep. I will see you all in the morning."

The others left to tackle their own final errands too. Skaal carried the half-empty pot away, and Lace disappeared into her tent.

"I would join you after my meditation," Miko told me quietly in one of her two native tongues, "but I do not wish to distract you from your duties."

"It's fine. We can talk tomorrow morning instead."

"Yes."

I didn't like leaving it there, and stopped her before she could head to our tent.

"You know that nothing in Mordecai's story, even if it *did* happen, is your fault, right?"

"Of course. I was not even hatched."

"Then what's wrong?"

"Many things. First, if my people summoned this Swarm when trying to reach Synos, what does it say about our celestial father's true fate?"

That... hadn't occurred to me.

"Second, how much of my own education, about not just our history but the Framework itself, is based on misconceptions or half-truths? Copper? Iron? Bronze? Every day deepens the realization that what I thought I knew was at best incomplete."

"Like you said back at the inn, it's an opportunity to learn," I said. "If nothing else, it's pretty easy to get Mordecai to talk."

"Most importantly, however," she said, barely listening to my words, "is the realization that I have reached these lands, the Great Wilds my teachers spoke of with such disdain and loathing, only to find that it is *my people* who are considered the villains of the tale. How can I make a place for our refugees if most people here see us as little more than beasts?"

"It's not something you have to figure out alone," I said. "Shan brought me here for a reason, remember?"

"Then what do you suggest? Because I am tired and I am troubled and even if we survive the next moon, I am at a loss as to what should be done."

For just a moment, she sounded her age.

"We're already doing it," I reminded her. "We're working on learning about the land while getting stronger and hopefully making both connections and coin. After that? We'll try making contact with the native synossians. If anyone's going to feel motivated to help prepare for the refugees' arrival, it'll be them. As for the other races?" I shrugged. "It sounds like this Grand Duke Willerton could be sympathetic. We just have to figure out a way to get to him."

"You make it sound almost easy. Is that your merchant training, coming to the fore?"

"Uh… probably not," I admitted. I hadn't learned any real lessons from my time at Pritchard's other than *the customer is always right and frequently an ass*. "But we have a joke back on Earth. How do you eat an ele—" I paused and changed the last word. "A sluthar?"

"Given that their meat is rancid even before death, I wouldn't suggest doing so at all." I could hear the disgust in Miko's voice.

"Bad example. Do you have any large beasts that *are* edible?"

"A thegar, maybe? They are several times the size of the dalysi."

"Ok. How do you eat a thegar?"

"I don't—"

"One bite at a time."

There was a long pause. "What?"

"It's a joke and a lesson," I explained. "When dealing with a problem that seems impossibly big, try breaking it down into smaller tasks that you *can* complete. By the time you've done enough of those, the problem's no longer quite so scary."

"*How do you eat a thegar?*" she repeated softly. "I do not perceive what makes this joke humorous, but there is wisdom there, nonetheless. I may have to rethink my opinion of your dirt planet."

"Personal power. Coin. Local contacts. High-placed connections." I ticked them off on my fingers. "If we focus on those four things, we'll be halfway there."

"Halfway through *eating the thegar*." The light from the fire made her sharp-toothed smile into something even more savage.

"…right." I wasn't *entirely* sure she was getting it, but at least she seemed happier.

"Then that is what we will do. And I will start by meditating. I am still too far from my next level, but perhaps I will see an increase or two in my skills today."

"Good luck."

"Thank you, Brian." She vanished into our tent.

Less than a minute later, Mordecai made it back to camp, the timing so perfect that I suspected he'd stayed away to give us privacy, even though we were speaking a tongue he couldn't understand. He nodded once to me, expression hidden by his cloth mask, and headed for his own tent.

And just like that, I was alone.

Mindful of what I'd been told, I found a seat slightly away from the camp, with the fire at my back where it wouldn't damage my night vision. As Mordecai had warned, there was no shortage of sounds to keep my attention. Grass rustled with the wind or the passage of something unseen. Birds called to each other in the distance, and larger beasts warned away rivals from trespassing on their domains. Now and then, the river's murmur reached me, just random enough to keep me on edge.

I didn't hear anything near enough or large enough that I would deem it a threat. Which didn't say a lot given how ignorant I was of the dangers on Eos. There were no trees above us, so the catosaurs and the treefolk were unlikely. And we were far enough from the river that any of those plant monsters seemed unlikely too. But giant carnivorous worms that burrowed through the soil and only emerged to swallow people—and tents—whole? Those were entirely possible, as were elephant-sized birds that might swoop down from the sky to pluck a man right out of his newly crafted boots.

Ignorant as I was, all I could do was keep my focus and make damn sure nothing snuck up on me.

"Greetings," said Skaal, appearing at my side from out of absolutely nowhere. "How goes watch?"

"I *thought* it was going pretty well," I managed, desperately hoping for my heart to find a path back into its chest, "but now I'm having some doubts."

"Is quiet. Is good."

"I guess." I blew out a long breath. "Is my watch already over?"

"Not yet."

"Shouldn't you be sleeping then?" I gave the much, much bigger man a second look and opted to rephrase the question. "I mean, aren't you tired?"

"I sleep little most nights. Decide to keep company."

"Well, thank you." It would have been easy to think the reaver simpleminded, if I hadn't heard him speak in an entirely different language—and seen the subtle, playful ways in which he liked to tweak Lace's nose. "I don't mind leaning on someone's expertise."

"Very wise."

For the next glass or so, we sat quietly together. Occasionally, he broke the silence to explain the nature and origin of the sounds we were hearing. By the end of those lessons, I wasn't *comfortable* yet, but I felt better prepared for standing watch.

"Wanted to ask on spear," Skaal said abruptly, when my traitorous eyes were threatening to droop shut.

I touched the weapon at my side. "What about it?"

"Is different."

"You mean the metal shaft?" He shrugged, which I took as a yes. "I don't know a lot about it. It belonged to a great Warrior."

"Oh?"

"Well, kind of? I guess he was only Tin, in retrospect, but... he seemed great to me."

"Rank is factor of level, not quality of person. Have seen honorable fighters never reach Tin. Have seen Coppers not worth dirt they tread."

After a moment, I nodded, oddly comforted by his words. "Riok was a good one."

Despite the language barrier, Skaal didn't miss my verb tense. "How did he fall?"

I wasn't sure how to answer that at first. *A necromancer's blood ate him alive* was a weird thing to say. It also opened me up to topics I didn't want to discuss. "Striking a blow against a stronger opponent," I said instead.

"Is a good death."

"I'd prefer a good life."

That won me a grunt. "Is not always possible."

That was dark. True, but dark.

"I'm not great with spears," I admitted, "but Riok taught me the basics. And while the weapon's not much to look at, it's traveled a long way with me." A very, very long way, not that I was going to explain as much.

"May I?" He gestured to the spear.

"I… yes, of course."

Skaal took the weapon and stood. Even at seven feet tall, he was smaller than Riok, but the spear that was practically a lance in my hands looked more appropriately sized in his. He went through a series of stances and attacks, each movement slow but filled with undeniable power. I could tell that Riok's *Spear* skill had been higher—maybe a lot higher—but the reaver clearly had some familiarity with the weapon.

Finally, he stopped and gave me back the weapon. "Is more than just shaft that makes special," he said. "Is broken but not broken. Clings to form and function in defiance of fate."

I paused. "I'm sorry?"

Instead of elaborating, he shrugged.

I badly wanted to switch to the language he was fluent in, to get a better explanation, but resisted that urge. "Have you ever seen anything like it before?"

"Yes." With the fire behind us, I couldn't see his face, but his voice had gone somber. "In reflection of glass, or lake, or slow-moving stream."

Before I could parse his words, he clapped me on the shoulder with an oversized hand. "Go sleep," he said. "Watch over. My turn now."

ooo

I didn't go to sleep. Not immediately anyway. First, I followed Mordecai's example, and… *watered the grass*, so to speak. Then, once I was back in our tent, with Miko's slumbering form a tangible presence, I did my best to meditate.

It was harder than usual. Skaal's odd comments kept rolling around in my brain. What on Earth—or Eos—had the reaver been talking about? Broken but not broken? Defiance of fate? And… assuming I'd interpreted his last words correctly, how did *he* have anything in common with a spear?

Eventually, exhaustion won out over confusion. As I reached that half-step just before sleep, I managed to nudge myself into a meditative state. Over the next half-glass or so, the day's events replayed in my mind. I tried to guess if there was anything that my soul might find valuable. Would the hours of walking net me a point in *Athleticism?* All of it had been done while also carrying a heavy pack; would that bring about a long-sought *natural* improvement to Strength? Even the night's lesson from Skaal on Eosian wildlife might count as training in standing watch, assuming there was a skill for that.

I let the blend of experiences filter through my mind, both participant and third-party observer to my own life. But when I woke, the Framework had somehow managed to surprise me yet again:

```
You have increased the following skills:

General skills:
Animal Behaviorism [+1]: 10/10
Deception [+1]: 1/10
```

Skaal's lesson had been enough to finally push *Animal Behaviorism* to its maximum rank, but my eyes were fixed on the second skill, one I'd apparently just earned by lying through my teeth about where Miko and I had come from.

Maybe Shan's faithful and I had things in common after all.

35

Sleeping in a tent beat the hell out of sleeping out under the moons and stars… but it still lacked the creature comforts we'd become accustomed to in Harborton. The thin blankets Valestia had included in our packs were sufficient to ward off the night chill, but those blankets didn't keep me from waking up stiff and sore. While some of that ache was from our hike the previous day, of course, most of it was from sleeping on the ground instead of in a cot, or—Gods forbid—an actual bed.

This adventuring stuff was going to take some getting used to.

Miko was back to her usual self when I woke, and though she remained anything *but* a morning person, she seemed cheerful enough as she helped Skaal prepare a cold breakfast while the rest of us broke camp. She gave me a hard biscuit and some sort of fruit jam that we had to finish before it went bad, and her smile held no traces of the uncertainty or concern she'd voiced the night before.

I didn't give myself all the credit for that transformation—sleep had its own healing magic, after all—but I had to believe our conversation had done some good.

As we set out, I adjusted my pack until the weight was evenly distributed across both shoulders. It felt even heavier than it had the day before, but nobody else was complaining, and I had just enough pride to not be the first. So, I swallowed my groan and fell in behind Mordecai as the five of us adopted Lace's suggested marching order.

The sun was just inching its way above the horizon when we reached the forest's edge. Lace paused to adjust the slim sword at her belt and the brace of daggers that charted a line from left shoulder to right hip.

"Mordecai and I will be rotating our auras to ward off predators," she reminded us, "but if you wish to talk, keep your voices low. It'll be good practice for the future when noise might get you dead. Miko and Brian, mirror the movements of the person in front of you and try to follow in their footsteps. Most predators here will hunt by sound or scent, but anything on two legs will be looking at our tracks."

Inspirational pep talk over, she nodded to Skaal and disappeared into the woods. About twenty seconds later, the reaver led us in after her.

Of the Marauder, there was no sign. No tracks, no sound, not even a swaying branch to indicate her passage. It was as if the forest had swallowed her whole.

Skaal marched on and the rest of us followed.

It was hot and sticky and tiring, for all that we were just walking through the woods. I did my best to ape Mordecai's movements but following in his exact footsteps proved impossible. While he was the second smallest person in the party, his stride was still significantly longer than mine.

It had only been a little more than a day and I was already missing Lomas.

At least my new boots made a difference when it came to hiking through the forest. There was a lot more underbrush than there had been to the east, and any attempts at navigating the terrain barefoot would have had me bleeding in a matter of minutes. Again. The trees close to the fringe were thin and tall, their branches reaching upwards instead of out, and sunshine filtered down through the open spaces to paint the ground in dappled patterns of shadow and light.

Over the course of the next few glasses, Lace made a handful of appearances to confer with Skaal before heading back out again. During one such moment, I approached Mordecai.

"What are they talking about?" I could've found out for myself if I'd just gotten close enough to listen in, but it had occurred to me that my *Speaker of Tongues* trait was the only real wild card I had… and it was most valuable when kept secret. As long as people didn't realize I could speak their language—maybe *every* language, even— they'd be that much more likely to speak freely in front of me.

Maybe it was just my *Deception* skill talking, but we were all effectively strangers, and Lace had already demonstrated a remarkable lack of concern with my continued wellbeing. I didn't think she or Skaal or Mordecai would outright betray us or anything, but *if* they did, my trait might let me see it coming.

As long as I kept it secret.

"Lace is providing directions and filling the reaver in on what possible dangers she has spotted during her scouting trips," answered Mordecai. "Skaal is, from my understanding, an equally accomplished explorer, but she is better versed in the forests and jungles."

"Why?"

"Have you heard of the blood-scorned amazons?"

I shook my head.

"Few have, this far north. They dwell mostly in the southern jungles, though a few clans have made their homes over the mountains and into the woods there instead." His soft laugh had a grimness to it I wasn't expecting. "It is said the southern lands contain great cities of awe-inspiring wealth, where the windows are made of diamond, not glass, and rubies are used to line the streets like cobblestones. Unfortunately, thanks to the reaver tribes in the southern steppes and the amazon clans beyond, the journey to confirm those tales is invariably fatal."

"The reavers and… amazons… are hostile?"

"And territorial, yes. If they didn't spend so much time fighting each other, they might be a legitimate force in the world. Their raids are the stuff of nightmares."

"How did Skaal and Lace come to be here then, and together?"

"Now *that* is a subject I have spent much time pondering." He tapped the bottom of his mask, where his chin was presumably located. "As someone whose education is far broader than most, it is my hypothesis that—"

"Mage," said Skaal, somehow only a few feet away and looming over us like one of the forest's own trees. "We move."

Mordecai flinched and I took some small comfort in the fact that he was as startled as me. "Quite right, lad. Lead on, and we will follow."

We pressed onward, deeper into the forest, the trees around us changing, not just in size but species. Twice, we encountered single trees with bark the color of dried blood, each situated in the center of its own clearing. Skaal led us in a wide arc around those trees, never entering the clearings themselves.

"Needles," he said, pointing to what I had taken for leaves on the blood-colored branches.

Mordecai shuddered and explained. "The whole clearing is the scarlet thorn's domain. If you could survive long enough to dig down, you'd find its roots spread from edge to edge. Nothing else is permitted to grow, and anything that enters is getting a hundred needles to the face and chest."

Skaal nodded. "Good poison if can survive to harvest."

"Better you than me, lad." The Flameweaver turned back to Miko and me. "The scarlet thorn feeds on blood rather than water or sunlight. And the remains of its prey are often used to lure in the next meal."

The reaver nodded again. "Smart hunter, for tree."

I met Miko's gaze and tried to look confident. I was starting to think we'd survived the eastern forest on sheer luck. Hell, Nikkaali's pursuit of us might have even *protected us* from other predators.

It was a sobering thought.

ooo

Perhaps the biggest challenge of the day was adjusting to Lace and Mordecai's steady rotation of auras. I still didn't know how the two hid their auras in the first place, but as we hiked, they took turns letting go, and each time, it came as a shock to my system. One moment, all was well, the next, the man in front of me seemed to have a physical weight and presence far beyond what was merited by his slim form. And then, a glass or so later, when I had almost gotten used to the pressure, it disappeared again, replaced by a vague sense of something similar far ahead of us.

Their rotation was just frequent enough that I never managed to adjust entirely, always either dealing with an unexpected sensation where my mind insisted none should be... or trying to come to grips with that sensation's disappearance.

By the time we made camp—no fire this time, with dinner being more of the hard bread from the morning and the last of the jam—I was almost as exhausted mentally as I was physically. I was even grateful that they would be hiding their auras entirely the next day. Sure, it was because we'd be in even *more* danger, but at least I'd be able to hear myself think.

Riok's steady, constant presence had never worn on me quite like this, and I didn't know if that made both Lace and Mordecai more powerful than him, or if I was just less comfortable with the two adventurers.

Before he went to sleep, the Flameweaver set wards around the camp for the first time. There was nothing to really see, other than Mordecai walking the perimeter, stopping every ten feet or so to murmur a few words, but by the end, he was visibly tired, so I could only assume something had happened. According to Lace, those wards would help mask our presence from anything in the vicinity. What exactly *fire* had to do with any of that was another question I didn't think of until I was falling asleep.

My watch—this time in the middle hours of the night—proved uneventful. The sounds in the forest differed from what I'd heard out in the fields, but between Skaal's lessons and my now maxed-out *Animal Behaviorism* skill, I remained confident as I identified and then dismissed each possible new threat. I even had time to think about how I could monetize the skill … if Scribe was a profession, surely there was something with animals too? Maybe Stable Master or Lion Tamer?

Of course, I'd first have to level up additional related skills before either profession became available. That was a concern, given that I didn't know what those skills were, or how to acquire them. It was also possibly a moot point, as I had the strong suspicion that neither profession was a pathway to overwhelming wealth.

Still… taming lions would be a pretty cool job.

Eventually, it was time to wake Miko, who this time had been given final watch. I kept the half-asleep and thoroughly grumpy synossian company until my own tiredness sent me stumbling back to our tent. The next morning we passed yawns back and forth like trading cards.

I would've killed for a Pop Tart and a lukewarm cup of Pritchard's shitty coffee.

I hadn't picked up any new skill gains from our second day of travel, despite finding moments to pepper both Mordecai and Skaal with questions about pathfinding and orienteering. There were apparently mosses that grew only on the eastern side of certain trees or stones, and wildflowers that only bloomed northward, and the combination of those and other details made cardinal directions simpler than they otherwise seemed. Or so they said; I was still struggling to distinguish one moss from another, and every wildflower looked the same to me.

Lace had the responsibility of planning our route. As we broke our cold camp that morning, she gathered us to her.

"Nothing above a whisper, from here on in, unless we're in a warded campsite," she said, the usual sardonic bite gone from her voice. "We're going to refill our water skins at the river, then press south again. Two days and then we'll cross."

"Not follow river?" asked Miko.

"We mostly are, already. But if you mean hugging the bank?" The Marauder shook her head. "Living things need water and that makes the river more dangerous than we can afford. Once we've refilled our skins, we'll parallel the river from a good distance instead. And pray that nothing truly aggressive comes across our scent."

It was her tone, more than the constant warnings, that had me shifting my pack nervously on my back. Lace and Mordecai, at least, were Tin. Probably Skaal as well, although he hadn't joined in the aura rotation the day before. If a bunch of Tin-ranks were concerned, then Miko and I should be outright worried.

"I won't be traveling as far ahead today," concluded Lace. "It reduces our scouting range, but we'll be in position to assist each other, if necessary."

We all nodded, trading more cold bread between us. Without the jam, I had to stick it in my mouth and wait for saliva to soften it before I could chew. Even after I got it down, it sat in my stomach like a hard lump.

Apparently, travel bread was the same across continents.

"Should we bathe at river?" asked Miko. "To cover scent?"

Skaal and Lace traded glances. "I wouldn't recommend getting into the river if you can avoid it," said the Marauder. "We do have oil that can be mixed with water from the skins to dampen your scent, but the supply is limited, and some creatures' noses are impossible to defeat. We're better off just avoiding those creatures if we can, rather than trying to sneak past them. The chances of them following a faded trail are small unless we intrude upon their territories."

Given that Miko and I had been hunted for literal days by a serpent the size of an Amtrak train, I wasn't reassured.

It took us a full glass to make it to the river, reinforcing just how much space Lace had been giving to keep us away from thirsty predators. I was still in the rear, still hot, still sweaty, and more than a little scared, my head on a swivel as I prepared myself for whatever might decide to rush us from behind. Instead, I bumped into Mordecai, as he and the others pulled up short, a dozen or more feet from the riverbank.

The Snake River was a lot smaller here than down by the sea, at most fifteen feet across. It made up for that by being significantly faster. The flow of water had carved a path through the rock and soil, and I crept forward with the others until we reached the bank, staring down at the water rushing by just a few feet below us.

"In the early spring and summer," said Lace, her voice a breath barely audible over the river's noise, "I'm betting the Snake overflows its banks, flush with the rains and melting snow upstream. This whole area would be underwater."

As it was, Skaal was the only one who could reach all the way down to the water, and only if he laid flat on the bank above. We passed him our skins, one after another, and he filled them in turn, careful to keep his hands from ever breaching the surface.

It took me far too long to see why.

"What are those?" I asked, pointing at the long dark shapes darting downstream. Between the water and the inconsistent light, it was hard to gauge their size; they could be anywhere from a foot long to half a dozen.

Lace shook her head uncertainly. This time, it was Mordecai who had an answer.

"Cutters," he said. "A type of fish, with teeth as long and sharp as Miko's and twice as plentiful. I once saw a school of them strip the flesh from a phloxl before the poor thing even knew it was dead."

Miko took a careful step away from the river.

"Their spawn need freshwater and cold temperatures, so they swim into the mountains upstream to lay their eggs. Now, I suppose they're headed back to the sea."

I looked at the cloud of writhing, tentacle-like creatures as they swept past us, and shuddered, remembering my own river crossing. The only thing worse than drowning would have been getting torn apart by monstrous eels.

Even as we watched, one breached the surface, all dark, glistening scales with a mouth almost as long as its body. It made no sign that it had seen us—I didn't know if the things *could* see at all— but a moment later, a second cutter leaped into the air, this one launching itself towards Skaal's outstretched arm.

It fared as well as the many-legged beast that had attacked two nights earlier... or the drunken farmer back at Lomas' inn. Skaal barely moved, but the cutter was suddenly thrashing about, inextricably caught in the reaver's free hand.

He turned to Mordecai, paying no attention to the long, barbed tail on one end of the cutter or the rows of needle-like teeth on the other that were each doing their best to reach his hand. "Can eat?"

Mordecai shook his head. "They have poison glands toward the tail. If you don't know how to remove them, cooking the cutter will spread that poison through its body."

"We can't risk a fire anyway," said Lace.

Skaal nodded thoughtfully to himself, and underhanded the cutter a good thirty feet down the river, where it landed with a splash. "Pity," he said, filling the next skin.

We'd only drunk a third of our water supply so far, and we were full up again a few minutes later. Presumably, we would top up our skins a second time when it came time to cross, but for now, we would avoid the river.

After seeing the cutters, I was okay with that.

Not that anybody had asked. Still, it was one more bit of knowledge that I could squirrel away. As Miko said, every day was an opportunity to learn.

ooo

More hiking, this time without any auras to distract me. Our water skins were full and our packs were too, and after two days of travel, my body was letting me know of its displeasure. It didn't help that each day seemed hotter than the one before, despite our path taking us up into the wooded hills.

I had three changes of clothes, thanks to Valestia, but if this kept up, they'd all smell as badly as I did.

At least I wasn't bleeding all over everything this time. And maybe our stench would act as a deterrent for those things not fooled by scent-free soap or oil?

The Marauder was far more visible throughout the day, her whispered conversations with Skaal never lasting more than a few sentences. Every time she showed up, my own complaints died in my throat. Lace was traveling half again as far as we were, and doing most of it alone, without anyone to save her if she stepped wrong. Her skin dripped with sweat just like mine, but she otherwise seemed immune to the heat. It was a testament to her people's lives in the jungle, I figured.

Skaal was… well, Skaal. The sickliest looking of us all, and the one any betting man would pick to collapse in a heap even *before* learning that his people had lived in the comparatively cool steppes, he continued to defy my expectations. The man seemed indefatigable, level gaze regularly scanning our surroundings even as he carried by far the greatest load.

If the reaver stood at the top of our endurance scale, and I staggered around at the bottom, Miko and Mordecai were somewhere in between, both closer to me than to Skaal or even Lace. Miko bore her load better than I did, but the heat seemed to slow her down, whereas Mordecai struggled mightily with both. I even saw him pull his mask off entirely at one point, though he was careful to keep his face hidden beneath the hood of his cowl.

I focused on breathing, on keeping one foot in front of the other, and on regular sips from my waterskin, although the last was as much to lighten my load as to replenish all the fluids I was losing. Miko and I had hiked just as much on our way to Harborton, but the pace Lace set was barely within our capabilities. Any thoughts of guarding our rear had faded sometime in the sixth hour, and now, the idea of an attack almost seemed appealing.

Finally, Lace manifested out of the trees ahead of us. Our four-person caravan ground to a halt.

"The way ahead is blocked, so we'll be stopping early today," she whispered. "I've found a campsite just over the next hill."

"Blocked?" I asked. We were in a forest, not some narrow mountain pass. As great as stopping sounded, my tired brain was struggling to understand how anything could block our route.

"Once we're set, I'll take one of you with me to see," replied the Marauder. "Skaal can guard the rest at camp."

"I plan to drink two skins of water and hearken back to the days of yore when my back was not on fire," muttered Mordecai. "If you want to go, lad, don't let *me* stop you."

I looked to Miko and she nodded.

Somehow, I had just volunteered for even more walking. I wasn't a cat, but curiosity was threatening to at least maim me.

The campsite Lace had chosen didn't seem all that different from any other spot in the forest… there were trees, some bushes, and just enough clear space for our tents. I looked around, trying to identify what made it more suitable than every other location we'd recently traipsed through. There were no scarlet thorn trees, of course, but we'd only seen two of those so far. I didn't see any obvious dens, nests, or even fruit-bearing bushes either, which meant less chance of an unexpected encounter. But still…

"What?" asked Lace, impatiently waiting on me.

"I'm trying to figure out why we're camping here instead of where you originally met us."

The Marauder tilted her head, silver eyes studying me. "No tracks or nearby game trails." She then nodded to the surrounding trees. "Old growth puts us out of a flood or fire zone, and the lack of scarring on the bark means nothing has claimed this area as theirs." Finally, she pointed downhill. "And we're up on the ridge here. Any wind should carry our scent up into the air, instead of down. That means fewer predators to scent us from below."

"Oh." It still just looked like a small clearing to me, but I tried to see it through her eyes, examining all the signs I had missed. "How did you learn all of that?"

"I had no choice. In my clan, it's the children who hunt for food. By your eighth cycle, you either graduate beyond gathering or your name and your place in the clan are open to challenge."

I didn't know what form a challenge against a child could take, and the expression on her face told me not to ask.

"If the children hunt for food, what are the adults doing?"

For a brief moment, her smile flashed into appearance, a touch more genuine than the usual half-snarl.

"Hunting people." That bright smile flickered and died, leaving something hollow in its wake. "Enough talk. Come if you're coming."

I looked back at our newest campsite, swiftly rounding into form, and shrugged. I *had* asked. Might as well see what was going on, now that I'd caught my breath.

Lace had already made it to the southern edge of the small clearing, impatience evident in every line of her body. I followed her into the woods.

Whatever small lessons I'd learned about woodcraft since coming to Eos were proven thoroughly inadequate after only a minute on Lace's trail. The woman moved like a wraith for all that she wore thick leather armor to my simple cloth. Meanwhile, every step *I* took seemed to find a dry branch, a leaf, or a root, the noises painfully audible even to my untrained ears.

Lace lasted another minute and then came to a stop, whirling on me. "Stand like me," she whispered. "Knees bent and feet closer together."

I mirrored her stance and waited.

"Take shorter steps," she continued. "Dirt farmers walk like they are forever falling. Out of control is clumsy and clumsy is loud."

She waited for my nod. "When you step, move directly forward, not outward, and place the blade of your foot down first. The outside," she explained, correctly reading my confusion. "Blade first, feeling where your foot will land, and then roll inward. Only place your heel after you've made full contact with the ball of your foot."

"And that's going to make me quieter?"

"In a way. It will let you test where you are stepping before you commit your weight. We were taught barefoot until we gained the skill, but it's possible in soft boots like yours as well." She demonstrated, moving soundlessly across the forest floor. "Try."

I tried. And when I failed, I spent another five minutes trying. The movement never felt natural, and I didn't see any signs of progress, but eventually Lace nodded.

"You have the sense of it now."

I… was pretty sure I *didn't* but opted to take her word for it.

"Follow behind and continue your practice," she said. "I will go even slower for your benefit. Better that we take too long and arrive unheard than we travel swiftly and attract attention."

As she turned and started back up the hill, it finally occurred to me that whatever was blocking our path, whatever it was I had *volunteered* to go see, was almost definitely dangerous. And I was trying to sneak up on it by walking on the outsides of my feet?

My mind screamed at me to turn back, but I was already lost at that point… and I *was* still curious. So instead, I took a long, slow breath and followed in Lace's footsteps, focusing on the mechanics she'd taught me and not how painfully slow I was going.

When I caught up to her, long minutes later, I had a moment of instinctive fear… that I'd sped up somewhere along the way and lost whatever flow she'd tried to teach me. Instead, the Marauder had stopped and dropped to a crouch. She pulled me down beside her, grip strong, but not entirely irresistible.

Interesting, the part of my brain fascinated with the Framework's numbers whispered. Lace's Strength attribute couldn't be much more than a point or two above mine. Which begged the question: where *had* she placed her points? And had it been a mistake to spend mine on Strength, given that it hadn't made me any taller?

My looming existential crisis was interrupted by Lace's lips at my ear. "We'll crawl to the top of the next ridge. When I stop, come up alongside me to the left, where I will have cleared out space. Whatever you do, do not go any further than me. Do you understand?"

I nodded, feeling my heart begin to race again. For the first time all day, I couldn't quite tell if it was fear I was feeling or excitement. If we were headed only as far as the top of the ridge, that meant whatever was blocking the way south had to be just beyond.

What was I about to see?

36

I t took me almost as long to crawl up the hill as it had taken to
sneak to its base. By the time I reached the summit, Lace was
already laid out on her stomach, a dark shadow in the
underbrush. As promised, she had cleared the area next to her, like a
parking space just waiting to be filled.

I eased my way in, still doing everything I could to keep my
inevitable noises to a minimum. Only when I was settled did I check to
see what she was looking at.

Ahead of us, the terrain dipped again before rising a few
hundred feet away into a hill that made my quads ache just by its
existence. But in the small valley between that hill and ours was a scene
of total devastation. Enormous trees had been upended and shattered.
Grass and soil alike had been torn apart. The evening sun, barely above
the treetops to our right, caught fire on the antlers of the two creatures
at the center of the wreckage.

Deer! my Earth-born brain insisted, for all that they were vastly
larger than anything that roamed the woods in Ohio, with antlers that
glimmered like rough-cut opals instead of bone. The smaller of the two
stags—this one the size of an SUV instead of an F450 Super Duty—
had bloody gashes across its flanks. The larger one, though untouched,

heaved for breath, eyes the size of dinner plates rolling as it pawed at the earth.

Both monstrous creatures were still for a moment. The dying sun etched their forms into my memory, and then they exploded into motion. The giant deer rocketed towards each other like cars playing chicken and driven by men too proud to spin the wheel. I felt the resulting impact all the way up the hill, felt it in my bones as much as in the cloud of dust and dirt and blood that filled the air.

The smaller stag got the worst of it, unsurprisingly, but instead of forcing the issue, it spun to one side, shedding some of its opponent's momentum. Antlers that had been pristine white were suddenly glowing a deep crimson, for all that it had yet to land a blow.

Lace sucked in a breath, savage joy stealing across her face.

The stag had a narrow window to drive forward and score a hit on its larger foe. Instead it rose up onto its back legs, the bloody glow of its antlers now pulsing like a heartbeat. When its forehooves struck the earth, a duplicate appeared from the stag's long shadow, its hide as blood red as its summoner's antlers.

The new stag moved with a speed neither of the others had displayed; it was on the much larger beast before a heartbeat had passed, tearing long, vicious rents in its opponent's side and hindquarters.

When the freshly wounded stag spun to face the new threat, its original opponent was already there, waiting. It drove the spikes of its antlers—opal white once again now that its technique had been cast— up into the larger deer's throat, spraying blood across the clearing.

The mortally wounded stag staggered and collapsed, its cry shrill and choking, and the earth and trees shook for hundreds of yards in all directions.

It was all I could do to keep the remnants of my half-digested biscuit from reintroducing themselves to the world. We'd done worse things—bloodier things—just trying to make it to Harborton, with catosaurs and treefolk both falling to my spear or Miko's club. But I'd been in the thick of the action then, in true kill or be killed mode. Here, I was just an observer, bearing witness to the overwhelming savagery of combat.

With the battle over, the blood-red copy of the victorious stag faded away, leaving only one creature upright in the clearing. It scanned the surrounding woods, its gaze far too intelligent for comfort. That gaze wandered our way, then paused, as if stuck.

A moment later, that gaze moved on again, leaving me desperate for oxygen. Neither stag had given off any kind of aura, but I knew, deep down in my bones, that the creature below us was at least the equivalent of a Copper.

I knew also that Nikkaali would have swallowed it whole and not even slowed. Which made the serpent Iron at a minimum.

It was a miracle we'd reached Harborton alive.

Lace stayed still and so did I. Eventually, the stag finished its inspection. It pawed the earth, making a piercing cry that bore no relation at all to deer noise back on Earth. The trees rustled and almost two dozen more deer came into the clearing. Many were as large as the stag, but none had antlers. They crowded around the victor, brushing up against its flanks as if to say hello. When the greetings were completed, the herd of does pulled back. They trotted off in the direction of the now-setting sun and the victorious stag followed.

The clearing below us was left behind, ruined and abandoned, empty of anything but the body of the stag who had lost its bid for breeding privileges.

Lace waited until the herd was gone, waited a few minutes more, and then motioned me back down the hill. This time, we walked instead of crawled, but the Marauder otherwise remained focused on stealth. It wasn't until we were at least halfway back to camp that she finally turned to me.

"That was unexpected!" Her voice was a whisper. "A stag with a blood aspect? Copper too? The herd will benefit from its potential."

"That was something," I admitted.

"I didn't see my first deer until we'd crossed the Waste, and now look at me." She shook her head. "One day, Skaal and I will reach Gold and no place on Eos will be out of reach."

"That sounds like a good dream."

As if remembering where we were and who she was talking to, she shrugged, closing herself off. "It's just an idle thought."

"I have those too." My legs protested at the shit my mouth was about to peddle, but I had to ask: "Now that the deer are gone, should we gather the others back up and press south?"

Lace shook her head. "The sun will be down by the time we make it to camp and a carcass that size will attract attention we do not want to deal with, especially at night. I'll scout things out tomorrow; either predators will have already taken their fill and moved on or we'll find a different path forward."

"Why couldn't we have done that tonight?"

She shot me a look. "The last thing you want to do is spook a herd when there's a challenge underway. The four of you trying to sneak your way around *that?* We'd have had *both* Coppers on our tail, sure as the Night Hag's venom kills."

It was a strange argument, given that she'd chosen to bring me up there anyway, but I was too tired to question her. Especially since it was painfully clear that Lace had more woodcraft in her pinky finger than I did in my whole body.

"Also," she added, almost as an afterthought, "Mordecai was on his last legs. The extra glass or two of rest tonight will do him good for tomorrow's push."

I almost missed a step, sparking an irritated glare from the Marauder. That was the last thing I'd expected her to say, given the disdain she regularly showed the masked spellcaster.

I thought on that a lot during the rest of our hike back to camp. It was so easy to buy into the images that people presented of themselves. I needed to do better than that. I needed to look deeper than just the surface to find allies Miko and I could trust.

Lace and the others weren't there just yet; truthfully, they were barely more than strangers. Still, between the impromptu lesson in stealth, and Lace's unexpected compassion for Mordecai, it was hard not to look at the Marauder differently.

"You're doing well," she said a few minutes later, interrupting my thoughts. "Now, try moving faster than an infant's crawl. The sooner we make it back, the sooner you can start your watch."

I buried my sigh and hurried along in her wake. At least I'd get some water before everyone else went to sleep.

○○○

By the time everyone turned in for the night, I was feeling a little less put upon. The others had set up camp in our absence. Even better, Mordecai had used his magic to warm our dinner meal without the risk of an open fire, and his efforts made the bread and hard, salted jerky almost palatable. A warm meal, a skin of water, and the chance to rest had gone a long way to improving my mood.

Plus... as brutal as the battle between the two stags was, it had *also* been really freaking cool.

My watch passed quietly again. If I hadn't gone with Lace, I might have thought the forest's reputation overblown. As it was, the devastation wrought by two Copper-equivalent beasts that were *technically* considered prey animals had me more than a little concerned about what predators would be capable of.

Despite the long day, I had no difficulties staying awake and alert until it was time for Lace's watch. I shook the tent from the outside to wake her—we'd been warned not to try to enter the tent itself—and waited. She emerged with a knife in each hand, and a murderous look that only slightly faded as she fully awoke.

"Your watch," I said brightly.

Her grunt would have done Skaal proud, but she nodded and sheathed her blades. "I'll walk the perimeter before I settle in."

"I'll be in my tent if you need me."

"I won't."

I waited until she was gone to roll my eyes. Miko clearly had competition when it came to hating early wakeups.

I was as quiet as I could be entering the tent, which was to say not very, and Miko stirred. Either she recognized my shape in the darkness, or had never fully woken up, because she immediately rolled over and drifted off back to sleep. I was too tired to meditate the normal way, so I adopted my unique hybrid stance, curled up on one side, a corner of my pack under my head as a pillow.

Sometime later, I emerged from meditation to find some seriously good news waiting for me:

```
You have increased the following skills:

Minor skills:
Athleticism [+2]: 12/15
Pain Tolerance [+1]: 11/15

General skills:
Meditation [+1]: 5/10
Stealth [+1]: 1/10
```

Two points in *Athleticism* was massive, even if it was only a Minor Skill. The improvements in *Pain Tolerance* and *Meditation* were great too, but the fact that I'd picked up the *Stealth* skill was on a whole different level. Lace's instruction had no doubt had a lot to do with it, but I was betting the evening's circumstances had played their part too. I had been forced to immediately put her lessons to use in a situation with life-or-death implications.

As everyone said, the soul grew best under pressure… and there were few pressures as intense as having your own life on the line.

I looked at the dialogue window, visible even in the darkness, and felt a warm glow of accomplishment. Miko and I had arrived on this continent underleveled and underequipped, but we had persevered anyway. And now, after all that time in Harborton, I was seeing concrete gains again.

At the same time, what I *really* needed was levels. Three increases in Minor skills helped me down that road, but when it came to my Major skills, I'd only seen a single skill-up in *Spear*, and that had been after weeks of night training in Harborton. I was still a very long way from capping the skills I'd need for level three, despite having reached experience satiation months earlier.

I hated to even think it, but it would be a lot more productive if this expedition stopped being so safe and peaceful. With a shrug, I dismissed the screen. That's when I got my second surprise:

```
You have increased the following attributes:

Vitality [+1]: 14
```

My Vitality had gone up on its own, *without* me reaching another even level. Excitedly, I pulled up my full character sheet for the first time in days:

```
Name: Brian Fieldings
Class: Warrior (Common) - 2
Profession: None
Deity: None
Ideal: Freedom

Attributes:
Strength: 11 [+1] / Finesse: 10
Vitality: 14 [+1] (+2) / Intellect: 12
Discernment: 10 / Will: 14 (+2)

Skills:
Major: Formations: 1/15, Light Armor: 10/15,
Spear: 11/15, Tactics: 5/15

Minor: Athleticism: 12/15, Avoidance: 8/15,
Pain Tolerance: 11/15

Professional: None

General: Animal Behaviorism: 10/10, Brewing: 1/10,
Caretaking: 7/10, Danger Sense (R): 5/10,
Deception: 1/10, Hunting: 1/10, Meditation: 5/10,
Mercantilism: 1/10, Riding: 3/10, Scribing: 4/10,
Stealth: 1/10

Techniques: Lunge (C)


Achievements: None
Titles: None
Traits: Speaker of Tongues, ???, ???
```

My list of skills was growing out of control, and as tired as I was, it took a distressingly long time to read through the whole record. There were no additional surprises but seeing everything laid out like that really brought home just how much I'd done, even in the down months of caretaking in Harborton.

Only four more points in *Spear*. Five in *Light Armor*, assuming neither of the other Major Skills rapidly advanced. Three points in *Athleticism* and either four in *Pain Tolerance* or seven in *Avoidance*.

That was all that stood between me and level three, when I'd upgrade *Lunge* into something more effective or add a devastating new technique to my arsenal.

I was tired. I hurt from my feet all the way up to my shoulders. I was alternately hot and cold, but always uncomfortable, and a part of me was *still* grappling with the idea of deer-on-deer violence that could uproot building-sized trees.

And yet the thought that kept running through my head had nothing to do with any of those concerns:

Sometimes, I love life on Eos.

37

The next morning, Lace decided the battle site was still too great a risk for us to approach. Instead, she took us on a circuitous path that avoided the area while adding at least an extra mile or two to the journey. When we paused for lunch, the most dangerous thing we'd encountered was an errant root that I didn't see until *after* I'd tripped on it.

The afternoon was a different story entirely.

I'd noticed the effects of my improved Vitality right away. Normally, it wouldn't have been any more obvious than my slightly upgraded Strength, but our pace so far had been pushing me to my limits. I'd spent three days sucking wind while trying to ignore the growing ache in muscles I'd barely used during our stay in Harborton.

An extra point in Vitality changed that. I was still tired, and still sore, but instead of feeling at death's door, I felt like I might have at the end of a tough but good workout. Things were hard, yeah, but my body still had a little more to give. Most of all, my own exhaustion no longer occupied the entirety of my mental process.

Which is probably why I noticed when some indefinable something inside me sounded an alarm.

I spun to the side. The awkward weight of my backpack turned that movement into a barely controlled stumble, but it was enough to get me out of the way of the large creature that blurred past, claws extended and mouth agape.

My first thought—a thought I would never, ever share with anyone—was that Miko had gone mad and attacked me. But in that moment between heartbeats, additional details trickled in… four legs instead of two, scaled feet as large as my synossian friend's head, and a maw in place of her comparatively humanoid face.

It wasn't a synossian. It was a big gods-damned lizard, like a Komodo dragon on steroids.

It landed softly, its movements terrifyingly swift despite its size. I hadn't even regained my balance yet when it turned and launched itself again with a hiss. There wasn't time to bring my spear to bear, so I just ducked a shoulder, putting my pack between the leaping creature and me.

Neither my augmented Strength nor my recently boosted Vitality were up to the task. I was bowled right over, landing hard on one side, with a significantly heavier creature scrabbling on top. To either side of me, frenzied claws tore deep furrows into the earth.

A fan of fiery darts streaked through the air and the lizard hissed again, its head turning to where Mordecai stood, one arm raised. I took that moment of distraction to get my hips under me so I could wedge my feet in against the creature's underbelly. Step one of my half-baked plan was to push the lizard away so that I could roll out from under it. Step two… would have to wait for me to think of it.

Even step one was problematic. As much as I strained, the lizard above me didn't even budge. Worse, my struggles reminded it that juicy, tender prey was already within claw's reach.

Pinned as I was, the only thing protecting me was the lizard's own size and the small pack I'd kept between us, but the creature was pivoting to bring its mouth to bear. If it was anything like Komodo dragons back on earth, its bite would be venomous… but given the size of its jaws, I doubted I'd live long enough for that to matter.

And then its weight was gone, claws flailing wildly as something tossed it into the air. Skaal stepped over me, one long stride easily clearing my body. The weapon on his back—Tempest—remained sheathed and shrouded, but in his hands were the axe and short sword from his belt.

Miko was at my side a moment later but it wasn't until warmth flooded through me that I understood I'd been injured. Claw marks, visible through gashes in my left pants leg, swiftly clotted, though blood had already soaked through the fabric. It was my turn to hiss as *Pain Tolerance* chose that moment to take a coffee break.

"Up, lad," said Mordecai. The masked caster was scanning the woods, not even paying attention to the showdown happening in front of us.

I grabbed Riok's spear and forced myself to my feet. My new backpack was a mess and *Minor Healing* or not, my left leg seemed engaged in a spirited debate about whether it wanted to hold my weight, but Mordecai's tone told me there was no time to worry about any of that.

"How do we help him?" I croaked.

"Skaal?" For a half-second, Mordecai stopped looking about and looked to me instead. "He doesn't need our help with a single gyr beast. But as soon as he puts it down, we'll need to go and fast."

"Why?"

"They travel in packs," said Miko simply.

As if the universe had just been waiting for her words, two things happened, almost simultaneously. First, the lizard facing Skaal charged forward, where it was met by both the reaver's weapons. And second, the trees beyond their bloody melee rustled and another scaled head poked its way out. I wasn't a herpetologist or anything, but the size of that head, and the fact that it was almost as high off the ground as mine, told me the newcomer was vastly larger than the one we were currently fighting.

More rustling came from the forest around us.

Skaal's battle with the first gyr beast continued, but even my untrained eye could tell it was almost over. He was slower than the lizard, but had the range, and seemed able to predict its attacks even before they were made, leaving him always in the perfect position to avoid them and counter. As I watched, his axe charted a lazy arc through the air that sent scales, flesh, and blood flying. The first lizard fell, and he turned to the newest arrival.

The problem was even more lizards were already emerging, and if they weren't all as large as the one Skaal was now facing, it was all too easy to picture the reaver being buried under multiple tons of scaled flesh.

"Take a Flameweaver into the woods at the tail end of summer," swore Mordecai, in the language that seemed uniquely his own. "Brilliant decision, as ever." He turned to us and switched to Trade. "Do either of you know the way to the river?"

I didn't even know the way back to the camp we'd left that morning, but Miko nodded uncertainly.

"Good. When I say go, you both need to run in that direction."

"I stay and heal," protested Miko.

"We'll be right behind you, lass," said Mordecai. "You can count on that."

"What are you going to do?" I asked him.

"Something I probably shouldn't." Flames gathered around his hands, but instead of the darts I'd briefly seen earlier, they coalesced into a spitting, snapping orb of fire between his outstretched palms. He raised his voice. "Skaal!"

The reaver took a step forward, accepting a hit from the behemoth he was facing, and lashed out with a booted foot. His kick lifted the thousand-pound lizard into the air and sent it flying towards its pack.

Unlike Lace, the man had *clearly* invested points in Strength.

As soon as there was separation between the two opponents, Mordecai unleashed his technique. Fire roared forward, striking the lizard while it was still in mid-air, and then flooding past. Flames exploded outward as the orb of flame hit the tree line.

That quickly, a swath of the forest was on fire, along with at least four lizards.

"Now!" said Mordecai, pushing Miko forward. "To the river!"

I didn't know where we were going, and Miko had longer legs anyway, so it only made sense that she took the lead. I followed as closely as I could.

We'd made it maybe fifty yards when Lace appeared out of nowhere, running easily beside me. "What happened?"

"Gyr beasts," I managed. "Pack."

"Skaal? Mordecai?"

"Behind us. Said to head to the river."

"Blood and ash. That explains the smoke." She clapped me on the shoulder, throwing me off stride. "Stop at the bank. Stay as still as you can. We'll find you there."

And just like that, she was gone again, veering away to head back towards where we'd come from.

Three Tins, I told myself. *They'll be fine.*

Only... if that were true, then why would Mordecai have told us to run? And risked setting the woods ablaze?

There's no risk. Flame Manipulation will keep it from spreading.

Then why does it seem like everything behind us is on fire?

I… didn't have an answer for that, which made for the second internal debate I'd lost in less than a week.

Somewhere into the run, my wounds opened back up. *Pain Tolerance* was back at work, but I could feel blood trickling down my leg, mingling with the sweat and dirt.

One more problem to add to the pile.

It was all I could do to keep Miko in sight. I focused on her form, willed my legs to keep churning, and desperately hoped she knew where we were going.

I don't know how long we ran. It felt like hours but could have been only minutes instead. When the Priestess suddenly slowed, my heart sank with the fear that she was as lost as I was. Then I heard it: water, rushing by at a breakneck speed from somewhere just ahead.

She hissed as I came up beside her. "You're bleeding again."

"Yeah. It opened back up as we ran."

Instead of casting another *Minor Healing*, she took off her pack and started rooting through it. An interior pouch held a small assortment of dried herbs.

"I'm sorry. I would heal it again, but…"

"I get it. You don't know how badly the others will be hurt."

"Exactly."

She took a greyish leaf from the pouch, ground it up between her clawed fingers, and paused. "Can you take off your pants?"

"We might have to keep running."

"This will only take a moment."

"Okay." I planted Riok's spear to the side and shrugged, as if disrobing in the middle of a forest fire while being hunted by giant predatory lizards was just another Tuesday. The wind was blowing east to west, so at least we didn't have to worry about the fire coming our way.

My leg looked a lot worse without torn fabric covering the damage, the re-opened wounds in my outer thigh jagged and bloody. I swallowed as I saw how close the gyr beast had come to the main artery in my leg. If I'd been lying at an even slightly different angle when it hit me…

I would have been dead before Miko could even reach me, and finding out if all of Shan's threats were real or just motivation.

"This will sting," warned Miko. She took the powdered herb in both hands and rubbed it directly into my open wounds, in a scene that would have given any medical doctor back home conniptions.

It *did* sting. Without *Pain Tolerance*, I'm pretty sure it would have outright hurt like hell, but the Priestess ignored my startled gasp.

"We need bandages too," she muttered. "Why didn't I bring bandages?" She dug back into her pack and eventually pulled out the robes I'd traded weeks of language class for.

"Wait!" I told her, waving to my pack. It was a shredded disaster, but the clothes inside were still mostly intact, and miraculously, nothing had fallen out during our panicked run. "Use the scarf instead?"

She hesitated, then nodded. "It's a good length. That will work!" Soon, she was wrapping Nala's gift around my bare and bloody thigh.

"That's a little bit tight," I wheezed, after she had tied it off.

"It has to be." When she looked up at me, I could see worry in her strange orange eyes. "The hangroot will slow the bleeding, but until I can spare another *Minor Healing*, your wounds have to clot on their own. We can't afford—"

"To leave a blood trail." I nodded, feeling lightheaded. "More than I already have, anyway."

"Yes." She returned the supplies to her pack and stood, scanning our surroundings as I pulled on what was left of my pants. "Do you think the others can find us?"

I tested my leg. It wasn't ideal, but it held my weight. I tried not to wince as I pulled Riok's spear out of the earth and held it at the ready. This close to the Snake River, the trees had thinned out, so I would at least see any man-eating lizards coming.

How that would help, when the beasts were almost definitely Tin, was yet another in a long line of problems for future-Brian.

"Both Skaal and Lace know how to track," I said, eyes drawn to the thick plumes of smoke now visible in the skies behind us. "I'm sure they'd already be here if they hadn't had to guard us from those things."

"Gyr beasts," she reminded me.

"Right. You have those back home too?"

"They have a different coloration and are much, much smaller, but yes. We should both be grateful that your wounds were inflicted by claw and not bite. Their venom is incredibly potent."

"Does *everything* on this planet want to kill us?"

"There's a reason our ancestors needed the Framework," she reminded me.

"The gods should have given you artillery instead," I muttered.

Miko ignored my complaints, eyes fixed on the forest behind us. "Is the fire coming this way?"

"I don't—" I stopped. The wind had shifted at some point during my bandaging, and the smoke rising into the air was a lot closer now than it had been. Worse, I could see flickers of orange, almost lost within the depths of the dense tree line. "Crap, you're right. Let's get as close to the river as we can. Watch out for cutters or anything else in there that might be eager to eat us."

She was way ahead of me, swinging her pack onto one shoulder and holding out her arm as she offered support.

I waved her off and used Riok's spear as a walking stick instead, carrying my now open-faced pack in my other arm. Together, we retreated across the fifteen to twenty feet of space we had, stopping only as we ran up onto the bank itself. The Snake River was much narrower here than it had been the day before, the current that much faster, and the sun's light was enough to spot the things wriggling downstream in its depths.

"Between the river and the reduced number of trees, this would be a decent firebreak," I said. "If—"

"If only we were on the other side," Miko finished for me.

"Exactly. As it is, if the fire gets much closer, we're going to have to figure out what to do."

"We should eat the thegar," Miko reminded me.

"That's not—" I sighed. She was right. One bite at a time. "Yeah. First, let's wait as long as we can and see if the others reach us first. If not, we can try to figure out a way across the river, or head further upstream and hope the wind doesn't shift again?"

She eyed the river. "I think I could make the jump."

"Are you sure?"

She considered it for a moment longer, then nodded. "I am not a great runner, but I can leap. However, with your leg..."

"I couldn't make that jump even if I was fully healthy." I shook my head. "I'm not a runner or a leaper, and all these points in *Athleticism* haven't changed that. Not yet anyway."

"You kept up with me, while wounded."

"Barely."

"Even so." Her transparent inner eyelids flickered as she looked up and down the river's bank. "There," she said, pointing to a slightly elevated outcrop jutting over thee river. "Maybe if I can leap from there, I can carry you with me?"

I started to reply and then stopped, as I realized for the first time, just how dumb I was being.

"Or I could just get across with Lunge."

"I…" She blinked both sets of eyelids rapidly. "I had forgotten your technique."

"You're not the only one." If I'd triggered it when the gyr beast leaped at me the second time, I could have avoided being injured at all. "I haven't used it in days and then when the opportunity came along, I forgot I even had it."

"We were ambushed by a hunting pack of oversized gyr beasts," Miko said. "Panic is understandable."

"If you say so." She was trying to make me feel better, but that wasn't going to happen. If I was going to survive on Eos, I had to use every gift I'd been given… and that included my brain.

Keep training, I told myself. *Train until using your techniques is a matter of instinct.*

It was a great plan… and one I wouldn't be able to implement until we were out of this godforsaken forest.

I was starting to think future-Brian really did get the shaft.

For now, there was nothing I could do but keep pressing forward. Spear in hand, I headed for the outcrop Miko had mentioned. "Let's cross there," I said. "We can stay in sight of the river so Lace and the others see us. And if the gyr beasts find us first, we'll at least have a piranha-filled moat between us and them."

If Miko could leap the river, the lizards would *definitely* be able to, but maybe I could skewer them in mid-air… or at least knock them into the river where they and the cutters would have a face-to-face?

38

We were halfway to the jumping spot when a shadow burst out of the woods a good hundred feet to our south. I clutched Riok's spear tightly, relaxing it only when a second shape appeared, this one long and frightfully skinny.

Skaal. Which made the first shape Lace.

As ever, Miko's eyes were better than mine. "Skaal has Mordecai," she told me, breaking into a run. "The caster is wounded."

The others spotted us almost as soon as we had spotted them and hurried over downstream.

"Are the gyr beasts dead?" I asked Lace.

"Not enough of them. I've never seen a pack even half this size before." There was blood on her black leathers, but none of it seemed to be hers. She held her slim sword in one hand and a dagger in the other. "We'll have to cross and hope the river's enough to shake them."

Miko was already at Skaal's side, her hands hovering above the still shape in the reaver's arms. I turned from the familiar glow of *Minor Healing* and pointed to the outcrop now behind us.

"We were thinking the same thing, just about escaping the fire instead. Miko is convinced she can make the jump from there."

"What about you?"

"I have *Lunge*."

She nodded, wiping her blades clean on the grass and sheathing them again. "Even in its base form, that should do."

"Will you and Skaal be able to make it? Especially with him carrying Mordecai? *And* two packs?"

"There's only one way to find out." She turned back to the other members of our party. "Is he healed?"

Miko shook her head. "It take more."

"Heal him again when *Minor Healing* is available. For now, we need to move."

Skaal looked like death warmed over, but… he kind of always did. He met Lace's eyes. "River?"

"Yeah. Cross and then cut into the trees on the other side. Hopefully, the pack will lose our scent or Mordecai's budding forest fire will drive them away."

The reaver looked to the river and back to the burning woods to our west. When he spoke, it was in the language they shared. "There is another option."

"No, there isn't," snapped Lace. "Not now and not ever."

For a moment, something shifted in Skaal's pale eyes, something cold and hard.

"Your life is mine, old man," Lace's voice was a low hiss. "I choose when and how you spend it. Not you. Do you understand?"

Miko looked between the two, picking up on the obvious tension, even if she couldn't understand the words being said. In Skaal's arms, Mordecai was still out like a light.

Finally, the reaver nodded. "Brian and Miko first," he said in his clumsy Trade. "Then me. Then you."

"What is going on?" asked Miko in the High Tongue as we headed for the outcrop.

"I have no idea." I switched back to Trade. "Be careful."

She nodded. As we reached the riverbank, she kicked into a run, one long stride after the next. Her third step took her onto the outcrop and then she was airborne, one arm holding her pack tightly as the other stretched forward in case she needed to grab onto the far bank's edge.

Instead, she cleared that edge by at least three feet, tumbling as she landed. When she stood and looked back, I could see the synossian smile break out on her face.

"Thank God I don't have to do *that*," I muttered.

"Which god?" asked Lace, appearing at my side.

"Take your pick, as long as it's not the one that would spit roast us for all eternity."

"It's just as well," she said. "The Night Hag *wants* us to fall."

Which answered the question of whether Hashoggath and the Night Hag were one and the same.

"And you worship her?"

"Why not? At least she's honest."

There was no mirth in the Marauder's grin. On top of whatever was going on between her and Skaal, I was starting to think our party leader might be clinically insane.

Which… was probably a valid survival tactic on Eos.

Needless to say, I wasn't loving this world quite as much as I had been a night earlier.

I clutched my ruined pack to my chest and stepped up onto the outcrop, Riok's spear in hand. I fixed my attention on a spot just to the side of where Miko had landed. It seemed well within *Lunge's* range, but there was no escaping the knowledge of what waited for me in the river's depths if I was wrong. Maybe there was a better spot to lunge from?

You're stalling.

I'm… preparing.

This is one of the few things you have *trained for.*

I blinked, nerves settling. That was actually true.

Before I could talk myself back into being afraid, I triggered *Lunge.* That momentary exhilaration returned as the world blurred around me, as momentum carried me forward at a speed my purely physical body still couldn't match. When it faded, I was on the far side of the river, feet planted firmly beneath me, only inches off from the spot I had targeted.

Practice really does pay off.

Before I could even pat myself on the back, Skaal was in the air, clearing the river easily despite the body in his arms and the two packs and large weapon on his back. He landed heavily, dropping to one knee, but was up again just as quickly, eyes now scanning the forest on our side of the river.

Lace was the last to make the leap, somehow almost as graceful in the air as she was on the ground. She made it a few feet past where Miko had fallen, landing on both feet and easily absorbing the impact with her legs.

"How long until your next cast?" she asked the Priestess.

"Soon."

"When you—"

Thunder cut her off, the rumble so loud it felt like it shook the ground. Dark clouds had appeared above us, where there had been smoke and otherwise blue skies. As I looked, more clouds manifested out of nowhere, blotting out the sun in a way the smoke from Mordecai's fire hadn't managed.

"Into the woods," hissed Lace, eyes suddenly wide. "Now."

This time, she didn't wait for us, but sprinted for the trees, her speed leaving everyone else in the dust. Skaal was next, then Miko, with me in the rear as always, courtesy of a low Finesse stat and legs more suitable for a dunsman.

Behind me, the skies shook again, and a downpour began.

By the time I made it into the woods, Skaal had laid Mordecai down and Lace was kneeling over the masked caster.

"Mordecai, wake up." When he didn't reply, she removed one of her gloves and slapped the unconscious man across the face.

Miko stepped forward. "What are—"

"We need him conscious," said Lace. "If you can help, help. Otherwise, stay out of my way."

For the first time in a long while, I saw the difference between a synossian smile and an *actual* snarl. The Priestess set her pack down and retrieved the same pouch of herbs she'd used earlier. Whatever she pulled out wasn't hangroot, but something shaped almost like a pod of peas. She held it above Mordecai's face and snapped it between her two clawed hands.

"Stimulant," she said, voice still a low growl. "Better than hitting already injured."

"Whatever works—" Lace stopped as Mordecai startled awake beneath her.

"What... where..."

"Flameweaver, we need wards. Now."

"I... what?"

"Moment," said Miko, tossing aside the used pea pod and holding her hands out above Mordecai's chest.

A second casting of *Minor Healing* washed over the Flameweaver and he stopped thrashing about.

"Are you with us, Adept of the Crimson Needle?" asked Lace.

"For now." Mordecai's voice was weak, but coherent.

"We need your wards," she said again. "And... overload them if you can."

"That will put me back out until morning, lass."

"It's necessary. Your little bonfire has attracted attention."

Another peal of thunder shook the forest, and Mordecai stiffened. "Gods above." He turned his masked face to Lace. "I'll need help to walk the perimeter."

"Skaal will carry you. Miko and Brian, join me in the middle."

We did so, my leg throbbing as I took a seat across from the Marauder.

"What attention?" asked Miko, her voice still tight.

"According to the Adventurer's Guild in Madea, there's an ancient Thunderbird that nests in the peaks at the forest's southern edge. I don't know what it's doing this far north, but…" She paused again, listening to the thunder, then cursed. "That was closer. It's coming this way."

"What rank is it?" I asked.

"The guild didn't know. They just posted a general warning, same as for that snake titan of yours: *avoid at all costs*. What in the nine demon realms is it doing down here?"

"Wards are done," said Skaal, lowering an unconscious Mordecai to the ground next to me.

"Not a moment too—"

Thunder pealed again, and just like that, rain fell upon us in sheets, forcing its way through the thin canopy of leaves and branches. In a matter of seconds, we were soaked to the bone.

That was when I felt it… a presence that flooded the forest just like the storm that had announced its arrival. The Thunderbird's attention was elsewhere, but steadily moving toward us.

Maybe it was *Danger Sense* or maybe it was just basic self-preservation, but I knew we did not want that focus falling on us.

"Form a circle," said Lace. "Clasp hands with your neighbor."

Miko and I exchanged confused glances but did as told. Mordecai was still unconscious and flat on his back, so I took his right hand in mine while Skaal did the same with his left.

The center of that terrible presence swept toward us, the river's sound lost somewhere beneath the greater storm.

"Don't move," said Lace, her voice tense. "And whatever you see or hear, don't speak."

Like an idiot, I opened my mouth to ask for clarification.

The rain vanished.

The forest vanished.

Only the Thunderbird's presence remained, but even that was muted, like when I had hidden from storms as a child under a shield of every blanket in the trailer.

This time, there were no blankets. No trailer. No bed. There was just darkness, all-consuming.

Except… even that wasn't true.

Because the darkness that had swallowed us wasn't empty. Shapes slid through it like cutters, twisting and turning in upon themselves, writhing in agony and ecstasy alike. I felt some brush by me, and even with Lace's warnings, it was all I could do not to scream or twist away.

Miko's hand, ten miles away for all that it was held in mine, squeezed tightly. I squeezed it back, not sure if I was giving comfort or seeking it.

Even in the darkness of another realm, I could feel when the Thunderbird passed by overhead, feel the killing edge of the creature's focus pierce Mordecai's wards. Those wards robbed it of some of its strength, some of its vision, but what remained fell upon us—

—and moved on, blinded by the darkness we had fallen into.

I waited until that presence had passed beyond Mordecai's wards and let out the long, slow breath I hadn't even realized I'd been holding.

The shapes around us froze. A thousand eyes turned toward me in the darkness, and then the largely unseen horrors scattered, fleeing into the unseen night of their realm.

Something shifted. It was too far away to see or sense, but I knew it was there anyway. Something that defied purely physical concepts like size and distance. Darkness rippled, an entire realm reshaping itself as something too large to be contained started our way.

I squeezed my eyes shut, but the glow that came from an unseen horizon—fiery and wet, malignant and bone dry—couldn't be unseen. Neither could the monstrous creature, as large as an ocean, crawling her way across terrain now revealed to be nothing but miles of broken glass.

She had tentacles instead of hair, every undulating strand ending in a grasping hand, and nine misshapen breasts, each crowned by a spike of black metal. Her eyes were raw wet pits, gateways to the darkness we had so recently been surrounded by.

Without pupils or sclera... without anything that resembled an eye at all... it should have been impossible to tell what she was looking at, but I felt it in my bones, when that unseen gaze landed on me.

And then we were back in the forest, drenched and sitting in inches of mud. To my left, Miko shuddered. To my right, Mordecai remained blissfully unconscious. But directly across from me...

Lace's silver eyes were locked on me. "What did you do?" she demanded.

"Nothing! Unless you count breathing."

"I felt her gaze, for the first time ever, but it was you she sought. She woke for you." Her words were iron. "She wanted you, and if I hadn't ended the technique, she would have had you. So the least you can do in exchange for me saving both your life and your soul is speak truly: *what did you do?*"

"I just *told* you. I breathed. If I wasn't supposed to do *that* either, you should have said so."

"Who is she?" asked Miko, white scales dripping in the rain.

"Hashoggath," I answered. "Lace's deity, the Night Hag. Am I right?"

"Yes," said the Marauder, her voice still hard.

"I thought gods weren't allowed to interfere with the physical realm?" I asked, ignoring that Shan had done just that for me.

"They aren't. My gift is Framework-given, and that wasn't the physical realm… it was hers."

Miko blinked both sets of eyelids. "You have technique to go to gods?"

"Just one god: mine. And we don't travel there so much as temporarily hide in her domain. Any large movement ends the technique."

"And sound?"

"Attracts the denizens." Lace scowled. "*Night Hag's Embrace* is the technique I gained in my Dreaming. No energy cost, but the maximum duration is five minutes, and I can't use it more than once a moon. I've never been offered an upgrade to it. Nor has Hashoggath herself ever stirred."

"I don't know what to tell you," I said. "You were there. I didn't do anything."

"Fire is out," said Skaal. "Gyr beasts likely scattered by Thunderbird. Camp?"

The Marauder nodded, finally releasing me from her death glare. "Mordecai isn't in any shape to cast fresh wards, and even pierced, his wards tonight will be stronger than usual."

"Because he overloaded them," I said. "What does that mean?"

"I'm not speaking with you, Brian Fieldings of some small town that nobody has heard of."

"*Overload is* technique," said Skaal. "Alter other technique. Make strong at big cost."

"Slightly stronger at more like quintuple the cost," muttered Lace. "Even if he hadn't been injured, he'd be unconscious from the drain alone after the wards and the battle with the gyr beasts." She caught herself and turned on the reaver. "And don't *you* speak to him either!"

Skaal inclined his head solemnly. "Was speaking to little Miko."

"Of course you were." She blew out a long breath and when she spoke again, her voice was almost calm. "We'll stay here for the night and make use of Mordecai's overloaded wards. Miko, use what heals you have remaining and then get some sleep. Brian has first watch. Skaal has second, and I'll take third. Anyone speaks to me before then and I'll gut them myself."

She stalked away, finding a space inside the perimeter to set up her tent.

"How did she get an ability like that in her Dreaming?" I wondered aloud.

"Should ask," said Skaal, blithely ignoring Lace's commands not to talk to me.

"Maybe later. She seems kind of angry now." It was as much a leading question as the mother of all understatements.

He took the bait. "Is responsible for party," he said. "Fears cost of decisions she makes."

"Maybe you should lead then?"

The reaver's pale eyes—sometimes blue, sometimes grey— hardened. "No. Is path for others."

He rose to his feet again, towering above us all. "Will set up tents while little Miko heals. Do not forget leg."

39-Interlude

Lace woke on her own, which was the first sign something was off. The fact that she could see without activating her *Night Eyes* technique was another. Biting back a sigh, she made her way outside to find the night sky a pale grey instead of its usual black, courtesy of the swiftly approaching dawn.

With no fire to circle around, the tents had been laid out more haphazardly than normal, but Skaal was exactly where she expected him to be, quiet and still in the early morning light.

"You were supposed to wake me for my watch," she told him, speaking the language of the south.

"You travel twice as far as the rest of us on the best of days." He kept his senses tuned to the surrounding forest, voice a low rumble. "You needed the rest more than I did."

"Still looking after me all these cycles later."

"It is not my place."

That stole the smile from her face. Lace sighed. "I shouldn't have said that yesterday. To you, least of all."

"It is forgotten."

"Is it?"

For the first time, he looked at her, his features fuzzy in the half-light. "Yes. I know your heart."

After all this time, she was pretty sure he didn't, but she just leaned against him, always taken aback by how thin he had become.

"However," he added, "the others in our party might not be as confident."

"You saw what I saw," she said. "Better than me even, given your vantage point."

"I saw."

"She woke for *him*. Hashoggath woke for Brian Fieldings."

"So it seems."

"And?"

"And I don't think he has answers to give you."

"Really? You think he and the scaled are just ignorant villagers from a town nobody knows exists?" She scoffed.

"Answers about the Night Hag," Skaal clarified. "As for the rest, it is clear they have their secrets."

"And?" she pressed again.

"And that is their right, just as it is ours. We have few enough things to call our own. Maybe our pasts should be one of them."

She hit him with a sharp elbow, not even eliciting a grunt. "I hate when you get philosophical."

"And yet here we sit, a new day about to dawn."

She snorted, hiding a laugh that would have shocked their two newest party members if they'd seen it.

"As for Brian," continued Skaal, "I have kept my eye on him. While raw, he is a quick study and a hard worker."

"So were a lot of the people we've buried over the cycles."

She took his grunt as an acknowledgment of her point.

"Even so, I can tell you at least one thing he is hiding from us."

She sat up straight, tossing a glance back at the tents even though she'd have sensed someone stirring. "What's that?"

"He speaks more than just Trade and the language of his supposed village."

"What do you mean?"

"Watch his eyes when we talk in Gorash."

She sucked in a breath. "He's not from the south."

"Agreed."

"Then an academy like Mordecai's Crimson Needle?"

"Maybe." He shrugged. "He did say he was a translator. Perhaps we should have clarified what languages he speaks."

She let her eyes drift shut as she tried to remember anything and everything they'd said freely over the past few days, confident that the newcomers wouldn't understand. "Are you certain?"

He gave her a long look that made her feel like she was sixteen cycles old again.

"Fine, but I'm going to make sure. Later. In the meantime, the wards should be breaking down soon. If you're going to stay on watch, I might as well go scout out our path."

She patted him on the shoulder, trying not to wince at the feeling of bone where there once had been hard muscle, and rose to her feet. A step later, she spun back to face him.

"I shouldn't have said what I said to you yesterday, but the message stands. I don't want to hear you asking to throw your life away. Not again. Not anymore."

For only the second time since she'd woken up, he looked at her, and if it had been anyone else, the storm in his eyes would have had her reaching for her blades.

"Next time, I will not ask."

"Skaal…"

"The choice is mine. It has always been so. Your life above my own. A fair trade, especially now."

She swallowed. "We'll find a cure. *I* will find one."

He nodded, the caged tiger of his soul vanishing behind a too-white mask of flesh and bone.

"I believe you."

"Then promise me that you will hold on until we do."

"I promise to try."

She wanted to be angry, to demand more. Instead, she nodded. "I'll be back in a glass. Stay well, son of the storm."

"Safe travels, daughter of dusk."

40

I woke refreshed, not caring whether I had my improved Vitality to thank for it or the early watch that had let me sleep the rest of the night through. We'd hiked for less than half of our usual time the day before, but between the gyr beasts, the Thunderbird, and Lace's terrifying goddess, it had been a *lot* to take in.

And my most recent injury hadn't helped.

I ran through my forms, and then checked on the wound before I got up, unwrapping the scarf bandage on my thigh. Miko's second *Minor Healing*, along with a good night of sleep, had transformed the lacerations into long, thin scars. The skin was still puffy, tight, and tender, but another casting would hopefully take care of that.

After a night of sleep, my friend should be back to full energy. I just hoped she leveled soon. A new spell or even an upgrade to *Minor Healing* would be huge for us all.

She was already gone from our tent, so I pulled my pants on—a new pair, if not exactly fresh—and headed outside. Mordecai was upright, looking tired but well as he spoke in low words with Skaal. On the other side of camp, Miko had donned the robes I'd given her and was greeting the dawn.

I waited for the ceremony to finish, then brought her a waterskin.

"It's not *kallnor*," I told her in the High Tongue. "But if you're thirsty…"

"You remember *kallnor*?"

"It's not every day you drink something made from fermented beetle feces."

"More's the pity." Miko exhaled. "I was asking for Aurea's blessing."

"Did she respond?"

"Sometimes, I wonder." She mustered up a smile as she took a drink from the offered skin. "And then I think how much worse yesterday would have been without her grace."

"I think the others are realizing Mordecai was right about needing to bring you." Meanwhile, I'd been essentially useless except as a basic watchperson, but that was neither here nor there.

"I hope so." She held a clawed hand to her lower belly. "I'm close. To level five, I mean."

"Have you meditated?"

She nodded. "Before you woke. A few skill-ups, but my soul is not quite ready. Still, another day like yesterday…"

"Let's not invite calamity down upon us." I grinned uneasily. "I somehow gained two points in *Light Armor* and *Avoidance*. I also got a point each in *Athleticism*, *Pain Tolerance*, *Danger Sense*, and, for some reason, *Formations*. Not bad for a fight where I didn't land a single blow."

"We were battling ranked opponents. Tin opponents," she corrected herself. "Simply surviving was an accomplishment our souls could resonate with." She passed back the waterskin. "Help me with the tent once I have changed for travel?"

"Of course." I watched her go. It had almost stopped feeling odd to me that she was, by far, the most alien person I knew, and still the only one I felt entirely comfortable with.

Familiarity is a weird thing. But so is common cause, I guess.

By the time Miko changed and we had stashed away the tent in her pack, Lace was back at camp. She darted a glance at me, and then visibly reconsidered whatever she had wanted to say. Instead, she gathered the group.

"The Thunderbird is gone, back to the peaks by the looks of the storm clouds. I didn't see any sign that the gyr beast pack had crossed the river either."

I let out a thankful sigh. The Thunderbird returning to its nest made sense, but for some reason, I'd expected the pack to continue hunting us.

"We crossed earlier than planned," Lace continued, "but should be able to reach the caves the day after tomorrow."

"Pray they are unoccupied," murmured Mordecai.

"It's possible that the Thunderbird's storms will have flooded out any inhabitants."

Miko looked up at that. "The nilwort?"

"Does well in wet places, lass," said the Flameweaver.

"It also might not be growing there at all," added Lace. "The caves we're headed for seem like the right sort of environment, but we have no confirmation the plant is actually there."

"What do we do if it isn't?" I asked.

"Keep looking, obviously. That's the mission."

As much trouble as we'd had making it through the forest with a concrete destination in mind, I didn't relish the idea of just wandering aimlessly instead.

"We'll still have to find shademoss."

"I might be able to help there." Lace finished tightening the straps on Skaal's pack, her hand lingering on the taller man's arm. "Thick clumps of moss with indigo flowers, growing only on the underside of rock formations, right?"

"Yes…" said Mordecai, drawing out the word.

"And *indigo* means dark purple?"

"More like bluish purple."

"Then I think I spotted some while out scouting." She gave her half-smile, half-snarl to the masked man. "The way you all have been talking, I thought herbalism was supposed to be hard."

"Get moss, head to caves?" suggested Skaal.

"That's the plan. While Mordecai and little Miko deal with the moss, I'll double-check our path."

"Miko," said the synossian in question.

"Pardon?"

"I am Miko," she said, careful to remember her verbs for once. "Not little Miko."

Lace stood there in silence for a moment, her eyes for some reason darting over to Skaal. Finally, she shrugged.

"It was meant to be affectionate, but sure. You've proven your value to this party; you deserve your respect."

"Thank you." Miko folded her hands together and bowed, somehow making the movement graceful even with a pack on her back.

ooo

The moss Lace had found was, in fact, shademoss, which was the first bit of good news we'd had in a while. Mordecai gave Miko the storage container and the two of them worked together to properly harvest the moss, taking chunks seemingly at random, and spraying them with a small vial of solution before they were secreted away again.

It was boring, and I didn't hate that.

When Lace returned again, the pair were still working. To my surprise, she came directly over to where I was keeping watch.

"Last night almost went very badly," she said.

Oh good. More of the same.

"I know," I said. "But like I told you—"

"I get it. You don't know what happened either. I'm just saying: I think you need to figure it out."

"*I* need to figure out why *your* goddess fixated on me?"

"Yes."

I called upon seven years of running a register in a cash-only business to maintain my calm.

"How am I supposed to do that?"

"I don't know." She watched the emotions run across my face. "All I'm saying is that if you two end up becoming a more permanent part of our party, we're going to need to know what's going on."

My irritation subsided, just a bit, as I realized what she was driving at. "Because otherwise you won't be able to use your technique when it refreshes."

"Or at least I won't be able to bring you in there with me." She scowled. "Hashoggath is a vengeful bitch. I love her for that, but I'm not so foolish as to end up on her bad side. Especially not when doing so would keep me from using my oldest and most unexpected technique."

That made an uncomfortable amount of sense.

"Figure it out," she said again, "and then we can talk about you and little—you and Miko accompanying us to Madea when this is done."

Unfortunately, I *had* already thought about the whole strange experience, and the conclusion I'd reached—that it had something to do with me being Chosen—was precisely the sort of thing I didn't dare tell virtual strangers.

Lace stepped in close, a head taller than me for all that she was relatively short. "In the meantime," she whispered, breath cool on my forehead and face, "you might want to avoid Skaal. Sometimes, reavers get a hankering for human meat, and last night I heard him saying something about Warrior dumplings."

I blanched, looking toward the stoic half-giant despite myself.

"Huh," said Lace, smiling brightly as she turned away. "I guess he was right. We'll want to talk about how someone from the pit end of nowhere knows Gorash too."

Shit. I closed my eyes as the realization set in. She'd kept me so off balance that I hadn't even recognized her story about Skaal was in a language other than Trade.

I was going to have to tell Miko my secret was out.

○○○

A full glass later, we were back underway. I was in the rear once again, but Mordecai and Miko were walking side by side, the taller synossian speaking in hushed whispers with the masked spellcaster. From the way the Flameweaver was rubbing his hands together, I was almost positive the two were discussing other herbs they could collect for sale.

As far as get-rich schemes went, it seemed like a good one, and Miko would both get her cut and earn valuable skills in the process. I tuned out their dialogue and focused instead on the world around me.

I was pretty sure *Danger Sense* had saved me from the gyr beast's initial assault, but if I'd been paying better attention, I might have been able to avoid being injured at all. So, I played rear guard, doing my best to utilize the walking style Lace had taught me, while also turning my senses to the woods around me.

The lack of birds was the first thing I noticed. They hadn't been plentiful west of the river, but we'd still heard them. Here, their song was almost entirely absent, while the clouds of bugs were that much thicker and obtrusive. Somewhere in the distance, something like a frog gave off a loud croak, and there were the occasional cries from unseen critters that my *Animal Behaviorism* skill alternately tagged as warnings, calls of distress, or even lonely creatures seeking mates.

I wrinkled my nose. Sometimes, the Framework's skills gave out *too* much information. It was a pity those undersexed forest animals couldn't waste their days on dating sites and social media like the rest of us.

After dropping her bombshell, Lace hadn't said anything more. She seemed content to once again scout ahead, leaving Skaal to lead our tiny column. In fact, we didn't see her again until long after another cold lunch; she materialized out of the woods to guide us around some sort of den or hive whose inhabitants I was deeply sure I didn't want to see, let alone encounter.

Mud aside, the rest of the day passed quietly and peacefully. Still, as we bedded down for the night, I had a hard time relaxing. The gyr beasts had taught me that death was ever-present here, and just because it didn't take the form of half-cat, half-dinosaur hybrids dropping down on you from above didn't make it any less threatening.

I had middle watch—which I was pretty sure was a punishment from Lace—but barely slept during first watch anyway. When I was done meditating—one sorely needed skill-up in *Stealth*, but nothing else—I lay awake in the dark, listening to Miko's quiet breathing. As much as I hated to admit it, Lace kind of had a point. Her technique had saved our lives, but I was under no illusions as to what would have happened if the Night Hag had reached me while we were still even partially in her realm.

If I was Chosen, as the synossians had insisted, what would that mean to the pantheons who *hadn't* been part of my summoning? Did my association with Shan make me a target of rival deities? And for that matter, how had *Lace* of all people gotten a technique so tightly coupled with her goddess, when Miko, as devout a worshipper as I'd ever met, just seemed to get the usual generic options from Aurea?

Ask her, Skaal had said. Like all good advice, it was mostly useless because it involved something I didn't want to do.

○○○

The next morning, I found myself walking just a little bit more naturally than I had the day before, the movements coming more easily on account of my raised *Stealth* skill. I wasn't any faster, and it still took more focus than I could really afford, but concrete evidence of the Framework's benefits had my mood soaring.

When we stopped for lunch, I approached our ever-present masked font of information, Mordecai.

"Hi."

As ever, the only parts of his face I could see were his eyes, brown and almost always bloodshot. They darted to my face and away again. "What can I do for you, lad?"

"I was hoping we could talk tonight after you set the wards?"

"Ah, I see." He took a careful step back and gave a bow that made Miko's seem primitive. "I am flattered, truly, but my heart belongs to another, and she is entirely female. Excessively female, some have been known to suggest, though I would never be so crass."

I stared at him. "I meant the Framework."

"What?"

"I wanted to talk with you about the Framework."

"Oh. Well, yes, I can understand that. There are few schools as well renowned as the Crimson Needle after all."

"Exactly." So far, he was the only person I'd met who'd seemed impressed by the name, but I wasn't going to argue. "As you know, Miko and I are from a small village."

"Yes, I do remember."

"While she knows some things about the Framework, I was never…" I coughed and gave him a self-deprecating smile. "Well, I was only ever interested in languages, really. Except now…"

"Now, you find yourself in the greater world and realize your ignorance and idleness might cost you."

"I wouldn't say idle—" I cut myself off. Why was I arguing about a history I'd invented on the spot? "Yes," I agreed. "I am starting to recognize that knowledge is power."

"Knowledge is power?" Mordecai muttered the words, stroking the lower portion of his mask like it was a beard. "I have never heard it said quite like that, but you are spot on, my boy. And I will be happy to help—" He lowered his voice, glancing around. "—once we are safe in camp, with the wards up again, of course. However, what you really need is a primer."

"A what?"

"Primers are a kind of book." He hesitated. "Do you… know what a book is?"

"I worked as a scribe during my time in Harborton."

"You're a Scribe?" I could almost hear the capitalization.

"Not officially, no… I don't have all the necessary skills, but I *can* read and write."

"Well, there you have it."

I waited in vain for him to continue.

"Have what, exactly?"

"Your solution, of course. Most cities and even some towns have archives. Access to the deeper stacks can be problematic, but if all you need is the fundamentals, you should have no concerns."

"There are books about the Framework?"

"Of course! Now, any knowledge with *real* value is either jealously hoarded away by greedy families, clans, and sects *or* painstakingly preserved for promising students in a few notable academies—"

I didn't even have to ask to know that he placed the Crimson Needle in the latter group.

"—but the basics? A copper plug will get you a day's pass to the first-level stacks of any archives outside of the capital city itself."

I smiled despite myself. We already had the equivalent of a plug and a half in bits, even before considering the money Miko would earn through the herbs she was gathering.

"I can tell that the seed has been planted." I couldn't see the Flameweaver's face, but his eyes were bright. "And lo, from lazy ignorance, a future scholar is born! Perhaps I *should* have stayed and become a meister!"

Skaal turned and gave us both a look that killed the conversation as swiftly as if he'd used the named weapon on his back. Still, as we marched on, Mordecai's steps were lighter somehow, as if my apparent interest in the academic arts had made his day.

Meanwhile, I was just annoyed I'd been called lazy again.

41

The rest of the day passed without incident, as did the night's watch. It seemed that the Thunderbird's passage had driven a lot of the forest's lesser predators into hiding. That would change soon enough—as instinct and simple hunger took over—but we used the unexpected peace to make good time.

My conversation with Mordecai was less illuminating than I'd hoped. He did confirm that most of what I had been taught about the Framework—ranks notwithstanding—was true, but he also tended to go on long, rambling tangents about things he'd learned, seen, or heard while studying at the Crimson Needle. By the time he headed to his tent, I knew more than I wanted to about a school I'd never see.

The next morning stayed quiet, although the forest's population seemed to be recovering from the Thunderbird's unexpected visit. Twice, Lace veered far to the east or west to avoid unnamed dangers. Thankfully, neither of those terrors appeared inclined to follow our trails. And just before we were planning to stop for a quick and cold lunch, she brought back the word we'd all been hoping for:

We'd finally reached our destination.

The caves weren't much to look at. Set into the side of one of the area's many hills, there were two openings, one near the bottom and one above. The lower one was partially blocked by dirt.

"Mudslide," Lace said, when I pointed it out. "That's also the entrance we'll have to take. The top one was an old den of some sort and ends about twenty paces in."

"Any signs of life below?" asked Mordecai. For some reason, his mask today was black instead of cream or grey, giving him an ominous look entirely at odds with his personality.

Lace shook her head. "A few tracks that I'll want Skaal to look at, but I didn't see any scat or markings in the cave itself. Although I only went deep enough to make sure it continues."

I traded looks with Miko. Now that we had arrived, the occasion felt almost momentous. Our first dungeon dive in pursuit of treasure and glory!

Granted, the 'dungeon' was a set of caves, and the 'treasure' was a plant, but still… it was the principle of the thing.

"Do we keep the same formation?" I asked.

Lace nodded. "For now. I won't be ranging far ahead, but even a little bit of scouting goes a long way in tight areas."

Which meant I would be at the back again waiting for something to creep up behind us. Lovely.

My pack only had a single functional strap after the gyr beasts, but Miko had used her single-ranked *Tailoring* skill and the remnants of the other strap to gather the pack's pieces up like a satchel. I shifted the burden to my left shoulder, leaving my right arm free to thrust with the spear.

Technically, I needed *both* arms, but it was the rearmost hand—the right one in my case—that delivered the power.

Don't forget Lunge *this time, moron.*

"Mordecai, the group will need a light eventually," added Lace. "Should Skaal make a torch, or will you provide?"

"Let's do the former, lass." He was all business. "I can grab the flame from the torch if need be, but I'd rather preserve my energy for when it's necessary."

That raised a question that had been troubling me since the lizard ambush. "Why weren't you able to use *Flame Manipulation* to control the forest fire's flames?"

"It's a question of scope, my boy. There are many considera—"

"He can't handle anything larger than his hand," interrupted Lace, "and even then, his range is about the same as his physical reach."

"Well, yes. I suppose that's a layman's explanation," harrumphed the caster. "Fire wants to burn, you see. It is far easier to unleash than to bring back under control."

While we were talking, Skaal took the hand axe from his belt and cut down a small branch from a nearby tree. He wrapped one end tightly in rags taken from his pack and handed the makeshift torch to Miko.

"Weapon and light," he explained.

"I have *Flare* as well," said Miko. "But does not—" She coughed. "*It* does not burn."

I gave her a stealthy thumbs up. Despite the challenges of our trip so far, she was still working hard on her Trade.

"Wait to light the torch until you need it," said Lace. "If there *is* anything down there, any light will tell them we're coming. With luck, I'll have found the dangers by then."

"You won't take a torch?" I asked.

"No." Lace traded glances with Skaal, then turned and disappeared into the cave.

"Eyes like a cat, that one," whispered Mordecai.

I just nodded. Honestly, I was more surprised that they had cats here on Eos than that Lace could see in the dark.

I had been expecting some sort of gently rounded interior like you saw in cartoons about bears, but once we squeezed through the partially blocked entrance, we found ourselves at the mouth of a winding tunnel instead, the floor a mixture of soil and stone.

Lace was already gone, and Skaal led us down as soon as we had all made it inside. Tempest remained sheathed and under wraps on his back, but the reaver had a metal gauntlet on his left hand and held the now-familiar short sword in his other. For the first time since we'd met him, he was even wearing armor, a padded vest that extended down past his hips, and a chain shirt above it. Even with the added bulk, he still seemed like he might disappear if he just turned sideways.

I looked down at my filthy clothes and sighed. At least they counted as light armor for the purposes of my skill gains. Still, something offering *actual* protection would've been nice.

That's what the spear's for, I reminded myself. *Stick them with the pointy end and keep them away and you'll never get hit.*

It was a nice fantasy… I decided I'd hold on to it for as long as I could.

ooo

Even with the recent rain, I somehow expected the tunnels to be dry and sterile. Once again, reality proved different. Puddles filled the nooks and crannies of the uneven floor, too often unseen until the splash that announced you'd found another one. Lichen and moss dotted the walls, floor, and ceiling, suggesting the Thunderbird's storms weren't the only ones that hit the region.

Underground, dark, and damp. This definitely had all the necessary criteria for nilwort. Now we just had to find some.

We made it around one bend before the already limited light from the distant opening went away entirely. I stood quietly in the darkness, listening to the scraping of Miko's fire-striker and trying to shield my eyes from the sparks that flew like short-lived fireflies.

Finally, the rags on the makeshift torch caught, and a warm glow lit the tunnel's interior. Ahead of us, the passageway bent and twisted again, but it unmistakably continued to lead down.

At least I wasn't afraid of tight spaces. Growing up in a trailer had been good that way.

"Keep torch behind," Skaal said in a quiet rumble. "Need preserve vision."

"Yes. Will." Miko cleared her throat. "*I* will."

The reaver nodded and started down the tunnel again, his head almost brushing the ceiling, the torchlight glinting off his chain shirt and the buckles of the padded vest below. Miko was close behind, followed by Mordecai, while I again brought up the rear.

We found Lace at the first intersection, almost fifteen minutes later. The tunnel continued down behind her while a second passageway stayed mostly level and split off to the right. She led us into the latter, a soundless shadow barely seen even with the light from Miko's torch.

A tunnel split made it that much more feasible for something to sneak up behind us, so I focused on my duties, listening for any noise that would suggest we weren't alone. Instead, I heard only the occasional drip, as water trickled through cracks and schisms in the hill above us to add to the puddles we'd been trying to avoid.

When the tunnel opened up into a larger cavern, I was the last to realize it. The low ceiling and cramped quarters gave way to a space as large as the chapel I'd first woken up in on Eos. Miko lifted her torch above her to broaden the reach of its light, revealing stalactites high above us. Ahead and to the right were the cave's walls, covered with fungus, and to the left was another puddle, this one so big it might be considered a pond.

I took a careful step to the right, away from the water. I'd seen enough horror movies to know that nothing good came from water in deep places.

"The other tunnel continues," whispered Lace, "but I thought we should check out this space before going further. If you can find nilwort here and now, we can be on our way back to Harborton this afternoon."

"I don't know about nilwort," said Mordecai, scanning the room, "but that over there looks like creeping fog, wouldn't you say, Miko?"

The synossian followed his gaze and nodded excitedly. "Yes. Is good for pain."

"Or for forgetting your troubles for a time or two." I couldn't see the Flameweaver's smile, but I could hear it. "Which is why certain people pay a premium for it."

"Be quick, but be thorough," said Lace. "The nilwort remains our priority."

"Perhaps the three of you can help look for it, while we secure goods for sale, lass? Remember, it's a green tuber, with black-edged, five-sided leaves. Just," he added, "try not to step on anything as you're searching."

"I can't see color in the dark, Mordecai, and the rest of us can't see at all."

"Oh. Quite right. Your torch please, dear," he said to Miko. She lowered it to him, but instead of taking it, he reached up to the fire atop, gathering a few tongues of flame into his hand. He moved those flames to a spot just above his right shoulder and then released them. "That should do. You can pass the torch to Lace now."

As he turned away, still intent on the thick grey moss he'd called creeping fog, the little ball of fire floated with him, like a drone set on auto-follow.

Lace took the torch from Miko, looked to Skaal, who had turned to face the tunnel entrance, then to me and the spear in my hands. She scowled. "I guess I will carry this for now," she said. "If you see anything, try to keep it at bay with that sticker of yours long enough for me to join the fray."

Just once, she was going to give me instructions that *weren't* ominous… but today was clearly not that day.

In a clear sign that Eos didn't have movies, the Marauder headed straight for the pond. In the torchlight, the water was black and opaque. It could have been a handful of feet deep or a thousand. The only movement I saw were ripples, caused by drops of water falling from a stalactite above.

Along the pond's edge, a handful of mushrooms had sprouted, as pale in the torchlight as the water was dark. I held my spear ready, but the shrooms didn't react as Lace bent down to examine them. When she stood again, she gave me an amused look.

"They're not going to tear their way out of the soil and attack you."

"You're not worried that you'll trigger some sort of spore attack or something?"

She shook her head. "These are nightcaps. They are harmless unless you try to eat them."

"And if you do?"

"You'll regret it. They're poisonous."

"Charming." I eyed the ugly mushrooms. "Do you want to collect a few then?"

"Who are you planning to poison, Brian Fieldings?"

"Nobody! I just figured your daggers might be that much more deadly with a little bit of poison on them."

"In an unrefined state, it's bad for the bronze," she said. "Causes pits and scoring while also being too diluted to really matter."

"And if it has been refined?"

"Then it can be dangerous. However, nightcaps are common and can be found above ground as well. There's no point in weighing ourselves down with something that won't bring much money."

"Okay." Movement caught my attention out of the corner of my eye, but when I turned, it was just another ripple, this one caused by a drip from a slightly more distant stalactite. "Should we move on then? I keep worrying this water isn't as empty as it seems."

"It's only a foot deep, and that's because of the storms. The things that live in there aren't going to be large or particularly aggressive. Even a level two Warrior should be safe."

"Still."

"All men are stubborn, even after they've been leashed," she muttered in the language she'd called Gorash.

"I beg your pardon?"

"You heard me, translator." She waved the torch ahead of her. "We'll check that corner next, away from your deadly puddle."

∩∩∩

It took a while to search the cave, and almost as long again for Miko and Mordecai to gather the potentially sellable herbs. Sadly, nilwort was not on that list. We returned to the intersection and headed deeper.

Underground, time was a malleable construct. I wasn't sure how long we descended. I knew only that we'd had to re-wrap the torch twice over that period, finally switching to the branch's other end as the first was chewed away by the constant flames. Eventually, we stopped lighting it entirely, left only with the small ball of fire still floating above Mordecai's shoulder, a sphere that grew and then shrank again as he fed it oxygen.

Three vastly smaller caves later, Miko and Mordecai had packs bulging with potential profit, but we had still come up short on the nilwort.

Lace met us again in the tunnel.

"One last chamber," she said. "This one big enough that Skaal can actually stand upright again."

Skaal grunted. I didn't know how he'd managed the narrow tunnels and low ceilings, but the man hadn't complained even once, in either language.

"Did you see anything that might be nilwort, lass?"

"I couldn't see much of anything, even with *Night Eyes*. But I smelled something musty, along with something rotten."

"Nest?" asked Skaal.

"Yes." Her teeth flashed yellow in the light of Mordecai's flame. "Whatever's down there stirred as I approached. Could be my scent, could be that the thing senses vibrations. Either way, going forward is a risk."

"What's the alternative?" I asked.

"We go back to the surface and search for other caves."

"Places like this don't happen accidentally… there's something about the mineral composition that lends itself to the formation," said Mordecai. "That means there *should* be other caves around. We'd just have to find them."

"That could take days."

Lace nodded at me. "It could. Which is why I'm calling for a party vote. Do we head forward into the unknown, dealing with whatever waits below, or do we go back to the surface and look for a new spot?"

"There is no… are no guarantees other place will have nilwort," said Miko. "Could be repeat of today."

Mordecai sighed but nodded. "She's right. And the next caves might not be as empty as these have been either."

"Two votes to press on then?" Lace turned to Skaal.

"Have come this far."

"Right. Brian?"

"I'll make it unanimous. The sooner we get the nilwort, the sooner we can get back to Harborton. Valestia's brother isn't *dying*, precisely, but time still matters."

"Okay." The Marauder leaned in close, her voice dropping even further. "Then we need a plan of attack."

42

Some time later, we reached the mouth of the newest chamber. We'd left our packs behind, and Mordecai had extinguished his light at the end, making the last several yards an unpleasant affair, each of us with one hand on the person in front. As the only one who could see, Lace had led the procession, and it was she who brought us to a halt.

I 'd hoped that my night vision would eventually adapt to the darkness, but there just wasn't enough light for that. And so, I felt more than saw Lace make her way over to Miko, tugging the synossian out in front. This had been my *least* favorite part of the plan, and that was saying something, considering the rest of the plan.

Still, I hadn't had any better suggestions.

Forewarned, I squeezed my eyes shut and put my free hand over those eyes even as I turned away. Around me, I could faintly hear Mordecai and Skaal doing the same.

Lace didn't say anything, but she must have squeezed Miko's shoulder or given some sort of sign, because a moment later, there was a burst of brilliant light from ahead, visible even through the barriers I'd erected. Something within the chamber gave off a high-pitched wail, and then Skaal was bellowing a war cry and charging forward. I cracked open my eyes to find Mordecai following the reaver, flame wreathing his hands. Lace was already inside, while Miko stood behind, holding her half-charred torch like a club.

Flare's light, combined with Mordecai's flames, caught upon something dark and chitinous, as long as the sluthar and with at least as many legs, although it lacked that horror's mutated bestial half. Pincers the size of my legs protruded from a bulbous insect-like head, but the creature seemed stunned by the sudden burst of light.

Mordecai unleashed his spell and darts of flame streaked past the charging Lace and Skaal to strike the monstrous centipede. Flame washed over the carapace, eliciting fresh, ear-splitting wails, but whatever damage was inflicted appeared minimal. As the creature pulled back, rising like a cobra preparing to strike, I finally spotted its mouth, an undulating circle of jagged spikes.

Just once, I wanted Eos to show me something beautiful. Instead, all I got was constant nightmare fuel.

Skaal didn't slow, crashing into the monster like a linebacker on way too many steroids. Lace flickered with her last step, and was suddenly behind the creature, a dagger in one hand, and her slim sword in the other. The creature's carapace seemed proof against her lighter weapons, but she switched targets on a dime, looking for gaps to stab into. Meanwhile, Skaal's bull rush had pushed the creature even further off balance. Axe and short sword in hand, the reaver was a slow whirlwind of bronze as he attempted to carve his way through the centipede's armor.

I tore my eyes away from the combat. I wasn't here to cheerlead. I wasn't even here to help. My role was to keep my eyes peeled. Because the word *nest* usually suggested…

There!

Whereas most of the caves we'd seen had been barren, the floor here was covered in an odd mix of fungus and debris. As I watched, some of that debris moved aside, and two smaller centipedes, each the size of a medium-sized dog, scuttled forth, approaching Mordecai from behind.

"Behind you, Mordecai!" I called. The bugs moved way faster than their oversized parent, and I kicked into a sprint as I tried to intercept them. I tossed my pack aside so I could grip Riok's spear in both hands.

As our only healer, Miko's role was to stay out of the fight, but I could hear her clawed feet slapping the stone behind me as she joined in anyway. Ahead, Mordecai finished his most recent casting and turned to face the new threat. I watched the eyes behind his mask widen as he realized the creatures were already almost on him. He slapped his hands together and then pulled them apart again, a strand of fire now dangling from his right grip like a whip.

He wasn't going to be quick enough.

Lunge took me across the intervening space in the blink of an eye. My spearhead caught the lead centipede from behind a moment before it lashed out at the caster, and the augmented thrust pierced right through its carapace armor to skewer the wriggling mass underneath.

It was still a long way from dead, but I planted my feet and whipped my spear about like a staff, the centipede still impaled on its tip making a simple maneuver into something that taxed my 11 Strength to its limit. I only grazed the second centipede, but it was enough to send it skittering to the side, and by the time it had righted itself, a whip of fire tore off one of its pincers. It surged forward again, but I'd bought Mordecai time and space; a wave of burning darts struck it head on. While those same darts had barely even slowed the larger creature, the smaller centipede writhed in pain. A second flick of the flame whip and it curled in upon itself and went still.

Miko had only now reached us. She waited for me to pin my centipede back against the ground and then darted in with her makeshift club, battering the creature's underside like a child faced with their first *piñata*. Something in the centipede broke before the synossian's weapon could, and the weight on the end of my weapon went limp, legs still twitching in that strange post-mortem dance.

More grateful than ever for my boots, I kicked the thing off the end of my spear and scanned the room.

Skaal and Lace had backed the mother—or father—centipede against the far wall, but the rest of the chamber was quiet. Given the lack of intelligence the dog-sized centipedes had shown in their attacks, I felt confident that we'd killed all the possible reinforcements.

With a tired sigh, Mordecai let his whip fade away. "Three more castings of *Flame Dart*," he called to the others. "Say when."

I had yet to see Skaal use a technique at all, but Lace seemed to have more than anyone could rightfully expect. She dodged the creature's thrashing tail and hurled one of the daggers from her bandolier. In mid-flight, one dagger became three, and then five, slivers of metal streaking through the air to hit the centipede from the side.

Only two of them struck true, and even they rebounded uselessly off that thick carapace. They clattered to the ground and then faded into smoke along with the other copies. The Marauder cursed. "Skaal?"

The half-giant was facing the brunt of the creature's attacks yet somehow holding his own. His short sword chopped down, failing to sever one of the creature's many thrusting legs, but the blow created an opening that the reaver took full advantage of. The half moon edge of his axe swept down—

—and rebounded, its bronze face warped beyond recognition.

"Gods below," breathed Mordecai. "That thing is at least Copper."

Skaal used his mangled axe to push the beast away, and then let the weapon drop. For the first time since we'd met him, he reached for the shrouded weapon on his back.

"No!" Lace used her short-range teleport again, but this time it was to tackle Skaal. She knocked his hand away and spun to face the centipede.

"Overload, Mordecai! Now!"

"I'm only Tin, you fool," murmured the Flameweaver in the tongue only he had ever spoken. Nonetheless, he raised his left hand. This time, I actually saw him trigger the *Overload* technique, the fingers on his other hand marching through a complex combination of patterns. The darts that streaked forth were half again as large as usual, crackling with heat and energy that dwarfed even the fireball he had tossed back in the forest.

One dart splashed uselessly against the cave's far wall, but the other four hit the centipede, and for the first time, the creature's screams sounded pained as well as angry. Unfortunately, whatever damage it had just taken seemed to energize it rather than sap its strength. It redoubled its assault, suddenly moving at a speed that matched or even exceeded its spawn.

Lace gave ground desperately, fighting to keep the creature from reaching her, as Skaal found his feet behind her.

Mordecai collapsed, exhausted by the overloaded spell.

"Watch him," I told Miko. I tried triggering *Lunge* again, but it wasn't off cool down, so I ran forward instead. The synossian said something, but her words were indistinct and hazy, trapped outside my bubble of focus as the world seemed to slow around me. The centipede slowly pulled back up onto its rear legs, and I was reminded again of the sluthar, of the first blow I'd ever struck with a spear. If I could hit something vulnerable, then maybe...

Two things happened, almost at once.

First, whatever state of focus I'd entered collapsed all at once, the world returning to full speed.

And second, I felt something inside of me shift.

Lunge was back.

I triggered the technique and then I was there, in front of both Lace and Skaal, spear not just positioned to receive its strike but actively thrusting forward on its own, the centipede and I recreating the head-on collision between stags I'd witnessed only days earlier.

This time, size really did win out. I was knocked to the ground like the half-grown teenager I was too often mistaken for, thrown onto my back with an impact that blasted all the air from my lungs. The only thing between me and the centipede was Riok's spear, one end propped up against the floor by my hip, the other driven no more than a quarter of an inch into the creature's body. The corroded shaft quivered under the centipede's full weight but held strong.

I watched the creature's horrible mouth undulate for a moment, and then the centipede spun, shifting its weight. The rear end of the spear slid free of whatever had been propping it up, and gravity did the rest, robbing me of my imperfect, ephemeral defense.

There was nowhere for me to dodge, as the centipede fell towards me. Instead, I reached for my weapon and my grasping fingers found nothing but air. I didn't have the time or the space for the spear to really matter, but somehow, it burned that, in the end, I was going to die without it in hand.

Lesson #1 is a killer, Riok.

For the second time in three days, death from above was averted by a too-tall man who looked like he belonged in a hospital's long-term care ward. Skaal hit the centipede from the flank, knocking it aside, and for only the second time, the creature shrieked in obvious pain.

I was crab walking backwards on hands and knees when I finally realized what had changed, and why my weapon was nowhere to be found.

Tempest remained wrapped on the reaver's back, but in his too-long hands was the long shape of Riok's stained spear, which had already proven stronger than the party's bronze weapons. Even with the aid of *Lunge*, I'd barely penetrated the creature's armor, but Skaal's strength was a difference maker. He used the reach of the borrowed weapon to keep the centipede on its back feet, and every strike he delivered tore through a carapace that had seemed all but impregnable.

It took the centipede far too long to realize this was a losing fight, and by the time, it tried to flee, it was too late. Without any techniques at all, Skaal dismantled the creature, leaving its corpse overturned, legs twitching spasmodically.

Miko was at my side before I could stand, but I waved her off. "I'm fine," I said. "It didn't do more than bruise me. Also, this is the second time I've been saved by a giant with a spear. One more and I think I get a free sandwich."

She gave me a look and I waved my hands. "Idiom. Sorry. I think I'm a little bit loopy." I could practically feel the adrenaline draining out of me, taking any semblance of energy with it.

She traded smiles with me, though hers seemed to vibrate with excitement. "I did it."

"Did what?"

"I will soon be level five. At last."

"That's the best news I've—"

"Skaal!" It was a struggle to even turn my head to look at the shouting Lace, but my tiredness washed away as the reaver staggered against her, dropping to one knee. The Marauder lowered him to the floor "Miko! Come!"

The reaver was flat on his back by the time we reached him, Riok's spear cast aside. For the first time, I realized he was bleeding from a dozen different wounds. The savage cut on his chest, from a strike that had torn through *both* chain shirt and padded vest beneath, seemed the most dangerous, but given the amount of blood being shed, even the smaller wounds might prove fatal.

Miko's orange eyes went wide. She turned to Lace. "Need bandages and hangroot from pack. Get stillblossom too."

"I don't know what either of those last two are."

"Get pack then! Hurry!" Any deference Miko normally showed was forgotten in the heat of the moment, her usually soft voice cracking like a whip. She was already kneeling over Skaal, the familiar glow of Aurea's blessing gathering about her outstretched hands.

"What can I do?" I asked her in the High Tongue.

"Help Lace when she brings my pack. You remember what the hangroot looks like?"

"Yes."

"Stillblossom is a spotted yellow mushroom. We have three we were planning to sell." Her *Minor Healing* finished, but she stared helplessly at the chest wound. It wasn't bleeding as profusely as it had been, but it was still a long way from healed… and it was just one of many lacerations. "His body doesn't want to heal; I don't know why. We'll need to stop whatever bleeding if we can and bandage everything else, but I don't…" She took a long breath. "*Minor Healing* can't fix this."

I didn't know what to say to that; she was our only healer. "Is there some other herb we can look for then? Miko?"

She hesitated. "I don't know."

"Then we'll just have to do what we can."

A rush of wind preceded Lace's arrival as she used her short-range teleport to shave seconds off her journey. She had two packs in hand, Miko's and Skaal's. "We'll help you bandage while you wait for *Minor Healing* to return."

Wonder of wonders, I *did* remember what hangroot looked like, and I fished it out of Miko's pack as the synossian triaged Skaal's many, many wounds. It took me longer to find the stillblossom, and by the time I did, Lace was making strips of bandages out of the reaver's collection of rags, muttering angrily under her breath the whole time.

"Crush hangroot and sprinkle dust into wounds," Miko instructed in her fledgling Trade. "Stillblossom grind into paste. Spread on larger wounds on top of hangroot. Bandage after."

We formed an assembly line of sorts. I applied the powder and paste while Lace was on bandage duty. Miko helped, in between castings of *Minor Healing* and repeats of *Flare*, but I watched her grow steadily more exhausted. By the time we were done, she was barely better off than the slumbering Mordecai.

Skaal still hadn't stirred.

"Bleeding is mostly stopped, but…" Miko shook her scaled head. "I sorry."

"This isn't the end," said Lace. "He didn't travel a thousand leagues to die to some overgrown bug. Heal him again."

"She's exhausted, Lace."

"Then rest up and recover your heals."

"No time." Miko's voice conveyed all the grief her mastery of Trade could not. "Body does not want to recover. Do not know why."

"He's cursed." The words slipped out of Lace like a dying man's last breath. "Because of me. It's why we came north. We needed a cure. That must be why."

Miko hung her head.

I didn't know much about curses—hell, I hadn't known they were a thing on Eos until just now—but even so… this wasn't my first centipede. "Are you sure it's not poison?"

"What?"

"Where I come from, centipedes are venomous."

"Did not bite," said Miko, gesturing to the wrapped wounds. "Only cut."

"Yes, but it was also at least Copper," said Lace, suddenly energetic again. "Who knows how it evolved? Would poison explain the trouble you've had healing?"

"Yes, but—"

The Marauder was already unwrapping the very first wound Miko had healed. When we'd applied the hangroot and stillblossom, the flesh around the wound had been ghost-pale, but now it was puffy and reddish pink beneath the yellow paste.

"That's either an infection or Brian was right. If it's poison, how do we treat it?"

Miko tore through the contents of her pack, tossing careful bundles aside in her haste. She gave out a small cry as she pulled forth a handful of seeds. "Is good for slowing blood toxin," she said. "Mordecai found near shademoss."

"That will cure Skaal?"

Miko shook her head. "No. Will slow poison only."

"For long enough to get back to Harborton?"

I winced. I had no idea *how* we'd get back to Harborton without Skaal's aid. Having to carry him the whole way would make a challenging trip damn near impossible.

Miko shook her head again. "Not enough seeds. And effects lessen with use." She cocked the man's head back and tucked three of her five seeds under an arctic blue tongue. "But will give me time."

"For what?"

I met Miko's strange orange eyes, finally understanding where she was going with this.

"For her to level."

The synossian nodded. "If Aurea hear prayer, Framework give cure ability. If not, maybe upgrade to *Minor Healing* will be enough."

"If you can save him…" Lace shook her head, the tears streaking down her night-black cheeks catching the light of Miko's still-burning *Flare*. "I will do all that is in my power to repay you."

Miko patted the other woman's shoulder and then settled back into a meditative pose. "Am Priestess," she said simply. "Is what I do."

43

Watching someone meditate didn't rank highly on my list of things to do. After a few minutes, I got up to look through the debris that the giant centipede had been using as a nest. Most of it was waste and as foul as expected, but there were scraps of cloth and even a few pieces of wood. I gathered them into a pile in the center of the room, Miko's fire-striker in hand, then hesitated.

"I'm not going to use up all our air or something if I start a fire, am I?"

Lace remained at Skaal's side but stirred enough to shake her head. "Can't you tell? The air here is fresh. If you check the ceiling and walls, I suspect you'll find cracks leading to the surface."

The air seemed stagnant to me, but I decided to take her word for it. After all, she *was* a seasoned adventurer… and I really didn't want to sit in the dark when Miko's *Flare* spell ended.

A few minutes later, a small fire was burning cheerfully in the cave, and we hadn't blown up or passed out, so all seemed well. One task done, I turned to Mordecai, who was still lying where he'd fallen after his final spell. The Flameweaver was out like a light, but otherwise seemed unharmed, his chest rising and falling evenly. After consideration, I decided to leave him be.

Overload seemed like a powerful supplementary technique, but the drawbacks were very real.

Lace's entire focus remained on Skaal, which left it to me to discover if this mess had been worth it or not. I made a slow circuit of the cave, this time ranging beyond the creature's nest. The Marauder had been right; as I approached a few of the walls, I could feel the gentlest touch of fresh air, filtering through cracks that I couldn't quite see. The fire cast dancing shadows against those walls, but I still saw a few different types of lichen and moss, including more of the creeping fog our two would-be Herbalists had collected earlier.

Moving on, I found what at first seemed like a second nest, this one against the cave's far wall. I wrinkled my nose at the faint stench of something I couldn't quite place... halfway between mildew and dry rot. Using Riok's spear, I sifted through the pile, already dreading what I would find.

"I think this is what's left of one of the centipede's past meals," I said, voice tight as I internally ordered myself to *not* throw up. I'd found remnants of a skull—too large to be human—and what appeared to be half of an arm bone.

Or maybe a leg bone. I wasn't sure which, really, especially since I didn't know what species it came from.

"Check for valuables," said Lace, not even looking my way. I could have found the crown of England and I don't think she'd have given a damn right then.

"Right. Valuables." My fantasies of treasure hunting had never included digging through dead bodies. Still, at least this one was almost entirely decomposed. The parts of it that hadn't already been... you know... eaten.

It took some time—and even more dry heaving—but eventually, I had a pile of loot separated from the rest. There was a small coin purse with seven copper bits inside. A set of tarnished rings that might sell for something. An opal pendant with a chain of copper links. And last, but definitely not least, a long-bladed dagger still in its sheath. The hilt was plainly wrapped in leather, but the blade, when I unsheathed it, was burnished bronze.

I took it all, tucking the dagger into the braided rope I used as a belt. This wasn't the piles of gold I'd been hoping for, but it was nice to get *something* for our troubles.

And speaking of something…

"Mordecai said the nilwort was a tuber, right? Green?"

"With black-edged leaves, yes." For the first time since Skaal had fallen, Lace showed some interest. "Did you find some?"

"I think so?"

"Then don't touch it! It needs to be harvested properly."

"Way ahead of you on that front." I marked the location in my mind and brought my loot back over to where Miko was sitting. I'd spent enough nights standing watch while she meditated to know that she would be done fairly—

The synossian opened her eyes, and a smile spread across her face, beautiful despite the sharp teeth and inhuman features. "I am level five," she said softly in the High Tongue, clearly energized by her advancement. "Let us see what my options are."

We waited as her orange eyes scanned text the rest of us could not see.

"Thank you, Bright Lady." Her inner eyelids slid shut as she turned her reptilian face to a sun none of us could see. "Under your light shall we grow."

"What did she say?" Lace's voice was tight, one hand still unconsciously clenched in the fabric of Skaal's sleeve.

Miko continued to speak in the High Tongue, so I translated for her. "She's been offered an upgrade to *Minor Healing* that makes it more efficient. An upgrade to *Flare* that adds a fire component. And…" I felt a smile break out on my face until it matched Miko's. "…*Touch of the Dawn*, an Uncommon technique that neutralizes a broad range of poisons."

By the time I had finished translating, Miko was at Skaal's side. The glow that coalesced around her clawed hand as she laid it atop his bandaged chest wound was golden, like the first touch of sunlight on the ocean.

"Now what?" asked Lace, eyes fixed on the puffy skin around that wound.

"Wait. Watch," said Miko.

Nothing happened.

"Is it not—"

"Look!" said Lace. "The red is fading!"

It took a few more seconds to verify her observations, but by the time a minute had passed, Skaal's skin had regained its usual white sheen. Lace unwound another set of bandages and found the same result.

"Technique targets whole body," said Miko in Trade, words slurring with exhaustion. "Should be good now. Will heal again when—"

"Thank you." Lace clasped Miko's hand in both of hers and bowed her head. "For your sacrifice and your goddess' blessing."

The synossian was already asleep.

"Sacrifice?" I asked.

"She chose a technique whose use is situational over upgrading her most powerful ability. The upgrades offered on leveling are random, and she may never see that one again." Lace cleared her throat, finally releasing Skaal. "I owe her. Both of you, in fact. Without your weapon, that monster would have been too much for us. It almost was anyway."

"That's what being in a party is all about, right?"

"Many in the Adventurer's Guild behave otherwise." She ran a filthy hand through her braids, not even noticing the dried blood that flaked off. "I will keep watch while you and the others sleep."

"Actually… is it okay if I take first watch?" I nodded to the fire. "That's only going to last a few more glasses, after which I'm not going to be able to see anything anyway. Better to have someone with night vision on duty at that point."

Lace gave me a long look.

"What?"

"When you ambushed us in the dunsman's inn, I didn't think much of you, let alone your scaled companion. But I was wrong. You have the makings of a good adventurer, provided you survive that long."

I looked away. "I'm just doing what I can."

"Keep doing it then, Brian Fieldings. We'll see you and Miko Naseri both reach Tin or even Copper someday."

◡◡◡

Standing watch at the bottom of a series of caverns was significantly less interesting than doing the same thing in the forest or even the fields south of Harborton. There just wasn't a lot to see or hear, beyond the soft crackle of our fire and the breathing of my party.

Miko, I couldn't help but notice, was snoring quietly, head turned into the robes I'd tucked under her head.

Before Lace went to sleep, I'd had her bring the rest of our packs down, and while nobody had erected tents, it otherwise looked and felt almost like a normal campsite.

I needed to meditate—was anxious to see my gains after that hellacious battle—but by the time I'd thought of it, Lace was already out. So I sat and listened to nothing and saw nothing as the night went on and our fire slowly diminished.

By the time that fire had dwindled to embers, I was wondering if I was too tired to even meditate. I pushed myself to my feet, feeling my knees pop. I turned to where Lace was sleeping, still next to Skaal, if not quite touching, took one step…

And stopped.

I wasn't sure what it was that stopped me. It wasn't *Danger Sense*, which remained flaky as hell for all that it was a Rare skill creeping toward its maximum rank. It wasn't anything I heard because I didn't hear a damn thing. Maybe it was a deity whispering in my ear, or that small, niggling voice in the back of my head from *Animal Behaviorism* that remained convinced some hunters would never give up the trail…

I took another look around the darkened cave, and saw a long shadow slip out of the tunnel, its clawed feet silent as it rushed Mordecai's sleeping form.

I yelled—not sure if I was trying to alert the camp or scare the thing off—but the gyr beast, large enough to be the twin of the one Skaal had fought and Mordecai had blasted, paid me no mind.

Thankfully, my weapon was, as always, in my hand, and the cave wasn't *that* big. *Lunge* got me to Mordecai before the lizard, and I let the momentum of that charge flow through me as I twisted my hips and thrust Riok's spear outward.

I was unranked, while it was at least Tin, stronger than me, faster than me, and equipped with four monstrous claws, a tail, and a venomous bite. There was no way I could fight it myself, and almost as little chance of me holding it off long enough for someone else to wake.

And yet, as I flowed into my thrust, feeling my body working in harmony with the spear in a way that had so regularly eluded me, as the gyr beast leaped through the air, claws extended and vicious maw open, I felt only calm, a brief moment of clarity. The man, the spear, and the opponent, combining to form a scene that could only end one way.

And so, when my body tried to shift, I let it, bringing the spear point up just an inch. My back foot turned of its own accord, adding stability to my stance. And the dark tip of Riok's spear, permanently stained with the blood of an unholy terror who would not die, slid past the heavy scales along the creature's snout, missed the equally thick ridge of scales that formed its brow, and found a path between, straight into its eye.

Even with the perfect stance—and mine was still far from perfect—that much weight was far too much for me to withstand. I slid backwards, tripped over something, and fell, the spear torn from my grasp. But as I scrambled back to my feet, pulling my new knife from its filthy sheath, I found the gyr lizard motionless on the cavern floor. My spearhead had been driven all the way through its eye and into its skull.

Someone stirred at my feet, and I finally realized what—and who—I'd tripped over. Mordecai's eyes were wide behind a slightly askew mask, as he looked from me to the creature that had collapsed mere inches away.

"I feel like I missed a few things, lad," he managed, voice hoarse and still fuzzy from sleep.

Behind us, Lace was rising from a crouch, blades in her hands. Skaal and Miko had somehow stayed asleep through my yells.

"Yeah," I told the Flameweaver. "Just a couple."

It took Lace and me both to drag the gyr beast aside. Mordecai had revived the fire, despite a lack of fuel, and its light showed the creature had taken serious damage recently, from scorch marks on its belly and foreclaws to cracked scales along its side where a half-giant's oversized boot had once sent it flying.

"Is that one of the—"

I was too tired to do much more than nod. "Yeah."

Lace gave me a look. "How many does this make?"

"I'm sorry?"

"Monsters who chased you for literal days."

"It was after Mordecai, not me."

"Because he was defenseless."

"Or because he tried to burn down their forest." I dropped my end of the body and straightened up with a groan. "I'm just glad the rest of the pack stayed home."

"And I'm glad you saw it coming." She dropped her half and then bent to examine the fatal wound. "That's quite the strike."

"I got lucky. *Really* lucky."

"I won't argue with you on that. Even so." A knife appeared in her hand. "Gyr doesn't taste half bad as long as it's well cooked, and fresh meat could make the trip to Harborton that much less tiresome."

"I'll leave you to it. I need to check in with the Framework and then pass out. Are you okay butchering that *and* standing watch?"

"If I'm not, you'll be the first to know." She paused and scanned the cave. "No, actually Mordecai will be, I guess. He's still closest to the tunnel."

The Marauder was a lot chattier than she had been when we first met, but I wasn't sure she was any funnier.

"Try not to let his screams interrupt my meditation," I said.

"I heard that," muttered Mordecai. The Flameweaver stood up, gathered his pack, and walked to the rear side of the cave, past Skaal and Miko both.

I sent him a grin. Okay, maybe it was a *little* bit funny.

ooo

I fell asleep somewhere in the middle of my meditation, leaving my soul exactly as unenriched as it had been to begin with, the

Framework correspondingly silent. I woke to find Skaal upright and huddled with Lace, cooking lizard bits over Mordecai's woodless fire. The caster and Miko were both up too, excitedly chattering as they gathered more creeping fog from the nearest wall.

"Did Lace show you two the nilwort?" I called.

"Already recovered, dear boy," said Mordecai, not looking up from where Miko was carefully peeling away grey lichen. "Three for the mayor's brother and two more for the stores, leaving enough behind for future growth to occur."

That was… more conservation minded than I'd expected from a man harvesting lichen because it sold well to drug dens, but I just nodded and turned to Lace. "I'm going to get my meditation done and then I'll be ready to go."

She nodded, one hand almost incidentally maintaining contact with Skaal as the sickly looking reaver instructed her on how to properly cook the meat. Even though I knew *exactly* where that meat came from, it smelled distressingly good.

I tried to push that thought out of my mind and took a sip of water instead, finishing off my second-to-last skin. I sat the way Riok had first taught me, palms on my knees facing skyward, his spear resting atop those palms, and closed my eyes.

Almost a full glass later, I opened them again, feeling oddly rested, the crick in my neck gone, along with the aches I'd accumulated over the previous day and night.

Miko and Mordecai had moved to another spot in the cave, this one almost all the way around to the centipede's nest, and Lace and Skaal were now packing cooked meat away. The Marauder threw me a slice, hitting me right in the chest.

I would have complained if I hadn't been too busy eating it. Gyr beast meat tasted… kind of like chicken, to be honest, if a little bit more gamey. I didn't hate it, especially after days of hard bread and salted jerky.

"Lizard tail," she said. "Far from the venom glands, since we weren't sure how to extract those safely."

I paused, mid-chew. I'd forgotten the gyr beast was venomous. "Has anyone *else* had any yet?"

"Yes. Mordecai frothed at the mouth a bit and fell over, but Miko was able to revive him." She rolled her silver eyes. "Everyone has had a piece. It's fine."

It was too late anyway since I'd eaten almost the entire slice. I swallowed the rest down and nodded.

"It's really good."

"Some herbs for medicine," said Skaal. "Others for food."

I traded nods with the reaver. He looked terrible… which was to say, almost normal.

"Get anything good from the Framework?" asked Lace.

"I haven't checked yet. One moment." It looked like I had at least one window waiting for me. I pulled it up.

"What the hell?"

```
Congratulations, Warrior.

You have reached level 3!
```

"Something wrong?"

"I… leveled." No wonder I felt so good.

"That's the opposite of wrong."

"Yeah, but…"

I frowned and dismissed the first window, finding another swiftly taking its place.

```
    You have increased the following skills:

    Major skills:
    Formations [+2]: 4/20
    Light Armor [+3]: 15/20
    Spear -> Spear (Uncommon)
    Spear (U) [+4]: 15/20
    Tactics [+2]: 7/20

    Minor skills:
    Athleticism [+1]: 15/20
    Avoidance [+4]: 14/20
    Pain Tolerance [+4]: 15/20

    General skills:
    Danger Sense (R) [+1]: 7/10
    Deception [+1]: 2/10
    Meditation [+1]: 6/10
    Stealth [+1]: 3/10
```

Okay, that explained it. I'd gotten a shit ton of skill gains.

"I'm surprised it wasn't more," said Lace when I told her. "Of everything we fought yesterday, only the baby centipedes were unranked."

"I got *four* points in *Avoidance*. My other skills must have run into the level cap."

She winced and pulled me away from the fire to a spot halfway between Skaal and our two amateur herbalists.

"If you want some advice for the future? Don't tell people what combat skills you have. Outside of the party, anyway. I mean *Avoidance* is practically a given for a Warrior with no armor, but still. The more your enemies know about you, the better they'll be able to counter your strengths."

"I assume the same goes for techniques?"

"It goes *double* for techniques."

"So… should I not tell you what my options are for level three? Because I'm pretty sure I'll need some advice."

To my surprise, Lace gave that question some serious thought. "You and Miko are planning to continue with our party, right? To Madea at least, so we can get you registered with the Adventurer's Guild?"

Two days earlier, and us even being permitted to accompany them to Madea had been an open question. I didn't have to look at the half-giant behind her to know how and why things had changed so dramatically.

"Yes. And for as long as you'll have us after that," I said. "Obviously, we're both under-leveled, but I think we can still be helpful."

"What are your goals? Ours is to gather enough money and prestige to buy membership in one of the better adventuring companies. We need high-end contacts to find a cure for Skaal's condition."

"I don't know anything about adventuring companies, but money and fame are at the top of our list too. We have a cycle or two to make as much progress on that front as we can. After that, we might have to turn our attention to something other than adventuring."

The look she sent me said she was aware just how much I was leaving out… but also that she wasn't going to press me on the issue.

"Then I'm happy to provide advice on your technique choices," she finally said, "and will keep the secrets of you and Miko both."

She did not, I couldn't help but notice, volunteer to share her own list of skills or techniques. I'd already seen some in action, and could guess others, but still… this felt a little bit one-sided. On the other hand, I'd only been on this world for a few months. I wasn't going to pass up the expert opinion of someone a full rank higher than I was.

Nor was I going to exclude the one person I trusted to my core. I switched to the High Tongue and raised my voice. "Miko, do you want to help Lace and me figure out my leveling options?"

The synossian left Mordecai to continue harvesting, taking a seat next to us both. She cocked her head, replying in her native tongue.

"You are level three? Already? How?"

"These last fights gave me the necessary skill gains."

"That much is expected," she said, confirming what Lace had told me. "But skills are always quick to improve at our levels. How is your soul strengthened enough to advance?"

"It's been ready since we hit Harborton, thanks to the quest."

"The *what?*"

I blinked. Had I seriously never told her about my quest to see her to safety? I thought back to our desperate week in the eastern woods, the long nights on watch, and our flight from the serpent king.

Huh. I really hadn't.

"Sorry," I said. "I just realized I never told you about that. I had a quest to escort you to safety."

"Given by… who?"

"The Framework?" It was my turn to give her a confused look.

"Should I give you two some space?" asked Lace.

"We must talk about this later," Miko told me, before switching back to Trade. "Is okay. Minor confusion. Should focus on technique choices now."

I did my best to hide my frown. I wasn't sure what was going on. Still, I had that window just waiting to be displayed…

I brought it up so I could see the contents.

```
Congratulations, Warrior.

Select your level 3 advancement option:

-   Upgrade: Lunge (C) -> Liberating Lunge (U)
-   New technique: Beast Skin (Passive - C)
-   New technique: Fueled by Pain (U)
```

The list was… underwhelming, to say the least. Especially since there wasn't any descriptive text explaining what the hell it meant.

I read the options aloud to my two advisors. "U means Uncommon, right?"

"Yes, it's a step up in quality," confirmed Lace. "Common, Uncommon, Rare, and Epic. Mordecai says there are tiers even beyond that—Ancient, Legendary, and Divine—but I have yet to see any proof of that."

I nodded. My *Spear* skill had just evolved from Common to Uncommon… something I was pretty sure I'd actually *felt* during the fight with the gyr beast.

"So, *Liberating Lunge*, whatever that is, is a direct upgrade to *Lunge*." The liberating modifier made it sound like my Ideal was involved somehow, but I had no idea what it did. The continuing lack of help text was going to give me an aneurysm. "And the other two techniques are new. But what do they do?"

"I've never heard of *Liberating Lunge*," said Lace as Miko tapped her left arm in agreement. "*Beast Skin* is new to me too, but it sounds like a spin on a fairly standard defensive ability."

"Make skin tougher," agreed Miko.

"Exactly. If so, it can be upgraded further as you level."

I nodded. Given that the Framework took skills into consideration, I was guessing my maxed *Animal Behaviorism* was why

I'd gotten a different flavor of the common technique. As someone who took more than his fair share of damage, the idea of something to reduce that was appealing, especially since it was a passive technique.

But it *was* Common, whereas my other new option was already Uncommon, much like *Liberating Lunge.* I just… didn't love the name.

"What about…" I sighed. "…*Fueled by Pain?*"

Miko shook her head, as ignorant as I was. Thankfully, Lace did know that one.

"It's a popular technique with the reavers. I'm guessing your *Pain Tolerance* skill must be high for that technique to have been offered."

"You don't even want to know."

She waited for more, then shrugged. "When triggered, any damage you take increases the damage you deliver. Like the *Skin* line of techniques, it can be upgraded, although since it's an active ability, those upgrades range from reduced cost to improved output." She looked over to where Skaal was putting away the last few cuts of cooked meat. "I once saw a reaver take a sword to the chest while using *Fueled by Pain.* His return blow obliterated the attacker, the wall behind him, and a good portion of the road on the other side."

"Huh." It sounded powerful, no doubt, but I didn't like basing my advancement path around me taking even *more* damage. If this had been a game, and injuries just an abstract concept, it would have been one thing, but getting hurt sucked, even with *Pain Tolerance.* I'd rather find a way to defeat my opponents that didn't involve my own pain.

Which left *Beast Skin* vs. *Liberating Lunge.* Defense or offense, presumably. *Lunge* had already proven its value a dozen times over as a technique, and upgrading it had a definite appeal, especially if it further improved my somewhat questionable effectiveness in combat.

And yet…

I could only use the technique a handful of times over the course of a day before I was tapped out of energy. Until I gained a lot more levels, I'd predominantly be fighting the normal way, spear in hand, following the basic patterns Riok had taught me.

And that made a *passive* defensive ability too good to pass up.

"I'm taking *Beast Skin*," I announced.

"Not a bad choice." Lace shrugged. "You can't do damage if you're dead."

Miko and I traded looks. We'd learned otherwise, sadly.

I confirmed the selection. Once again, there was no obvious sign that anything had changed. That was both good and bad. Good, because part of me had been concerned my skin would physically change to resemble an animal's… and rhino hide would make me look like the world's smallest Teenage Mutant Ninja Turtle villain. Bad, because there was no confirmation it had even worked.

"Miko, can you heal me after I test out the change?"

"Yes, I hea—I *will* heal."

I unsheathed my new dagger and placed the sharp point against the back of my other arm. Even with heals available, I wasn't going to risk cutting into the delicate workings of my hand. I took a breath and slowly pushed down on the blade.

I had never made a habit of cutting myself, but there was a lot more resistance than I would have expected. It took about half of my full strength to push the blade's tip through the outer layers of skin. Almost immediately afterward, blood welled to the surface.

"Not bad," said Lace. "Active techniques tend to be stronger, but with the obvious tradeoff of costing energy per use. You'll still have to watch for direct hits and any opponent significantly more powerful than you are, but as a first line of defense, that seems solid."

"Like *Bronze Scales* technique," agreed Miko. She waited for me to wipe the blade clean and return it to its sheath before she leaned in and extended her hands.

Lace interrupted. "Maybe you should just bandage it instead, Miko? It's a tiny pinprick of a hole, and we don't know what we'll encounter today as we head back north. Might as well preserve *your* energy if we can."

The synossian looked to me for confirmation, and I swallowed my sigh and nodded.

I was going to get *another* point in *Pain Tolerance*, wasn't I?

44

My new defensive technique didn't do anything to help me heal, but the hole I'd poked in my arm was small, and between firm pressure and my Vitality, it was clotting almost before we finished applying the bandage. I ate a second slice of hot gyr beast tail, drank some water, and by the time I was done, everyone else was ready to go.

Mordecai had stolen a single orb of flame from the fire and extinguished the rest. Both the Flameweaver's pack and Miko's were stuffed full of herbs and fungi and whatever else they had harvested, though the nilwort and shademoss had been set aside and tucked into Skaal's pack instead. My pack, meanwhile, remained a haphazard bundle of scraps and straps, just whole enough to keep my clothes and the now bloodstained scarf inside.

Our trip out of the cave was surprisingly quick. As we'd already explored all the side tunnels on the way down, Lace led us straight out into sunshine and a forest practically bursting with new growth after the Thunderbird's recent passage.

There were no signs of any other gyr beasts. It was possible the rest of the pack had staked out an ambush somewhere else, but I was confident that wasn't the case. And since I had no rational *reason* for my confidence, I was pretty sure *Animal Behaviorism* was at work.

I still didn't know how I'd earned the skill to start with, but damn if it hadn't been useful so far. *Especially* for a General skill.

We made good time heading back north. It was almost like the forest, as a whole, had decided we'd dealt with enough danger for any one trip. Even the creatures Lace had previously had to circle around were gone. By the time night fell and we made camp again, we were more than halfway back to where we had crossed the river.

I had first watch, which I was starting to realize was my favorite of the three. Instead of bunking down in our tent, Miko came to sit with me. The day had been clear and sunny and the night sky was thick with stars, more than I'd ever seen back on Earth, even in photos. Eos' two moons hung like ornaments within that backdrop of darkness and light. The trees rustled as a light breeze swept in from the south, and even without a fire, the camp felt almost… pastoral.

Every now and then, this new world I'd found myself in liked to remind me that it *could* be a thing of wonder… that there was more to it than monsters and mud and pain.

The others had long since gone to sleep when Miko finally spoke, her words quiet for all that they were in the High Tongue.

"What did you mean earlier, when you said the Framework had given you a quest?"

In the thrill of leveling up, I'd almost forgotten that strange exchange. I kept my face and senses turned to the darkness surrounding our campsite but responded in kind.

"Exactly that. Back in Whitehall, when we first charged down toward the garrison and I was doing everything I could just to stay on the back of our dalys—"

Miko giggled. "You were pitching side to side like a sack of grain instead of a rider. I was doing all I could to keep your arms wrapped around me."

That wasn't *quite* how I remembered it, but I'd been panicking at the time, to be fair.

"Well, in the middle of that, the Framework popped up a new window. It offered me a quest." I did my best to remember the exact phrasing. "'*Escort Priestess Miko Naseri to safety.*' I was given the option to accept or decline it. Obviously, I accepted. At the time, I assumed it just meant getting you to Whitehall, so it seemed like a no-brainer."

"A what?"

"An easy choice," I clarified. "Only then… well, *everything* happened. Honestly, I forgot all about the quest until we reached Harborton, where I was notified of its completion."

"And the Framework rewarded you for this… quest?"

"Yeah. I had only just reached level two, remember? As soon as the quest completed, I felt satiated again." I frowned. "Are quests that rare of a thing?"

"They are not *rare*… they are *impossible*. That's not how the Framework functions." She adopted her scholarly tone. "Actions that correspond with our given class progress our soul, amplified by any strain or pressure the soul is under at the time, and the Framework exists as conduit, qualifier, and quantifier for that progression." Another pause, and then she was speaking normally. "It doesn't… *give quests*, and it certainly doesn't then provide rewards for completing those quests."

"I mean… it kind of did?"

She shook her head. "I'm not questioning your experience, Brian. But while there is some basic intelligence baked into the overall system—there *must* be for it to manage the millions of permutations of advancement—one thing that every text agrees upon is that it has no will of its own."

"Do you think this might be another thing your people forgot?" I asked, feeling oddly rude for the question.

"I…" She sighed. "Perhaps? And yet surely, over the course of a thousand cycles, one of us would have been given a quest by the Framework, if that was how it worked? Especially if you were given one at level one."

"And at level two."

"What?"

"I got a second quest, before we left Harborton."

I couldn't really see Miko in the darkness, but I could feel the weight of her stare.

"Is there a reason you didn't tell me? And do you trust me enough to tell me now?"

I coughed. "Honestly? I forgot. That was the night I gave you your new robes and told you that there were other synossians on this continent. Another quest didn't seem as important."

"*Didn't seem as—*"

"As far as I knew, they were just a part of the Framework you had never gotten around to teaching me! How was I supposed to know otherwise?"

Her sigh could have filled a half-dozen balloons. "That's fair."

"We're in this together," I told her. "Whether I'm truly Chosen or just plain Brian, you're the only friend I have. I'm not going to abandon you and I'm not going to hide stuff from you either."

"You're right," she said. "And I am being unkind. I truly didn't think you would. I'm just… it feels like ever since I met you, the earth has been constantly shifting beneath me."

I turned my senses to the ground we were sitting on, just in case she *wasn't* being metaphorical, but it was calm. No giant dirt worms digging their way up beneath us.

"I know how you feel," I finally said. "Probably better than anyone."

"Of course you do. The entire world is new to you."

"I can try to sound out Mordecai tomorrow on the idea of quests. See if they are a known phenomenon here in the Great Wilds? If they aren't—"

"Then this may be related to your status as Chosen," she finished. "Which honestly makes more sense."

"How so?"

"We know that the Framework was built by the gods. All of them, working together, if sometimes at cross-purposes. And while it was Shan who spoke to you, we can presume that my entire pantheon was involved in bringing you across the Veil. Perhaps *they* are the will behind the quests you have been given?"

"So, you think they're using the Framework as a way to influence the physical realm without touching it directly?"

"Through their Chosen, yes, who they have a connection with. And in doing so, they abide by the letter of the celestial law."

"But… Shan broke that rule once already," I reminded her. "When he stopped time and saved us both."

Saved *me*, not that I was going to split hairs. Besides, Shan must have known I was going to save Miko anyway. After all, if her theory was right, he'd given me the quest in the first place.

"Yes, he did," said Miko, voice clearly troubled. "And I wonder what his intervention cost him."

It wasn't a question I'd thought to ask. Breaking a law almost had to have consequences, right? Yet Shan had done it anyway. For me. Maybe the Trickster god wasn't quite the ass I'd taken him for.

As if he'd heard me—and as a god maybe he had—a dialogue window filled my vision:

```
NEW QUEST: Find out more information on the celestial law
                of non-interference.

                 [ Accept | Decline ]
```

"Huh."

"What is it?" asked Miko.

"I just got *another* quest." Until now, I'd assumed I could only have one at a time.

"How? What does it say?"

"It wants me to research the law that Shan broke in helping us."

"There's nothing more?"

"No. The other quest I still have—the one I received in Harborton—is to help you contact the local synossian population. There's never any explanation or itinerary provided, but these both seem fairly straightforward at least?"

Miko was quiet for a long while. I hit *Accept*, dismissed the window, and waited for her to gather her thoughts.

"Do you know what this means?" she finally asked.

"Yeah. If I keep getting quests and completing them, skills are going to be the only thing slowing down my progression."

"Well, yes… and I would find that unfairly broken if you weren't a Chosen, but that's not what I meant." Out of the darkness, her clawed hand found mine and squeezed it. "We are not alone, Brian Fieldings. The pantheon is doing all they can to guide us."

I squeezed her back but said nothing. On the one hand, divine guidance fell just behind divine intervention in terms of cheat codes, and we needed any help we could get. On the other, I'd spent the last decade on Earth realizing that *my* god either didn't exist or didn't care… that whatever happened happened, and we had only ourselves to rely on or to blame.

I couldn't quite decide if this sudden attention was welcome, overbearing, or some unholy hybrid of the two, and a part of me wanted to resent it, no matter how badly it was needed.

But Miko was holding my hand and humming softly, and there was a lightness to her that I hadn't felt since before Whitehall's fall.

I held my peace and let her have the moment.

Above us, the stars followed suit.

ooo

The next two days passed just as swiftly. We did encounter a brief issue when we reached the site of our river crossing though. The rains had caused the Snake to overflow its banks and although the water had since subsided, both sides were a muddy mess that made getting back across that much more difficult.

Thankfully, I had *Lunge.* Lace's teleport didn't have the necessary range, but the Marauder's Finesse attribute proved more than equal to the task. Miko and Mordecai, on the other hand, had to resign themselves to being passengers on the Skaal express. Fully recovered now, the Reaver cleared the gap without any issue, taking multiple trips to ferry both passengers and their packs across.

The scars left by Mordecai's fire were impossible to ignore, but the Thunderbird had kept that fire from spreading more than a few acres. Soon, we were back under the green canopies of untouched trees. I kept a wary eye out for the rest of the gyr beast pack, and Lace hovered around the party like a wary sheepdog, but the lizards never showed. By nightfall, we had left the ambush site far behind us.

The next morning, we were up at first light to continue north. The nilwort would stay potent for six days after being harvested, and if our current pace held, we'd reach Harborton with one to spare, but everyone moved with a sense of urgency.

Maybe it was just that we were all tired of smelling ourselves. Before we'd refilled our water supplies at the river crossing, we'd used whatever was left in the skins to try to remove our outer layers of dirt and caked blood, but it would take warm water and an awful lot of soap before I even began to feel clean again.

Hell, I'd have settled for one of the synossian scale brushes. Yeah, it would remove a layer of my skin, but at least it'd remove everything on top of that skin too.

On the fourth day after our night in the cave, we broke free of the forest, grassy hills slowly descending in front of us toward the distant sea. Out from under the thin canopy of leaves, it was that much hotter, and the bugs returned *en masse* to greet us, but I still felt a smile creeping across my face at the most random of times.

We'd done it. We'd plumbed the depths of the forest, survived its dangers, and emerged stronger, treasure in hand. Even Lace was all smiles, needling Mordecai enthusiastically as the five of us followed the river down to our eventual destination.

The next afternoon, the sight of the desolation left by the Swarm stole some of that joy—the crunch of brittle grass and crystallized soil under our boots—but soon after that, we were being ushered into Harborton, greeted by the same guard who'd watched us leave. By the time we made it to the siblings' house, Valestia was outside, waiting with Tantalas.

"Did you get it?" she asked, and though her face was carved from stone, I could see the tiredness in her eyes.

"With over a day to spare," said Lace. "Three sprigs of nilwort and the shademoss you requested."

Skaal was already pulling his pack from his shoulders. He handed the carefully wrapped bundles to the mayor, who passed them on to Tantalas.

The Herbalist unwrapped both and studied their contents, his alien face breaking out into a gentle smile. "These will do perfectly," he told Valestia. "With your permission?"

"Please. Get started right away." She watched him leave, long strides taking him down the road toward his shop and home and turned to us. "If it is agreeable with you all, I will book you rooms at the inn for the night. While the Herbalist works on my brother's cure, I would hear the tale of your journey."

"Throw in baths, and you have a deal," said Lace, as if we'd otherwise have set off for Madea even with night ready to fall.

"I can do that." For the first time since I'd met her, Valestia cracked a smile, deepening the lines around her eyes and mouth. "I might even be able to convince Lomas to part with some of his latest batch of ale."

"You drive a hard bargain, lass," said Mordecai, "but we accept."

A glass later, Miko and I rotated in for our turns in the two copper tubs Lomas had set out upstairs, each full of water pulled from the well and heated over the fire. At the innkeeper's insistence, we'd scrubbed down even before entering his inn, and so the water only turned beige instead of black. I groaned as the warmth worked its way into knots I didn't even know I had, knots I should have had Miko heal once we'd left the forest behind.

"Do you think," asked Miko, her words so languorous they were almost slurred, "that Lomas has a stiff-bristled brush, perhaps?"

I forced my eyes open. The soap they made and used in Harborton was harsh stuff, but it had done the job for me. A synossian's scales were another matter entirely. "I'm just about done here. I can ask."

Lomas didn't, but Halletia knew someone who did, and if that brush's usual purpose was to remove burrs from phloxl coats… well, it still did the job for Miko.

A glass after that, we were all in the common room. As Lace and Mordecai gave a properly embellished account of our journey, I spoke with Lomas in the words of stone and wind. After hearing about the origin of the Waste from Mordecai, I was more curious than ever about the dunsman, but he kept the conversation focused on general town gossip and his newest achievements in brewing.

Merchant Jessup, who Lace and the others had escorted to Harborton, had ended up staying in the village a good seven-day longer than expected after one of his mounts had fallen sick. Tantalas had fashioned a tonic to flush the illness from the creature's body, but between the illness and the cure, the merchant had found himself in Harborton with little to do.

Rumor was Jessup *could* have left a few days earlier than he eventually did, but he and Agnes the Tailor had found more than a few interests in common; it had taken the merchant's second-in command to finally pull the other man away. The latest gossip was that the merchant was planning to sell his business when he returned home, and that he'd be back for good sometime in the next few moons.

Lomas didn't give much credence to the possibility.

"Man has a good job," he told me gruffly. "Just enough danger to keep it interesting, but not so much to keep him from making profits. Why would anyone give that up just for a woman?"

The dunsman, I couldn't help but note to myself, was a very *ineligible* bachelor.

By the third glass, I'd lost count of the number of toasts that had been made. Lomas' special reserve was seriously strong—reminding me of my dad's Wild Turkey back home, if quite a bit sweeter on the finish. When Nala showed up out of nowhere, part of me was surprised to find there were two of her. I just stared for a bit, not sure which one I was supposed to address.

Moments later, a cool energy rushed through me and the inn stopped swaying. I blinked my suddenly sober eyes and looked over at Miko, who had come up beside me.

"This is a conversation you should be fully aware for," she said in the High Tongue.

"*Touch of the Dawn?*"

"No matter what the others say, alcohol *is* a poison."

There wasn't much I could say to that, given that the spell had just proven her right. Fully sober, I turned back to Nala, who had watched our unintelligible conversation with wide eyes.

"Hi."

"Welcome back." She pinked up as she met my eyes. "I'm glad you're safe."

"Thank you for the scarf," I told her. "Believe it or not, it helped save my life."

"It… did?"

"Yeah." Rather than explain, I cleared my throat and reached for the coin purse I'd tied to my makeshift belt. "And I have something I'd like to give you too. Both as a thank you and as a goodbye gift."

I watched exultation be replaced with consternation and did my best to remember that she was way too young for me, that we barely knew each other, and that I ultimately could never give her what she wanted or deserved. And it helped, because it was all true, but even so…

I'd been in her shoes before, and it sucked.

"Of course," she said, swallowing as she said it. "Of course you'd be leaving."

"I have to," I said.

"And do you think you'll come back someday?"

The truth was I didn't know, but this was one of those instances where the truth would do more harm than good.

"I don't think so," I said instead.

"I see." She glanced down at the coin purse in my hands. "You don't need to pay me off, teacher."

"What? I'm not." I opened the purse and drew out the pendant I'd found in the centipede's cave. It looked small and kind of cheap in the inn's dancing firelight. "It's the one beautiful thing I found out in the wilds and I thought you should have it. I know it's not much, but…"

Nala blinked down at the simple necklace in my hands. Just when I had convinced myself she was going to laugh at my shitty present, she snatched it away, holding it to her modestly covered chest. "Thank you," she said, her voice almost lost beneath the hubbub of the room. "I need… I should… Goodbye."

She whirled about, so sharply that her skirts flared about her, slapping against my legs and Miko's both. And then she was almost running out the door, head down, and hands to her chest, slipping between two farmers arriving late to the party.

"Did that go well or poorly?" asked Miko.

"I think a bit of both," I replied in Trade. "But it would have gone a lot worse if I'd been drunk. Thank you."

"Am Priestess," she said, grinning a toothy synossian smile. "Is what I do."

45

Much like Merchant Jessup before us, we stayed in Harborton longer than expected. It took Tantalas a full day to make Erlund's cure, and as soon as it had been administered, Mordecai and Miko were meeting with the Herbalist to get the rest of the nilwort processed before it could expire.

Valestia didn't invite Miko or me to see Erlund when her brother finally woke. After taking care of the man for more than a month, that was a bitter pill to swallow, but I got it. Just because he'd been cured didn't mean he was *better*; the Swarm had taken literal years off his life and we were, in some small way, ultimately responsible. And while the rest of the village might have warmed to us in the interim, Erlund had been comatose the whole time. In his mind, everything would still be fresh.

Whatever hurt feelings I had were soothed pretty quickly when Lace came back to the inn with our rewards. As promised in the commission, we'd earned a full tower and five plugs, along with a letter of recommendation that the Marauder said would be worth almost as much when it came to getting new jobs.

To my surprise, she handed me five plugs.

"Two and a half each for you and Miko," she said. "Something tells me I can trust you to give the Priestess her share."

"This is honestly a lot more than I expected."

"It's a six-way split. You both did the work of full party-members, so you should get paid as such."

Which was great, but… "There are only five of us, not six."

"That's right; you're new to the life." She ran a hand through her dark braids, making the red beads she'd put back in dance. "Any adventuring party—any good one anyway—has a general fund for handling party-wide expenses like supplies in the field or basic food and board in town. Anything extra comes out of the individual's purse."

So, two and a half plugs for each person in the party, and another two and a half for the party fund. I could live with that.

"Still, I appreciate it. We both do."

Lace shrugged with clearly forced casualness. "It costs a plug just to join the Adventurer's Guild. You'll find coin goes faster than you expect in Madea. That is, if you're still coming?"

"To Madea? Definitely."

"Good. I wasn't sure. Rumor has it you gave the Tailor's daughter quite the courting gift."

"Excuse me?"

"Moonstone pendant, about yea big?" She held her index finger and thumb a little less than an inch apart.

"That wasn't a *courting gift*. It was a goodbye."

"Expensive way to say goodbye."

"I'm sorry?"

"Moonstone that size and clarity? It would have earned you at least a plug, maybe more."

So much for it looking small and cheap. A copper plug was more than most people in Harborton would see in a moon.

"I didn't realize."

"I figured. And since you're new to this life, I *also* figured you just forgot to check in with your party members before giving away what you found out in the field."

I sighed. "Shit. I should have split the loot, shouldn't I?"

"That's how it's usually done. Even Miko and Mordecai will give the rest of us some of the proceeds from their herb gathering. We won't split it evenly, as they did most of the work, but a party where everyone profits is a happy one. A party where only one person profits… not so much."

"I wouldn't want that." I tried not to cry as I took a plug from the stack she had just given me and handed it back. "For everyone else's share of the pendant."

She took it from me and made it disappear. "That's a nice dagger you found there too."

"*Seriously?*"

She grinned. "It *is* nice, but you don't have to pay us for it. We took a vote last night and decided you should keep it. You need a close-range weapon anyway."

"What about a *party where everyone profits?*"

"The better prepared we are individually, the more capable we are together. If someone needs something we find *and* the rest of the party agrees they can have it, what's there to fuss about? Now, currency on the other hand… that's something we'll *always* split."

She gave the coin purse hanging from my rope belt a long, meaningful look.

"Are you sure you're a Marauder?" I asked as I fished seven copper bits out of the purse I'd found them in. "This feels more like highway robbery."

Five of the seven bits disappeared, just like the plug before them and Lace's smile grew.

"In my homeland, banditry's an ancient and honored profession."

Because of course it was.

Another day passed. Miko and Mordecai dragged me to a meeting with Tantalas and I put my fledgling *Mercantilism* skill to work selling the herbs they'd gathered in the field. *Some* of the herbs, anyway… there were quite a few that the Herbalist had no interest in, and others that he openly admitted we'd get better prices for in Madea. Even so, our party walked away with another handful of plugs, far more than what Miko had made working for the man.

Some of that coin went to the party's general fund, but the rest was split among us. My share wasn't anywhere near Miko's, but it *was* larger than Lace or Skaal's. After all, my skill had played a role in the sale. As confirmation, I received a point in *Mercantilism* later that night, the first new one I'd gotten since my Dreaming.

I spent some of my money on a replacement pack from Agnes. She even threw in an extensive lecture on the do's and don'ts of gift giving for free. By the time she was through, I wasn't sure whether she considered me a possible future son-in-law or a bad influence who needed to get as far from Harborton as possible… but I *had* learned, in excruciating detail, exactly what would happen if her daughter disappeared one day and I was somehow involved.

I didn't think the Tailor had ever been an Aspirant, but the way she wielded a needle gave her threats all the dramatic emphasis they needed. Nala, I couldn't help but notice, remained conspicuously absent throughout my visit.

I'd washed my other clothes—and my gifted scarf—at the inn, but I purchased a few more changes of clothes, a real belt, and a cloak that the Tailor swore would keep the rain off. The woman was all smiles again once coin changed hands, but I felt her eyes drilling into my back as I walked away.

Merchant Jessup, I decided, *has balls of solid brass to even* think *of dating that woman.*

Afterwards, I headed to the town's general-purpose store. I bought a rudimentary bag of toiletries—it didn't have a razor for the bird's nest that was my beard, but Lace had said there were barbers in Madea—and picked up the stiff-bristled brush Miko had already paid for. Just like that, I had a pack full of clean clothing and travel gear, two weapons, *and* my boots.

I was also almost broke somehow—or would be once I paid for my enrollment in the Adventurer's Guild. If Madea really *was* more expensive than Harborton, I was in trouble.

Surprisingly, Miko had a solution for that. In our room that night, she poured out the contents of her own purse onto the bed. Including the money she'd made from working for Tantalas, she had the equivalent of four plugs, even after her purchases. She pushed two plugs aside and split the remaining twenty bits into matching piles of ten.

"What are you doing?"

"One plug for the guild registration fee and one to purchase a weapon when we arrive in Madea," she explained, nodding to the two heavy coins she'd set aside. "The rest we will share."

"That's not…"

"We are in this together, Brian Fieldings, yes?"

"We are." I emptied my coin purse onto the bed too. One plug and four bits didn't have quite the same impact.

She pushed my plug back over to me. "Your registration fee. Everything else, we split evenly."

And just like that, I'd gained eight bits for nothing.

"I feel like I'm getting the better end of this deal."

"This is not a merchant's transaction." She flashed her increasingly charming smile. "And if it were, I would still owe you for my robes, remember?"

She wouldn't owe me anywhere *near* what she was giving me, but I nodded my acceptance. "Okay. But just because I'm carrying half of the coin doesn't mean you can't use it if you need to. Given what Lace said about the prices in Madea, I'm not sure a plug will get you the sort of weapon you're looking for, especially one made of bronze."

She tapped her left forearm in agreement. "We will eat that thegar one bite at a time."

The next morning, we finally left Harborton.

◦◦◦

In the stories, the whole village would've turned out to see us go. In reality, Harborton was still teetering on the precipice of survival. The farmers and fishermen were off doing their very necessary jobs, and so was most of the rest of the population. Valestia, however, waited next to the western gate, and she had a familiar yet unfamiliar face with her.

Erlund.

The mayor's brother looked *different*. He wasn't the imposing middle-aged man I'd met atop Harborton's wall, but he wasn't the broken-down invalid I'd cleaned and changed either. He looked old—older than Val now, as she had predicted—but steady and strong in a way I couldn't have imagined even a seven-day earlier. Someone had cropped his white hair and beard short and he squinted against the rising sun as we made our way to the gate.

His eyes never left my face as he came toward me. Miko dropped into her usual bow, while Lace took a few steps to the left, something my *Tactics* skill told me put her in the other man's blind spot. Mordecai shifted his pack from one shoulder to the other, while Skaal, as was his wont, did nothing at all.

"I'm told you looked over me while I was ill." Erlund's voice was one thing that hadn't changed, still strong and imperious. "I wanted to thank you for that."

I felt something inside me unclench. "Your sister didn't give me much choice."

"That's Val. Toughest older sister a man can have, for all that she's now the younger of us."

"I'm glad you're on your feet again. And I'm sorry for any part we may have played—"

"My knees will curse you every morning, but my heart knows better. Your fellow adventurers say that you and the scaled were instrumental in retrieving the medicine that broke my sleep."

"It was a group effort."

He just nodded and offered his weathered hand. "Be that as it may, I wanted to speak with you before you left. May this parting be a clean one, with no ill will between us."

I took his hand and shook it. "Can you pass that sentiment on to your nine demon gods while we're at it?"

Erlund's smile was almost lost within the white of his beard. "I would not dare speak for such as they."

Which, I realized as he walked away, wasn't all that reassuring. Especially with me already on the bad side of *Lace's* goddess.

Valestia was next. She kept her speech short and to the point, thanking the party for their contributions and wishing us well on the road to Madea. At the end, she pulled Miko and me aside with a curt flick of her head.

She turned to my friend first. "There is no suitable penance for what your people did to this land, though the cycles turn and turn and turn. Nor is there forgiveness to be had from those of us who dwelled near the wasteland your ancestors unleashed." For a moment she stopped, mouth twisting. "But you are not responsible for the sins of long-dead fools. In your time in Harborton, you have proven yourself trustworthy and hard-working, considerate even to those who show you none. You are welcome within our walls and if others of your kind ever come this way, their reception will be warmer because of your actions here."

The bow Miko gave the older woman was deeper than any I'd seen from her since greeting Riok himself.

Valestia turned to me next and for just a moment, her cold mask slipped. "I have never seen someone so visibly hate something they are clearly skilled at as you over these past two moons. I suspect you will never willingly serve as caretaker again, and that is your choice. Still, I hope you will remember one thing."

"What's that?"

"Your final patient *lived.*"

I nodded, struggling to hold her bright-eyed gaze.

"Now get out of my village," she continued, voice brisk, "before Nala gets it in her fool head to chase after you. I can't have our only Tailor wasting her days hunting you both down again."

Mordecai was wearing a mask as always—back to the grey one he'd first arrived in—but his coughing sounded suspiciously like laughter.

ooo

The road to Madea had one detail that immediately made it distinctive from every other trip I'd taken on Eos...

It was an actual road.

Well, it was more of a wide pathway, really, made of dirt rather than asphalt or even cobblestones. Still, it had been cleared to allow passage to wagons back and forth from Madea, and it was a hell of a lot easier to traverse than the hills, forests, and even caves I'd become accustomed to.

By midday, when we stopped briefly for lunch, Harborton was already far behind us. Lace had pushed the pace harder than before, but the combination of the road and my extra point in Vitality meant I was handling it just fine. Tired, yes, sweaty, always, and sick of bugs like you wouldn't believe, but still far from the exhaustion that had plagued me previously.

Lace continued to scout ahead, but the rest of us had adopted a looser formation. Miko and Mordecai were even keeping their eyes peeled for anything harvestable along the road, though the chances seemed slim that Merchant Jessup or his men would have missed a potential sale.

As they conferred about the latest shrub, Skaal dropped back beside me. He nodded to the old dagger hanging from my new belt.

"Should learn use," he said.

I eyed the half-giant. "You can just speak to me in your native tongue; I know Lace told you I understand."

"It was the other way around, actually," he said, swapping easily. "And it seemed impolite to do so without your permission."

"Is that a reaver thing? Politeness?"

He snorted. "It is not."

"A Skaal thing, then?"

"I would prefer it be a person thing."

I shook my head. "You would have gotten along well with Riok. Berys too."

"Your training master and…?"

"His friend and, I guess, advisor."

Skaal nodded and went quiet. Ten minutes later, long after the conversation had ended, he continued.

"The spear is a good weapon, but you should adopt at least one other to address its flaws. If not the dagger, then the short sword. Something to utilize when space is an issue."

"Isn't it hard to maintain multiple weapon skills?"

"Many, yes. A few, no. And better to expend that effort than find yourself in a situation where the lack will get you killed."

I grinned. "I can't help but notice that most of your and Lace's advice comes hand in hand with premonitions of certain doom."

"Yes."

"That was a joke, Skaal."

"Yes."

It wasn't until I gave the reaver a look that I saw the mischief dancing in his cold blue eyes.

"Shouldn't you be teasing Lace, not me?" I asked, switching back to Trade.

"Lace not here. Secondary target must suffice." This time, he outright smiled, the expression deeply disturbing on his sickly face. "But when she return, should ask to train."

"Why her? Why not you?"

"Better with small blade." He switched languages. "And she needs a friend."

"She's got you," I pointed out.

He lost his smile. "For now."

It was my opportunity to ask what exactly was going on with him, but something in the half-giant's expression stilled my tongue.

"I'll ask her," I said instead.

ooo

Lace was a terrible teacher. Three nights later, and all I'd learned was how to stab an unarmed man in close quarters: angle the blade up so it slides between their ribs and hits the heart.

Because *that* was something I'd ever want to do.

Everything else was basically gobbledygook.

"It's easy," she said for the hundredth time. "When you strike, they'll react, even if they're just a trumped-up dirt farmer with dreams of competence. So, you want to read their reaction and respond accordingly. You won't know what they're going to do until they do it, so you need to just feel your way through the flow. Take whatever opening they give you and try not to give any yourself."

"Okay…"

"Your turn," she said, also for the hundredth time. She held out her blade in a ready stance and waited.

"I didn't really get all of that," I admitted.

"Which part?"

"Everything after 'It's easy.' What does *feel your way through the flow* even mean?"

She rocked back on her heels, sheathing her knife without even looking. "Maybe this isn't the weapon for you."

Right. Because it was the *weapon* that was the problem. I'd tried asking the Marauder to just focus on teaching me individual strikes or moves—eating the thegar as Miko would no doubt call it—but for a seasoned hunter and scout, Lace had all the patience of a toddler.

Which was to say, none at all.

"Maybe you're right," I agreed. According to Mordecai, adventurers sometimes leant their services to the guild as trainers; I could probably find one in Madea once I had the money to spare.

"I've noticed you and Skaal talking lately." It wasn't a question, but she looked at me expectedly.

"Yeah. I guess learning that I can speak your language—"

"Gorash," she reminded me. "And it's less our language than the language of the south. My clan—" She trailed off and shrugged. "There are many languages."

"Good to know." It was an easier name to remember than *the words of stone and wind,* for all that it lacked a certain poetry.

Another impromptu knife lesson had ended with me almost certainly no closer to actually gaining the skill. I turned back to camp. There were no concerns about campfires here on the comparatively safe road to Madea, so dinner would be hot tonight. Miko's *Cooking* skill had been climbing steadily as she worked with Skaal, and tonight he'd given her the reins to cook solo. I didn't want to miss a bite.

Lace fell in beside me, moving silently through the foliage. "How does someone learn to speak a language without even knowing its name?"

I tripped on a root that I was sure hadn't been there a second earlier. "I told you: our village had all sorts of information, but most of it was fragmented."

She cut in front of me like I hadn't even been moving, bringing me up short. Though smaller than Miko and Skaal, she still managed to loom over me in a way I hated. "I'm not a fool. I'm not even sure this *village* of yours exists."

"You think the two of us just lived out in the wilderness by ourselves?"

Lace huffed. "Well, obviously not."

If I'd had the *Deception* skill back on Earth, I might have been unstoppable.

Unfortunately, the Marauder wasn't so easily deterred. "You're not from the south," she said, "yet you speak like a native. Nobody gets that from schooling. It's not a technique, because you have *Lunge* and were only level two when we found you."

"I'm not—"

"Which means it's either an enchantment—unlikely, given that you again had virtually nothing to your name—or..." Silver eyes sharpened in the twilight gloom. "Do you have a trait?"

Unfortunately, I only had two points in *Deception.* "Why would you think that?" I tried.

"You do! What is it?"

Since lying clearly wasn't working for me, I tried a new tactic.

"I'll tell you everything if *you* tell me Skaal's story."

She lost all expression. "It's his story to tell, not mine."

"Are you sure?"

"Mostly."

"And would he tell it if I asked him?"

"Blood and ashes, no. He'd say something like '*What was done is done and I will live or die with the consequences.*'"

"I kind of figured," I lied. "Which is why I'm asking you."

"And you won't tell me about your trait otherwise?"

"You're the one who's convinced it *is* a trait. I haven't said a thing."

She chewed on that as the woods got progressively darker around us. Finally, she sighed. "Keep your secrets then. I'm hungry."

○○○

We were one day out of Madea when Lace finally broke. We hadn't trained in knives in two days, which would have been a real punishment if I'd been learning anything in our sessions. As it was, I still didn't have the skill. I'd filled my free time each evening with some homebrew calisthenics trying to level up my *Athleticism* skill—or any of my physical attributes—but so far, the Framework was being stingy.

Maybe if I added more danger into the mix? I could have Miko throw things at me or something.

It was worth a try.

I'd been given middle watch in another not-so-subtle indication that our party leader was still pissed at me. So far, the road to Madea had been almost blissfully peaceful, and I couldn't decide if that made standing watch more of a pain or less of one. I mean… I wasn't worried about the Thunderbird dropping out of the sky to swallow me whole, but that just made multiple hours of sitting around that much more boring.

So when Lace sat next to me, sometime well after midnight, I was happy to see her. I was even happier when she sighed and finally spoke.

"This story is for your ears only."

I shook my head. "Miko too."

"What?"

"I'm not keeping secrets from her."

I couldn't see her face, but I could hear the exasperation in her voice. "What is it with you two? I'd think you were bonded if it wasn't for your little romance back in Harborton."

"Would you rather hear about that or how I can speak your language? The choice is yours."

She sighed. "Mordecai *told* me you had the *Mercantilism* skill, but I guess now I have proof of it. I'll stick with my original question. And fine, you can tell Miko. The way she and the old man are getting on, I don't think he'd mind anyway."

"It's a deal." I waited, letting the silence build between us.

"You want me to go first?"

"Let's just say trust is in short supply. After all, I've heard your thoughts on banditry."

That surprised a laugh out of her, which was a first.

"Fine. But only because I know that you know what will happen if you welch on our deal." There was a rustle of movement, where she presumably drew one or more daggers.

"You know I can't see what you're doing, right?"

"Shut up." She cleared her throat. "Just… shut up and listen."

So, I did.

46

For a long while, Lace just sat there in the darkness, her slow breaths the only sign she was still present. Finally, she stirred. "To understand Skaal's story, you must first hear mine. What do you know of the clans?"

"The blood-scorned amazon clans?"

"Asked and answered." She sighed. "That's not our name for ourselves. It's a name given by fools up here in the north, dirt farmers and cowards who'd never even dream of crossing the Waste."

"What do you call yourselves then?"

"It doesn't matter. What does matter is that we're not a nation or even a confederacy. We share similar cultures and beliefs, but each clan stakes out their own territories and is led by their matriarch, their witchmother, or both. Clans skirmish against one another all the time, and while true war is rare, it does happen. Two clans lost their names when I was but a child."

"What does that mean? A clan losing its name?"

"It means the heart of the clan's strength fell in battle and those who remained were unable to hold their lands. The survivors were taken by neighboring clans as laborers, servants, or in very rare cases, potential recruits."

"What about the reavers?" I wanted to know.

"You follow orders poorly, Brian Fieldings."

"Right. Shutting up again. Sorry."

She stayed silent for a few seconds, as if to test my resolve, then continued. "For all that the clans fight among themselves, they reserve their true enmity for those who do not share their beliefs. To the west are the kithrizal prides, dwelling in the deepest reaches of the shade-touched jungle. To the south, the longbeards in their stone cities. To the east…" I could hear her shake her head. "We do not speak of the east. But to the north, in the steppes and the mountains beyond, live the reaver tribes. The blood that has been spilled along each border could fill the Snake River, but it is in the north that the fighting has always been fiercest."

"Why?"

"We are both warrior peoples. While there are those in clans and tribes alike tasked with livestock or even dirt farming, they are the unnamed. Some failed to claim a place of honor as they aged into adulthood. Others were taken as captives on raids. Strength reigns and strength must forever be proven through action."

The image I was getting was one of regular conflict, clans raiding each other while also attacking or fending off attacks from neighboring species and nations.

"You were one of the raiders, I take it?" I asked.

"No. I had only sixteen cycles and was one of my clan's lead hunters. Old enough to have gained my class and my name, of course, but not yet considered worthy of joining the raids. It burned me every time I was left behind, left with a few others to watch the daughters and the unnamed, while those just a cycle or two older went forth to claim their glory."

"That was the season our oldest allies, the Nightstalker clan, turned on us," Lace continued. "There is no worse blood than among those once considered family. War erupted between our clans."

"Do you know why?"

"It was over a man, believe it or not. An unnamed who was famously fair of face and form. Our matriarch claimed him as breeding stock from the joint raid on a third and rival clan. The matriarch of the Nightstalkers had designs of her own and claimed rights of seniority, demanding that the man be delivered to their clan and her bed instead."

Matriarchal society, I thought to myself. *Check. Men seen as chattel and breeding partners. Check. Enforced captivity as laborers or servants. Check.* It wasn't my place to say anything, but I didn't think a whole lot of Lace's upbringing, and I sure as hell wasn't ever traveling that far south if I could help it.

"Naturally, our matriarch refused. If she had backed down, she could have prevented war, but only at the cost of her own authority and life. There are always those in the clan watching and waiting for the leader to show weakness."

"And so you went to war."

"Yes. Both clans suffered, but the Nightstalkers had underestimated our strength. Over the course of a cycle, our victories slowly mounted, while theirs vanished like smoke on the wind. The day came for the final strike. Our matriarch led the war party into the jungle and I watched them go, one of the dozen or so hunters left behind in camp." Lace's voice went quiet. "It was several glasses later, as the bloody sun was rising in the east, that the reavers came. I was one of four on guard at that time and I… had fallen asleep."

I could practically feel her fierce-eyed glare on me, waiting for me to say something, anything at all, but I wasn't a complete idiot.

"I woke to screams," she said, bitterness filling the air. "There was less than a score of them, but they swept through our thinly defended camp like a plague of black-skulled cursewings. I joined a sister and together, we brought one reaver down, but his dying blow literally cut her in two."

"And Skaal?"

"Led the raid as the son of his tribe's war chief though I did not know it or him yet." She coughed and cleared her throat. "None of us were even Tin. We had no chance, but we fought anyway, as we had been taught. We fought and we died, by axe and sword, by boot and fist. I didn't even see the blow that felled me, but it broke my ribs, one arm, and my hip. As I struck the ground, I used *Night Hag's Embrace* to hide like a coward."

"What was the alternative? Dying? For nothing?"

"You are not of the clans. You wouldn't understand."

"Damn right I wouldn't."

She sighed and moved on. "It was all I could do to hold on to the technique with the pain wracking my body, and even then, my movement ended it early. Whichever reaver had struck me down was already gone, and the sound of battle had been replaced with the moans of the dying. I couldn't move. I could barely breathe, but I watched as the reavers rounded up the unnamed, along with our livestock and our young. Words were said and two of the unnamed were cut down by a reaver in black furs, silenced with a stroke of his greataxe. The others fell into line, as the unnamed always do, but the children…"

I shut my eyes, wondering if she could see it. *You wanted to hear this story*, I reminded myself. *Bargained for it even.*

"Daughters of the clan are raised to be future warriors. There is no greater shame than to be taken captive and lose one's name. Even those fresh off their mother's tit know that truth. And so it was no surprise when the eldest of the children, eight cycles old and tall for her age, waited like a dusk panther for the black-furred reaver to approach. He crouched to claim her, hand to chest, and she struck true. The blade she used was meant for skinning, not battle, but the reaver never saw it coming and lost an eye because of it." Another sigh. "She died, of course. Then and there, thrown to the ground, and crushed beneath the reaver's boot, but the half-giant's bloodlust wasn't satisfied. He turned on the rest of the children, bloody axe sweeping upwards to blot out the sun, and then down again like a falcon on the hunt."

"I get it," I finally croaked, throat dry and hoarse as if I'd been the one speaking.

"No, you don't." Her voice was hard. "Nor did I at the time. Because as that axe swept downward, another reaver interposed himself between the axeman and his prey. And though this new reaver was the smaller of the two, he stopped the strike cold."

I thought back to Lomas' inn, when a too-thin half-giant had immobilized a drunken farmer with one oversized hand.

"Skaal."

"Yes. The two men argued in the language of the reavers, one waving his bloody axe about, the other calm like the eye of a storm. Finally, they appeared to settle. The smaller one patted the larger on the shoulder and then both stepped away." She paused. "I don't know what changed things after that. Maybe one of the daughters said something, or maybe the black-furred reaver had only told Skaal what he wanted to hear. Either way, he turned again on the children and this time nobody was close enough to stop him. Two more daughters fell, one of them no older than four."

"What did Skaal do?"

"Something I still struggle to believe. He turned on his own tribesman. One strike took the reaver's arm at the elbow, the other pierced his heart. If I was surprised, the other reavers were stunned.

There was a moment of silence, and then they went after him. Every single remaining half-giant."

"Why?"

"One tribe, one blood," said a deep-voiced Skaal in Gorash from behind us. "To raise a blade against your own tribe mid-raid is to spit in the face of the ancestors. To kill one? The only fitting punishment is death."

"Skaal, I—" Lace trailed off. "Brian asked," she finally finished, sounding defensive.

"Is your choice to tell story," he said, switching to Trade. "I gave up choice long ago. Only one left."

Lace stiffened.

"If you knew what it would mean for you, why did you do it?" I asked the reaver.

"No strength in killing unarmed. No honor in Skolgur hurting helpless for own mistake." He settled in on my left, putting me between the two. "Continue."

Lace cleared her throat. When she spoke, her voice was subdued. "There were thirteen reavers left in total, including Skaal, and the other twelve all went after him, howling for his blood."

"Had just reached Copper," added Skaal, voice a low rumble. "But twelve was too many. Five, maybe. Twelve? No. Had just broken ties with family for sake of children. What was one more shame to add to pile?"

"There was plenty of shame to go around that day," said Lace sharply. "None of it was yours."

"What happened?" I wasn't sure who I was asking.

"Unleashed Tempest," said Skaal. "Ancestors were not pleased."

"What?" I turned to Lace this time.

"What do you know about enchanted items?" she asked me.

"Nothing."

"Why am I not surprised?" She sighed. "I don't have the energy to teach you tonight, but let's just say they come in tiers."

"Like technique ratings?"

"Yes. At the bottom are bound enchantments, single-use items that release their effect when triggered. Above them are relics, items that were inscribed with runes as part of their crafting, and which maintain their enchantments as long as the runes remain unbroken. At the top, so rare a normal person would never encounter one, are artifacts. Some say they're relics that have lasted long enough to accrue power and will of their own. Others say they are their own type of crafting entirely."

"Tempest is artifact," said Skaal. "Handed down from war chief to war chief for generations."

"The other thing that differentiates artifacts from relics is that artifacts always come with a cost," added Lace. "Tempest's is… extreme."

"Uses Vitality of wielder." The reaver could have been discussing the price of tea in China for all the emotion in his voice. "Not safe to use before Bronze or maybe Gold. Should not have even had with me but brought on raid for luck."

"So when you used it…"

"Gave me strength to destroy tribe turned enemies. Consumed Vitality in return."

"One reaver against twelve," said Lace, "yet it was the twelve who fell, one after the other, cursing Skaal's name. And with each death, his body withered, muscle and mass melting away like ice in the noon sun. At the end, they were all dead but him, and he was skin and bones, unable to even hold his weapon.

"The warriors of my clan returned soon after to find the carnage. The unnamed had hidden away the children once the danger was gone, but they left Skaal in the center of our clan grounds and skipped over me entirely, likely thinking me dead."

"Warriors found one living reaver in middle of slaughter," said Skaal. "Made only smart choice. Matriarch herself came to end life. But young hunter was not dead, merely broken. Claimed *she* had defeated me. Claimed me as captive. Should have let me go."

"You had just turned on your own tribe to save our daughters," snarled Lace. "I didn't know why, but I wasn't going to watch you die."

"Yes. Made choice. And then paid cost. There is always cost." The reaver pushed himself to his feet and headed out into the night.

I waited until I was sure he was gone. Or… reasonably sure.

"Why did he switch to Trade? He knows I speak Gorash."

"That was about me, not you. For someone who claims he has neither will nor desire, he always finds ways to let me know when I misstep." She sighed for at least the fifth time in as many minutes. "Still, I've started the story so I might as well finish it. Where was I?"

"You… claimed Skaal as captive."

"Right. A hunter who couldn't even stand claiming a reaver who lay twenty paces away. It was a laughable thing, but the matriarch couldn't disregard it. It helped that two of the daughters backed my story, though I was never sure why."

"Maybe they didn't want him dead either."

"Maybe. Regardless, I earned my second name and a seat at the raid table. Skaal and I were both healed, although there were limits to what could be done for him."

"I'm still not sure I understand what Tempest did. It permanently drained his Vitality attribute?"

"Yes. His natural Vitality dropped to zero, and most of the Vitality he earned through levels, something that is usually untouchable, was similarly drained. Such is the power of an artifact. He had enough left to live, but not much more than that, and without Vitality, his techniques were all but unavailable to him."

Because Vitality was one of the determining factors on someone's energy levels. I remembered that much at least.

"Things went well enough for a few cycles. Skaal was not loved around camp, but he was a hard worker. With the Nightstalkers destroyed, there was relative peace. As he regained strength, we spent our days together, and I learned more of who he was and why he had done what he had done. As his owner, I decided it fell upon me to see him returned to health. Our witchmother had no cure for his condition, but every two levels..."

"He'd gain one point in Vitality automatically... and a second point he could also add to it."

"Yes. Leveling in Copper is anything but swift, but even so, I had hope. And for the first time in my life, I had someone to share my burdens with, someone who would not strike me down or send me to burn in the Night Hag's fires for perceived weakness."

"So what happened?"

"We have a saying: *when mortals plan, Hashoggath smiles.* There were always those in the clan who resented Skaal's presence. Others who resented that I had claimed him as mine. Still others who believed an artifact like Tempest had no place in the hands of one as young as me, let alone the hands of my unnamed. As the daughters aged into adulthood, the story of what really happened that day leaked out. I had long since proven my skills as a member of our war party but lost my claim to both Skaal and Tempest overnight. I had no choice."

"You ran," I realized.

"The matriarch would have used him, would have drained him dry, and then sacrificed whatever was left," she snarled. "I had no choice. We killed no one on our way out, but still the clan took offense. They sent my sisters after us, wielding weapon and spell. They took my names from me and alerted the other clans. But Hashoggath's spite can blind even the most watchful eye. We escaped the jungle. We survived the steppes and the bitter cold of the mountains that came after. By the time we reached the southern edge of the Waste, I knew we had at last eluded pursuit. I chose to press on anyway, across the Waste, to the lands of the north, where maidens wet their cheeks with honey and even dirt farmers live like kings."

"I haven't seen a lot of honey so far," I admitted.

"No. The north is soft in many ways, hard in many others, and nothing at all like I expected when we first set out four cycles ago. Yet we are here now and here we will stay. I gave Skaal back his names and took a new one to replace those I lost in the jungle. And that, in far too many words, is his story and mine. Let's never speak of it again."

"He gave up his tribe to save your clan's children, and you gave up your clan to save him. That's somehow both sad and beautiful."

"As the old man would say, it is what it is and no more. We are adventurers now. Every even level grants him some of his lost Vitality, while the coin and renown we gain will one day open doors that are otherwise closed to us. We require access not just to the rich and powerful, but to the Priests and Mages among them."

Something she had said days earlier finally made sense. "Because you're still hoping to find a cure."

"Every hex has a counterspell, every curse a blessing that should counteract it. If there is anywhere to find such, it will be here, where soft people worship equally soft gods."

Between Miko and me, I already had way too much on my plate, but something about her story struck home. Maybe it was that she was so clearly in love with Skaal that it hurt to see. Maybe it was that neither she nor Skaal seemed to realize it. Or maybe part of being a Chosen was finding myself drawn to lost causes.

Either way, I couldn't help but respond.

"I don't know how long Miko and I will be with the party. We have responsibilities that will come due sometime in the next few cycles. But as long as we are here, I will help however I can."

"You can start by speaking with Skaal and convincing him to forgive me. That man has made an art of passive aggressiveness, and I will not have guilt chasing my every footstep."

"Uh, yeah. I can do that." I wasn't sure why I'd expected anything else from the hard-eyed Marauder. Emotions and sympathy were clearly best left to the so-called soft northerners.

"And I believe you also owe me an answer," she added, "in exchange for my story."

I nodded, trusting that her *Night Eyes* technique would let her see it. I also lowered my voice, even with Mordecai asleep and Skaal… well, somewhere else. "I do. And you were right before. It *is* a trait."

"I knew it! What is it called? How does it work? Is it active or passive? No, it must be passive."

"It's called *Speaker of Tongues*, and yes, it's passive. At least I think so. I'm still figuring it all out, but so far, it seems like if I hear a language, I can understand it and speak it back. Fluently, in the proper accent for whoever I'm speaking with."

"Any language?"

"I'm up to six so far." Seven, including English, but she didn't need to know that.

Her voice dropped to a quiet hiss. "So, you will understand me when I tell you that you are the worst knife trainee I have ever had?"

I responded in kind, letting my trait handle what was almost definitely its eighth language. "I will and while you're not the worst teacher I've ever had, that's only because Mrs. Snowdon was eighty-four, senile, and called half of the men in class by her dead husband's name."

She paused. "Perhaps she was speaking to his ghost?"

"I don't think so."

I could just barely hear the timbre shift as she swapped back to Trade. "That is an incredible trait. It has little value in combat, of course, but for an explorer, or a merchant—"

"Or a translator."

"Yes, or that… If not for being limited to speech, I would almost call it *too* powerful."

I coughed. "So far, it's worked for reading and writing as well."

"And yet the Night Hag must make do with only nine breasts."

I wasn't sure what that was supposed to mean—other than the obvious, which I'd already seen for myself—so I stayed quiet.

"There is profit to be made from a trait like that," Lace continued. "The north prides itself on the knowledge it locks away in books, but to hear Mordecai speak, many of those books are mysteries even to their owners. Noble houses with ancient tomes they cannot read. Advancement paths written thousands of cycles before the Endless Empire ever rose, in languages nobody has heard of since. Even the duke is reported to have a collection of oddities and no understanding of their use. The potential is staggering."

"I don't think any of those people—or even the owners of the public archives—are going to let me access their rarest books on faith. Hell, I'm not sure they'd even agree to see me at all."

"They wouldn't. They'd summon their guards and have you ejected from the gardens you had just managed to climb into, all because you lacked the proper connections to this or that fool in over-fluffed finery."

"That… sounds pretty specific."

"We did not begin our time in the north out here on the fringe. But connections require money and power, and making either in the inner cities requires even *more* connections. We came to Madea and then Harborton to start that slow process of building." Lace slapped me on the shoulder, the impact even more sudden because I couldn't see the movement. "But those connections will come quickly with your bookcraft and Miko's healing. And once they have, your absurd trait might just be the key to unlocking our future."

I felt like she was skipping some steps in the process—and not just a few of them either—but I didn't say anything. After all, Miko and I needed money too, and while adventuring was the short-term solution to that need, Lace's ideas had real merit.

I went back to my shared tent with dreams of Scrooge McDuck-sized piles of gold flooding my brain and was halfway asleep before I remembered I was supposed to talk to Skaal.

Tomorrow, I sleepily told myself. *The best day to start something is* always *tomorrow.*

Book 4: Adventurer

"There are few things on Eos more dangerous than an adventurer with too much time on their hands and treasure on their mind."

-Old Proverb

47

From the road above, Madea looked a lot like Harborton… just significantly larger. It was a town instead of a village, with the buildings inside its perimeter wall ranging from one story to three or even four, but it still gave off a provincial vibe. The forest that bordered it on two sides contributed to that impression, although the trees had been cut back to create large open fields outside the wall. The hills that rose to the north and west added some charm. With the sun shining down from above, it might have made for a pretty postcard, had cameras been a thing on Eos.

This close to town, we weren't the only ones on the increasingly well-traveled road. We encountered a handful of hunters, both heading out and returning with game, local farmers bringing their produce to market, and even two different merchants, their wagons drawn by horses instead of dalysi. Shortly after leaving camp, the road from Harborton had merged with a larger and better maintained road angling in from the south. Given that we hadn't seen anyone before then, I assumed almost all the traffic we were now encountering came from that other road.

Valestia and Erlund clearly had their work cut out for them if they wanted to make Harborton a destination.

We received our share of looks from the other travelers, especially the guards on the merchant wagons. And by *we*, I mostly mean Skaal, Lace, and Miko. Walking next to a seven-foot-tall gaunt reaver, a cold-eyed woman with skin as matte black as her clothes, and a white-scaled, orange-eyed synossian, Mordecai and I might as well not have existed.

I was more than okay with that, but our esteemed Adept of the Crimson Needle spent a lot of time muttering to himself under his mask.

Like Harborton, Madea had two gates, named—in a stroke of undeniable genius—the Forest Gate and Hill Gate, based on whether they faced south or west. We entered through the first, where we were stopped by a guard in a chain shirt and conical helmet. His sneer did unpleasant things to a face that didn't need that kind of help.

"I see you're all still alive somehow." He directed his words toward Skaal, but it was Lace who stepped forward to respond.

"Don't look so disappointed, Henrik."

"That's Guard Henrik to you, amazon."

"Guard Henrik then." She didn't roll her eyes, but nobody would miss the edge of mockery in her voice. "And you know who we are, as you have already demonstrated by greeting us. Can we be on our way?"

"Not until you state your business in Madea."

I tried not to look at all the people who were streaming past us into town, unchallenged.

"It's the same as the last four times, *Guard* Henrik. Guild business. We have two new recruits to register."

"A scaled and a…" He eyed me up and down, eyes not even lingering on the spear. "…feral half-man?"

Half-man was enough to set my blood boiling. Feral, on the other hand… I'd caught a glimpse of my own reflection in a stream, and it kind of fit. It was a wonder Agnes hadn't run me out of Harborton even sooner… and it said truly terrible things about the village's dating pool.

"Best of luck claiming any sort of recruitment bounty for that riffraff," Henrik continued. "No offense intended to either of them, of course."

"How could calling us riffraff *not* be considered offensive?" Miko asked me in the High Tongue.

"I'm pretty sure he was just being facetious."

"I see." She looked the guard over. "I will pray for him tonight."

"That's enough talking in… whatever language you were speaking," blustered Henrik.

"Why?" asked Mordecai, speaking up for the first time. "Has Madea's mayor outlawed foreign tongues? If so, I'll need to make a note of it. I can only imagine the chilling effect it might have on trade."

"That's not what…" The guard scowled and stepped aside. "Get your recruits registered and see if you all can avoid starting any brawls this time. All it takes is one property owner complaining and I *will* bar you from entry in the future."

"Don't threaten me with a good time." Lace bared her teeth as she led us around the armored man.

"So, you're on good terms with the local authorities then?" I asked.

"Some of them, yes," the Marauder replied. "Henrik, on the other hand, is a failed adventurer and successful pain in the ass."

"He has no power over the guild," added Mordecai, "but you'd never know it to hear him prattle on."

"Is bitter and angry," Skaal said simply.

Lace shot me a look, reminding me that I *still* needed to talk to the reaver, who had stuck to Trade all day. I was pretty sure he was just doing it now to tweak Lace's nose, but still… I *had* promised.

I sidled up to him as Lace led us through town. Whereas Harborton's streets were often empty during the day, with most of the village out working, there was a steady flow of traffic down Madea's main thoroughfare.

I spoke in Gorash, leaning in toward the other man even though my head barely came up past his elbow. "I wanted to apologize for last night. I asked Lace about your shared pasts when I should have respected your privacy instead."

For the first time all day, he replied in the same language. "History is just that. It does no harm for you to know the truth of those you walk beside."

I felt a small but undeniable twinge at his words, considering that Miko and I had been anything but honest with them.

"Is it true that you speak any language?" he asked.

"Lace told you already?"

"Just as you no doubt have told little Miko our tale."

I couldn't argue with that. "It's true."

He nodded slowly, pale eyes in a too-white face, and though I couldn't tell exactly how, I knew his next words were in a language other than Gorash. "Good. Then we can speak freely."

I scanned the crowd around us. While a few were gawking at the reaver, nobody seemed to be listening. When I opened my mouth, I knew I was speaking the new language. Officially my ninth, although much like Mordecai's, I didn't know its name. "What was wrong with Gorash?"

"Lace speaks it, of course." His smile looked like a death's head grin but his eyes sparkled. "Not being able to understand us will drive her crazy."

I blinked. Crazy seemed to be going around. "You're not worried she'll just stab you at some point?"

"She *is* skilled with her knives…" He gave it about half the consideration I thought it deserved and then shrugged. "Still, it will be worth it."

As the other potential stabbee, I was less sure, but I *had* just learned a new language for free. I ignored the glare Lace threw at both of us and settled in to talk.

○○○

It took almost twenty minutes to reach the Adventurer's Guild, which was double the time it would take to cross all of Harborton. The building was a three-story wooden affair with narrow windows on all three floors. A sign hung above the oversized door bearing a crossed blade and hammer.

"That's the sign of the guild, lass," Mordecai told Miko. "You'll find one in every city and at least some of the larger towns. As a hub for the region, Madea has the privilege of hosting the guild."

The door burst open, and a man and a woman staggered out, both reeking of alcohol. The man took one step, tripped, and fell flat on his face in front of us, while the woman took three steps to her right, vomited noisily, and passed out.

Mordecai cleared his throat. "Sometimes, it's less a privilege than others, admittedly."

Through the still-open door came a middle-aged man with a sour face and a bucket in both hands. He sighed but otherwise ignored the man sprawled in the street before him, turning to the woman instead. With a grunt, he upended the bucket over the prone woman, targeting both her and her spilled vomit with equal prejudice. She didn't stir, but the puke was at least partly washed away.

That duty successfully performed, the man turned to go inside, only to pull up short when Lace cleared her throat. His eyes floated past Miko and me to land on Lace and Skaal and his expression somehow soured even further.

"Nylessa help us all, I see you made it back."

"Hello, revered Deputy Keeper Carlson." This time, Lace's smile seemed genuine.

"It's just Carlson. I've told you that." For a second, a thin smile threatened to break through his vague irritation. "Merchant Jessup stopped in Madea a day or two ago and said you'd reached Harborton without issue. Were you successful in completing the mayor's task?"

Lace pulled a scroll from her pack and beamed. "Of course we were. She even threw in a letter of recommendation."

Carlson took the scroll with a nod. "I'll see it added to your records. Perhaps this will go some ways to helping people forget the prior debacle."

"You know that wasn't our fault, lad," put in Mordecai.

"Given that everyone else involved ended up dead and the premises burned to the ground while the errant mercenaries escaped mostly unscathed, we have only your words to take for that, Adept of the Crimson Needle." He ignored Mordecai's garbled protests and knelt to remove the coin purses from the two unconscious adventurers' belts.

"Now then," he said, tucking both purses and scroll under one arm, "enter and be welcome once more to the Adventurer's Guild. As always, we make no promises as to the safety of you or your belongings on these premises. I will say, however," he added, with a wrinkle of his thin nose, "that it at least *smells* better inside."

ooo

We followed Carlson inside and while he wasn't *lying* about the smell, per se, we were hit with a strong wave of what might have been Pine Sol if we were back on earth. An improvement? Yes. Mildly cloying? Also yes. A handful of tables sat empty in the main room, while a small bar stood against one wall. At the rear of the room, where Lomas would have placed *his* bar, was a staircase leading up, and in front of that staircase were two desks. The left one had papers scattered haphazardly across the breadth of its surface while the right one looked like it had just been professionally cleaned by a team of forensic scientists.

I wasn't *too* surprised to see Carlson lead us to the second desk, nor by the irritated look he reserved for the neighboring desk and its absent owner.

He opened a drawer and deposited both coin purses within, then removed his stiff-necked jacket and draped it over the back of the tall chair behind the desk. Only after he was seated and the neat stack of papers to his right had been needlessly adjusted did he favor us with another glance.

"What will it be? Lodging? Spoils? Another mission?" For the first time, he turned to Miko and me, and I felt myself swiftly evaluated. "Or are some of you looking to join the kingdom's premiere organization for the accomplishment of tasks and the eradication of dangers?"

I blinked. Between the man's officiousness, efficiency, and yes, verbosity, it was almost like talking to another Mordecai.

"All of the above," said Lace. "We'll need three rooms for the duration of our stay, and Skaal and I will want to look at the mission board."

"Noted." Action followed words, as he dipped a quill in ink and logged our requests. "And the spoils?"

Mordecai took over. "Most of it we'll deal with ourselves, but we have two bundles of prepared nilwort, and a few other less common herbs that the guild's patrons might be interested in acquiring."

"Patrons?" I asked Lace, speaking in Gorash.

"The guild is partially funded by retired adventurers, wealthy merchants, and the nobility," she replied. "They pay a premium for certain items. It takes longer, and the guild gets a cut for serving as middleman, but the profit is significantly higher than we'd get on the street."

"And you improve your reputation with those in power."

"Exactly."

"Need I remind you both," said Carlson, "that we are in the Kingdom of Elthor? While Grand Duke Willerton of course welcomes all species, religions, and… backgrounds, it *is* considered polite to use Trade when conducting business."

"I was just telling our new recruit that," Lace assured the man. She turned a scowl on me. "It's like I always say: *politeness is the truest foundation of a society.*"

Apparently, stabbing *wasn't* her only way of getting back at Skaal or me.

"Of course," I said, as Miko did her best to stifle a giggle. "It won't happen again."

"While we handle that business, revered Deputy Keeper Carlson," continued Lace, in a voice as pure as snow, "perhaps your assistant could register these two as new guild members? They are rough around the edges, but their hearts are in the right place."

Carlson nodded and lifted a bell that had been carefully positioned about an inch from the far corner of his desk. He rang it, waited, then rang it again. After about a minute of waiting, he sighed. The bell went back in its spot on the desk, and he spread his open hands instead, palms facing each other. The air became slightly opaque and started to shiver.

"Melligula," he said, voice ice cold as he spoke into the space between his hands, "your break time elapsed precisely a quarter-glass ago. You are needed at your workstation forthwith."

I traded glances with Miko. Was that… the magical equivalent of a telephone? And if so, how did I get one?

"Melligula will be present shortly," said Carlson. "You two may wait in front of her… *desk* while I handle the rest of this business with your seniors."

It was only five feet, but it felt like being sent to the kiddie table or the principal's office. I tried not to slouch as I followed the synossian over.

"This is exciting," said Miko in the High Tongue, "although it seems less efficient than just having the legions handle security."

I gave Carlson a careful look, but he didn't seem to have any issue with us talking in something other than Trade now that we weren't *doing business*. And that worked for me.

"From what I've gathered," I replied in kind, "the kingdom doesn't really have large standing armies like your legions. The dukes and their vassal nobles each have small forces of their own, but they only come together in times of war."

"I'm not sure how I feel about that, but it does give us more opportunities here." After a moment's thought, she nodded more firmly. "Opportunities that we sorely need."

A clatter on the stairs stole our attention. We both looked up as a large creature in a brightly colored dress pounded her way down to the main floor. She skidded at the bottom, but caught her balance, and was over and seated in the desk in front of us within three long strides.

"Hello!" she said, the gold jewelry in her nose, lips, and ears twinkling. "Welcome to the Adventurer's Guild. My name is Melligula."

For too long of a moment, I just stared. Thankfully, Miko was quicker on the uptake than me. She brought her hands together and gave the other woman a bow.

"We greet," she said in her still-improving Trade. "I am Miko and this—this *is* Brian."

"And is Brian mute or just too busy staring to speak?"

I winced and finally dropped my gaze. "I can speak. And I'm sorry, I didn't mean to stare. I just—"

"Never met a turbinga before, I take it?"

"I haven't." I cleared my throat and offered her my hand. "But that's no excuse. It's a pleasure to meet you."

"Aww, see? And here I thought you *weren't* going to be a charmer. First impressions aren't always correct, I guess!" With a toothy grin, she took my hand in both of hers and tossed her head like a high schooler attempting their first flirtation.

Her *head* because she didn't have hair. Instead, above two sets of eyes, she had a cowlick of coarse black fur, and above that cowlick, two ivory horns pointed to the ceiling. The reason for her near slip on the stairs was likewise suddenly apparent. Instead of feet, Melligula had hooves.

I didn't know what a turbinga was, but if someone had ever asked me to draw a voluptuous demon cow person in a muumuu, I'm pretty sure my crude sketch would have been a dead ringer for the woman seated in front of us.

"What can I do for you cuties?" she asked, still beaming.

A desk over, Carlson cleared his throat noisily, and the cow woman rolled all four of her eyes.

"What I *meant* to say was… as the assistant to the deputy keeper, it is my honor and privilege to serve the loyal members of our guild. What can I assist you with today?"

One pair of eyes stayed on us, but the other pair turned toward the officious man in her periphery. When he returned to dealing with Lace and the others, Melligula's smile widened.

"We'd like to register as new members of the guild," I told her.

"Oh!" She finally released my hand so that she could clap both of hers together. "I haven't gotten to do a member intake since the youngest Johannesburg." Her expression fell. "I'm sure things will go better for you though."

"What do you mean?"

"He... well... he died on his first mission. But that's rarer than you might think!" she assured us. "And besides, he was unranked and trying to fight way outside his means. Now, where did I put the forms..."

"Right-side drawer," said Carlson, not looking up from the bundle of nilwort in his hands. "No, that's your left."

"And here we are!" Melligula regarded the mess on her desk and then shrugged, pushing one pile into another until she had cleared space. While her feet were hooved, her hands were human enough, albeit with only three fingers and a thumb. She took up a quill, leaned across the way to dip it into Carlson's inkwell, and beamed at us. "We'll start with you, Brian. Full name if you have one. We also accept aliases, but the guild makes no guarantees that your true identity won't be discovered."

"Brian Fieldings," I said.

"How many F's is that?"

"Just one." I spelled it out for her. Despite her appearance and general behavior, the turbinga's handwriting was every bit as neat as Carlson's.

"Class and rank?"

"Really?"

"We need the basic information," she explained. "Your level and your techniques are your secrets to keep, but we try to avoid giving missions to those who aren't qualified for them."

"We are with them," said Miko, nodding to the others. Her sharp teeth flashed in a proud smile at a sentence that had been grammatically flawless.

"And I'll add that into your profile, believe you me, sweetheart. But there may come a time when one of you, or both, decides to go their own separate way. That's why we keep records on all our member's classes and ranks and not just their party leader's."

"I'm a Warrior," I said. "Currently unranked."

"That's okay," said Melligula, reaching across the desk to pat my cheek. "I'm sure you'll reach Tin in no time. Assuming you don't die, of course." She made a note on my form and then her second pair of eyes looked back up again. "Anything else to report? Pets? Next of kin? Hobbies?"

"Hobbies?"

"I like sewing and thank you for asking! I'm not going to make a profession of it or anything, but it's something to keep the hands busy while my mind is whirring away, you know?"

I did *not* know, but she seemed absurdly nice in a kind of freaky way, and the last thing I wanted to do was offend her. Again.

"That sounds nice. Uhm, what was the question?"

"Pets, next of kin, or hobbies, dear."

"Right. No pets or hobbies. As for next of kin…" I turned to the synossian at my side. "I guess Miko?"

The woman in question swallowed and dropped into a deep bow. When she rose, her orange eyes were suspiciously bright. "I would be proud to consider you nest-brother."

"Aww!" Melligula put down her quill and wiped a hand across all four of her eyes. "You two need to stop that or I'll start crying a river. It's been that kind of season, you know?"

While she was composing herself, I offered Miko my best version of the bow she'd just given me. Given the resulting giggles, I must have screwed it up somehow.

"Okay, there's just one more space on the form," said our attendant. "Are there any special skills—small S, not big, mind you—that you would like to have recorded?"

"For what purpose?"

"Sometimes, we get missions with specific parameters. A seek-and-destroy mission might also need someone versed in runic inscribing. That sort of thing. Having our member information readily available means we can reach out directly to the adventurer that best fits the need rather than just having them find it on the mission board themselves."

That made sense. And it dovetailed well with what Lace had said about using my trait for good and profit.

"I'm good with languages," I said. "Really good."

"Speaking, writing, reading, or all three?"

"All three. I'm not a Scribe but I worked as one in Harborton."

"Well, *that's* different." She wrote it all down. "And done! Now there's just the matter of your registration fee."

I slid a copper plug—my second-to-last—across the desk.

"Excellent! Thank you for making this so easy! Now, if you don't mind, I'll take care of your next of kin over here before I give you both the welcome spiel?"

"Of course. And uhm… she is only just learning Trade. She's really good with it now," I added, "but I'm here to help if anything needs translation."

Melligula put down her quill, all four eyes trained on me. "Definitely a charmer," she cooed. "I could just eat you up!"

ooo

Miko's registration went a lot more quickly than mine and I didn't have to help even once. The only minor confusion came from when Melligula asked whether the name Naseri came from Miko's mother or her father, and the synossian said neither, that it was a name shared among all the hatchlings in her nest that season.

Four vaguely bovine eyes had blinked, only to be met by a pair of eyes with two fluttering layers of eyelids. When all the blinking was done, Melligula had continued with the intake.

Miko's herbalism and gathering skills were added to her profile, with the turbinga assuring her that there would *definitely* be missions where they were a bonus. Ten minutes earlier, my language abilities had only merited a *that's different*, but I tried not to take it personally.

Another copper plug crossed the desk and disappeared into a drawer, and then Melligula stood again, towering above everyone in the room that wasn't a reaver. She passed us each simple badges, carved from a light-colored wood, and strung on a rawhide cord.

"With that done, I'd like to welcome you both as new members of the Adventurer's Guild, the kingdom's premiere organization for the accomplishment of tasks and the eradication of dangers! Membership in our guild is tiered. New recruits start at the bottom, of course, as provisional members. The badges I've given you will identify you as such to any who ask."

I examined my badge. There wasn't much to it… just the crossed blade and hammer of the guild atop an ornately carved P.

"Complete two or more missions in a satisfactory manner and you can trade those in for badges signifying your status as full members of the guild. Two missions a cycle along with payment of your annual dues will maintain that standing. To become a *senior* member, you'll need to be ranked at least Iron. Dues are waived for Iron members, but they must commit to at least three higher-grade missions a cycle. There are a few tiers beyond that, but…" she shrugged her massive shoulders.

"Well, Madea hasn't seen someone that's Iron or above since it was founded. If you get that far, you'll probably go somewhere with a little more action, you know?"

"What do the different roles get you?" I wanted to know.

"Provisional members can only take missions if they are accompanied by a full member. Full members have no such restrictions, but in cases where multiple parties want the same mission, past performance determines who gets priority. Senior members, on the other hand, are usually sought out directly rather than having to pull from the board."

That explained why Valestia's letter of recommendation mattered. The party's last mission before Harborton had apparently gone badly, so we needed the reputation boost if we were going to be able to claim any decent missions from the board.

"We're done if you both are," said Lace, manifesting behind my shoulder just for the sick pleasure of seeing me flinch. "Rooms are upstairs and paid for. Your meals and your first bath will come out of the party funds too, but everything else, alcohol included, is your responsibility. Tonight, I suggest you rest. Tomorrow, we'll hit the merchants and resupply. And the day after that, we'll be on the road again."

"You found a mission already?"

"Two of them, but the first one's not available just yet."

"And the other is a wild goose chase," said Mordecai. "Still, now that you're both full members of the party, it'll be good to get our ducks in a row."

Which told me two more things I hadn't previously known… apparently, some idioms did translate… and Eos had both ducks *and* geese.

Who would have thought?

48

Miko had already left our small room when I woke, which was surprising given how much she hated mornings. Her bed was neatly made, but her pack was still in the corner. Wherever she had gone, she'd be back before long.

I went through my morning forms—fingers, hands, arms, toes, feet, legs—but everything was still functioning normally. The previous night's bath, combined with the nicest bed I'd slept on since coming to Eos, had me feeling cozy and a little bit lazy, so I lay there a while longer as I ran through my list of things to do.

Some of my day would be spent helping Miko and Mordecai sell their wares. Another portion would be dedicated to lunch and dinner—served not at the guild house but in a tavern just down the street, thanks to a deal between the two businesses. I didn't think I had enough money for any kind of armor but wanted to at least browse the local shops to get an idea of what I'd need to save. And of course, I needed someone with teaching experience who could instruct me in the knife. It would be even better if they also knew the spear; while skill gains happened fastest in real combat, I still wanted to improve my foundations.

Upgrading my *Spear* skill to Uncommon had been a qualitative difference rather than a quantitative one, and there were still many tiers to go. While my single remaining plug seemed unlikely to buy me armor, it *might* net me a glass or two of training.

Lastly, I needed to follow up on my two quests. Miko had gotten fewer looks than Skaal on our way to the guild, which told me synossians might not be completely unknown here. If I found some local so-called *scaled* and introduced Miko to them, we would not only be able to start laying the groundwork for her people's arrival, I'd be that much closer to my next level.

I also wanted to check if Madea had any sort of archives, and what the requirements for using them would be. A better understanding of the Framework would be helpful to both of us and information on the divine rule that Shan had broken would complete yet another quest. The amount of experience needed to level climbed as we progressed, but if one quest had gotten me all the way to level three, I hoped two of them might take me a long way toward level four.

Another point in Vitality and whatever other attribute I chose was a pretty powerful enticement, but it was the level after that truly excited me. There was something about technique choices being offered every odd level that I couldn't help but obsess over. Maybe it was the thrill of not knowing what those options would be. Or maybe it was that they offered such a huge potential change in tactics and combat flexibility, in a way that simple attribute improvements could not. Either way, I wanted more. And the fact that Miko had only *just* hit level five herself wasn't enough to blunt my enthusiasm.

Keep fulfilling quests as you get them. Find ways to accelerate your skill gains, complete enough missions to become a full member of the Adventurer's Guild... and the levels will come.

At some point, I really needed to spend some time thinking about my Ideal, Freedom, too. Tin rank was a very, very long way away, but any progress I could make now in understanding myself and my purpose on Eos—not just my god-assigned tasks, but my fundamental goals—would surely help when it came time to break through.

A key rattling in the door's lock told me I wouldn't have time for that kind of introspection today. Miko entered, wearing the colorful robes I'd had made for her and carrying a wooden tray.

I sat up, eyes locked on that tray. "If that's breakfast, you might just be my new favorite person in the world."

"Are you saying I'm not already your favorite?"

"Well, there's always Lomas…" I teased.

"And Nala?"

I rolled my eyes "Don't start. Did you know the pendant I gave her was worth more than a copper plug?"

"Really? Even though it was so small?"

"According to Lace, yeah."

"No wonder everyone thought you were interested in mating with her then." She placed the wooden tray down on the floor between our two beds. We both took seats on the floor and dug in. It was just bread and some type of… porridge… I thought, but the bread was warm, and the porridge was sweet.

"Did you go down the street for this?"

"No. I uh… I didn't want to leave the guild on my own. After hearing Mordecai's story about the Swarm, the looks I've gotten in the Great Wilds make a lot more sense, and Madea is so much bigger than Harborton…" She tore her way through a piece of bread, not meeting my eyes.

"I don't think any of us should go anywhere alone," I agreed. "We're strangers here and there's safety in numbers."

"Exactly! Thankfully, while the guild doesn't have a full kitchen, they do provide simple breakfasts."

Simple or not, I had no complaints; the porridge was thick and nourishing, with some sort of cinnamon on top to keep it from being too bland. When I was done, I used my bread to sop up the last bits from my clay bowl. A cup of water washed the whole thing down, leaving me content and sleepy. I could almost feel my bed calling my name.

Sadly, I had *just* finished putting together a list of all the very many things I needed to do.

"When do you and Mordecai want to sell your herbs?" I asked.

"He said to wake him whenever we were ready." Miko yawned, showing off her rows of sharp teeth.

"I was surprised you were already up. You're not usually a morning person."

"It's the bed," she said. "I think it was *too* soft."

I looked from my bed to hers. Their mattresses were maybe an inch or two deep and stuffed with straw rather than memory foam. Yeah, they were the nicest beds I'd slept on since coming to Eos, but... *too* comfortable?

Someday, with every Eosian god as my witness, I'd get someone to craft us both those adjustable smart beds I'd seen on TV.

And speaking of crafting...

"Are you still planning on trying to pick up the Herbalist profession?"

She nodded. "I think so? My *Herbalism* skill is almost maxed out after helping Tantalas process the nilwort, and *Gathering* isn't too far behind. I need to increase at least one more profession-related skill to ten, and I'd need space and equipment to do anything complicated, but it seems like a useful profession to have."

"Maybe you can talk to the town Herbalist after we sell them your stock? As long as we're not going to stay here long term, they might be willing to teach you if you pay."

"That's what I was thinking too. Do you mind staying with me for that talk, just in case? My Trade is still not where I want it to be."

"Of course. We're not walking the streets alone, remember? And afterwards, I was thinking we could do some shopping. You want a weapon, right? And we'll both need some kind of armor, eventually. We can even get lunch on the way back."

○○○

Our day in Madea was a mixed bag. The first of the town's two Herbalists kicked us out as soon as Miko walked through the door. The second Herbalist was marginally more welcoming, but despite my two points in *Mercantilism*, the prices I negotiated never rose beyond the lower midrange of what Mordecai had been anticipating. Worse, the Herbalist flatly refused to teach Miko, saying she already had one apprentice and wasn't interested in creating more competition for herself.

Mordecai returned to the guild after that, but Miko and I stuck together. The synossian was doing her best to stay poised, but without Skaal to draw the eye, she was getting a lot of looks, few of them pleasant. The people of Madea were even less friendly than the villagers in Harborton had been at the beginning.

"They don't know you," I reminded her after a passerby muttered a curse in our general direction. "And they're blaming you for something that happened nine hundred cycles ago."

She shook her head. "Mordecai says most people don't even remember the story of the Swarm. Now, they just hate us on principle."

"The ones that get to know you will learn better, and the ones who don't were never worth your time in the first place." It was advice my dad had given me in elementary school… and I think it was just as useless now as it had been back then.

We kept walking.

Madea had an open square in its center where the weekly market was held, but more established merchants had storefronts on side streets flanking that square. It took three tries to find someone willing to give us directions, and then almost ten minutes of wandering, but eventually, we found our destination.

We'd been warned that the smithy focused more on farming implements than adventuring gear, and that was all I saw when we entered. There were a few tools that might double as weapons in a pinch, but no armor at all. It made me wonder how the town guards replaced or repaired their equipment.

When thinking *Smith* with a capital S, I'd been expecting a massive bear of a man, soot-stained and streaked with sweat. Instead, we were greeted by a cat-like creature: whip-thin and short even though they stood on two legs instead of four, their fur striped grey and black. A mohawk of a mane was also black, spilling down in a straight line between two prominent twitching car ears. A vest hung open on their slender frame, making it clear that, whatever the species, the shopkeeper was male.

His voice confirmed that. "Come in and be welcome," he said, voice soft. "My name is Mrrl and contrary to rumors, I neither bite nor claw."

"Rumors?" I asked. Next to me, Miko performed her little bow.

"Ah, you must be new in town. Adventurers?"

"Yes and yes." Behind the counter, something swayed back and forth. It took me a moment to realize it was the man's tail.

Mrrl followed my gaze and caught his own furred tail in one paw, lifting the tip above the counter and waving it at me. "I'm guessing I am the first kithrizal you have met as well?"

"I'm sorry; I didn't mean to stare." It was a habit I needed to break.

"There are worse things than staring." Almond-shaped eyes flickered to Miko and back. "As I'm sure you and your companion have discovered. Few have it harder than the scaled, in my experience, even here in the duke's lands."

"It's their loss," I said, and if I was a little bit forceful about it, well, it *had* been a long morning dealing with idiots.

For the first time, Mrrl smiled, his teeth every bit as sharp as Miko's, if more like the cat he resembled.

"That's not the sort of sentiment that will win you many supporters in the streets of Madea," he warned, "but within these walls, we could not agree more."

"I'm glad to hear it. I am Brian and this is my friend, Miko."

His smile widened further at the word *friend.*

"Well met. What can I do for the two of you this morning?"

"I need weapon," said Miko. "Sorry, *a* weapon."

"Of course. May I see your Adventurer's Guild badges please? Per the mayor's orders, weapon sales in Madea are restricted to town guards and members of the guild. We do have an assortment of small knives and tools for everyone else."

Glad that we'd already registered for the guild, we fished out our badges, Miko's from her inner pouch, and mine from where it was hanging under my shirt.

"Wonderful." He rang the bell on his counter, a twin to the one Carlson had in the guild. "Seanna? Customers! Special customers!"

A second kithrizal limped out of the back room. It was immediately clear which of the two was the Smith. Seanna was only a few inches taller than Mrrl, but she was half again his size, with furred arms as thickly muscled as any bodybuilder's. Like the shopkeeper, she wore a vest, the garment only loosely laced in front, and I did my best to keep my eyes on her orange-furred face. Unlike the synossians, the kithrizal were *clearly* mammals.

"This is my mate, Seanna, and the secret to our success," said Mrrl, blithely ignoring that the shop had been empty before we entered and remained so except for us. "Dearest, these are Brian and Miko, provisional guild members, companions, and… friends."

"Well met," said Seanna. For all her size, her voice was lilting and sweet, her accent heavier than her mate's. "Allow me to show you our wares."

She took us behind the counter and into a small room. Through the open door in the far wall, I could feel the heat of the forge, even if I couldn't quite see it. A rack to the left held smaller weapons, while the rack to our right had a variety of polearms.

My eyes went to the spears first. Two of them nestled between what I thought were a halberd and a glaive. They each had similar wooden shafts, but different bronze heads; one was almost a cylinder, rounding down to a point, while the other was closer to Riok's leaf-shaped blade, possessing both a point and sharp edges.

When I turned back, Seanna was standing next to me, inhuman eyes scanning the spear I carried everywhere with me.

"Metal shaft?" she mused, tail swaying back and forth. "Interesting approach. I'm guessing you gain stopping power at the cost of elasticity and weight. Durability's likely a wash, given that wood bends before it breaks, whereas metal either shatters or dents. But what sort of alloy is this? It's not bronze."

"I'm not entirely sure," I said. "It's an heirloom."

I was almost amazed at how smoothly the lie rolled off my tongue, especially since I hadn't come up with a story in advance. My gains in *Deception* were paying dividends.

"May I?" She gestured to the spear.

I shrugged and handed it over. It wasn't like there was a shortage of available weapons in the room if she wanted to attack us, to say nothing of her teeth and what I was sure were retractable claws in her hands and feet.

Seanna hmmed as she took the spear. "Lighter than expected. And still solid despite what looks to be some kind of corrosion. Is it stronger than bronze?"

I thought back to the fight in the cave. "Yes."

"Fascinating. I wouldn't try to forge anything like this, not with the materials we have, but I bet I could find a buyer. I'll give you seven plugs *and* the glaive for it if you're interested."

Apparently, she'd noticed me eyeing the glaive. I could see myself swinging that thing around like a pool noodle, carving my way through a small mob of enemies while theme music blared in the background. *Glaive* almost definitely being its own separate skill did surprisingly little to dispel that fantasy. Seanna's offer was also more money than we'd seen since coming to the Great Wilds. But still…

I shook my head. "Thank you, but it's not for sale."

"I thought you'd say that." She shrugged her massive shoulders and handed the spear back over. "It was worth a try. What do you need then? Between that spear and the dagger on your hip, I'd say you're already armed. Maybe a longer blade for the other hip, or something with real stopping power? If you want armor instead, I have a few pieces, but they aren't cheap, and it will take me time to resize them."

Given what little I knew of armor, I was pretty sure that *wasn't* a shot at my height.

"Do you supply the guards as well?" I asked, thinking again of the hauberks we'd seen them wearing at the gate and on patrols.

Her ears flattened, and her tail went still. "No. That'd be Ragyar Nial. Half the Smith I am and one quarter the man, but he's got Mayor Aulson's ear and a license to be the guards' exclusive supplier." She looked from me to Miko and back. "He also… doesn't sell to those he considers undesirable."

Miko shrank in on herself, just a bit.

"Then it sounds like we came to the right Smith," I said, putting as much cheer into my words as I could. "I don't think we can afford armor yet, but I'd still love to see what you have. Meanwhile, it's my friend Miko who's looking for a weapon."

I doubted Seanna knew or had even met many synossians, but she picked up on Miko's reaction anyway, and swooped in on the taller woman.

"And well she should! Beautiful pearl scales like that, I bet you need a stick just to beat off unwanted suitors, don't you, dear?" Before Miko could reply, the Smith wrapped a heavy arm around her. "You just tell me what you're looking for. Do you want a spear like your friend over there? You certainly have the height for polearms."

Miko, who had flinched when the kithrizal moved in, perked up under the woman's attention. "Short staff," she said, holding her hands up about four feet apart.

"A woman after my own heart," said Seanna. "Sometimes, you just want to get up close and personal and beat a problem into submission." She waved to the second rack of weapons. "Why don't you look through our offerings there? If there's nothing that suits your fancy, I do custom orders, but they cost more and take some time. In the meantime, I'll bring our armor selections out for you and your friend to see."

I joined Miko at the other rack, leaving the spears—and the glaive—behind with a not inconsiderable amount of regret. "She and her mate seem nice," I said in the High Tongue.

She nodded. "With the kingdom predominantly populated by the children of Corros, Tantalas says those who look different should stick together. I had never met one of their species before though. And did you see their tails? So soft! Maybe my people should not be so sensitive on that subject."

By the time Seanna limped back to us, struggling under the weight of several different pieces of armor, Miko had pulled three different weapons down from the rack. One was exactly what she had asked for… a short staff, its wooden shaft capped on both ends with bronze. The second was half the size, closer to a baton than a staff. It had a core of bronze within the wooden shell, though I couldn't figure out how that had been done without burning the wood. The last weapon wasn't a staff at all, but a mace, with a short shaft and a heavy, weighted metal end on the opposite side.

Miko swung the mace around a bit then put it back with a sigh. "Is different skill than club or staff."

"It is," confirmed Seanna, setting down armor pieces on the floor with a muffled yowl instead of a grunt. "The others you selected should work for your skills though."

Miko nodded. "I like this one," she said, spinning the wooden staff in her hand. "Is better length. What is wood?"

"That's Elthoran ironwood, hand-crafted by my mate. You're not going to find anything tougher for sale outside of Trynfall and even then, only in specialty stores that deal in blackwood, scarlet thorn, or a few imported species. The bronze caps on both ends give it better finishing power. An enemy in heavy armor or with a large shield will still be problematic, but I assume you have techniques to get around that."

Miko didn't, but she nodded anyway. "How much?"

"A full-length staff sells for four bits. This is smaller, of course, but given the quality of the wood and the forged caps, I can't take less than eleven."

In other words, a full copper plug and a bit. And my fledgling *Mercantilism* skill told me there was no budging on that price. Any hopes I'd had of buying armor died a swift and painful death. Even with my cut of the herb sales, and Miko once again insisting that we split everything beyond the money she'd set aside for her weapon, I barely had three plugs in total. If just the caps on the staff's ends could inflate the price that much, I didn't want to even guess how much something like chain mail would be.

Unaware of my internal monologue, Miko nodded. "Will take."

"Excellent. Mrrl will handle the payment in the front room. But first, you wanted to see armor, Brian?"

"Please." If nothing else, it would be useful to see how much things cost. And given my lack of familiarity with medieval-era armor, having a Smith walk me through the available options was a no-brainer. As I had told both Mordecai and Nala, knowledge was power.

○○○

A short time later, we were done. As expected, the cheapest piece, a sleeveless half-shirt made of crude iron chain links, was still five plugs all on its own. The rest of the armor on offer was significantly more. If I wanted some, I'd have to save for it… or hope we got lucky enough to find functional pieces in the right size while adventuring.

The chain was lighter than I'd expected it to be from movies and fiction, but heavy enough that a second issue occurred to me. So far, *Light Armor* was one of my two highest Major skills, but I was pretty sure everything Seanna had on offer counted as medium or even heavy armor instead.

Did I want to have to earn one of those skills from scratch and advance it all the way up to match my existing skills? On the one hand, it would slow down my leveling process significantly. On the other, it would potentially help keep me alive, which seemed even more important. As they said back on Earth, slow and steady wins the race. Fast and dead, however…

Miko and I volunteered to help Seanna carry the armor back to her forge. The heat I'd sensed only magnified as we stepped through the door and found ourselves outside again, in a small, walled yard dominated by its forge and an anvil. An oversized bucket of water sat between anvil, bellows, and forge and a table held both smithing tools and a variety of molds.

"Under the table, please," said Seanna. "I'll sort this all back out again some other time." When we were done, she smiled at Miko. "Congratulations on your new weapon, dear. I know I don't have to tell *you* this, but weapon usage inside the town is a swift way to end up on the guards' bad side. And for people like us, our natural weapons count too."

"Will remember," said Miko, considerably happier than she'd been a glass earlier. "But have one more question for you, if do not mind."

Seanna shot me a mystified glance that I returned with an unsubtle shrug. "Of course. What do you need?"

"May I see leg?"

The kithrizal stiffened, her hackles literally rising. "My shame is mine and mine alone."

"Is not about shame," said Miko. "Am Priestess. Am healer. Only small still but can maybe help."

It was the first time all day that I'd seen the Smith look vulnerable. Her eyes flicked in my direction then away again. "I…"

Seanna clearly wasn't modest, given her choice of top, but if my presence made her too uncomfortable to have Miko look at her leg, there was an easy solution.

"Why don't I go pay for Miko's weapon up front?" I suggested.

"Thank you," said Seanna, the relief obvious even on her cat-like features. "Tell Mrrl that I said it was okay to greet the sun."

That was obviously some kind of code, but I just nodded. Everything about the two kithrizal so far had suggested they were good people. Besides, while I wouldn't give myself more than a stabber's chance against Seanna if things went bad, I was pretty sure I could at least hold off Mrrl with my spear.

I carried Miko's short staff to the front room and paid for it with my own coin, knowing the synossian would repay me as soon as she was done. When I also passed on Seanna's words, some previously undetected tension drained out of the other man.

"The two of you must have impressed her." He reached under his counter and pulled out a glass decanter and two clay cups. The liquid he poured was glorious amber light, straight from the finest of color-corrected beer commercials, but it tasted like alcoholic honey.

"Our people's contribution to the kingdom's drinking problem," he said, fangs fully on display. "One cup won't even give you a headache. Two will have you flat on your back for a seven-day."

I decided to stick with just one. Each sip went down like water but filled me with warmth. The light filtering into the shop through its two front windows seemed to strengthen until the otherwise serviceable interior was awash in sunlight.

We sat there for at least ten minutes in silence, taking turns with small sips as we waited. Maybe it was the alcohol talking, but I couldn't remember the last time I'd felt so relaxed with a total stranger.

I took a mental step back and reviewed that thought.

Okay; it was *definitely* the alcohol talking.

"Any advice for a newcomer to Madea?" I asked.

"Stay off the back streets, especially at night. Things are better here than in larger cities, but also worse."

"How so?"

"Less crime, particularly of the organized variety. But also less oversight. The guards are here to keep the mayor's peace, but don't particularly care how it's done."

"Guards like Henrik?"

"You've met?"

"He was on gate duty when we came in."

Mrrl took another sip, whiskers quivering with pleasure at the taste. "He's not the absolute worst, but he's up there. The point being that you're best off not relying on any of them."

"What about other adventurers?"

His eyes, almost a match for the alcohol in our glasses, glowed in the light. "Depends on the adventurer, really. In a frontier town like this, you need to be able to stand on your own or have enough allies with you to make potential predators reconsider. And if you're beastkin, that goes triple."

"Beastkin?"

"That's what these northerners call people like me and your friend, Miko, as if we weren't all separate species created by the gods, just like them. Kithrizal, lupine, corbins... the scaled get it the worst, of course, but it's often just a question of degrees. I'm surprised you and Miko made it through the gates at all if Henrik was on duty."

"We have a reaver in our party."

"That would do it." He shook his head, staring at the bottom of his cup. "All I'm saying is—"

The door to the back room burst open and Seanna hurried through, dragging a flustered Miko behind in her wake. The Smith still limped but was moving at almost normal speed. She stalked over to Mrrl, plucked the cup from his paws, and downed the remainder in one gulp.

"Dearest?" asked the confused shopkeeper. "Are you feeling well?"

"Am I feeling well? I could almost dance!"

He stilled. "Your leg?"

"Metal in old wound," said Miko in her best Trade. "Spell forced metal out and cleared poison. Will need more and stronger healing than mine to fix remaining damage, but—"

"But it barely hurts, Mrrl. Look!" Seanna shifted from foot to foot as if she was doing something profound… and by the look on her mate's face, she was. The Smith turned to Miko. "Please, take your staff in exchange, with our blessing."

Miko shook her head. "Price was agreed upon. Bronze and hardwood not cheap. But if can direct us to tailor or leather shop…"

"Of course," said Mrrl. "Are you looking for armor or clothes or both?"

Miko turned to me, putting me on the spot.

"I need gear that qualifies as light armor," I said. "If it can work as a base layer for when or if I add something heavier on top, so much the better."

Mrrl's smile widened. "I know just the person. Head toward the Hill Gate and turn south along the main road there. You'll find Datha at his shop. Let him know we sent you as honored friends and he'll give you a fair price."

"How will we recognize his store?"

"He does the tanning out back," said Seanna, wrinkling her cat-like nose. "You'll smell it before you see it."

49

Datha was what Mrrl had referred to as a *lupine*, but where I'd expected a humanoid with doglike characteristics, he looked a lot more like a werewolf, tall, overmuscled, and scary even before you added in the thick black fur, claws, and jaws that looked like they could snap a leg in half. He was much gruffer than Mrrl had been too, even after we told him the kithrizal had sent us, but his basic wares were as well-made as anything I'd seen in Agnes' shop back in Harborton.

A glass later, I was the slightly poorer owner of a brand-new gambeson—a quilted leather jacket that extended all the way down to my thighs. It would add some protection on top of my passive *Beast Skin* technique and could even serve as an underlayer if I did eventually buy a chain shirt or something heavier.

On the way out, I almost tripped over three little blurs of fluff and fur streaking in through the open door. It wasn't until they tried to tackle the much larger Datha and the lupine's stern demeanor dissolved into a wolf-like grin that I realized they were his children. Or… cubs. Or whatever the proper term was. There was a lot of mock growling going on, but otherwise they seemed a lot like rambunctious children everywhere.

Meeting other non-humans had done Miko a world of good. She walked tall the rest of the day, ignoring the looks and the comments, and making a point to greet anyone who seemed even halfway courteous. We ate lunch late in the mostly deserted common room of the tavern nearest the Adventurer's Guild, and then headed back out.

Madea did have a public archives, of sorts, but the small building was closed for some sort of private function with the mayor. On the opposite end of town, not far from the primary guardhouse, we found a training arena, but it was closed too, so I escorted Miko back to the guild house.

Carlson was on duty once again, but Melligula was standing over by the bar, mixing something that smelled kind of like asphalt on a hot summer day. I waved, Miko bowed, and we headed upstairs to our room. While the Priestess napped, I took the opportunity to meditate.

```
You have increased the following skills:

General skills:
Mercantilism [+1]: 3/10
```

It wasn't much, but it was progress.

Dinner that night was a quiet affair. Miko was still sleepy, and I was just plain tired. Lace was the only one who drank at all, although I wasn't sure if everyone else was as poor as me, or if they were simply being responsible. After all, we were headed out the next morning and hiking with a hangover sucked.

I'd learned that much already from experience.

"We should ask Seanna where to find others of my kind," Miko said much later, her voice carrying through the darkness of our bedroom.

"When we come back," I agreed. "Maybe we'll be able to afford armor for both of us after this next mission too."

"I don't need much." I heard the now-familiar tapping of claws on scales. "And I don't want to be weighed down either."

"Maybe we'll see if we can buy you some equipment for mixing herbs and making poultices then? I bet Melligula can find us a place if we ask."

"She is nice, isn't she? Nothing at all like she looks."

"That seems to be a common truth on Eos."

"Unless you consider the sluthari. Or that creature we fought for the nilwort."

I shuddered. "On that horrible note, I'm going to sleep. Happy meditating."

Minutes later, I was still trying to get comfortable when she spoke again.

"Brian?"

"Yeah?"

"You are a good friend and a credit to your species."

It would've probably hit harder if I hadn't already been half asleep. Instead, I just nodded, eyes still closed. "So are you, nest-sister. Sleep well."

∘∘∘

We left Madea with the rising sun, packs once again empty except for supplies, Skaal's chain shirt, and my gambeson. We took the Forest Gate, trading nods with some guard who *wasn't* Henrik, and followed the road south to its first junction. We'd come from the southeast, originally, and Lace turned down the western path instead.

We were in civilized lands—or what passed for them this far out on the frontier—and walked in pairs rather than our usual formation. At such an early hour, there weren't a lot of people on the road, but it wasn't deserted either. We crossed paths with yet another merchant heading to Madea, and while the guards flanking the wagon rode with their eyes on us and their hands on their weapons, the encounter was peaceful.

"What is our mission?" I asked Mordecai. Ahead of us, Miko and Skaal walked together, the first asleep on her feet, the second as silent as stone. Lace wasn't scouting, but still ranged ahead of the rest of us, as if irritated by the party's pace.

"Didn't we tell you, lad?" The Flameweaver's mask was blue, the eye holes slightly larger than normal.

"No. You just said it was a wild goose chase."

"It's the sort of thing usually left to provisional members," he admitted. "Reports of some minor disturbances from the outer farms. A chicken or some other animal goes missing and suddenly it's a clear sign that there are monsters about."

"Are there? Monsters, I mean?"

"Occasionally, yes, which is why the guild accepts the missions at all. That and the posting fee, of course. Most of the time though, the chicken has simply wandered off, or a neighbor is responsible. A party like ours is overkill."

"Then why take it?"

"Politics," said Skaal, half a dozen feet ahead.

I waited for the reaver to elaborate, but he never looked back.

"He's right." Mordecai pulled his hood down lower over his eyes, even though the rising sun was behind us. "Like many other large organizations, the Adventurer's Guild runs on politics as much as coin. The administrators will tell you there are only three tiers within the guild, but the truth is more complex. Parties compete against each other for the better assignments and favor with the guild carries a lot of weight in that competition."

"So, we're doing a low-end mission, one that other parties have skipped, to improve our standing?"

"Exactly." He examined me for a moment. "You have an agile mind. If you ever wish to retire from the life of an Aspirant, I could give you a referral to the Crimson Needle. You'd still have to be accepted, of course, but I think you would do well."

"It's not just for Mages?"

He blew out a long sigh, the mask on his face rippling with his breath. "I sometimes forget how little you and our would-be Herbalist know about the greater world. The Crimson Needle is an institution of *learning*, one of the greatest in the kingdom. While each of the four duchies has its highly touted Aspirant training academies, the Crimson Needle is both independent and an entirely different beast."

"How so?"

"Those other academies are essentially finishing schools for the adult children of noble families. They focus on training those on the path of the Aspirant, offering progression to Tin within a comparatively safe environment."

I wasn't going to say it, since I knew Mordecai wanted to talk about the Crimson Needle instead, but that sounded *amazing*.

"The Crimson Needle, on the other hand, is a place of *true* education. Yes, we have Aspirants, and yes, many of those are Mages— after all, several of the base class's Major and Minor skills touch upon scholarly pursuits—but there are also commoners and Dedicated among the student body and even the faculty. When the dukes seek not just information but understanding, their retainers make the long trek to our mountain school, to the gates of the academy founded three hundred cycles ago by Olmithor Sezan the Unknowing."

"The *Un*knowing?"

"It was his belief that no matter how much knowledge one might amass, they should always approach new things from a position of humble ignorance. For it is the knowledgeable man who knows how little he truly knows." He sighed again. "While the school he founded has had its struggles with internal politics, it remains one of the few places in the north dedicated to so pure a cause."

"I'd like to see it someday," I decided, "once we're all a little bit better off."

"I'll take you there myself, lad." Mordecai adjusted the pack on his back, his voice thick with satisfaction. "One day, I will retire from this life and return to the Crimson Needle, this time as a meister rather than a student."

○○○

It took us a full day to reach the first farm, situated on a large plot of land that had been carved out of the surrounding wilderness. On seeing Skaal and Miko—and to a lesser extent, Lace—our initial reception was less than cordial. Mordecai helped calm their fears somewhat and our guild badges did the rest. When the father realized we were there to investigate their complaint, he even unclenched enough to smile. Lace and Skaal followed him out to their pasture and the henhouse nearby, while Miko, Mordecai and I broke bread with the remainder of the family—an elderly woman, three full-grown men and their wives, and almost a dozen children.

We ate outside at a weathered table instead of in the farmhouse itself. The whole dinner was a noisy and chaotic affair, but there was an energy to it, different from the crowds we'd seen in taverns across the past several months. We were the only strangers here, the only real outsiders. Everyone who lived on the farm knew and loved each other. They worked together and got by on the support of their family and community.

Bug would have half-jokingly accused me of *indiscriminate Amish leanings*, but honestly, I was just impressed and encouraged by their very different, infinitely more wholesome, concept of *family*.

And then one child dumped her cup of water on another's head, prompting fresh screams and mayhem, and I found myself looking to the smelly but quiet barn we'd be sleeping in for the night. Family was great… right up until the point it wasn't.

Much later, Lace and Skaal reported back, saying that the traffic around the henhouse over the past seven-day had obliterated any tracks of note. For now, the chicken's fate remained a mystery.

"I'll walk the perimeter tomorrow morning, when signs should be clearer," said Lace, "and then we'll press on to the next farm. Their complaint was more recent at least."

Skaal grunted and Mordecai swallowed his sigh.

"How many farms in total are we going to?" I asked.

"There were three on the mission request. We should hit the remaining two tomorrow."

Two days out and two days back? That wasn't too bad. I wasn't getting anything in the way of skill-gains, but at least Miko and I would be halfway to becoming full guild members.

"I'll take third watch," said Lace. "Skaal will take first. Brian, you have the middle."

I waited for everyone to disperse and then approached the Marauder. "You do know I spoke to Skaal, right? Like I promised?"

"Yes? The old man and I put that argument behind us on our first night in Madea."

"So, the middle watch *isn't* a punishment?"

"No, it is."

She said it so smoothly and sweetly that I had already started nodding before her words sank in.

"For what?!"

"For dragging your feet. If something needs to be done, it should be done as soon as possible, not a full day's march later." She patted my shoulder. "*Or* you might just be being paranoid and not realizing that I picked up the rotation from where we left it."

Again, I started to nod, and again, I stopped, mid-motion.

"I had middle watch the night before Madea."

She hmmed thoughtfully. "Are you sure?"

"Yes!"

"Well, thank you for your sacrifice then. Now, if you'll excuse me, I need to get some sleep. I'd advise you to do the same while you can; the middle watch is a tough one."

Since I'd come to Eos, Miko had gone from the closest thing I had to a friend… to actually *being* one. Mordecai was starting to feel like the chatty grandfatherly type I'd never gotten in my first life. Skaal was… well, I was still figuring the reaver out.

But Lace?

I didn't like Lace.

Some of the time anyway.

ooo

The second farm visit went down much the same as the first, even if we reached it mid-morning instead of late afternoon. This family had lost a phloxl, and even Mordecai perked up a bit at that revelation. It wasn't until I saw the phloxls that I realized why… the creatures were three-quarters the size of a full-grown cow, slow to move, and stubborn as all hell. The carcass of one would have been impossible to miss. Without a body, natural predators seemed an unlikely culprit, unless the phloxl had been carried away by something the size of the Thunderbird. The pen remained in good condition, and the family swore the gate had been latched.

Lace came back from walking the fields and shared a long look with Skaal. "Did you see them too?"

The reaver nodded, holding his hands about fourteen inches apart. "Boots. Bigger than any in family."

"They match a few of the older tracks I found at the last farm."

"Someone is stealing animals?" I asked. "Who?"

"Could be a rival family? Maybe the last farm ate their own chicken and claimed it lost to avoid suspicion?" She shrugged. "We'll see if I can pick up the trail when we reach the woods again. If not, we'll press on to the next farm and get more information."

"Can I come with you?" I asked.

"If this is about the watch, I was just making a joke. You'll get early watch tonight."

"It wasn't but I'm glad to hear it."

"Then what?"

"I still don't have the *Knife* skill, but you helped me with *Stealth*. I'd like to see if I can pick up *Tracking* too."

"Fine. Stay behind me and keep your spear pointed elsewhere. I'm not going to slow down on your behalf."

It took her only a few minutes to pick up the trail outside the farm—several sets of footprints instead of just one, and strange indentations that were apparently the phloxl's hooves. As we followed, Lace explained the basics of what we were doing. Having just gone through the joy of multiple days of having her tell me things like *just feel the flow* and then whipping her knife around like she was a carnival worker, I was surprised to find her instruction on tracking clear and even relatively concise.

"Why are you able to teach this so well and not knives?" I murmured, a glass later when we stopped and waited for the others to catch up.

"Maybe you're just not suited for small blades?" I gave her a look and she ran a hand through her braids. "I'm teaching you how I was taught as a daughter of the clan still hoping to earn my name. Woodcraft was something we all had to learn."

"And knives?"

"Have always come easily to me. The sharp side goes in. Angle to avoid hitting bone. Be fluid and never stop moving. Cut whatever is within reach." She shrugged. "Nobody ever taught me, and it seems like I can't teach you what I instinctively know."

"Honestly, the four things you just said seem like they'd have been a great place to start."

"Huh." She cocked her head, listening to something I couldn't hear. "Skaal's almost here. Let's keep moving."

Unfortunately, a half-glass later, the trail disappeared entirely. We searched the surrounding area but couldn't pick it back up again. I looked about, trying to figure out how they'd managed it.

"Did they climb the trees or something?"

"With a phloxl? I don't think so." She eyed the nearby trees anyway, then shook her head. "More likely, they met up with someone here and that someone has better woodcraft than the people we've been following. That or a technique to hide their trail."

"So what do we do?"

"Once the others arrive, I'll ask Skaal to double-check. Between his height and his background, he sometimes sees things I don't."

Unfortunately, the reaver came up empty too.

"We've wasted enough time," Lace decided. "Thankfully, we're not *too* far from the road. The third farm should be only a few glasses away."

I didn't have a watch—or an hourglass—but her estimates ended up being right on point. Or at least they would have been, if everything hadn't gone sideways. Again.

Miko spotted it first. She'd been chattering away with
Mordecai when she suddenly went quiet, looking past him at the
darkening sky.

"Is that smoke?"

Skaal's head snapped up and he turned to look in the direction
she was pointing. "Yes."

It had been a mostly cloudy day and with the sun setting, it was
hard to see, but Miko was right… a dark plume of smoke was rising to
the sky.

"Too much smoke for campfire," added the reaver.

"I think that's the Maris farm," said Lace, rejoining us.

"Maris?" I asked.

"The third family we're visiting."

I traded worried glances with Miko, visions of Whitehall's
burning somehow still fresh in my mind despite the past two moons.

"First theft, now arson?" Mordecai shook his head. "Sounds
like bandits to me, lass. Their ill fortune that a Flameweaver stands
ready."

"Follow me," said Lace. "We're going in as fast as the unranked
can manage."

It took ten minutes to reach the farm. Three minutes in, the
wind shifted and though the trees above us blocked any view of the fire,
we could smell it; thick, and hot, ash starting to fall out of the sky like
rain. Seven minutes in, my legs were mush, already tired from a
morning of following Lace around trying to earn a new skill. Nine
minutes in, we could see the glow in front of us, indistinct through the
trees but undeniable, waiting like the open gates of hell.

And in the tenth minute, we emerged into pandemonium.
Both a house and a barn were on fire, the former having already seen its
roof and one of its walls collapse inward. Livestock—chickens and
sheep, but also some strange things that looked like a cross between a

goat and an alligator—were running in all directions, senses overwhelmed by the conflagration, but my eyes went to the shapes on two-legs, silhouettes against the burning eye of the fire.

As I watched, one tumbled to the ground in a flurry of what had to be skirts. Another shape loomed over her only to be knocked aside by a third. The clash of weapons was there, barely audible above the crackle of flames or the screaming animals.

"Put down anyone with a weapon," shouted Lace. "We'll make identifications later."

The next few minutes felt like an hour, felt like a seven-day trip into the heart of insanity. I played rear guard as Mordecai and Miko followed the other two into the melee. Shapes appeared out of the smoke and darkness, and I had only a heartbeat to tell if they were man or beast, let alone bandit or victim. I flagrantly violated Riok's rule #2 and exclusively used the butt end of my spear, striking down anything that seemed poised to charge our small party from behind.

Mordecai called the fire's flames to him as we moved, orb after orb summoned to his waiting hand. Most, he extinguished, but a few were sent back out, streaking toward targets I couldn't see. Ahead of him, Miko was crouched low, cloak over her face as she tried not to breathe in smoke, and ahead of her was Skaal, made even taller by the fire's light.

Lace was nowhere to be seen, but I took comfort in that fact. If she wasn't with us, she was out there somewhere, doing what her clan had taught her: hunting.

Finally, we reached an open space between the two burning buildings. Two women and a handful of small children huddled there, guarded by a soot-covered man with a bloody blade in his hands. He saw us a moment after we saw him, and then he was a literal blur, streaking toward Skaal as the women behind him cried out in fear.

I recognized *Lunge* when I saw it.

Skaal barely moved, but the other man's blade missed, slipping through the tiny pocket of space the reaver had just vacated. Before the attacker could adjust, Skaal had trapped his wrists, tossing the sword aside and pinning the other man to the ground.

"Calm!" he shouted. "Be calm!"

Miko hurried past the two, headed for the women. With a curse, I sped up to join her, leaving Mordecai with the reaver. The presence of children made it likely that this was what was left of the Maris family, but until we knew for sure, they were all threats, and I needed to keep the Priestess protected.

One of the women had fainted, but the other held a knife in her hand, sharp and dangerous for all that its usual purpose was clearly cooking. She reeled back as Miko's scaled visage was revealed, her free hand trying to corral the children behind her.

I pushed between Miko and the people who I was now almost positive were farmers, fishing my guild badge from around my neck. "It's okay!" I yelled, planting my spear and waving the badge like a madman. "We're from the guild!"

Miko, belatedly realizing she'd scared the people she was trying to help, found her badge too.

The knife-wielding woman looked from badge to badge blankly until comprehension set in.

"My friend is a healer!" I told her. "Are any of you wounded?"

"I... I... Papa!" she waved at the burning main building. "He held the door when we tried to escape out the back. And Berys...!"

I winced at the last name. Realistically, it had only been a matter of time before we ran into someone with a name we knew, but even so...

A shape moved up beside me, and I whirled, Riok's spear leaping back into my hand, but I recognized that shape at the last seconds and pulled my swing. It was the man Skaal had taken down—a teenager, really—eyes wide and pale in a face streaked by ash and tears. I looked past him, but both the reaver and Mordecai were gone.

"Your companions went into the house," he said, voice cracking with adrenaline and fatigue. "The big one said… the rest of us should get away… from the fire. He told me to tell you…" He paused, coughed, and carefully sounded out the syllables. "*Is okay.*"

I didn't need my Speaker of Tongues trait to tell me that the stranger had just tried to phonetically repeat two words in a language he didn't understand, or that the language was one only Skaal and I had ever spoken. The fact that he was upright and free said everything; if the reaver hadn't been convinced he was one of the victims, he would never have gotten up at all.

"Miko will carry the unconscious woman," I said, bowing to her superior strength, "if you and the other one help with the kids."

He visibly started as he finally saw Miko for the first time, but to his credit, he just nodded tiredly. "You'll keep us safe?"

I didn't tell him I was level three and every bit as tired as he was. I was older and must have looked halfway competent, and that was the only thing that mattered.

"I will. Stay low if you can," I said. "Try not to breathe too much smoke. Miko will want to save her heals for injured survivors."

The knife-wielding woman's face twisted at my use of the *s-word*, but she mirrored the teenager's weary nod, tucking the weapon into her belt. There were five children, all younger than ten, but the pair of farmers got some of them moving in the right direction, picked up the remaining two, and headed for the woods. Miko slung the second, unconscious woman over one shoulder, and I followed behind, spear in both hands, and head on a swivel as I looked for danger.

The closest we came was a sheep, bleating as it charged out of the darkness. It sprinted right past me on a course only its tiny brain could understand and disappeared again into the night.

The air was fresher by the tree line, and it wasn't until I looked back at the burning farm that I realized we were on the far side of where we had originally come from, the wind still blowing ash and smoke in the opposite direction.

We had a heartbeat to relax and then two children screamed. I spun, ready for anything, only to see the teenager crumple to the floor. At first, I thought I'd missed an attacker somehow, but Miko was already kneeling next to him, peeling back his shirt to reveal a bloody wound. The glow of her *Flare* spell showed a shirt that had been soaked through.

"Stupid phloxl," she muttered angrily in the High Tongue. "If you need healing, you say so!" She turned to the hovering woman and switched back to Trade. "You. Come. Put pressure."

"Can you heal Bryant?"

"Need stop bleeding. Pressure helps. Come."

I reminded myself I was supposed to be standing guard and turned away as the light of *Minor Healing* blended with the ongoing illumination of *Flare*.

Which… now that I thought of it kind of made us a target.

"Miko," I suggested, my voice low now that we were far enough away from the burning buildings, "do you need to keep *Flare* up, or can you cancel it? If anyone's on this side of the fire, they're going to see our location pretty easily."

"Good thought," said a voice just a few inches from my ear, "but a little bit slow." Lace slid past me to crouch next to Miko and the others. "They're gone. All but a few had left by the time we made it here. Skaal and Mordecai are salvaging what and who they can, so keep some heals in reserve, Miko."

The Priestess nodded sharply, eyes not leaving the man under her hands. Her murmured prayer was too quiet to catch, but the warm glow of Aurea's light surrounded her hands for the second time.

"Will live," she said, as much to herself as the rest of us. "Will see it so."

50

The teenager's name was Jalen. We got that much from Kira, the woman at his side who was also the eldest sister of the Maris family. It took two *Minor Healings*, some hangroot, and a lot of makeshift bandages just to stabilize him, and even then, he wasn't out of the woods, literally or figuratively.

All but one of Miko's remaining heals went to the first of the two men Skaal and Mordecai had recovered from the burning farmhouse. Berys was a few cycles older than Jalen, husband to Kira, and had broken his leg sometime *after* a bandit ran him through. Heals and more hangroot stopped the bleeding, and some sort of powder had been sprinkled over his burns, but we couldn't do much more than set the leg for now. Kira sat at his side, unwilling to let him go.

Darragh was the farm's patriarch, older and balding and the only reason he hadn't bled out from the loss of his arm was because the fire had cauterized his wound. He was unconscious when Skaal carried him in and remained so, every breath a coughing wheeze thanks to the smoke in his lungs. Miko had one *Minor Healing* left, but after examining him for a few minutes, she shook her head.

"Am sorry."

Kira clutched tighter to Berys, fresh tears leaving streaks through the ash and soot on her face. The children, mostly too young to understand what Miko was saying, picked up on the mood anyway, and fresh wails filled the air, finally waking the other unnamed woman. For his part, Jalen didn't move, but I could see the anger in his eyes, mixed with a sense of helplessness and even shame. That emotion intensified when Skaal and Mordecai returned again, this time empty-handed.

"Where are the others?" he demanded.

Lace was conferring with Skaal, their voices too quiet to overhear, while Mordecai had slumped down next to Miko, almost as tired as the Priestess. It was left to me to respond.

"What others?"

He turned to me, wincing in pain. "Mom. My other sisters. Little Cain. There are thirteen of us in the family. Fourteen, with Berys."

"One other body in farmhouse," said Skaal, as he and Lace joined us. His voice was solemn and empty. "Could not reach, but was small and already gone."

Kira's silent weeping turned to low, racking sobs, but Jalen's face only hardened, aging cycles in a matter of seconds. "And the others?"

"Taken," said Skaal.

I turned from all those faces filled with grief and despair and looked at Lace, standing in the half-giant's shadow. Rage bubbled up inside of me. "*Tell me again about the* honored profession *of banditry*," I spat in Gorash.

Silver eyes met mine in the darkness and she looked away.

"We'll hunt them down," she said, and I couldn't tell if she was speaking to me or the family or both. "There are at least twelve in the main group and they have a half-glass lead at least, but they're traveling with captives. That means they'll be slow. We can catch them. Kill them. Free the prisoners."

"Must have camp somewhere in area," said Skaal.

The Marauder nodded. "We'll need to hit them before they make it there. I'm not attacking fortifications unless our casters are fully restored."

Miko motioned to the injured farmers. "What about wounded? Cannot travel."

"We'll wait here," said Kira, her tears giving way to something between cold rage and bitter acceptance. "At least until morning. Keep the little ones warm. Stay with Papa until he…" She took a long breath. "If we don't see you by mid-day, we'll try to make our way over to the Campbells."

I wasn't sure how they'd manage that, given Jalen's injury and Berys' broken leg, but Miko just nodded. She removed several clean bandages from her pack and gave them to Kira.

"Remember," she told the woman. "Pressure on wound if bleeding starts again. Will heal again when back."

"We need to go." Lace hauled Mordecai to his feet. "What do you have left?"

The Flameweaver coughed, trying to clear smoke from his lungs, but when he spoke, there was steel beneath the exhaustion. "Enough. I have enough."

"Of course you do." The Marauder clapped him on the shoulder and turned to the rest of us. "Carry only what you need. Leave the rest here. We travel light and we travel quick."

I pulled my gambeson on, tossing the rest of the pack aside. "How will we find them in the dark?" We'd already failed to track them once in the daylight.

She didn't look my way. "I have that covered."

We left the farmers behind, nine scared and injured people clustered around a man who would likely be dead by the time we returned. They were lost to the darkness within a matter of breaths, but I carried some of their grief and their anger with me, knuckles white on the dark shaft of Riok's spear.

Catosaurs, gyr beasts, treefolk… even Nikkaali and the predatory Thunderbird. They had all done their best to kill us, yes, but they were beasts or monsters. It was in their nature. But this? Preying on farms? Stealing livestock was one thing, but pillaging was another entirely, to say nothing of the man and *the child* the bandits had killed and the women they had taken for reasons I didn't want to think about.

People like this needed to die. They needed to be wiped from the earth, their fate a warning to future generations about what awaited any who went down that road.

I was only level three. I had all of two techniques to my name. But I had a spear in my hands, a knife on my belt, and vengeance in my heart, and I vowed that all three would have their fill by the time the night was over.

I didn't see Skaal slow, but he was suddenly running beside me. "Stay calm," he said in the unnamed language of the reavers. "Be cold like the wind out of the mountains. Calm and cold and merciless."

"I don't *feel* calm," I replied.

"That's when it matters most."

"How are we tracking them?" The pace Lace had set for us was brutal, but as far as I could tell, our course hadn't changed even once. "Another technique?"

"Yes. Lace marked one of the bandits and let them go. We will follow them to the main group." He was breathing easily, despite the curse that had stolen most of his Vitality. "The Night Hag made her a hunter of men. She will not falter."

I nodded, ducked my head, and ran faster.

For once, I wasn't the weak link in our party. That was Mordecai, who couldn't seem to shake the smoke from his lungs. He slowed the longer we ran until there was a twenty- or thirty-foot gap between him and Miko. I was starting to think we'd be forced to leave him entirely but Lace and the others had stopped, barely visible in front us even with the light of two moons and all those stars.

"Just ahead," she whispered.

"I hear," replied Miko.

I didn't, but both women had already proven their senses were far superior to mine. I'd take their words for it.

"Skaal and I will circle around," said the Marauder. "Get in front and cut them off. Mordecai, can you hold the rear?"

He strangled another cough. "I have maybe three casts left, lass. But if Brian and Miko can keep them off me…"

"We will." It was an almost ludicrous thing to say, given both my own lack of power and the numbers we faced, but I meant it.

"Yes," agreed Miko.

"Miko, lead them forward along this line," said Lace, her gesture lost to me in the darkness. "Half speed and as quiet as you can be. Surprise is our greatest weapon. Wait for the screams and then strike fast and hard. We don't know how far their camp is, so we have to be wary of reinforcements."

Mordecai blew out a long breath, the dark mask on his face barely rippling. "When we hear the screams," he confirmed.

ooo

One thing I'd never quite realized from Bug's games was just how dark a non-modern world could get at night… and how difficult that would make damn near everything. If I was offered a technique at level five that let me see in the dark, I was going to be hard-pressed *not* to take it, whether it was something like Lace's night vision, or some kind of *Predator* infravision.

While Mordecai was in charge of our three-person group, it was Miko who led the way, her vision by far the best among us. She kept to the line that Lace had given her. Mordecai followed on her heels while I stayed to the rear as usual, doing my best to move quickly and quietly as I adjusted to my armor's unfamiliar weight.

It was another minute or two before I heard our targets, but after that, I no longer needed Miko's help to guide me. The bandits were traveling in darkness, just like us, but ten people of varying levels of woodcraft made a lot of noise, even before you included the prisoners they had with them.

The bandits didn't have horses or dalysi—maybe because of the cost of feeding and caring for the larger animals—and the moonlight was bright enough to see that two of the Maris women were slung over their captors' shoulders. The third was bound and barely managing to keep upright, lagging even as the bandit in front of her tugged on her leash and the bandit behind pushed her ahead.

Another push and she fell with a strangled cry, struggling back to her feet just in time to avoid a boot in the ribs from the man who had pushed her. I marked that bandit as my target and waited for the signal.

It came, as Lace had promised, with screams of pain. Two shapes at the front of the small group went down to hurled blades, and then Skaal was there, a mountain lion among dogs, cutting down people in his path.

We didn't have time to stand and watch. Mordecai sent his fiery darts into the back of the bandit carrying the leash, and as that man fell, dragging down the woman with him, I rushed at my target.

The light was far too weak to see what sort of armor the bandits had on, but Riok's spear struck the bandit in the small of his back and carried right through. The man crumpled forward, his roar of pain lost in the noise of the greater battle. I changed my grip, twisted the spear as I pulled it out, and thrust it down again. This time, the bandit went still.

Another enemy went up like a torch, and that light showed five men already down, wounded if not all dead. Unfortunately, that left seven opponents and our element of surprise was gone. One bandit grew until he was as large as Skaal and twice as wide, his massive sword now wielded in one hand instead of two. Another activated a defensive technique and his shadow blurred, becoming that much more difficult to track in the night.

What had been a disorganized column had just as quickly become a disorganized defense, the enemy individually triggering whatever special abilities they had energy for after the slaughter at the farm. Most focused on Skaal and Lace at the front, but one turned back toward Mordecai, summoning his own orb of flame. A blade came hurtling at the enemy Mage's back only to be deflected by a crackling shield of energy that went visible then slowly faded away again. Crooked teeth shining in the light of his own technique, the caster sent his fireball streaking toward Mordecai—

—who reached up and simply caught it. A heartbeat passed and then the flaming orb was speeding back, not at the original caster, but at one of the bandits who had stepped aside to nock an arrow to their bow. The would-be archer went up like a Roman candle.

Assuming he'd just used *Flame Manipulation*, that meant Mordecai had energy for one more technique. After that, he'd be at the mercy of the enemy Mage... or anyone else who could get past Miko.

But my charge had brought me to within a half-dozen paces of that caster and the man's attention was fixed on the Flameweaver who had just turned his spell.

In a movie, that was when I'd have hurled my spear, but the damn thing was taller than I was; assuming I could throw it at all, I had virtually no shot at hitting anyone. Instead, I triggered *Lunge.*

The familiar feeling of exhilaration filled me as I rocketed forward, Riok's spear leading the way, but a moment before my strike, that shield of energy reappeared around the caster. Where Lace's thrown dagger had rebounded, the spear that had once pierced a Copper centipede's armored hide simply embedded itself in the Mage's shield and ground to a halt, the point mere inches from the other man's body.

I don't know which of us was more surprised, the Mage or me, but we both reacted at the same time. He spread his hands, summoning a fan of fire to scorch the air between us, while I turned my shoulder, ducked, and pushed forward.

Flames washed over me and either *Beast Skin* didn't offer protection against fire, or that protection was rapidly exhausted, because it *hurt.* Even with a *Pain Tolerance* way higher than I'd ever wanted to level it. As I tried to hold back my screams, I barely noticed that my feet were still churning away in the ground beneath me... until there was a sudden pop of air and the Mage's shield vanished.

I stumbled forward as much as stepped, driving Riok's spear into the body of the man who had just tried to roast me alive. As he fell, I was on top of him, pulling the knife from my belt and stabbing at anything in reach.

By the time he stopped moving, I could barely think from the pain. My left shoulder and side felt like they had been dipped in acid, but at least I had preserved my face and eyes. I reached out for my spear, found it, and forced myself back to my feet.

Another bandit was just a few feet away, a rusty cutlass cutting horizontally at my head. I tried to pull my spear in front of me, putting the point between us to stop his charge, but my body was moving slower than it should have. My knife had been left buried in the caster's body, *Lunge* was still on cooldown, and that left me out of defensive options.

So, I just dropped instead, the one thing I *knew* my body could do even with nerves screaming and limbs otherwise unresponsive. The cutlass slashed through the space I'd just been standing in and then the bandit was standing above me, shifting his stance so that his backswing cut down toward where I had fallen.

Instead of more pain, there was an audible impact. The incoming cutlass deflected off an ironwood staff, the bandit's shabby blade visibly getting the worst of the exchange. Miko stepped across me, white scales shimmering in the starlight. She spun her short staff around to crack a bronze-capped end against the other man's wrists and then redirected its rebound up and into his unarmored throat.

He staggered, but didn't fall like he should have… which was when another wave of darts streaked past the Priestess and me, burning holes in our attacker. I saw starlight through the man's body, and then the bandit's corpse fell to the earth.

Even the heat from those darts' passage had been enough to trigger new tremors of pain in my body, but Miko was kneeling next to me, hands outstretched as she cast her last *Minor Healing* of the day. The warmth that swept through me was the antithesis of the fire, healing instead of burning, soothing instead of inflicting pain.

"Stay with me," she said in the High Tongue, and either the battle around us was starting to fade or I was, because her voice was suddenly perfectly audible. Unlike the rest of the party, she'd kept her pack, and I realized why as she pulled out a handful of different herbs. "Crushed emberbark," she continued, sprinkling the last of the powder she had used on Berys, "is good for fire and better for burns. Stillblossom will prevent infection and help with pain."

I didn't feel the dust *or* the paste, which was quite possibly the best thing I could say in either herb's favor. Instead, a numbness spread through the left side of my torso and the world snapped back into focus around me.

The battle *was* over, and it seemed we had won. Nearby, Lace was flitting between bodies, scavenging for loot as she made sure each bandit was well and truly dead. Skaal was a silent figure in the distance, almost lost within the shadows, and Mordecai was doing his best to calm the three women we'd just rescued.

Miko cast a glance at those women and then back at me, the indecision clear in her body language.

"Go," I told her, surprised to not be hoarse. "I'll survive. Thanks to you."

She nodded and went to join the Flameweaver. Between the darkness and the shock of their capture and then rescue, nobody seemed to care that she was synossian.

After a few moments, Mordecai left and came over to me.

"Are you okay, lad?"

I was… I thought. Just not okay enough to sit upright quite yet. And definitely not okay enough to risk assessing the damage to my left arm and side.

"We will have to teach you how to fight a Mage," he continued, when it became clear no reply was forthcoming, "or you'll wind up dead long before Tin."

"So, charging directly at them *isn't* the recommended approach?" My voice was almost as dry as my mouth.

"It is not." He matched my dryness with both ease and flair. "The dead Mage you're currently lying on must have been low level. Otherwise, his *Fan of Flames* would have left you with more than just mild burns."

Nothing about my burns felt mild, or even moderate, but a quick glance at my exposed forearm showed the skin *wasn't* cracked, peeling, and ready to slough off the bone.

"It still sucked," I finally said.

"Fire wants to feed. Appetite is both its blessing and its curse."

Having just experienced that appetite firsthand, I wasn't in the mood to get philosophical about it. Instead, I tested my legs, starting with the toes as if I was doing my daily forms. I'd already stood once, but that had been mid-battle, when adrenaline was high, and *Pain Tolerance* was presumably at its best. I wasn't taking anything for granted.

Thankfully, everything seemed to be in working order. The flames had caught me above the waist and, thanks to my last-second turn, mainly been restricted to the left side of my upper body. And that meant I could walk.

But before that… I found my knife buried in the caster's thigh, wiped its blade on the man's pants, and returned it to the sheath at my belt. I was literally on top of the dead man, but the thought of also searching him seemed a bridge too far.

"Do you mind looting this one?" I asked Mordecai "I'm still adjusting to not being dead."

"Of course." He helped me to my feet, moving to my right side instead of my injured left, and then, as I stepped carefully away, started searching the enemy Mage for a purse or travel pouch.

"Are you going to make it?" Lace had materialized out of the darkness, a bandit's pack slung over one shoulder and bulging with items.

"I'll survive, yeah." There was no way Miko would have left me otherwise. I felt confident in that much.

"Charging a Mage was—"

"Dumb. I know."

"I was going to say gutsy, but dumb works too. If you live long enough, we might just make something out of you and Miko both."

"That feels like a pretty big if sometimes."

"Welcome to life as an adventurer. Or even an Aspirant in general." She patted my shoulder and thankfully, it was my right instead of my left. "Skaal will escort you all back to the farm. Heal up, skill up, and get some rest."

"Where will you be?"

She turned and pointed in the direction the bandits had been headed. "These rotters were headed somewhere. The lack of any additional outcry tells me their camp is either empty or a good distance away. Either way, I aim to find it. This isn't over."

"You want to stomp them all out?" My mind kept going back to what she'd said about her own clans, and banditry in general. The latter line both had and hadn't been a joke.

"If we don't, they'll just cause more trouble down the line." She paused and in the darkness of the clearing, I could feel her eyes searching my face. Her voice was soft, in direct contrast to her words. "Clan life was clan life. We were born into it, as were our rivals, and I make no apologies for that fact. If who and what I am troubles you, we can part ways in Madea with nothing more said. But even though I still think you northerners are soft as the silk your nobles swaddle themselves in, there *is* a difference between raiding an enemy clan and what these men did tonight."

Message delivered, she turned away.

"You're right," I said, catching her before she could leave. "I have no business judging you or your background. This is…" I licked my lips and tasted blood, with no clue if it was mine or someone else's. "A lot of this is new to me."

"You're only level three. Of course it is."

"Fair enough. Be safe, and we'll see you back at the farm."

"I guarantee I'll see you first."

As if to prove her words, I couldn't see the smile I so clearly heard.

ooo

Soon after Lace left, Skaal brought the rest of us together. The three women—Darragh's wife, Elsbeth, and her two daughters, Neesa and Shale—were bruised and battered, but still better off than me. Miko volunteered to carry Elsbeth, and Skaal carried Shale. Neesa declared she'd walk, but Mordecai stayed close by to lend an arm if necessary.

The numbness from the stillblossom started to wear off about halfway back and by the time we had reached the farm, I was doing my best not to hiss with every step. The combination of the enemy caster's low level and Miko's *Minor Healing* had likely prevented me from third-degree burns or even complete immolation, but fire still hurt in a new and deeply disturbing way.

My mood plummeted even further as we returned to find that Darragh had died. As expected as that event was, it cast a pall over the family reunion. In the fields beyond us, the fires had mostly burned out; luck as much as a favorable wind had kept the conflagration from spreading. Here and there, a few hot spots still glowed, illuminating what was left of the Maris farm.

It looked like a graveyard... and not *just* because there were actual bodies out there.

I found a quiet spot to be alone with my pain, but Miko hunted me down anyway. There was no emberbark left, but she slathered on another layer of stillblossom paste and sat beside me.

"We did a good thing," she said in the High Tongue, long after I assumed she had lapsed into meditation or simply gone to sleep, "so why does it feel bad?"

"Because that's how the world works. You do your best and it's never enough." The bitterness in my own voice shocked me back awake. "Sorry. That was grim."

"Even when unwelcome, the truth remains true. I read that in the Archives when I was studying to be a Scholar. But I don't believe it is never enough, Brian. If we can make any difference at all, does the magnitude of that difference really matter? "

"I don't know." I shook my head. "I think I'm just angry and hurt and tired. People on Earth were cruel and violent and wasteful too, but it all mostly happened in the distance. I had my own troubles to worry about. Here, it's… just right out in the open. It's upsetting, and for some reason, it's even more upsetting when it's humans instead of monsters… like we should be better somehow, even though all evidence makes it clear we're not."

"That sounds like someone who *does* believe in moral justice."

"Maybe I'm coming around to your way of thinking."

She was silent for a long while. "I cannot save everyone," she finally said. "Not even *we* can do it together. But when the dawn does finally come, I will focus on those who live because of our actions, and not all that they have lost in the process."

I let the words roll around in my head, finding a bit of comfort in their simplicity. "Did that come from the Archives too?"

"No. That one is direct from the mind of Miko Nesari, a former shrine keeper turned refugee turned adventurer."

"Huh," I said. "She sounds pretty wise."

○○○

A glass later, I finished my meditation to the sounds of a quietly snoring Miko. My usual excitement about numbers was missing, buried under tiredness and melancholy and yes, pain, so I dismissed the skill-up window without reading it and rolled onto my right side to go to sleep.

The Framework would still be there tomorrow and so would all that came with it, the traits and the titles, the skills and the levels. For one night, for at least a few hours of sleep, I just wanted to be Brian.

51

T hings were different the next morning. Better in some ways, worse in others. On the positive side, my anger and unhappiness had subsided, and my arm was feeling a little bit better. On the less positive side, I had a lot to unpack when it came to my recent behavior… not just the anger I'd felt—which still seemed warranted—but the outright bloodlust.

I didn't want to deal with any of that first thing in the morning though, so I brought up my dismissed skill-up window from the night before. That was another thing I now regretted… the dialogue screens were my only connection with the Framework, and it had been the height of stupidity to ignore them just because I was feeling tired or down.

Thankfully, the screen appeared without issue.

```
You have increased the following skills:

Major skills:
Formations [+1]: 5/20
Light Armor [+2]: 17/20
Knife [+1]: 1/20
Spear (U) [+3]: 18/20
```

```
    Tactics [+2]: 9/20

    Minor skills:
    Athleticism [+2]: 17/20
    Avoidance [+1]: 15/20
    Pain Tolerance [+3]: 18/20

    General skills:
    Deception [+1]: 3/10
    Stealth [+1]: 4/10
    Tracking [+1]: 1/10
```

That was… a lot of skill gains. Again. We hadn't fought anything on the level of the Copper centipede, so it must have been a matter of quantity rather than quality… the chaotic march through the fire at the farm followed by the ambush of and battle with the bandits.

Avoidance had only gone up one point. Meanwhile, *Pain Tolerance* and *Spear* were the big winners of the day, having both gone up three.

Having survived another battle where I was once again injured, I was starting to regret not taking *Fueled By Pain*. If *Avoidance* kept lagging behind, the one thing I knew for sure was that I'd keep taking hits, and so far, *Beast Skin* wasn't really holding its weight.

A few other things jumped out at me. I'd gained points in both *Knife* and *Tracking*. The first just showed how much combat leant itself to skill gain… after multiple days trying and failing to learn the skill from Lace, I'd picked it up with a few stabs of an enemy Mage. The second, on the other hand, was all thanks to the Marauder. With Lace and Skaal both in the party, *Tracking* was a bit of a redundant skill, but it would be useful once Miko and I split off on our own.

The other thing that surprised me was *Deception's* improvement. I couldn't remember telling any real lies in the past day, so why had the Framework rewarded me with another point?

After a bit, I shrugged internally. Numbers had gone up and that was a good thing all around. Even better, I was halfway to level four with some of my skills.

As far as experience went, though… I didn't feel anything even vaguely approaching satiation. It was like Miko and then Riok had originally told me… at the lower levels, skill gains were swift, and experience was the true bottleneck.

When we returned to Madea, I needed to finish my two quests.

Numbers dealt with, I fished some travel bread from my pack. The camp was stirring, the Maris family making enough noise for thirty people instead of the twelve that they were, but Lace wasn't back yet, and I had some thinking to do.

I'd killed two men yesterday. Not beasts or monsters or reanimated zombies, but living, breathing men. The first bandit had been quick, dispatched at the end of my spear, but the Mage had gone down hard and up close. If I closed my eyes, I could feel his body under me, the way my side had flared with burning agony and the impact of blade meeting flesh as I stabbed blindly again and again and again. I waited for the inevitable feelings of nausea and regret, or shock and horror at what I had done, even to someone who deserved it, who had been trying to kill me and had killed before.

Those feelings never came, and *that* concerned me almost as much as the overwhelming need for vengeance that had arisen the moment we'd learned Darragh was going to die. That Cain—a child—already had. That the bandits had taken not just food and lives but women for their enjoyment.

I didn't regret the bandits' deaths. I didn't regret my part in those deaths either. But I was a kid from Midton, Ohio. I wasn't supposed to be running around killing people.

They had it coming, I reminded myself.

Of course they did. But what happens when things aren't so black and white? Are you going to act, react, or actually think?

I didn't know.

Stay calm, Skaal had told me, and while that had been advice for the battle, it felt like a lesson I could apply to more than just combat. Anger was good, healthy even sometimes, but letting it control me… seeking justification in my emotions… was a fool's game.

Stay calm. Be cold like the wind out of the mountains. Calm and cold and merciless.

I wasn't going to run from my anger. I wasn't going to run from my need for payback, or even the knowledge that two men were dead at my hand, and I felt… nothing… for their loss. But I needed to channel those emotions, those desires, in a controlled manner. Otherwise, it would be all too easy to find myself justifying my own atrocities down the line.

Of course, what I needed even more than all of that was someone I could trust to tell me if I ever went astray. Someone who *did* believe in moral justice.

Miko nodded when I finished explaining my thoughts to her. "Is good discussion to have," she said.

I raised an eyebrow. "Why are you speaking in Trade?"

"Must get—*I* must get better at it. Using High Tongue is a…"

"Crutch?"

She nodded again. "Yes. That."

"Whatever works best for you." Once again, I thanked the gods—or at least Shan—for my *Speaker of Tongues* trait. As much as I would have preferred something that helped me in battle, the trait had proven its immense value time and time again. Even better, it had saved me from all the work that Miko was having to do.

"Thank you," said the synossian. "As for concerns? Are valid. But emotions also valid. Is no—*there* is no rule for all situations."

That was less helpful than I'd hoped. "Meaning?"

"If must act in moment, then do so. Examine motives after. Make changes if needed. Try again."

"What about law? And order?"

Mordecai, walking by with a freshly filled water skin, scoffed. "Out on the frontier and beyond the walls of towns or villages? *We're* the closest thing there is to that, lad. Adventurers."

"Then who keeps us in line?"

"The guild. I've read of parties who thought they could play king out in the countryside, only to find themselves stripped of membership, bounties placed upon their heads. The guild operates with the permission of the rulers of each land. We police ourselves because the alternative is to risk losing our independence."

I nodded and the Mage continued on his way, bringing water to the Maris matriarch as Skaal put the finishing touches on whatever he was cooking. It was good to hear that the guild provided some sort of structure and law, but that seemed like the nuclear option that only came when someone had completely lost their way. I was more concerned about the ten thousand individual steps that would take someone down that path in the first place.

"You are..." Miko looked around and lowered her voice. "*Chosen*. Do not think you have to fear."

"My Ideal is *Freedom*," I reminded her. "Historically, a lot of bad things have been done in the name of freedom."

"Have regrets about yesterday?"

I shook my head. "Just that we didn't get here sooner."

"Is good. Was justice. But understand—*I* understand concern. Is easy to fall."

"That's what I'm worried about. Not now or next moon or even this cycle, but..."

"Can watch each other. Help each other. Talk and think. Always together."

That was exactly what I'd been looking for. "Thank you."

She just flashed her synossian smile.

○○○

By the time breakfast was over, the Maris family was preparing to head to the nearby Campbells. They'd gathered what they could from their ruined farm but needed to regroup and decide what to do next. After listening to their hushed conversations, I thought they'd choose to come back and rebuild.

Lace appeared out of the forest, looking surprisingly fresh. Skaal was the first to greet her, something unspoken passing between the two before she made her way over.

"Why does it look like you got a better night's sleep than we did?" I asked.

"Probably because I did? I slept before I came back. None of us can afford to be tired or sloppy today."

"You found them?"

She nodded. "It wasn't easy. They've got a Tin with them who has some kind of technique for hiding things. Tracks, trails, even camps. If the dead men last night hadn't been marching straight toward that camp, I might have walked right past."

"Just one Tin?" asked Mordecai.

The Marauder shook her head. "There are eight people in total. Two are unarmed, either camp followers or former prisoners, but three of the remaining six are Tin. The leader is a half-breed of some kind, almost as big as Skaal. Second in command is a turbinga."

"Like Melligula?" asked Miko.

"Yeah. Not sure on their classes, but those are the other two Tins."

I nodded to myself. Technically, the numbers were almost even. Six versus five, assuming the unarmed camp followers didn't join in, and three Tins versus two Tins and a Copper who couldn't use his techniques.

That left three unranked bandits for Miko and me. It wasn't ideal, especially with only one offensive technique between us, but we'd again have surprise on our side.

"Could there be more?" asked Miko.

Skaal shook his head. "Almost too many already. Hard to support group of twenty. Explains theft and kidnapping if not attack."

"If we're going to hit them," said Lace, "it needs to be soon. They'll be starting to wonder where the other men are."

Mordecai nodded, and while his face was hidden as always, his voice had gone hard. "It must be done."

Miko tapped her left forearm, even though nobody but me understood the gesture's meaning. "Am ready," she said.

Skaal just gave the Marauder an even look, so she turned to me. "Brian?"

"Sorry; I didn't realize we were taking a vote. I'm in."

We saw the Maris family off and then headed in the opposite direction, following Lace. It took two glasses to reach our destination, and like the Marauder, I ended up almost walking right by it. The camp wasn't *invisible* or even *blurry* like the defensive technique I'd seen last night… it was just easy to miss. My eyes didn't want to focus on it or register the details they saw. A number of tents had been set up across the clearing, most of them haphazardly ringing the firepit in the center.

There were still only eight people present, but the leader was currently conferring with the turbinga—a male judging by its bare chest and lack of udders—off to one side. Their body language screamed wariness and concern.

"Looks like they're starting to think something's gone wrong," I whispered to Lace.

"Yeah." She turned to Skaal. "Thoughts?"

"No fortifications." He pointed to the fire where the camp followers were grilling meat, and then to a small pen where one bandit was trying to keep the captured phloxl from mindlessly banging its head against a wooden gate. "Leaders wary but others still scattered. Bad defense."

The Marauder nodded. "Go in hard and go in fast."

"The usual then." Mordecai sighed. "Targets?"

"You take the turbinga, Skaal has the half-breed." She pointed to one of the men by the fire. "I've got the last Tin."

"And Miko and me?" I asked.

"Stay back with Mordecai again. Once the Tins are down, you can help us mop up the rest."

I nodded. I didn't like sitting out most of the battle, but I'd nearly died the night before to an unranked Mage. Staying out of a battle between Tins just made sense.

Miko nodded too, even as she scanned the camp. She paused. "Wait. Only see seven."

"That's—" I redid my count and came up one short. "There were eight."

"The Tin by the fire," said Mordecai. "What happened to him?"

Sure enough, the one Lace had been targeting was gone, though none of us had seen him move.

"Blood and ash," swore the Marauder. "I guess we know which of them has the hiding technique."

"If he suddenly decided to use it…" I started.

"Then something tipped him off." The camp was suddenly in motion, unarmed women running for a tent even as the other bandits came to their feet, weapons in hand. "We're out of time."

And with that, Lace was gone, a black blur as she streaked down the hill, blades in each hand. Beside her, Skaal's long legs made up for the difference in their respective speeds.

Apparently, charging the enemy was only a bad idea when I did it.

Mordecai waited until our companions had almost reached the bandits' defensive line, and then sent a flaming orb arcing over their head. It touched down just behind the bandits and erupted, sending two of the unranked opponents to their knees and staggering the rest.

Lace took one more step and then reappeared behind the turbinga, blades dancing. Somehow, the cow demon thing reacted in time, spinning to catch her blows on metal vambraces, and his greater Strength sent the Marauder skidding backwards. Mordecai sent a wave of flame darts into the creature's back, but where they'd perforated my cutlass-wielding attacker the night before, they barely singed the turbinga's skin, eliciting a howl filled more with rage than pain.

The bandit leader was a head shorter than Skaal but built like a brick wall, mottled green skin and what looked like tusks giving hints to his ancestry. He stepped forward to meet the charging reaver, stone-like armor shrouding his body as a defensive technique activated. Skaal's first blow sent him stumbling back, but the armor held. The bandit activated a second technique and suddenly there were three of him, spreading out to surround the reaver even as one of the unranked bandits crept in from the side.

Another wave of darts from Mordecai took out the sneaking bandit and left glowing holes in one of the illusions, but the other bandits were back on their feet, one joining the turbinga to menace

Lace, while the other replaced his recently downed compatriot to approach Skaal from behind.

Never one to pass up a free target, Mordecai summoned another cluster of flame darts.

I had only a heartbeat of warning, a sudden twisting of my guts as *Danger Sense* finally remembered it existed. Instead of dodging away from the danger my skill was warning me of, I spun toward it, spear darting out in the sort of fluid, instinctive thrust I'd only managed once before, back in the nilwort cave.

There was a ring of metal on metal and the third Tin appeared out of nowhere. He brushed my strike aside with a parrying dagger and attacked Mordecai, the rapier in his other hand a blur.

My intervention had spoiled the bandit's sneak attack, but his speed was terrifying. The Flameweaver was still turning to the threat in our midst when the bandit struck, weapon piercing the Mage's cloak, clothing, and flesh with equal ease.

Behind his mask, Mordecai gasped in pain, but he sent his summoned darts into his attacker's face and chest. I flinched, my own experience with fire fresh in mind, but the bandit didn't even pause. A ring on his hand glowed brilliantly then faded just as quickly and the fire darts vanished, leaving him unscathed. He withdrew his rapier and struck again.

Miko was there now, and while she was too slow to stop the man's second thrust entirely, her staff caught him in the shoulder, spinning him about. Before he could regain his footing, I came in to harry him from the side, using my spear at a distance as I tried to pen the bandit in.

Mordecai was down to one knee but took advantage of the space we had given him. Still clutching his injured side, he sent a third wave of darts forward with his other hand.

Again, the ring on the man's hand glowed, and again the darts vanished even as they struck their target. This time, however, the ring's glow took longer to dissipate. Even better, I could smell something burning. He shook his hand, dropping the parrying dagger it held.

Whatever defense he had, it was starting to overload.

A fourth wave of darts burst toward him and the bandit dodged aside for the first time. With a growl, he slid under Miko's strike and past her, lashing at the back of her knee with the ridge of his free hand. The synossian barely stumbled, taking one step forward and then pouring that momentum into her return strike, sweeping back around with her staff a blur.

Having natural armor apparently didn't suck.

The bandit dodged Miko's blow but had to abandon his planned counterstrike when a whip of pure flame nearly took his head off. Mordecai was back on his feet, and though his shirt was soaked through with blood, the fiery weapon in his hand crackled and glowed with an intensity that made it hard to look at.

The bandit's morale wavered. I watched the thought of flight cross his sun-bronzed face, watched his eyes momentarily shift from the three of us to the trees beyond. If he could get away, his techniques would make it unlikely we'd ever find him again.

Maybe he'd settle down somewhere and give up his life of crime. Maybe he'd even join the Adventurer's Guild and make something of himself instead. Or maybe he'd find a new group of thugs and criminals and arsonists and some other family would pay the price.

I wasn't willing to take that risk.

I came at him from behind, steps measured as I sent my spear ahead of me in a series of thrusts. Miko took her cue from me, and moved in on the flank, short staff a blur. Mordecai didn't look up to walking, but his whip lengthened as needed, cracking as its fiery tip filled the space the bandit had just vacated.

Even then, the enemy was too fast and we were too slow. I traded glances with a panting Miko and then thrust again, not at the bandit but at where he was headed. He stopped, avoiding the strike easily, but that decision froze him for just a moment, and in a battle like ours, mobility was key.

A *Flare* burst in front of the bandit's face.

I didn't know if the man's fire defense had collapsed entirely or if it failed to react because Miko's technique lacked any sort of damage component. Either way, the man reeled back, temporarily blinded. Mordecai's whip answered my question about the bandit's defenses as it curled around the enemy's arm, tugging him forward and off balance as flesh smoked and seared.

My *Lunge* took the bandit in the back. Riok's spear pierced through padded cloth, bone and flesh… and then kept going, driving through the other side of the man's ribs and out his chest.

A loud thump announced the fall of the bandit's now-severed arm, both stump and limb smoldering from Mordecai's whip, but the enemy was already a dead weight on the end of my weapon.

52-Interlude

The turbinga was a nightmare to fight. It had been a long time since Lace met an opponent as agile as she was and none of those had also been both taller and stronger than her. Even though the bandit fought unarmed, he still had the reach on her, and the technique he was using left his fists as impenetrable as his vambraces. Worse, his horns, twisted sculptures of yellowed bone, had started to crackle with an energy that reminded her of the Thunderbird's storm.

Needless to say, Lace was having the time of her life. A grin stretched wide even as she spat out blood from a blow she'd taken earlier when ridding herself of the unranked adder-on.

Another punch barely missed her, too fast to be so strong. She used *Shadow Step* for a second time and came out of the darkness behind the turbinga, where her passive *Backstab* technique would end the fight in a single blow, but the enemy had already spun about, reacting even before she struck. Her attacks were parried yet again and this time, the riposte almost took her head clean off.

A backwards roll brought her out of range and back to her feet, but the bandit was right on top of her. She burned *Echo* and used it to trigger *Shadow Step* again before its cooldown had expired. The enemy's sphere of awareness only seemed to extend to within a few feet of his body, and she used that weakness to merciless effect, stepping out of the shadows five feet away and off to his side. Her fighting knife went back into its sheath and she drew and threw a throwing blade in the same motion, triggering the second-to-last of her active combat techniques as she did so.

One flying blade became three, then five, as *Hive of Hornets* took effect, all of them streaking toward the other fighter.

He had only just located her again, but still got both hands up, deflecting three of the five blades. The fourth missed him entirely, while the fifth cut a thin line across his face. Horns now glowing, he roared and took a step forward.

Lace was already there, fighting knife back in her hand along with her longer blade, weaving together into a storm of steel that was nothing but instinct and lightning-quick reactions.

At first, the turbinga was more than up to the task, but as one second turned to two, he started to slow. She watched his two sets of eyes widen in surprise, watched the realization set in even as the flesh around the one cut she'd made turned black and rancid.

It would have been a sick joke if Skaal had died to poison, given that it was one of the Night Hag's signatures.

Cuts started to mount as she found holes in the slowing bandit's defenses. Without her *Hive of Hornets* technique, they were just normal wounds, but their ever-increasing number made it clear how much the tide had turned.

The turbinga lashed out with one fist, missing wide, but as she moved aside, it lunged forward, bringing its head down, the energy in its horns reaching a fevered pitch.

And that was when her *Venom Spit* took him right in three of his four eyes.

Shadow Step was still on cooldown for the next minute, *Echo* for the next three days, but dodging the poisoned and three-quarters blinded turbinga's lightning-infused headbutt was child's play. She buried a blade in his back, *Backstab* increasing the likelihood of hitting something critical, and followed it up with a second one for good measure.

The combination of poison, venom, blood loss, and two catastrophic blows was more than the turbinga could take. As his corpse hit the ground, Lace scanned the battlefield and found Skaal overwhelming the half-blood bandit leader. She thought about sending a throwing dagger—her last until she retrieved the rest—into the bandit's back, but the reaver could get prickly about those things. Instead, she kept looking about.

Two women cowering by the tents. One dead turbinga, one soon-to-be dead leader, and three unranked rotters.

There was one Tin still unaccounted for.

It wasn't until she heard the cry that she realized where the man must have gone. She left Skaal to finish his fight and raced up the hill to where Mordecai and the others had been. She *should* have realized something was up when the Flameweaver's rain of fire suddenly ended, but she'd been too caught up in her own fight to make the connection. And her battle obsession might have just cost some of her party members' lives…

She reached the tree line at a dead sprint, only to find the missing Tin bandit—some variant of Rogue, she was guessing—retreating from Miko and Brian. Mordecai was injured but on his feet, that *Flame Whip* he was so proud of in one hand.

Before she could *Shadow Step* into position, Brian thrust outward with that strangely scary spear of his, a spear that had no business being in the hands of an unranked from a village nobody had ever heard of. The bandit dodged away and right into a *Flare* that Miko had ready. Mordecai pounced with his whip, and then there was a blur as Brian impaled the Rogue from behind, killing the man as neatly as she could have managed with *Shadow Step* and *Backstab*.

Lace came to a halt, reflexively cleaning her blades and re-sheathing them. She watched as Miko rushed over to heal a groaning Mordecai and as Brian tried and failed to pull his spear back through the body of the man he'd just ended.

The pair were unranked but pulling their own weight already. It was like she'd told Brian: she had high hopes for what the two could eventually become. And that meant good things for the party, for her, and especially for Skaal's eventual recovery.

For the first time in a very long while, the future looked bright.

53

I'd been in almost a dozen battles now, and I was starting to realize that, as scary and sometimes painful as the combat itself was, it was the aftermath I hated most. Adrenaline dumps left me exhausted and covered in gore—too frequently mine—and yet there was always a ton to do. I had to help with our wounded, assuming I wasn't one of them, confirm the dead, and even just gather up the weapons and loot.

At least it was daytime, which lessened the chances of stepping in something disgusting or mishandling a weapon that probably hadn't been cleaned since my arrival on Eos. When I finally got the Tin bandit's body off my spear, I found Lace behind us, a silent spectator. The man's ring had vanished, leaving only a burn scar on his finger, but Lace patted down the corpse on my behalf, tossing anything of potential value into her pack for a later inspection. Afterward, she went back down into the camp to do the same with the many bodies they'd left below, while Skaal watched over the two unarmed women.

Neither Lace nor Skaal had emerged unscathed from the battle. In fact, in a weird twist, Miko and I were the only two who *hadn't* been injured. Mordecai took two of Miko's *Minor Healings*, Lace one, and Skaal the remaining two, but then the synossian had me sit down so she could check on my mostly healed burns from the night before.

I hadn't felt any pain from those wounds during the fight, so I wasn't too surprised when she unwrapped the bandages to find fresh new skin underneath a layer of scabs and the hints of a few blisters that had never quite formed.

What *did* surprise me was the color of that new skin.

"That's... odd," I said.

"What is?"

"My new skin." I stared down at the small swath of visible skin. It didn't match my normal skin color at all.

"I don't understand... isn't new skin normal for your kind when you heal?" Miko was gentle as she checked my shoulder and the left side of my torso.

She had switched to the High Tongue, seemingly forgetting her earlier decision to speak only Trade. I switched along with her.

"Yeah, but it's normally pinkish, not... cream or beige or whatever that is." Bracing myself for possible pain, I pushed against the new skin with my index finger. "Huh. It feels different too. A little bit firmer maybe?"

Miko had the same thought I had. "*Beast Skin?*"

"I guess?" There was no fur or excessive hair growth, but assuming the color stayed, I was going to look like someone suffering from reverse Vitiligo. *Especially* if this happened every time I was hurt.

"Is it *actually* tougher than it was?" asked the synossian.

"That's a great question." I unsheathed my knife, wincing at the state I'd left it in after the previous night's battle. In the darkness, I hadn't cleaned it thoroughly, and it showed. I held the tip to my shoulder.

"Keep the wound small," Miko reminded me. "I don't have any heals, so we will be binding it again."

That had been my plan all along, but I just nodded, and slowly increased the level of pressure I was applying. I didn't have any way to measure it, but it clearly took more force to pierce the skin than it had previously.

"Definitely tougher," I confirmed. "I guess *Beast Skin* is a progressive thing then?"

"It seems so?" She held a small wad of bandages to the pinprick incision I'd made. "We should observe this wound as well, in case the new skin changes yet again."

That was a thought.

"At the rate I get wounded, I could be a walking tank by the end of the cycle," I said. "And also dealing with a serious identity crisis."

"Tank?"

"Sorry… it's an armored vehicle on Earth that can take a lot of damage."

Her eyes widened and she darted a look at the rest of our party. They were all either resting or searching the camp, but still well within earshot. After a moment, her inner eyelids flickered down as realization set in.

"I switch to High Tongue again, didn't I?" she finally asked, the switch from eloquence to broken speech as jarring as ever.

"Yeah."

"Is good for… reasons. But also bad."

"Do you want me to point it out when you lapse?"

"Please. Will cause problems otherwise. Cannot always fall back on native tongues when need to speak clearly."

Around me, she technically *could*, but I knew what she meant.

"If it helps, your Trade is getting better. There's just an occasional issue of missing words or subject-verb agreement."

She nodded as she finished re-wrapping my bandage. "Basics are—*The* basics are easy. Mastery is harder. I may look for teacher in Madea."

"I need to do the same." I patted the spear at my side. "For this instead of language though. My skill keeps going up, and I can *feel* the difference, but I also feel like I'm missing a lot."

Miko cocked her head. "Strong foundation is important for higher levels when skill gains slow."

"She's right, lad," said Mordecai, coming to join us. "The broader your understanding of a skill, the more avenues you'll have to explore to keep pushing it higher. The scions of the kingdom's elite have their academies for that, but Madea should have at least one weapons master available for paid training."

"I found the training hall before we left but ran out of time and money. Do you think we'll be heading back to town soon?"

"I'd say we're about to find out." Mordecai nodded to Lace, who had finished speaking with the two camp followers and was now coming our way. The Marauder was smiling broadly.

"I'm guessing they had some good loot?" asked Mordecai as the other woman reached us.

Lace shrugged. "Most of it would have been garbage even if they had maintained it, but we can sell that for scrap. There are also a few items we can divvy up or sell for a small profit."

"Only a *small* profit?" The Flameweaver frowned. "Then why are you so happy?"

She tossed an item to him. To my surprise, Mordecai caught it as neatly as any baseball player would have back home. He frowned down at it. "Why are you showing me your—Wait. Was this one of theirs?"

In his hands, he held an Adventurer's Guild badge. Unlike the ones Miko and I had, it was ringed in bronze, confirming the owner as a full member of the guild.

"The leader and the turbinga both had them," confirmed Lace. "Either they took them off the dead and the guild will pay us for their return, or—"

"Or they were guild members themselves, in which case the guild will reward us for policing their own."

Lace nodded happily. "There might even already be a bounty. More money *and* more influence. And all because we took a mission nobody else wanted to bother with."

Mordecai laughed. "It seems our luck has finally turned."

"Who are women?" asked Miko, gesturing to the two camp followers, still huddling by themselves.

"They say they're sisters and victims," said Lace, sobering. "Not sure I believe them on either front, given that they look nothing alike and seem well fed, but we're bringing them with us as far as the Campbell farm, so they can be locked up. When we get back to town, Carlson can alert the mayor to send the law to pick them up and investigate further. Innocent or guilty, they'll be Madea's problem, not ours."

I glanced over at the two women. One was clearly older than the other, but both were dirty, heads down and shoulders hunched. "And they're okay with that?"

"Given the alternative?" Lace barked a laugh. "Yes. Looks like Skaal is ready with the phloxl. If we head out now, we might reach the farm by dark. I wouldn't hate a roof over our heads and eating someone else's cooking for once."

I waited for her to leave and then turned to Mordecai.

"Alternative?"

He shook his head, masked face giving away nothing. "You can't afford to leave enemies alive behind you, lad. It's a good way to end up with a knife in your back."

"Ah."

No wonder the women had agreed to come with us.

ooo

It was late by the time we reached the Campbells—the second farm we'd visited on our investigation. The Maris family was already there, and by the red eyes and long faces, more than a few tears had been shed in our absence. Still, that mood lifted, just a bit, when we arrived, hale and hearty, and bearing news of the bandits' destruction.

The return of the other family's missing phloxl was somehow even more of a hit. I could only assume the things tasted good, because after a single day hiking through the woods with one, I understood exactly why Miko used their name as an insult.

Our prisoners got a mixture of hard and uncertain looks. The Campbell patriarch and his two eldest children escorted the women to a shed near the phloxl pen. They provided blankets and a small amount of food and drink, but also locked that shed as soon as the women were within.

"They will be safe and will get two meals a day and water," the eldest told us, "but they're also staying in that shed until the mayor's men come to get them. I'm not risking my family."

Two meals a day was twice what I'd gotten in Harborton, so it seemed fair to me.

With the farm already overflowing, Lace did *not* get that hoped-for roof over her head. Even the food was somewhat meager, stretched thin by so many guests. We set up camp outside the barn, just far enough away that we could pretend we didn't hear the occasional weeping from the Maris family.

I caught Mordecai coming back into our small camp, a glass or so after the rest of us had retired from dinner. He had a small object in his hands.

"Is everything okay?"

The Flameweaver started. "By the unwritten book, lad, you scared me! I had thought everyone was already asleep."

I shook my head. "I'm keeping watch while Miko meditates. She'll do the same once she's done."

I could feel his masked gaze on my face. "These are good people, you know. Simple but genuine. You do not need to fear them."

"It's really just a habit now."

"I see. Well, far be it from me to get in the way of good habits. However, *I* am exhausted and will be going directly to bed."

I eyed the object in his hands. All but one of the farm's few lanterns had been extinguished, but there was still enough light to see. "Is that your coin purse?"

He paused, sighing. "The Maris farm was destroyed. The land is theirs, but they'll need supplies and labor to rebuild, especially with Darragh dead. I can't solve that problem for them—I'm neither an Earth Mage nor a Carpenter—but I can help in other ways."

"You gave them money?"

"I gave Elsbeth some of my coin, yes. With luck, I'll earn that much back and more from our share of the bounty. If not..." He shrugged, tucking the mostly empty purse back into his pack. "We choose as we must."

"You're a good person."

"I can afford to be. A cycle from now, we'll be elsewhere, and these families will only cross my mind on quiet, lonely nights where I've had too much to drink. Meanwhile, they will still be here, working to make something of the land."

"You make it sound like you envy them."

"Envy or pity, I can't quite tell which it is. I don't want their life, not when there is so much to see and learn, but I respect the commitment it requires."

I hesitated. "Should I give them money too?"

"Save your coin. You and young Miko are at the start of your journey. You need that money as much as Elsbeth and her family. And now," he added, stifling a yawn, "I am going to sleep. With luck, I will dream of something other than almost dying. Goodnight, lad."

"Goodnight."

It was another half-glass before Miko was done. I waited for her to get settled and then it was my turn to meditate. The day's events filtered through me, the lessons learned and not learned, as I waited for the Framework to render its judgment. When I opened my eyes again, long minutes later, the skill-up screen was waiting:

```
You have increased the following skills:

Major skills:
Light Armor [+1]: 18/20
Spear (U) [+2]: 20/20
Tactics [+3]: 12/20

Minor skills:
Athleticism [+2]: 19/20
Avoidance [+2]: 17/20

General skills:
Danger Sense (R) [+2]: 9/10
Stealth [+1]: 5/10
Tracking [+1]: 2/10

The following skills have decreased:
Riding [-1]: 2/10
```

Spear was already maxed for my level, *Light Armor,* *Athleticism,* and *Avoidance* were all getting there, and I *hadn't* seen an increase in *Pain Tolerance.* All of that was great, as was the fact that *Danger Sense* was now almost to *its* cap. Even so, I couldn't help fixating on the bottom two lines.

I had lost one of my hard-earned points in *Riding.*

Miko and Riok had warned me that skills could deteriorate, of course, and I hadn't been on a mount in months, but still… seeing a skill go down instead of up was a gut punch.

At least you still have *the skill,* I tried telling myself. *Getting it is the hardest part. Leveling it again once you have access to a mount should be comparatively easy.*

What I was saying was true, even if it ignored the unlikelihood of us being able to afford mounts any time soon, but it didn't change how I felt. I should have tried to ride the phloxl instead of simply leading it. At least then, the beast would have contributed more than a series of incredibly foul dumps along the way.

I frowned and settled down to sleep under the stars.

Just take this as a lesson learned, as Miko would say… whatever else happens in the future, don't ever let any other skills regress.

I wasn't sure exactly *how* I'd manage that…

I just told myself I would.

∘∘∘

We made faster time the next morning without our prisoners or the phloxl to slow us down. The Campbells promised to spread the word about the bandit's demise, and so we skipped the first farm on our circuit and followed a path straight through the forest instead. The family didn't take it often but said it eventually would intersect with the road to Madea.

That path was badly overgrown, but it was still better than breaking our own trail or wasting most of the day going north to the road and only then following it east. The sky was clear, and it was cooler than the last few days had been, another sign that summer was finally losing its grip on the land. We kept to our usual marching order and the most dangerous thing Lace encountered was a small family of tuskers—oversized boars that were apparently as common here as they were on Miko's home continent. For the most part, it was an idyllic day, helped significantly by the fact that we'd been able to bathe before leaving the Campbell farm.

Days-old body odor was one thing, but body odor plus dried blood and all the other fluids that came out of a dying body?

None of Bug's games had ever mentioned that.

I idly wondered if adding a point to Discernment would make me *more* aware of the smell or make it easier for me to filter it out.

Another thing to ask my companions or research when I had access to a library.

We were still a glass or so out of Madea when Lace came back. "Brian and Miko, as newcomers to this region, there's something you should see."

We traded glances and then added shrugs for good measure. If Lace said we needed to see something, we probably did. I left my pack—heavier than ever now that it carried a portion of the bandits' gear—and followed Lace off the path and into the woods.

We stopped about forty feet in, though I couldn't see why. I scanned the surrounding forest, looking for anything of interest or significance, but I could almost have been back in Ohio for how mundane the setting was.

"These look like… trees?" I offered.

"Because they are. But if I wanted to show you trees, we wouldn't have needed to leave the path. Look at the ground beyond those two ironwoods." Lace pointed to a series of low and wide bushes.

We were almost twenty feet away, but I could see they had some sort of bright-red berries or fruit.

Miko had spotted them too. "Berries edible?"

"Not if you want to live."

I gave Lace a look, but she was uncharacteristically grim. "Poisonous?"

"No. Up here, they call that shrub something pretty like false dawn. Down south, it's known by a different name: creeping doom."

Miko gasped. "Tantalas mentioned false dawn in Harborton."

"I'm not surprised. Anyone who goes out into the wilds around here knows it. We'll have to mark this spot on the trail and notify the guild when we reach Madea. Someone better qualified than us can come to eradicate it."

"Why? What does it do?"

"By itself? Nothing. But wherever you find a patch, a nest of lurkers is almost certainly underneath."

I waited for her to elaborate.

"Lurkers are bugs." She held out one hand and spread the fingers wide. "Biggest get to about that size, with claws and mandibles that can shred bronze. Unlike most insects, they spend a lot of their lives in hibernation. When they do wake, they'll eat anything and everything, but otherwise, you could walk right past a nest and never know it."

"But what do the berries have to do with anything?"

"I'm getting to that. Only… let's make some more space first." She led us back another dozen feet until the shrubs were out of sight. I was starting to think she was worried they could hear us or something. "Lurkers have a kind of connection to creeping doom. The plant is fertilized by their nests, and somehow, they get sustenance right back from it. That's what allows them to hibernate for so long. But if the plant itself is food, the berries are a kind of alarm system."

"Crush berry, wake nest," said Miko, nodding.

"If by wake, you mean enrage, yes. It's said that lurkers can detect a single crushed berry at a range of a hundred strides. An entire shrub's worth of berries at a league. The whole nest—and any other nests in scenting range—will swarm the location." She shivered. "I saw an attack site once out in the woods. Just dirt and bones and a few pieces of metal left from whoever or whatever had stepped wrong. Until we visited your village, it was the most desolate thing I'd seen outside of the Waste."

"Don't the berries fall on their own?"

"Not until whatever's in them that sets off the nest has been drained. You could probably find a few husks on the ground by the shrubs if you went over there, but I wouldn't recommend it."

"How do we clear away?" asked Miko.

"That's a question for Carlson or maybe Melligula. All I know is that it requires special equipment and training and even then, it's still as dangerous as the nine demon realms. *We* don't worry about clearing it… we report it to the guild and then stay the hell away."

It was Miko's turn to shiver. "Will do so."

54

Henrik was on duty at the Forest Gate again, but this time, he just waved us through without stopping, too busy conferring with one of his fellow guards to harass a party of adventurers. Lace cast an uneasy glance at the man as we left and shook her head.

"That's odd. There must be something going on."

Skaal grunted. "Politics."

"Maybe. Watch your backs, everyone. We'll meet back at the guild at sundown."

That gave us about one glass, give or take, but we'd had ample time on the walk to Madea to discuss our immediate plans. Lace headed off for the Adventurer's Guild with the two recovered guild badges in her hand. The rest of us followed the reaver to a line of shops Miko and I were already familiar with.

Mordecai looked doubtfully at the exterior of Mrrl and Seanna's storefront. "You know there's a perfectly good smithy on the other side of town, right?"

"I thought they only served the guard?"

"Officially, yes, but for a nominal fee…" The Flameweaver smiled at me, spreading his hands. "All things are possible under the sun."

"Is true," murmured Miko, casting her orange eyes skyward and sketching a bow to her distant deity. "But we know owners here. Serve freely instead of make pay to enter."

"In that case, I will bow to your expertise, lass."

I couldn't see Mordecai's face under the mask, but I was pretty sure he was smiling.

Mrrl was inside, manning the counter. His ears twitched at the sight of Skaal's tall, gaunt form, but he relaxed when he saw Miko and me in the reaver's shadow.

"Welcome, friends! It is a delight and a pleasure to see you again. What can we help you with today? Some armor to wear atop your new gambeson, perhaps?"

Miko bowed but looked to me to take the lead.

"Hi, Mrrl." I did my best to copy Miko's bow. "Today, we're mostly looking to sell."

He eyed our very full packs and the travel dust on our clothes. "A successful expedition then? We're a small shop, as you know, but I'll be happy to look through what you have brought. Although I know Seanna would love to see the two of you if you have a moment."

"Go ahead, lad," said Mordecai, patting me on the back. "We'll be sure to call you back out here before any deal has been struck."

Mrrl's ears twitched again. He gave me an inscrutable smile. "It sounds like I'm not the only one with the *Mercantilism* skill? No wonder I felt compelled to share the good brew last time!"

Mordecai handed his pack to Skaal and stepped forward, offering a bow of his own "Good brew? I like the sound of that! Tell me, Master Kithrizal, have you ever heard of an elixir known as sunlight? I had a sip when I was but a young man at the Crimson Needle and have never forgotten it."

Mrrl's smile widened. "I should have known bright souls like Brian and Miko would only spend time with others of similarly excellent character. Let's see what you have brought and then we can speak more on greeting the sun." He motioned Miko and me to the door behind his counter. "Seanna is out by the forge. If she's actively working, just strike the gong by the door. She'll make time for you."

We took him at his word and entered the small chamber where Miko had found her short staff. I didn't see any new weapons on the walls, but everything Miko had tested but not bought had been returned to the proper places on the wall rack. The rear door was open, and we passed through it and out to the forge room, where the heat made me wish I had removed my gambeson.

Seanna wasn't working, but standing at the nearby table, tail slowly lashing back and forth as she examined an item in her hands. Either I needed to work on my *Stealth* skill or kithrizal senses were just as good as Earthborn cats, because she turned as soon as we entered. She gave out a happy yowl and hurried over, moving even more easily on her injured leg than when we'd last seen her.

"If it isn't my favorite two new friends! I wasn't sure when we'd see you again, if ever. Chala knows that adventurers come and go like the birds in the skies."

I wasn't sure who Chala was, but my best guess was they were yet another god I hadn't heard about. They could have been one of the infamous demon gods or, if the kithrizal had their own pantheon, someone totally new.

"Came to sell, but wanted to see you also," said Miko, happiness suffusing her every word, "How is leg?"

Seanna smiled, the shame she'd shown last time nowhere to be found. "Stiff in the morning and the evening, of course, but otherwise? I feel like a new person!"

Miko's smile warmed the room. "Is good to hear. Can make—*I can* make a poultice to help with stiffness. Would like to heal again too, if is okay?"

Seanna shook her head, cat-like eyes blinking. "You've already done so much and taken nothing in return."

Miko took a deep breath and carefully enunciated each word as she said it. "The Bright Lady Aurea give... gives me her blessing freely. Is.. *it* is only right that I do the same."

It was one of the best things she'd said yet in Trade, and not just because her grammar was nearly perfect.

Seanna blinked again and bowed her head, tail wrapping itself around one of her legs. "I would not be so foolish as to refuse that grace, Priestess Miko."

"I can head back out to join Mrrl and the others," I offered.

The kithrizal woman turned to me, shaking her head. "I have nothing to hide. Not anymore. Not from friends."

"Will only take moment anyway," said Miko. "Do not even have to sit."

She knelt in front of the heavily muscled Smith and held her hands out. First came the golden glow of *Touch of the Dawn*, followed by the softer light of *Minor Healing*. When Miko stood again, she was still smiling.

"No new poison to cleanse, which means metal is all gone. *Minor Healing* should help with aches and stiffness—"

"It did," said Seanna, her smile a twin to Miko's, for all their obvious physiological differences. The kithrizal swayed back and forth, tail dancing around her. "It truly did. Thank you!"

"Am Priestess," Miko reminded her. "Is what—"

"Yes, yes I remember. But it must be said anyway: thank you." She stepped toward Miko and then stopped. "May I hug you? My people express gratitude… well, most emotions, really, through physical contact."

Miko glanced at me, as if asking for advice.

"*It's okay to say no*," I told her in the High Tongue.

I read the gratitude in her sclera-less eyes, but she turned back to Seanna. "Will accept hug, with thanks."

○○○

By the time we left the smithy, our packs were light and our coin purses correspondingly heavy. Mrrl had ended up purchasing all the weapons we brought him. Those that could be repaired fetched a higher price, while the rest were sold as scrap to be melted down and reused. In addition to the two guild badges, Lace had kept a few items with her that we'd look over as a party, but for now, we were out of merchandise and flush with cash.

Kind of flush with cash… split six ways, any sum shrank quickly.

Still, I was confident I had enough to both hire a trainer *and* pay whatever fee might be required to access Madea's archives. As for armor… well, Seanna had volunteered to make us each a piece of our choosing at cost, but even that was expensive. It would also take time I wasn't sure we had… Lace had mentioned a second mission, and something told me she'd want to get started on it as soon as possible.

Walking back to the guild, we found Madea busier than it had been on our last visit. Flimsy stalls were being constructed in the main square for the coming market, and while it was already evening, the streets were choked with people. Skaal's presence helped clear a path for the rest of us, but I could only imagine what a madhouse the town would be when the market was underway.

We were about halfway back to the Adventurer's Guild when the crowd packing the street in front of us seemed to melt away, people scattering into the side streets. A heartbeat later, I felt it; a domineering presence sweeping toward us.

For the first time since leaving the smithy, Skaal raised his head.

The man stomping down the street was a foot shorter than the half-giant, but massive, the layers of dirty hides only adding to his bulk. His exposed arms and legs were slabs of heavy muscle, the skin bronzed by the sun and heavily scarred, and the club resting on his shoulder was so oversized it made Miko's staff look like a fidget spinner.

He stopped a few feet away, that aura threatening to drive us to the ground. Still, I'd felt the Thunderbird's presence, and before it, the Buried necromancer. This man was a candle to their bonfires.

To my right, Miko stiffened but held her ground.

"Reaver." The stranger's face was mostly hidden beneath a forest of black hair and an equally overgrown beard, but his voice matched his appearance, powerful and brutish. A hand the size of my head tightened its grip on the monstrous club.

"Arrius." Skaal's voice, by contrast, was empty and emotionless.

"I thought you'd be dead by now."

"Someday, yes. Maybe soon. But not yet."

Arrius grunted. "I guess we'll see."

Their exchange apparently over, he moved on. Miko earned a dismissive glare, but he didn't appear to even notice me or Mordecai. As his presence faded behind us, the street came back to life.

"Was he Copper?" I asked.

"Yes," said Skaal. "A bully and one with cracked foundations, but still Copper. Dangerous."

"I didn't expect to see him here in Madea," said Mordecai.

The reaver nodded. "Will need to be careful. More careful."

I turned to see where Arrius was heading, but the street had already filled in behind him, and with everyone in it taller than me, any vantage I might have had was lost.

"Come," said Skaal. "Should return to guild."

"You lead and we'll follow, lad," said Mordecai. "The sooner we collect your Marauder, the sooner we can eat."

When we finally reached the guild house, it was equally busy. Carlson and Melligula were both on duty, and the few tables available were already occupied by a half-dozen people of varying species. Few were wearing armor, but all were armed, and most looked a hell of a lot tougher than I felt.

"What is going on?" murmured Mordecai.

"We got screwed. That's what's going on," said Lace, the woman's face a thundercloud as she came to meet us.

"The guild's not paying a bounty?" I asked.

She scowled. "No, they are. A tower for each of them."

That seemed pretty good to me, even split six ways. "Then what…"

"Our next mission. It got taken off the board while we were gone."

"What?" That was Mordecai. "I thought we had already told Carlson we wanted to claim it as soon as it was available?"

The man in question looked at across the room, shook his head, and went back to his paperwork.

"We did," said Lace, pulling our party aside, "but the other group had *higher priority*. They don't anymore, now that we finished our mission *and* caught two guild traitors in the process, but…"

"But the mission had already been taken." Mordecai sighed.

"Exactly. They rode out this morning."

"Where does that leave us?" asked Miko, nailing a full sentence in Trade for the second time in a glass.

"Fighting for scraps, especially with three other parties in town now, those thieving dirt farmers not included." Lace scowled. "Whole group of adventurers descended on Madea like a school of cutters."

"Why?" asked Skaal.

"I figured you'd have already heard. Apparently, it's the talk of the town. Grand Duke Willerton's daughter went missing more than a moon ago. Word only just reached Madea while we were gone. The duke has posted a reward for her return."

Mordecai scoffed. "And someone thinks she'd be all the way out here?"

"She hasn't been found yet, and there are adventurers and mercenaries scouring the duchy's interior lands. I guess a few people thought the frontier seemed a more likely option."

"Morons," said the Flameweaver. "The best reason to kidnap the heir to a duchy is ransom, and you can't hold a ransom hundreds of leagues from the intended payee." He harrumphed as we all turned to stare at him. "What? I'll have you know I studied *history* while at the Crimson Needle."

"When this is over," said Lace, "you and I should sit down and see what other… lessons… we can glean from history. But for now, what matters is that we have some unexpected time on our hands."

"Should we tell the mayor about the prisoners at the Campbell farm?" I asked.

"Carlson already sent word. A small contingent of guards will head out on the morrow. The guild will also officially post the false dawn removal mission tonight; maybe one of these other parties will be dumb enough to take it. In the meantime, we should distribute the rest of our earnings. We might be stuck in town for a while waiting for a worthwhile mission to come along."

"What was mission that got taken?" asked Miko.

"Ruins were recently discovered by a family of wanderers, somewhere deep in the marshes and crawling with beasties. Mission was to clear them out and report back on anything else we found."

I perked up. Actual ruins? That sounded promising. "Couldn't we still go there even without the mission?"

"Not if we don't know where to go. Information like that is provided only to the party who receives the mission. Besides, the value of doing missions is that you get paid twice... the guild's reward *and* whatever loot you accrue along the way. It's bad business to do something for free."

"It also risks conflict with the party who actually took the mission," added Mordecai. "We're all part of a guild, yes, but accidents do happen..."

I looked at the cast of hard characters busily drinking their way through the guild house's stores.

"Okay, yeah. I wouldn't want to step on any toes or anything."

"Right." Lace pinched the bridge of her nose. "Anyway, we will be here for a few days at least, so if there's anything you ever dreamed of doing in Madea, you'll have your chance, starting tomorrow. For now, we need to split our funds and review the few items of value we found at the camp."

"And eat," said Skaal.

"I wouldn't say no to a drink either," said Mordecai, who hadn't been able to get a glass of sunlight out of Mrrl despite his best attempts.

"Might as well." The Marauder gave a heavy sigh. "Everything was going so well too..."

ooo

We had sold almost everything we found in the bandit camp to Mrrl and his mate, but Lace spread the remaining pieces on the floor between her bed and Skaal's. Their room was the mirror to the one I shared with Miko, complete with entirely separate sleeping arrangements, something I hadn't seen coming. I'd never heard Lace say a single halfway loving thing to Skaal, but the way she felt about him was evident in every line of her body… the way she unconsciously turned to keep him in view, the emotion that seemed to fill her silver eyes when she thought nobody was looking. Even the fact that she'd fled her own clan to keep him safe… it was all there, spelled out as plain as any daytime television relationship.

But… two beds.

I didn't get it.

"I'm thinking we take the jewelry to get appraised," said Lace, pointing to the set of copper bangles and a gaudy necklace that made the pendant I'd given Nala look like the height of elegance. "If there aren't any enchantments—and I'd be surprised if there were—my vote is to sell them."

We all nodded our agreement and she moved to a pair of vambraces. They were nicked and unlovely but made of some metal other than bronze.

"Some sort of iron-based alloy, I think," said Mordecai. "It's not as brittle as the poorer stuff usually is."

"They did a good job of blocking my attacks," admitted Lace, "but they don't fit my arms and would slow me down even if they did."

We turned to Skaal and Miko, the only two people even close to the same size as the turbinga. The vambraces would be a tight fit on Skaal even now; if he ever regained his Vitality, they'd be unwearable. But Miko…

The synossian slid one of the vambraces onto her wrist, lashing it shut. It extended up her forearm to the elbow, looking downright dingy next to the brilliance of her scales.

"They look good on you, lass," lied Mordecai.

"Will take, if is okay?" said Miko.

"More protection for the party healer?" Lace handed over the second vambrace. "I'm not going to argue with that."

Everyone else gave their assent, and just like that, Miko was the owner of some ugly new armor that put my recently purchased gambeson to shame.

The rest of the loot was divvied up almost as quickly. Mordecai claimed a new bedroll that the turbinga had kept remarkably clean. The spellcaster was still going to use *Flame Manipulation* to do his own one-man fumigation routine, but he seemed pleased with both the thickness and quality of the padding. Skaal asked for and received several packets of spices, some of which had apparently been imported from neighboring nations. Lace didn't take anything and neither did I, leaving the remaining items to be sold in the next day's market.

"Skaal and I will handle the sales," said the Marauder, before shooting me a glance. "Unless you want to?"

I shook my head. I wouldn't have minded the possible *Mercantilism* gains, but I had stuff to do.

And speaking of stuff to do… As Lace swept the items she'd be selling back into her pack and the others split our proceeds, mission reward, and bounties six ways, I had to ask:

"Does Madea have a bank or something?"

"They do," said Mordecai, "and I'd suggest we all head there to deposit our funds. *Before* we lose our heads and possibly our wallets drinking."

"Don't want a repeat of last time, I see," said Lace, grinning.

"Once was enough," retorted the other man, "although I hope she's very happy with her ill-gotten goods." He dismissed my evident curiosity with a wave of his hands. "Suffice it to say, there are some lessons you can't learn at school, even a place as revered as the Crimson Needle."

Lace snickered. What little I could see of Mordecai's face behind the mask had gone beet red.

"Bank, dinner, drink, sleep, sell," said Skaal. "Ready."

And that was that.

ooo

Thankfully, the bank was a short walk from the Adventurer's Guild and thus a short walk from the tavern as well. I still kept three plugs in my purse, but it was less than half my current fortune.

It was hard to believe that Miko and I had arrived in the Great Wilds just two moons earlier with little more than the clothes on our backs. We were a long, long way from reaching our goals—both in terms of power and wealth—but I couldn't help but be impressed by what we'd already accomplished. At the top of that list was finding a party that had not only agreed to take us on—admittedly, with a bit of persuasion—but which seemed well suited to help us grow for at least the next cycle. That they were all at least halfway decent people was an unexpected bonus.

Dinner was simple fare, but it was paid for out of the party's shared coin, and it made for a nice change from Skaal's solid but sometimes monotonous meals. I bought a mug of ale with my own funds, found it every bit as inferior to Lomas' as the dunsman had said it would be, and nursed it as the night went on. There were two barmaids, one younger and one older, and they did their best to navigate the increasingly crowded space. Contrary to my expectations, there were no handsy customers, no bar fights, and no mysterious strangers spying on the people from the corner.

Unless *we* were the mysterious strangers—our table was past the stairs, and kind of wedged into a corner between the kitchen and the bar. I wasn't sure if we'd been given that out-of-the-way table because of Skaal or because of Miko, but since neither one seemed offended, it didn't seem worthwhile to ask.

Mordecai drank a steady parade of ales from the bar and ended up absolutely plastered. As we were preparing to head back to the guild, Miko suggested using *Touch of the Dawn* to cleanse at least some of that alcohol from his system, but Lace shot the idea down.

What surprised me was the reason why.

"Man came very close to dying the other day. If it hadn't been for you two, he probably would have. Sometimes, we all need to get out of our heads a bit, let the memories dull on their own."

Miko clearly disagreed, but I was reminded of a poster I'd once seen back on Earth:

I don't have a drinking problem.

I have a drinking solution.

I guess we'd have to see if Mordecai's solution worked.

55

The day after Mordecai's drinking binge, my plan was to start knocking items off my to-do list. Unfortunately, the town market made that difficult. The town's archives—a small, visually unimpressive building a block from the mayor's residence—were closed for the day. Again. And so was the training hall, on the opposite side of town.

It was like they didn't *want* my business.

Miko and I ended up visiting with Mrrl and Seanna instead. Mostly, we just talked, but toward the end, the Smith reminded us about her offer to make armor. Miko was still thinking about what kind of armor she wanted to use, but I placed an order for a chain mail shirt that could be worn over my padded tunic. It wouldn't be done for a long while, despite profession-given techniques that simplified several stages of the construction, and even at cost, it was going to eat up most of my funds. Still, *not bleeding* sounded like a win to me. When we finally left their shop and home, it was with an invitation to come back for *dinner the kithrizal way*, whatever that meant.

Despite the general public's bias against the scaled, Miko was kind of a cheat code to making friends with quality people.

I also stopped in to see the lupine, Datha, to get some of the padding in my gambeson replaced. When Seanna was done with my armor, I'd have to ask Datha to remove the excess padding, but for now, I was pleased with more protection. And with the weather finally changing, it wasn't even overwhelmingly hot to wear anymore.

The following day was another market day, and Miko and I spent it with a still-queasy Mordecai, following the Flameweaver from stand to stand as he offered his take on the quality of the offerings. It was kind of like a swap meet combined with a farmer's market in Midton… there was a lot of food, some hand-crafted wares, toys for the children, and so on. Miko and I shared kebabs from a stand manned by a bird-like thing that I thought must be a corbin and spent the rest of the afternoon licking outrageous spices off our respective fingers. I bought a brightly colored ball to replace the tattered one I'd seen Datha's cubs kicking around and was mobbed by three hyperactive balls of black-furred fluff when I delivered it later that night.

Children had always made me sad back on Earth, but damn if the lupine cubs weren't cute.

I ended the day with a visit to the barber, shaving my awful beard off, and cleaning up what had become of my hair. I even picked up my own straight razor for the future, although shaving with it would be an adventure. That night, we ate again at the tavern. This time, Mordecai stuck to water.

The day after was the start of the new seven-day, and that meant the archives were finally open. I woke up, went through my forms, and headed down to have a small breakfast at the guild house, all before Miko woke up. The rest of my morning was lost working through the archives' admissions process, first proving my literacy, then proving my trustworthiness, and finally, handing over a bribe of two bits when the first two actions proved insufficient. Even then, the ancient woman in charge only gave me access to the first of two rooms.

As Mordecai had warned, information was jealously guarded even out here on the frontier.

In lieu of the book stacks I'd expected, there were long shelves with cubbies, each cubby containing one or more scrolls. Markers had been painted with a number and a letter in some antiquated version of the Dewey Decimal system I was only vaguely familiar with from school, and it was here that my earlier bribe paid off in spades; the archivist was more than happy to help me find what I needed. After the first glass, she even graced me with a smile, apparently reassured by my scholarly dedication.

I *really* wanted to dive into the fundamentals of the Framework, but I started instead with the history of what was commonly referred to as the Godswar instead. Two glasses and way too many scrolls later, I had a better grasp on the history Miko had only covered with me in passing.

History, because gods really did exist, which meant all of this mythology reflected events that had occurred in one form or another.

As Miko had told me, Corros, the head of the human pantheon, had led a civil war against the other gods shortly after the creation of the Framework. That war had begun with assassinations, with Synos being only one of three elder deities lost to the void that day. Several dozen gods, elder and younger, had then flocked to Corros' banner. A few came from the human pantheon, including Corros' youngest son, Arkos, the human god of chaos, but they were joined by members of almost every celestial family. And not all were strictly evil, as I would have expected, either. There were other chaos gods and goddesses, storm gods, war gods, nature gods, and even one fertility goddess, although the texts didn't even hypothesize as to her reasons for joining the war.

The synossian pantheon had stuck together throughout the conflict—Synos' children helping rally others of the younger gods to join the fight—but they were more the exception than the rule. Pantheon infighting was apparently at least a common as cross-pantheon rivalries. The kithrizal, for example, had once worshipped a mated pair, Chala and Kerso, but Kerso had been one of the first to join Corros' side, and in the process, had tried to depose his own mate.

The war had taken place on Eos as much as out in the cosmos, with the gods using their own mortal creations as puppets and avatars. Over a hundred cycles of battle had reshaped the world, creating mountains where there had been plains, deserts where there had been oceans, and oceans where there had been snow-covered peaks. When it was done, Corros and his co-conspirators were locked away in their own private dimensions and set adrift in the void between stars. The remaining gods looked upon Eos and saw the consequences of their war: many of the myriad species they had created had been wiped out, and of those who remained, none could be called prosperous.

I paused in my reading there. The story was like a fusion of the Bible's Great Flood and the Ten Plagues… except it was also somehow real. Between that realization and the hours I'd spent squinting at handwritten scrolls, my head hurt even worse than when I'd gone through caffeine withdrawal.

Gods are real, mythology is history, and judging by the quest you were given, all of it has some relevance to your present situation.

It wasn't any easier to wrap my mind around on a second or third try, so I just went back to reading the scrolls instead. At least I was finally getting to the part that mattered for my quest.

With the war over and its devastating costs recognized, the remaining gods formed a pact: they would withdraw from the physical realm entirely. The Framework—a system of great flexibility and often contradictory designs thanks to the myriad gods who had created it—would remain, providing the mortals a means to forge their own paths to greatness, but the deities would never again reach beyond the spiritual realm.

And… that was it. Roughly five lines out of more than a dozen scrolls. Worse… my quest hadn't updated.

I flagged down the archivist. "Do you have anything more on the pact of noninterference?"

She bestowed another smile on me, transforming the lines on her face into deep canyons, but shook her head. "There might be more at one of the cities. As much as the mayor prizes learning, Madea *is* a small town, and our archives reflect that."

"It's still really impressive," I told her, and I wasn't just trying to butter her up. Eos didn't seem to have a printing press yet, which meant every scroll had been handwritten and carefully preserved. My fingers and wrist just ached at the thought of filling even one of the shelves.

"Well, I do try my best." Something in her face softened even more than it had with her smile. "What specific questions did you have? Maybe I can help? I received my education at Neveah after all."

I didn't know what Neveah was, but I was guessing a city. Either that or another academy or university.

"I'm curious about the nature of that pact," I said. "Was it a handshake agreement, or did they attach a punishment to it? Did anyone vote against the whole idea? And has it ever been broken?"

"Those are very specific questions."

"I'm hoping to become a Scholar," I lied. "The pact is an area of particular fascination to me."

"Madea could *use* another Scholar!" said the archivist, buying my lie so swiftly that I almost felt bad about the point in *Deception* I was no doubt earning. "As for your questions… the gods do not make handshake agreements. By their very nature, they are a part of the cosmic weave, you must remember."

I nodded sagely. "Of course."

"That means divine will quite literally becomes cosmic law," she continued. "With the traitor gods gone, there was no longer anyone actively working at cross-purposes, as there had been during the Framework's creation and then again, more viscerally, during the Godswar itself."

"So, they all agreed, and just like that, it became an immutable law?"

"Precisely. And as such, it has never been broken. Since that day in Eos' primordial past, the gods have only ever been able to reach us through the spiritual realm or the conduit of the Framework itself."

"That's fascinating." And it really was, but less because of the history behind it, and more because I had proof that it was untrue. Shan had broken that law when he'd saved me and Miko outside Whitehall. He'd even said something to that effect... what had it been?

One more chance. That's all you get, and all I can manage.

And even earlier, in the Dreaming that I could still only remember bits and pieces of...

Rules. There are always rules.

Somehow, Shan had found a loophole in the cosmic law, a technicality in a rule that every remaining god had willed into existence. It was the sort of thing only a Trickster—a chaos god—could have done, and it had clearly cost him, but even so...

He had managed it. He had reached Eos directly, frozen time, and sent me thousands of leagues across the ocean.

And that meant the physical realm wasn't as free of divine interference as everyone wanted to believe. Was *that* why I'd been given this quest? Were Miko's gods trying to warn us of something? And if so, would a little more detail have killed them?

The archivist spoken on for a while longer, and I listened intently and then thanked her as she went back to her duties, but the dialogue window obscuring my vision made it clear I'd already found out what I needed to know, courtesy not of the archives themselves but the old, somewhat lonely woman who worked among their shelves.

QUEST COMPLETED: Find out more information on the celestial law of non-interference.

As with the last quest, there were no physical rewards… no treasure chests materializing out of thin air with glowing artifacts of untold power and minimal complications or even stacks of silver towers or gold crowns, piled as high as my head. But when I checked the strange sensation that I now associated with my experience rather than hunger, it had grown significantly. Not enough to level me—I wasn't that lucky—but still… *significantly.*

And I still had a quest left to complete.

ooo

By that time, I had spent most of the day in the archives. I left with a promise to return when I could, a promise made to both the archivist and me. After all, while their shelf on the Framework was small, and most of the cubbies contained only a single scroll, it was still knowledge I desperately wanted.

But while knowledge was power, as I had told people, power was *also* power. And that meant I needed to find a trainer.

The training hall was a bit of a misnomer as the whole thing was open to the sky. I walked through the open doorway into a wide arena, the only shade to be found that which was cast by the surrounding wall. It was evening, so those shadows were long, but I could imagine what it would feel like training out there at noon, let alone during the summer.

I wasn't always a fan of winter, but fall? Fall I liked.

Contrary to my expectations, the floor of the arena wasn't entirely flat. *Most* of it was, but to the left, dirt had been mounded into several piles and then baked hard by the sun. I was still trying to figure out their purpose when a balding human wearing a kithrizal-like open vest came over.

"We mix up the terrain so our students can learn to fight in varied situations," he said, voice surprisingly melodic for a man who looked like he'd been dragged behind a dalys for ten leagues, been cut loose, lost himself in a barrel of tequila, and then reported to work. "Uneven ground, higher terrain, lower terrain, and transitioning between them all."

"That makes sense."

"I should hope so." He looked me up and down, eyes flicking to the spear I carried with me. "Here for instruction?"

"Yes. In the spear and knife both, depending on availability and price."

He scowled but nodded. "Walks like a Rogue, talks like a merchant," he muttered in some language I clearly wasn't supposed to understand. "The spear's not a bad choice for someone of your size," he allowed, reverting to Trade, "but that one's a little large, don't you think?"

"It's a family heirloom," I said.

"Still hoping to grow into it then? Fair enough. I can instruct you in the knife, but my usual spearman's gone out adventuring. Some sort of ruins or something he wanted to explore with his party. I should be able to source a replacement though, especially since you don't seem to be Tin. What's your timeframe look like?"

"The sooner the better. I'm not sure how long we'll be here."

"Another adventurer?" He shrugged at my nod. "Figured. You people are everywhere all of a sudden. Good for business, bad for when a man wants to sit and hear himself think. Do you really think the grand duke's daughter is all the way out here?"

"We only just heard about that," I told him. "We came into town from Harborton a seven-day or so ago."

"Harborton?" He squinted at me from under the bushy eyebrows that were his only visible hair. "Don't suppose you met a dunsman named Lomas while you were there? Crazy enough to want to build a tavern in a village the size of my thumb?"

"I know him, yeah."

"He still waxing poetic about how great our beer is in Madea?"

I gave the other man a flat look. "He says the stuff your town's Brewer makes is nothing but watered-down vermin piss. And after comparing it to his special reserve, I'm inclined to agree."

"Ha! I guess you do know him then." He slapped me on the shoulder. "It's good to meet you. I'm Caleb. When I'm not running this here training hall, I moonlight as Madea's one and only Brewer."

I winced. "Sorry, I wasn't—"

"Nah, you're right, and so is that little bastard. Man can brew circles around me, and it's not just a function of level either. He's got a nose for things, while I'm mostly just muddling along. Still…" He eyed me up and down again. "Maybe you can try a few sips of my latest batch sometime? Give me a pointer or two on how it compares to the dunsman's best? All I ask for is an honest opinion."

"I'd be happy to."

"Great! I'll let you know when. But in the meantime, you were looking for training. It's two bits a session. One bit goes to the hall, and one to the trainer. If you're going to be here a while, I'd suggest getting a package instead… it's more money upfront, but less per session."

I bought a package of five sessions for nine bits… then got him to chop off one more bit in exchange for my tasting notes on his beer.

"I'll let you know when and if I find an instructor for your spear, but in the meantime, we can get started with the knife."

"Now?" We'd been talking long enough that evening was turning to dusk, leaving the arena awash with shadows. It seemed like a great way to roll my ankle or trip and fall on my own blade.

"Got to learn to fight in all conditions," he said, "but I guess that depends on what your *Knife* skill's at. I could test you and adjust my lessons to my best guess of that skill, or you could just come out and say it. Choice is yours."

Lace had warned me to be cautious about who I shared my Framework-granted numbers with, but his logic made sense.

"I only just gained the skill," I said. "It's still at 1."

"Then we should save the night-fighting until much, much later." He nodded. "Come back tomorrow. I've got the morning free and can fit you in whenever you show up, as long as it's not too close to lunch."

And just like that, I was a student of the knife.

○○○

Miko was back at our room in the guild house. She bounced up to her feet as I entered, chattering away in the High Tongue. "How did it go? What did you find? Did you bring back anything to eat?"

"You wanted me to remind you to use Trade," I pointed out. "And... did you stay here the whole day?"

She dropped her gaze and swapped languages. "Lace and Skaal are out and Mordecai was—is?—was busy. I thought about going to Seanna, but..."

"I get it." And I did. The looks Miko got hadn't improved any over our few days in Madea. In fact, some had gotten worse. "You don't want to be out on the streets alone."

"Don't want bring trouble to their home," she corrected. "Or their business."

"Is that a risk? Really?"

She sighed. "I don't know. I'm not… used to this."

"The people that matter know your worth," I reminded her, "but we can talk to the kithrizal… kithrizals?"

"Is kithrizal for single and plural, says Seanna."

"Right… the kithrizal about your concerns. In the meantime, you can't just stay cooped up in here for however long it takes us to get a new mission."

"I trained and also prayed," she said, and I couldn't tell if the slightly sullen tone in her voice was from emotion or her continued struggle with Trade. "And ate bread in guild house after wake."

"Waking."

"After *waking*. Was not—It was not a bad day."

"Well tomorrow, I'm going to start learning how to fight with a knife. Caleb, the man in charge, knows Lomas, and if you want lessons to help improve your staff skill, I suspect he'd welcome the business."

She nodded. "Will go with you."

"Good. Because I'm also planning to ask him and the kithrizal both where we can find other synossians in Madea. Assuming you're still interested in meeting with them?"

This time, her nod was more assured. "Yes. Is important, and not just because of quest."

"Then we'll make a day of it and—" I stopped as a loud noise filled the room. "Uhm… was that your stomach or mine?"

She looked away guiltily. "Yours, I think."

"I see someone else is working on the *Deception* skill." I grinned. "If all you had was breakfast, then no wonder. I should have gotten you another kebab on my way back—there are still food stalls out, if not as many as when the market was going. But since I didn't… how do you feel about going to the tavern for dinner? It will be my treat."

The look she gave me was vintage Miko. "Dinner at tavern is free as part of our stay at guild house," she reminded me.

"How strange," I teased. "I had forgotten."

That finally won me a sharp-toothed grin. "Fine. But I pay for drinks."

"On that subject," I said, escorting her out into the hall, "you'll never guess what this Caleb does in his free time…"

○○○

The tavern was almost always busy, and this night was no exception. With there only being two of us, we ended up seated at a long communal table with other customers. While one or two gave the white-scaled synossian pointed looks, nobody seemed keen to start anything. Maybe it was the guild badges we'd chosen to wear openly over our clothes, or maybe it was the stained spear I leaned against the wall behind me, within reach at all times.

It probably *wasn't* the hard-eyed look I gave to each of the haters, but I wanted to believe that had played its part too.

About halfway through the evening, a bard took the stage, his features so delicate I at first wondered if he was human. The voice that poured out of his throat only added to that question—fine and rich, like Mrrl's sunlight given audible form. He sang a song of two lost lovers, filling the tavern with the story of their exploits, their meeting, their passion, and ultimately their tragic endings. He sang of a love that outlived them both, finding immortality in song, and when he was done, several of our tablemates were openly weeping.

Before the mood could settle, the bard launched into a second song, and while it started out soft and quiet and sincere, it took a turn halfway through into a bouncy, comedic tale about a hero—a bard, to nobody's surprise—and his raunchy exploits as he traveled through the Waste and beyond. The cheers that followed that song's end echoed almost as loudly as the emotional silence that had preceded it.

We stayed late, eating and drinking. I switched to water once the food was gone, mindful of the fact that I'd be swinging a live blade around the next morning. Miko was less conservative, but her mood steadily improved as the glasses kept coming. By the time I convinced her to switch to water, she was well on her way to being drunk. A glass or so after that, our table had cleared out, but the younger of the two barmaids came by again to fill our waters.

"Can I get you anything else?" she asked. She was the same general age as Halletia back in Harborton, far less modestly dressed, and had a way of swishing her skirts around as she walked that inevitably drew the gaze of the tavern's patrons. Her eyes sparkled as she leaned over to fill my cup, but I saw the weariness lurking underneath.

Serving in a tavern was a hell of a lot harder than manning a register at a coffee shop, and she'd been doing it all night. She was probably wondering how long we were going to sit there and not spend any more money.

"I'm good, but thank you," I told her. "And I'm sorry; we'll be out of the way soon."

"You don't curse, you don't leer, and you smile when you say thank you, like you really mean it," she said, leaning even closer. "You and your friend can stay here all night as far as I'm concerned, honey, especially if you're going to keep looking at me like that. Besides, I have to work for another glass anyway. As for after that? Who knows?"

She gave me a wink, then leaned across the table to fill Miko's cup instead of walking around to the side, brushing up against me as she did. As she straightened again, I felt a soft hand squeeze my shoulder. Then she headed back to the bar, skirts swaying with every step.

"I think I'm beginning to grasp your species' mating rituals," said Miko, and for once I was glad that she had accidentally lapsed into the High Tongue.

"I…" I coughed. "So I wasn't just imagining that then?"

"First Nala and now this woman. Are you considered attractive for your species? It is hard for me to know what aesthetic traits are valued among you soft skins." Her orange eyes went wide, and she hid a burp. "I am so sorry! I shouldn't have called you that."

"It doesn't bother me, remember? And to answer your question… not really? I mean Kate said I was good looking, but it's not like I had women beating down my door or anything, even before… Maybe politeness just goes a long way in the Great Wilds?"

Or maybe one of my still-hidden traits made me more attractive somehow. God, I hoped not. Not only would it make for a potentially gross cheat—touching on all sort of issues like consent—but it would also be a total waste for me.

"If you wish to mate with her, I can find my own way back to the guild house," said Miko, with a combination of bluntness and honesty brought on by one too many dark ales. "I know you humans do not like to go so long between copulation."

I nearly choked on my water. "First of all, *how* would you know that?"

She blinked owlishly over at me. "I listened to the bard's song. Did I… did I not understand it correctly?"

"I mean… no, you got it. You definitely got it. But…" I sighed and changed my approach. A sober Miko knew the difference between stories and reality, so there was no reason to try to explain. "I'm not going to mate with her."

"Why not? Is she not pretty?"

"No, she is. She really is." Maybe I'd had too much to drink too because I found myself opening my mouth again. "It's just… do you have contraceptives here?"

"Do we have what?"

"Devices or herbs to prevent pregnancies."

She made the synossian equivalent of a frown. "My people have medicine to prevent our fertile cycle, but I don't know about the children of Corros. Tantalas didn't mention them."

"That's what I figured. I'm not risking it."

"You don't wish to further your line?"

"You mean having children?" I shook my head. "When I was growing up, all I wanted was to be a dad, believe it or not."

I didn't see the glow of *Touch of the Dawn*, but Miko suddenly seemed almost sober, orange eyes intent upon my face. "What changed?"

"My dad's father died." I sighed, and took another sip of water, wishing it was ale or something even stronger. "They were estranged, and had been since well before I was born, so the first thing I even knew of him was when we got a call saying he was gone. And the woman who called—my grandfather's nurse, I guess?—didn't call because she thought we would care. She called because of what had killed him."

"A monster?"

"Not in the way you mean it. You have diseases on Eos, right?"

She nodded solemnly.

"Well, this one has a fifty percent chance of getting passed down to the carrier's children and a one hundred percent chance of killing anyone who has it." I swallowed. "My dad got tested the next day. He had it too. It took four or five years more for me to learn what was going on, but then I got tested. I wanted to know. I needed to."

"You also have the disease," she breathed.

"Yeah. At some point, I'm going to start losing muscle control function. I'll have memory lapses or mood swings. I'll lose who I am, and I will eventually die. On Earth, we do have ways to prevent pregnancy, but they're not foolproof. I wasn't going to risk someone else being doomed with this disease just because they had the misfortune of having me as their parent. That hasn't changed just because I'm on Eos."

"I'm sorry," said Miko, laying her hand atop mine. "I did not know your pain."

"There's no way you could have. That's the thing about disease; it's invisible right up until the point where it's not."

The synossian nodded, inner eyelids flickering. She looked away for a long minute, blew out a sigh, and then patted my hand.

"You should get it cured."

"I… what?"

"Your disease. You should have it cured. Aurea has already given me the ability to remove poison. Surely someone out there in this land of terrifying Aspirants will have been given a technique to cure disease?"

I just stared at her.

"If we cannot find such a person," Miko continued, "then I will pray to Aurea that she grants me that blessing one day instead. You are a Chosen of the gods, Brian Fieldings. A Chosen of *my* gods. More importantly, you are my nest-brother and friend. I will not sit back and watch you fade away."

56

Over the next few days, we settled into a routine in Madea. Miko and I would wake up to train, I would spend some time in the archives with Julla the elderly Scholar, and then we would either visit with the kithrizal or meet up with others in our party for dinner at the tavern.

Caleb had confirmed that there were other 'scaled' in Madea but neither he nor Seanna had had more than vague suggestions on where to find them. In the end, it was Datha who pointed the way, taking us down the street from his shop through a series of progressively shabby buildings on the hill-facing edge of Madea. In the smallest of those houses, four synossians lived.

"Maybe I speak with them alone?" suggested Miko as we stood just outside the shack's door. Even with an eleven Strength, I was pretty sure I'd be able to kick the thing in. "If is okay?"

"Of course," I agreed. "They're your people. I'll just wait out here in case you need me."

"Thank you, nest-brother."

I spent upwards of a glass standing in the streets of Madea's slums, one hand on the knife at my belt, the other on Riok's spear.

Contrary to my expectations, there were just as many humans living in the area as beastkin. Poverty remained the great equalizer.

I got my share of hard stares and a group of younger kids even set up on a nearby corner to watch me, but while Madea had its share of Tins, the slums didn't seem to have any at all. The inability to inspect someone's level worked in my favor for once, and my readily available weapons proved to be sufficient deterrents for anyone interested in making trouble.

When Miko finally emerged, she was shaking her head.

"Is everything okay?"

She tapped her left arm a single time, speaking in the High Tongue once again. "I will tell you on the way. For now, let us just go."

We left the slums behind, heading for the kebab stall that we'd already hit twice since the market ended. Miko's inner eyelids were fluttering and the ridges around her eyes had tightened, signs of high emotion or concern. It wasn't until she'd finished her first kebab that she finally settled down.

"They were not what I expected."

"How so?"

"They were a *family*." She paused. "Blood-mother and blood-father and two hatchlings raised alone. Without dedicated nest-mothers, it must be left to them to raise the young. This I can understand, but they do not even remember who we are as a people."

"What do you mean?"

"I asked for their history, and they wanted coin in return." She sounded vaguely incensed. "One bit bought me their story, but it did not extend beyond a single additional generation. They know nothing of their ancestors, of the Waste, the Swarm, or even our people's flight from the Great Wilds."

"It might be harder to hold on to your history and culture when you're a persecuted people and education is in short supply," I suggested.

"I do not blame them for their circumstances or their greed. They needed that copper bit more than me. I am simply shocked to witness their fall. I spoke to them of Synos and his celestial children, and they did not even know the names. They call themselves the scaled. The Father would weep to see what has become of his people."

A dialogue window popped up, but I minimized it, focusing on Miko. I was pretty sure I already knew what it said.

"Did they have any ideas on finding others of your kind?"

"Trynfall," she said. "There is an enclave in the Grand Duke's capital city, where my people gather under the only ruler who grants them any rights at all. I think… I think we need to go there."

A second dialogue window appeared, but I waved it away. Trynfall would be a big step up from Madea, both in size and expense, but I just nodded. "I can talk to Lace about heading there. I know she and Skaal are trying to work their way back toward the cities anyway."

"What if the enclave is like this family?" asked the Priestess. "What if none of them remember their origins?"

It was a good question. When we'd heard that there were synossians on this continent, it had seemed like an easy way to gather allies before the refugees arrived. But if the so-called scaled didn't even consider themselves synossians, would they want to help? Would they be able to?

"I don't know," I admitted. "Maybe you could teach them their history or bring worship of your pantheon back to this continent, but that honestly seems like an even bigger task than preparing for the Synossian Primacy's arrival."

"I am just one Priestess," said Miko, and I couldn't tell if she was agreeing or simply voicing her frustrations, "and this is so much bigger than a thegar."

We ate in silence for a while. When we were done, she sighed.

"All is not lost," Miko decided. "The gods would not have sent you your quest if there was not some value to be had in meeting with my lost kin. Perhaps the enclave will have more information or will be able to support us in some unforeseen way. I will keep my faith in the Bright Lady and her siblings."

I didn't say anything. I still wasn't big on faith, but sometimes it was hard not to envy Miko for hers.

"Did you finish it at least?" asked Miko, finally switching back to Trade. "The quest?"

I nodded and pulled up the first window I'd dismissed earlier:

```
QUEST COMPLETED: Help Miko Naseri make contact with the
                native synossians.
```

I'd already known what I would see, of course, known by the feeling of satiation that had filled me, mid-conversation.

"I did, and I'm ready to level too, once my skills catch up."

"Truly, the gods are good."

"They seem to think you have the right idea too."

"What do you mean?"

I pulled up the second dialogue window and read it aloud:

```
NEW QUEST: Help Miko Naseri make contact with the
           synossian enclave in Trynfall.

           [ Accept | Decline ]
```

I hit *Accept* and shrugged.

"Divine guidance doesn't get clearer than that."

ooo

Over the course of the next few seven-days, Miko continued to visit the synossian family, and if our shared stash of funds dwindled a bit each time, I wasn't going to say anything. She came back from every visit disheartened and yet showed no signs of giving up. There wasn't much I could do but try to buoy her spirits.

And when that didn't work, we tried Mordecai's solution instead.

Weapons training continued. Caleb hadn't been able to find a spear trainer for me, but I worked out with my weapon in the arena every day, the older man offering general advice on my footwork. My *Knife* skill, meanwhile, was rapidly improving under proper instruction, and Miko had almost maxed *Staff* for her current level.

On the fifth day of training, we both stayed late and sampled Caleb's latest brew. It wasn't anywhere near as good as Lomas', but the trainer and apprentice Brewer already knew that. Our feedback was received well and as he walked away again, I could almost see the wheels turning in the bald man's head. Every seven-day or so, he tried again, each new batch a mild improvement over the old.

Hopefully, Lomas wouldn't be too put out to learn that we'd been in some small way helping his competitor. Knowing the dunsman, he would just be happy *someone* was improving the quality of the brew available in Madea. Besides, his special reserve was still far and away the better of the two.

On our thirtieth and thirty-first days in Madea, two things happened that finally shook us out of the lull of our routine.

First, I emerged from meditation to be greeted by the notification I'd been waiting for:

```
    Congratulations, Warrior.

    You have reached level 4!

    You have one point to allocate to an attribute of
your choosing:

    Strength: 11 [+1] / Finesse: 10
    Vitality: 15 [+2] (+2) / Intellect: 13
    Discernment: 10 / Will: 14 (+2)
```

My two quests and our battles against the bandits had gotten me the experience I needed to level, so the skills had once again been the main obstacle. Without Caleb's instruction, I was pretty sure I'd have still been toiling away at raising everything to its necessary rank.

Miko was asleep in her bed, so I kept my celebration quiet. Vitality had gone up another point with my level, as expected. Interestingly, the point that I'd earned naturally while questing for the nilwort wasn't called out in the brackets, but instead merely reflected in the attribute's overall score. From what Miko had said and what I had since confirmed through my own study, that was because natural gains—and losses—were distinguished from those earned through levels.

Still, I'd gone from a 12 Vitality to 15 in less than four moons. I felt kind of like a superhero.

I'd already put a lot of thought into how I'd allocate my one free attribute point. Part of me wanted to keep dumping points into Strength until I was some sort of walking behemoth like Arrius, but Skaal's comment on broken foundations had given me pause. This wasn't a game, where min-maxing always made sense and so-called dump stats just gave you a penalty on a roll of the dice. This was reality… a reality I had to live in. I wanted to ensure I was addressing my needs and not just my desires.

Intellect had been my second attribute to increase on its own, thanks to weeks of long hours of study in the archives and maybe even the help I'd given Miko with learning Trade. There were hard limits on *natural* gains beyond just the time and dedication they took—you couldn't improve any stat more than five points above its starting score—but that one-point increase had pushed Intellect from 12 to 13, making it my third highest stat. I'd want to upgrade it again at some point, just to improve my memory and reduce my technique cooldowns, but for now, I had bigger needs.

Needs like Finesse. I had wrongly assumed that Strength would be the single most important attribute for wielding a spear, but what I'd learned was that Finesse was every bit as important, if not more so. Putting the spear where I wanted it would do me a lot more good than simply hitting harder with it, especially with Riok's spear proving tougher than bronze or high-quality iron.

As for Discernment…? The attribute had its advantages too. Between identifying discrepancies in the wild and navigating social constraints with the social elite, Discernment had a lot to offer. And, much like Intellect, it helped with cooldowns.

Still, the choice was clear to me. The spear was my primary weapon, and having passed up *Fueled By Pain*, I desperately needed ways to improve my damage output. Finesse and Strength would both help me do that, but being able to thread my weapon through the narrow gaps in an enemy's armor would be of more immediate value than simply hitting that armor a little bit harder.

I spent the point and dismissed the other windows that had accompanied my level-up. As usual, there was nothing immediately noticeable to say that I was now better than I had ever been before… but I trusted it was true.

I pulled up my full character sheet:

```
Name: Brian Fieldings
Class: Warrior (Common) - 4
Profession: None
Deity: None
Ideal: Freedom

Attributes:
Strength: 11 [+1] / Finesse: 11 [+1]
Vitality: 15 [+2] (+2) / Intellect: 13
Discernment: 10 / Will: 14 (+2)

Skills:
Major: Formations: 5/25, Knife: 7/25,
Light Armor: 20/25, Spear (U): 20/25, Tactics: 14/25

Minor: Athleticism: 20/25, Avoidance: 19/25,
Focus: 1/25, Pain Tolerance: 20/25

Professional: None

General: Animal Behaviorism: 10/10, Brewing: 2/10,
Caretaking: 7/10, Danger Sense (R): 9/10,
Deception: 7/10, Hunting: 1/10, Meditation: 5/10,
Mercantilism: 4/10, Riding: 2/10, Scribing: 4/10,
Stealth: 5/10, Tracking: 1/10

Techniques: Beast Skin (C), Lunge (C)


Achievements: None
Titles: None
Traits: Speaker of Tongues, ???, ???
```

Over the course of our lengthy stay in Madea, I'd gained the *Focus* Minor skill and added points to *Light Armor, Knife, Tactics,*

Athleticism, *Avoidance*, and *Pain Tolerance*, all through training with Caleb. I'd also earned an extra point in *Brewing* from giving halfway-qualified feedback, a point in *Mercantilism* through my daily haggling—mostly at the kebab stand—and… well… *four* points in *Deception* on account of my continued lies.

I didn't feel great about that last one, but if it wasn't safe to tell the truth, I figured I might as well be getting skill gains for lying.

The second big thing didn't happen until the next morning. At least that's when we found out about it. It had truthfully happened many days earlier, but Madea's position out on the frontier made the town almost the last to hear about anything.

War was the word on the streets.

Reparations was the word in the guild house.

Absolute disaster was what one drunk merchant had been muttering to himself in the tavern, mere minutes before passing out in his own bowl of stew.

The truth was somewhere in between. By all accounts, the grand duke's men had finally traced his heir's kidnappers to Zaris, a small mountain nation which sat to the distant southwest and shared no more than twenty leagues of border with the duchy and the Kingdom of Elthor at large. The duke's daughter herself had *not* been found, and the prevailing theory seemed to be that she had been dispatched somewhere along the way.

Willington had sent an emissary to demand answers from Zaris' elected rulers and summoned his nobles to the capital to assemble an army if the answers received were unsatisfactory. Given the regions' respective sizes, it was thought that any resulting military campaign would be over in a moon or two after it began, with Zaris the inevitable loser.

The conflict—and the plight of the murdered heir—was all anyone wanted to talk about, and even though we were multiple seven-days from Trynfall, and the relevant decisions had likely already been made, everyone seemed to have their opinion on what would happen next. Even market days became as much an opportunity to spread fresh gossip as a time to buy and sell.

Or maybe they'd always been like that. In my experience, gossip was a small town's greatest industry.

The adventurers had a different take on the whole thing, one voiced not so much in words as in the swiftly declining numbers in Madea's guild house. Parties who had traveled to the town thinking they would stumble across the heir out in the wilds soon drifted away again. The mission board, which for the past moon had been picked over like a five-dollar buffet, finally started to accumulate some new tasks.

By our thirty-fourth full day back in Madea, there were a dozen missions up on the board, including the false dawn purge that nobody had shown interest in even when competition was at its most fierce. Mordecai was entirely out of coin, I was getting close, and we were collectively eyeing the board like it was a Sudoku puzzle, trying to figure out ways to chain multiple missions together to minimize travel and cost while maximizing potential profit.

But the thirty-fifth day, it turned out, was significant in ways I couldn't have anticipated.

I finished my morning forms and headed downstairs, leaving Miko slumbering in her bed. She'd maxed out her staff for level five a few days earlier, ending her training sessions with Caleb, and I knew better than to wake her up early if it wasn't necessary.

I was done training too… for now, anyway. What money I had left was earmarked for the second half of my payment to Seanna. The Smith had promised she'd be done with my new armor in just a matter of days now, and the last thing I wanted was to not have the necessary funds.

Lace and Skaal were both up and standing together in the nearly empty common room, but that wasn't too unusual. The surprising thing was that Mordecai was with them, and all three were at Carlson's desk.

"What's going on?" I whispered to a sleepy Melligula.

She blinked two of her four eyes, leaving the other set closed. "What? Oh, it's been a full moon since the party from Steppin's Skirmishers left to complete their mission."

Steppin's Skirmishers, I'd learned, was the name of a well-known adventuring company based out of the western half of the kingdom. It was one of their parties that had come all the way to Madea and sniped our mission while were out killing bandits and saving the day.

"And? Why does that matter?"

"They're still not back," said Lace, cutting in.

I waited for her to elaborate.

"A party can only hold a given mission for one moon," said Mordecai. "Two, if the destination's far enough to warrant an extension."

"Which isn't the case here," added Lace.

"The ruins?"

She nodded sharply. "The mission is ours again. Only now, we have a finder's fee stacked on top if we can find out what happened to Sleepy's Sunchasers."

"Steppin's Skirmishers," murmured Melligula.

"Whatever." The Marauder's smile was entirely too bright and bloodthirsty for however early it was in the morning. "Carlson's getting the information we need now. We'll be on our way before lunchtime."

Which meant I *wouldn't* have my new armor. That sucked, but after a moon in Madea, I was just as ready to leave as anyone else.

"I'll wake Miko," I volunteered. "And we'll get packed."

57

According to the provided map, the ruins we sought were a full seven-day's journey out in the wild. The first day was familiar as it was an almost exact repeat of the path we'd taken when investigating the thievery at Madea's neighboring farms. We traveled another two days on the road, meeting almost nobody, and then cut south. A fire had ravaged the forest there at some point, and in place of the old giants, there were a lot of young trees and overgrowth, as nature tried to fill the vacuum that fire had created.

The trip had been quiet so far. Fall had fallen and while it impacted the number of daylight hours we had, it also made for cooler days on the march. The nights were already downright cold, but the heavier blankets we'd brought from Madea were up to the challenge. I kept one of those blankets wrapped around me even on watch, while promising myself that I'd find winter coats for Miko and me if we were going to do any true cold-weather adventuring.

On the fourth day, we reached the marsh, and I learned there were worse things to experience than cold. Mosquitoes the size of Skaal's fist charted lazy paths above the scattered pools of water, while the unseen creatures below were noticeable only by the noises they made. *Animal Behaviorism* didn't tell me what those creatures were, but common sense told me not to wade through waters so murky they were practically opaque.

The trees became sparser as we traveled deeper into the marsh, and the pools of muddy, vegetal water became both larger and more common. Where Lace had initially led us around such obstacles, charting courses that stuck to dry land, that quickly became an impossible task. So, instead we pushed straight through. By the time we stopped for camp that night, my pants were soaked and filthy from the waist down, as much muddy water inside my boots as outside.

The only good news was that so far, nothing had attacked.

Our camp that night was on a cramped stretch of higher ground, rising above the water-logged terrain around it. I had my boots off and drying by the fire while Miko scrubbed at her mud-brown scales with the brush she'd bought in Harborton.

"You know you're just going to get dirty again tomorrow, don't you?" asked Lace. Though taller than me, the Marauder was somehow even *filthier*, testament to the effort scouting a viable path had taken.

"Yes," said Miko. "But at least I will be clean when I sleep."

"Your Trade has gotten quite good, lass," said Mordecai. The man had swapped his mud-spattered mask for a fresh one from his pack, and it looked oddly out of place… clean where everything else was stained from the journey. "I know Brian here is the linguist, but I think you might have talent in that area too."

Off to the side, Lace shook her head but said nothing.

"It has taken longer than I want—wanted," said Miko, "but thank you. Am trying."

"Can one of the two of you take last watch tonight?" asked Lace. "I am tired, and we have two more days of this slog ahead of us."

"I will take," said Miko.

"Why don't I handle last watch instead?" I suggested. "You can have first watch if Skaal takes the middle."

The half-giant grunted in agreement, while Lace frowned.

"I don't really care which of you takes which, but why?"

"I do not like mornings," said Miko, carefully stringing the words together. "Or waking up early."

"Exactly. Whereas I'm used to it. Deal?"

The synossian sent me a sharp-toothed smile. "Deal." She looked me over and that smile faded. "Please try not to track mud into tent."

I… didn't see how that would be avoidable.

The next two days were somehow even worse. Rain fell steadily, drenching the parts of me that weren't submerged in water despite my cloak's best efforts. The absence of trees meant more than a lack of shelter… it also left me feeling exposed, and the fact that we never saw any living thing other than bugs somehow only heightened the sense of danger. While I used my spear as a walking stick as much as a weapon, I made sure it was always in hand, and every time Lace led us into water that was waist-high on me and knee-to-hip-deep on everyone else, I prepared myself for an attack.

Still, nothing came. No alligators. No mutant anacondas. No land-bound second cousins to Godzilla. The marsh felt nearly as empty as the Swarm-stricken fields east of Harborton, and equally foreboding.

Not even the two points in *Athleticism* I gained from multiple days of walking/swimming through sludge cheered me up.

On the seventh day, we reached a large lake. Its banks were choked thick with algae and vegetation, but inward, water shifted from murky green to sapphire blue. The rain had finally stopped, and wan sunlight peeked through the clouds to reflect off the lake's surface.

A body of clean-looking water in the middle of a marsh suited for Lace's nine-breasted demon goddess? I distrusted it immediately… which was problematic given the land mass at the lake's center and the crumbling remnants of some kind of fortifications that perched on top.

"*Please* tell me we aren't swimming there," said Mordecai, unknowingly echoing my innermost thoughts.

"Not if the Night Hag herself told me to do so. Thankfully, it's not a true island." Lace pointed off into the distance, her dark finger following the curve of the lake's shoreline. "According to the map, there's some kind of pathway across the water from the southern shore."

"Where did these ruins come from?" I asked.

"I have no idea." She shrugged.

Mordecai squinted at the ruined fort, eyes slits behind his mud-spotted mask. "The Endless Empire? No, this would have been beyond the edges of their frontier. An outpost for some neophyte country that died before it could grow into anything larger, perhaps? It's too large and remote to have simply been an estate, but it could have been some sort of purposefully isolated institution. Or even a monastery."

"In other words, you don't know." Lace nodded. "That's fine. What matters is we found it."

"See movement," said Miko, pointing one clawed finger at the barely visible fortifications.

Lace peered in that direction. "You're right. The wanderers who reported this place saw evidence of the blighted. Irkonnen, they thought."

I must have looked confused because the Marauder sighed. "Mordecai?"

The Flameweaver cleared his throat. "Irkonnen are somewhat similar in appearance to the lupine, but about a third of the size, and—with apologies to our delightful Priestess friend—often partly scaled."

So... scaled little dog people? If I hadn't already experienced catosaurs up close and personal, they would have sounded almost cute.

"They and the rest of what we commonly refer to as the blighted were not created by the gods, but by mortals," continued

Mordecai, "each species magically bred as weapons of conquest in a time long before even the Endless Empire. Sadly, those ancient Mages appear to have been more concerned about winning wars than what might come after. Now, you can find pockets of them throughout the wilderness."

Lace nodded. "Irkonnen are bloodthirsty little bastards and clever, if not particularly smart. A place like this would be perfectly suited for their kind."

"And we're here to clear them out?"

"And rescue or find out what happened to the party from Stubby's Shortcomings," she confirmed.

I liked some of her mock company names more than others.

"The previous party was Tin," pointed out Skaal, sticking to Gorash for once. "To defeat them would require either many irkonnen or something far stronger."

I translated quietly for Miko, who hadn't started trying to make inroads on yet another language just yet.

"Right," agreed Lace. "Which is why we're crossing at night. Unlike some of the blighted, irkonnen are daywalkers. We'll find somewhere to hide by the causeway, and then I'll get the lay of the land. For now, let's pull back from the shore as we make our way around. There aren't a lot of trees to hide behind, and I'd rather they didn't know we were coming."

By the time we had circled the lake, it was dark anyway, making our concerns about being spotted moot. A few lights could be seen from the ruins, but the causeway that kept our destination a peninsula instead of an island was pitch-black, the stars and one half-full moon doing little to illuminate the passage. Even knowing Lace was out there didn't enable me to spot her.

Miko meditated while Mordecai napped, but Skaal and I stayed alert and on guard, the reaver's eyes trained on the darkness Lace had disappeared into. I tried making idle conversation as we waited, but it was like talking to a wall.

A glass or two passed before the Marauder materialized out of the darkness. Miko had long since joined us, but we woke Mordecai to hear her news.

"It's what we thought," she said, voice pitched not to carry. "A whole den of the things has moved in. Twenty or thirty, at least. Irkonnen don't believe in things like standing guard, but the numbers will make things difficult."

"Any sign of the other party?" asked Mordecai.

She shook her head. "The den has made one of the broken towers their nest, so it's possible the bodies are stashed in there, but… since when have so few irkonnen been a match for a full party of Tins?"

Skaal shrugged. "Kill irkonnen, check tower, return to Madea."

"Agreed." She sketched something in the mud at our feet before remembering we couldn't see it. With a sigh, she tossed the stick aside. "There's the wreckage of a second tower to the right where we can set up. Mordecai and Miko, I want you to save your spells. I'll make a path to the tower."

"Easy to get boxed in," warned Skaal.

"That's true of the whole island. I'd rather have walls at our backs than irkonnen crawling up our asses because nobody saw them coming," she shot back. "No offense, Brian."

I wasn't offended. It was a hell of a lot easier to defend a space than to run around in the dark..

∘∘∘

The first irkonnen I saw was already dead, a still form slumped where Lace had left it. It was the size of a child, but with the wiry musculature of an adult and the long snout of a wolf or dog. A scattering of scales across its scarred hide was faintly visible in the moonlight. I couldn't tell if it smelled or not, because I'd smelled nothing but marsh for three days and everything else—even wet, dead, humanoid dog lizard—paled in comparison.

Between Skaal's ghost white skin and Miko's shimmering scales, I had spent the entire crossing convinced we'd be spotted immediately, but either the irkonnen were even less vigilant than I'd thought, or Lace had thoroughly cleared the way forward; we made it to the 'island' without any outcry.

I saw three more bodies on our way to the tower Lace had designated our base of operations. In truth, I was pretty sure it was a safe spot to keep the more fragile members of the party protected while she and Skaal took out the trash. And while I wasn't *opposed* to that strategy, my character sheet said I was a Warrior. A part of me felt like I was supposed to be fighting, not hiding.

Skaal stayed with us for a while as Lace did what she promised to do. When she returned this time, her blades were dark with blood and her smile was unfit for civilized company.

"There are several clusters of three or more left," she whispered. "And then however many dwell in the tower."

"Still no sign of the other party?" It was my turn to ask.

"No." We could hear her frown. "None of these irkonnen have been Tin, and their equipment is trash, even for low-level blighted. Skaal and I should be able to clear them out on our own, to say nothing of a full party."

"Maybe they never made it here?" suggested Mordecai. "Who knows what horrors we might have slipped past in the marsh?"

Lace and Skaal exchanged glances. I'd heard from both that tracking anything in the marsh had been difficult, between the ever-shifting terrain and the regular rainfall. Gods knew my own *Tracking* skill had been next to useless... and stuck at only one point.

"There's only one way to find out for sure. You three hole up here while Skaal and I tackle those last few clusters."

Yep, I'd called that one. "And the nest in the other tower?"

"We'll take that as a group when I don't have to worry about anything coming at our less-defended party members from the sides or rear."

She disappeared into the darkness and Skaal followed. Despite the half giant's size and color and Lace's ongoing complaints about his lack of stealth, he moved quickly and quietly, an overly large pale shadow.

"Hurry up and wait, as ever," muttered Mordecai. "I'm taking a defensive technique next level, and then we'll see who is left behind."

"Whereas I'm doing just the opposite at level five. Assuming I get the option." I sighed. "At least you know *your* path, Miko. Uh… Miko?"

The Priestess wasn't at my side where she'd been standing. I looked wildly about before spotting her, moving deeper into the confines of the partially collapsed tower we'd taken as shelter.

Patting Mordecai on the shoulder, I left my post to see what she was doing. "What is it?"

My voice was hushed, but she held up a scaled finger to her mouth anyway, in a gesture she'd taken from us soft skins as a call to silence. She slowly walked me around one pile of rubble and gestured at another, near the back of the fallen tower's wall.

I couldn't see a thing. The remnants of the wall made the flickering light from the irkonnen's nearby campfires barely sufficient to even see my companions, let alone… whatever it was she was trying to show me.

Apparently, Miko realized that too. She pulled me back to the front of the tower, where Mordecai was keeping watch.

"We have problem," she said, and if the rest of us had been speaking in whispers, her voice was a breath on the non-existent breeze.

"What is it, lass?"

"Stairs."

In unison, the Flameweaver and I both looked up at the tower that would have once risen above us.

"Not up," she hissed, switching to the High Tongue in her worry. "Down and hidden beside the rubble. They look like they have been repaired recently, and I think I spotted something moving below."

I translated for Mordecai, who fiercely rubbed his chin beneath the mask. "You're saying the irkonnen have a bolthole, and we're sitting right on it?"

Miko shook her head, answering in Trade. "Irkonnen are small. Why would they make stairs big enough for Skaal?"

"The stairs are probably as old as the ruins themselves, and sized for whoever built them," I reasoned. "Still, I'd have expected the irkonnen to keep the entrance small when clearing them again. That would prevent larger predators from entering."

I wasn't sure if that was *Animal Behaviorism* speaking, or if I was talking out of my ass, but Mordecai was shaking his head.

"It doesn't matter who did it or why, lad. If these ruins have a subterranean level, we can't risk sitting on top of the only known entrance and exit. We must join the others."

The three of us exchanged looks and then nods. Lace would blow a gasket—another idiom that would make no sense here on Eos— but the fact was we would be safer with them than alone next to unfamiliar but apparently well-used stairs.

This time, I led the way, Riok's spear in hand, with Mordecai on my heels and Miko bringing up the rear. The Priestess had her bracers on and the purchased short staff in her hands, and while she wasn't a Warrior class, she still made for an imposing figure. I sure as hell wouldn't have wanted to run into her in a dark alleyway.

We had a general idea of where to go to reach the second tower, helped by the fires the irkonnen had set around the ruins to keep themselves warm. I stepped over another body and started to weave around the next decrepit shell of a house or stable or—as Mordecai insisted—library, when something caught my eye.

More fire.

In and of itself, that was nothing unusual—we'd woven our way through at least four of the things on our way to the first tower, and another two so far on our way to the second—but there were two big things that made this particular flame special.

First, it was a long way away.

And second, it was moving.

I pointed it out to my two companions. "That's the shoreline, isn't it?"

Before they could reply, that single flame had seemingly multiplied, becoming five, then a dozen, then even more.

Another forest fire, insisted the part of my brain that lived for snap judgments.

No, said the more sober part of me, as the flames neared the unlit causeway leading from shore to island. *Torches.*

Mordecai had realized it too, eyes wide in the dancing light of the closest campfire. "One torch per group of irkonnen," he murmured. "Three at the best, seven at the worst. Multiply by the number of torches, carry the—"

I'd done my home's budget since I was twelve; I'd already finished the math. "We have to get to Skaal and Lace. Now."

We raced through the ruins. It was Miko who found the other two, a hissed word in the High Tongue changing my direction so I didn't overshoot them.

"What are you three doing here?" Lace sounded as annoyed as I'd expected as she rose from a low crouch. Four bodies lay strewn around another fire, and the second tower loomed ahead, just a few shattered buildings away.

I looked back to the shoreline only to realize it wasn't visible from here. Even someone of Skaal's height couldn't see over the broken eggshell walls.

"Reinforcements. A *lot* of them, already crossing to the island."

"What?"

"Hundreds of them, lass."

"Dens don't get that large—" She cut off as Skaal rose from where he'd been examining the bodies. The half-giant handed her scraps of torn cloth. "What is it?"

"Bloodline crest," he said, his voice a low rumble. "Three. All different."

"More than one den," she breathed. "That *doesn't* happen."

"Must go. Now."

"Where? This island isn't big enough to hide us from hundreds of enemies, even if we hadn't left rotters everywhere." She glanced my way and I saw the realization hit her. We didn't dare *Night Hag's Embrace* unless she abandoned me entirely.

"Water?"

Lace shook her head, the firelight just bright enough for me to see her night-black skin go grey. "You wouldn't suggest that if you could see what I see."

"Stairs," said Miko, finally joining the conversation.

"What?"

"The lass found stairs leading down," said Mordecai. "Hidden at the rear of the tower you left us in. That's why we left."

Skaal locked eyes with the Marauder and nodded. "Enclosed space better than open. Easier to be trapped, but harder to be overrun." Somehow, a bit of humor leaked into his voice. "Keep from crawling up ass."

"Stop throwing my words at me, old man." Lace grinned and for just a moment, she was almost beautiful. "We've got places to be."

Of the five of us, only the Marauder was silent as we raced back to the original tower, although it might have just been hard to hear her over everyone else's noise. The lead torches were already nearing the island when she led us back into the ruined tower. Miko pushed past her and revealed the open stairwell like it was some kind of magic trick.

"I should have seen that," hissed Lace.

"Past is past," said Skaal.

She nodded. "Standard formation. We'll find a spot below where we can regroup. If it's a dead end, we'll make a stand there. If it's not... I swear I'll find a way forward."

We headed down into the darkness, two dozen dead irkonnen behind us, and several hundred live ones on their way.

58

The further we went down, the darker it got, but any hopes I had that the way ahead would be clear ended long before we'd reached the bottom. From below, there was a low snarl, a squeal, and the sound of something heavy hitting the ground.

"More of them down here," said Lace, her quiet voice carrying.

I kept one hand on the wall as I descended, my gaze trained behind and above us. The rubble in the tower above blocked any light from the nearby fires, but hopefully, I'd catch the motion of any irkonnen entering the stairs in pursuit.

And if not… well, *Beast Skin* and *Pain Tolerance* would get put through their paces.

We made it to the bottom without being attacked.

"It's an intersection," whispered Lace, the only one of us who could see in the dark. "Stay here and watch the stairs and the passageway to our left. I'm headed right."

Less than a minute later, she was back. "Another den. Only a dozen or so sleeping irkonnen, but there's no way we're sneaking through. Follow me to the left."

"Need light," Skaal reminded her.

"We need distance more. If we can make some space—"

A chorus of yipping howls interrupted her, echoing down the stairs.

"They found the bodies." I tightened the grip on my spear, listening for the sound of clawed feet on worked stone.

"Is that a guess, or…"

I shook my head, knowing she would see it. "That's literally what they're saying."

Apparently, *Speaker of Tongues* worked for dog things too.

"Move. Now."

At Lace's urging, we headed down the hallway only she could see. Another two irkonnen died under her blades, but these two had apparently been armed and alarmed, moving to see what the noise above was about. My trailing hand told me we had passed at least two doorways, but the Marauder led us on, down the hallway, around the corner, and into a larger room.

"Shit." The worried expression on Lace's face concerned me. That I could see her face at all concerned me even more. Light was coming our way from ahead, moving toward us from what appeared to be another hallway. As it neared, the details of the room we'd found ourselves in became clearer: mounds of refuse piled between elaborately carved stone columns. Above us was an arched and tiled ceiling that wouldn't have looked out of place in a palace or hotel ballroom.

Lace wove between the trash and the columns, leading us to the far end of the brightening hallway. She tapped Skaal on the chest, nodded to the hall, and then darted to the other side. Moments later, I could hear the coming irkonnen, their barks and growls translated into words by my trait, words that barely fit together to form coherent sentences.

Five seconds of listening was enough to banish any lingering concern I might have had about our recent one-party crusade against the creatures. Every other word out of their mouths was something foul, something bloodthirsty, or some unholy combination of the two.

The first three irkonnen passed between us. One carried a torch in its scaled grip, while the other two were armed with sharpened bones and their own natural weapons. Matted black fur covered the portions of them that weren't scaled, and their misshapen maws struggled to form the words I'd been listening to.

The fourth irkonnen took one step into the room, then stopped, its head turning up as it sniffed suspiciously at the air.

By then, it was too late. Skaal's axe took its head right off its shoulders as Lace jumped the other irkonnen from behind. Her slim sword pierced the throat of the farthest enemy, while her dagger buried itself in the back of the other. The torchbearer was still spinning about when my spear took it full in the chest. As it fell, Miko caught the torch.

I'd never impaled something so small before, so light that my strike lifted it clear off the ground. It was an uncomfortable feeling, like our roles had suddenly reversed and *I* was somehow the monster.

By the time I had recovered from my brief bout of existential guilt, Lace and Skaal were dragging the bodies behind one of the piles of trash, hoping to both hide them and mask their scent. I joined in, but it took a kick to remove the body from my spear.

"Another den," said Skaal, nodding to the trash piles.

"That makes three." Lace looked down at the bodies we'd stacked. "And a fourth crest too. What is going on?"

"Keep torch?" asked Miko.

"Yes," Mordecai and I said at the same time.

"I can't help if I can't see," added the Flameweaver.

Lace nodded. "That's fine. We're far enough away from the stairs that any pursuit won't see the light anyway. And if they did, they might think it was just another patrol like this one. But we must keep moving."

The ballroom we had found ourselves in had only two exits, the hall we'd come in through and the one our latest victims had traveled down. Lace took us into the latter, blades still in hand. Skaal was a wall at her back, followed by Miko and the torch, Mordecai, and then me. Now that I could see, I realized the halls had been built to a different scale, wide enough that Riok's spear wouldn't touch both walls, and tall enough that Skaal could walk without hunching over.

As the others had said, the irkonnen must have moved in sometime after this place had fallen.

A long time after, I decided, passing another doorway that was missing its door. Every open room we encountered slowed us down, with Lace darting inside to inspect it before we passed. I could hear more distant yipping, irkonnen calling to each other with messages of blood and pain. So far, we had stayed ahead of pursuit, but I didn't know how long that would last.

Stripped of furniture and decoration, there was no way to know what purpose the basement level might have once served. All I knew was that it was at least as large as the island above. The whole space was despoiled, not just with trash, but urine and feces and tufts of fur left like territory markings on the floor and walls.

We passed through a half-dozen more intersections before our hall ended in another open space. Light from Miko's torch spilled across cracked tile floors and more of the same columns we'd seen before. The obvious difference between this room and the banquet hall was the lack of piles that I had come to realize served as communal beds for an irkonnen den. Even the usual supplementary filth was gone, the tile floors clear even of dust.

We stared at that strangely clean floor for a solid minute as the baying of our pursuit slowly strengthened.

"Do you see anything?" Mordecai asked Lace.

She shook her head. "Nothing. The floor's swept clean even past the entrance."

"Maybe we've made it past the irkonnen territory?"

"That doesn't explain the lack of dust."

Skaal spoke to me in Gorash. "May I see your spear?"

It would leave me with only a knife, but I passed it over. Whatever plan he had was probably better than listening to Lace and Mordecai argue some more.

The half-giant gripped the spear near the bottom of the shaft and extended the weapon into the room, letting its head lightly scrape against the tile in a short arc a good eight feet from the door. When nothing happened, he pulled the spear back and repeated the motion at five feet then two then at the hallway's threshold.

"Is solid," he said in Trade, handing me back my spear.

"And if anything's waiting to jump out at us, it's smart enough to recognize a spear instead of a meal," added Mordecai.

Lace nodded. "We're headed in and through. Keep quiet."

We were halfway across when the bundle of nerves I associated with *Danger Sense* lit up. Lace was already darting ahead, but Skaal and the others heard my hissed warning. They turned and looked at me as I tried to identify where the sensation was coming from.

Not ahead, where Lace had already abandoned the circle of Miko's torch. Not behind, where the irkonnen could still be heard. It was more… to the right, but also…

Up.

I waved to Miko who raised the torch in the direction I indicated. About fifteen feet away, wedged between ceiling and wall, was a bulbous mass, like a cancerous growth somehow extracted from the body and grown to superhuman proportions. It twitched under the light of Miko's torch, and it took me far too long to realize those twitches were black eyes, opening and closing.

The mass peeled itself open, and something emerged, something with a hundred staring eyes and no legs. It started to slide down the wall with an audible slorp, the movement almost hypnotically smooth.

"Run," whispered Mordecai, eyes wide behind his mask.

Even as he spoke, a similar squelching noise came from the other side of the room, like a wet mop being dragged across a cracked laminate floor. Then a third, from the far corner.

We had never been a particularly stealthy group to begin with, but we abandoned all efforts on that front as we tore our way across the room. Lace was waiting for us in the hallway, her eyes momentarily reflecting the light like a cat's. She blanched at whatever she saw in the darkness behind us.

"Fire barrier, Mordecai."

"There's no fuel! It will burn itself out in less than a minute."

"We need that minute!" She was already sending Skaal past her and down the tunnel.

The Flameweaver nodded and ran his hand through Miko's torch, scooping up a handful of fire. The flames in his hands quickly grew to dwarf that of their original source, and then he spun back to the room we had just departed.

Dark, disfigured shapes slithered toward us, each different from the next. Despite our speed, they were only a dozen feet away.

Mordecai passed the flame from one hand to the other and those fires doubled. "Back away," he warned us. "Fire wants to expand. I'll do my best to push it toward them, but…"

We scurried down the hall. The encroaching *things* were now ten feet away, now eight… each a mass of glistening skin and too many eyes. There were no mouths to see, but I could almost hear a whisper above the sound of their own locomotion, discordant consonants chained together into syllables that made no sense but scratched and clawed at my brain.

Mordecai didn't say anything. He didn't even stand up straight. He just flicked his wrists and unleashed the fire in his hands, not at the monsters creeping closer, but at the stone between him and them, at the mouth of the hallway we'd retreated down. Flames struck the cracked tiles and sprouted up like weeds, weaving together to form first a gate, then a wall.

Then he turned and sprinted after us.

"I didn't use *Overload*," he wheezed, slotting back into his place in the formation. "Something tells me we're going to need it later."

We ran. Deeper and deeper we ran. On and on, taking turns at random as we tunneled into the unknown. Minutes passed with nothing but harsh breaths to accompany the sound of boots on stone. It started to feel like we'd somehow slipped into a parallel dimension of endless halls and empty rooms… right until the wall in front of us put an end to that fantasy.

"Double back," said Lace, turning away from the unanticipated dead end. "We'll go straight at the fork this time."

"What *were* those things?" I asked. My fifteen Vitality had kept me upright through our desperate flight, but Miko and I were both sucking wind, and Mordecai was clutching his side.

The Flameweaver found it in himself to answer. "There were far worse kinds of blighted created than irkonnen, lad. Now you've met one of them, gods help us all."

"Less talking, more running," snapped Lace, heading back down the passageway we'd just taken.

We were almost to the mentioned fork when something lashed out at Miko from the door of a room we'd already cleared once. The synossian barely dodged, throwing herself to the floor, and her torch fell, scattering hot sparks. Before she could climb back to her feet, one of the creatures we'd been fleeing oozed into the hallway. Its rubbery skin secreted some kind of fluid even as the greater mass of its body reached with makeshift limbs toward the fallen Priestess.

A wave of fiery darts struck, and the pseudopods shivered, the almost inaudible whisper in my mind swelling into a cacophony of voices shouting nonsense. A flood of new tentacles darted toward Mordecai instead, and the Flameweaver had to abandon a second casting to dodge the assault coming his way.

I used every bit of my eleven Strength to haul Mordecai back, pulling him out of the way of another two tentacles he hadn't seen. I heard him stumble and fall behind me, but didn't have the time to check on him, not with the creature amping up its assault. For the first time since entering the ruins, the length of my weapon became an advantage, allowing me to strike at incoming tentacles while staying out of range of the blighted's counterattacks. The monster didn't bleed, but it did seem to feel pain.

Given the way its tentacles shaped and shifted and reformed at will, I had to assume any vitals the creature might have would be in the center mass, where all the eyes were located. Unfortunately, even with the spear, I couldn't commit myself without getting in range of those tentacles.

A looming figure announced Skaal's entrance into the fray on the creature's far side, the axe in his hand humming as he wielded it one-handed, whipping it back and forth to hack apart the tentacles coming their way. Lace was a smaller shape in the reaver's shadow. She threw one of her daggers, multiplying it in mid-flight with her unnamed technique, and all five weapons hit home, eliciting fresh spasms from the monster in our midst.

A *Flare* burst into existence almost right in front of the creature, but other than a few bulbous eyes squeezing shut, it didn't react at all. Still, Miko was in motion, scampering toward me where she dove and rolled past my constantly shifting spear. She'd left her pack behind, next to the fallen torch, but the creature seemed disinterested in either.

Another wave of darts, this time coming from over my shoulder, landed home with far greater effect, the attacking tentacles slowing for just a moment as the voices that weren't voices swelled in my head.

And that gave me a really shitty idea.

"Can you hit it again, Mordecai?" I was shouting, trying to be heard over the auditory hellscape the creature had unleashed on us. If the man replied, I couldn't hear it, but I felt him pat my shoulder. Heat bloomed along my left side as more burning darts streaked forward, but this time I charged with them, a half-second behind their flight.

It was a lot like rushing headfirst at a hornet's nest—only even dumber than that—but as a dozen tentacles reoriented on the target I presented, Mordecai's spell struck home. Those same appendages stiffened, for half a second, and I slid between them to drive my spear home.

Center mass, bulging clusters of eyeballs, lots of momentum, and a weapon far tougher than bronze… even without *Lunge*'s force multiplier, my thrust drove deep into the creature's body.

Unfortunately, despite the damage I'd done—and I hoped like hell it was significant—the gelatinous monster was still alive. All those tentacles that had gone rigid with Mordecai's attacks surged back into motion, collapsing on me like a fisherman's net.

I dropped to one knee, dodging the first of too many blows to even see, let alone count, and looked back over my shoulder. Miko was just taking a step past Mordecai, short staff in her hands as she rushed to my aid, while the Flameweaver was beginning a spell that would arrive far too late.

But next to them both was an empty space, clearly visible, with nothing between me and it.

I triggered *Lunge* and flew backwards, pulling my spear with me as I went. I reached my target destination, caught my heels, and tumbled to the ground, but I was whole, and I was out of the blighted thing's trap.

Practice might not have made perfect, but it had kept me alive.

Skaal and Lace took advantage of my distraction, crowding in close and cutting through wayward tentacles. Before the creature could regroup, Lace's slim sword pierced the main mass and at least two clusters of black, staring eyes, followed almost immediately by her dagger. Then the reaver's axe swept in, tearing a rent in the creature as long as one of my legs.

Those strange voices in my head hit a fever pitch then went blessedly silent. The blighted collapsed like a popped balloon, the stone beneath it hissing as it the creature consolidated into a single mass and then slowly spread across the tunnel.

Before I could so much as slump over in relief, Miko was pulling me to my feet. "We must go, nest-brother," she murmured in the High Tongue. "There will be more on the way."

We retrieved her pack and the still-burning torch, stepped around the spreading corpse of the latest monster sure to figure prominently in my nightmares, and headed on. Nothing awaited us at the fork, but we could hear the war cries of enraged irkonnen creeping ever closer.

"Will they enter the territory of the other blighted?" I asked Mordecai, steadying him as he stumbled on loose stone.

"I don't know," came his reply. "Irkonnen bloodlines are bred to hate each other, yet here they seem to be working together. Who's to say if the same holds true for the essoli?"

Essoli was a pretty name for something that looked like the byproduct of a giant slug and an extra-dimensional hell beast with nothing but eyes.

I tried keeping all my senses active as we ran… not just my hearing and sight, but also *Danger Sense*. I didn't think the blighted counted as animals, but I tried tuning in to *Animal Behaviorism* too, just in case I was wrong. Any warning or hint might be the difference between life and death.

When our tunnel terminated in a small room with no other exits, it started to feel like we were just delaying the inevitable. The chamber we had found ourselves in was roughly ten by ten and empty of furniture. The far wall was decorated by a faded mural, while the near walls were simple, unrelieved stone. Above us was more of that blank stone.

Lace went to check the mural, while Skaal removed his pack and turned to face the hallway. The threshold was narrower than the hall itself had been, about five feet wide instead of eight or nine.

"Make stand here," he said.

That wasn't a plan, it was a death sentence. I wracked my brain to think of an alternative. There were other intersections we'd flown through on the way here, but all of them were back on the other side of the essoli nesting room, and to get there, we'd have to fight through more of those monsters plus hundreds of irkonnen. We could try to bring the tunnel down… but then we'd just have to deal with tons of rock and limited air in addition to all our other problems.

"Lace should use *Night Hag's Embrace*," I suggested instead.

"And when Hashoggath comes for you? What then?" asked the Marauder.

"I guess we'll find out. It's better than *everyone* dying, right?"

She shook her head, turning back to the mural. "The technique lasts five minutes… ten at the most. When it fades, we'll be right here, in the exact same situation, but down a party member. That's not happening."

"Is not," agreed Miko, shooting me a hard look.

A hiss drew our attention to Skaal, who was examining his axe. The weapon's half-moon edge was warped and pock marked. Even as I watched, it eroded further.

"Sorry, lad," said Mordecai. "The essoli's internal fluids are acidic in nature. I suspect our fearless leader's blades are similarly damaged."

A sudden bout of cursing, in a language that was neither Gorash nor Trade, confirmed that fact.

I looked to my spear, but it remained unchanged… dark, stained, and unlovely, but unchanged.

"If we live long enough to reach a city, you *have* to get that thing identified by an enchanter," said Mordecai, following my gaze.

Skaal nodded in agreement, hooking his ruined axe back on his belt. "Miko, can I use staff? I have skill."

"Yes, of course." She passed him her short staff, which looked like a baton in the half-giant's huge hands.

"Thank you. I will take front. Brian, use spear to strike from left side. Mordecai—"

"Wait!" Behind us, Lace had dropped to one knee, fingers tracing the mural's surface. "I think I found something!"

"What?"

If the answer was *more ancient artwork*, I was going to be deeply disappointed.

"One second."

I held my breath, eyes fixed on the dark hallway as my senses tried to gauge how far away the sounds we were hearing might be. They were unquestionably coming closer, and the irkonnen sounded like they might have already passed through the essoli nest.

Somehow, we'd discovered the one place where all the blighted had found common ground in their hatred of people like us.

I almost missed the click, but Lace's cry of delight had me spinning around again. A vertical crack in the wall had appeared, running from the floor to about three quarters of the way up the ceiling. The Marauder eyed the crack for a second, took three big steps to the left, and pushed on the wall.

The crack widened, becoming a massive pivot door. Behind it, more stairs descended into the darkness. A breeze from below carried the scent of something sweet and vaguely spiced up to us, a callback to better times, when I wasn't permanently stained with swamp sludge and standing in an underground warren filled with monsters.

"I told you I'd find a way forward," said Lace, smile briefly reaching her eyes.

"Can we close it behind us?" asked Miko, ever practical.

The other woman nodded. "It looks like it. We might even be able to jam the mechanism so nothing can follow us. Neither the essoli nor the irkonnen seem particularly smart, but who knows what *else* might be lairing up here."

"Or waiting below," said Mordecai.

"Better the danger we don't know than the certain death on our heels."

That... wasn't how the idiom went on Earth, but it was hard to argue with.

"Come on, old man," she called to Skaal. "Save the desperate last stand for another day."

59

When we'd first seen the ruins from afar, I would never have suspected there was a subterranean city below… and now we were on the second level of that city. With the secret door wedged shut behind us, and our pursuit at least momentarily lost, I felt the first stirrings of excitement. We were entering a level that had seemingly escaped the blighted's presence to this point. Which meant two things: less disgusting filth… and a high possibility of treasure.

I wasn't sure which of the two excited me more.

Both Lace and Skaal were down their primary weapons—the Marauder's blades having fared even worse against the essoli's acid than the reaver's axe—but she still had her brace of daggers, while he held Miko's short staff. The reaver also had Tempest on his back and a long knife at his belt. Mordecai had used up a fair bit of his energy fighting the essoli, and we were all varying levels of tired… but we were also all uninjured. And Miko had so far only cast a single *Flare*.

As a party, we were about as prepared as we could hope to be, three levels into a dungeon none of us had anticipated.

By the time we reached the bottom of the new stairwell, Lace was already gone, ranging ahead to look for potential dangers. She came back soon after and huddled up with the rest of us. "There's a hallway leading off to the left and right," she said. "It extends twenty or so paces each way before turning right and left, respectively. There are doors—intact and wooden—on what would be the outer wall of the hallway, but I haven't checked inside any of those rooms."

"Any sign of people?" asked Mordecai.

"It's clean, and there's light coming from around the bends. Between that and the doors that must have been replaced, it's a sure bet something lives here, but who or what I couldn't say. If I'm going to scout through well-lit corridors, I want the party at my back."

Skaal's grunt made it clear he approved.

We followed the Marauder into the hallway. It was dark, but as she had mentioned, light spilled around the far corners. The floor here was tiled, just like the previous level, but clean in a way that the irkonnen warrens would never be again.

Lace took us left. There were two doors on the outer wall, about halfway between the stairwell and corner, and we stopped at the first. No light or sound came from within, which I'd recently learned meant nothing at all. I focused on *Danger Sense*, straining to feel if there was any threat within.

Either the room was empty, or my skill was as flaky as ever. I gave Skaal a nod, and the reaver carefully turned the handle. It wasn't locked and the door swung inward.

Lace darted past the reaver, blades at the ready, but the room was empty except for a low cot and the crudely crafted chest at its foot. A padlock held the container shut.

"A bedroom?" Mordecai's frown could be heard if not seen. "What is this place?"

Honestly, the size and lack of furnishings reminded me of the living quarters back at Miko's shrine.

"Miko, please hold the torch close by so I can see. The rest of you, watch the hall," said Lace, returning both daggers to their respective sheaths and kneeling at the chest. After a brief examination of its lock, she pulled a small cloth square from under her leathers. It unfolded several times to reveal carefully stored bronze wires of varying sizes. She picked up one of medium thickness and inserted it into the lock.

"What are you doing?" I asked her.

"Getting this open. Locks like this exist to keep out idiots, not talented amateurs, let alone true professionals."

"Is there a *Lockpicking* skill associated with it?"

She sighed and gave me a look. "Yes. It's a Major skill for Rogues, but even with it nearly maxed, it requires focus."

"Right." I coughed. "I'll watch the hall with the others."

"Good."

"…but if we make it back to Madea, I want to learn the skill."

She paused, considering. "Only if you pay for my drinks for the next seven-day after our return."

I traded glances with a silent Miko.

"The next seven-day after I learn the skill," I countered. This could get pricey—and I was already starting to rack up enough skills that simply keeping them all from degrading would be a full-time job—but *Lockpicking* seemed too valuable to pass up. I just hoped Lace was better at teaching it than she had been with knives.

"Deal." Her smile caught the light of Miko's torch. "Now get out of the way. You're blocking the light."

Mordecai was seated on the floor opposite the cot, leaning back against the far wall, but Skaal stood at the door. I joined him there.

"You should have talked her down to a single night of drinking," he murmured in the language only he and I knew. "Most locks require far more than ten points in *Lockpicking*… and those that *can* be picked with the General skill succumb to a high Strength just as easily."

"That would have been good to know ten seconds ago," I murmured back. "Still, you never know when it could end up being useful. And I'm curious how or if it will impact the technique or class evolution choices I'll eventually be offered."

I don't know what the reaver thought about that, because before he could reply, there was an audible click behind us, and an even more audible scraping of metal against metal, as Lace undid the padlock.

"Robes," she said, and we could all hear the disappointment in her voice. A soft jangle of metal changed her tune. "And a purse. Looks like it's all copper bits, but there's also…"

"Also what?" I left Skaal at the door, abandoning my assigned post for the second time in as many minutes. The Marauder had tucked her lock picks away and now held a threadbare velvet pouch in one hand, a handful of glittering copper bits in the other. Among those bits was a small copper ring. She poured the bits back into the pouch and held up the ring. It was a simple band, but there was an inscription on the inside:

Steppin's Skirmishers.

Lace wiped away a fleck of what appeared to be dried blood. "The other party must have made it this far. Either that or whoever dwells down here has figured out a way to trade with the blighted above."

"We didn't see any bodies in the warrens," I reminded her. "Other than the ones *we* created."

"Nor would you," said Mordecai from his slumped position against the wall. "The blighted eat the dead. Theirs and anyone else's. And the essoli don't even leave behind bones."

If reincarnation was still a real thing on Eos, I hoped whoever had created the blighted was forced to spend their next seventy lifetimes as a phloxl.

"Should assume inhabitants hostile," said Skaal.

"I was going to do that anyway." Lace tucked the ring back into its pouch and added the pouch to her pack. "Let's go. If all the side rooms are like this, I suggest we come back and hit them once we've cleared the floor."

That made sense. I didn't want to pass up any copper, especially given that I'd just agreed to pay Lace's bar tab, but we needed to deal with potential threats first. *Especially* threats that had possibly wiped out the entire party from Steppin's Skirmishers.

Lace replaced the clothes in the chest and clicked the padlock shut again, then slipped past Skaal and back into the hallway.

I pulled Mordecai to his feet. "How are you doing?"

"I could do with a nap, lad, but I'll survive. I had harder days than this just preparing for exams."

If he could talk about the Crimson Needle, he was doing just fine. I followed Miko and him out the door, and the four of us trailed Lace down the hall.

The second door was also unlocked and opened onto a room that could have been the twin to the first. Lace hmmed as she looked over another locked chest but left it alone to continue down the hallway.

We stopped just before the turn. The Marauder lowered herself to her belly and crawled forward. Her lockpicking pouch came back out and this time she folded back another layer to reveal a piece of mirrored glass. Holding it cupped in the palm of her hand, she angled the glass so it pointed around the corner.

A moment later, she stood back up, glass still in hand. "Empty," she said. "For now anyway."

"Should I douse torch?" asked Miko. The passageway ahead seemed well lit enough to make it redundant.

"Yes. We don't need it and the smoke could give us away."

Instead of using even more of his energy to trigger *Flame Manipulation*, Mordecai simply wrapped his bare hands—fingers bronzed and callused—around the burning torch head, smothering the flame and robbing it of oxygen. When he opened his hands again several seconds later, only smoke remained.

He shrugged at my look. "I would be a poor Flameweaver if I hadn't made passive fire resistance a priority."

I'd read that elemental Mages got resistance skills pertaining to their element, just like I, as a Warrior, had been blessed with the joyous experience that was *Pain Tolerance*, but this was the first time I'd seen it in action… or realized Mordecai had advanced his skill.

Next time I had an overly hot plate, I knew who to call.

Miko retrieved the torch, now just a smoldering stick, and we finally turned the corner. The new hallway looked a lot like the old, only more visible, thanks to the two globes of light floating about eight feet above the floor. Far in the distance was another corner with another right-hand turn.

"They have Mages," warned Mordecai, pointing at the globes "And enough of them to waste at least one person's energy simply keeping the area lit."

"Then where are they?" I wanted to know.

"There's only one way to find out," said Lace. "Keep moving."

This time, there were a half-dozen doors on the exterior wall, and still none on the interior. Lace checked each room as we passed it but found them to be clones of the first and equally empty.

Meanwhile, I was doing the math. Not counting the stairwell door, the previous hallway had had four doors—two on each side—all of which had presumably opened onto similar rooms like these. Added to the six in our current hallway, that made ten. If the other hallway was the same, that would make for sixteen small bedrooms on this level alone. *Twenty* if the hall we were approaching mirrored the first. To say nothing of what, if anything, was in the inner space the halls were skirting about.

Twenty rooms meant twenty chests, all with some small chance of treasure, but it also meant twenty *people*, at least some of whom were, as Mordecai had said, Mages. Unless we could split them up and ambush them like we had the bandits, I wasn't liking those odds.

It only made my original question that much more pertinent. *Where were they all?*

We stopped again at the corner, mindful of the way the lights sent our shadows skittering in front of us, and Lace repeated her mirror trick. When she stood, she was shaking her head.

"Still empty."

She was right. We turned the corner and found more light globes, another hallway, and… no people. There were five doors in the outer wall, mirroring the hall we'd first found ourselves in on this level, but they were joined by an open set of double doors at the midpoint of the interior wall.

We'd made it about ten feet when Lace stopped again.

"I hear something," she said.

It was another few feet before Miko nodded that she heard it too, and even more feet before I joined the party. It sounded like… chanting?

"Is coming from the inner door," said Miko.

The Marauder nodded. "I think we've found our missing inhabitants. Stay quiet and I'll investigate."

There wasn't anywhere for us to go, so the four of us just kind of lurked there, out in the open, as Lace crept toward the open doors. She came back moments later, eyes wide.

"Thirty or forty people, mostly human, wearing robes. I don't know what language they're speaking, but they seem to be holding some kind of a ceremony. There's an altar up on a platform, a disfigured body lying on that altar, and channels in the floor carrying the body's blood towards a hole in the center."

"Cultists." I breathed the world like a curse. It had been months now since I'd wrongly believed I had been kidnapped from my Ohio double-wide by cultists… and yet here they were.

"Certainly sounds like it, lad," whispered Mordecai, turning back to Lace. "Any indication of which god or gods they worship?"

She shook her head. "The room's otherwise a lot like the quarters we've passed. No decoration at all."

"Thirty is too many to fight," said Skaal.

The Marauder nodded. "I think at least half are Tin too. And the person standing at the altar might be higher. We need to be gone before the ritual ends."

"We can't go back to the warrens," said Mordecai.

"Unless the hall we skipped branches off, thirty people would require more rooms than exist on this level," I said.

"Which would mean there's yet another level below us," agreed the Flameweaver. "But I haven't seen any more stairs."

Miko pointed to the door opposite the open double doors. "If is like stairs up, then stairs down would be there."

She was right… if this hall mirrored the first, the four rooms on either side would be bedrooms, but the fifth door in the middle would hide a stairwell.

"How do we get there without being seen?" I asked.

"Only the leader is facing the doors," said Lace. "And he's up on a raised platform with the altar. If we hug the far wall and keep silent… maybe we can sneak through? That's assuming there *are* stairs there."

"We could take the long way around and check to see if that other hall is different, but—"

"But we don't know when this ritual is ending. I know." She blew out a breath and nodded at me. "Okay. Follow my lead and stay as close to the left wall as you can."

We crept down the hallway, and the noises became more distinct: wordless chanting and above their murmur, a commanding voice. *Speaker of Tongues* had no problem translating the latter, and I listened intently, trying to remember the words in case they would prove important later on.

For the most part, it was like being back in church, post-communion, listening to the priest give his homily. A *sermon*, if one that seemed more focused on bloody payback and some kind of return than anything I recalled from my time at St. Augustine's. There were a few words that *didn't* translate, which almost had to be names.

I kept one ear tuned to the sermon and watched Lace slow as we neared the open doorway. The Marauder was a wraith, flitting through shadows that shouldn't have hidden a dust bunny. She slid past the closed door, the meeting room and all its occupants at her back, and eased the portal open.

It pulled outward, which was far from ideal, but she widened it just enough to slip inside. A moment later, she was back, face still turned downward to hide the whites of her eyes. She gave us a single nod.

We had our path forward.

We crossed in front of the open double doors one after the other. Skaal went first even though he was the most obtrusive. As soon as he had cleared the sightline of the double doors, Lace was urging him in through the partially open stairwell door. Miko, with her white scales, was next to go, and I held my breath the whole time, certain the sermon-giver would look up, or one of the other cultists would happen to look behind them at that precise moment.

Instead, she, too, disappeared into the stairwell, and I remembered to breathe again. Mordecai didn't have any issues either, and then Lace and I were the only ones left in the hallway, the Marauder on the far side of the doors, with me still having to cross.

A loud sound rang from within the meeting room, like a clash of cymbals or…

Or a gong, I realized, as it came again.

The chanting had risen to a crescendo and was starting to die down, which could mean only one thing. The ritual was almost over.

Lunge was many things, but subtle wasn't one of them, so even though it would get me to where I needed to be faster than anything else, I couldn't risk it. Instead, I scuttled forward, hunched over to try to minimize my size. With each step, I tensed, waiting for the scream or shout that would signal my discovery. Then Lace's hand was on my arm, and she was turning me about and pushing me in front of her as we both entered the stairwell. The door shut behind us again.

Another bong rang out, now faintly muffled.

"We have to go," whispered Lace. "Down. Now."

60

Thankfully, *this* stairwell was well lit. We rushed down past two landings, curving around as we went, and burst out the door at the bottom, where Skaal bowled over two robed figures who had apparently been left to stand guard.

I don't know if they were unranked or just unprepared, but before either had found their feet again, we swarmed them like the cutters that called Snake River their home. One died without making a sound. The other managed a choked gurgle as he tried to scream through a throat Skaal had just collapsed.

"There's no hiding this mess, lass," said Mordecai, looking down at the scrapheap we'd made of two people. "Our presence here won't be a secret for long."

"We'll go left again," said Lace, barely listening. We were in another hall, almost identical to the one we'd just left, right down to the four other doors. "With luck there won't be anyone else down here, but that advantage ends with the ritual. Kill anything that moves."

Skaal paused to toss Miko her staff, retrieving both of the spiked maces the dead cultists had been carrying. One went into his pack, but the other he held in his right hand. Like Miko's staff, it looked small when the half-giant equipped it.

I was beginning to wonder just how many weapon skills Skaal had advanced. He'd told me that maintaining a few wouldn't be problematic, but if you included his limited ranks in *Spear*, he was up to at least five.

There were fewer lights down here than on the floor above, with only one glowing orb per hallway, but otherwise the layout was eerily similar. We turned the corner and found the expected hallway with six doors on the outer wall. Nobody even suggested we stop and check them; we just pushed on, down to the next corner, where we made another sharp turn.

Five doors in the outer wall, one in the inner. It was a dead ringer to the hall we'd left on the floor above, just flipped. I pointed to the middle door of the five.

"Take the stairs again?"

Lace nodded, already racing towards it.

The problem was… when we reached it, it was locked.

The Marauder reached for her tools then shook her head as she got a better look at the lock. "Skaal?"

The reaver stepped forward, hefted his borrowed mace, and smashed it into the locked door. I wasn't sure which got the worst of the impact, weapon or hardwood, but a second blow told the story as wood splintered. He followed that blow with a kick from his size-twenty boots, and the door finally gave way, flying forward into the stairwell.

Only… it wasn't a stairwell.

"What the hells?" asked Lace.

Instead of yet another series of stairs, taking us ever deeper into the dungeon, we'd found a chamber that put the previous bedrooms to shame. Thick rugs covered the floor, still partly visible beneath pieces of door. A desk was set against one wall, a bed practically festooned with blankets sat by the other, and a small shrine stood between them, a single obsidian hand sprouting from the rough stone base to hold a copper bowl.

Miko looked in the bowl and then away again, just as quickly. Synossians didn't get nauseous, as far as I knew, but the Priestess looked positively green.

"This must be the leader's room," I said, stating the obvious.

"Does that mean there *are* no other stairs?" Mordecai almost definitely had a higher Vitality than I did, thanks to his level, but the man had also used a half-dozen techniques in the past few hours. It was no wonder he sounded tired.

"Could wait here, try to ambush leader, but…" Skaal nodded to the door he'd just bashed into pieces.

"What is in center room?" asked Miko.

We traded glances. According to Lace, the blood from the body on the altar was being channeled below… and that central room was directly below the space where the ritual was taking place…

So, the answer was almost definitely: nothing good.

On the other hand, it *did* have a functioning door.

Lace was already heading over, but I paused to scan the cult leader's quarters one more time. The chest by the bed had a lock as thick as my wrist, but the papers on the desk? They were out in the open, and I had a feeling that it wouldn't really matter what language or even cipher had been used to write them.

I'd made a habit of telling everyone in this strange new world of mine that knowledge was power; I wasn't going to change my stance now.

I swept the papers into a pile, shoved them into my pack, and checked the desk's two small drawers. One was empty, while the other held a velvet black pouch. It jingled when I shook it, a flash of silver inside, so I tossed it into my pack too. The party would thank me if we somehow survived. And if we didn't? Well, I would at least die rich.

I returned to the hallway to find the others clustered around the interior door. Lace was on one knee, running through a variety of key-like shapes with her bronze wires as she tried to trigger the lock's spring.

Someone shouted in the distance. They were too far away for me to decipher their words, but the alarm in that voice carried.

"I think we've just been found out."

"Then let's hope this room leads somewhere." The Marauder rose back to her feet, opening the now-unlocked door. "In. Now."

We rushed in and she turned to latch the door behind us. "Now then, what do…"

Her voice trailed off as she saw what we had.

The room we were in was wide and mostly empty. Blood poured through a hole in the ceiling, a thin waterfall that splashed into a deep basin in the floor. There were four obelisks around that basin, a chain and manacle bolted to each. Those chains reached all the way to the bloody basin, but for the moment at least, nothing was being held. Carved pictographs covered the walls around us, depicting scenes of violence and grotesquerie, and above us, circling the bloody waterfall, floated four glowing orbs, their light crimson rather than the soft white in the halls. The room had everything you'd want for performing some sort of deeply twisted ceremony.

What it didn't have were any other doors.

○○○

Lace cursed and turned back to face the hall. "I guess it's time for that desperate last stand, after all. Skaal, help me brace this door. The rest of you, look for anything else we can use."

Again, the parallels to my brief time in the Shrine of the Family were startling. It was almost like the last few months hadn't happened, and I was back in Miko's small chapel to Aurea, looking desperately for anything to help barricade the door with. And just like then, there wasn't anything that would help.

I looked over at Miko, curious if she was having the same bit of déjà vu, and found the synossian standing dead still, a few feet from the basin that already contained more blood than any one body could provide. Her bald, scaled head was cocked, and her transparent inner eyelids had come down over her orange eyes.

"What's wrong?" I asked her. "Beyond the fact that we're trapped in some sort of evil secret room with a few dozen cultis—"

"Shh!" She took a step away from the basin and cocked her head again, speaking in the High Tongue. "Do you hear that? I hear falling water."

I coughed. "There's literally a blood waterfall right there."

Her inner eyelids snapped open, and she shot me a look. "The noise comes from below, not above, nest-brother."

"Well, we're in the belly of a dungeon built into an island," I reasoned. "There's probably water beneath or around us. But it shouldn't be making noise like that, unless—"

"Unless it is finding its way inside somehow. Which would suggest another room nearby." She headed to the back wall and switched to Trade as she called out. "Lace! Can you look for secret door with me?"

"Another one?" The Marauder looked back from the door she and the half-giant were bracing. So far, nobody had attempted to enter. "I can try."

The two women hurried to examine the rear wall, running fingers or claws over the carved reliefs of terrible atrocities.

"What even *is* all of this?" I muttered, heading to the left wall to do the same.

"They are scenes from stories, lad," said Mordecai, coming to join me. "Either history or mythology, I know not which." He pointed to a series of carvings. "There is Prisoleth the Unclean, Goddess of Putrefaction. It tells the story of the plague she unleashed on Eos during the Godswar." He pointed to another series. "And that's Anno, one of many deities of warfare, slaying his own celestial children when they joined forces against Corros' revolt."

"These are all gods who rebelled?"

He scanned our wall. "Yes. Unsurprising to find in a cult that practices ritual sacrifice, I suppose."

I thought back to the words I had heard above. "Does the name Khamani mean anything to you?"

"Another banished deity." Once again, the mask hid his frown, but I could hear it in his voice. "I believe he was called the Ever-Hungry. A god of foul creatures, if a lesser one."

Eos had too damn many deities.

"Would the blighted have worshipped him?"

"They were created long after his banishment. Why?" he asked.

"Just trying to piece things together. The cultists were saying that name in the ritual above. And chanting something about his return and a new avatar."

He scoffed. "Dating back to the Godswar, there have been people trying to bring about their deities' return, lad. It hasn't happened yet, and it won't happen here. However…" He turned to Lace and Miko, his voice just loud enough to carry. "Look for images of Khamani, lasses!"

"Who?" asked Lace.

"A humanoid figure with no head, a mouth in its chest, and two more mouths in its palms." He dropped his voice, almost muttering to himself. "What story would a cult worshipping him want to memorialize on their wall of horrors?"

"Found him!" hissed Miko.

"What is he doing in the carvings?"

"Swallowing the sun?"

"Well, of course he—" Mordecai froze. "That's not right."

"What isn't?" I asked.

"In the stories, Khamani tried to devour Lakshi and Tirsa instead."

"The moons?"

"Exactly."

"Are you *sure?*"

"I am an *Adept of the Crimson Needle.*"

At the back wall, Lace was examining the carvings Miko had discovered. By the look of things, she wasn't finding anything.

"It's a puzzle," said Mordecai. "It must be! Look for a carving of the moons."

We passed the message on to Miko and then examined our wall of carvings. About halfway down and two-thirds of the way to the left, the sliver of a moon was represented in a carving of animals devouring one another.

"The turning of the beasts," murmured Mordecai. "Once their own creator was banished. But that was reputed to happen in a time of darkness, where neither sun nor moon dared to shine." He pressed on the crescent moon, and it slid into the wall with an audible click.

Nothing else happened.

"That didn't work," I told him.

"Because Eos has two moons. Look for the other!"

We found it on the third wall, sandwiched between two scenes that my mind refused to even comprehend. Mordecai didn't explain what either story was about, and I didn't ask. I just pushed the moon carving and waited.

A soft sound came from the back wall, and a door opened, thick stone sliding back to reveal another stairwell leading down.

Outside, the muffled pounding of boots could be heard, but nobody had tried our door just yet. Skaal abandoned his post and entered the stairwell with the rest of us. A panel on the far side of the door shut it again.

"I don't see a way to jam the mechanism," breathed Lace, "but if we're lucky, they'll canvas the rest of the floor before checking their secret chamber. And if the Night Hag chooses to spite our enemies instead of us, there'll be an exit below. Somehow."

Unlike previous stairwells, this one only had a single flight. The first landing was also the last. Lace and Skaal darted through the entryway, weapons at the ready, but there were no guards. As we joined them, I finally heard the water Miko had been talking about, trickling as if from a fountain.

That sound was almost enough to drown out the low moans coming from our right, where a series of barred doors had been built into the rough stone wall. I didn't want to go anywhere near whatever was making those noises, but the chamber, more cave than room and far smaller than either of the two ritual chambers above, had nothing else to see. And I *still* couldn't find any water.

"Blood and ash." The strange note in Lace's voice got me moving, joining the Marauder at the first of the cells. Inside lay a man, but his hands and feet had been removed, and every inch of his naked form was inscribed with bloody runes.

For a moment, we just stood there, staring in horror.

When the handless, footless body turned its head toward us, it was all I could do not to scream.

"He...lp..." His voice was weak, and the breaths he took turned a single syllable word into two. His eyes were open but would never see anything again. "...me."

Lace cursed again. "I know him. Jessup Ilsarn."

"From Steppin's Skirmishers?" asked Mordecai.

"The same." She fished out her lock picks and started in on the lock. "Brian and Mordecai, see if you can find the source of that water noise. Another false wall, a pit in the floor, anything. Skaal, guard the stairs. Miko, we're going to need your healing."

"I can't…" The synossian swallowed. "*Minor Healing* won't fix. No matter how many times I cast."

"I know." The Marauder's voice was hard, unflinching in the face of death and pain. "But maybe you can stabilize him. We don't know what he has seen or heard, but if any of it can help us…"

I squeezed Miko's shoulder, offering what comfort I could before I left to help Mordecai with our latest search. If this was what dungeons were like, I wasn't sure I wanted to be an adventurer anymore. Maybe I could lean into the whole *Scribing* thing instead and try to help the synossian people as a wealthy and influential Dedicated.

"What are we looking for, lad?" Mordecai asked me, his voice hushed.

"I have no idea. A way out, but…" The surrounding walls were rough stone, more cavern than room, as I had already noted. The floor was smoother, but empty of furnishings or décor. Other than the six cells in the near wall, there was nothing to see.

Almost nothing.

"What is that?" I pointed to an indentation in the far wall. From a distance, it looked like nothing more than a chip in the stone, but as we approached, I realized it had been shaped by human—or at least sentient—hands. It looked almost like a miniature version of the shrine we had seen in the cult leader's room.

It was Mordecai's turn to curse. "I've seen devices like this before."

"What is it?"

"It's a lock, keyed by blood, not a physical object."

"You just bleed on it, and it opens?"

He shook his head. "It would be a poor lock, if so. It's keyed to a specific person's blood. Or multiple people. In a place like this, it's probably keyed to the leader or to worshippers of Khamani in general. Either way, we're not opening it."

To prove his point, he took the dagger from my belt, pricked his own finger, and let a single drop of blood splash into the miniature bowl.

Nothing happened.

"Which means," he added, suddenly sounding ancient, "that we are trapped here. Come along; we should tell Lace before we join Skaal at the stairs."

The Marauder had the cell door open and Miko was inside, the glow of *Minor Healing* just starting to fade. The man—Jessup—wasn't breathing any more easily, but he seemed halfway coherent.

"Do you remember me, Jessup?" asked Lace.

"The… amazon?" He coughed and nodded, limbs twitching. "Should not have… taken your mission."

"It's a little late for that."

"My… party?"

Lace shook her head. "We've only seen one of them. I'm sorry."

The man sagged.

"We need to know if you saw or heard anything that can help," said the Marauder. "We need a way out."

"There's a tunnel… beneath," said the man. "The cult uses it to reach the mainland when they… don't wish to deal… with the blighted."

"Deal with the blighted? You mean they *are* working together?"

"They have… some sort of control… over them, but…" he coughed again, and this time, blood came up instead of phlegm. "…it's limited."

"We found the lock for the exit," I told Lace, "but Mordecai says it's blood bound."

"Then we'll have to bash our way through." She raised her voice. "Skaal! Leave the stairs. Look for a part of the floor that could be a trap door. We'll need to break through."

"If… you can… flee… take her with you." Jessup gave a small sigh and his head rolled back.

"More heals won't save," said Miko, her voice tight. "Might not even wake."

"What did he mean by *her*?" I asked.

"Another party member, maybe?" Lace shrugged. "I haven't heard anyone else stirring down here but check the other cells just in case. I'll help Skaal find our exit."

I gave Miko a hand and pulled her to her feet, and even though she was taller, heavier, and stronger than me, she let me do so.

"I will look, nest-brother. You join Mordecai by the stairs."

61-Interlude

Miko watched Brian turn away, the spear of Riok Diocil in his hands, and felt something in her soul twist. She and her nest-brother had come a long way, come further than any synossian in her era. It seemed unjust that their journey might end now, down in the darkness, at the hands of people worshipping a god long banished.

I am your servant in all things, Bright Lady, she prayed, *but I cannot see why you have brought us here or how the death of your Chosen will serve a purpose.*

Lace had found a thin, almost invisible crease in the floor, and marked out the wide edges of what had to be the tunnel door the other adventurer had mentioned. Unfortunately, even Skaal's tremendous strength was proving insufficient, his borrowed mace deforming against the floor. He called to Brian and tried with the Wind Walker's weapon instead, but though the spear held where bronze had given way, it was not the right tool for shattering stone. It would take days to carve a path through the floor when they didn't even have a glass.

Scales tight around her eyes, Miko tore her gaze from the tableau of futility. She'd been given a task, and she would see it done, even if it served no purpose. Even if it was the final thing she did before her demise.

The second cell was empty of anything but a smell. Death and blood and pain, much like Jessup's cell. The third cell was cleaner, but also empty, as were the fourth and fifth.

The sixth and final cell was different. It held a small bed and on that bed was an even smaller figure. She lay still, caked in dried blood, but her tiny chest rose and fell.

"I found…" Miko cleared her throat and tried again, switching to Trade so everyone would understand. "I found a child. A daughter of Corros, I think. She is alive."

Lace joined her a moment later, the Marauder's steps soundless even now. "What is a little girl doing in a place like this?"

Miko shook her head. "You think—*do* you think this is who Jessup meant?"

"It must be." Lace was already working on the lock. "Maybe we can't offer her the kind of escape he was thinking of, but Hashoggath take me if I leave even an unnamed in this cult's grip."

The door popped open and Miko followed the other woman inside. Beneath the blood, the girl's dress must have once been fancy, but it was torn now as well as stained. There were no visible wounds, but her pulse was thin and reedy.

Lace shook the little girl, the motion curiously gentle for someone like the Marauder, but got no response.

"What's wrong with her?"

"Know not," said Miko, too focused to worry about putting her words in the right order—or the wrong one, from her way of thinking. "Will try healing."

The Marauder stopped her. "How many heals do you have left?"

"Not enough for battle against so many enemy," Miko said simply. "Maybe girl can tell us more than Jessup."

Lace sighed and nodded. "Do it."

Dawn Maiden, prayed Miko, as she held her hands above the child's still form, *please give this little one your grace.*

Minor Healing triggered, and a glow formed, as usual, but as Aurea's blessing rushed through her and into the child, it was met by an opposing force, something slippery and slimy to Miko's metaphysical senses, almost like a concentrated form of the swamp sludge they had waded through to reach these ruins.

It wasn't poison—Miko knew what that felt like now. It wasn't disease or infection or anything natural. It felt almost like another god's presence, but for all that it had spread through the girl's body, it was thin and weak, more the film atop a cooling mug of kallnor than the kallnor itself. Miko focused and the energy of her spell surged forward, forcing the sludge back into the child's core, a finger's width below the ever-curious human navel. There, the foreign energy rallied, forming a walled fort even Aurea's light could not breach.

Minor Healing faded, and with it her connection to the child's body, but not before she could feel that dark energy trickling back out of the little girl's core. Its progress was slow and weak, but within a day or less, any gains from her healing technique would be undone.

A notification from the Framework formed in Miko's vision but she blinked it away, lifting the still slumbering child in her arms.

"Is she—" began Lace.

"Is alive. Has something wrong with her. Come. Quick." She carried the girl out into the small cave, past where Brian and Mordecai had turned to face the stairwell and where Skaal was still trying to open the trap door, now banging with his gauntleted hand instead of the spear Brian had reclaimed. The lock her nest-brother had spoken of was in the far wall and she carried the little girl to it before turning to the trailing Marauder.

"Prick finger. Use blood."

Lace sighed. "Your blood's not going to do anything, Miko. It's—"

"Not me. Her."

"What? You think *she's* a worshipper of this Khamani god?"

Miko shook her head. "Do not know. But has energy in her like when I use goddess-given blessings. Do not know where it come from or how, but—"

"But it might be enough to fool the lock."

Miko started to nod, then froze.

"Do fast," she said. "Think enemy just opened puzzle door."

Lace cocked her head, listening, and her eyes widened. "Skaal, we have incoming." A blade appeared like magic, and she extended the unconscious girl's hand over the lock's bowl. The tip of the dagger met the tip of a tiny finger, and a drop of blood welled forth. For a moment, it hung suspended, as if refusing to hear gravity's call… then it fell, splashing delicately into the bowl.

There was a click and then a rumble. Skaal's grunt sounded startled, as the floor he'd been trying to force his way through fell away of its own accord.

"I could kiss you right now," Lace told Miko, her grin wild and savage.

"Please don't," said the Priestess. "Am filthy."

62

I didn't see how Miko and Lace opened the locked door, but it couldn't have come at a better time. Okay… technically, any time *before* then would have been better, but I wasn't going to look a gift horse in the mouth.

A part of me wondered what Miko would do with *that* idiom.

As it was, the first pair of boots had only just appeared on the stairwell we were guarding. The cultists came slowly at first, perhaps uncertain if we were even down there. I literally speared the robed figure in the lead, Riok's weapon piercing cloth, leather, and the flesh beneath. The man's scream turned into more of a wheeze as I hit something vital, but as he stumbled, I withdrew the spear and thrust again.

Flame darts took the second cultist in the chest, and he fell back, trailing smoke. "We need to go before more come, lad!" said Mordecai. "I'll put up a barrier while I can."

I nodded. Miko and Skaal were already below, and as I watched, Lace emerged from the first cell with a storm in her eyes and blood on her blade. I wanted to join the others, but our experience with the essoli had taught me that Mordecai's barrier technique took more time than we had. "I'll guard you until it's up."

He swallowed and nodded, gathering fire in his hands. The stairwell was starting to fill with smoke, but I spotted another silhouette rushing down toward us. Whoever they were, they weren't Copper, and they weren't going to live long enough to reach Tin either… they ran onto my spear and died cursing.

I bent to pull my spear loose and dark, crackling energy blew through the space I'd just occupied. More figures appeared above, and the discordant glows told me techniques were being triggered.

"Mordecai!"

"Move!"

I ducked aside, and a wave of fire struck the base of the stone stairway, splashing upward to fill the entryway. The Flameweaver was panting heavily, but he helped pull me to my feet.

We ran to the hole in the floor where a worried Miko was waiting below. I ignored the ladder entirely and jumped down, my fall arrested by the synossian's strong arms.

"They are *right* behind us," I told her.

We both turned to watch Mordecai descend. He leapt like I had, only to go strangely stiff in mid-air. Instead of a controlled landing, he hit hard, his ankle giving way beneath him.

I was there in an instant to help the man up, but he staggered and leaned against me.

"Miko!"

She knelt before us both, hands stretched toward an ankle that was already swelling above the lip of Mordecai's boots. *Minor Healing* fixed what it could, and we dragged him along with us, down a tunnel lit by strange lichen rather than summoned orbs. Water trickled down the walls, seeping in through cracks that I kept expecting to suddenly widen and burst.

"We need to hurry," said Lace, manifesting out of the gloom. Skaal was a pale figure beyond her, and either I was going mad, or he was carrying a small child in his arms. She peered at Mordecai. "What's wrong with him?"

"He rolled an ankle," I said, "but Miko healed—"

The Flameweaver coughed and fell forward, dragging me down with him. I rolled him over and found the eyes beneath his mask had gone wild and unfocused. My nest-sister made a noise somewhere between a gasp and a sob, pointing to Mordecai's side.

There was a hole in his shirt and the flesh beneath, but it wasn't bleeding. Instead, it was *growing*, devouring tissue, bone, and clothing alike.

The glow of *Minor Healing* lit the tunnel, but nothing changed. The golden light of *Touch of Dawn* followed, with similar results.

"Leave it, lass," said Mordecai, his eyes regaining focus despite the pain. "The Ever-Hungry may be long-banished, but his magics remain as puissant as ever."

"How do we stop it?" Lace turned the man's masked face her way. "Use your book learning, damn it, and tell us what to do!"

"You need to *go*. All of you."

"What?" I stared down at him.

He twitched and when I looked down, I saw that the hole was still spreading. "There's no curing this, lad. No cure and no escape. Get yourselves to safety."

"Not without you," said Miko.

"I have only minutes left. And this is as good a place to end it as any. On my terms, the way it should be." He scowled at the water dripping down the walls, then shrugged his only working shoulder. "Take my pack, prop me up, and leave me behind. I will do what I must."

Lace's expression went empty as she helped the Flameweaver to a seated position, turning him to face back the way we had come. "Give us what time you can, Adept of the Crimson Needle. I swear your name will not be lost."

Mordecai's right arm dangled limply to the side, but his left rose to point down the tunnel, flame gathering about the outstretched fingers. The wound in his chest continued to widen. Still, he held steady, his voice a hoarse breath on the non-existent breeze.

"Go."

Lace went first, pulling Miko with her, the synossian carrying both her pack and the Flameweaver's. I moved to join them, but Mordecai's voice stopped me cold.

"Lad."

"Yes?"

The distant roar of his summoned flame barrier went silent, replaced by the angry shouts of cultists entering the room we'd just left.

"So little time", he muttered, eyes darting back the way we had come. "Still. I wanted to know…." His breath had deteriorated into wheezing, but the fire swelled, no longer orange but white, and so hot I could feel it in my lungs. "There is something… about you. Something… different."

It wasn't really a question, but I answered anyway, pitching my voice so it carried over the murmur of fires building. "I'm Chosen. Chosen by Miko's gods to save her people."

I could hear more sounds back down the tunnel, people climbing down after us.

"Huh." With a hole in his side, fire in his hand, and a mask covering his face, I could *still* hear the smile in his voice. "I always wanted… to meet a Chosen."

"This one owes you his life."

"Only if… you make it out. Use that… technique of yours to catch… the others." His cough this time was weirdly dry and hollow, echoing where it shouldn't. "This will be… a big one, lad, fueled by life as well as energy. I'll do… what I can to focus it, but fire… resents control. *It wants to be free.*"

The Flameweaver's outstretched hand had started to shake and the flames around it were changing from white to blue, too hot for me to withstand even a half a dozen feet away.

I didn't dare approach, so I just gave my best approximation of a Miko bow.

"Goodbye, Mordecai."

I turned and fled.

Lunge took me down the tunnel in a heartbeat's time and I continued on at a dead sprint. Moments later, fire erupted behind me, scorching everything and everyone in its path, and the man who had brought it into existence and then set it free breathed his last.

○○○

By the time I staggered out of the tunnel, scorched by hot smoke and nearly boiled alive by steam, the others were in combat, cutting down a small batch of irkonnen that had either been posted as guards or had the misfortune to be patrolling nearby. It was now Miko who was inexplicably carrying a small, sleeping, blood-covered girl, while Lace and Skaal swept through the overmatched opposition like a plague.

I'd barely finished coughing by the time they were done.

"Into the marsh," said Lace. "Follow my lead but stay close. We'll kill who and what we must but speed matters more."

I didn't have the breath to argue, not that I wanted to. Nothing that made it into the tunnel could have survived Mordecai's dying blast, but there were almost definitely still cultists alive. They'd have to either wait for the tunnel to cool or head back upwards through the multiple levels of dungeons and then through the ruins themselves, but if they *did* have some sort of control over the blighted, they had more than enough troops to just roll right over us.

We needed to get the hell out of here while we could.

The next few glasses blurred together into a few scattered scenes… wading and swimming through the marsh, hiding from the patrols Lace spotted, and killing the ones she didn't. I lost count of the number of dog-like humanoids I fed to Riok's spear, my arms moving of their own accord, every motion scraped to the bone as I pursued efficiency in the face of my own exhaustion.

Twice, we were forced to stop when the child in Miko's arms started to spasm. *Minor Healing* settled her down each time, but the blood-caked girl never looked any better, and Miko herself just grew more and more tired.

It had been morning when we emerged, somehow having spent a few glasses plumbing the depths of that terrible dungeon, but Lace led us late into the night. She might have kept going forever, but at some point, I took a step and my other foot refused to do its part. I face-planted into the murky marsh water, and only the reaver's grip kept me from slipping under completely.

After that, we found a spot to camp.

"Do what you need to do to commune with the Framework," said Lace, her voice hard and empty of emotion. "Then get some sleep. We'll rest long enough to regain our energy, but once we have, we're gone again."

Skaal looked like death warmed over, which was to say, his usual self, but any spark of mischief was gone. "Will keep tonight's watch."

"You need sleep too, old man."

He switched to Gorash. "Less than you, daughter of dusk, and what scant energy I have remains undiminished. There are some small advantages to my state."

"Fine." Lace didn't snap or growl. She didn't do much of anything. She just found a spot on the ground and closed her eyes. I couldn't tell if she was asleep or meditating.

Skaal looked down at her and shook her head. "Both should meditate and rest," he told Miko and me in Trade. "Long day. Hard day. Tomorrow will be brighter."

"Will you watch child?" asked Miko about the girl that nobody had bothered to explain to me yet. "Will heal again before sleep but if she stirs, wake me. Please. *Minor Healing* is only thing keeping her true."

The reaver nodded. "I will watch her and you and the camp. Whatever changes, I will be here."

I waited for Miko to settle into her meditation and then turned to Skaal.

"What did any of that mean? Keep her true? Who is the girl and where did she come from?"

"They found her in one of the cells," he replied in Gorash. "As for the rest… I don't know."

I blinked. "You don't?"

"All I know is that she was a prisoner of our enemy, her blood opened the lock, and she has none but us to keep her safe. That is enough."

I was way too tired to point out all the very many ways that that *wasn't* enough.

Instead, I nodded and copied Miko, finding a seat on the ground. I closed my eyes, offering a silent prayer to none and all of Eos' many and frequently horrible gods, asking for my meditation to go faster than usual so I could finally get some sleep.

Spoiler alert: meditation took exactly as long as usual.

Still, when I cracked open my weary eyes a full glass later, it was to find a now-familiar window in front of me:

```
You have increased the following skills:

Major skills:
Formations: [+5]: 10/25
Knife [+3]: 10/25
Light Armor [+2]: 22/25
Spear (U) [+4]: 24/25
Tactics [+4]: 16/25

Minor skills:
Athleticism [+3]: 23/25
Avoidance [+5]: 24/25
Focus [+7]: 8/25
Pain Tolerance [+2]: 22/25

General skills:
Danger Sense (R) [+1]: 10/10
Stealth [+3]: 8/10
```

I didn't have the energy to wonder why I'd gained points in *Knife* when I hadn't even used the weapon. I just dismissed the window, toppled over, and went to sleep.

And probably not in that order.

ooo

We slept through the night, and if anything threatened the camp, it didn't survive long enough to disturb us. The sun wasn't even in the sky yet when Lace roused us again.

A groggy Miko shot the other woman a glare before remembering the situation. The first thing the Priestess did was to check on the girl we had freed, another *Minor Healing* swiftly followed by a slow shake of her head and the tightening of scales around her eyes that I knew meant concern.

The second thing she did was to come check on me.

"Are you okay, nest-brother?"

I nodded. My lungs still felt like they'd been slapped on a grill and cooked low and slow for at least a day, but my cough had faded sometime in the middle of the night. "I'll be fine."

"Good," said Lace, handing out hard rolls from her pack. "Because it's still two days to the road and I want to make it in one and a half. We haven't seen any sign of pursuit yet but until we're free of this marsh, I'm not leaving anything to chance."

The Marauder sounded… better, if not great. Her voice was still hard, but emotion had started to seep back into it, like paint coloring the edges.

I planted my spear in the soggy terrain and pushed myself upright. "Agreed. Along the way, maybe one of you can tell us who the girl you freed was and why Miko has to keep healing her every few glasses too?"

"Will explain," promised Miko.

We adopted our usual formation, but even with me closing ranks so I was on the synossian Priestess' heels, there was an undeniable hole in our middle. I kept finding myself looking up, expecting to see Mordecai trudging along, the masked Flameweaver as eager to discuss the knowledge he'd gained at school as he was to find a way out of watch duty. Instead, he was gone. Only his pack, added to Skaal's usual burdens, showed that Mordecai had even been a member of our party. His body was lost forever, along with whatever else he'd had on him, burned to ash in the funeral pyre of his final spell.

At least he took a lot of them with him.

It didn't make his loss hurt any less.

Over the course of the next few hours, Miko explained what she could about the little girl, feeding me snippets of information whenever time and space allowed.

"I don't think *Minor Healing* is actually healing her," she admitted during a long stretch of halfway dry land, "so much as using the energy of the blessing to keep the… whatever it is… the taint… at bay."

"What does that mean?"

"I don't know." Miko shook her head. She was as tired as I was. More so, since she had to keep casting *Minor Healing* every few glasses just to keep our unconscious rescuee… well, *true*, as she had said to Skaal. "But," she added, her voice dropping to a whisper even though she was speaking in the High Tongue, "I received a Title for doing it!"

"You what?" Titles, I'd learned from Madea's deeply limited section on the Framework, were kind of like Traits, except the latter were granted at birth and revealed in the Dreaming, while the former had to be earned. "What was it?"

"Hand of the Dawn Maiden." For just a second, pure joy leaked out across her reptilian features, her smile wide and beautiful. Just as quickly, that joy was gone. I saw her eyes dart to the side, where Mordecai should have been. Her next words were sober. "I don't know what it does, but Aurea approves of our actions."

"She approves of *your* actions, Miko. And she should. You're a credit to the very idea of gods, just like those people back there were the absolute opposite."

A dialogue window appeared in front of me, cutting off my view of the white scaled Priestess.

NEW QUEST: Return the unnamed child to her home.

[Accept | Decline]

"Ok," I admitted. "Maybe she approves of *both* our actions."

"I am certain she does," said Miko, giving a firm nod as the matter was resolved in exactly the manner she had expected. "Wait… why did you change your mind?"

"Because I just got another quest." I shared the contents, limited though they were, then hit *Accept.*

"That means she still *has* a home," said Miko.

"That's true." Despite the brevity of the quest descriptions, Aurea—or more likely, Shan—did sometimes find a way to sneak in information we could use. "It also means you saving her was something your gods wanted us to do."

"Well, obviously." Miko cocked her head, looking at me so long that she almost tripped over a root for the first time since we'd left Madea. "We save who we can, when we can, and however we can."

"*Is what we do,*" I finished for her.

Synossians couldn't blush, but she dropped her head. "Is that really what I sound like?"

"I mean… kind of? But it's a good thing."

"How do you know?"

"Because I wouldn't be talking to a brand-new Hand of the Dawn Maiden if it wasn't."

Whatever she was going to say in response was cut off as we reached yet another stretch of marsh where everyone else had to wade and I had to swim. Still, the look she sent me was 50% gratitude, 50% humble satisfaction, and 100% Miko.

○○○

Another night passed, and all I gained from it was a single point in *Athleticism* and another in, for some reason, *Pain Tolerance.* Either I was blocking my aches and pains so well I didn't even notice them anymore, or the Framework was giving me unearned credit for dealing with *emotional* pain.

I was pretty sure it was the former, but who knew for sure?

On our third day, with the end of the marsh in sight figuratively if not yet literally, Lace finally decided we had left behind any possible pursuit. She didn't slow our pace, but she did relax enough to speak in more than short bursts of sentences.

When we finally reached the road, she even handed out extra rolls. They were hard and by that point even staler than usual, but I appreciated the gesture.

We got some seriously odd looks on our way back to Madea from the other travelers we encountered. I wasn't sure if it was the mud that was only now starting to dry and flake away, the blood stains then revealed beneath, or the eternally sleeping little girl in Miko's arms. Hell, it could have just been that we were a party consisting of a snow-white reaver, a so-called scaled, an obsidian skinned amazon, and a suspiciously short human with an overly long spear.

Add a masked Mordecai to the group and we really were a traveling menagerie, weren't we?

I gave myself a mental kick. I needed to bury Mordecai's memory in my mind, like I had my father's.

Grief could wait its time.

I didn't have to ask Miko to know what she would say to that… but she had her ways of dealing with things and I had mine.

63

Before we reached Madea, Lace finally agreed to us using the rest of the water to make ourselves halfway presentable. Only *halfway*, because some of that stuff wasn't coming off without a bath, a scrub, and possibly a power wash.

Of us all, Miko fared the best, thanks to her scales and stiff-bristled brush. Skaal fared the worst, because he'd been in the thick of most of the fighting and we didn't have anywhere near enough water for his seven-foot-frame.

Maybe being tall wasn't *always* a good thing.

We still got our share of reactions as we entered the town, but at least nobody was looking at us like we were returning home from an overly exuberant serial killer convention anymore. Henrik wasn't on duty and the guard who was just waved us through. We headed straight to the guild hall and found it even more sparsely populated than when we'd left.

As usual, Deputy Keeper Carlson was at his desk. The keeper looked as tightly wound and as sour as ever. He greeted us with a short nod.

"Another successful mission, I take it?"

"No," said Lace shortly, "and also yes."

He frowned. "Further explanation might be prudent."

Our party leader reached into her pack and tossed a guild badge onto the other man's desk. "We found Jessup and what was left of the party from Steppin's Skirmishers, but weren't able to clear the ruins. It would take a dozen parties to do so, or a literal army."

"There are only three parties left in Madea, including yours, and the duchy's sole army is currently invading Zaris," murmured Carlson. For the first time since we'd met him, he seemed concerned instead of just vaguely irritated. Sharp eyes scanned our party, and while Miko and I were mostly hidden behind Skaal, the fact that we were four instead of five was apparent. "Your Mage?"

"Mordecai didn't make it."

"My condolences. Truly. He was a man of education and intelligence." He cleared his throat and waved to the seats in front of his desk. "Sit. Please. The guild will want to know exactly what happened."

There were only two chairs and Skaal and Lace claimed them. Before the Marauder could speak, however, Carlson peered over them both at Miko.

"Why is your party member carrying a child?"

"We rescued her from the ruins," said Lace. "She was—"

The keeper raised his hand, cutting her off. "Start at the beginning, please. Leave nothing out."

When she was done, Carlson stared off into space for a long time. A frown sat easily on his narrow face.

"The wanderers who reported the ruins to the guild either vastly underrepresented the number of creatures at the ruins or more have gathered in the interim."

"The blighted had been there a long while," said Lace. "The cult even longer, by the looks of it."

"Is surprising wanderers survived finding ruins," added Skaal.

"Surprising… or suspicious," agreed the Marauder.

Carlson raised an eyebrow. "You think the reports were designed to lure adventurers to their death? For this cult of… who was it… Khamani?"

"They were gathering blood for something," she replied. "We saw one sacrifice, and I'm pretty sure Jessup would have been next."

It wasn't until Lace had recounted the story that I had understood the significance of her leaving Jessup's cell with a bloody dagger. Unable to bring the man with us, she'd at least ensured he wouldn't suffer any longer.

"And yet a small child somehow survived."

"She needs healing," said Miko, stepping forward. "Am—*I am*—helping as I can, but *Minor Healing* cannot cure what is wrong."

"There are two healers in town," said Carlson, voice softening slightly as he took in the sleeping girl in Miko's arms. "I'll summon one of them shortly. Do any of you have any idea what was done to her?"

We shook our heads. Lace had already described the room with the blood pool, the obelisks, and the manacles. Given that the sacrifices had occurred in the room above, it seemed likely that the second room had been used for something even more diabolical, but what it was, we didn't know.

Although…

"I have some papers I stole from the leader's room," I said, surprising everyone. "I don't know what information they might contain, but they could be useful."

"Well done. Unless we're truly lucky, those notes will require translation and even deciphering, but it is a start. In the meantime, please place the child on my desk."

"Are you sure?" Miko asked. "Is dirty. Girl, not desk," she hastily clarified, as the keeper's eyebrows rose in seeming affront.

"It's quite alright, though I appreciate the courtesy." The keeper moved two careful stacks of paper to another spotless portion of his desk, opening a space for the little girl.

"Carlson has a technique for cleaning," said Lace, and though the smile that crossed her face was small and short-lived, it was an improvement over the stone mask she'd worn since Mordecai's death.

"I am an Administrator," replied Carlson. "Cleanliness is a fundamental aspect of organization."

I could hear the capital-A in Administrator, which suggested he was speaking of his profession. Lace had said both he and Melligula were Dedicated, not Aspirants.

Miko laid the girl down on the table, one clawed hand brushing back curly hair that was now visibly blonde with most of the blood removed.

"Most of my gifts center around communication and management," continued the keeper, "but I have some small capabilities in analysis as well. With luck, I will be able to determine what is ailing the child without us having to decipher the notes your companion secured."

There wasn't a glow like when Miko used her blessings. Carlson just placed a hand on the little girl's forehead and closed his eyes. A moment later, the blood drained from his face. He opened his eyes again and stared down at the girl on the desk.

"Is it that bad?" asked Lace.

"What?" He shook himself, looking rattled for the first time. "No. I mean… I have no idea what is wrong with her."

"Then why do you look like you just found two dusk panthers mating in your tent?"

"Like *what?*"

"Surprised," said Skaal. "And also scared."

Carlson took a deep breath and finally tore his eyes away from the girl on the desk. "I suppose I'm both. Because while my abilities may not have told me what is ailing this girl, they *did* tell me who she is. And with Grand Duke Willerton's forces currently marching on the country of Zaris in retaliation for his heir's death, I did not expect that heir to be lying upon my desk, alive if not well."

"*What?*" asked Lace, speaking for all of us.

"This is Wilhemina Annerose Lakesia Willerton, the duke's eldest child, who has been missing and presumed dead now for over two moons. And not only is she not dead, she is nowhere near Zaris, and has—according to you—been held by a cult of the Ever-Hungry for an indeterminate length of time." He shook his head. "You want an army to cleanse the ruins? I guarantee this girl will get it for you. And her health has suddenly become my hall's top priority."

He took two blank sheets of paper off the rightmost stack, dipped his quill in the inkwell, and wrote out identical notes. He tapped both messages with his index finger, and in the sort of display that would have made an origami enthusiast faint, each page folded itself into the shape of a bird and flew off through the guild hall's open door.

"I've summoned *both* of the town healers," he said. "In the meantime, let's take a look at the documents you recovered."

Carlson still seemed like the kind of guy who would report you to the principal if he even suspected you of cheating, but I was beginning to understand why Lace didn't hate him. I put my pack on the floor and knelt to rummage through it, thankful that my pack was waterproof even if my clothes were anything but.

All told, I'd *rescued* almost two-dozen pages, far coarser than the paper Carlson was using, fronts and backs covered with hand-written script. I passed them over.

The keeper took one look and sighed. "As expected, it is written in an unfamiliar tongue. Likely a secret language known only among the sect. Deciphering it at all will be difficult, if not impossible."

Lace gave me a look.

"Actually…" I cleared my throat. "I should be able to read it."

Carlson stared at me over the slumbering body of the duke's heir. "Are you saying you're affiliated with the cult of Khamani?"

"Absolutely not. I just have a… knack for languages."

"He was originally planning to be a Scribe," said Lace, as if that explained my ability.

"I see." The keeper didn't look like he bought the explanation, but he always seemed borderline suspicious, so I didn't take it personally. "We should move Lady Willerton into a room upstairs, so the healers can treat her privately. And I will take another room with…" he looked at me, waiting.

"Brian. Brian Fieldings."

"Yes, Brian Fieldings, to review these pages and see what information can be gleaned from within."

"I go with girl?" asked Miko.

"Of course. We *know* your god's magic works to at least contain her condition. Until we determine whether the town's other healers can cure her or not, I want you with the heir at all times. The rest of you—"

"Are exhausted and fresh from the road," said Lace.

"Of course." He looked at us again and made a decision. "In fact, all three of you should bathe first… provided your Priestess is willing to wait with Lady Willerton?"

Miko nodded.

"You and I," added Carlson, speaking to me, "will reconvene in room seven upstairs, after you are washed, and the healers have arrived. Lace and Skaal, you may rest or join either group as you see fit. We will discuss the bounties you have earned soon enough, but for the moment, the duke's heir takes precedence." He paused, losing his brisk efficiency for just a second. "And I suspect Melligula will want to hear the tale of Mordecai's passing whenever she deigns to show up. The two were close in their way."

ooo

By the time I was done with my bath, I had gone through three tubs of water and almost a full chunk of what passed for soap in Madea. I was clean and warm and extremely sleepy. Nevertheless, I went to room seven, as Carlson had requested. Or ordered… I wasn't entirely sure how much the keeper's position gave him authority over the guild members.

If my *Speaker of Tongues* trait could help us figure out what was wrong with Wilhemina, I was going to put it to use. Mordecai hadn't died *for* the girl—not really—but her rescue and eventual return to Trynfall might be the one good thing to come out of the Flameweaver's sacrifice.

Carlson was waiting. He had spread the recovered pages across the room's wooden floor, and even though he couldn't read any of the text, had somehow arranged them in what appeared to be chronological order. Sharp eyes watched me as I picked up the first page.

"Translate it for me as you go," he ordered, "as close to verbatim as you can manage. We do not know what secrets might be locked inside specific word choice or usage."

A glass later, my throat was dry, my eyes were drooping, and the keeper looked significantly more disquieted than when we had started. According to those notes, the cult had been attempting to turn Wilhemina into a vessel, a physical anchor and avatar through which their banished god might return to Eos.

Why the duke's heir? That wasn't entirely clear, but the leader seemed to think that the nexus of two ancient bloodlines in Grand

Duke Willerton and Wilhemina's mother—the duke's now-dead first wife—held a special significance to the Ever-Hungry… making the little girl both a particularly suitable candidate and an attractive lure.

"There hasn't been a divine avatar walking the physical realm since the Godswar," Carlson had said, staring so fiercely at the page in my hand that I halfway expected it to burst into flame. "It has been over five hundred years even since the last Chosen was found, and *they* died without ever achieving their unknown goals. For mortals to believe they could create an avatar on any god's behalf, let alone a god who was banished and locked away? It defies reason."

"Well, they *are* cultists of a deity whose main theme seems to be eating things." I shivered. "Not to mention their choice of neighbors and the whole human sacrifice thing. Nothing about them screams rational to me, or even halfway sane."

The good news was that the process had failed miserably so far. In true cultist fashion, the leader had placed the blame not on himself or the missing deity, but on the quality of the sacrifices provided. Jessup's party had been the start of a new phase for the cult's experimental rituals, and the leader had seemed far more optimistic about their chances.

According to the notes, we had rescued the duke's heir in time. Still, the dark essence Miko had detected in Wilhemina's body meant the rituals had produced *some* kind of result. We just didn't know what.

Nor, as Carlson pointed out, did we have any explanation on how a cult all the way out in the frontier had managed to kidnap the duke's heir, when all signs reportedly pointed to Zaris being responsible.

"Were you able to recover anything else?" he asked, after I'd read the notes aloud for the third time. "Anything at all?"

"Lace found some copper bits in one of the flunky's rooms," I said. "And I found a pouch in the leader's desk. I didn't have time to check, but I think it might have included a silver tower."

"I meant actionable intelligence. Any coin or items recovered are your party's by right, per guild charter." He sighed and rubbed his eyes, as if *he'd* been the one reading cramped handwriting in a secret language for the past glass. "The mystery of the heir's kidnapping might have to wait for a more exhaustive search of the ruins. No doubt, the grand duke himself will want the entire place torn apart, top to bottom."

"How long will it take a messenger to reach Trynfall?" I asked.

"Three seven-days." He gazed off into the distance as he tabulated numbers and dates. "At least one day to receive an audience. Another seven-day or more to put together a force capable of taking on the numbers Lace described—likely formed from our guild house in Trynfall, with the assembled nobility already marching on distant Zaris. And then four seven-days back."

"Four?"

"An army moves slower than a lone traveler."

I did the math. "That's… more than one and a half moons. Can you use your bird-note technique to get the message to Trynfall faster and at least shave off the first three seven-days?"

Carlson gave me a look. "It is called *Winged Messenger*, and its range is limited to a league in any single direction. Although…" He trailed off and the look he was still giving me turned speculative. "Is it true that you have spent time in the town archives?"

"Yes? I was researching history."

"And Julla did not kick you out, which suggests you were appropriately respectful of both her and the archives' inventory," he said, referring to the elderly archivist.

I wasn't sure where he was going with this, so I just nodded.

"There are several tomes in the restricted section," said the keeper, "that are reputed to include rituals that might augment non-combat techniques. The cost of creating such a ritual would be significant, but…"

"But if it's true, you might be able to send a message all the way to Trynfall?"

"Or at least to a closer guild hall, yes."

"Sounds great. Where do I come in?"

"The reason we have only rumors about these tomes is because they are written in a language that Julla has only been partially able to decode. But if your *knack* for languages is as well suited for ancient scholarly texts as it is the secret code of unholy, human sacrificing cultists…"

The level look he gave me said a lot without words. It said I might be able to help, and in doing so, prove both my value to the guild *and* the grand duke… or I might be exposed as someone who *only* knew the language of the cult of Khamani, for reasons that would almost necessarily be explored in great and possibly painful detail when the duke's men eventually arrived.

I liked the first part of that a lot better than the second. Thankfully, it was also the truth.

"I can do that," I said.

"Excellent. I will dispatch a rider to the capital tonight, regardless, but if you can translate the books *and* their contents justify the rumors, the duke might receive word that his daughter lives in one or two days, rather than twenty. A war might be averted, and the assembled army could instead be sent here to wipe out this cult and their nest of blighted."

"But no pressure," I muttered.

Carlson's gaze sharpened. "There is in fact, a considerable amount of pressure. As I just said, a literal war is at stake, to say nothing of—"

"I get it. It was a saying from my… village. A sarcastic saying." I pinched the bridge of my nose. "Sorry. I'm exhausted."

"Understandably so. I will order food to be delivered to your room, so that you may eat and then sleep. You have been moved to room six, just next door."

"Why?" Miko and I had previously been sharing room two, just a few feet from the stairs down.

"Your scaled companion insisted." He read the confusion in my face, and it was his turn to sigh. "I forgot to tell you. That is unlike me. Perhaps I will insist Melligula take the night shift so that I, too, can sleep."

"Forgot to tell me what?"

"Neither healer was able to cure Lady Willerton. Worse, while they could sense the taint your Priestess spoke of, they were unable to calm it, let alone drive it back in the way she continues to do."

"How's that possible? Aren't they higher level than Miko?"

"One is Tin, so presumably yes." He shrugged. "It could be an aspect of the deity providing their blessings, it could be that the heir has unconsciously attuned herself to your companion's specific energy, or it could even be that Lady Willerton's body is incapable of supporting the divine energy of three different, perhaps antagonistic, deities at a time. I do not know and neither did they. All they could say was that your companion's actions seemed to be beneficial to the duke's heir. In the absence of alternatives, the scaled must continue attending to Lady Willerton personally."

"And room six?"

"Is, like this one, larger than your previous room. Large enough for three beds. Lady Willerton will, by necessity, bunk within a few steps of your companion, but the Priestess also insisted you continue to share rooms." He let that sentence hang in the air, clearly seeking an explanation.

"I watch her back," I said lamely. "And she watches mine."

"Your personal business is not the guild's concern. With permission, I will store these pages in our vault?"

"Of course." It seemed a little silly since I was the only one who could read them—homicidal, god-summoning maniacs aside—but the less I had to carry, the happier I was. Even if my bed was only a single room away.

"Then I will let you go." Carlson stood and, to my shock, offered me a nod almost deep enough to be the world's shallowest bow. "Food will arrive shortly. By the time you wake, Julla will have granted you access to the necessary volumes in the restricted section. I ask that you head to the archives immediately after breaking your fast."

I just gave him a tired nod.

Food sounded good.

Hot food sounded even better.

But I wasn't sure I'd stay awake long enough for it to matter.

64

I woke up the next morning and ran through my forms. My body was still functioning as it should, but I ached far more than normal. It took a few panic-filled moments for me to remember why: with Miko tasked with keeping the Wilhemina stable, she hadn't had enough energy to cast *Minor Healing* on herself or me.

A week of hard travel and harder fighting meant I was even more sore than after my first ride on the back of a dalys.

Still, it was better than suddenly turning symptomatic. A lot better. I climbed out of bed and pulled on a shirt. Wilhemina remained comatose, or ensorcelled, or whatever it was that was going on with her, and Miko was asleep. I let the synossian be. She'd gotten up in the middle of the night at least once to recast *Minor Healing* on the duke's heir.

Downstairs, the guild hall remained largely empty. Carlson was nowhere to be seen, but Melligula manned her far messier desk, horns lowered as she gazed into the bottom of the cup on the table in front of her. One set of eyes glanced in my direction as I came downstairs, but she said nothing further.

Clearly, she'd been told about Mordecai. I hadn't even realized the pair were on a first-name basis, but grief looked the same on a demonic cow-like turbinga as it did a human.

Before turning in the night before, Miko had told me we'd be meeting with Lace and Skaal the coming evening to go over our minimal loot and whatever rewards we'd earned for discovering the fate of Jessup's party and uncovering a significant threat to the region. Those were the only payouts the guild would be providing... we hadn't completed our mission to clear the ruins, after all. And while I knew we all had high hopes for what Wilhemina's safe return might net us, any reward would be forthcoming from the duke or his men instead.

In the meantime, I had more research to do. It seemed unlikely I'd earn another point of Intellect in the process, but I could always hope.

I checked the mission board on the way out. Someone had taken the messenger mission Carlson had promised to post. No other new missions had popped up and I was irritated to see that the false dawn cleansing mission was *still* on the board. Maybe it was *Animal Behaviorism* talking, but I found myself more and more concerned about the burgeoning potential apocalypse only a glass or two outside town. Did the guild just need to up the reward on offer or what?

The streets of Madea were never quiet, at least in comparison to Harborton, but there were fewer people out and about as I made my way to the archives. Julla was up—I wasn't convinced she slept at all— and while she gave my spear a dirty look, she didn't comment on its presence.

We'd been down that road already... twice.

Besides, I was here on official guild business.

She led me to a table near the back of the first room and motioned to the seat. I gave her a confused look.

"I thought I had access to the reserved section?"

"You have access to some of the *volumes* from the reserved section, but I will bring them out to you. Our collection is not as grand as you'll find elsewhere, but there are scrolls—and even a few tomes—that require careful handling. It takes more than partial clearance to be permitted entrance to the section itself. If you'll sit, I will fetch the requested texts."

Librarians were the same in every world… efficient, educated, and more than a little terrifying. I nodded my acceptance and took the seat as directed.

A few minutes later, Julla returned with five scrolls and two leather-bound books. I knew from experience how long the scrolls would take to go through, even with my trait, and one look at the significantly larger books had me swallowing a groan. As much as I loved *Speaker of Tongues*, it would have been nice if it had also made me a speed reader.

Three glasses passed in tedious fashion. Julla stopped by a few times, and I translated brief passages from whatever I was reading for her. She copied those words down along with the location or page, no doubt building her own Rosetta Stone for future translations when I was gone. Given that the seven resources she'd brought me included three different languages, I wasn't sure the cheat sheet would be as useful as she hoped. I didn't tell her that though.

I liked Julla well enough, but I had the *Mercantilism* skill for a reason. I wasn't going to just give out translation keys for free.

One of the scrolls she'd brought appeared to be a personal diary whose contents were almost entirely focused on the author's sexual conquests, but the other scrolls and both books focused on the expected topic: rituals. Two were primers, written by two very different authors, with very different takes on the subject. I read through both a few times, just to get a better understanding of the subject matter.

Rituals were a Framework-supported construct. In fact, Ritualist was a well-known profession—and the most honorable of them all, according to the author, who almost definitely spent hours preening in front of a mirror each morning. At their heart, rituals were like techniques, except that they were single-use and required significant and often-costly setup by an adequately leveled Ritualist. Most of the time, the Ritualist did not actually trigger the ritual… instead, they set it up on behalf of the person who would be using it.

Many rituals were used to modify a user's existing technique in one way or the other. They were largely useless for combat purposes, both because of the time and expense of setup and because of the delicacy of the rituals themselves. It was hard enough to get the construct right at all; it was that much harder to invoke it correctly with arrows and spells flying about.

I bit back a sigh. This wasn't easy reading, and it didn't help that I found it hard to focus. My mind kept replaying those last few minutes with Mordecai. The Flameweaver's hand outstretched, wavering as he tried to hold it steady. The fire that gathered around that hand, the heat that sucked the moisture right off the tunnel walls. Mordecai's eyes, the only thing ever visible of his face, wide and pained and… something else I couldn't quite grasp, something that not even *Speaker of Tongues* could help me interpret.

But most of all, it was his final words that rattled around in my brain, constantly derailing my thoughts.

Fire resents control and restraint. It wants to be free.

The Ideal given to me in my Dreaming, the Ideal *I* had chosen for myself, if my memories of that dream were correct, was Freedom. But what did that truly mean? Did I want to be free like fire? Free of responsibility or constraint, expanding across Eos like a primal force?

I had lived my time on Earth chafing at the restrictions that life had set for me. At the need to take care of Dad, both because of his illness and because Mom had long since left. At what that meant for my free time, for my future, for any dreams I'd thought to have before one diagnosis changed everything. *Freedom* meant not being stuck in Midton. Not being told what to do. Doing whatever I wanted, whenever I wanted, and however I wanted, and telling the world to go to hell if it dared to disagree. I had wanted to be free like the fire Mordecai had dedicated his life to.

But as much as the Flameweaver's words rang both familiar and horribly and undeniably true, that didn't feel like *my* truth anymore. It felt less like freedom and more like callous detachment. I'd stepped from Earth right into a whole host of new responsibilities on Eos, but as much as those responsibilities worried and wore on me, they also motivated me. They provided structure and purpose, Miko's infamous thegar that we continued to break into bite-sized pieces.

And Miko herself wasn't a constraint at all. She gave as much as she took, often even more. We were stronger and better for each other's presence.

So, what *did* freedom mean to me?

I needed to figure that out sometime before Tin.

In the meantime, I reminded myself, I had more scrolls to read.

It was somewhere around the fourth glass after lunch when I finally found a ritual that seemed like a good match for what Carlson was seeking. It could be set up in less than a day, the ingredients all were—as far as I could tell—at least somewhat available, and it added significant range to a single usage of a non-combat technique. Increasing the value of the components used in the setup increased the magnitude of the effect... although the author admitted there were severely diminishing returns after a point.

What point that might be, they hadn't opted to share.

"Is that it?" Julla hadn't so much walked over to me as materialized directly beside me, curious eyes scanning my notes. It had been a weird thing to have to consciously write those notes in Trade, even though I was reading in several totally different languages.

"Yes, that's it. I think so anyway."

"Excellent." She piled her own notes—all taken directly from my translations—into a small stack. "If you are done, I will return the scrolls and books to their shelves."

I couldn't stop myself. "You know… the translations I gave you were from multiple languages."

She blinked. "They were?"

"Yes. So, I'm not sure they'll be as helpful as you might expect." I watched the old woman try to hide her wince and then sprang my trap. "However, for a small fee, I might see my way to helping you sort them out. You'd have three incomplete language keys instead of one jumbled mess of one."

I'd halfway expected the archivist to be angry, but her eyes sparkled, and her smile was the grin of someone half her age. "And here I thought you were an innocent. Very well. What are your terms?"

That was a surprisingly good question. The truth was, I hadn't really thought that far ahead. Any amount of coin would be useful, especially without knowing what rewards our party would be seeing over the next moon or two, and yet I found my mind flashing back to the guild mission board and the task nobody would take.

"I'm looking for books on invasive plant species."

"Like prowler's moss or false dawn?"

My smile grew to match hers. "Exactly."

○○○

By the time I made it back to the guild hall, night had already fallen. Lace and Skaal were in the room Miko and I shared with the duke's daughter, trading words with my synossian friend. It said something about Miko's improvements in Trade that she felt comfortable using it when I wasn't around to translate. And yeah, she still got a lot of words wrong—especially when she was excited, scared, or emotional—but it was far better than I'd have managed without my trait.

"Welcome, nest-brother," said the woman in question, rising from her crouch to give me a bow.

"About time," said Lace. She tossed a coin purse in the air and then caught it again with a clink from the coin inside. "Carlson finally woke up and paid us the bounty for finding the party from Steppin's Skirmishers."

I didn't point out that she'd gotten the company name correct for the first time ever. She knew that as well as I did. And the joke wouldn't have been funny anymore anyway.

"Between that and the miniscule amount of copper we retrieved from that first chest, we… well, we have enough to stay here until the duke's men arrive, if not exactly in style."

"Should we get another mission?"

She shook her head. "Not yet. Carlson or Melligula will want to speak with each of us about Mordecai's death. It's something the guild does to make sure parties aren't just murdering members in their sleep as soon as the nearest city is out of sight."

"Need rest too," said Skaal. "Recovery."

"Grieving," added Miko, sending Lace a defiant glare for some reason.

"Yes, all of that."

"I will hold a memorial service for Mordecai tonight," said Miko, choosing her words carefully. "Have already told Melligula. Would like all of you to come."

"The Night Hag doesn't believe in memorials…" I watched the objection form on Lace's lips and then watched it blow away again with the Marauder's sigh. "…but I told him his name would not be forgotten. I'll be there."

Skaal grunted.

Miko turned to me.

"Of course. Don't we have to wait for both moons to go dark though?"

She shook her scaled head. "Is only for long dead. For newly dead, is best to do memorial whenever can." The Priestess met our eyes, one by one. "Will meet you all downstairs, five glasses after supper. Melligula says guild will provide space for ceremony."

"Fine. But first, the money." Lace upended the purse and a small stream of copper poured out… the thirteen bits she'd stolen from the cultist's chest as well as fifteen heavier plugs.

"Two plugs a piece," she said, "and two bits, with the extras of both going into the party pool. I'll add Mordecai's share to his possessions and see if Carlson has any listed next of kin."

She glared around the circle at all of us, as if daring anyone to argue and seemed disappointed when nobody did.

"Should get his share of reward from duke too," said Miko. "If there is one."

Skaal nodded.

"Agreed," said Lace, clearing her throat. "In the meantime, I think we should—"

"Oh, wait!" I stood and went to retrieve my pack. I'd given the pages I'd stolen to Carlson, but I still had the leader's small velvet pouch. I tossed it in the air, like Lace had, watching the Marauder's eyes widen at the satisfying clink it made when it landed back in my palm.

"What's that?" she asked.

"I stole more than just papers from the leader's room."

The look she gave me was long, considering, and mostly discomfiting. "Are you *sure* you're not a Rogue?"

I shrugged. "The desk was unlocked."

"Was good find," said Miko supportively.

"I guess we'll see." I emptied the pouch on the floor next to Lace's small pile. I'd already seen a flash of silver when I stole the pouch, but watching the first tower hit the rug, bounce, and flop over onto one side still compared favorably to memories of Christmas as a child. One tower, two towers, a handful of plugs, a small gemstone that might have been a ruby if it hadn't looked wet, and last but not least...

"Huh." I picked up the ring that had fallen out of the pouch. It was a thick band of silver, with a crest on its flat bezel—some sort of bird, surrounded by fire. A phoenix, maybe? Or... an animal being sacrificed? Hell if I knew. What I did know was that the ring was worth more than just the metal it had been made from... because I'd just gotten a quest:

```
NEW QUEST: Find the owner of the crest ring.

         [ Accept | Decline ]
```

When Shan said *owner*, did he mean the cult leader we'd already crossed paths with? Because if so, this was one quest I wouldn't be completing for a very long time. And if Khamani's dedicated psycho *wasn't* the ring's owner, then who was, where would I find them, and how had the ring made it to the sub-basement of those blighted-infested ruins in the middle of a marsh?

As usual, the quest generated more questions than answers.

I hit *Accept* anyway because I wasn't an idiot.

I showed the ring to a curious Miko, but otherwise held onto it, as Lace reviewed the sum I'd just added to our tiny pool of earnings.

"Three towers, four plugs, a bloodstone, and..." Her silver-eyed gaze went unerringly to the ring in my hands, "one silver signet ring of uncertain origin. I'd say that trinket's worth at least a tower on its own. Excellent find."

"Can I take it as my share? I'd like to find who it belongs to."

"May I see?"

I nodded and passed the ring over to Lace, who examined the signet and then showed it to Skaal. After a moment's consideration, she tossed it back.

"I don't have a problem with it," she said, "but the math doesn't add up. A bloodstone of this size will go for three or four plugs, at best. Say forty-eight plugs, all in, including the ring. What's that six ways?"

"Eight plugs." Which was two less than she'd said the ring was worth. I tried not to grit my teeth. "I can give up two plugs of my share of the other rewards to make up the difference."

Lace's nod was just starting when Skaal spoke.

"Are not mercenaries or merchants. Are party. Maybe friends too. Can have my plugs to make up difference."

"Or mine," agreed Miko. I could read the curiosity in her face in a way I'd never have been able to do even as recently as Harborton. She knew *something* was up.

Lace, on the other hand, just looked exasperated. "I wasn't going to *rob him of his plugs*, old man. I just wanted to make him sweat a bit." She turned to me. "The rest of us will split what remains, but the ring is yours. If you do ever choose to sell it, just buy us all a round with the proceeds. Deal?"

"Only water for me," said Skaal.

Lace bit back a growl.

○○○

Much later that night, we gathered behind the guild hall. The cold wind cut through the alleyways, sending the flame of Miko's memorial lantern whipping back and forth. With its buildings a mixture of wood and stone, Madea had forbidden open flames outside of hearths, and the lantern had been Melligula's best attempt at a compromise.

The turbinga stood with us, crying in silence, and if the occasional lowing that spilled from her mouth was anything but quiet, nobody saw fit to comment.

The first part of the ceremony was the same as I'd seen in Harborton, even if the setting and components were wildly different. Miko called upon each of her gods in turn, from Kal to Aurea to the twins, Etriska and Shan, asking them to listen, to watch, and to welcome the recently dead. But this time, there was only a single name to be remembered.

Miko's voice filled the air. She had performed the entire ceremony in the High Tongue, and continued doing so, even now.

"I honor Mordecai Callus na'Mezzari, Adept of the Crimson Needle, second in his circle, endowed with the secrets of flame and the greater power that is knowledge. I never saw his face, but I carry his voice in my heart. We live through his sacrifice and that means a piece of him lives on with us. Like the fire in this lantern and that which became his pyre, I will use his memory to bring light to the darkness. In his honor and in honor of his final gift. "

She bowed her head once, then twice, then turned to the rest of us, switching to Trade. "If anyone else wishes to speak of Mordecai, they can do so now."

After a moment, Lace stepped forward, dark face a mask.

"When Skaal and I first met Mordecai, he was drunk off his ass, and I thought he was the most obnoxious human I'd ever encountered. The north was soft, but he was somehow even softer, nothing but flesh and hot wind. I called him a dirt farmer in a language I didn't expect him to speak, and he responded in that same tongue. He asked what clan I'd grown up in, and when I told him Dusk Panther, he pulled flames from the tavern's fireplace to give me cat ears and a tail." She shook her head, voice wavering. "He was the first friend we made in the north and the one who stuck with us through success and failure. He was *not* soft, and he was not weak, and he was and forever shall be worthy of all his names."

Lace stepped back and to my surprise, Melligula took her place. All four of the turbinga's eyes were wet and bloodshot, but her voice was steady.

"I have not known Mordecai as long as some of you, but I might have known him best, for he greatly enjoyed a sympathetic ear and I like hearing educated people speak. What none of you know is that he never wanted to be an adventurer. He was to become a meister at the Crimson Needle upon graduation, only for his relationship with a female instructor to be revealed by a jealous rival. While Mordecai was permitted to graduate with the honors he had accumulated, he was expelled from the school and separated from the woman he loved." She cleared her throat. "He didn't dream of wealth and fame, like most adventurers, but of one day returning to that mountain school, not as an exile seeking forgiveness but as a man of enlightenment and erudition who would willingly share the knowledge he had earned in the deep and dark places of the world. The school he held in such high regard is lessened by his loss, and so are we."

I didn't step forward, but simply bowed my head, listening as Miko brought the ceremony to a close.

Goodbye, Mordecai. Rest in peace, Adept of the Crimson Needle.

May you one day live and learn again.

65

The next day, the Ritualist got started on the rite I had translated. The setup would take almost a full day to prepare, so after verifying that the Ritualist had what he needed, Carlson sent me away. And if the keeper had looked a little bit green at the time, well, he'd just seen—and agreed to—the bill. The material costs alone had been so exorbitant that the guild had paid with credit rather than coin.

I was starting to see why rituals weren't an everyday occurrence.

Miko and I spent our morning at the training hall. Caleb worked with me for a few more glasses on the knife after introducing the synossian to a wiry human woman who fought with a pair of spiked gauntlets. Those weapons weren't quite a parallel for Miko's combination of bracers and claws, but I could see how at least some concepts might cross over.

When we were done—sweaty and exhausted, but also satisfied—I wanted to stop by the smithy to check on my long-awaited armor. Unfortunately, Miko needed to be at the guild hall to watch over the duke's heir. So, I escorted my nest-sister back, left her with a kebab I'd splurged on, and then headed out again to see Mrrl and Seanna on my own.

I ran into Lace on the way downstairs.

"Going out?" she asked.

"Again, yeah. I'm hoping my armor will be ready."

"That's the kithrizal Smith, right? Skaal mentioned you and Miko had made some friends."

"Speaking of Skaal, where is he?" It was odd to see her without the reaver at her side.

"Sleeping. He doesn't sleep often or regularly, but every now and then, his whole body shuts down for a day or two. I'll stuff some food down his gullet tomorrow and see if that wakes him." She shrugged. "Anyway, don't let me keep you."

I nodded, started to move away, then hesitated. Skaal's words on the road to Harborton replayed in my mind, as fresh as if he'd only just spoken them:

"*She needs a friend.*"

"*She's got you,*" I had pointed out.

"*For now.*"

I turned back. "Do you want to come with me to the smithy?"

"You need a guard?"

"No. But I wouldn't mind the company."

She looked at me for long enough that I started to feel self-conscious, and then finally nodded. "I'll come. Skaal and I need our weapons repaired anyway."

I waited a few minutes for her to gather her pack, Skaal's warped axe, and her equally battered sword and dagger. Then, we made our way across Madea.

"Do you think the ritual you deciphered will work?" she asked, eyes straying to a food stand whose offerings weren't even half as good as Miko's prized kebabs.

"I don't really know. The author seemed to think so, and so did the Ritualist that Carlson found, so I'll bow to their expertise."

"We're lucky a town like Madea has a Ritualist at all."

"It doesn't. There's not enough money here for a Ritualist to advance, apparently. He was visiting his niece from out of town."

"Good timing, that."

"I guess not all our luck is bad."

"No. Just most of it." She shook her head. We'd been back in Madea for multiple days now and yet she still hadn't added the red beads back into her braids. I wasn't sure what that meant, but it almost had to mean *something*. "Still, the sooner the grand duke receives word, the sooner his daughter will be taken off our hands. And with the backing of someone as powerful as him, we'll be one step closer to finding a cure for the old man."

"Is Skaal anywhere close to another level?"

"I have no idea. One moment, he'll spout poetry that would make a northerner weep, and the next he's silent and still as the steppes he grew up in. I would pity reaver women if I didn't despise the whole species."

"*Almost* the whole species."

She shrugged. "He's different."

"I won't argue with that."

I studied the Marauder out of the corner of my eye as we crossed Madea. Three moons in, she was still a confusing mix of characteristics, sometimes brash and quick to anger, other times thoughtful and measured, like the hunter she had once been. Her words at Mordecai's memorial had hinted at the inner self she so rarely exposed, but I knew better than to bring any of that up uninvited.

So, we walked in silence the rest of the way, passing through the mostly empty market square and on into the shabbier neighborhood that housed even Madea's better-off beastkin.

The smithy was empty of customers, as it almost always was, and Mrrl rose with a cat-like smile to greet me. He froze halfway out of his seat, tail going still as he caught sight of my companion. His green eyes were hard and fixed upon the taller woman next to me.

"May I know your clan, amazon?" It was the first time I'd ever heard the kithrizal speak Gorash, but he was every bit as fluent as Lace or Skaal.

"I have left both clan and name behind," said Lace, "and with them old debts and grievances."

"She is a friend of both me and Miko," I said, joining them in the language of the south, and escorting Lace over to the counter. "The leader of our adventuring party."

Mrrl shot me a look. "I did not realize you spoke Gorash."

"Yes, we all go through that period," said Lace, voice dry as a desert. "Brian does enjoy his surprises."

The kithrizal looked between us and some of the stiffness went out of his form. "I bid you both welcome. As young Brian might have told you, I am Mrrl, mate to Seanna. We are formerly of the Swiftstep tribe but are now citizens of the duchy."

"We fought them once," murmured Lace. "A worthy opponent."

"Yes, perhaps." Mrrl cleared his throat. "Brian, Seanna has been waiting for your return."

"It's ready?"

"Almost." His smile returned. "She needs a test fitting with your gambeson on, but if no adjustments are needed…"

"I can do that."

"You will find her out back, as usual." He turned back to Lace. "As for your companion… if you have relinquished your names, how would you like to be called?"

"Lace."

"Like the fabric?"

"Like the plant."

"Ah." Mrrl read the confusion in my face and explained. "Widow's lace. It is poisonous enough on its own, but when concentrated and distilled, creates a toxin that will paralyze a body and consume it from within."

I side-eyed the Marauder, but she said nothing. That plant *hadn't* been in any of the books on invasive flora Julla had found for me in the archives.

"You are welcome to browse our wares, Lace," continued Mrrl, "but if there are specific items you need or services you require, I can assist with the pricing."

In response, she pulled out both mangled weapons, taking care to place them on the counter so they never faced the kithrizal.

"These need repairs," she said.

"The sword needs repairs. That axe head needs to be melted and recast entirely."

"How much?"

"Is it okay," I interjected, "if I go back to Seanna now?"

"Of course," they both said.

"And you two won't attack each other the second I'm gone?"

"This is commerce," said Mrrl. "It trumps ancient history."

○○○

A glass later, I walked out with a shirt of chain links that Seanna had called a hauberk. It fit perfectly over my gambeson… or would once Datha removed a small amount of excess padding. The shirt covered me from shoulders to waist, and while its short sleeves left my forearms as bare as my legs, it still represented a massive upgrade in protection for me. The hauberk's links were made from iron instead of bronze, but the Smith swore they didn't suffer from the same brittleness that made so many weapons of that metal inferior to their bronze counterparts.

If I'd known a damn thing about metallurgy, I would have taught her how to make steel instead. Eos had an assortment of foreign ores that were almost definitely stronger, but their rarity and expense made them inaccessible to anyone outside the nobility or master craftsmen who headed up their own manufacturing empires.

Meanwhile, iron was cheap and plentiful. The riveted rings Seanna had used in my hauberk would be a potent defense against getting stabbed or shot with an arrow, two things that ranked low on my list of dream activities. The new armor was also heavy as hell, but I'd bear the discomfort as long as it kept me alive.

If the lupine and amazons had their own combative history, neither Datha nor Lace seemed compelled to mention it. I made small talk with the Leatherworker as he undid several stitches in my gambeson, removed a small handful of padding from the areas Seanna had indicated, and stitched it all back up. Neither of us said a word about the cubs doing their best to terrorize the agile amazon's ankles.

Not until we were on our way back to the guild hall anyway.

"I didn't know you liked children," I said.

Lace sniffed. "I'm not sure that I do."

"I see. It must have been a different amazon wrestling with Datha's cubs then."

That won me a look that I was all too ready to ignore. After another block or so, Lace shrugged. "Neither the adult nor his two male cubs would have been granted names in my clan, but the girl… she could've made a fine daughter, fierce and true." Lace's smile was sharp. "Although a lupine as a dusk panther would've caused a stir."

"That was the name of your clan?" I asked, remembering her words at Mordecai's memorial service.

"Yes. The Dusk Panther Clan, as old as the jungle we dwelled within, if not quite so deadly."

"Do you miss it? Your old life, I mean?"

She raised a dark eyebrow, silver eyes meeting mine. "Do you?"

I almost missed a step. "I'm sorry?"

"You told us you lived your life in a tiny remote village with Miko." She waved a hand at Madea's semi-urban setting. "Now, you are an adventurer, braving the dark places of the world. That is quite a shift."

Oh. That. I tried to keep my face neutral. "Yeah, it's been an adjustment. Miko has been a huge help."

"Well, she has a lot riding on you, it seems."

"What?"

Lace shook her head. "It is as they say. Some people choose this life, while others are instead *chosen*."

In combat, the Marauder was swift, stealthy, and subtle, invariably finding ways to strike when least expected. In conversation, she lost some of that subtlety. I swallowed my first reply, walking in silence for another block. *Deception* wasn't going to help me here. "I take it you heard what I said to Mordecai."

"You are a member of my party. I stayed behind to assist you as needed. And my senses are sharper than most."

I dodged aside as someone dumped the contents of their chamber pot into the street, not even sparing a thought as to whether the risk of being splashed by bodily fluids would increase the chance of a skill-up in *Avoidance*.

"It explains many things," continued Lace. "My people have their own legends of those brought across the Veil. The one thing they all agree on is that wherever those individuals walked, their trail was marked in blood."

"Are you blaming me for Mordec—"

"If I did, you would never have survived to leave the marsh. The blame for his death lies on those who killed him, and on me, for allowing us to become trapped in the first place."

"That's not—"

"But I see now why the Night Hag might have her eye on you, and why both the Thunderbird and Nikkaali stirred at your presence. You and Miko have done well in your time with us, but I will not walk into danger blindly. If you two wish to continue in this party, we will need to know everything."

"And if not? You'd just kick me out? And Miko, your healer?"

"Skaal and I have spent cycles surviving as a lone duo," she said, and there was no give in her words. "We can do so again."

"I see."

"I told you our story," she added, voice softening. "All I ask is that you tell us yours."

"Let me talk to Miko first," I finally said. "If she agrees, I'll tell you everything tonight."

"Tonight?"

"After Carlson sends his message. The keeper wants me stone cold sober for the ritual, and I'm going to need *at least* one ale before I dredge up the past."

I took a left at the next street.

"The guild hall is back that way," Lace told me.

"I know."

"Then where are we going?"

"The sun's not down yet," I told her, "and that means there are a few vendors still out in the streets?"

"And?"

"And I'm getting a kebab."

"There *are* other foods in Madea." I had started walking faster, but she simply lengthened her stride to stay even with me. "Better foods, even."

"Other food, yes. Better food?" I shook my head. "Sounds like a lack of enlightenment to me."

○○○

I observed the ritual from within the room itself, under strict orders *not* to speak at all unless I saw something go wrong. I wasn't sure how I'd know something had gone wrong, or what I'd be able to do if I did notice it, but my post at least earned me a bit of breathing space from Lace, who'd stuck to me like a shadow the whole way to the kebab stall and back.

Given that she'd basically threatened to kick us out of the party, I wasn't sure why she felt compelled to make sure I didn't run, but as Mordecai had said—

I shook the thought away with a sigh that earned me a sharp look from the Ritualist. Like me, he was there as an observer. *Unlike* me, he was old, more than a little snooty, and had more jewelry on one hand than most Earthborn goths collected in a lifetime.

The kebab, I was starting to realize, hadn't taken the edge off my irritation at letting something slip where Lace could hear it. It wasn't that I didn't trust the Marauder and her reaver companion, really. It was just…

Actually, I wasn't sure *why* I was so annoyed, except that I was once again in a situation where I was being forced to do something I didn't want to do.

I swallowed my second sigh and watched as Carlson stepped within the ritual circle that had been painstakingly drawn, its loops and borders filled in with a pinkish red sand that cost a silver tower per ounce. Along the outer edge of the large circle, three smaller ones held the items that would be consumed by the ritual: a bronze and silver bell, the enormous feather of some ancient bird the book had called a cloudwing, and an inkwell that had been carved out of a semi-precious gem instead of being formed from glass or clay.

Carlson had his note already written. It was far fancier than what he'd used to summon Madea's healers, complete with guild seal and several dozen lines of looping calligraphy. He held the letter in one hand and reached toward the ceiling with the other.

This was where lots of metaphysical weirdness was supposed to happen, but it took longer than I'd expected from my reading. The sand marking the permutations of the circle eventually started to shift. As time ground on, that movement became a visible current, flowing around the ritual circle and even forging a connection with the three smaller circles.

The bronze and silver bell rang. The feather ignited, its flames blue instead of orange. Ink within the crystal well spun, counter to the sand's clockwise rotation. When Carlson activated *Winged Messenger*, the note in his hand folded at lightning speed, but the origami bird that resulted had a wingspan as wide as the circle, and its paper beak was the length of my knife.

Ink-filled eyes scanned the room in a distinctly avian way, for all that the creature was anything but flesh and blood, and then the bird hopped straight into the air. A flap of its mighty wings was enough to blow the Ritualist off his feet, but it didn't matter anymore. The bird and its message were gone, streaking through the open window at a speed that might have made even the Thunderbird jealous..

Carlson turned to the two of us. "Thank you, Master Ritualist, and you, Brian. The courier dispatched last night will be overtaken in a glass at best, and Grand Duke Willerton should have notice by no later than tomorrow night. With luck, we may have just averted a war *and* saved the duke's heir in a single night."

"Gods be praised," murmured the Ritualist.

Considering Miko was the one keeping Wilhemina stable, thanks to the healing spells granted by Aurea, and *I* was the one who had deciphered the ritual, thanks to a trait given by Aurea's younger brother… I knew which particular gods deserved the Ritualist's praise.

ooo

Dinner was a quiet affair. I'd spoken to Miko, and after some debate, she'd agreed to share our secrets with Lace and Skaal, but that was for after the meal. While we were in the tavern, we'd committed to talking of other things. Yet the looming specter of my story hung over everything. A second ale didn't help. Nor did the fact that our meal and drinks were delivered by the older of the tavern's two barmaids. The one who had propositioned me weeks earlier seemed fixated on another table, laughing delightedly at the story a merchant's son was telling her.

"I think you missed your chance there," said Lace, following my gaze. "I guess she got tired of waiting."

I shrugged, not so much hurt as simply *tired*. "There are other fish in the sea."

Miko looked about, frowning. "What fish?"

"It's… never mind. Just a saying."

"Oh." She nodded and delicately cut another slice of tusker free. "Would not mind fish to eat. Miss it a bit after Harborton."

Much later, after Miko had checked on her charge and cast another *Minor Healing*, we crowded into Lace and Skaal's room.

"What do you want to know?" I asked them both.

"Start at beginning," said the reaver.

"Start with the interesting stuff," disagreed Lace.

"Just start," said Miko. "Is easier to explain once talking."

That made sense to me.

"Okay. I guess the first thing to say is that what I told Mordecai was true. I am—"

A heavy knock set the wooden door vibrating within its frame. "Lace? Skaal? Are you in there?" asked Melligula's voice. "Because we have a problem."

Lace closed her eyes and appeared to be murmuring a prayer or a curse… although I wasn't sure what the difference would be for the Night Hag's faithful.

"We'll continue this shortly." She raised her voice. "What do you need, Melligula?"

"Carlson wants you downstairs. A family of farmers just arrived in Madea. They say there are blighted in the forest and on the roads. They're marching on the town."

66

We knew the farmers. The Maris family had lost their farm to bandits and now the Campbells had lost theirs to the blighted. Most of the survivors had been sent to the two nearest taverns, where they were being looked over by the town healers, but Jalen Maris and his mother Elsbeth were in the guild house, sitting across from a well-dressed woman and staring vacantly into the cups in their hands. Across the room, Carlson stood with a heavyset man who wore a beaded shirt and a worried expression. Henrik and two guards leaned against the far wall, eyes alert and hard.

"Mayor Aulson," said Carlson, as we approached, "these are the adventurers who brought word of the blighted infestation."

"And now that infestation is bearing down on my town." The man scowled as he waved a thick-fingered hand at the two farmers. "And bringing fresh harm to our loyal citizens. What are you and your guild going to do about it?"

"Are you sure they're coming this way?" asked Lace.

Carlson nodded. "The Campbell farm was overrun. The survivors fled here and encountered blighted outriders on the road ahead of them. They're coming this way, and in significant numbers."

The Marauder exchanged glances with Skaal. We had focused on speed not stealth, but it sounded like the blighted had ignored our tracks entirely to make a beeline to where we had ended up.

"Wilhemina?" she asked.

Skaal nodded. "Must be."

"Who?" asked Mayor Aulson.

The guild's keeper cleared his throat and spoke in a low tone. "Our adventurers did more than just identify a threat to the region, Mayor. They also found Grand Duke Willerton's missing heir."

"Impossible! She's dead, and in Zaris, I hear."

"Apparently nobody told her that," said Lace.

"Is sick," added Miko, "but am keeping her well."

The mayor scowled at Miko but turned on Carlson. "Why wasn't I informed of this?"

"It was considered need to know."

"I'm the mayor!"

"And my guild is one of the only reasons your town even exists." Any sign of deference had left the keeper's voice. "The heir's safety was my main concern, and that seemed best achieved by limiting those who knew her identity and location. If you have complaints regarding my decisions, I invite you to register them with our primary branch."

The mayor harrumphed. "I may just do that, Keeper Carlson. I may indeed."

The keeper was too much of a professional to roll his eyes, but he turned back to us. "You think the blighted are tracking the duke's heir somehow?"

"Either the blighted or the cultists of Khamani," said Lace. "We didn't pass by the farms, which means they took a more direct route to Madea."

"Something they could only do if they knew where she was or where you had gone," agreed Carlson.

"If you take Lady Willerton and run, will they then pass by Madea entirely?" asked the mayor. "From the sounds of it, you stayed ahead of the blighted once already!"

"Was different," said Skaal. "Had advantage of surprise and confusion."

"We didn't see any outriders then either," agreed Lace. "If they have mounts and are already canvassing the region, we wouldn't last a day."

"Even if these cultists passed the town by," added Carlson, "an army of hungry blighted wouldn't. Your farmers can attest to that fact."

"What if Lady Willerton was already dead? Would they have a reason to keep coming?"

"You'd sacrifice the duke's heir?" asked Lace.

"The needs of the many outweigh a single life. That is reality."

I hated that phrase in Earth and I hated it on Eos.

"Will not abandon girl child," said Miko, steel in her voice.

The mayor sneered. "You and your kind may have rights under the duke's law, but they do not include inserting yourself into a conversation of your betters. Be silent or be gone."

I stepped forward. "Miko is the only reason Wilhemina is alive. Right now, she's a lot more valuable than you are."

The man puffed himself up, looking down on me from a distance even though he was only of average height. "I don't know you, boy, but I could have you and your pet thrown into jail with a snap of my fingers."

I wanted to see him try. I doubted the man was even an Aspirant, and the guards who clearly were would never reach us in time. My hand tightened on the shaft of Riok's spear, and I saw that realization appear in the mayor's eyes, along with a spark of sudden fear.

Carlson inserted himself between us.

"To even speak of harming the duke's blood is treason, Mayor Aulson, as you well know. For your sake and ours, I'm going to pretend I did not hear your suggestion, and I will ask all those present here to do the same."

"It's…" The mayor sighed. "I'm trying to *save* lives, keeper."

"Then you can't afford to deprive Madea of any Aspirants. Especially one of your town's only three healers." The keeper turned to me. "Stand down, guild member. Madea will need your spear, too, in the days to come."

It was Miko's hand on my back that calmed me more than anything the keeper or mayor had said. *Touch of the Dawn* washed the alcohol from my system and took at least some of my anger with it. "Rest easy, nest-brother," she told me in the High Tongue. "As you have told me, we are not responsible for his fear and ignorance."

I shook myself. "I'm… angrier than I thought."

"Yes." She patted my shoulder, the gesture almost as soothing as her spell.

The mayor had already dismissed us both. "His spear, Carlson? Does that mean the guild will aid in Madea's defense?"

"It is our home too. A moon ago, we could have fielded an army of our own, but the news from Zaris put an end to that. We still have three parties in town, and the other two are primarily Tin."

"Not enough," said Skaal. "Even with guards."

"I don't see any better option, reaver." Carlson glared up at the much-taller man. "Die on the road or stand, fight, and maybe live in Madea. Those are the choices."

"There are others in town who were once Aspirants," said the mayor, speaking slowly as his brain kicked into gear. "I can order Smith

Nial to open his doors and provide weapons to those who need them. And we have our walls, of course, walls that have never been breached."

Lace tried and failed to keep her opinion of those walls off her face. Madea's walls were maybe twelve feet tall at best; *I* could climb them and I was pretty sure at least the blighted could too.

But Carlson was right: what better option did we have?

The keeper nodded, although I couldn't tell if he was agreeing with the mayor's words or just placating the man. "I sent two Scouts out already to check the roads. We'll have a better idea of our timeline when they return, but I suspect it will be a day at least before the enemy arrive in force. Maybe another day after before they attack, assuming the blighted truly are under control. In the meantime, can I suggest we establish a war council for Madea's defense? We'll need more than just the six of us to plan the town's defense."

"Yes." The mayor snapped his fingers. "Henrik! Rouse the men. I want guards on the walls and a full squad at each gate. Tell your captain and his senior lieutenants that their presence is required here within the glass."

The sour-faced guard saluted and left.

"It's late, but I've sent Melligula out to summon the leaders of the other two adventuring parties," said Carlson. "We also have a Master Ritualist in town. He helped send a message to the duke earlier today."

"The grand duke knows we've found his heir?" The mayor's voice went pale at that realization.

"He will by morning." Carlson didn't point out the obvious, that his letter had included no mention of an army of the blighted bearing down on the town… and that even if it had, the duke's men were far too far away to help.

"Will also speak to Mrrl and Seanna," said Miko.

"Who?" asked the mayor.

"Other Smith in town," said the synossian. "And Woodworker mate."

"Oh. The kithrizal." The mayor shrugged and nodded. "May as well. We can use their wares too."

"May know other retired Aspirants too."

"And I can reach out to Caleb at the training hall," I added.

"Now hold on here." Aulson addressed Carlson instead of Miko or me. "We can't have people running around telling everyone about the blighted, keeper. It will generate a panic that will do more harm than good."

"You just roused your entire guard," pointed out the other man, "to say nothing of all the people who have seen the farmers already." He turned back to Miko, including me with a glance. "Tell them to keep things quiet if they can, but any who can fight should prepare themselves. And those whose homes border the wall can bring their young and defenseless here. We have rooms, if not many."

My estimation of the man went up almost instantly. In Madea's southern and western boroughs, it was almost exclusively the poor and the beastkin who lived right up against the walls.

Miko gave the keeper a deep bow and held it. "Yes, Keeper Carlson. Will do."

∘∘∘

A little more than a glass later, we were back in the guild hall. The mayor stood with a stern-looking man with a sweeping grey mustache and crisply pressed guard uniform. A few paces behind both was a long-limbed, plain-faced woman of the same species as Tantalas, Harborton's Herbalist, also wearing a guard uniform and carrying a bow. A tired and at least slightly tipsy Caleb had brought his hand-to-hand trainer with him as well as a woman with shoulders like a linebacker.

Lace, Skaal, and Carlson had been joined by Melligula and two hard faces I recognized from the occasional guild hall encounter. Both were men and each was the leader of their respective party. We were the only party whose members were all present… maybe because we had been the impetus for the whole unfolding crisis.

Next to Miko stood Seanna. Datha had come too, but Mrrl was watching the lupine's cubs. The two feathered figures with them were corbins, although I didn't know their names or stories. Miko had even stopped in to speak with the native synossians, only to emerge moments later, shaking her head. Either they had never been Aspirants, or they just weren't willing to come.

It should have been reassuring, looking around the room at the small force we had assembled in a single glass, knowing that each represented not just themselves but others of their kind. But I remembered the torches I'd seen making their way to the island ruins. I remembered the sheer scale of the warrens underneath, and the power of both the cultist leader and the essoli. I'd even spent a few minutes with a heartbroken Jalen Maris, and if his reports were true, the army marching toward us was even bigger and more diabolically diverse than I'd feared.

I kept my silence as the leaders of the various town factions all gave their two cents, all offered their advice on how to best defend the town. The truth was, I didn't have anything to contribute… I was growing comfortable with the spear, but whatever my *Tactics* skill might say, I'd never fought in a battle that involved more than a handful of people. The Buried attack at Whitehall had been the closest thing to large-scale combat I'd participated in, and we'd lost that. So instead, I listened to the plans being formed, and tried to internalize what those plans would mean for us… how Miko and I would fit in when the time came, and what, if anything, I could do to augment my limited impact.

The town had almost a hundred Aspirants, all told. Unfortunately, two-thirds of them were retired or, like Jalen, only advanced and leveled as a hobby in their free time. They were kind of like US military reservists back on Earth, and while that was a hell of a lot better than nothing, it was also a long way from people who spent their lives out in the field.

I was *still* only level four, but I was likely higher level than many of the hobbyists… and I'd seen action far more recently than the rest. One-on-one against an irkonnen, I thought they could hold their own. Outnumbered or against something stronger?

I was far less optimistic.

When he wasn't suggesting murder or putting his foot in his mouth, Mayor Aulson seemed relatively competent. As the mustached guard captain organized the town's actual defense with the other Aspirants, the mayor worked with Carlson to deal with things like supplies and support.

The town's two Smiths agreed to open their inventories and help arm those who could wield a weapon. The town's Fletcher had a handful of bows on hand in addition to the crossbows carried by Madea's guards, but there was a severe shortage of trained archers to use them. Nevertheless, he had agreed to put his assistants to work making new arrows and bolts to augment the town's ammunition stores. As soon as Datha was able to retrieve his cubs, Mrrl would be heading over to help. Seanna's mate was a Woodworker, not a Fletcher, but apparently there was enough crossover for him to be more help than harm.

There was less concern about a possible siege than I'd expected—apparently, the blighted weren't the type to sit around and wait—but even so, water and food were being stockpiled. The guild hall, with its central location, would serve as the temporary headquarters for the town's defenders, and a nearby warehouse was being hastily converted into a clinic for the casualties that were sure to come.

One or two days wasn't enough to prepare for an entire town's defense, especially against a foe like the one we were facing. Still, we accomplished more in the span of a few glasses than I'd thought possible, and as people filtered back out of the guild hall, they moved with a sense of purpose.

"A quarter of them will be gone before the sun rises," Lace told me, her voice a quiet murmur.

"Gone?"

"Out the Hill Gate and hoping whoever sticks around can hold off the blighted long enough for them to reach some kind of safety." She shook her head. "You can see it in their eyes."

"Really?"

"The guards will have orders to stop them, but we'll see how well those orders fare. Hell, I bet there are a few guards right now questioning whether their jobs are worth it."

"What about you? Are you staying?"

"I wouldn't still be here if I wasn't."

"Why though?"

Lace scoffed. "Good luck convincing Skaal to do anything, let alone abandon a town of mostly defenseless dirt farmers. And protecting the duke's daughter is the fastest way to getting the old man cured. Also…"

"Also?"

"Hashoggath's a vengeful bitch and Mordecai was party."

I didn't have anything to say to that.

"Do you think they'll make it? The ones who do run?" Miko and I had briefly discussed doing just that, only to come to a similar conclusion as Lace: Wilhemina's safe return was our best path forward.

Not that my nest-sister had been willing to abandon the little girl anyway.

"Some, maybe. But if the blighted really are only a day out, that means their outriders are even closer. If I were an irkonnen in search of easy meat, I'd go for the defenseless prey first, and then tackle the bigger challenge with a full stomach."

Another of her uplifting pep talks delivered, she wandered over to exchange words with Melligula, leaving me to reassess my earlier pessimism about the town's defense. If having only a hundred Aspirants, many of them greener than me, was problematic, having only seventy-five was even worse.

As Riok had said on the road to Whitehall, numbers mattered.

That thought struck me and I scanned the slowly emptying hall. I was looking for one person in particular and not finding them.

Numbers matter, Riok had said, *but strength matters more.*

I pulled up the hood of my cloak to ward off the chill and stepped out into Madea's empty streets.

○○○

It took a full glass to find Arrius, and even then, I only managed because of the aura he never seemed to bother restraining. The massive Copper was outside a windowless house, his primitive club upright on the road next to him, and a pack that could carry a dead man open at his feet. As I watched, he placed a small chest in that pack, wrapping it within clothes.

He froze as I entered the alley and then relaxed again.

"I know you, boy. One of the reaver's companions. What do you want?"

It was the second time that night that someone had called me boy. I didn't know if people were just keying off my height or actively trying to be disparaging. Unfortunately, this time, I couldn't afford to care.

"I take it you've heard the news?"

"Horde of blighted. Whole place will be rubble in a matter of days."

"Not if we drive them off."

He had yet to even look in my direction, but that finally changed. It was dark out, but I could read the disdain in eyes as black as his overgrown beard.

"We?"

"You're Copper, right? Worth more than ten Tins put together?"

"More like twenty."

I nodded. "Twenty then. I bet you could swat irkonnen away like they were flies."

"The reaver send you to beg on his behalf, boy? I know what you're doing."

"Trying to get your help? You're right; I am. We can't hold this town without you. Not even with Skaal. But with you up on the wall with us…"

"Forget it. Madea's a graveyard. It just doesn't know it yet. And you're not going to change that with your lies or your flattery or a spear that'll probably snap three minutes into the fight."

"The spear's stronger than you think it is. So am I."

He grunted and heaved the pack onto his shoulders. "Boy, I could break you in half over one knee and then do the same to your spear, and not only would nobody stop me, nobody would even care."

I tried again, leveraging *Deception* for all it was worth. "We just have to hold out for a few days."

"I've known dogs that yapped less than you. Probably tasted better too."

I wasn't going anywhere near *that* comment.

"Three days," I said instead. "Four at the most. And then reinforcements will be here."

Arrius coughed up something gross and spat it onto the road. "Madea's the only place of any size out here, boy. Ain't no other towns sending help." He pushed past me, heading for the main street.

"I'm not talking about towns," I said. "I'm talking about Grand Duke Willerton."

That was enough to get him to stop.

"What?"

"The duke's on his way."

"He and his army are in Zaris. Everyone knows that."

"Right." I swallowed, trying not to let the gamble I was about to take keep me from acting. "Because everyone knows his heir was killed there."

"Exactly."

"Unless she wasn't."

Skaal had described Arrius as brutish and a bully, and he seemed to be both things, but he also wasn't altogether stupid. He put together the pieces I'd handed him.

"The duke's daughter is in Madea? Your party found her?"

I nodded. "Which is why he's already on his way. I have to imagine a Copper who played a big role in defending the town—and the heir to the entire duchy—would get any reward they asked for."

I waited with bated breath. The problem was, I didn't know Arrius at all. I didn't know who he was, what he'd done in his life, or what he wanted, so I didn't know if my enticements would work. But unlike Skaal, he was a Copper who could use his techniques. We needed strength, and the man had it in spades.

"Who else knows?" asked Arrius.

"Just our party and a few others," I said. "You don't know who you can trust when times get tough."

I winced at my phrasing. The last thing I needed to do was talk about trust when I was lying my ass off.

"True," he finally agreed. "Three days… and I get your party's reward as well as mine."

"That's—"

"That's the deal. Take it or not."

I waited just long enough to make it seem real and then sighed. "Fine. You get our reward as well as yours, but the three days start tomorrow."

"Deal." He grunted again and left, his steps taking him back into town rather than towards the exterior wall.

I waited until he was out of sight and then let the shakes wash over me. The duke didn't even *know* about his daughter yet. And by Carlson's estimates, it would be at least a moon after the message's arrival before any troops reached Madea. But the blighted would be here in less than twenty-four hours, and this deal would give us two full days of Arrius fighting on the wall.

I had to hope that would be enough.

And if we both somehow survived long enough for my lies to be exposed…?

Well, maybe future-Brian would have a plan for that.

○○○

The guild hall was still a hive of activity when I returned, although there were now only a handful of people instead of twenty. Miko was gone, almost definitely back up in our room with Wilhemina, but Lace was drinking by herself in a corner.

"Ale?" I asked her.

She made a face. "I wish. Madea's stores of alcohol have been *requisitioned* for the town's defenses. Apparently, being a vital part of that defense doesn't count. Are you looking for Skaal? He's helping that Smith of yours move inventory."

"Actually, I was looking for you. I need your help."

"With what?"

I watched the blood drain from her face as I explained. When I was done, her eyes were wide. "Forget *Chosen*, you're actively insane. My clan would burn you alive to make sure the madness didn't spread."

"Is that a *no*?" The truth was, I couldn't do it without her.

"Do you really think it'll work?"

"I have no idea, honestly. But I read it in a book."

"A *book*." She scowled, sighed, and stood. "I'll get my coat."

67

The sun was already in the sky by the time we made it back to Madea. We didn't enter, but walked a slow perimeter around the town, three hundred yards from the exterior wall, starting just past the western Hill Gate and proceeding counterclockwise until we reached the road to Harborton.

When we were done, the north, northeastern, and most of the eastern approaches were still untouched, but there was no helping that. The blighted were coming from the southwest, and hopefully they'd focus on the town's two gates instead of trying to encircle the entire town.

There were guards on the walls and guards at the gates, as the mayor had ordered. The latter shook their heads as they let us in, questions in their eyes.

"Wasn't sure if you two were coming back," said one, voice gruff. He glanced at the blood on my spearhead and splattered across Lace's leathers and came to the obvious conclusion. "Good hunting?"

"Passable," said Lace. "Did the guild Scouts return yet?"

"About a glass ago, aye." He waved us into a street where more than a dozen people were helping to assemble wooden frames with long spikes. We'd already seen several in place outside the walls. "By midday, the mayor wants both gates shut. We'll be barricading them from within after the defenses are set."

"To keep people in or the blighted out?" asked Lace.

The guard gave a quick glance to the working townsfolk and lowered his voice. "Some of both, I'm guessing. We had more than a dozen Aspirants leave last night. Five were from our own guard."

"Any adventurers?"

He chewed on something, then spat to the side. "Huh. With you two back, I guess not."

Unnoticed and mostly ignored as usual, I breathed a sigh of relief. Arrius was sticking to his word so far.

We left the guards and the gate behind, making our way to the guild hall. Despite the early hour, Madea's citizens were working away, filling buckets of water, cutting bandages, or even blocking off certain side streets in case the attackers made it into the town. It would have been inspiring if it wasn't for the thick blanket of dread that overlaid everything and everyone.

Lace and I got some looks as we made our way, and I thought at least a few people perked up at the sight of two adventurers who had clearly been out taking the fight to the enemy. I wondered if the truth—that the kills we *had* made had been purely incidental—would reduce their already paltry enthusiasm.

The core of the blighted army was still many glasses away, but the farmers hadn't been wrong either; the land southwest of Madea was already crawling with the enemy. We'd done our best to avoid them as we could, but even Lace's *Stealth* had frequently proven insufficient.

Thankfully, they had only been irkonnen, and we'd encountered them in clusters of two or three at a time. Lace could have probably handled them by herself, but with the addition of my spear, they had fallen that much faster. Our biggest challenge had been two of the so-called outriders... scaled irkonnen perched on the backs of largely feral tuskers. My spear's range had proven its value yet again, impaling the tusker who charged me and keeping its natural weapons from tearing me to pieces even as I switched to my knife to deal with the irkonnen on its back. Lace, on the other hand, had danced around both of her targets, emptying her bandolier of throwing blades before she shadow stepped onto the back of the mortally wounded tusker, killing its rider with one blow.

I wasn't at peak satiation yet, but even without any quest completions, I could tell I was getting close. A part of me had wanted to stay out in the fields until I managed it, but common sense had prevailed. Every passing minute brought new irkonnen into the vicinity, and we could have found ourselves boxed in and overrun all too easily.

Also, we'd gotten what we had gone out into the wilderness for. While the book had been right, as evidenced by the fact that we were both still alive, neither Lace nor I had been willing to risk combat while carrying the packs we'd just filled.

Those packs had been empty again after our circumnavigation of Madea, but we'd left them in the fields anyway. It paid to be sure.

Carlson was speaking with the guard captain and one of the other party adventurers when we entered the guild hall. Sharp eyes assessed us both, pausing briefly on the bloody spear. "I heard the two of you disappeared last night."

"We had things to do, Assistant Deputy Keeper," said Lace, with the savage smile that almost never reached her eyes.

He nodded to my spear. "I can tell."

The guard captain interjected. "My men reported seeing you walk the town's perimeter before reentering. What was that about?"

He directed his question to Lace, just as Carlson had, and the Marauder shrugged.

"I just hope nobody else tries to leave the town," she said. "I wouldn't want them to encounter the surprises we've left for the blighted."

"Traps?" At Lace's lazy wave of acknowledgement, the captain nodded, stroking his long grey mustache. "I'll pass the word, not that anyone should be leaving the walls at this point anyway. Three hundred strides?"

"Let's say two hundred, just to be safe."

"I don't know how much good they'll do," I told them honestly, "but it should be something to see."

Carlson had already written two quick notes. He waited for the guard captain to read and approve them and then sent them winging through the air. "I've informed the guards at the gates," he said. "They can pass on word to the rest. Have either of you slept?"

"Sleep is what happens when there's nothing to do," said Lace.

"Then this seems like the appropriate time for it. Our Scouts made it back a glass ago. The bulk of the blighted army will be here by late afternoon. Guard Captain Pike will review the strategy for Madea's defense with everyone before then, but I want you both rested and replenished."

I didn't bother to hide my yawn. Even with a fifteen Vitality, the last few hours had been exhausting, physically and mentally.

"I've moved all of you into room six," added Carlson, carefully avoiding further mention of the duke's heir. "We'll need the other rooms to accommodate the townsfolk who will be sheltering here."

Lace just nodded and waved. She headed for the stairs, and I followed on her heels. The empty rooms we saw still only had two to three beds a piece, but blankets had been laid in the spaces between. We'd have five people in our room, but most other rooms looked like they'd be holding ten or more.

Miko was asleep next to Wilhemina. The girl didn't look any better than when we'd rescued her—outside of being a whole lot cleaner—but she didn't look any worse either. My nest-sister, on the other hand, looked deeply tired.

I found a seat and closed my eyes, doing my best to block out the noise from the streets and the even more persistent noise in my mind. It must have worked, because some time later, I opened my eyes again to see a familiar window.

```
You have increased the following skills:

Major skills:
Knife [+3]: 13/25
Light Armor [+3]: 25/25
Spear (U) [+1]: 25/25
Tactics [+4]: 20/25

Minor skills:
Athleticism [+1]: 25/25
Avoidance [+1]: 25/25
Focus [+3]: 11/25

General skills:
Deception [+3]: 10/10
Diplomacy [+1]: 1/10
Gathering [+1]: 1/10
Stealth [+2]: 10/10
```

As I saw my gains, I had to bite back a curse. I'd maxed out the necessary skills already. If I'd fought just a few more irkonnen on our way back, I could have been level five, with another technique or upgrade under my belt. Instead, I'd been cautious and was paying the price for it.

As for the rest of my gains? *Knife* continued to level at near meteoric speeds. The increase in *Tactics* had presumably come from listening to defensive discussions the night before as well as the few steps I'd taken to help bolster Madea's defenses. And *Deception…* well, lying to a Copper's face was clearly worth a few points.

Diplomacy and *Gathering* were both new and welcome, but less important than maxing out *Stealth*. I would never match Lace's sneakiness, given that it was a class skill for her, but if *Beast Skin* had been any indication, there was a chance that the upgrades or techniques I would be offered would have a stealthy facet to them now.

Given that I was *still* stuck at level four, I couldn't know for sure.

I dismissed the window and looked over at Lace, lying flat on her back on the blanket between my bed and Wilhemina's. "Are you asleep?"

"Yes," she replied. "Why?"

"I was hoping we could spar some? I'm close to a level."

She didn't even open her eyes. "How close?"

"Feels like a few fights away?"

"That'd be several *days* of sparring, even at your level. We should've killed more blighted when we were out in the wilds."

"Yes, I'm realizing that."

"Good thing there's a horde of the rotters on their way here. Now go to sleep. And Brian?"

"Yeah?"

"Don't think I've forgotten. You and Miko owe us your story."

"I could tell you now if you want."

"I really don't. Some maniac had me out wandering the forest all night because of something he read in a book."

"Sounds like a smart guy."

"I guess we'll find out soon enough."

○○○

I opened my eyes to the soft light of *Minor Healing*. Miko was awake and standing next to the duke's heir, orange eyes closed and hand hovering over the little girl's forehead. The synossian turned to me as I stirred.

"I thought I might have to wake you."

I yawned. I felt refreshed if not exactly rested. Lace had apparently already left again. "It was a long night."

"But successful?"

"I hope so. We'll find out for sure when the blighted show up." I went through my forms and found nothing amiss beyond the aches and pains of *not* getting *Minor Healing* cast on me. "I'm sorry you couldn't come with us."

"*Stealth* is not a skill of mine, even if I had not had other responsibilities…" Her eyes strayed to the little girl. "I am more concerned that I will not be at our party's side for the battle itself. I have met the other healers, and they are strong and seem trustworthy, but…"

"I know. I'd feel better if you were with us too. But Carlson is right… you need to preserve your energy for keeping Wilhcmina safe and alive. And it's not like they're letting the other healers up on the wall either."

"You have seen where the clinic was established, right?"

"Yeah. It's just a block away."

"If you get injured, promise me you will go there to be healed."

"I'll do what I can."

"If they are too busy, come to me. Unless the pattern of Lady Willerton's malady shifts, I should have energy for a few extra casts of *Minor Healing* each day."

I'd never really had someone fuss over me like a mother hen before. It was kind of nice. Not as helpful as the Priestess fighting by our side, but... *nice.*

"Are you sure we're doing the right thing by staying?" I asked her.

"In the absence of a quest from the gods..." she waited for me to confirm I still hadn't received anything, "then we have only our own morals to guide us. I do not understand how this child's life became linked with mine, but I will not abandon her."

"And our chance of slipping away *with* her was always close to zero." I nodded. We'd been through all of this at least twice, but the very real possibility of death in the next few days had my mind going back to the debate.

"And from a more utilitarian standpoint," she continued, "few things will be more directly beneficial for my people than the friendship of a grand duke. One bite of the thegar we have both mentioned was forming connections. This one would be undeniable."

"And if we both die?"

"I don't know." She swallowed. "I am as scared as you are, Brian. Not just of death but of making the wrong decision and what it might mean for others. But we can only do what we think is best. All else is up to fate or chance or both."

"You're right." I finally stood, reaching for the spear at my bedside. "I'm just wallowing. We're going to both be fine and we'll come out of this even stronger."

"Speaking of which..." A sharp-toothed smile bloomed on her face. "All of this healing has had its benefits; I leveled this morning."

"Level six?"

She nodded happily.

"Which is why you have the excess energy for healing."

"Precisely. The last few moons have been… hard, but two levels in less than a cycle would have been almost unheard of back home."

"We'll both be Tin by the time your people arrive," I said.

"Tin?" Miko didn't have eyebrows, but the ridge of scales over one eye twitched. "I plan to be Copper!"

ooo

Within a glass, the war council gathered to discuss final details of their defensive strategy. The spiked frames we'd seen the townsfolk making had been placed around the town's exterior wall, blocking the gates and funneling attackers into kill zones where guards and other Aspirants would stand ready with weapons. Buckets of ale had been stored on the ground just inside the wall to be poured down on attackers, and several Cooks from the town's taverns waited nearby, their techniques to boil water just as effective on ale.

Including the guards with crossbows, there were only a dozen or so defenders with ranged weaponry, but thanks to Mrrl and the town Fletcher, they would have ample ammunition. If the walls were overrun—*when* the walls were overrun, one of the guards had muttered darkly—there were established choke points to fall back to. If *those* were overrun, well… we'd be fighting in the streets if not already dead.

Carlson kept one adventuring party and a small group of Aspirants in reserve, but the rest of us were up on the wall. Arrius and Skaal, as our only two Coppers, would roam the wall as needed, buttressing the defense. That left Lace and I as the world's smallest and least impressive adventuring party, all two of us assigned above the Forest Gate, where we'd have a fantastic view of the horde coming to kill us.

Once we reached our post, I walked my section of the wall a few times, and then reviewed the pathways between wall and fallback position, wall and clinic, fallback position and clinic…

Eventually, I realized I had long since memorized my routes. Now, I was just tiring myself out. And maybe psyching myself out too.

I rejoined Lace on the wall.

"Got all of that out of your system?" asked the Marauder.

"I think so."

"Good. You were making Lissiana nervous."

The lanky alien archer who was one of Guard Captain Pike's lieutenants snorted. Her bow was unstrung, and her eyes were trained on the distant forest. We could see blighted milling about, but they had yet to emerge into the open space.

"I'm Brian," I told her.

"Yes, I know." Where the captain was gruff and no-nonsense, his lieutenant was just no-nonsense. "If you don't mind, I'm trying to stay alert."

I glanced at the distant tree line, back at Lissiana, then shrugged. "Irkonnen aren't *that* fast, even on tuskers, but I get it. I'll leave you alone."

"Thank you."

I wandered back over to where Lace sat with the rest of our small group of defenders. "She's a little bit testy."

"Everyone handles nerves differently. Miko fusses over her friends, you start randomly socializing, and Skaal monologues about ice and mountain winds."

"And you?"

"I point out everyone's blindingly obvious flaws or bad habits." Her smile came and went. "You're clear on what to do when they come?"

"Defend the wall, Lissiana, and our two other archers. Use my spear to stab anyone climbing toward us. It's straightforward enough that I doubt I'll even get a point in *Tactics* for it."

"I think you'll be surprised." For the first time in a glass, the Marauder stood. "Do you see that, Lissiana?"

"Yes." The woman's voice was as brisk as ever, but I could tell some unknown emotion lurked just beneath. "They're gathering."

A call went up along the wall and more defenders surged to their feet. A few minutes later, irkonnen poured from the forest, their numbers too great to count, a tide of scaled humanoids that seemed likely to wash right over Madea without even slowing.

I waited for the traps Lace and I had painstakingly laid to bear fruit, but the irkonnen just charged right through.

"We forgot to account for travel distance," I told the Marauder.

"Fight now, talk later," she told me.

That was fair.

I turned back to the onrushing wave of enemies. They'd separated into multiple ranks, with only the first batch, maybe three hundred irkonnen in total, headed our way. According to Carlson's briefing, that was a *bad* sign, as it meant the blighted really were under the cultists' control. The blighted weren't known for their strategy. Or their restraint.

Meanwhile, *I* was just grateful to be facing a few hundred irkonnen rather than the thousands still waiting behind.

Three hundred yards was a *lot* of ground to cover, and it was almost ten seconds before our archers started loosing their arrows and bolts. Lissiana was one of the first to fire, barely pausing to aim between shots. I watched irkonnen fall, one after the other, to be trampled by the greater mass.

She wasn't using any techniques that I could see, just her bow and the associated skill. Here and there, spells exploded in the midst of the charging irkonnen as Madea's few Mages entered the fight, but mostly it was arrows that told the tale of those first few seconds. Pike had instructed us all to be judicious with our spells and abilities, but it was a difficult balance to find. The numbers of the blighted were such that rampant technique usage would exhaust us long before we ran out of enemies. On the other hand, it didn't do any good to save energy while being completely overrun either.

The closer the irkonnen got, the more concentrated the volleys became, and by the time the foul creatures reached our makeshift defenses outside the walls, almost a hundred of the creatures lay dead, many of them struck non-fatally by an arrow only to then be torn apart by the clawed feet of their own kin.

The barricades slowed the blighted some and more enemies fell to point-blank shots, but then the rest were at the wall, leaping higher than anything their size should be capable of. Clawed hands and feet found purchase in mortar and sometimes even stone.

Lace and I rushed forward, our movements echoed along the wall by the other defenders. I stabbed down with my spear, trying to strike climbing irkonnen without getting pulled over the edge. It was a losing tactic. I couldn't get the right angle to put force behind my strikes without leaning out, and that left me vulnerable, not just to the irkonnen swarming up the wall, but to their fellows, lurking below and hurling sharp-edged stones up at us.

I pulled back instead and focused on stabbing the irkonnen as they clambered over the battlements. Timed just right, I could knock them back off again, and while my initial strikes were rarely fatal, damage was both done to and delivered by my targets as they fell back down.

An unnamed Aspirant collapsed next to me, blood fountaining from his throat, but Lace was there, long blade piercing an irkonnen through the eye as she drove her knife into the spine of another. I impaled the creature creeping up behind her, withdrew my spear, and whipped the butt around to crack a climbing irkonnen in the skull.

There was a thunk I couldn't hear over the battle, but could feel in my hands, and the blighted fell away again.

It felt like we'd been fighting for hours, not minutes, when a call went up behind us. Lace pulled me back to where Lissiana and the archers had retreated and a wave of townsfolk pushed past us, bearing not weapons but buckets of boiling ale. One slipped in the bloody mess atop the wall, his screams mercifully brief as he fell, but the others reached the edge unscathed and upended their buckets, shrinking back from the steam that rose from the mass of suddenly screaming irkonnen below.

And then it was our turn again, replacing the retreating bucket brigade as we prepared for the next wave.

Only… the next wave didn't come.

Out in the field, far beyond the range of anyone on the wall, the irkonnen ranks had devolved into chaos. Cries of anger and pain had replaced the usual yipping, and techniques flashed as the blighted spun about, tearing at the ground, the air, and each other.

"What in the cold heavens?" asked Lissiana. She made a series of gestures with her long-fingered hands, gestures that I recognized even before a viewing window appeared in the air before her. Magnified a hundred times, the distant irkonnen were larger than life, and so were the small creatures that flitted between them doing their level best to devour everything in the area. "Are those…?"

"Lurkers," I confirmed, scanning the field where the scene was being repeated across the blighted army's overly long lines.

"But how?"

"It's strange what you can find in books. It turns out there was a farmer once who saw false dawn as an untapped resource, a cash crop that nobody had thought to leverage. He learned how to harvest the berries without crushing them and alerting the nest beneath."

"I've never heard of anyone selling false dawn."

"Well, no. Even when harvested safely, it turns out the berries erupt on their own after a seven-day. Given the amount the farmer had stockpiled, his whole farm *and* the nearby town were wiped out. I'm pretty sure the author meant the story to be a warning, but…" I shrugged. "The harvesting method worked."

"You used false dawn to trap the town." I couldn't tell if Lissiana was horrified or impressed. "You're a madman."

Lace snorted. "That's what I said."

68

I'd been hoping that the lurkers would wipe out the opposition for us, but it seemed Madea had been doing *too* good a job of clearing out nearby nests before our arrival. It took a blessedly long while, but order was eventually restored to the invading army, every lurker torn to pieces or—in cases unhelpfully highlighted by Lissiana's *Farseeing* technique—literally eaten.

Still, several hundred more of the blighted were down, and I was pretty sure I'd seen one or two dead essoli among the masses of irkonnen. As far as traps went, ours beat the hell out of pits with spikes or even *Indiana Jones*-style crashing logs. Downsides notwithstanding.

"You'll probably have to burn the fields to make sure no new nests take root," I admitted. "But that's something to worry about if we survive."

The good news was that they hadn't mounted a second assault just yet. The better news was that the sensation in my core told me I'd done enough to reach level five.

"I doubt you're the only one," said Lace when I told her. "The longer this goes on, the stronger the survivors will get."

She wasn't wrong, but this too was a case where numbers mattered. We'd lost three Aspirants just from our section of the wall, and while one of them had been carried off to the clinic for healing, the other two were simply gone. If that casualty rate continued, we were screwed. There was no way the rest of us could advance fast enough to make up for the people we were losing.

It was early evening when the next attack came. If the first had been a berserker rush, this one proved *someone* was at the wheel. The Khamani cult leader, I was guessing, though we hadn't seen anything but blighted so far. The irkonnen didn't have shields, but they came in a looser formation, giving each other space to dodge, and for our archers to frankly just plain miss. It took them longer to reach the wall, but they lost maybe a quarter of their number instead of a third.

And that meant significantly more bodies to climb the wall.

We were busy fighting for our lives, more and more techniques firing off around me, when a boom sounded below us and the entire structure shook. The irkonnen we couldn't see must have clambered over the fortifications to get to the gate. I stabbed another irkonnen, kicked him off my spear into a second creature just climbing up, and ran to our side of the wall. "We need another round of ale!"

Turns out they were way ahead of me on that front. Maybe because people who *aren't* engaged in life-or-death struggle are a little more attuned to everything else happening around them. Four men and one sturdy woman were already on their way up the stairs, arms straining with their steaming burdens.

I grabbed the two closest Aspirants, one a guard, the other a sharp-faced fellow who fought with a short staff like Miko, and pointed to the part of the wall that overlooked the Forest Gate.

"We need to keep that area clear!"

I wasn't sure if either could hear me, or if they just wondered who I was and why I had decided to give orders, but as the bucket brigade reached the wall, realization set in. The three of us headed for the section of wall, bolstering the two people fighting there, and clearing a circle of space for the townsfolk to occupy.

More screaming. More steam. This time, none of the unarmed bucket carriers died. Best of all, the battering down below came to an immediate and precipitous end.

A scream rang out, and I spun, to see a different guard go down in the area of wall I'd just vacated. There were five irkonnen up on the wall already, with more climbing behind them.

Lace appeared in a blur and two irkonnen went down, but even with those deaths, five had become nine just as quickly. The Marauder took one hit, then another, and slowly gave way.

I picked my target and prepared to trigger *Lunge* when a large shape brushed me aside. In two great strides, they were among the irkonnen, each swing of their weapon literally launching the smaller creatures back off the wall. In moments, nine irkonnen had become five, then three, and then that section of the wall was clear again.

I couldn't hear Lace, but I could read her lips. "Thanks, old ma—" The Marauder cut off as she realized it was Arrius who had saved her not Skaal. The Copper didn't even look her way, heading to another section of the wall that looked in danger of being overrun.

By that time, I had joined Lace. Along with the staff-wielding Aspirant, we returned to our bloody game of whack-a-mole, striking down irkonnen as they appeared.

They didn't try the gate again, and it was only a matter of minutes before the irkonnen still alive turned and loped back toward the core of the army, running on all fours like the beasts they resembled.

I was exhausted. My hands were cramping around the spear they held, my mind was fuzzy from the lack of sleep and the intense focus needed to fight in sheer chaos, and for some reason my *feet* hurt too.

"Please tell me that was the last attack of the day," I said, examining my boots to make sure nothing had stabbed me through them. As far as I could tell, they were whole and unharmed. The soft soles that were so useful for sneaking through the woods, however, were a lot less comfortable when fighting atop a blood-soaked stone wall.

As if in answer to my prayers, a bird landed in Lissiana's open hand and unfolded into a note. She nodded my way. "Make way for the reserves coming up. Pike says the rest of you are off until a few glasses after midnight. Register your gains with the Framework and then get some sleep."

"What about you?" I asked.

"When you all come back, you'll be replacing me. We need at least one person in each section with clear sight."

"Meaning night vision," Lace told me, as we headed for the guild hall. "I guess I volunteered to be that person for the second half of the night."

"That explains your inclusion. What about me?"

"Party sticks together." She scanned the wall, almost definitely looking for Skaal, and sighed. "Or at least that's how it's supposed to work. You watch my back, I'll watch yours."

"He'll be fine."

"Of course he will… unless he does something stupid and selfless again." We passed through a guard post where a handful of irkonnen bodies had been piled to the side, a clear sign that there'd been at least one short-lived breach atop the wall. "I hate to say it, but it's a good thing you convinced Arrius to stay. The man's an ass but he's worth a hundred irkonnen all on his own."

"Yeah well… we only have two days left of his help."

"And then what happens?"

"He realizes the duke isn't showing up when I said he would, and either kills me or leaves or both."

"Are you *looking* for ways to commit suicide?"

I decided it was a bad time to tell her I'd also promised our party's share of the duke's eventual reward.

"It was the only way to keep him here," I said instead.

"Then I won't complain. Likelihood is, we'll both be dead tomorrow anyway. Blighted aren't known for their patience and I can't imagine the followers of a god called the Ever-Hungry are either."

We passed through the door of the guild hall, finding a tired Captain Pike standing with the seemingly indefatigable Carlson. Messengers were streaming in and out, and the keeper was using his technique to dispatch notes to recipients on the wall in response. Neither looked our way as we headed for the stairs.

Miko was awake when we entered the room, light from a single lantern glimmering off her white scales. "Is it over?"

"It's barely begun," said Lace. The Marauder winced as she pulled off her leather breastplate and set it aside. Her shirt underneath was soaked. Most of it was sweat, but there was also visible blood.

"You're hurt." Miko intercepted the other woman.

"They're just scrapes. Nothing a bandage or two won't solve. Save your healings for the little girl. If we survive all this, she's our ticket to a better life."

"Miko said earlier she has some energy to spare," I said. "Courtesy of a new level."

"Another level already?" Lace shook her head and stopped resisting. "I forgot what it was like to be unranked. So weak and yet progress lurks around every corner."

Instead of casting her spell, Miko sent me a glance. "Are *you* injured, nest-brother?"

"Just sore." I'd taken a few hits, although I couldn't precisely remember when or how, but between my hauberk and my gambeson, I'd come through with little more than bruises. "I don't need healing."

"You know," said Lace, gritting her teeth as she peeled her shirt away from the two bloody wounds she'd taken, "it's impolite to offer to heal someone and then turn around and prioritize someone else."

"Indeed? I am learning much about impoliteness here," said Miko, in nearly flawless Trade. "I think it comes from the company I keep."

Before the Marauder could reply, a glow gathered around Miko's clawed hands. *Minor Healing* did its thing and Lace's *scrapes* stopped bleeding, one of them closing up entirely.

"Next level," said Miko, "I will take either a new heal or something offensive."

"Speaking of next level…"

"Already?" Miko asked, unconsciously repeating Lace's earlier response. "Truly, the gods have blessed you."

"I'd hope so." Lace said it before I could. The Marauder lay down on her bedroll, pausing to spear the Priestess with a look. "We're expected back on the wall in about five glasses. Can you get us something to eat and drink before then?"

"Yes. Sleep and heal."

The other woman nodded. Either she had nothing to communicate with the Framework or she meditated differently than the rest of us, because she was out in a matter of seconds.

As for me… for the second time in a day, I closed my eyes and let my recent experiences flow through me. The hours atop the wall. The seemingly endless wave of small scaled dogs coming to tear us to pieces. The screams from the unseen irkonnen as they boiled alive, and the sheer mayhem unleashed by the false dawn trap we'd so painstakingly set.

I couldn't decide whether to be annoyed that Lace and I had literally risked our lives for a nature-born scourge that only ended up killing a small fraction of the total enemy force… or elated that the plan had worked at all. In the end, we'd killed hundreds of irkonnen without having to fire a shot, and in doing so, cost the enemy time for a third attack before dark.

When I opened my eyes again, however many minutes later, all my minor aches were gone. Even my feet felt like they'd just spent a long weekend in one of those spas that only exist on television or in fancy resorts that real people never get to visit.

I knew exactly what that feeling meant.

```
Congratulations, Warrior.

You have reached level 5!
```

I swiped the screen away and pulled up the next one:

```
You have increased the following skills:

Major skills:
Formations [+2]: 12/30
Medium Armor [+3]: 3/30
Tactics [+4]: 24/30

Minor skills:
Focus [+4]: 15/30
Leadership (U) [+1]: 1/30
Pain Tolerance [+2]: 25/30
```

Not a ton of skills had advanced, because my main ones had already been capped for the level, but still, there were some interesting finds. Like Lace had said, *Tactics* had taken another sizable leap, maybe just for me not completely losing my mind in my first large-scale battle.

Focus continued to grow, as did *Pain Tolerance*. More interestingly, I had two new skills: *Medium Armor* and *Leadership*. The first answered my question about what the hauberk qualified as… and probably explained why I'd felt so much less comfortable in it, but the second?

I'd never been a leader growing up. I'd never been much of anything other than an outcast and the kid with no mom whose dad had started acting weird in public. I wasn't sure I cared about being a leader on Eos either, but… if it helped convince people to do what I wanted, or even better, helped make up for the automatic loss of prestige that inevitably came with my less-than-optimal height?

Yeah, I could live with the *Leadership* skill. And it being an Uncommon skill had to mean good things too.

But now it was time for the main event, my level five advancement option.

Except… when I dismissed the skill-up window, I got a totally new dialogue screen instead.

Congratulations, Warrior.

You have earned a new title: Agent of the Wild

I didn't have any idea what that meant. It didn't take a genius to guess I'd somehow earned it thanks to my trick with the false dawn, but did it *do* anything for me, or was it just kind of a soul trophy to remember that I had once done something incredibly insane that actually sort of paid off?

I wasn't sure. Titles had been a very limited section in the Framework books I'd found in Madea's archives. Some scholars swore they were the key to unlocking secret paths, where others thought they were worth little more than the lines of text they added to your personal record.

I'd have to figure out which category mine fit into, but for now, I just wanted to see my freaking technique options. Thankfully, the Framework was done serving me random windows:

```
Congratulations, Warrior.

Select your level 5 advancement option:

-    Upgrade: Lunge (C) -> Liberating Lunge (U)
-    Upgrade: Beast Skin (C) -> Beast Hide (U)
-    New technique: Deceptive Strike (U)
```

This time, I had two upgrade choices, and only one new technique. I was half relieved and half irritated to see that *Fueled by Pain* wasn't on offer anymore. As for the choices I *had* gotten…?

I opened my eyes. Lace was asleep, a still shape in her bedroll, but Miko was kneeling in an open space in the room, engaged in her distinctly one-way dialogue with Aurea. She stirred as I approached, orange eyes blinking in the lantern's flickering light.

"Did you level?" With everyone else asleep or unconscious, she had reverted to the High Tongue.

"I did. Do you feel like helping me make my pick?"

"If I recall correctly, you ended up ignoring everyone's suggestions last time and making your own choice."

"I was younger then, and dumber." I ran down the options available to me. As usual, without any descriptions or help text, it didn't take long.

"*Beast Skin* has already been useful," I admitted, "but I've got armor now too. I'm not sure I want to upgrade the technique when what I really need is more offense."

"Lace may have heard of *Deceptive Strike*," said Miko, and if there was a tiny touch of disapproval in her tone, I was pretty sure it was reserved for the technique's name and not the sleeping Marauder. "It is not an ability that I recall from the primacy."

That was understandable, assuming that I'd been given it because I'd maxed out *Deception*… or *Stealth*… or both. The synossians—at least *Miko's* synossians—were big on honor and honesty. Even the Rogues in Riok's band had been the sort of people you'd happily take home to mother.

Assuming you had a mother… and that she wouldn't totally freak when presented with seven-foot-tall lizard soldiers.

"*Liberating Lunge* we have already discussed," continued Miko. "I don't know what it does, but if it interacts with your Ideal…"

I nodded. I'd had a lot of time to think about that technique since I'd rejected it in the centipede cave. "*Lunge* is as much a movement technique as an attack. I'm thinking it either expands those capabilities or removes some of the restrictions."

"How so?"

"Like maybe it'll let me *Lunge* to places I can't see, as long as they're in range, or will let me travel even when I'm somehow pinned or bound?"

She tapped her left forearm. "So, will you take that then?"

"I don't think so. Not now anyway. I've been offered it twice, which is a strong indicator I might be offered it again. And as much as *Lunge* is a staple in my arsenal, what I need is another ability I can chain with it."

"For when *Lunge* is unavailable."

"Exactly. What I think—"

I staggered as a chorus of whispers assaulted my mind. Whispers I hadn't heard since the ruins where Khamani's cult had set up shop.

"Brian? Are you okay?"

I winced through the pain of voices that spoke of horrors unseen but felt. "Can't you *hear* them?"

"Hear what?" said Lace, awake in an instant.

I had my spear in hand and was already heading for the door.

"Essoli," I gasped. "Somewhere in town. Somewhere near."

It turned out that neither Lace nor Miko could hear the insane muttering. It shielded them from the assault I was currently undergoing but left them blind to the essoli's presence. And if I had *Speaker of Tongues* to thank for this particular… let's call it *gift*… that meant the rest of Madea was similarly blind.

Which was a problem for multiple reasons, the biggest being that the volume of those mental whispers meant the essoli should've been in the room with us. As that clearly wasn't the case, it left only one other possibility.

There was more than one in town.

Lace pulled her breastplate on, turned for Miko to tighten the straps, and then tugged me downstairs where Pike and Carlson were still standing and strategizing. Nobody in the guild hall seemed aware that the blighted were stalking the night.

"There are essoli in town," said Lace, cutting through the two men's conversation. "They must have made it over the wall somehow."

"How do you know that?"

She waved to me. "Brian can sense them."

"Are you—"

"Yes," I interrupted. "I'm sure."

Pike barked an order and the small contingent of guards who had been resting in the common room climbed to their feet.

"Can you tell where they are?" asked the guard captain.

I closed my eyes. It made the whispers worse, but I'd been through this before. I tuned out the words that made no sense and focused instead on where they were coming from. I took a half-step to the right and turned, finger coming up to point of its own accord.

"There."

I opened my eyes and found I was pointing at a wall. A bare wall. Thankfully, Carlson was quicker to the punch than I was.

"Not in here, but outside. What's in that direction?"

Pike went as gray as his moustache. "The clinic. Men, form up. You," he said, pointing a gauntleted hand at me, "come with us."

Lace started to follow, only to be stopped by the guild keeper. "We need you here," he was telling her, as I followed Pike out into the darkness, "in case they double back and come at the hall."

Lace must have lost the ensuing argument, as she stayed inside.

The clinic was less than a block away, and even from outside, we could see something was wrong. The lanterns were out, and no sounds emanated from within. Meanwhile, the essoli speech was echoing all around me, so thick I could have drowned in it.

"Light!" snapped Pike, and one of his guards responded, summoning an orb that was eerily similar to the ones we'd seen in the cult's dungeon. She sent it ahead of her, in through the open doorway.

There were bodies on the floor, and while most appeared to have been laid there for healing, their half-dissolved remains told me they would never be getting up again. And near the back of the room, the misshapen, amorphous form of an essoli was lashing out at a flickering energy shield. Behind it, one of the town's healers had dropped to one knee. His mouth was open, but we couldn't hear his scream.

The guards rushed in, Pike at their lead. The guard captain's sword glowed a brilliant blue and then arced down, almost too fast to follow, cutting a deep gash in the essoli's central mass. In response, a fusillade of tentacles came at him and the other guards. One man stumbled and fell but was dragged out of danger before a tentacle could strike. The rest worked as a unit, parrying tentacle strikes to create spaces for Pike to counterattack.

I was pretty sure this essoli was stronger than the one we'd faced in the dungeon, but the environment was less favorable, and the numbers it faced too great. The outcome of the fight was clear, even to a level-five Warrior like me.

Only… hadn't I thought there were *multiple* essoli?

Danger Sense screamed a warning that would have been far too late if I hadn't immediately triggered *Lunge*, blurring a half-dozen feet to the side. Behind me, another essoli came out of the shadows, half again as large as the first. A dozen tentacles whipped at me again and with *Lunge* now on cooldown, my dodge to the side was just a shade too slow. Burning pain traveled up my leg from the point of impact, but I kept moving.

I brought up my technique selection window, made my choice, and shut it again, all within the space between heartbeats. And then, before I could think better of it, I triggered *Deceptive Strike* and thrust.

Riok's spear lashed out, but as it did so, it blurred and I blurred with it. I was suddenly a few feet to the side, watching myself strike, even as I mirrored the action.

The tentacles I'd only partially avoided the first time struck the image of me, trapping it and tearing it to pieces, but as the illusion faded, my unseen spear drove deep into the creature's body from my new position, deeper than it had in the caves despite stats that remained the same. I withdrew the spear, sidestepped the tentacles that emerged from the side of the mass I'd just struck, and thrust again.

This time, the essoli was slower to respond. Maybe it was the wound I'd just dealt or maybe its tormented excuse for a mind remembered what had happened the last time and thought I was another illusion. Either way, I landed another, slightly less punishing blow.

That woke it up, and once again, my *Avoidance* proved insufficient. I tried to roll with the blows that hit me, creating space between the essoli and me as I held to Riok's spear, but the creature filled that space in an instant. The whispers crescendoed in my mind and though the words still made no sense, still felt like cracks in the world rather than the building blocks of communication, I sensed something like triumph behind the creature's speech.

I did the only thing I could do.

I spoke back.

I don't know what I said, because even with *Speaker of Tongues* granting me knowledge of their language, I still lacked the understanding of it, lacked the necessary frame of reference for it to make sense. But I spoke anyway, and the essoli paused, mid-strike.

And *that* gave Guard Captain Pike just enough time to reach us both. His sword was white now, not blue, and his armor was scored by hits from the other essoli, but his overhead slash tore into the central mass of the creature, met the gaping hole my *Deceptive Strike* had made, and continued on through to bury itself in the cobblestone road beneath.

Blessed silence filled my mind. It took me a moment to realize Pike was even speaking to me, took me even longer to convince *Speaker of Tongues* to swap back to a language that didn't torture reality through its very existence.

"Are there any more?" he asked.

"No." I wanted to collapse, the wound in my leg and the newer one in my side both suddenly burning beyond *Pain Tolerance*'s ability to mute, but I forced myself upright, forced myself to hold on to my spear. "That's all of them."

69

We were already on the wall when the next day dawned. Both Lace and I had been granted a few hours of sleep after the essoli attack, but for the first time in months, I found myself desperately missing coffee. My eyes were dry, irritated, and heavy, and the sight of the teeming horde of blighted awaiting us didn't do anything to perk me up.

After our return to the guild hall, Carlson had taken me aside. "I'm not going to ask how you can sense essoli, just like I'm not going to ask how you learned the secret code of the cult of Khamani. Your past is your past, and your actions have proven that you're not with them anymore. What we *are* going to do, however, is rotate you off the walls in the afternoon so that you can help us watch for any future assaults at night."

He'd made the perfectly wrong assumption about why and how I could do the things I did, but I let it slide. It was safer than sharing my trait, especially if that trait led him to dig into the rest of my past. I'd be an ex-cultist for however long it took to be done with Madea, and then I'd reinvent myself when we headed to Trynfall with the duke's men.

Unfortunately, any relief I had in knowing that I only had around eight hours on the wall before I got a break was completely undercut by the knowledge that I'd once again be staying up for most of the night.

The sun was just clearing the tree line to our left when the blighted horde finally stirred. Chanting arose in the distinctive yipping language of the irkonnen, and Lace leaned in my direction.

"What are they saying?"

"You don't want to know." Despite my exhaustion, I felt a snarl forming on my face. The blighted weren't entirely at fault for what they were—they had been created as monsters, after all, according to Mordecai—but they'd had centuries to grow and change and instead seemed to have only gotten worse with each passing generation. I wasn't sure what other sub-species there were beyond the irkonnen and the essoli, but I was more and more convinced that they all needed to die.

I didn't realize I'd said that last part out loud until Lace clapped me on the back. "Hold on to that feeling," she said. "You'll need it today. Spite will keep you going long after hope is gone."

It was something I'd expect a devotee of the Night Hag to say.

I just nodded, eyes fixed on the enemy I could only vaguely see. I'd sacrificed a full glass of sleep to squeeze in yet another meditation that morning—my third in the last day. It had only amped up my desperate need for sleep or coffee or both, but the tradeoff had been worth it:

```
You have increased the following attributes:

Will [+1]: 15
```

Dealing with the excruciating pain of the essoli's speech had been enough to boost my Will a point all on its own. My energy pool for techniques would now be at least a little bit larger, but just as importantly, I'd have a better chance of avoiding soul-crushing migraines if I encountered any more of the monsters. I'd also seen gains in *Spear*, *Medium Armor*, *Athletics*, *Avoidance*, *Focus*, and, yes, *Pain Tolerance*, bringing me almost halfway to my next level.

Skill-wise, anyway. As for the experience side of things… I was already there, though neither Miko nor Lace could explain how or why. The Marauder's best guess was that I'd gotten credit for the irkonnen the lurkers had killed the previous day. A Rogue's mechanical traps gave them experience when used in battle, and a Mage or Priest's summons did the same. The lurkers didn't technically count as either… but maybe the Framework had decided to see it otherwise? Or maybe Shan was somehow interceding on my behalf again?

Hell if I knew. All I knew was that after I'd spent months working my way to first level three and then level four, level six was already in view. And all it had taken was a small war and the likely death of everyone I knew.

I shook off the maudlin thought, realizing I'd gone silent for far too long. "Did you speak with Skaal?"

Lace pretended I *hadn't* zoned out in the middle of our conversation. "Yeah. He held the wall all night. Plans to do the same today and tomorrow."

"Won't he have to crash after that?"

She nodded. "Soon after, anyway. He says it won't matter. That things will be decided by then. The loss of our wounded and one of our three healers last night only accelerated things. Either Pike's new plan works, or we'll all be food." She gave me some serious side eye. "Unless you've got any other tricks to play?"

"I'm afraid I'm out."

"Then we hold to the plan. Whatever else happens, today will be different."

She wasn't wrong, and it started with the very first irkonnen assault. Much like the second wave, this one made it to the town without losing more than a small fraction of its numbers. Some of that was the enemy learning how to defeat volleyed fire, some of it was that we'd lost several archers in the previous assaults, but the rest of it…

…well, that was by design.

Atop the wall, a half-dozen men and women in light armor stepped forward, each accompanied by a single guard with a shield. Techniques triggered, one after the other. One large swath of land turned to a pool of mud that dragged down the irkonnen who had been passing through. In another spot, the scraps of one of the wooden barricades came to life, tearing through another cluster of blighted. Spikes sprouted from the earth outside of the Forest Gate, making an approach all but impossible.

The spellcasters retreated and now our archers stepped forward, each triggering their own techniques on the stalled irkonnen advance. Where individual arrows had failed to make much difference, the abilities unleashed in rapid succession absolutely ravaged the horde. In our section only a dozen survived to even reach the top of the wall, and the rest of us were waiting there to dispatch them.

In less than twenty minutes, an entire wave of attackers had been annihilated.

Of course, half the people on the wall had used a good chunk of their energy in that same stretch of time. But our first day of battle had shown Pike and Carlson that we couldn't survive a war of attrition. The numbers arrayed against us were simply too great. The blighted had lost at least a thousand of their kind over their first three assaults, corpses thick in the fields all the way out to the tree line, but it was just a fraction of the greater whole, of a throng whose numbers seemingly continued to swell.

Our best strategy was to make a show of overwhelming strength, to convince the minds behind the blighted assault that our resources were greater than they knew… that *they* were the ones who needed to change their plans.

To misquote a certain fictional superhero back on earth… we needed to make them think we could do this all day.

Ten minutes later, the second wave hit, and though it was dispersed almost as easily as the first, some of the casters and at least a couple of the archers were already looking haggard. Another wave, maybe two, and our bluff would be obvious.

Thankfully, the enemy blinked first. Something emerged from the forest, unfolding into a shape far taller than the town's walls, each of its legs as thick around as the trees it had left behind.

There were eight of those legs, because no fantasy nightmare would be complete without an enormous terror of a spider. And because Eos was a special brand of horrible, the creature's massive, distorted face was almost human.

A few feet away, Lissiana sucked in a breath. "A shadeweaver," she said, voice cold and empty. "I didn't think any were left."

"Another species of blighted?"

She nodded. "One of the few that were truly sterile. They were used as siege breakers in the wars."

It kind of felt like overkill for a town as small as Madea.

The third wave started forward, bigger than the last. This time, I spotted essoli among the irkonnen. In the daylight, the horrific creatures would be less effective, but still devastating if they could gain the wall. And behind them stalked the shadeweaver, black hairy hide, bulging spider eyes in an oversized human face, and legs that made Riok's spear look like a sewing needle.

"Use what abilities you can," said Lissiana, and those near her passed the command down the line. "Defeat this wave, kill the shadeweaver, and the leadership will have no choice but to show themselves or give up the fight."

I saw nods and renewed optimism among the guards on our section of the wall. We'd just crushed two waves with barely any casualties, and the appearance of the essoli seemed to motivate the men and women around me. They'd all heard of the sneak attack the night before, and this was their chance at payback.

"Try to kill the essoli before they reach the wall," I added, and if a few of the Aspirants seemed confused why I was giving advice, the others nodded. "Their blood is hell on weapons."

Pike's sword had come through unscathed last night, as had my spear, but the guards who had joined us in our late-night defense had all needed new weapons when the fighting was done. That sort of loss could be just as devastating during a battle as any actual damage the essoli might wreak.

"You've come a long way," murmured Lace, her eyes trained on the slowly approaching horde. "I wouldn't advise ever crossing the Waste."

"Why's that?"

For once, her grin reached her silver eyes. "A woman of the clans would take you to her tent in a heartbeat."

"And that's a bad thing?"

"Depends if you like keeping your name and freedom."

"Right." I swallowed. "I'm not planning on going south, but thanks for the warning."

"It was more of a compliment, really."

Sadly, it probably had been. But if we survived all of this, I had things to do and an entire species to help save, and even if I hadn't

been the carrier of an awful disease, I wasn't going to spend the rest of
my days as someone's bed servant.

Across the field, the blighted moved from a walk to a run.

This was nothing like the first two waves of the day. Long-
ranged abilities and spells went off all around us, adding to the chaos,
but the blighted pushed through. They died in droves but even those
bodies provided problematic for us. Stacks of the dead made for
barriers other blighted could duck behind. Up against the wall, corpses
made for ramps the blighted scaled even faster than the stone.

The more that we killed, the less effective our next attacks were.

I found a rhythm fighting next to Lace and the unnamed staff
wielder from the previous day. My spear darted forward like an adder,
each thrust measured, calibrated to cause damage without over-
committing me and exposing me to the blighted swarming the wall.
Irkonnen fell, some dead or dying, others simply crippled as I moved
on to the next opponent.

If I'd been by myself, I'd have been overrun in the first minute.
With Lace on one side and a capable Aspirant on the other, I held, and
they did too.

I heard the first essoli before I saw it and spun to face its awful
bulk. I met its whispers with a scream in the same language and was
gratified to see my words take effect again. The creature hesitated and
that gave ample time and space for Riok's spear to strike.

Lace followed up my hit, one thrown dagger becoming five, all
of them sinking into the creature's mass, but it was the staff-wielder
who finished things off. The world seemed to warp around him as he
brought his weapon down in an overhead strike. The staff grew, now
six inches thick, now a foot, now as wide as a building for all that it was
still held in two hands. It landed like a meteor, blasting through
whatever defense the essoli tried to erect, and sent pieces of the creature

splattering into the irkonnen climbing over the wall. Scales and flesh alike sizzled and another wave of attackers fell to their death.

When I looked again, the staff was just a staff, the man just an Aspirant, and visibly tired, but the space in front of us had been swept clean of enemies.

I needed a technique like *that*.

Along the wall, others were faring less well. Pockets of irkonnen had made it to the top, and the essoli slipped through the cracks in their formation, bringing additional death and chaos. I saw Skaal for the first time in two days, now wielding an axe almost as big as he was, each sweep of the great blade leaving carnage in its wake. Further down, the unmistakable shape of Arrius was a wall of resistance the blighted couldn't break. But otherwise?

We were losing.

Irkonnen started to slip over the wall and into the town. I was heading for the stairs when a fresh wave of techniques erupted. Our reserve unit—guards and adventurers both—pushed forward from their posts deeper in town, crushing the irkonnen in their path as they fought to join us on the wall.

Just that quickly, our defenses firmed, but Pike and Carlson had committed the entirety of their reserves. Madea's future hinged on the next few minutes.

And there were still hundreds of blighted on their way, the shadeweaver only now reaching the wall.

As luck would have it, the shadeweaver came straight at our section above the Forest Gate. I didn't know if it had been instructed to clear the gate, if it had heard me speaking in the essoli tongue, or if it just thought we looked particularly weak, but either way, it was soon looming over us, not having to climb the wall at all when it could simply step over it.

Lissiana unleashed an ability and the air filled with arrows that glowed gold like the sun. A dozen of them hit, one even sinking into the smallest of the shadeweaver's eyes, but the creature didn't seem to notice or care. It opened misshapen human lips to reveal a mouth as black as the night. Dog-sized spiders issued forth, pouring across the wall toward us like a wave. The creatures weren't flesh and blood, but shadow instead; I watched the staff wielder's weapon slip right through them without causing any damage.

Riok's spear didn't have that problem. It tore through shadow as easily as flesh and armor, and I couldn't help but wonder if it was the spear itself or its baptism in the Buried necromancer's blood that made such a difference. Around me, the other defenders switched tactics, triggering techniques that damaged what their base weapons could not.

I speared two spiders climbing the back of the staff-wielder, slung their bodies at the irkonnen coming up over the wall, and ducked aside as Lace appeared behind two blighted I hadn't seen, stabbing one from behind and then cutting the legs out from the other. The Marauder was laughing as she fought, covered in blood, her teeth and eyes the only light visible in the darkness.

But of course, the shadeweaver wasn't *just* a delivery system for shadow spiders.

A leg as thick as Arrius and twice as tall thundered down at me and I burned *Lunge* to get inside it, triggered *Deceptive Strike* to dance to the side and drive my spear into its bulbous belly from the optimal angle. For the first time, the weapon failed me… or my body did… or both; even with the technique optimizing my strike, the spearhead barely penetrated, skittering off the layer of hardened bone beneath.

It was the centipede all over again. I didn't have the Strength to penetrate its armor and lacked the Finesse and reach to find a vulnerable spot.

I dodged a second strike and stumbled over the staff-wielder's corpse, his torso split from shoulder to pelvis by a blow he hadn't seen coming. Lace danced away from another series of attacks and Lissiana slowly retreated toward the stairs, the bow in her hands reduced to kindling.

A domineering aura erupted from further down the wall, as Arrius fought his way toward us, but our section was already full of the dead and dying, empty space rapidly being filled by more spiders or the blighted from below. *Lunge* wasn't off cooldown yet, so I ran instead, barely ducking past another building-sized leg. I stabbed one of the shadow spiders in the back with Riok's spear and bowled it over. Came up with my knife in my other hand and tore through the throat of an irkonnen neither Lace nor Lissiana could spare attention for.

The first of the shadeweaver's legs touched down on the other side of the wall and then it was directly above us, finally able to bring the rest of its natural weapons to bear. Lace blurred into the air, like a bird trying and failing to take flight, a full ten feet up before gravity started to reassert itself. As she fell, she spun about, torquing her body until she faced the shadeweaver's giant human face. She spat a stream of liquid that struck the creature's hide and clung to it like napalm without the fire.

I couldn't see what her spit was doing, but for the first time, the shadeweaver screamed, the sound a physical force as much as the essoli's had been mental. It ignored the fleeing Lissiana, ignored the gnat with his spear and knife, and turned all its attention to the woman just now landing cat-like on her feet below.

Three legs thundered down like a dark god's furious vengeance. Lace dodged the first, was batted to the ground by the second, and couldn't do more than bare her teeth and snarl at the third as it drove down to end her story.

A bronze axe met that leg, four feet from its target. Metal bent and warped, but the axe just kept going, severing the limb at its first joint. Skaal threw his ruined weapon at the shadeweaver's face like a javelin, a gaunt, sickly presence standing against the nightmare that dwarfed even him. Arrius arrived a moment later, the Copper's club shattering a second leg as he triggered a technique I'd seen twice before, growing until he could almost look the shadeweaver in the face. The survivors of one of the other adventuring parties followed in his wake, falling upon the shadow spiders and blighted with a vengeance.

"Skaal!" I did the one thing Riok had taught me never to do and tossed the reaver my spear, knowing he'd put it to better use than I had. I then hurried to Lace to pull her out of danger. Her face was a mask of pain, her right arm broken in at least two spots, but she drew a throwing knife with her left hand and hurled it at the shadeweaver's face where great boils had started to appear. Once again, one blade became five, and all five landed, creating fresh wounds that festered even more quickly than whatever her spit had done.

Hashoggath, I reminded myself for the hundredth time, was scary as hell, and her faithful weren't all that much less so.

The shadeweaver had been forced to turn its attention from Lace to the two Coppers bent on removing its limbs. It blocked a crushing blow from the giant-sized Arrius, then spun about, lashing out with one of its remaining legs. Two of the newly arrived adventurers went flying, one into the battlements with a sickening thud, the other out into the fields of dead irkonnen, but those casualties were just an unfortunate side effect; the move had been designed to bring the creature around to face Skaal and Arrius both.

The mouth opened again, misshapen lips now cracked and bleeding as fresh sores sprouted from nowhere. Darkness billowed within its open mouth, but instead of more shadow spiders, that darkness remained amorphous, a cloud that swept over the two Coppers.

The barest hint of it neared us. I felt my heart shiver and almost stop, until a stiff wind arose out of nowhere, stopping the darkness cold. Lissiana had returned. She had a new bow in hand, but her lips were pursed as she blew, and the wind rose to reinforce her breath.

The shadeweaver's cloud of death couldn't resist the elements, dispersing even as it was blown through the massive spider, and then out over the battlements. Our two Coppers were revealed again. Skaal had dropped to one knee, shoulders heaving, while Arrius had lost his size and was clutching an arm and shoulder. Both were alive but seemed lessened by the experience. Meanwhile, the shadeweaver remained alive and dangerous.

Another avalanche of golden arrows took the creature in its face, projectiles finding purchase in the open wounds that Lace's spit had spawned. A dozen mad, staring eyes squeezed shut, and a second earthshaking scream came forth, but before the shadeweaver could do more than voice its rage and pain, someone leaped from Madea's streets below, flashing into the air like the bird Lace had failed to emulate.

They hung in the sky for a single moment. Even the wind Lissiana had summoned seemed to still and a long blade caught fire in the mid-morning sun. Then, blade and figure both streaked down toward the shadeweaver below, the air igniting with the force of their passage. They struck the creature's main body and tore right through, bursting from its belly less than a second later and landing heavily onto the wall in a flood of blood and fluids.

I stared wide-eyed at Guard Captain Pike, as the man picked himself back up and dodged out from under the collapsing body of the dying shadeweaver.

"Are you *sure* he's not a Copper?" I asked Lace.

"Tin," she said. "Must be a rare class and damn close to ranking though. And even then, I'm guessing he's entirely built for offense."

"I'm not going to hate on him for—"

A series of calls came from further down the wall, as clusters of defenders finished off their vastly smaller foes. They were pointing toward the forest, where another wave of irkonnen were already racing toward Madea. There were several dozen taller figures among them, figures in familiar robes and wielding weapons where the blighted had only their claws and teeth.

Our strategy had succeeded in luring the cultists out into the open… and we weren't in any way prepared to meet them.

70

A large army *still* stood on the forest's edge, hundreds now instead of thousands, but instead of advancing, the other blighted seemed content to watch. It was almost as if they were waiting to see whether Khamani's cultists could succeed where their own kin had consistently failed.

Even that was more thought than I'd been told to expect from the blighted, but it renewed my faith in the shift in strategy that Pike and Carlson had endorsed.

The cult clearly has some sort of sway over them, the captain had said. *Cut off the head and the rest will scatter.*

Now, with more than half of our defensive force dead, we were going to see if he was right.

There weren't enough of us left to truly hold the walls, but the cultists drove the irkonnen straight at the pockets of resistance that remained, as if by crushing us, their dominance would be reasserted. I helped Skaal to his feet, retrieving my spear in the process. The reaver's armor was torn, wounds beneath showing where weapons had found their way through his defenses, but it was the darkness still clinging to his flesh that had me concerned. It didn't eat at him like the Ever-

Hungry's curse had Mordecai, but his snow-white skin had gone grey in places, robbed of the Vitality that usually kept him going.

He bore it with his usual stoicism, unsheathing two new weapons. Beside him, Arrius had taken far less damage, but the man's eyes were wide and white, and his breath came in short, sharp gasps.

He's a bully, Skaal had said, and looking at the other Copper made me think of what often happened when bullies were finally punched in the face.

I went to talk to him, either to use *Diplomacy* or *Deception* or both, but Pike was there first.

"One last stand," he said, mustache drenched in gore that he had clearly failed to notice. "Crush the Ever-Hungry's faithful and the day is ours."

Arrius' grunt echoed Skaal's, as both Coppers turned back to the charging army.

"Watch their spells," I said. "They've got something that can eat right through a body."

Pike nodded. "Do you see the leader?"

I turned to Lace, who was scanning the oncoming horde. After a moment, she shook her head. "It's hard to say. They all look the same to me."

"Then we'll just have to cut every one of them down." Pike turned to Lissiana. "Pick your targets, lieutenant. Let them know we're still here."

The woman already had an arrow nocked. She pulled back the bowstring, muscles in her slim arms now impossible not to notice, and waited. One breath, two, and then she loosed, the arrow catching fire as it took flight.

Two hundred yards flew by in a second and a cultist dropped, not even seeing the projectile that had taken them in the head.

"Two more, captain," she said, nocking another arrow.

"That's two less than will make it here. Go ahead."

Another two fiery arrows split the air, each separated from the other by a handful of seconds as the archer picked out targets for her technique. The second cultist died just like the first, but the third one, forewarned, had just enough time to trigger their own defenses. *Something* appeared in the air between them and devoured the arrow whole.

And then both blighted and cultists were on us.

Anyone with energy called on their abilities and their spells. I recognized a few... another Warrior with *Lunge*, a Rogue with Lace's strange ability to shadow step. There was even a Mage who specialized in fire, although their output paled in comparison to what an overloaded Mordecai had done.

I killed a dozen irkonnen and helped end another essoli, but it was Pike and the two Coppers who did most of our damage. As the fight went on, I saw that Lace was right... the captain relied entirely on his armor and attributes for defense, with his techniques all oriented toward offense. It made him a whirlwind of bronze, faster than Skaal or Arrius, if not nearly as powerful.

Without his usual cadre of guardsmen as support, it also left him far too open to reprisal. A downward slash from his long blade cut an irkonnen in half, the backswing quick enough to block the cultist who had come from the side. But when that same cultist threw himself on the captain's weapon, there was nothing protecting Pike's right side.

I shouted a warning, unable to reach him, the creatures between us blocking both my path and *Lunge*'s effective usage. Pike pushed the dying cultist aside and tried to duck under a blow from the second cultist who had appeared in the first's shadow.

It wasn't enough. The attacker's hammer caught the guard captain in the collarbone, blasting through already battered armor, and driving him to the floor. An arrow from Lissiana killed the cultist before he could follow up his attack, but by then, irkonnen were swarming the fallen guard.

Nobody could reach Pike to save him, and the man didn't get back up.

I fought my way to Lissiana's side instead, working with Lace to protect the archer as she sent death at point-blank range into every robed figure she could see. There were tears in the woman's inhuman eyes. Even without the energy for techniques, every arrow found its mark, but at least half encountered defensive techniques or spells and were overcome.

Danger Sense flared and I swept Lace aside, taking the two of us to the floor and likely further damaging the Marauder's broken arm. Above us, Lissiana's upper half simply disappeared, leaving just a pair of legs and half a bow behind. A figure took shape behind her, and though he wore a robe like all the others, the aura that flooded out of him told me exactly who it was.

It wasn't domineering, like Arrius' aura, or solid and dependable like Riok's. It wasn't even cold and deathly like the Buried at Whitehall.

It was *hungry.*

A gauntleted hand stroked the severed end of one of Lissiana's still-standing legs, and the entire limb shriveled, drained dry like a mug of beer. A three-tailed whip manifested in the cult leader's free hand. Perhaps the most horrible thing of all was the leader's face, visible for the first time beneath his hooded robe. It was… normal. Pleasant, even. The sort of face you'd expect to find on a non-adulterous milkman in Earth's '50s and '60s. Even his smile seemed friendly, somehow.

"We've come to collect what is ours." His voice, at least, was as I remembered it, harsh and biting, a better reflection of the man inside.

As he took a step toward Lace and me, I triggered *Lunge* from the floor, picking a spot behind him and to the side. I landed, spun, and thrust in a single motion.

Deceptive Strike.

He effortlessly parried my initial blow… the one my technique had transformed into an illusion, but I had been shifted two feet to the side now, and Riok's spear drove into the man's back.

Only to come to a dead stop, a few inches from my target. The sense of hunger intensified, and the weapon vibrated in my hands, subjected to pressure I could sense but not see.

A second passed, and the cult leader frowned, turning to face the spear still caught in his defensive technique.

"Now, that is—"

I drew my knife and threw it at his face.

I didn't have the *Throwing* skill, and my lessons in *Knife* had never involved willingly discarding my own weapon, so the chances of the blade going where I wanted it to were infinitesimally small… but that didn't matter, because the blade hit that same defensive sphere. Where my spear had held strong, the knife was simply consumed.

The cultist didn't notice, eyes still fixed on the quivering spear. He reached out a hand to touch it, then winced, pulling his hand back.

"What is one of Corros' faithful doing *here,* of all places?"

I didn't know what he was talking about, but I was pretty sure he wasn't talking to me.

"A question for another day," he decided, still blissfully unconcerned in the middle of an ongoing battle. He took a deep breath and then exhaled again, and a wave of force washed over me. It drove me to the ground and the air from my lungs but sent the spear arcing through the air to clatter off a rooftop and fall into one of Madea's distant streets.

So much for Riok's lesson #1. I'd just lost my spear.

There was a roar and a massive club hit the cultist from behind. Size and momentum did what even Riok's spear could not. The club was consumed as it passed through the leader's defensive shield, losing mass with every inch, but enough remained to strike the man, knocking him away. There was a flicker and then Lace was crouched behind the enemy, one arm still hanging loosely at her side. She stabbed out with her slim blade and either the shield was gone or she'd used a technique to pierce it as her blade caught the man in the side.

The cultist stood, pulling the Marauder up with him, and almost negligently tossed her away, sending her body careening over the wall just like my spear. He turned to Arrius, warm eyes glancing at the whittled-down toothpick in the Copper's hands, and then at the man himself.

"You," he said mildly, "would feed Khamani's vessel for days."

His aura swelled, nothing but hunger and *need* filling the air, and whatever was left of Arrius' own energy vanished, gone like it had been run out of town.

Skaal stepped up beside Arrius, and the cultist's smile finally faded. "*Two of you?* In a bottom-feeding town like this?"

A battle was going on around them, around us, townsfolk, cultists, and blighted alike dying on each other's weapons, but it all seemed curiously distant. There were only the three Coppers, facing each other, and though the cultist was outnumbered, his confidence seemed undiminished.

I didn't have any weapons, but I forced myself to my feet anyway. I was surrounded by the dead. Maybe I could find…

I froze. I'd seen Skaal fight before, of course, but I'd never seen multiple Coppers going full out. Weapons blurred. Techniques I could barely even see, let alone identify, were tossed back and forth between Arrius and the enemy cultist, while Skaal had little choice but to dodge what he could and bear what he couldn't. The cultist leader made

Arrius seem slow and the reaver weak. Worse, he seemed to be growing in strength as the battle continued, whereas the others had already been fighting for the better part of two days.

I saw trouble coming before it happened.

I watched the cracks appear in Arrius' demeanor, watched the doubt take hold, as the Copper encountered a foe that could go toe-to-toe with him and more than hold their own. In that moment, he was closer to animal than human, and *Animal Behaviorism* was one of my maxed skills. I knew fear and a desperate need to survive when I saw it.

But I *still* didn't expect him to step to the right, trap an unsuspecting Skaal by the arm, and hurl the reaver toward the cultist. Arrius spun away and sprinted down the wall, leaping over the edge to land in the fields below. Just that quickly, he was out of sight.

Skaal took three hits before he could recover, and though none of those wounds ate at him the way Mordecai's had, I could see the strength draining from the half-giant's body. He staggered back, barely avoiding a lash of the cultist's whip. Cold blue eyes scanned the wall, and though I think he was looking for Lace, he found only me.

Blood pooling beneath him, he tossed his axe aside, and reached for the shrouded weapon on his back.

His opponent didn't give him space to draw it. The space between them disappeared and a gauntleted fist drove into the reaver's chest, tearing through already-broken links of chain, then flesh, then the bone beneath. Skaal staggered, but didn't fall, abandoning Tempest to wrap his arms around the cultist's body. He lifted the other man into the air and smashed his forehead down into that smiling face. Bone and cartilage broke, and I couldn't tell whose it was. Something finally *did* begin to eat away at the reaver's body, but Skaal stayed standing somehow, smashing away at the cultist with the only weapon he had left.

Unfortunately, no matter how it had felt, we *weren't* alone on the wall. Another cultist hit the reaver from behind, and then the last of the nearby irkonnen followed, driving Skaal to his knees.

Finally breaking free of my paralysis, I picked up the closest weapon… Lace's rapier-like sword, and *Lunged*, skewering the second cultist. I soccer kicked the irkonnen, and even if I didn't send it flying like a Tin might have done, I folded it in half. My follow-up strike broke Lace's sword but ended the blighted's life.

I turned back to Skaal just in time to catch the cultist leader break something new in the reaver's body. When the half-giant rose again, it was only because the other, vastly smaller man had picked him up. He tossed the body over the wall's edge, I heard it hit one of the spiked wooden barricades Madea's townsfolk had assembled, and then, there was nothing more.

Skaal's killer turned on me, and with the damage he had taken, his pleasant mask had finally slipped to expose the hunger lurking within. He took a step toward me and then blinked.

"Khamani sees you, Chosen. A vessel already prepared on our behalf. A cup waiting to be filled and then consumed."

I crab-walked backwards, looking for another weapon, looking for anything that could help against a Copper, even one who had clearly had a screw knocked loose by Skaal's dying blows. But the cultist devoured the space between us, moving without moving. The next thing I knew, I was pinned against the wall.

"The girl-child can be bled," he told me, "flesh and blood both sustenance for the Ever-Hungry, but you, you will be Khamani's return, as the scriptures prophesied."

Riok had given me three rules when we first trained.

Rule #1: The spear goes where you do.

Rule #2: The spear points at your enemy.

And Rule #3: there was a time for talking, and there was a time for killing, and mixing the two was a great way to end up dead.

I'd lost my spear, which made the first two rules moot. And given the situation, I decided I had nothing to lose by breaking the third.

I swapped to the speech of the essoli and spat a series of unintelligible curses up at the man effortlessly pinning me.

He... was neither shocked nor impressed.

"You already speak one of the sacred tongues, I see. That will serve you well in your new role."

I kept the curses going, not because I expected any change in the result, but because I had realized something else: we were *both* breaking Rule #3, and that... well, that was his mistake.

A *Flare* burst into existence in front of the man's bloody face, bright and fiery as the goddess who had given it. Even as it faded, a flock of paper birds swarmed the cultist, causing chaos if not damage. He staggered, hands flying up to protect his face, and just like that I was free.

I still didn't have any weapons and I had less than a moment before he realized that neither attack had done even a bit of damage. So instead of running or punching or doing something halfway intelligent, I lunged forward, wrapped my arms around his waist, and suplexed the bastard right off the wall.

It would have been cooler if I hadn't gone over with him.

The walls of Madea were twelve feet at their tallest, designed more to keep out wild animals and the occasional bandit than for serious defense. At the Forest Gate, there were fewer bodies piled up and more of the hedgehog-like fortifications that Skaal had hit on his way down. I spun as we fell, each fraction of a second an eternity, trying to end up on top of the cultist, trying to skewer him on one of the wooden spikes. We were halfway down, the cultist only now reacting to his sudden fall, when *Lunge* returned.

I held onto it until the last moment, until wood bit into the writhing body beneath me, and then triggered the technique for a spot a mere two feet away, an empty space amidst the manmade briar patch.

The thunk of a body impaling itself on multiple spikes blended with the air being driven out of my body as *Lunge* caused me to belly flop onto packed earth and no less than two of the sharp stones the irkonnen had brought as throwing weapons.

Midton Brian would have laid there and moaned. Whitehall Brian would have hoped like hell Shan might show up again to save him. Even Harborton Brian would have taken a second to bitch about the blatant unfairness of life.

I forced myself back to my feet, pulled one of the sharp rocks out of my side as I turned, and triggered *Deceptive Strike*.

My blind stab would have caught the cultist leader in the side of the head. Maybe it would have penetrated his skull, maybe it wouldn't have. But *Deceptive Strike* did more than just hide my true attack… it shifted me to a spot that would do optimal damage. So while my illusory self struck the cultist leader's temple and did nothing, I found the serrated stone in my hands burying itself into the cluster of nerves at the base of his neck.

And that made one hell of a difference.

Khamani's voice on Eos went limp, with only the two wooden posts through his chest and pelvis keeping him upright, but I wasn't taking any chances: I pulled back his head by his Mayberry haircut and dragged the bloody stone blade across his neck.

And just like that, he was *definitely* dead.

"Brian!" I looked up to find Miko leaning over the wall above me, Carlson and Seanna at her side. Madea's Dedicated had come at the pivotal moment to bolster the town's defense. "Are you okay?"

Orange eyes darted to Skaal's still form a dozen feet away, and she gasped.

"I'm alive," I called back weakly. I was pretty sure more of me was going to be bronze than pink when this was all over, *Beast Skin* changing me even as I healed, but it was better than the alternative. Better than Skaal or the unnamed staff wielder. Better than Pike or Lissiana. Better than… "Did you find Lace?"

"She's being healed! We think—"

A chorus of yipping drowned her out, as the remainder of the blighted emerged from the forest. You didn't have to understand their language to know that Pike's strategy had failed, that without the cultists to control them, the blighted had chosen to follow their natural instincts instead of fleeing.

You just had to watch them come, loping toward the largely defenseless town.

"Climb the wall with *Lunge!*" shouted Miko.

I didn't bother telling her I'd used the technique on the way down, that I was a solid forty or more seconds away from triggering it again, or that that would easily be twenty seconds too late. It didn't matter. The blighted would hit Madea's walls like an avalanche and bury whoever remained inside.

Miko wasn't dumb. She knew all of that as well as I did.

"Get to safety," I yelled back at her, looking about me for anything I could use as a weapon. The cultist's whip had faded long before I threw him over the wall, and that left only the irkonnen's makeshift weapons.

Except…

Skaal lay face down, one of his long legs sticking out at an angle that would've hurt to look at if he weren't already dead. I limped over as fast as I could. The reaver had one weapon left on his belt, a dagger as long as my arm, but bronze wouldn't do a damn bit of good against what was coming for us.

I could run and die. I could stand and die. For the thousandth time in my life, fate had trapped me, pinned me down, and made me cry uncle. Eos had conspired to make a mockery of my supposed Ideal, the gods pushing me about like a pawn on a board, and I had nothing to show for it.

But I wasn't Mordecai's fire, wild and unrestrained. I wasn't a child, sheltered from the world and responsibility. Freedom didn't mean callous hunger to me, and it didn't mean blind ignorance either.

Freedom was simply the ability to choose.

I skipped the bronze dagger at Skaal's belt and instead dragged Tempest from its sheath on his back. The irkonnen cries grew in my ears as I unwrapped the cloth shroud to reveal a simple ivory rod, four feet long, and carved with images instead of words. It felt impossibly heavy in my hands, and cold like ice cream straight out of the freezer.

"Stop."

The voice was thin and weak and spoken in a language few in the north knew. I turned to find Skaal looking up at me through one bloodshot eye. The other was gone entirely, as was a good portion of his chest and shoulder. I didn't understand how he was alive, let alone talking.

"Help me sit," he said, each word quieter than the last, barely audible over the sucking sound in his chest or the irkonnen now only seconds away.

I did what he told me to, trying not to wince as even more damage was revealed. There was more blood on the ground beneath him than there could have been left inside, and all the broken bones were somehow the *better* part of what had happened to him.

"Now... give it to me."

"Skaal, you're—"

"Tempest is… too much for you, Brian Fieldings." His smile was filled with blood and missing quite a few teeth. "Allow me to greet my ancestors… one last time."

I blinked and nodded. Above us, Miko was shouting something, and I thought I heard Carlson's voice as well, but it was all I could do to place Tempest into the reaver's one remaining hand.

"And now… step behind me. Reavers are not… by our nature… a discriminating sort."

I blinked again and for a moment, it was Mordecai lying there, dying there.

Go, the Mage had said.

Step behind me, said the reaver.

I obeyed them both, moving past Skaal and then turning to watch the oncoming horde. They were fifty feet away now, then forty. They were thirty feet and still nothing had happened. I blocked out their foul words, blocked out my nest-sister's cries above me, and waited.

For the first and the last time in my life, I felt Skaal's aura. It wasn't domineering. It wasn't hungry. It wasn't even solid and quietly reassuring like another dead hero's.

It was a cool wind out of the mountains. It was wan sunlight reflected off snow. It was an icy peak, unassailable and remote, and a hidden stream, offering respite to the weary. It was a man who had sacrificed everything for his values and then watched someone do the same for him.

It was simply Skaal, and in his hands, Tempest came to life.

One moment, there was a broken half-giant, propped up against the barricade he'd landed on. The next, he was whole and standing strong, healthy as I'd never seen him, a sword of crystalline ice in his hand as he faced the coming horde. Another flicker of a heartbeat and he was no longer alone but surrounded by others of his kind, men and women both, dressed in grey furs or armor as pale as their skin.

The nearest reaver looked at Skaal—the Skaal who was alive and standing—from a face more ice than flesh. No words were exchanged, but he clapped the other man on the shoulder.

Fifteen feet away, the irkonnen screamed their war cries, and I couldn't hear them.

Twenty-five reavers, twenty-four of them long dead, turned on the coming enemy, baring weapons as varied as they were, and the battle was joined.

○○○

I don't know how much time passed. It could have been a minute, a glass, or a cycle.

I know at some point Miko made her way down to me, and a *Minor Healing* swept through my body curing at least some of my wounds.

I know that the irkonnen died by the tens and then the hundreds. I know that the essoli's whispers were silenced, one by one. I know that the few blighted who remained at the end broke and ran, leaving a silent tribe of reavers standing tall.

I know that those reavers faded, one by one, and that Skaal was the last to go, turning back to look at Madea with eyes that saw nothing and everything.

And I know that when it was over, there was one half-giant's corpse, withered and broken, left in the field, for a partially healed Marauder to find and claim.

The battle of Madea was over, and we were still standing.

It wasn't victory, but survival.

EPILOGUE

Lace didn't speak for a full seven-day. She just worked and ate and trained and slept and then woke and did it all over again, with Tempest wrapped but always at her side. Miko held a memorial for the many, many dead and the entire town attended, except Lace. Miko held a party-only memorial for Skaal, and Lace was there but stayed silent.

We gave her what space we could as we cleaned up the damage and buried the dead, as word arrived that the duke's men were on their way, that he'd left his army behind to finish conquering Zaris and would somehow be in Madea in two seven-days instead of five.

I trained alongside Lace, together but alone. My life on Eos so far had been others sacrificing themselves for me, from Niaci to Riok to Erlund to Mordecai and now Skaal. Whatever growth I had managed, whatever strength I'd amassed, wasn't enough, would never be enough until I could stand beside my friends and not behind them.

Gain the duke's favor. We were almost there.

Get stronger. I would do everything I could.

Make a safe haven for the synossians. We still had multiple cycles before the first ship would arrive. We'd be ready.

Protect those who matter. It was a new bite of the thegar, to use Miko's broken parlance, but I would etch it into my soul, because if freedom meant being able to make a choice, it also meant being strong enough to survive the consequences of that choice.

And then, on the eighth day, Lace bared her teeth and finally spoke.

"I'm going to find Arrius," she said, each word dripping with her patron deity's venom. "I'm going to find him and end him."

"We'll do it together," I told her, carefully looking away as she finally began to weep. Seated next to Wilhemina's comatose body, Miko bowed her head in agreement.

Because sometimes, protecting your friends meant helping them find peace, and sometimes *that* meant killing those who really, really needed it.

I wasn't surprised when the screen appeared before me. The timbre of its text differed from what I'd seen before, as if this had come straight from Kal, the god Riok had worshipped. It was simple and to the point, and exactly what I'd expect from a god of honor and duty:

```
NEW QUEST: Deliver justice for a fallen brother.

            [ Accept | Decline ]
```

I hit *Accept.*

Brian's Personal Record at the End of Speaker of Tongues

Name: Brian Fieldings
Class: Warrior (Common) - 5
Profession: None
Deity: None
Ideal: Freedom

Attributes:
Strength: 11 [+1] / **Finesse:** 11 [+1]
Vitality: 15 [+2] (+2) / **Intellect:** 13
Discernment: 10 / **Will:** 15 (+2)

Skills:
Major: Formations: 14/30, Knife: 17/30, Light Armor: 25/30,
Medium Armor: 15/30, Spear (U): 30/30, Tactics: 29/30,
Throwing: 1/30

Minor: Acrobatics: 1/30, Athleticism: 29/30, Avoidance: 29/30,
Focus: 24/30, Leadership (U): 4/30, Pain Tolerance: 30/30

Professional: None

General: Animal Behaviorism: 10/10, Brewing: 2/10,
Caretaking: 7/10, Danger Sense (R): 10/10, Deception: 10/10,
Diplomacy: 1/10, Hunting: 1/10, Meditation: 5/10,
Mercantilism: 4/10, Riding: 2/10, Scribing: 4/10,
Stealth: 10/10, Tracking: 1/10

Techniques: Beast Skin (C), Deceptive Strike (U), Lunge (C)

Achievements: None
Titles: Agent of the Wild
Traits: Speaker of Tongues, ???, ???

Author's Note

When I first decided to write a LitRPG, I knew I wanted it to be just a little bit different from the mainstays in the genre that I know and love. Slower progression. Smaller numbers and more intelligible power scaling. A greater focus on parties and D&D style adventuring instead of a single overpowered main character. A system of progression that was grounded in the lore of the fantasy world, rather than forced upon an unsuspecting Earthborn populace.

I also wanted a setting where even information about that system was valuable… where in lieu of help text or snarky commentary from some sort of all-knowing entity, mortals had been left to figure those things out for themselves. And then I wanted a protagonist who was thoroughly unprepared for all of it.

The result is something I haven't really seen before in the genre. I hope you've enjoyed reading *Speaker of Tongues* as much as I've enjoyed writing it because I can promise you one thing: there's a lot more to come.

So far, we've only gotten the smallest of hints of the greater picture, of the people, and forces, and conflicts that will come to define future books. The challenges that await will either drive our protagonists to untold heights, or see them forgotten in unmarked graves, like so many other would-be heroes before them.

Because Eos is a world shaped by war… and even the gods who built it are restless.

About the Author

Chris began life as a gleam in someone's eye, but birth and childhood were quick to follow. He's been fortunate enough to live in Spain, Germany, and all over the United States of America, and is still planning a tour of the distilleries of Scotland.

A graduate of the Johns Hopkins University's Writing Seminars program, he put that degree to ill use for twenty years as a software engineer but has finally circled back around to the idea of writing for a living.

Chris currently lives in Nevada with his angelic wife and ever-expanding whisky collection and occasionally ventures outside to peer upwards, mutter to himself about 'day stars', and then scurry back into the house.

Speaker of Tongues is his tenth novel and the first book in his epic LitRPG series, *The (Second) Life of Brian*. Chris frequently shares updates on his author website at https://christullbane.com.